William H. Dixon, James Raine

Fasti Eboracenses

Lives of the Archbishops of York. Volume 1

SALZWASSER
VERLAG

William H. Dixon, James Raine

Fasti Eboracenses

Lives of the Archbishops of York. Volume 1

Reprint of the original, first published in 1863.

1st Edition 2022 | ISBN: 978-3-37500-675-4

Verlag (Publisher): Salzwasser Verlag GmbH, Zeilweg 44, 60439 Frankfurt, Deutschland
Vertretungsberechtigt (Authorized to represent): E. Roepke, Zeilweg 44, 60439 Frankfurt, Deutschland
Druck (Print): Books on Demand GmbH, In de Tarpen 42, 22848 Norderstedt, Deutschland

FASTI EBORACENSES.

LIVES

OF THE

ARCHBISHOPS OF YORK.

BY

THE REV. W. H. DIXON, M.A.;

EDITED AND ENLARGED

BY

THE REV. JAMES RAINE, M.A.,

VOLUME I.

LONDON:

PREFACE.

WHEN a work like the present emerges from the press, a work long-promised and long-delayed, on which the toil of many years has been lavished, the reader may naturally wish to know somewhat of its origin and progress, and it is only right, in this instance, that his curiosity should be gratified. These explanations may be appropriately prefaced by a short account of the beginner of these biographical annals, to whose industry and judgment the present volume is intended to be a memorial.

William Henry Dixon was the son of Henry Dixon, vicar of Wadworth, in the deanery of Doncaster, and was born at that place in the month of November, 1783. His mother was the half-sister of the poet Mason, who basked for many years in the favour of the family of Darcy at the neighbouring rectory of Aston, which he has immortalized in his verse. The estates of that well-known writer came into Mr. Dixon's possession, together with some literary treasures of much interest and value, including several volumes in the beautiful handwriting of Gray. These have now found a resting-place in the minster-library at York.

Mr. Dixon received his education at the grammar-schools at Worsbrough and Houghton-le-Spring. In 1801 he was matriculated at Pembroke college, Cambridge, and in January, 1805, he graduated in arts. In 1807 he entered into orders, and with the curacy of the pleasant village of Tickhill he began his clerical career in the diocese of York, with which he was connected during the remainder of his life. Throughout the whole of Yorkshire there were few clergymen more useful than Mr. Dixon, and none, perhaps, more generally beloved. He passed through all the grades of clerical life, and did his duty in each, whether he was acting as a parish-priest or a canon, or in the weightier and more delicate position of adviser to the primate, for he was domestic chaplain to two archbishops. For many years he was a prebendary of Ripon, but he gave that office up in 1852, and he held also, in succession, the perpetual curacy of Mappleton, the vicarage of Wistow and curacy of Cawood, the vicarage of Topcliffe and the rectory of Sutton-on-the-Forest. At the time of his decease he was prebendary of Weighton and a canon residentiary at York, rector of Etton, and vicar of Bishopthorpe. In the last-mentioned position he was brought frequently into daily contact with the primate, who had the greatest confidence at all times in his wisdom and discretion.

In his private life no one merited or won more universal respect and regard than Mr. Dixon. Gifted with ample means, and with a heart as open as his purse was large, he was never appealed to in vain, and he rejoiced to do good. In almost every parish in which he laboured he left behind him some substantial token of his munificence, and in everything that he did he exhibited the considerate kindness and the courteous demeanour of a Christian gentleman. His unobtrusiveness made these points in his character more observed and valued, for he was singularly modest and retiring, and yet when from the necessities of station he was brought prominently before the public eye, he never shrank from doing his duty in a position to which he was naturally averse. The refinement of his manners threw a charm over everything that he said and did. Nearly ten years have passed away since his decease, but even now there is no one in York who does not speak of Mr. Dixon with an honest warmth of feeling which is beyond the suspicion of affectation. An almost universal homage is still paid to his courtesy and goodness. In this brief tribute to his character the writer can only give the echo of the popular voice. It is a matter of deep regret to him that he never even saw the gentleman of whom he is now speaking, and whose literary labours it has been his privilege to take up and enlarge.

In the glorious choir at York, surrounded by carving and colours such as no other Christian temple can exhibit, a pious hand has erected a memorial of brass, enriched with the cunning workmanship of the graver, to an uncle and a nephew. Upon it the names of William Mason and William Dixon are inscribed, although neither of them is sleeping in that sacred dust over which you walk. One is resting in a neighbouring graveyard, the other is lying in "Aston's secret shade," which he loved so well. Yet in the noble fane at York, in which they were both sometime dignitaries, how appropriately are these two kinsmen commemorated and connected! That shrine in which they worshipped gave to each of them of its inspiration. It evoked Mason's verse, and the choir of the cathedral and its music were almost his chief care: it induced Dixon to recount and recall the great deeds of those who had ruled and ministered in that sanctuary of which he was so proud.

The worthies and the annals of the church of York have at all times excited an unusual amount of attention. Putting aside many historical works of a general interest and bearing in which the capital of the North and its ecclesiastical superiors are mentioned very frequently and fully, there are many pieces which are specially devoted to the Fasti of that cathedral. From the writings of Beda and Alcuin we may learn the history of Paulinus and Chadd, of Egbert, Albert, and the Eanbalds, but we have separate and distinct lives of as many as five of the early primates, Wilfrid, St. John of Beverley, Oswald, Thurstan, and St. William. In the twelfth century the famous chronicler, Symeon of Durham, addressed a brief but interesting letter to Hugh, the dean of York, in which he gave him a short account of the archbishops up to his day, and about the same time, or a little later, the poet, Hugh de Sotevagina, wrote down the lives of the first four primates after the Conquest, and his work is as yet unpublished. The historians of the church of Hexham record many interesting particulars relating to the archbishops and the cathedral of York, with which they were officially connected. In the fourteenth century, Thomas Stubbs, a Dominican friar, compiled his well-known chronicle containing the biography of the heads of the Northern province from its foundation to the end of the reign of Edward III., and this was subsequently continued by an unknown hand to the period of the Reformation. In addition to this there is more than one poem in which the glories of the church of York are described in lively verse, ascending from the middle of the fifteenth century until the mists of antiquity conceal all historical information but that which suggests itself to the imagination of the enthusiastic bard. After the Reformation there is a long pause in the annals of York, broken only by the biographies of the Northern archbishops which occur in the great work of Godwin, by Hacket's delightful life of archbishop Williams, and a work by another hand on the same theme. Towards the close of the seventeenth century we come to a man of whom no Yorkshireman ought to speak without respect and admiration, James Torre, the York antiquary.

He was a scion of a good Yorkshire family, and in his zeal for antiquity he was not unworthy of the county which was the mother of Roger Dodsworth and many other scholars of repute and fame. His powers of application must have been prodigious, for although he was but a middle-aged man when he died, he had filled scores of folio volumes with materials for history, biography, and genealogy, all written in that curiously minute hand which was one of the characteristics of the literary men of that age. The nerves and the heads of those who are now living shrink from the very thought of what persons like Prynne, Dugdale, Dodsworth and Torre could effect and endure. I do not think that James Torre of York was inferior in application to any of the scholars that have been mentioned. If we form our estimate of him merely from the three or four volumes of his manuscripts which are preserved at York in the registry of the dean and chapter, we can see that he was a man of extraordinary powers. In the space of three or four years he literally made an abstract of most of the official documents in the registers of the archbishops and the chapter. The succession of clergy in every living in the diocese, up to the time in which he lived, is given as far as he could ascertain it. The testamentary burial of every person of importance, all instruments and deeds connected with endowments of livings and chantries are mentioned, and in many instances church notes are added besides. These are some of the contents of these wonderful volumes.

The most extraordinary, however, of them all, is that which is specially devoted to the minster at York. There is in it a history of the church from the earliest times; there is a perfect survey of the fabric, all the glass is described, every monument is measured and drawn, and its inscription and decorations are given in the most minute way, by which many things are preserved which have long since disappeared. The endowments of the church are all given: there is even an abstract of the leases. There are full lists of the parsons, vicars, and chantry-priests. But the greatest wonder in the volume is that part which may appropriately be called the Fasti of the Cathedral. It is a list of all the archbishops, deans, dignitaries and canons of the church to the time in which Torre lived; all their preferments in the diocese are specified; the exact dates are given, with references for each statement, but here, as a general rule, the compiler ends. These things are merely the dry bones of a skeleton, but each is in its proper place, and Torre has left to others the more difficult and laborious task of clothing them with flesh and blood. He has made the framework of the Fasti himself, and in doing that he has accomplished a great deal.

Torre died at a comparatively early age, and little has been since done to illustrate the biography of the dignitaries of the minster. His lists appeared with a few additions in the works of Le Neve and Browne Willis, and the *Fasti Ecclesiæ Anglicanæ* have been still more improved in the recent edition by Mr. T. D. Hardy. The antiquary, Francis Drake, wrote the lives of the archbishops and published them in his *Eboracum*, but they contain little information of any novelty or value, and they are disfigured in several places by those caustic remarks of which that historian was too fond. There are memoirs also of archbishop Sharpe and of several of the later primates, but the Fasti of the industrious Torre still occupy the first position in importance. They are not free of course from errors of omission and commission,—the character of the work precludes the possibility of that—but on the whole these unrivalled collections are marvellously exact.

Mr. Dixon's connection with the church of York, the taste for letters which he inherited, and the natural bent of his own mind, induced him many years ago to turn his attention to the manuscripts of Torre, and the history of the minster and its officers. As he was unable to decipher the mediæval hands, he took the greater interest in the more modern period, and with much industry and perseverance he drew up a volume which he entitled, "Fasti Eboracenses; or, A catalogue of the Members of the Cathedral of York from the Great Rebellion to the present time." These are written in a stout folio of five hundred and fifty pages, drawn up with much care, and illustrated with information derived from many persons and sources. The work is by no means a dull and dry catalogue of names, but it contains numerous extracts from printed books, and many facts which could only have been ascertained by personal enquiry, and with much trouble and research.

For many years Mr. Dixon confined himself to the limits which have just been mentioned, but at the suggestion of the late learned and amiable Archdeacon Todd, he subsequently determined to take a wider range, and to attempt the biographies of the worthies of the minster from the very earliest times. This extension of his subject seems to have suggested to Mr. Dixon another method of arranging his materials. In the first portion of his work he had marshalled the dignitaries in regular succession under the offices which they occupied; in the latter he adopted a purely chronological order, with no regard to offices at all, and at the head of each century he placed a short essay on the general history of the church during that period. This plan was an intelligible and a good one, but the great length to which the lives of the primates alone have extended, has rendered its rejection necessary. Between the first and the second portion of Mr. Dixon's work there is no comparison in value and importance. The latter part (in point of time the earlier) was commenced far too late in life to present any appearance of the industry and research which are apparent in the other, and which would have been evident to a great extent in this if a longer career had been vouchsafed to Mr. Dixon. As it was, through the aid of the manuscripts of Torre, he had laid down a pretty substantial framework for his book. From the same invaluable collection he had derived many notices of the livings and offices which each dignitary enjoyed, and he had added, besides, some extracts of his own from other sources. There was no attempt, however, at composition, and for the most part Mr. Dixon's collections for the mediæval portion of the Fasti are little more than a bare catalogue of names and dates.

Soon after Mr. Dixon's lamented decease, which occurred in the month of February, 1854, his widow, acting under the advice of Mr. Canon Harcourt and the late Dr. Raine, resolved to prepare for publication the *Fasti Eboracenses* as a memorial to her husband. In compliance with his father's wishes, the charge of the work was undertaken by the editor, who was at that time a mere stripling as well in years as in literary experience. Neither he nor any one else who was interested in the book had at that time any idea of the real extent and weight of the burden which he was fastening to his shoulders. It was obvious, in whatever light the undertaking was regarded, that much toil and research would be required from the editor. In what form his labours were to be connected with those of his predecessor was not so evident. Dr. Raine, in the first instance, was of opinion that Mr. Dixon's manuscript should be made use of as a text, and that the additions of the editor should appear in the form of notes, but he soon discovered that this arrangement was impossible, as it would be mere folly to have ten and often twenty or thirty lines in note-type to illustrate only one of text. Mr. Harcourt, by whose advice, together with that of Dr. Raine, the editor has been guided in any case of difficulty, at Mrs. Dixon's request, stated from the very first that Mr. Dixon's manuscript should merely be used as a foundation on which the work should be constructed. At all events the general understanding was that what was wrong should be struck out, and what was wanting added. To do all this was a very weighty and serious office. No one, I believe, was at that time conscious of the toil that it would entail, least of all the writer of these words.

Ten years have almost passed away since this resolution was arrived at, and the present volume at least will shew that the editor has tried in all honesty and honour to adhere to it. These ten years have brought great changes to him as well as to others. They have removed from his sight one in particular, whose memory he can never dwell upon with aught but love and reverence, who before his decease had begun to look with some regret and fear upon the labour entailed by the work which he had counselled the editor to undertake. Those fears, however, have been happily belied, and the hopes and aspirations that ever accompanied them, as the writer humbly trusts, would not have been entirely disappointed, had his sire been spared to look upon this volume. The old words, *Spartam nactus es,* have been continually in the editor's mind, and he has been animated throughout his work by a wish, and why should he be ashamed to own it? that he might do some little honour to the name of a father of whom his children have so much reason to be proud. But the editor has been upheld throughout his labour by a higher motive still. He was requested to add to and correct Mr. Dixon's manuscript, supplying as far as he could whatever was deficient; a commission as unlimited as the labour which it necessitated. He accepted it voluntarily and cheerfully in its fullest and widest sense, and in its fullest and widest sense, as a matter of duty, he has endeavoured to fulfil it. He felt at all times that he could not conscientiously do otherwise, and in spite of labour which, in one word, has been tremendous, in spite of sacrifices as severe as they have been various, in spite of several very heavy discouragements, under which many would have shrunk and fainted, he has persevered in doing his duty by his work. He could never have done so if he had not been strong in body and stout in heart, and he cannot be too grateful to One who orders and sustains both, that his health has been uninjured, and his resolution, although sometimes sorely tried, still buoyant and undaunted.

The whole of the present volume has been written by the editor, and nineteen-twentieths of the materials have been collected by him. It was his wish to have issued the two volumes, in which the lives of the archbishops are to be comprised, at one and the same time, that the second, in which Mr. Dixon's work will be more apparent, should appear contemporaneously with the first, which the editor, owing to the paucity of the materials collected for it, has been obliged to write himself; but, at the request of Mrs. Dixon, the first volume has been issued without its intended companion. The editor has also been desired by the same lady to write or re-write the whole of the second volume. It will not be necessary, however, for him to do that entirely. Mr. Dixon's own collections for the later portion of his work will save the editor much trouble and research, and the public before long will have an opportunity of fully estimating the merits of an undertaking which, but for

Mr. Dixon, would never have been begun, and which is offered up as a memorial to his industry and judgment, not less sincere and lasting, it is to be hoped, because so much of it has been constructed by an alien, although a friendly, hand.

The perusal of this volume will shew the reader that this is not a work that has been hastily or carelessly constructed, and will at once explain the delay in its appearing, although it contains the lives of only forty primates. Many, however, will be surprised when they are told that the editor has made contemporaneously, in behalf of the Fasti, collections, *on the same scale,* for the biography of some seventeen hundred other persons, extending over a period of twelve centuries, and comprising, among the very greatest men in the Church and State, three hundred English and foreign bishops, three popes, and at least sixty cardinals. It is not too much to say that almost the whole range of the history, biography, and topography of England, and, in part, of other countries, has been ransacked for these Fasti. This, as every student knows, could not be done without great labour. He is aware, also, that for mediæval biography mediæval documents and annals must necessarily be examined, and that few have the inclination, still fewer the ability, to have recourse to them. Some may, perhaps, smile when the editor tells them that he has given up nearly a whole year to daily toil among original evidences in the public offices to make his work as complete as possible. New matter is what is wanted in these days, and that can only be derived from repositories like these. We wish also to hear of new men—not of persons like Wolsey and Cranmer, to whose biography there are perhaps few additions of any importance to be made; but of bishops like Thurstan and Thoresby, Bek, Skirlaugh, Hatfield and Langley. We want to know what they did and how they worked, who were the officers and clergy that were under them, what was the discipline of the church in their day, the state of the monasteries, the private and public life of the parish priests and canons. At present we know almost nothing about our early church history and biography, and for the simple reason, that men will not take the trouble to seek for information where alone it can be found. In preparing the Fasti the editor has made an honest, although very imperfect, attempt to fill up and supply a manifest defect, and he has not shrunk from the drudgery which the nature of his work required. He may venture to say with bishop Hacket, "I drew the knowledge of those things of most moment which I shall deliver from the spring-head, and I trust in God that I have incorporated them into this frame with integrity." In these days of book-making, one work with a loud-sounding title succeeds another, repeating the old errors and the old conclusions, which the absence of new evidence prevents the writers from discarding. All that they can do is to put the old materials in a new and a more pleasing setting, although this is not often the case. The book is the old dish served up again, the "*crambe repetita,*" against which the great Roman satirist shot his arrow.

No one is more sensible of the great defects of this work than the writer. What exertions can be worthy of so noble and so grand a subject! The editor's sensations are like those of the scholar who comes into a vast library, or of a person who finds himself suddenly introduced into the presence of a great multitude of men. The one regards himself as a dot or an unit in such a concourse, the other sees what a pigmy he is in genius when he gazes on those ponderous tomes which express the thoughts and the feelings and the deeds of the almost forgotten dead. The editor is well aware of the grandeur of his theme, although he has not risen to the high level on which it ought to have been placed. He does not believe that he has gathered together a third of the information which may be discovered about many of the primates whose lives he has been bold enough to attempt, and of this volume one third, perhaps, will be found to be incorrect. The very nature of the work precludes the possibility of complete accuracy and exactness, and if the writer had waited for them, his labours would never have been ready for the press. It is a great thing to lay a foundation for future research, and to give people something to correct. It is a matter of deep regret to the editor that so few of the national documents, especially the Close and Patent Rolls, are in the hands of the public. He is well aware that they may destroy many of his conclusions, and supply facts of which he is completely ignorant; but he must throw himself in this respect on the consideration of others. All will allow that he has not shrunk from toil, and he has been equally anxious to avoid harsh criticism and controversy. Of course he has not refrained from expressing his opinion about men and things, but he has endeavoured to make his way by stating what he believes to be the truth, and not by shewing where others are in the wrong. He is so well aware of the hidden fires that are smouldering under his own feet, that he has no wish to evoke them by censuring or attacking others.

One great difficulty that the writer has been obliged to contend with is this, that this work is restricted to a certain limited space, and he has thus been unable to do full justice either to his subject or himself. The strong hand of compression will be apparent in every page of this work. The life of more than one primate, were it fully entered into, would form a volume of itself. On account of this want of room many things have necessarily been omitted; facts have been stated, but the conclusions to be drawn from them have been left to others, and many critical remarks upon difficult and disputed points have been abbreviated or abandoned. But with all this compression the lives of the archbishops alone will occupy the space which was intended at one time to be filled by the whole Fasti of the cathedral; and with these lives, to be completed, it is expected, in another volume, this work will come to a termination. The reader will not be introduced to those many hundreds of other dignitaries, about whom such a mass of information has been collected. It would require ten or twelve volumes like the present to do justice to their biography, and the annals of the archiepiscopate must not be ruthlessly curtailed. It is with no little regret that the editor is obliged to throw aside five-sixths of the materials which he has gathered together, especially as a third volume, comprising the lives of the deans, sub-deans, chancellors, precentors, treasurers and archdeacons of York, would not only constitute the history of the cathedral to which the biography of its remaining members could easily be appended, but it would also disclose a vast body of information about many good and great, although hitherto unknown, dignitaries, which would be of greater novelty and interest than that which is now laid before the public. It would be a matter of much concern to the editor to see the subject continued on a scale less extensive than the present, but flesh and blood, somehow or other, cannot but shrink from the thought of the labour which such an undertaking would require, although in this case it would be merely the construction of an edifice out of the materials that have already been collected. It is certain, however, whatever people may say or think, that until the Fasti of one cathedral or diocese are exhausted in the way that has been suggested, we can know but little of the true history of the English Church. At present we are only catching at straws and pursuing shadows. We want to see what the ecclesiastics of other days believed and did, how they lived and wrote and died. At the present time we scarcely know their names.

This book professes to be nothing more than biography. It is not the history of the English Church or of any part of it. It has nothing to do with what are called "the times" of the archbishops or of any of them,—that vague and unsatisfactory term which is almost invariably the title of a bad book. It has simply to do with the men themselves with whom the work professes to deal, and collateral information is brought in only with the intention of setting off their characters and history. This book is addressed *ad clerum* rather than *ad populum,* to the bees and not the butterflies. It is written to bring out truth, and not to please fancy or prejudice, or merely to attract the popular eye. Too many sacrifices have been made to these already, and scholars who are worthy of better things have been frightened by the bugbear of popularity. Popularity of course must have its due weight in the mind of every one, reader or student, and it is but folly for the scholar to kick against the pricks by professing to despise it, but it must not be everything. If this is to be a book of reference,—and it can scarcely expect to rise to that dignity,—why should it be made a bad one, merely to gratify the taste that shrinks from dry details. This is an enquiring age, and what it wants are new facts from which new conclusions may be drawn. The true gold of literature and learning is far below that surface on which too many in these days are content to work. In quest of that gold the editor has not been ashamed to dig, and he has tried to do so in an honest and a kindly spirit. He is well aware that the main reason why people shrink from early biography and history is, that they cannot realize those times, they cannot think and feel as the men of those days thought and felt, of whom they know so little. You may see their portraits, if you wish, in the memorials that they have left to us. You may trace out the finer features of their character in their works, and rise up a better man than you sat down. The editor would fain hope that he has sojourned not altogether in vain among those great and holy men with whom he has endeavoured to surround himself, that he has drawn their true portraiture, and ascribed to them thoughts and words and deeds that are not unworthy of them. His labour has shewn to him, and he trusts to others also, that in those ages which many pass by as unenlightened and uninteresting, there were learning and true greatness, and a spirit of devotion and self-sacrifice of which few in these days can fully and properly conceive. Men like these belong not to one party, but to all, and they are England's noblest and greatest sons. Their very presence seems to act as an inspiration in the places which they once haunted. Who can enter the glorious fane of York without feeling this, although he is a stranger to its history and its fortunes? A kind of sacred influence seems to hang around you there, a legacy to the present from the past. Associations throng around you, for great things have been done within those walls. Roman emperors walked over this ground when as yet this temple was not. It was here, in the dayspring of Christianity, that the Northumbrian monarch stood with Paulinus at the font, and made vows and promises which he was not long spared to keep. On this sacred site was the church of which Wilfrid was the founder, lovingly enshrining in its heart the little chapel which had witnessed the baptism of the king. Recollect that Bede was in it twelve centuries ago, and that in this place were the home and the school of Alcuin; of which he spoke with true filial gratitude and enthusiasm among the Paladins of Charlemagne. Kings and nobles have stood where you now stand, and many of the princes of Northumbria, Norsemen, and mighty men of renown, are sleeping beneath your feet. What sights and scenes have these time-honoured walls beheld! They have seen, speaking only of more recent events, and what I may call only modern days, they have seen the great king surrounded by his court when St. William's bones were placed in a new tomb. They have looked upon the minions and the reprovers of his unwarlike son, Lancaster and Bohun, Clare, Argentine, Gaveston and Despenser. They have seen the marriage of Edward III. to Philippa of Hainault. They have witnessed the triumphant progress into the North of the victor at Agincourt, that he might pay his orisons at the shrine of the great saint at Beverley who had given him, as he thought, his victory. They have seen the mutilated remains of Harry Hotspur laid at last in the cold earth, and the presence of Richard III. and his youthful son, on a day of short-lived triumph, among his rejoicing Northmen. This is the transept which Walter Gray erected, and there in it he is reposing under that high-towering tomb. That is the monument in which Scrope's bleeding corpse was laid, and there on the screen is the image of the cruel king who slew him, still bearing upon its face a puerile token of the disgust which his injustice aroused, and almost by his side is his unhappy grandson's statue, to which the foolish and impassioned Lancastrian in after days paid a fruitless worship. No one can look on that nave and on that glorious window, the finest perhaps in the whole world, without thinking of the great primate who filled it with those glowing colours which, after the lapse of five centuries, look down upon you with a softer and a more solemn light, and then go into the choir, and forget Thoresby if you can. Stone and marble and glass are voiceful there, and they tell you with one tone of the good deeds of him who, with no memorial but themselves to preserve his name, is sleeping in front of that eastern window before the old altar of St. Mary, which he once reared, and which he loved so well.

In conclusion, the editor must acknowledge, and he does so with pleasure and gratitude, the aid which he has received from others during the progress of his work. Many a helping hand has been held out to him, and he has met with much sympathy which he cannot easily forget. To the Dean and Chapter of York he is under the deepest obligations: he has had unrestrained access to all the muniments they possess, as well as to their choice library; and from the chapter-clerk, C. A. Thiselton, Esq., he has received far more than merely formal courtesy, the unvarying attention and kindness which have extended over many years. To Messrs. Hudson and Buckle he is equally grateful for the readiness and the pleasure with which they have allowed him at all times to consult the records in the archbishop's registry, without which permission this volume would have been comparatively worthless.

The editor's most sincere thanks are due to Mr. Canon Harcourt, one of the greatest promoters of literature and science that York has ever known. If it had not been for him, this work would never, perhaps, have appeared in its present form, and he has been at all times most desirous, not only to smooth away any difficulties which may have arisen in the writer's path, but to give, what has been still more valued, many a kind word of encouragement and advice. The editor is also wishful to express his acknowledgments to Archdeacon Churton for his assistance, which few are as competent and none more willing to bestow. He cannot but feel that the lives of the archbishops of York would have proceeded from Archdeacon Churton's pen more appropriately than from his own, and that no one could do greater justice to the worthies of a cathedral among whom he himself occupies so high a place.

It would be impossible for the editor to enumerate and thank, as he could wish, all those who have helped him in his work. He cannot, however, pass over the Rev. William Stubbs, J. R. Walbran, Esq., and W. H. D. Longstaffe, Esq., who have afforded valuable assistance in securing the accuracy of this volume; nor must he omit two tried and always kind friends, Robert Davies, Esq., and the Rev. John Lees, who have been good enough to examine every sheet as it issued from the press, and to render aid and counsel with a readiness and a pleasure which he cannot prize too highly.

It is painful to speak of those who are not, but it would be unjust to pass those by who took no little interest in the progress of a work, the completion of which they have not been permitted to behold. To none would the sight of this volume have afforded more sincere gratification than to two beloved kinsmen, scholars themselves of repute and fame, who have gone into the new country, and the writer's fondest recollections are centred in a father and an uncle. But there are others, also, now no more, whom the editor cannot forget. From Joseph Hunter, Esq., the historian of South Yorkshire, he received at all times an almost parental kindness, and the aid which a master of his art is so pleased to render to the son of an old fellow-labourer in the great cause of letters, when he adopts his father's tastes and manifests a desire to make them hereditary. Of the Rev. Charles Wellbeloved the writer can only speak and think with affectionate regard, and he will always remember one who at an age, which few are permitted to reach, retained unimpaired the wisdom of the *constans ætas*, together with the warm zeal and buoyancy of youth. Nor must the editor pass by the late Archbishop Musgrave. He will always be deeply sensible of the considerate sympathy of the late primate, and of his overflowing kindness, of which he was frequently the recipient.

The writer must also express the great obligations he is under to the printer, Mr. Mitchell. He does not think that any house in London could prepare more creditable proofs than those which Mr. Mitchell has submitted to him.

J. R.

YORK, *April* 25, 1863.

REFERENCES AND AUTHORITIES.

The editor, for several reasons, has not placed his references at the end of each life, but has appended them to the fact to which they especially refer. Their number may perhaps be reprehended, but the writer has wished to put in each note an exhaustive list of the authors who have mentioned the particular circumstance to which it refers. The reader may not, perhaps, have access to every work that is referred to, but when many authorities are given, it will be in his power, if he wishes to do so, to test the accuracy of the narrative by examining at least one of them.

Exact references have been given to everything but the manuscripts at York. Any fact can be found without difficulty in the registers of the archbishops, which are arranged chronologically, and divided into archdeaconries, etc. Into the Act-books of the Dean and Chapter it is not so easy to enquire. Torre's fanciful titles, if given here, would only bewilder the enquirer, and a new system of lettering must be adopted when they pass, as they soon will, through the binder's hands.

Where there is a variety of editions of the same work, it will be necessary to mention those which the editor has made use of. This will assist the reader and facilitate investigation.

Alcuini Opera. 2 vols. Fol., 1777.

Baronii Annales. 11 vols. Fol., 1589, and the Continuation, 3 vols. Lyons, 1678.

Beda, ed. Smith, Fol., Cambridge, 1722.

Dugdale's Monasticon. The new edition.

Fœdera. The new edition.

Florence of Worcester. 4to, London, 1592. The continuation from the new edition by the Engl. Historical Society.

Peter Langtoft. Ed. Hearne. The reprint.

Chron. de Mailros. Ed. Bannatyne Club. 4to, Edinb., 1835.

William of Newburgh. Ed. Hearne. 2 vols. 8vo, Oxon., 1719.

Matthew Paris. Ed. Wats. Fol., London, 1684.

Chron. Petrib. Ed. Giles.

Polydore Vergil, Historia Angliæ. Fol., Basileæ, 1556.

Savile's Scriptores post Bedam. Fol. London, 1596.

Saxon Chronicle. Ed. Ingram, 4to. London, 1823.

Triveti Annales. 8vo, Oxon., 1719.

Wendover. Ed. Giles, 2 vols. 12mo.

A LIST OF THE LIVES CONTAINED IN THE PRESENT VOLUME.

FASTI EBORACENSES.

INTRODUCTORY CHAPTER.

THE history of the archiepiscopate of York commences with the mission of Paulinus. The lamp of truth begins at that time to shed abroad its full light, although several centuries had passed away since it was first kindled. An enquiry into the origin and progress of the Northern Church will be a necessary and appropriate introduction to the biography of its leaders. This, however, must be made in the briefest and the most summary manner, and I shall not pursue it after the arrival of the Norman conqueror.

It is not easy to say to whom we are indebted for the first preaching of Christianity in Britain. No one has as yet given any satisfactory solution of this doubtful point, and the bigotry of contending partizans has enveloped it in additional obscurity. It seems evident that there was in the British church an Eastern as well as a Western element; indeed it is quite possible that Judaic traditions had been brought to England before the birth of the Redeemer. The Eastern origin of the inhabitants of these islands, the frequent visits which they received from Asiatic merchants, could not fail to make the Britons more or less acquainted, at a very early period, with the truths of Christianity, and there are traditions which such a supposition can alone explain. We must either take it for granted that Greek forms and opinions, the Græcanitas of which Mabillon speaks, were at one time the tenets of the universal church, a point which will not be readily conceded, or that there was some direct communication at a very early period between Asia and Britain, which originated those peculiar variations from Roman discipline and ceremonial that were once rife in England. However this question may be settled, it is equally certain that Christianity would flow into this country from the Eternal City. It is very probable that our little group of islands, which were so well known at Rome for their fertility, their mineral wealth, and the valour and independence of their inhabitants, would be honoured with a special visit from some of the early propagators of the faith; but, even if they had never reached our shores, we may be sure that the truths which they inculcated everywhere, with such energy and success, would come to Britain sooner or later from the emporium of the world. The early Christians shunned neither the camp nor the forum; every place and profession was thronged with converts to the true faith, and we may be certain that there would be many of them in this country, in attendance upon the imperial court, or in the ranks of the Roman armies. Wherever there were Christians they would have their assemblies and congregations, and they would probably imitate, as far as possible, the example of their brethren at Jerusalem, where "all that believed were together, and had all things common."

From little beginnings a church would gradually be established. I do not mean to say that Christianity would at once become the national faith; very far from it; but still it is remarkable that we find no trace of any opposition being made to the new creed by the professors of the native religion. Into no country could Christianity be introduced with greater chances of success. It would soon encounter Druidism, and it does not appear that the meeting produced any angry collision. The Eastern origin of both creeds, the sacred mystery that enveloped them, the retired lives of their teachers, would disarm the suspicions of even the gifted critic. A kind of alliance seems to have been made between Christianity and Druidism, and, as is generally the case, the new and more active religion stepped before long into the place of the old. It became, in this way, more or less the national faith. Securing the favour of the native princes, and encountering little opposition, if any, from the Druids themselves, the Christian religion got possession of their holy places and consecrated them to a more exalted worship. Bangor, a name appropriated to several ancient monasteries, signifies "the great circle," thus connecting the place at once with Druidical worship and Druidical remains, and shewing how Christianity had occupied or superseded them. And on other occasions the Christians in Britain have displayed a similar adroitness. As soon as they gained the good opinion of the ruling powers, they have quietly taken possession of the holy places of the lately recognized creed, keeping a firm hold of their new position, but, nevertheless, disarming criticism and conciliating public opinion, by adopting, to a certain extent, all that was good and politic in the preceding system. It was one of the pieces of advice which Gregory gave to Augustine, that he should use the temples of the Roman deities, and in this respect that sagacious prelate only followed the example of Arcadius and Honorius. A little purification was enjoined, and then these heathen shrines might be dedicated to God. The cathedral church at Canterbury occupied the site of a Roman temple, so did old St. Paul's and Westminster Abbey. The crypt of the monastery at Hexham exhibits workmanship of very great antiquity.[a]

It must have been a great boon to the Saxons to have cities ready built for them, as the Britons had too great a regard for the Romans to destroy their works. Beda speaks with admiration of the memorials of their skill and energy that were standing in his time, temples, aqueducts, and bridges; but how grand they must have been nearly three centuries before his day, when the Saxons first arrived. They had all their public buildings ready, a mighty step towards civilization for a nation that was ignorant of everything but war. They were sheltered from their foes by Roman bulwarks; they could sleep, if they chose, in Roman houses;[b] they could pray, when they had learned the value and the need of prayer, in a Roman temple. It was from these edifices that the Saxons themselves learned how to build. What is now called Saxon architecture is only a rude imitation of the work of Roman masons. Nor were the Saxons indebted to Italian art merely for the shrines in which they worshipped —it gave them also the sacred vessels for the sanctuary. In the ancient Ritual of the church of Durham, and in the Pontifical of Egbert, archbishop of York, there are special forms of prayer for the consecration of vessels that were found in heathen places. This tends to shew that every nook and cranny in the Roman cities and camps has been ransacked long ago for hid treasure. And that the Saxons carried off everything of value, the paucity of the Roman remains discovered at the present day is a sufficient proof. No one who examines the seals that

[a] There are no remains of this antiquity in York. The minster stands within the old Roman camp, but there is nothing to shew that it either occupied the site, or was constructed out of the remains, of any heathen temple. The old name of Christ's Church, was the church of the Holy Trinity in the king's court. What king? Did it stand within the precincts of the palace of the monarchs of Northumbria? The recent restorations of the two churches upon Bishophill, disclosed some very early fragments of masonry and sculpture, and the two buildings, as they stand at present, exhibit several features of remarkable interest. They occupy the highest ground within the city. Is this the hill on which the earliest bishop that visited Eburacum set up his tent, and which, after the fashion of our spiritual ancestors, was crowned at once with a Christian temple? There are precedents for such a step, and the supposition will explain a name about which there has been some doubt.

[b] The Saxon remains which have been occasionally discovered in Roman camps in the North of England, seem to shew that these places were inhabited after the departure of their builders.

are appended to the earliest charters can fail to see how many of them are impressions of Roman gems. The seal of the great monastery of Durham is a remarkable instance. On the one part is the well-known cross of St. Cuthbert, but on the other, now lost, the monks wished to represent the head of their benefactor, king Oswald, so they graved upon a rim of brass the legend, *Caput Oswaldi Regis,* and fastened to it in the centre a fine gem, the spoil of some Roman camp, a magnificent head of Jupiter Tonans!

We cannot accept unreservedly the statement of Beda, that Britain was first converted to Christianity by missionaries who were sent from Rome by Eleutherius at the request of the British chieftain Lucius, about the year A.D. 180. It is plain that glimpses of the truth must have previously reached these islands; however vague and uncertain they might be. It was probably the wish for some more definite and accurate teaching, suggested perhaps, as Dr. Lappenberg observes, by the differences of opinion between the followers of the Eastern and the Western ceremonials, that tempted Lucius to send to the bishop of Rome for his assistance and advice. With the advent of this mission the British episcopate is said to have commenced. How it was distributed and arranged it is impossible to say. The traditionary account asserts that there were twenty-eight prelates, one for each of the greater British cities, who occupied the position of the Roman flamines. Over them were three presidents.

The cities which were governed by an archbishop were London, York, and Caerleon-upon-Usk, or the City of the Legions. What the duties or the exact rank of these high officials were we are not informed, only we are told by William of Newburgh that there was no archbishop, that is in the sense of a later age, in the early British church. York is the only city of the three that has preserved its ancient honours, and one of its mediæval chroniclers has proudly recorded—

> "Deficiunt reliquæ, primo frustrantur honore,
> Ast Eboracensis sola manet stabilis!"

The origin of Eburacum is concealed in the mists of antiquity. Far be it from me to dwell upon the fables of which the chroniclers of the past ages were so fond. I shall leave to them the glories of king Ebrauc, and the prestige of a city which was the seat of a monarch at least twelve centuries before the advent of Christianity! Eburacum may be satisfied with a humbler and yet a nobler origin. It is from the pages of the Roman annalist that we must learn the story of its grandeur. It is not probable that the Roman armies were well acquainted with

Eburacum before the expedition of Agricola into the North, which took place towards the close of the first century after Christ's birth. There the great captain would discover, what the name imports, an ancient Celtic city. Could we see the place as the intrepid Italian then beheld it, we should be loth to dignify it with such a title. There would be before us a collection of dirty hovels crowded together within an enclosed space, and a population of half-naked and painted barbarians living among their flocks and herds, and surrounded on all sides by wild-wood and water. But wretched as Eburacum must then have been, it could never have been so great under the Roman rule had it been of little consequence before. The Romans knew well how wise it was, in a strange and savage country, to take possession of a place of antiquity and note; where, probably, there was the only market in the district, and towards which all the forest paths converged. Here they could have a rendezvous for their armies in the North, and a direct communication with the ocean by the waters of the Ouse. It is scarcely possible to exaggerate the importance of Eburacum during the greater part of the first three centuries after Christ's birth. It was one of the most important places, if not the capital, of Roman Britain, and as Britain became more potent in the councils of the Empire, so did Eburacum become one of the greatest cities in the great Roman world. It is probable that every emperor who visited this island took up his abode in that city, and when he was absent the legate was the occupant of the imperial palace. Two emperors, Severus and Constantius Chlorus, died within its walls. Two claimants of the purple, Carausius and Allectus, were connected with the district, and the former is said to have been nominated Imperator at Eburacum. How magnificent must have been the city which was thus connected with stirring incidents and men of enterprize and energy! Thronged it would be with that noble soldiery which was as yet invincible, and filled with all the luxury and pomp that nestle about a palace or a court. Fortifications of the most massive character were around it, and within were public buildings, as fair and as grand as those which Italian architects had reared beneath the softer skies of their own delightful country. The historian, in a later age, when he gazed upon their ruins, accustomed though he was to more striking outlines and more delicate forms of beauty, could rebuild in fancy the shattered fabrics of Eburacum, and say proudly to himself that the noble city must indeed have been another Rome.[c] With what amazement would the Briton look upon

[c] Richard of Cirencester tells us that Verulamium and Eburacum were the two Roman municipia in Britain. Alcuin, in his poem *De Sanctis et*

the magnificence that Alcuin admired. The very sight of such grandeur would captivate the simple-minded savage, and in the fascinating luxury that encircled and ensnared him, Eburacum would be to him, as his conquerors desired, a second Capua.

It may be safely assumed that there was a Christian congregation at Eburacum presided over by a bishop, if indeed the episcopate were established at that time in Britain, which there is no reason to doubt. How the good seed that was brought from Rome ripened to the harvest it is impossible to say. Among the Romans themselves it is not probable that the new creed experienced less success than it met with at their hands in other countries; nay, it is likely enough that they would look upon it with greater favour, as they were here removed from all those dangerous fascinations of place and form that attracted them in other lands to their idol-worship. Among the Britons it would be the more readily accepted, as it chimed in with their traditions from the East, which must have been cherished even by those who had no intercourse with the merchants from Asia or from Gaul. However this may have been, it is evident that Christianity obtained a sure footing in this country whilst it was in the possession of the Romans. We know, also, that its professors were for a long time unmolested.[d] The persecutions that desolated the adjacent continent, and gave to the church of Lyons many a noble martyr, never reached these shores. There is no record of Severus, an apostate from Christianity and an active opponent elsewhere of the true faith, raising his hand against any believer in Britain, although he was for some time a resident in the island. The Romans were more tolerant here than they were in Italy and Gaul. They were less secure, and consequently had less time to spend in religious controversies. Perhaps the Britons were so attached to the Christian faith that the Romans did not dare to ruffle them. Perhaps the British church was so insignificant that it was entirely overlooked.

In the great persecution of Diocletian which began in the year 294, the British Christians were not spared, and the emperor would not be disposed to favour the island on account of its recent revolt. The care of this country was at that time

Pontificibus eccl. Ebor., says that the Romans built the city.

Ut foret emporium terræ commune marisque;
Et fieret ducibus secura potentia regni,
Et decus imperii, terrorque hostilibus armis:
Esset ab extremo venientibus hospita portu
Navibus oceano, etc.

Harrison, in his *Description of Britain*, speaking of Roman treasures, observes, "What store hath beene seene of them in the citie of London,—and likewise in Yorke, named also Victrix, of the legion Victoria, or altera Roma (because of the beautie and fine building of the same), I myselfe can partlie witnesse, that have seene and often had of them; if better testimonie were wanting."

[d] "Susceptam fidem Brittani usque in tempora Diocletiani principis inviolatam integramque quieta in pace servabant." *Beda.*

entrusted to Constantius Chlorus, one of Diocletian's associates in the empire. When the order for the persecution was communicated to him, Constantius was probably at York. Eusebius in his laboured panegyric upon his son, Constantine the Great, would lead us to believe that the wishes of Diocletian were disregarded, and that Constantius was most liberal and tolerant in his views and conduct. Beda, however, a more trustworthy authority, gives us a very different account. He tells us of the number of the martyrs and confessors that there were at that time in Britain—how the churches were thrown down, and the trembling believers were obliged to flee for refuge to the deserts and the mountains. And yet, in spite of all this cruelty and intolerance, the great Saxon historian speaks of Constantius as "vir summæ mansuetudinis et civilitatis," and Theophanes bestows upon him the flattering epithet of *χριστιανόφρων*, thus justifying, to a certain extent, the praises of Eusebius. He was, in all probability, the unwilling executor of the wishes of Diocletian, and, like Obadiah, could spare when he was ordered to destroy. And this is the more probable from the fact, that when he became a free agent he embraced that faith against which, in bygone years, he had been compelled to set his face. When Diocletian put off the purple in 305, Constantius divided the empire with Galerius. He then professed himself a Christian. The desolated churches were rebuilt, the sacred ceremonial was restored, and the joyous worshippers emerged at length from their hiding-places in the forests and the mountains.[e] There was peace at last for the scattered and affrighted flock, but after reigning for a few months the peace-maker was removed from it, and his ashes were laid to rest in the city of Eburacum. The first of his two consorts is still remembered for her virtues and her sufferings. She is said, on very slight authority, to have been a British lady, and it was this belief, together with the memory of her excellence, that caused three churches in ancient York to be dedicated to the sainted lady whose husband died within its walls, the good empress Helena.

The fame of the mother and the sire pales before the merits of the son, for to whom does the Christian church owe a deeper debt of gratitude than to Constantine the Great? The statement that he was born in Eburacum rests upon no better authority than the assertion of the English ambassadors at the councils of Basle and Constance in the beginning of the fifteenth

[e] "At ubi turbo persecutionis quievit, progressi in publicum fideles Christi qui se tempore discriminis silvis ac desertis abditisve speluncis occulerant, renovant ecclesias ad solum usque destructas, basilicas sanctorum martyrum fundant, construunt, perficiunt, ac veluti, victricia signa passim propalant, dies festos celebrant, sacra mundo corde atque ore conficiunt." *Beda*, i., 8.

century; but it was in Eburacum that some period of his early life must have been spent, and it was in Eburacum that he was saluted as imperator. At that time he was not a Christian, but soon afterwards he deliberately adopted his father's faith. Eusebius tells us that he was influenced by the good example of his sire, and any Englishman may be proud to think that the faith of one of the great regenerators of the heathen world may have been strengthened, if not kindled, by the sight of the piety and fervour of the imperial household, and the Christian congregations in Eburacum.

We should naturally expect that Constantine through his connection with our island would take some notice of its church, and, accordingly, we find that three British bishops, including one from the city of York, were present at the council of Arles in A.D. 314. The same episcopate was also represented at the councils of Nicæa, Sardica, and Ariminium. And from the accounts that are preserved of the deliberations at these sacred meetings we may gather that the British bishops were thoroughly catholic and orthodox. They were not afraid, also, of standing up for the faith when it was imperilled by the machinations of heretics. Against the Arians they took so decided a part that they are mentioned with honour by Athanasius; and Hilary, writing from his place of banishment to the bishops of Germany and Britain, says of them, "Gratulatus sum in Domine incontaminatos vos et illæsos ab omni contagio detestandæ heresios perstitisse."

Tradition has handed down to us the names of several of the early bishops of York, for, as Weever observes, "I finde a succession of British archbishops long before the time of Paulinus." The evidence on this point is very scanty and unsatisfactory, and there is no possibility of acquiring any accurate information.

A person of the name of Taurinus is said to have been bishop of York in the beginning, apparently, of the second century, and to have suffered martyrdom. A clerical error is the origin of this statement. Taurinus was not "episcopus *Eboracensis*," but "*Ebroicensis*," *i. e.*, of Evreux in France, with which place his name is still honourably connected. He must be expunged therefore from the Fasti of the English Church, as with Fuller, we must be "conscientiously scrupulous not to take or touch a thread which is none of our own."

Archbishop Ussher mentions an assertion made by a chronicle of York in 1460, to the effect that Fagan was the first bishop of Eburacum. Fagan is said to have been one of the Christian missionaries who were sent from Rome by Eleutherius. If Fagan really presided over the church of York, Lucius must have been king of the same city, an honour which the metrical chronicle of Eburacum ascribes to him when it says,

> "Sanctus Faganus, collega suus Damianus
> Regem cum populo mundificant lavacro.
> Templo mundato, consecrato, reparato,
> Metropolis sacra conditur ecclesia."

The temple which was thus purified is stated by the poet to be the shrine in which king Ebrauc and his descendants had observed their pagan rites for twelve hundred years, and which, on the arrival of the Roman missionaries, had been given up to Christ. The whole statement is probably fabulous, and the assertion that Lucius appointed Theodosius to the see of York rests only upon the authority of Harrison's description of Britain which is prefixed to the well-known chronicle of Holinshed.

For the name of Eborius, who is stated to have been present at the council of Arles, in A.D. 314, as "episcopus de civitate Eboracensi, provincia Brittannia," there is somewhat stronger evidence. Arles was one of Constantine's councils, and we must remember that we may expect to find British bishops associated with an emperor who was almost a Briton himself, and that of all those prelates he would, we should think, be most of all disposed to invite a bishop of Eburacum. The presence of Eborius is mentioned in an ancient catalogue of those present of very fair authority. The name is so closely akin to that of the city over which he presided that we cannot consider it to be the same that he usually bore. He had, in all probability, some uncouth British name which was changed by the Roman officers at the council for one more euphonious which bore a special reference to the city which he represented; so that *Eborius* Episcopus may be considered to be the same as *Eboracensis* Episcopus. A grave doubt, however, is thrown upon the connection of Eborius with York, as in another list of those who were at Arles he is said to have presided over a different city in the province of Byzantium.

The next name that we find in connection with the see of York is Sampson, or St. Sampson as he is generally called, and it seems probable that he was actually the bishop of that place. He is said to have lived in the fifth century. The metrical chronicle of York asserts that Sampson was brought to Eburacum by king Aurelius, who rebuilt the church which the Angles had destroyed, and made Sampson its ruler. It is by no means easy to discern the track of real history among the mists of fable; but it is probable that before the Saxons obtained full possession of Eburacum they had plundered and injured the city in some of their flying excursions, and that the British chieftains recovered it for a time, and restored what had been destroyed or changed. The life of St. Sampson has been more than once written,[f] but the account that is given of the saint is by no means clear and satisfactory. We are told that he was a native of Glamorganshire, and a student in the monastery of the celebrated Iltutus. Here he made such progress that in course of time he became the president of the house, and as years passed on, after various changes, he was induced by king Aurelius, or Ambrose, to become bishop of Eburacum. It is not probable that he held that office long. We are told that he was driven out of the city by the Pagans, and that he fled to St. David's and became the bishop of that see. But even here there was no rest for him. A dreadful plague that was ravaging Wales obliged him, much against his will, to cross the seas into Brittany, where he became archbishop of Dol. At that place Sampson died and was interred. This is the sum and substance of the accounts of St. Sampson. They abound, however, with conflicting statements into which there is no necessity to enter. It is probable that he was at York, and, singularly enough, there is a church in that city dedicated to him; the only one, I believe, in England of which he is the patron.

The old chronicler of York, relying upon the fabulous account of Geoffrey of Monmouth and Wendover, mentions another bishop of the name of Pyramus or Pyrannus. The legend about him runs as follows. The famous king Arthur, the last tower of British strength, visited York one Christ-tide after the departure of St. Sampson and his clergy, and grieved at finding the holy places desolated and the churches half consumed by the fires which the Pagan invaders had kindled, he ordered them to be restored; and made Pyramus, his chaplain, bishop of the city. Although the whole of this story is probably fabulous, we can well imagine what a struggle there would be in the North between the Britons and the Saxons. The latter were heathens, and would studiously desecrate the holy places of their enemies, in many of which, for centuries, worship of some kind or other must have been paid. The sacrilegious invasion of a time-honoured shrine would make the Briton sorrow over the injury as deeply as the pagan Roman would bemoan the loss of the tutelary deities of his household. There are probably the germs of truth in the traditions that have been mentioned. They give us a vague and indistinct picture of confusion and change. York must have been lost and recovered several times before

[f] One life, by an anonymous author, has been published by Mabillon in his *Benedictine Acts*. There is another in the *Bibliotheca Floriacensis*. A third was written by Balderic, archbishop of Dol, in the twelfth century. I have thought it unnecessary to go minutely into the subject.

the Saxons won it, and we may be sure that as often as the Britons regained their lost position they would re-establish the religion which their enemies had despised. At last the torrent of invaders became so strong that it swept them out of York for ever. The last British bishop is said to have been Tadiocus, and when he saw the hostile armies pouring in he joined Theonus, bishop of London, and fled for his life to Wales.[g] After this time the names Welsh and British are identical. Thenceforward for a gloomy century there is deep night hanging over the North, and it lasted until Paulinus dispelled the darkness by rekindling the old light in the new kingdom of Northumbria.

Of the condition and extent of the British church it is impossible to speak with certainty. Some are disposed to think that the absence of any early memorials of Christianity is a token of its insignificance or nonentity. The argument, however, proves too much. By the same course of reasoning you might shew that the neighbouring establishments in Gaul, and the seven Asiatic churches themselves, had no existence. Every relic of the faith that illumined these in the earliest ages has disappeared, but who can say that the sacred light had not once shone? The accordant testimony of the fathers chimes in with the narratives of our own chroniclers and the voice of tradition, when they assert the zeal, the sufferings, and the piety of the old British church. It is painful and yet cheering to be obliged to trace the progress of Christianity by heresies and persecutions. Melancholy although they are, they can still purify and ennoble. Diocletian was, in one sense, as great a benefactor to England as Constantine the Great. The British Church had its bishops, who were stalwart champions of the faith; it had its confessors and its martyrs. Chrysostom tells us that there were British versions of the Bible. We know that heretical teachers found their way to this island; their very presence shews that there was something to corrode. But what real and satisfactory progress could any church make when change and violence were on every side of it? Its bishops could only be missionary bishops, and we know from the records of the council of Ariminium that they had no regular endowment. Its clergy could only work ineffectively, if they worked at all, when their lives were endangered by the inroads of foreign marauders and the petty warfare of the native chieftains. Organization would be impos-

[g] The following passage is a fair sample of the metrical chronicle of York, from which it is taken.

"Turbatis rebus Archipresul Tadiacus,
Ecclesiæ sedem deserit et patriam
Archipontificum Tadiacus sedis Eborum,
Ultimus ex Britonum gentibus ille fuit.
Corpora Sanctorum, simul omnia vasa sacrorum,
Cunctas res reliquas transtulit ille sacras.
Expulsi Britones nomen patriamque relinquunt,
Dicti Wallenses nomine barbario."

sible, and we cannot be surprised therefore at the existence of that deterioration of morals and manners among the clergy which Gildas so strongly reprehends. Discipline alone could prevent this, and how was it to be enforced? Life was to be first protected and secured. As the wave of Pagan violence broke slowly over Britain, the ministers of Christ fled as it drew near them; they rested not till they were behind a barrier which the waters could not penetrate or overthrow—the secluded valleys and the mountain fastnesses of Wales.

In Wales the trembling fugitives were secure: there was an asylum for them in that noble province which has so frequently been the home of freedom and independence. The cradle of Christianity in Britain was destined to be its sanctuary. The earliest glimmerings of the sacred light illumined the country of St. David. The Asiatic merchant, who braved in his little bark the perils of the seas, found in that land the descendants of those Cimmerians who, restless like himself, had sought for a new home beneath another sun, and he would boast himself of the same lineage, and recognize a kinsman in the host that entertained him. Between the Welsh and the Asiatic churches there was a marked similarity, and time did not obliterate the resemblance but increased it. When Constantine had ascended the imperial throne, and after his decease, the news was brought out of the far East to Britain, how the pious Helena and her illustrious son had decorated the holy places in Palestine, and erected shrine after shrine to commemorate Him whose divine presence had consecrated that land, and from every corner of the West there were pilgrims setting forth to visit those hallowed abodes of which such great things were spoken. There were holy men in the East already, whose love and labours had added to its renown, if any supplement were needed. The sight of the pillar on which Simeon had watched and died was enough to tempt the devout Briton across the storm-swept seas. With what delight would he listen to the fervid eloquence of Chrysostom! With what reverence would he gaze on Jerome in his cell at Bethlehem! Every city and hamlet had its associations and its memories. Some holy presence that had ennobled it seemed to linger in it still. There was another lesson, also, which the British pilgrims would learn during their sojourn in the East. All along their route they would observe the retreats for pious and self-denying men that were springing up around them. Here was a cavern in which some impassioned zealot was striving to obliterate, by solitary penance, the offences of the past. Here a band of devotees had crowned some frowning precipice with their tabernacle, where their only companions were the raven and seagull, croaking and screaming as they swooped through the clear blue air above the foaming breakers. They could see the fearless inmates of these awe-inspiring shrines as they descended from their home among the clouds down the face of that insulated peak which raised them out of the world beneath, and then their thoughts would pass away to their own wild fatherland, and they would long for such sanctuaries there which the spoiler could never reach, where the world-worn sinner could strive to forget the past, and the pious enthusiast could muse in lowly pride upon the perfections of Him who is the God of the hills as well as of the valleys, and securely devise some great scheme of love and labour to enhance, if possible, His glory. They came home and erected in their own land the great monastery of Bangor, which was once the residence of above 2000 monks. There is no trace of it remaining now:

"Tantum ævi longinqua valet mutare vetustas."

But shortly before the Reformation you could mark the decaying walls looking down upon the "sacred Dee."

It was this great sanctuary that fed the streams of Christianity which watered Wales and Ireland. In the beginning of the seventh century it was divided into seven portions, each of them containing at least 300 monks who supported themselves by manual labour. In this and in other points there was a striking similarity between the British monks and those in the Thebais of Ægypt and other parts of the East. The positions chosen for the monasteries and the habits of their inmates were identical. The learned Selden, no mean authority, speaks of the Alexandrine rule being introduced into Britain at a very early period, and Rudburn says that in the second century Fagan and Dervan filled the church of Winchester with monks professing the rule of St. Mark. William of Malmesbury asserts that the monastery of Glastonbury, the origin of which is encircled with Eastern traditions, was governed after the Ægyptian fashion. The Culdees of Iona always looked up to St. John as their founder. These, assuredly, are signs and tokens of a very early connection with the East.

Between Wales and Ireland, the British and the Scottish tribes, there would at all times be a direct communication. Ireland is said to have been converted by St. Patrick who was sent from Rome. It is most probable, however, that the Christian faith had reached that country before the time of that saint, and Mabillon himself confesses that the peculiarities of the British church, in spite of better teaching, were dominant in early times in Ireland. My readers must not be led away by the ingenious and fallacious arguments of modern partizans, and imagine that these peculiarities involved any material difference in doctrine. There was nothing of the kind. In faith they were as firmly united as they were in the great councils in the fourth century; the only discrepancies were in comparatively trivial points of discipline and form, and the persistence of the Britons and Scots was mainly nourished and kept up by their old feeling of national independence. It would be idle, however, to deny that between the Roman and the old Welsh, Irish, and Scottish churches there were many differences in form and discipline. St. Bernard, in his life of Malachy, bishop of Connor, gives strong evidence on this point. The monasteries which he describes as existing in Ireland followed the same rule that was observed in Wales. The peculiarities which that rigid disciplinarian censured may be briefly enumerated. In the first place, as a general rule, there seems to have been a secular and a married clergy resulting in the evils of worldly-mindedness; and, as at Armagh and St. Andrew's, in an hereditary sacerdotage, the greatest bane by which any church can be afflicted. Another, and a famous, point of difference was in the manner of observing Easter, to which allusions will be subsequently made. In the mode of administering baptism, in the form of the tonsure, in the celebration of matrimony and episcopal ordination,[h] there were also variations. The Scottish people, also, gave no tithes or firstfruits, and they neglected or despised confession and the rite of confirmation. Several of these peculiarities may be traced to other countries than our own, and there is no one point that has been alluded to which would make the Briton or the Scot either a heretic or a schismatic in the full sense of those terms.

The name generally ascribed to the early devotees in these islands was Colidei or Culdees, the origin of which is involved in some little obscurity. It is probably equivalent to Cultores Dei. By them Wales, Ireland, and Scotland, were in the earliest times, to a great extent, overspread. In their observances and rubrics they were guided by the traditions of their spiritual forefathers, and it was the feeling of ancestral and national pride that tempted them to despise the invitations to full conformity with the church catholic which were so frequently held out to them. To the Culdees the early Christian memorials in Ireland and Scotland are, in all probability, to be ascribed. We owe to them that delicate interlacing work, itself of Eastern origin, by which the earliest crosses and manuscripts are adorned. In working with their own hands they shewed to others the utility of labour; they became the patrons of industry and agriculture.

[h] The Culdees have actually been held forward, by modern Scottish writers, as the originators of Presbyterianism! It is unnecessary to allude further to such absurd and unfounded statements.

In this manner they were the promoters of civilization as well as of religion. That the system of the Culdees was a popular one is shewn by the success that attended it. Its professors were, socially, but little different from those around them. There was nothing in it that baffled imitation; it so nearly resembled Druidism that it seems to have supplanted it. It taught the people useful and necessary arts, whilst, at the same time, it raised their thoughts to higher and better things. It did its work. It was just the system to attract the attention and the sympathy of a rude and ignorant people; but something more decisive and more refined would be necessary for the social and religious advancement of a more civilized nation. A body of secular clergy like the Culdees would have but little influence there.

It was in the middle of the sixth century after Christ's birth that the Culdee Columba passed over from Ireland to Iona, and planted there a little colony of holy men, which growing in influence and numbers, exercised in after years such a mighty influence over the kingdom of Northumbria. This was not the first visit that Christian missionaries had paid to Scotland. I shall say nothing of the journey of the abbot Regulus from Greece with a few of the relics of St. Andrew. We are told that some of those who escaped from the persecution of Diocletian fled for safety to Mona and Albania—the Isle of Man and the southern part of Scotland; and at the close of the same century, the fourth, Ninias or Ninian, as he is called, preached the Gospel in that district, and erected a church of stone, the first that had been seen in that country, at Candida Casa, or Whithern, in Galloway. Thus there were believers in Scotland, and thirty or forty years after this, Pope Celestinus sent Palladius to be their first bishop. But it is to St. Columba and his followers that the credit of evangelizing Scotland is to be especially ascribed; and the home that they selected for themselves, with the leave of king Connal, was the island of Hii or Icolmkill, better known in these days by its more modern name of Iona, or the Island of the Waves.

Close to the western shores of Scotland lies that solitary island, hallowed still by the noblest associations that any Christian sanctuary can boast of. A thousand years have passed away since the Culdees were there, but their great leader and his followers are not yet forgotten. The ruins that you see around you are the remnants of the shrine which a foreign order of monks erected, and not of that in which Columba prayed. But still at Iona you never think of the Cluniac but of the Culdee! You are treading upon holy ground. This is the cradle of the Christianity of the North; and here, beneath your feet, are the sea-kings sleeping! Rob it of its associations, and there is nothing to attract you to that island. It could be no selfish motive that drew Columba over the storm-swept channel to a place like that. A nobler impulse led him there than the quest of pleasure or the promptings of waywardness or caprice. It was the love of God that guided the bark of that apostolic brotherhood to their sanctuary in the sea. The memories of the happy past, the thoughts of others who were loving and praying for them in the home that they had deserted, could not wean them from their high resolve. The winds might howl around the frail tabernacle that they had set up, the spray might drench them through and through, but they remembered that they had devoted themselves to Him "whose way is in the sea," and they cared not for the tempest or the waves. Here they could pass away in peace, without a dread of that dissolution for which they had made a lifelong preparation! Here they could train themselves in deep seclusion for a higher reach in holiness, or meditate upon new victories over the unenlightened hearts that were beating with no love for them upon the adjacent continent! If the Pagan held out to them a friendly hand, they could reach him in a few minutes in their little boat. If that hand were threatening destruction, the timid evangelists could flee again to their old home across the protecting water.

How peaceful and how happy must have been the life of that devoted brotherhood in their sanctuary at Iona! Every day had its varied occupations, and in each there was a charm. Without, there were their nets and boats, for the sea was their meadow and their tillage. Within, there were the voices of supplication and praise, rising heavenwards even in the watches of the night—the sacred page rich with some divine story—the class room with the little knot of pupils to listen and to learn. Brighter and brighter shone the holy flame that was kindled at Iona, and to distant shores was its radiance diffused. There were not wanting intrepid evangelists to carry it with them among the rock-bound Hebrides; they were not afraid of encountering even the icebergs of the Baltic and the seas that rolled around the shores of Iceland. A halo of sanctity hung around Columba and his isle. The abbats who succeeded him were the greatest ecclesiastics in the North.

Whilst the lamp of truth was thus burning in the North, as well as in Ireland and in Wales, there was thick darkness hanging over Northumbria and the other provinces of England. The Saxons did not even tolerate Christianity, and its professors fled in terror as they drew near. It was to convert them that the pious Gregory sent forth Augustine, encouraged by the fair youthful faces of some natives of Deira or Yorkshire that he saw in the slave-market at Rome. The history of that mission and its success need not be dwelt upon here. A few years after the arrival of Augustine, Gregory addressed to him a letter in which he recommended him to make York a metropolitan see, with twelve suffragans under it. This is quite enough to shew the importance of that city more than twelve centuries ago. As a personal compliment to Augustine he was to have control over the new see and its prelates during his life; but his successors were to inherit no such authority, and the question of precedence was to be determined by priority of election. And to shew that the new episcopate was to be invested with the power of a metropolitan, it was to receive a pall from Rome without which no one could have suffragans under him.

Some time elapsed before any opportunity occurred of attempting to carry this scheme into effect, as Northumbria was dark with pagan idolatry, which the Culdees of Iona, strange to say, seem not to have endeavoured to remove. The enterprize was undertaken in the beginning of the seventh century by the missionary Paulinus, who was made the first primate of Northumbria. Of his labours and their fruits I have elsewhere given an account. But the question may be asked, and it is a very interesting one, how is the great success of Paulinus to be accounted for? Even under the teaching of an apostle, converts did not rush into the arms of the church by tens of thousands. It may be said, and plausibly too, that the people did but follow the example of their monarch; but it is observable in the conversion of king Edwin and Coifi, the high priest, that they were guided to a great extent by the *popularis aura*. Why, let me ask, should the people be favourably disposed towards Christianity? I can scarcely believe that an intolerant rule, even though it lasted for eighty years, could have obliterated every trace of a religion which seems to have had a strong hold on the North before the Saxons reached it. Wilfrid, at a later day, strove to recover as many of the holy places of the Britons as he could trace, and if there were traditions then, would they not be much stronger when Paulinus was at his work? Christianity had been the religion, it may be conceived, of the defeated party, and would it be forgotten by the remnant? It is a most curious circumstance also that the Pseudo-Nennius ascribes the conversion of Edwin and his subjects, not to Paulinus, but to Rum the son of Urien. Urien was a well-known British chieftain who had struggled long and stoutly against the Saxon usurpation. Can his son, after his father's fall, have gone to Rome and become a priest, assuming on that occasion the Latin name of Paulinus, by which we know him? What person more likely to be sent by Gregory from Rome to the country of his birth? What person more likely to be ordered by Honorius into the North to evangelize a people that had suffered and bled with his sire?[i] If these suppositions are correct the success of Paulinus is a matter of no surprise. His career, however, as a missionary was a short one, for it ended with the death of Edwin in 633. The land was scarcely ready for the seed when the sower was taken away.

With what curiosity must the Culdees in the North have watched the progress and the fortunes of Paulinus! The novelty of the enterprize and the zeal of the missionary could not fail to interest them. There is no record of any meeting, or of any intercourse between them. The interview between Augustine and the Welsh Christians had been anything but satisfactory. The Britons regarded the Saxons with the bitterest animosity. Charity was forgotten in the memory of national wrongs. Before there could be any cordiality there were many injuries to be wiped out. Even after their conversion, Beda boldly says that the Britons set the Saxons at nought, and treated them like Pagans. It is sad to think that Cadwalla, the Cumbrian prince, who drove Paulinus out of his diocese and slew Edwin, was a Christian in name. The Irish prelate, Dagan, refused to eat bread or to come under the same roof with archbishop Laurence, and we can easily imagine that a little of the same feeling would actuate the Culdees of Iona, when, whilst they were active in every other direction, they made no attempt to convert the Saxons in Northumbria. A more favourable opportunity for missionary exertion was soon offered to them, and under different auspices. The year after Paulinus left the North, Oswald ascended the Northumbrian throne, and he had been converted to Christianity whilst he sought protection across the Tweed. Accordingly, when he became king, he longed to propagate his recently acquired creed, and he sought for that purpose the assistance, not of Paulinus, who was in Kent, but of the Culdees from Iona. A missionary of the name of Corman was the first person who was sent into Bernicia, but he could make no progress with the rude inhabitants of the district, and he returned to Iona to give a piteous account of his mission, and to discourage the efforts of any future evangelist. He seemed to be quite unaware that the fault had been in himself rather than in the natives, and that a little more tact and patience might have effected a conversion which he now considered to be impossible. Another inmate of the same monastery, of the name of Aidan, was listening whilst Corman told to his

[i] This has been pointed out for the first time by Mr. Hodgson Hinde.

brethren the story of his own failure, and he criticized the method and the plan that Corman had adopted with so much wisdom and judgment, that he was himself prevailed upon to take up the holy cause that had been abandoned, and to go forth as a missionary into Northumbria.

The place on which, with the king's permission, he set up his tabernacle was a characteristic one. It still bears the name which the piety of its inmates won for it, the Holy Isle. Rock and sea and sky there were on all sides, enhanced by that dread charm of solitude which captivates the saint. As the evangelist looked towards the south he could see before him king Ida's tower, the Joyeuse Garde of story, crowning the grey cliff of Bambrough, in which his patron was residing, and near them across the angry waters of the frith were the bleak rocks of Farne, which St. Cuthbert has immortalized. Reared he had been himself on another island amid the western seas, and now, mindful of his old home, he chose for his abode in the strange land that he was to convert, a scene that would daily remind him of a place with which he had been long familiar, yea, another Salamis in the bosom of the deep, that was to be consecrated for ever by grander and holier memories than any earthly victory can evoke. Twice a day did a belt of living water encircle that little sanctuary; and when it was ungirt, there were the quicksand and the shoal, the scream of the seagull and the curlew. Here there was a safe retreat; for what spoiler could venture to approach? Here there was that solitude without which no great work for God can be conceived or matured. And in the evening, when the sea mists were away, the devoted bishop could see in the distance the lights in king Oswald's castle, and pray that they might long be fellow-workers in the path of Christian duty. Thankful he might indeed be for such patrons as Oswald and his brother Oswin, and his spiritual children inherited the gratitude of their sire. When the news was brought to Bambrough of that disastrous field in which Oswin had been slain, the saintly Aidan laid himself down to die, and expired with his head resting upon one of the buttresses of that little church of wood in which they had worshipped God together, and when the monks of Durham enshrined in after years the body of St. Cuthbert, they placed reverently upon his breast, as one of their most precious treasures, the mutilated head of Oswald.

On the career of Aidan in Northumbria, Beda, who had no partiality for the Scottish school, is eloquently minute. The life of the brethren at Iona was imitated at Lindisfarne. Humble, patient, intrepid, Aidan was the very man to win his way with such a monarch and such a people. His whole time was given up to his great work, instruction, prayer, and preaching. Two entire days in each week did he pass in abstinence and penance. He visited his diocese on foot, and all his worldly substance was surrendered to the poor. How pleasing it must have been to see him endeavouring to explain to the rustics, as well as a foreigner could, the promises and the claims of Christianity, uncouthly it may be, but still with words and gestures that shewed the earnestness of the speaker, whilst, whenever there was any obscurity in what he said, the good king Oswald, who was a listener also, was the interpreter and explainer.

" 'Tis a picture for remembrance."

It was not forgotten by the Northumbrians who gazed on it. The simple piety of Aidan, his love and labours, were copied implicitly by his successors in his see and the holy brotherhood that obeyed them. They acted like a spell upon the warm and unprejudiced hearts of the people of the North.

The influence that these men exercised in Northumbria was very great indeed. For thirty years they were paramount within that vast district. The large tracts of land that were given to Aidan and his successors by the kings stood in need of cultivation, the monasteries that they erected required inmates, and, therefore, at the instigation of the bishops of Lindisfarne, the Scottish Culdees came pouring daily into Northumbria, preaching and teaching, building churches and occupying religious houses. They penetrated, also, into the southern provinces of Britain. We can trace them in Iceland and in the Baltic. We find them in France and on the Rhine, at Cologne, Würsburgh, Ratisbon and Vienna. Those who assert that the Culdees were despisers of missionary exertion are egregiously misinformed.

With the churches and ministers of the Culdees there spread at the same time their discipline and ritual, which after the advent of Augustine were subjected to much hostile criticism. The Italian monks could not but dislike those differences in form which separated the native clergy from themselves. All attempts to bring about an amicable arrangement were unsuccessful. In vain did Augustine and his successors speak of the vast benefits that would result from unity, how undesirable it was that the common voice of Christendom should be set at nought by a little party in an obscure island, but they spoke to deaf ears. Dislike of the Saxons, with whom the foreign missionaries were allied, embittered the opposition of the Culdees; they clung to their peculiarities with an obstinacy worthy of a better cause. The bitterest controversies in religion are generated by little things.

As the influence of the Italian missionaries increased, a

collision between the two religious parties became unavoidable. Finan, the successor of Aidan, had a sharp dispute with a Northumbrian of the name of Ronan, who denounced the views of his superior in no measured terms. Soon after this an event occurred which brought prominently before the people of the North the necessity of union or compromise. Oswy, the Northumbrian monarch, took for his wife a princess who observed the Roman mode of keeping Easter. Thus, in point of fact, the festival was observed twice in one year in the same court; whilst the king was celebrating the feast with merriment and joy, the queen was still busy with the fasts and the prayers of Lent. Taking new courage at this obvious inconsistency, and aided by the active co-operation of prince Alcfrid and the queen, the Italian party prepared to strike a heavy blow at the system that thwarted them. Oswy summoned a great council at Streonshal at which the question was to be decided. The result of that meeting is well known. It ended in the triumph of the Roman party, which was completed by a hasty and inconsiderate step which bishop Colman then took; he gathered his Culdees together, and found a refuge eventually in Ireland. Some attempts were subsequently made to recover for them their lost position, and they were temporarily successful. When Wilfrid, at Alcfrid's request, had accepted the bishopric of Deira, and had crossed the seas to receive there the rite of consecration, Oswy, disliking that step, advanced Chadd to the see of York. The vacancy had been made by the decease of Tuda, who had succeeded Colman. After a brief tenure of office, Chadd voluntarily resigned it, and thenceforward no Culdee was ever the president of the see of York. All the intellect and the energy of the North were, for the future, on the side of Rome. Wilfrid, Benedict Biscop, and Cuthbert, introduced the Benedictine rule, or some modification of it, which seems to have worked efficiently for a time. Theodore and Egbert refused to recognize the ordination of the Scottish or British prelates without some proper confirmation of it. Egbert wrote, for the benefit of his clergy, several works on discipline and ceremonials. Eanbald probably introduced into his diocese the Roman service books. In spite of all this organized and continuous opposition, the system of the Culdees was for a very long time not entirely obliterated in Northumbria. The brethren in the monastery at York retained the name of Colidæi, or Culdees, until the time of Henry I. The spiritual descendants of the old Scottish monks flourished for a long while after this beyond the Tweed, in spite of the war that was being constantly waged against them by the regular orders. The archbishops of York could do but little against them there, although on one occasion Thurstan was bold enough to send the prior of Nostell to be bishop of St. Andrew's. He wished, no doubt, to obliterate all traces of the Culdees, but the destroyer found himself in a nest of hornets.

The ancient title of the prelates, upon whose biography I shall soon enter, was merely that of bishop of York, an appellation borne by all the presidents of that see between Paulinus and Egbert. The possession of the pall gave them the power of having suffragans under them, and they were then called archbishops of the Northumbrians. The two titles were subsequently combined. The right of electing the prelate seems to have rested, according to Alcuin, in the brethren of the monastery of York; and that distinguished scholar congratulates them upon the possession of that right, and the honest and excellent use that they had made of it up to his time. In the eleventh century the canons rejected Egelric of Peterborough, who had been nominated to the see. The Northumbrian monarch seems to have had the power of approval, and, on one occasion at least, there was a popular element in the election. It is curious also to observe that Wilfrid II. and Eanbald I. were marked out for the primacy by their predecessors, to whom they seem to have acted for some time as coadjutors. This step was in all probability taken with the consent of the brethren of the house. For several generations the archbishops were school-masters, having been exalted to the see from the class-rooms in the monastery: after the Conquest, when the power of the state became paramount, they were generally the chaplains of the king.

Many of the Saxon primates of York were courtiers and statesmen, and their biography is intimately connected not only with the annals of the church, but with the history of England. Paulinus was a royal chaplain, and left the North in the same suite to which he was first attached. The great Wilfrid basked in the smiles of a court before he suffered from its scorn, and during his whole life he was the favourite or the foot-ball of kings. Egbert was son and brother to a monarch of Northumbria. Wulstan was an intriguing politician, and played, with varying success, a very conspicuous part in the perils of his time. Oswald shared with Dunstan the responsibility of advising Edgar, and pushing the scheme of ecclesiastical reform. Adulph was chancellor to the same prince, and Alfric was either the prompter of some of the wicked deeds of Hardicanute or his tool. Aldred, with the exception of earl Godwin, was probably the greatest man in England in his day, and his influence with Edward the Confessor cannot be exaggerated. He steered the Saxon church successfully through the perils of the Norman conquest, and it was only after his decease that William could obtain his full ends. The archbishops of York held a very high position among the great men of England. They had a diocese extending from the gates of Lincoln far into the North, and to which another see in the South was temporarily united. They had a mint and other privileges of their own. They were the lords of many a broad acre, and moved about with an almost royal retinue. The number of regal grants which they witnessed shews how frequently they were in the presence of the sovereign.

It must not however be imagined that, although they were thus occasionally occupied, the northern prelates were oblivious of the high calling to which they were especially devoted. It was a duty as well as a necessity for them to conciliate the favour of the great, but public offices and employments did not interfere with the urgent claims of the flock, or the studies and devotions of the shepherd. The lives of the northern bishops present to us many a noble trait of piety and zeal. The missionary work of Paulinus and Wilfrid is not yet forgotten. We remember the patience and loyalty of the one, and the self-sacrificing toil of the other. We can see the humble-minded Aidan, unkind to no one but himself, deserting the table of the monarch, and hastening to the crowd that was waiting for the good news from God. Chadd is before us, wandering through his diocese on foot, or prostrating himself in lowliest obeisance amid the roaring of the thunder. We hear St. John observing, "It is more suitable for a bishop to be at his monastery, in attendance upon the poor, than revelling at the tables of the wealthy!" How noble were the fruits of the labours of the scholar-prelates, Egbert and his three successors: the first, a prince in birth and energy, toiling with his pen as well as with his lips, and all glorious advancers of the cause of Christian education! A sacred light still encircles the memory of Oswald. In the holy time of Lent, Kinsius went from village to village, preaching and bestowing alms, very frequently with bared feet. But in the midst of all this active employment hours were still found for solitary devotions and solitary penance. Of all the characteristics of our early Christian prelates this is perhaps the most remarkable. Each of them seems to have had an oratory, or some secluded spot, the predecessor of the private chapels of our bishops, to which he could resort.

> "Wisdom's self
> Oft seeks to sweet retired solitude."

Aidan devoted two days in each week to solitary prayer. Cuthbert ended his life upon that barren island which he had been so unwilling to desert. Chadd was in his oratory when the heavenly messengers arrived to tell him that he was soon to leave it. John, who in his earlier years had been a hermit on the Tyne, gave up his bishopric at York to watch for his end at Beverley, and two of his successors, Wilfrid and Albert, following his example, devoted the latter portion of their lives to seclusion and prayer. In a later age, when the light of holiness was less bright, there were to be found some good men who in their solitary devotions had not forgotten the practice of Christian antiquity. Archbishop Sharpe is said to have walked very frequently from Bishopthorpe to Acaster Malbis in the early morning, and to have knelt down and said his prayers to God in the porch of that little church. In the grounds of his own palace at Bishopthorpe he caused a labyrinth, as he called it, to be constructed, and that was his oratory. Thither would he resort many times a day. The book was closed, the friends were left behind, the cabinet of coins was locked, and the devout prelate sought the privacy of his cell, to banish the cares of earth and to meditate upon heaven.

The most influential of all the means by which the North of England was evangelized was undoubtedly the establishment of monasteries,[j] and the archbishop of York could wield no more effective weapon for the overthrow of paganism and vice. People in these days are too apt to depreciate the debt of gratitude which we owe to the early monks. The best interests of church and state were by them nurtured and advanced. The pious devotee could in the monastery pray and meditate; the scholar could think and learn; the world-worn pilgrim could at length repose. Two monarchs of Northumbria, Coenwulf and Eadbert, ended their days in a convent. Within those walls there was a sanctuary from the world and the vengeance of the pursuer. The rescued fugitive would there gaze upon a scene as fascinating as it was new. He would witness the devotions of the inmates in their never-pausing but never-wearying round. He would see the labours of the school-room, shared in by the children of the neighbouring nobles and the instructors of another generation. He would visit the library and the scriptorium, and observe the care with which each precious tome was treasured up and copied; and how music, architecture, painting, and caligraphy had their imitators and admirers. If there had been no monasteries we should have had no books, and we should have lost the Latin language, the noblest legacy that antiquity has bequeathed to us. And if we regard monasticism in its effects upon the outer world, we shall soon see how it softened and ennobled it. I pass by the humanizing influence of a life

[j] It is my intention to enter at greater length into this subject in the introduction to the lives of the Deans of York.

devoted to worship and literary pursuits, and turn to other points in which the monks advanced, if they did not originate, the cause of civilization. When they were not engaged in the services of the church or cloister they were generally busy with some manual employment. There was a saying among the Egyptian devotees that a labouring monk was only tempted by one devil, and in the English monasteries there were none to depreciate the usefulness of labour. The inmates were regularly trained to it, and even the bishops were obliged to be acquainted with some handicraft. And what they professed and practised themselves they taught to others. One of the reasons for the selection of the desert or the wild-wood as the site of the earliest retreats was undoubtedly the desire to bring the country into cultivation. The founder usually endowed the house with a portion of land sufficient to maintain a certain number of families. Upon it the monks were regularly employed. They tilled and sowed it with their own hands, reclaiming the moor from the heather, and clearing away the wood and water. They chased and killed the wolves, which were then abundant. They hunted and snared their own game, they caught their own fish. Before Wilfrid arrived in Sussex, the inhabitants were ignorant of the gentle art. They won their own hay, and reaped and ground their own corn. Agriculture was thus advanced and commerce followed in its wake. The progress of the early civilization of the North is coincident with the growth and influence of the monasteries. How many of these retreats there were in Northumbria prior to the Danish invasion it is scarcely possible to say. Mr. Hodgson Hinde makes out a list of twenty-one. The very site of some of them is forgotten. They were overthrown by the savage men whom they tried in vain to soften. The situations which the earliest houses of religion occupied are a sufficient index of the perils of the times. Many of them were on the banks of some stream on which the inmates could launch their little barges and escape from the invader, or in some pathless desert that no stranger could approach. Even in the days of Henry VIII. the royal commissioners were unable to discover the abbey of Blanchland, in the county of Durham, till they were recalled to the search which they had given up by the tones of the convent-bell which the monks were ringing, too prematurely, for joy at their escape! The sea was the defence of such wild and lonely retreats as Lindisfarne, Tynemouth, Hartlepool and Whitby. It was in a later age, when peace and law were at last paramount, that the ecclesiastical orders were able, in the sites and construction of their abodes, to blend together in one sweet union the beauty of nature and of art. Then it was that they deserted the sea-beaten cliff and the little strip of green turf among the moors for a fairer resting-place, the charmingly sequestered valleys and the wood-embosomed haughs which are washed by the Coquet and the Wharfe, the Swale and the Rie.

It is difficult to say at what time the earliest churches in the North of England were erected. Wilfrid, in his oration at the dedication of Ripon minster, speaks of the holy places which the British Christians had deserted, and that he succeeded in his attempts to recover some of them seems to be partly evident from the fact, that under the walls of one or two Saxon churches in the North Riding of Yorkshire, human remains, belonging to a very early period, have been disinterred. The church of Whithern in Galloway, a building of stone, is said to have been erected by Ninian in the sixth century. Alcuin, whilst speaking of king Edwin, tells us that he began the minster of York.

"Ecclesiasque suis fundavit in urbibus amplas."

The first temple between the Tees and Tweed was that at Lindisfarne, and to the energy of Aidan and his successors is due the erection of most of the early churches in Bernicia. Their dedications are very suggestive. Several of the houses of God in Cumberland and Westmerland shew the names of Irish and Scottish saints, which were brought into the country by their founders. Brancepeth, in the county of Durham, owes its name not to an idle legend, but to St. Brendan, to whom the church is dedicated. St. Columba presides over Warcop and Topcliffe. At Whitby, the ancient Streonshal, St. Ninian had once a shrine. The name of Patrington in Holderness is derived, not, as Mr. Kemble suggests, from the Patringas, but from the patron saint of Ireland who presides over the church; whilst the neighbouring shrine of Winestead, as well as the abbey of Selby, the creation of a later age, are dedicated to St. Patrick's friend, Germanus, the sainted bishop of Auxerre. All these names seem to point to a very early Christianizing of the country, in all probability by the Culdees. The churches themselves were of the rudest possible description. They were made of planks of wood, and were thatched with reeds or turf. Stone, if attainable, seems to have been very rarely used. The perils of the times were a bar to anything like expense or ornament. It is curious also to observe how many of the early churches are on the margin of some stream. One great reason for this propinquity was that which induced St. John to take up his abode upon the banks of the Jordan. When the word had been delivered and received, the preacher and his audience went into the water, and the convert was there admitted a member of that church to which he was eager to belong. As the population migrated or some enemy approached, the little church of wood could easily be deserted or removed, and the minister could retire to some monastery or fastness. His usual abode, in the earliest times, was within the walls of some convent, where he was under the eye of the superior, and subject to the control of the bishop, and he left it at their bidding to visit his flock in the wilderness, and to officiate in his little feld-kirk. In course of time, as peace and order became more firmly established, parochial arrangements began to be made, and the country was gradually divided into properly-endowed ecclesiastical districts. The present state of the church in several of the English colonies will throw some light upon their progress and formation. In New Zealand and Australia one clergyman has frequently a tract of land thirty or fifty miles in circumference under his charge. So it must have been in Saxon England. Those large parishes which are gradually disappearing from Lancashire and Yorkshire owe their size originally to a scanty population and a paucity of teachers.

In many other ways, also, did the Saxon primates of Northumbria endeavour to advance the spiritual welfare of their charge. The school, the teacher, and the church were not allowed to languish for want of encouragement and support. Proper endowments for them all were gradually made by the wealthy and devout, in addition to the regular contributions of the faithful. The aiding of the ministry, the maintenance of the fabric and services, and the feeding of the poor, were the objects for which these offerings were made. Over their appropriation and use the archbishop exercised a salutary supervision. Any defect in discipline or ritual was remedied by his own independent authority, or by the agency of a council. Synods also were occasionally convoked. The personal character of many of the archbishops added strength and potency to their official acts. They were men of piety and learning, of splendid tastes, and courtly influence. Their munificent gifts to the monasteries must have been copied and admired. The commons would gaze with wonder and yet pleasure upon the introduction of new arts and treasures, at the glazing, sculpture, painting, and embroidery which they saw before them. The train of masons and artizans by which Wilfrid was accompanied would surely have some good fruits. The Italian music that James and Benedict introduced was not forgotten. The sight of such temples as Hexham and Ripon, Beverley and York, could not fail to produce a marvellous effect and devotion: civilization and taste would necessarily be fostered by it. Each familiar shrine would evoke the memory of some once potent name. A holy influence seemed to linger around it still.

Beauty there was there, and between the creative and the sympathetic mind there is a strong bond of union. Great men long since gone down into silence, who had been reverenced by their contemporaries, would survive in the gratitude and for the weal of posterity. The aged and withered staff seemed to blossom and bear fruit again.

In spite of all this attention and activity on the part of the Northern primates, it is impossible to say that the church made any marked and efficient progress in Northumbria prior to the Conquest. Their labours were practically as fruitless as those of the Danaides. I can scarcely think that the cause of these shortcomings is to be ascribed to the listlessness or opposition of the people. There must have been among them many Pagan usages and traditions such as were reprobated in the time of Eanbald, but the presence of those relics of heathenism did not mar the progress of the church in other districts where they were equally rife. A thoughtful mind will detect several more probable reasons for the failure. One is, without doubt, the size of the district which the archbishops professed to moderate. Gregory's recommendation about the appointment of twelve suffragans had never been carried out, and the primate, therefore, had a diocese which the intellect and the energies of the strongest man were unable to direct. Good work indeed was begun, but there were none to foster and encourage it. Monasteries sprung up in which, as Beda says, worldliness and vice dressed themselves in the garb of religion. The archbishop, with his many avocations and his frequent presence at the court, was unable to check this. There were many parts of his diocese which he could rarely, if ever, visit. How could any newly-introduced faith advance when there was such a want of supervision and direction? This state of things would not be improved by the feud which was long maintained between the Culdees and their religious opponents. Wilfrid and his party carried the day, and introduced a stricter rule, but his subsequent misfortunes impeded its nurture and its growth. He pulled down the house of his enemies, but could erect little in its room. One system neutralized the other. Christianity, if it is to prosper, cannot long dwell in tabernacles in the wilderness. It must have fixed places, discipline, and rulers. All these were more or less wanting in Northumbria. The church, therefore, kept wavering to and fro like a storm-tossed ship. Practices crept in which Catholicity rejected, and there were none to check them. At the time of the Conquest the canons of Durham, with the example of St. Cuthbert before them, retained but one point of the Benedictine rule which they once observed. They sang the hours in a peculiar manner. At Hexham, Whalley, and Bedlington an hereditary sacerdotage obtained. Confession seems to have been much disregarded. Many of the clergy were married men, and several bishops followed their example. There was great need indeed of ecclesiastical reform. And even if the diocese of Northumbria had been smaller, and less subject to religious contentions, the troubled state of public affairs would have precluded or retarded improvement. What could Christianity do when chief was warring against chief, and race against race? It required a kindlier soil and more gentle airs. The troubles which Briton, Saxon, Dane, and Norman caused in Northumbria are matters of history. Can we wonder, then, that the light of religion was so feeble, and its influence so partial? Paulinus fled for his life from the spiritual province which he had begun to plough and sow so earnestly. Many years of Wulstan's life, fearless although he was, were spent in exile. The dangers which beset Eanbald robbed Northumbria of Alcuin. The Danish incursions checked the usefulness of Oswald. The troubles of Wilfrid and Aldred are too well known to be repeated. It is still more mournful to turn from the disasters which befell the pastors to the sufferings of their flocks, and the ravages of the fire and sword. The Danes destroyed almost every monastery in Northumbria. The wanderings of the monks of Lindisfarne are full of thrilling and romantic incidents. Their pilgrimage with the body of their saint has been described by historian and poet. A talisman it was dearer far than life itself which they bore along with them. The very existence of the Northern church depended upon their safety, and they knew it. A resting-place was long denied to them. They sought for it in vain beyond the seas. They sought for it in vain among the hills and green glades of Yorkshire, and it was very late in their day of trial that they found a sanctuary at last, the wood-embosomed crag which they have crowned with the grey towers of the English Sion. "A fair place" indeed it is, and memory's most binding charm attaches me to that "holy hill." May peace be within thy walls, oh my nursing mother! A wandering, but still loving child, bids thee prosper and be blessed.

The archbishop of the Northumbrians had in the earliest times the control of the whole of Northumbria, extending from the Mersey to the Clyde on the one side, and from the Humber to the Frith of Forth on the other. The power of the prelates kept pace with the growth or curtailing of the kingdom, although they occasionally asserted and maintained a still wider spiritual empire. These claims, as will be seen hereafter, were frequently the cause of much controversy and bitterness.

It was the wish of Gregory that England should be divided

into two large provinces; the Northern to be under the rule of an archbishop, who was to act as metropolitan over twelve suffragans. This arrangement was subsequently confirmed by Leo III., but for various reasons it was never carried into effect. The following sees were in existence in Northumbria, or were under the control of the Northern primate anterior to the Conquest.

LINDISFARNE. The seat of sixteen bishops, beginning with Aidan in 635, and ending with Eardulph. It was then transferred to Chester-le-Street. The first four bishops of Lindisfarne had the sole charge of Northumbria after the flight of Paulinus.

HEXHAM. This see was founded in 678, when the diocese of York was divided by Theodore. It had a succession of thirteen bishops, the last of whom was Tydfrith, who died in 821.

LINDSEY. Established by Theodore in 678. The seat of the episcopate was probably at Sidnacester or Stow, and Eadhead was the first and the last bishop. Lindsey, although a part of Mercia, was at that time under the rule of the Northumbrian monarch by right of conquest; it was soon recovered by the Mercians, and Eadhead retired to Ripon. The claim, however, to Lindsey was not surrendered. When the see of Lincoln was established soon after the Conquest, archbishop Thomas asserted that Lincoln, Stow, and a great part of Lindsey belonged to the province of York, and resisted the appointment and the acts of Remigius and his successor, Robert de Bloet, in the most determined way. The primate seems to have been in the right. The dispute was arranged, much against the will of Thomas, by pope Paschalis and William Rufus. Lindsey was to be henceforward a part of the diocese of Lincoln, and the see of York, in the place of it, was to have the abbey of Selby and the monastery of St. Oswald at Gloucester. The bishop of Lincoln became thenceforward a suffragan of Canterbury.

RIPON. Founded in 679 (?). Eadhead went there when he retired from Lindsey. He was the first and the last bishop.

GALLOWAY. A see established in 681, the district having been added to Northumbria by Ecgfrith. Trumwin was the first prelate, and he was called the bishop of the Picts. The seat of the episcopate was at Whithern or Candida Casa, where there was a succession of six bishops. Shortly before the year 800 Galloway came again into the possession of the Picts, and several centuries elapse before we hear again of Christianity at Whithern.

CHESTER-LE-STREET. The bishopric at Lindisfarne was removed to this place about 880, and continued here for nearly a century, when it was taken to Durham. There was a succession of nine bishops at Chester.

Durham. The series of bishops began here in 990, and is still going on. There has been much controversy and wrangling between the sees of Durham and York on the question of subjection. The bishops of Durham were men of too great influence and spirit to be suffragans to any one, but they ought undoubtedly to have paid ecclesiastical obedience to York. The contest was carried on for a long time with varying success, and even at the present day the power of York over Durham is not altogether admitted. The temporal power of the bishops of Durham was greater than that of the archbishops of York, and their appeals to the sovereign were frequently listened to, on that account, with the greater favour.

Glasgow. Magseu and John, bishops of this see, were consecrated by archbishop Kinsius shortly before the Conquest, and acknowledged themselves the suffragans of York. Their profession was disowned by their successors, nay, their very names are excluded from the fasti of the church of Glasgow by Scottish writers.

It will be seen that at no period anterior to the Conquest were there more than five prelates within Northumbria. On the arrival of the Normans the archbishop of York had only two suffragans, the bishops of Durham and Glasgow. In 1132, Henry I. established a bishopric at Carlisle, and subjected it to York. Cumberland, Westmerland, and Lancashire, with the adjacent islands, had been a part of Northumbria from the time of Ecgfrith in the seventh century, and were probably visited by the chorepiscopi, or the Scottish and Irish missionary bishops. The see of Sodor and Man was not formally subjected to York until the year 1458, although it had formed a portion of the old kingdom of Northumbria, and had on several occasions been connected with York. The see of Chester was founded by Henry VIII., and since that period only two bishoprics have been erected in the North. The suffragans of the archbishop of York at the present day are the bishops of Durham, Carlisle, Sodor and Man, Chester, Ripon, and Manchester.

With regard to the Scottish bishops and their subjection to York there has been much angry contention. It was undoubtedly designed in the first instance that the Scottish prelates should be suffragans of York, and before the Conquest such of them as were canonically appointed rendered their obedience to that see. The rest that we hear of were, probably, merely the chorepiscopi. After the arrival of the Normans there seems to have been for some time a desire for unity, and we find the bishops of St. Andrews, Glasgow, Whithern, Orkney, and the

Isles, recognizing the supremacy of the archbishop of York. A change, however, soon sprang up. The influence of the Culdees and the chorepiscopi, and their increasing dislike of the English, soon made the Scottish bishops break off their connection with an ecclesiastical head whom they never saw in their own country, and from whom their own national feelings more and more alienated them. They began to receive consecration at the hands of their brethren at home, and the bishops of St. Andrews began gradually to take the lead. At the commencement of the twelfth century pope Calixtus urged upon the Scottish king and his nobles the duty and the propriety of having their bishops properly consecrated by the metropolitan of York to whom they were subjected. In 1175 the question was again mooted at the council at Northampton, and the result of the debate was that the bishops and abbats of Scotland rendered their submission to the archbishop. The practice was soon given up, and in the reign of Edward I. pope Alexander took the Scottish bishops under his protection during the struggle with England. The wars which now ensued were an effectual bar to the claims of York, and in the fifteenth century the pope formally exempted the Scottish church from any obedience to an English metropolitan, and made the bishop of St. Andrews primate. The decree was vigorously resisted by the archbishop of York, but the pope told him that no enemy ought to be metropolitan of Scotland. In the following century it was the intention of archbishop Lee to have revived the claim, and to have submitted it to a general council, but the ecclesiastical troubles of the age were an effectual bar to any legislation. The church of Scotland is altogether exempt from any English jurisdiction, but that freedom has been the greatest curse which has befallen it.

The last point to be remarked upon is the relation that has existed between York and Canterbury, which has not always been of the most amicable kind. The original intention was that the two metropolitans should be entirely independent of each other. When one died the survivor was to consecrate his new brother, and until that event took place he was to consecrate all bishops, crown the sovereign were it necessary, and sing high mass before him on the three great festivals. It was intended that the Northern primate should have twelve suffragans under him, and the pall, which he was to receive from Rome, was to be the title-deed as it were of his authority. In position and power the two archbishops were to be exactly equal.

It was not so. For a century after the departure of Paulinus from the North no bishop of York either sought for or obtained the pall. Without this he could have no suffragans, and he was himself in point of fact under the authority of Canterbury. It was the absence of the pall from York that accounts for the successful interference of Theodore with Wilfrid. Egbert, however, at Beda's suggestion obtained that privilege which was continued to his successors. The position of the two primates was now equal, although the influence of York even then must have been less than that of Canterbury, on account of the few suffragans that it had, and the disasters that fell upon Northumbria. Soon after the Conquest Lanfranc made a successful attempt to subject York to Canterbury. He refused to consecrate Thomas of Bayeux unless he made his profession of obedience. Thomas, unfortunately, made his submission at the request of the king whose chaplain he was, but the controversy was immediately resumed. The result was unfavourable to York, as the Northern province was formally subjected to Canterbury at a great synod held in 1072. This decision, however, was as formally reversed by pope Honorius, fifty years afterwards, at the request of archbishop Thurstan, and the two metropolitans were henceforward independent of each other. Peace and amity were not so speedily restored. I shall mention, in their chronological order, the scenes and animosities which this want of friendly feeling occasionally produced.

These prefatory remarks are merely introductory to the biography with which I profess especially to deal; and many of the points which have been already briefly alluded to will occur again to my readers in their proper sequence and position.

THE ARCHBISHOPS.

THE ARCHBISHOPS OF YORK.

Paulinus was the first missionary from Rome that preached the Gospel in the Saxon kingdom of Northumbria. We are told that he was a Roman by birth,[a] and this statement is strongly corroborated by Beda's description of his personal appearance.[b] The words of the famous historian are thus rendered by a Christian poet:—

> "Who comes with functions apostolical?
> Mark him of shoulders curved and stature tall,
> Black hair and vivid eye and meagre cheek,
> His prominent feature like an eagle's beak,—
> A man whose stature does at once appal,
> And strike with reverence."

On the other hand, however, we have the assertion of the Pseudo-Nennius that it was not Paulinus who baptized king Edwin and the many converts in Bernicia and Deira, but Rum, the son of Urien, who was the well-known opponent of the Saxons in the North.[c] Can we identify him with Paulinus, and regard the latter name merely as the Latin title which the missionary assumed when his patronymic was discarded? If this were the case, Paulinus was a Briton. An able historical writer[d] observes that "the following sequence of events is far from improbable:—that on the death of Urien of Reged, and the expulsion of his family from the throne, his son Rum retired to Rome, and there entered into holy orders; that when Gregory was looking about for missionaries to send to Britain, he should gladly avail himself of the services of a British priest highly connected, more especially when we know how anxiously

[a] Alcuin de SS., etc., Ebor., apud Gale, i., 709.

[b] Beda, ii., 16: "Vir longæ staturæ, paululum incurvus, nigro capillo, facie macilenta, naso adunco pertenui, venerabilis simul et terribilis aspectu."

[c] Gale, i., 117. Lel. Coll., iii., 49, who says, "Run mapur Beghen., *i. e.*, Paulinus."

[d] Mr. Hodgson Hinde, in the first volume of the History of Northumberland, 77. It may be asked, Why should the son of a British chieftain go to Rome?

Augustine strove, though without success, to obtain the co-operation of the British clergy in the work of converting the Anglo-Saxons; lastly, that when the Kentish king had to select from the ecclesiastics about him a chaplain to accompany his daughter into Northumberland, he should make choice of a native of the district."

Paulinus left Italy in 601,[e] at the bidding of Gregory, whose disciple he is said to have been,[f] to labour in the harvest-field of England, where there was a great lack of reapers.[g] His companions were persons of repute, and the names of the members of the party make up, singularly enough, an hexameter line[h]—

Mellitus, Justus, Paulinus, Rufinianus.

They bore with them a missive to Augustine, in which Gregory announced his desire that York should be a metropolitan see,[i] with twelve suffragans. Little, perhaps, did Paulinus at that time think that his own shoulders would be decorated with the pall.

Many years elapsed before the intentions of the chief pontiff could be carried into effect, and during this period Paulinus was, probably, one of the coadjutors of Augustine and Justus in the evangelization of Kent. A wider field of duty was before him—the great Saxon province of Northumbria.

The monarch of Northumbria between 593 and 617 was Ethelfrith, the slaughterer of the monks of Bangor. He succeeded his father Ethelric on the throne, which properly belonged to Edwin, his wife's brother. The reign of Ethelfrith was a very prosperous one, and yet he was by no means free from care. As the brother-in-law, whom his father had wronged in his infancy, grew up to manhood, the "destrictus ensis" seemed to hang over Ethelfrith by a more slender thread, and his anxiety aroused the fears of Edwin, who, trembling for his life, fled at last to the court of Redwald, king of the East Angles, after he had sought for protection in other kingdoms and other hiding places. Thither, also, do the hate and fears of Ethelfrith pursue him. Bribes are freely offered for the fugitive, but without effect, and then comes the more potent threat of war, which induces the timid Redwald to pledge his word to

[e] Saxon Chron., 28. Asser, apud Gale, i., 143. Stubbs, col. 1687. Fl. Wigorn. (232) makes the date 626. Vita S. Gregorii, apud Mabillon, Acta SS. ord. S. B., sæc. i., 422. Vita S. Aug., apud Angl. Sacram., ii., 62.

[f] Ric. of Hexham, col. 285. Acta SS. mense Oct., ex Laur. Surio. The life of Paulinus in the Acta SS. is an uninteresting compilation.

[g] Beda, i., 29.

[h] Beda, i., 29. Hist. Mon. S. August. Cantuar., 96. Anglia Sacra, i., 1, 65. Baronii Annales, viii., 147.

[i] Beda, ut supra. Vita S. Augustini, apud Mabillon, Acta SS. ord. S. B., sæc. i., 515. Labbe, Concilia, v., col. 1558. Spelmanni Conc., 90.

the monarch of Northumbria that he would either put to death or surrender the unfortunate refugee. The news of this decision was brought to the unhappy Edwin by a friend, who promised to shew him a safer place of retreat, but he would not avail himself of his offer. Fortune had been so unkind to him that he cared not now whether she smiled or frowned. Redwald had welcomed him to his halls—why should he question his good faith by fleeing from them? He would stay where he was and await the end.[j]

It was night, and the homeless wanderer was seated on a stone bench before the royal palace, musing on his unhappy lot, and very sad at heart. Suddenly there stands before him in the gloom a wondrous visitor; his features were unknown, and his attire, like his face, was strange. Who could he be?

> "Frigidus horror
> Membra quatit, gelidusque coit formidine sanguis."

The stranger was the first to speak: "All men are now asleep; why art thou awake and sitting sorrowfully in this place?" Edwin gave a hasty answer, deprecating the intrusion upon his privacy; but the questioner heeded not the angry words, and told him that he knew well the cause of his anxiety. "But what," he said, "would be the reward of him who should banish all thy sorrow, and persuade Redwald neither to injure thee himself, nor to give thee up to thy foes?" "Any good that I could do him," was the reply; and the speaker again resumed, "What reward should be his were he to pledge his word that thou shouldest be restored to thy lost throne, and that thou shouldest become a greater monarch than England has yet seen?" "Anything that I could give and do for him to shew my gratitude," was Edwin's bolder and more grateful answer. "If all this is granted to thee," said the mysterious stranger, "and he who now speaks to thee has proved himself a true prophet, wilt thou listen to his words and his advice when he shews to thee a better rule of life than any of thy sires have known before thee?" "Yea, that I will, in all things," was the reply of Edwin; and then the stranger's hand was laid upon his head,—an act of authority not likely to be forgotten by the speaker or the promiser,[k]—and the striking words fell upon the exile's ear, "When this sign shall come again to thee, recollect then this hour and these words, and delay not to do as thou hast promised." The injunction was scarcely uttered

[j] The whole story is in Beda, ii., 12. Alcuin de SS. Ebor., apud Gale, i., 704, 5. Bromton, col. 781. Roger of Wendover, ed. Giles, i., 76. Mabillon, Ann. Ben., i., 332, 3.

[k] "Vatis signum," as Mabillon calls it. Cf. Æn., ix., 300. Juv. Sat., vi., 17. Ovid, Trist., v., 4, 45.

before the speaker had vanished like a spirit through the gloom, and Edwin, trembling and astonished, found himself alone in the friendly darkness.

Paulinus, in all probability, was the stranger who thus spoke and acted, and the whole scene is just such a one as an Italian monk would devise to influence an impressible mind. Redwald was at that time half a Christian, and the missionary would, perhaps, be flitting about the court in the hope of subjugating him entirely to the true faith. The event surpassed Edwin's most sanguine expectations. The friend who had counselled him to flee had acquainted the queen with his determination, and she, in pity for his sufferings, had moved her husband, who had probably been influenced by the mysterious stranger, to take up the exile's cause. Not only did Redwald protect the distressed fugitive, but he restored him to his lost inheritance, slaying the intruder Ethelfrith in a battle near the sluggish waters of the Idle.

Thus, in 617, Edwin became the monarch of Northumbria. The words of the mysterious stranger were accomplished, but no one asked him to fulfil his promise, and he thought, no doubt, that it was a spirit that he had seen. The end had not yet come. In 625, Edwin, still a pagan, wooed for his second consort Ethelburga, a daughter of Ethelbert, king of Kent, who had been converted by Augustine. Her brother, who was the king, rejected the proposals of the Northumbrian monarch with the scornful answer that a Christian virgin could not take to herself a pagan husband. This difficulty was soon met by Edwin. He not only promised to allow the lady, if she became his wife, to worship God with all her suite, but he professed his readiness to listen to the arguments of Christianity, and to adopt them, if they were deemed irresistible by men of prudence and discretion.[l]

The marriage takes place, and Paulinus accompanies the princess as her chaplain, having been consecrated bishop of the Northumbrians by archbishop Justus on the 21st of July, 625,[m] to preside over the mission. No one could go into the North with greater chances of success. He knew a token that would

[l] Beda, ii., 9. Stubbs, col. 1687. Mabillon, Ann. Ben., i., 332.

[m] Beda, ii., 9. Saxon Chron., 32. Flor. Wigorn., 232. Roger of Wendover, ed. Giles, i., 74. Chron. S. Crucis, apud Wharton, i., 153. Hist. Mon. S. Aug. Cantuar, 153. Rad. de Diceto, col. 437. Bromton, col. 740, 80. Stubbs, col. 1687. Mabillon, Ann. Ben., i., 332. Baronii Annales, viii., 268. In Gosceline's life of Augustine in the Anglia Sacra, ii., 66, 7, it appears that Augustine paid a visit to York after the massacre at Bangor! Two of his miracles are recorded. At the same time he is said to have baptized an extraordinary number of converts in the Swale! Cf. Smith's Beda for the explanation of this story.

soften the king's heart when everything else had failed, but that was a resource not to be lightly or incautiously made use of. The most potent argument was to be the last. In the meantime he could make but little progress. He gained no converts. All that he did was to preserve the queen's suite by his daily teachings and celebrations from the pagan superstitions of the country.[n]

Neither the arguments of the preacher nor the entreaties of the queen could induce Edwin to adopt the Christian faith. But Paulinus was patient and observant. He could read the king's feelings, and he saw that time alone could change them; when once converted, he knew that Edwin would act boldly and consistently, and the missionary, grieved and yet hopeful, was waiting for the event. It was precipitated by one or two remarkable circumstances. An unsuccessful attempt was made upon the king's life by a minion of a king of Wessex, and, on the same evening, Edwin's queen gave birth to a daughter. The king thanked his gods, but Paulinus poured forth his praises to his Creator, to whose agency he ascribed these two signal favours, with such fervour, that Edwin, struck by his earnestness, promised that if the God whom Paulinus worshipped would enable him to vanquish the king of Wessex, he would renounce his creed, and, as a pledge of his sincerity, he allowed his new-born daughter to be baptized. Eleven members of the royal household accompanied her to the font.[o]

The victory was Edwin's, but still the conqueror believed not. He talked about the new faith to Paulinus and his nobles, but he did nothing. A letter arrived from pope Boniface at this juncture, exhorting him to embrace the creed of his wife, but it was ineffectual.[p] Ethelburga spoke to no purpose. The words of Paulinus were listened to, but rejected. The king was dissatisfied with himself, for he had made a promise, and he had not kept it. The fear of giving offence deterred him from revealing what were the convictions of his mind. "He durst not entertain truth, a lawfull king, for feare to displease custome, a cruell tyrant."[q] He was moody and careworn, sitting by himself and musing over what was uppermost in his thoughts.[r] The crisis had at length come, and the preacher knew it. Well might he say with Ulysses,—

[n] Beda, ii., 12. Stubbs, col. 1687. Malmesbury, apud Savile, 9, a. Baronii Ann., viii., 269.

[o] Beda, ii., 9. Flor. Wigorn., 232. Chron. S. Crucis, apud Wharton, i., 153. Bromton, col. 781. Nennius, apud Gale, i., 114, 15. Roger of Wendover, i., 76, who says that thirty were baptized with the princess. Baronii Ann., viii., 275.

[p] Beda, ii., 10. Hist. Mon. S. Aug. Cant., 155, 162-3. Bromton, col. 781. Labbe, Concilia, v., col. 1659. Spelmanni Concilia, 135. Baronii Ann., viii., 269.

[q] Fuller's Church Hist., book ii., 72.

[r] Beda, ii., 12.

"ἦ μάλα νῶϊ
γνωσόμεθ' ἀλλήλων, καὶ λώϊον· ἔστι γὰρ ἡμῖν
σήμαθ', ἃ δὴ καὶ νῶϊ κεκρυμμένα ἴδμεν ἀπ' ἄλλων."

Alone the monarch was when Paulinus passed into his presence, and the well-known sign was again made; the hand was laid upon the head which it had touched twelve years before amid the darkness of the night. "Rememberest thou this?" said the missionary to the king: Edwin would have cast himself at his feet had he not been prevented; and then, at last, there sounded in his ears the tones of a voice no longer unfamiliar to him, "Behold, thine enemies have fallen in the battle; that is the Lord's gift to thee; behold, the kingdom that thou didst covet is thine, that hath the Lord given thee likewise; remember thy third promise, and welcome the faith and the rule of Him who hath done for thee such great things: an earthly throne He hath given to thee already, hearken to His will that I declare to thee, and thou shalt share with Him His kingdom in the heavens."[s]

There was no resisting an appeal like this. The king gave way, and told Paulinus that his wishes coincided with his duty, and that he should become a Christian. He desired, however, to confer with his council before he made any public announcement of his conversion. To this Paulinus would willingly assent, for the subject was not a new one to many members of that assembly. The bias of Edwin would now be known and would have its due weight. The opinions of the councillors were taken individually; and although the king cautiously spoke of the new faith as a "doctrina eatenus inaudita,"[t] the answers that were elicited, if they did not prove that the speakers believed in Christianity, still tended to shew that they had no confidence in their own creed. The speech of Coifi, the pagan high priest, was a very striking one. He said plainly, that in his own religion there was neither merit nor use. He, he observed, had served his gods more faithfully than others, and what had they done for him! Coifi took a very utilitarian view of religion in general, but it was the popular one, and the council assented to his wish to hear more of the new doctrine, and to adopt it if it were approved of.

Then it was that Paulinus had the opportunity for which he waited so many years. "Exspectate venis!" Right in front of him, perhaps, was the great idol-temple of Northumbria;[u] around

[s] Beda, ii., 12. Roger of Wendover, i., 77.

[t] Edwin would become acquainted with Christianity at the court of Redwald. Beda, ii., 13.

[u] Dr. Hook imagines that the Council was held at York, and describes the ride of Coifi to Godmundham,—the whole scene being a pleasing invention. Coifi did not mount the king's horse because

him were the great men of the province eager at length to hear the good tidings which they had so long rejected; there was the monarch, deaf no longer to his entreaties, but a listener and a believer. Well might Paulinus speak with eloquence and fervour, before an audience like that. There is no record of what he said, but he must have spoken with the dignity and the power of an apostle. The result was a most marvellous one.[v] Coifi was the first to renounce his idolatry, and wildly eager to atone for his past blindness, he vaulted, by permission, on the king's steed, and girding on his sword, rode, lance in hand, to desecrate the idols and the shrine that he had so long revered. When the people saw him on horseback and in arms, as no priest had ever been before him, they thought that he was mad. But soon, *more vulgi,* they were carried away by his impetuosity; they burst into the temple and its enclosures, profaning and destroying what they could. All this was done at Godmundham near Market Weighton, a place which in after years came into the possession of the church of York by the gift of the famous Ulphus.

This important event occurred, I believe, in the spring of 627, and upon Easter day (April 12) in this same year a most striking ceremony was witnessed at York.[w] This was the baptism of Edwin. A little church or chapel of wood was hastily constructed at the bidding of the king,[x] and dedicated to St. Peter, and in it did the monarch become a member of the true faith. Two of his children were baptized at the same time, together with Iffi the son of Osfrid, and many other persons of distinction and royal birth.[y] Around that little oratory, which he had so much reason to remember, the grateful monarch, at

there was any journey to make to the temple, but simply to shew his contempt for the pagan rule that a priest should only ride upon a mare!

"Templo, lucisque sacratis
Cornipedes arceantur equi."

[v] Beda, ii., 13. Hist. Mon. S. Aug. Cant., 163-4. Henry of Huntingdon, apud Savile, 187-9. Bromton, col. 782. Alcuin de SS. etc., Eccl. Ebor., apud Gale, i., 706.

[w] Chron. S. Crucis, apud Wharton, i., 153. Roger of Wendover, i., 77. Chron. Cantuar., col. 2230. Flor. Wigorn. places the baptism in 628.

[x] Saxon Chron., 33. Hist. Mon. S. Aug. Cant., 165. Anglia Sacra, i., 153, The altar at which Edwin was baptized was afterwards dedicated to St. Paul. Cf. Alcuin de SS. Eccl. Ebor., and Symeon, col. 113.

[y] The Ps. Nennius (Gale, i., 115) says that 12000 persons were baptized with Edwin in one day, and that for forty days Paulinus "non cessavit baptizans omne genus Ambronum, *i. e.* Ald.-Saxonum." Roger of Wendover, i., 78, goes farther, and says that soon after there was not one unbeliever left. Beda, ii., 14. Angl. Sacra, i., 153. Rad. de Diceto, col., 438. Bromton, col., 782. Stubbs, col., 1688. Lel. Coll., iv,, 69. Gaimar, l'estorie des Engles, apud Mon. Hist. Brit. 777, 9, says:

"Li reis Edwine estreit donc reis;
Si prist les Cristiene lois:
De Everwic ert: ico savon,
K'il estorat religion,
E un muster restorat,
E a Seint Pere la donat.
Icist reis fu del linage Elle,
Ki a Seint Pere fist sacelle.
Uns eveskes le baptizat,
Paulins out non, Deus mult l'amat."

the instigation of Paulinus, began to erect a church of stone which he never lived to complete.

"Euboricæ solidis suffulta columnis
Nobilis illa manet celso speciosa decore,
Qua statione sacra fuit ille lavatus in unda."[z]

It was in the form of a square with the shrine in the middle. However unsightly the latter may have been, we cannot but admire the feeling which prompted its preservation. Amid the temples and the gorgeous buildings on the Capitoline hill the Romans lovingly preserved the straw-thatched cottage of their founder; in the ancient church of York you could see the oratory of wood in which the sacred water had been poured for the first time upon a monarch of Northumbria.

A glorious field was now opened to Paulinus, and every one was ready to listen and assist. Edwin fixed the seat of his episcopate at York,[a] and, at the request of that monarch, pope Honorius rewarded the zeal of the good bishop by the welcome gift of a pallium.[b] The labours of the great missionary during his residence in the North must have been prodigious.[c] The kingdom of Edwin stretched from beyond Lincoln and Southwell far into the lowlands of Scotland, and the whole of this immense district seems to have been traversed by Paulinus. Tradition has preserved some traces of his footsteps. In Northumberland there is a Paulin's well, and Pallinsburn in the northern part of the same county is the burn or rivulet of Paulinus. There are still ancient crosses with which his name is connected at Dewsbury and Whalley, and there was another near Easingwold in the time of Edward I.[d] They were memorials, in all probability, of a visit of the archbishop whom the people of Bernicia and Deira had good cause to remember. He moved about with the court, for he was the royal chaplain, and wherever it halted there was work for him to do. Rarely has any missionary had so successful a career. There were no oratories or baptisteries when he begun his work,[e] and he needed them not; for wherever there was water he could baptize, and he could find a pulpit anywhere. At Adgebrin or Yeavering near the Cheviots he is said to have spent thirty-six days in catechizing the converts and baptizing them in the waters of

[z] Alcuin de SS. etc. Eccl. Ebor., apud Gale, i., 706. [a] Saxon Chron., 33. Angl. Sacra, i., 153.

[b] Saxon Chron., 34. Beda, ii., 16, 17. Hist. Mon. S. Aug. Cantuar., 170. Bromton, col. 783. Stubbs, col. 1688. Labbe Concilia, V., col. 1683. Spelmanni Conc., 138, 9. Baronii Ann., viii., 326. Mabillon, Ann. Ben., i., 336.

[c] "Per sex annos continuos verbum Dei in Northanimbrorum provincia predicabat." Symeonis Ep. de Arch. Ebor., col. 77.

[d] Archæol. Æliana, n. s., i., 154. Nichols' Collect. Topogr., i., 149-54. Walbran on the Saxon church of Ripon, 70. Whitaker's Whalley, 50. Loidis and Elmete, 299. [e] Beda, ii., 14.

the Glen.[f] In the province of Deira, where a great portion of his time was passed, he would generally be baptizing at Catterick or Tanfield (Donafield) in the Swale and Yore.[g] It was, doubtless, at the instigation of Paulinus, that Edwin prevailed upon Eorpwald, king of the East Angles, the son of his old protector Redwald, to become a Christian;[h] and hence it is that he is traditionally connected with the infant-university of Cambridge.[i] Hilda first heard of Christianity from Paulinus.[j] We hear, also, of the missionary in Lindsey and Nottinghamshire. In Lindsey[k] he was the earliest propagator of Christianity, and Blecca, the prefect or reeve of Lincoln, was his first convert: he erected a church, the predecessor of that glorious temple with which that "sovereign hill" is crowned, and in it, in 627, did he consecrate archbishop Honorius.[l] He is said to have founded the church of Southwell about the year 630,[m] and, nearly a century after this, Beda heard from a Lincolnshire abbat a description of the personal appearance of the great evangelist as it was given to him by one who had been baptized by him, with many others, in the presence of king Edwin, in the waters of the Trent.[n]

The support and countenance of Edwin must have been a great aid to Paulinus, but, unfortunately he did not long enjoy them. Cadwal, a British sovereign, aided by the fiery and savage Penda, broke into Northumbria and slew its king in a great battle at Haethfelth or Hatfield Chase in 633.[o] The loss of her protector was a sad blow to the Northern church. His bloodstained head was brought to York, and was interred in the porch or chapel of St. Gregory[p] within the minster that he was building.[q] His sufferings and his zeal have enshrined his name

[f] Beda, ii., 14. Bromton, col. 782; Stubbs, col. 1688.

[g] Beda, ii., 14. Archdeacon Churton (Hist. of Early English Church, 53) thinks that Donafield was near Doncaster. I agree with Mr. Hodgson Hinde in placing it at Tanfield on the Yore.

[h] Beda, ii., 15. Wm. Malmesbury, apud Savile, 14 *a*.

[i] Sprotti Chron., 271, ex Cantelupi Antiq. Univ. Cant. Fuller's Ch. Hist., bk. ii., 74.

[j] Beda, iv., 23.

[k] Beda, ii. 16. Saxon Chron., 34. Roger of Wendover, i., 78, Bromton, col. 782; Stubbs, col. 1688. Archdeacon Churton and Dr. Hook speak of Blecca being the founder of the church of Lincoln, but Beda's words may bear a different construction. Cf. Hist. Mon. S. Aug. Cant., 169, and Henr. Huntingdon, apud Savile, 188. Lel. Coll., iv., 69.

[l] Beda, ii., 16. Sax. Chron., 34. Roger of Wendover, i., 78. Anglia Sacra, i, 154. Hist. Mon. S. Aug. Cantuar., 170. Rad. de Diceto, col. 438, Bromton, col. 782. Stubbs, col. 1688.

[m] Dugdale's Monast., vi.. 1312.

[n] Beda, ii., 16, ed. Smith and Mon. Hist. Brit., 168. *n*. Lel. Coll., iv., 100.

[o] Beda, ii., 20. Bromton, col. 784; Stubbs, col. 1688. Harpsfeld, 89. Lyfe of Saynt Werburge, ed. Chetham Soc., 16.

[p] Beda, ii., 20. Bromton, ut supra. Roger of Wendover, i., 81.

[q] It was finished by king Oswald. Beda's description of this church is an interesting one (ii. 14). "Curavit majorem ipso in loco & augustiorem de lapide fabricare basilicam, in cujus medio ipsum quod prius fecerat, oratorium includeretur. Preparatis ergo fundamentis in gyro prioris oratorii per quadrum cœpit ædificare basilicam. Sed

in the calendar,[r] and few people are perhaps aware that the capital of Scotland is the burgh of Edwin, who shewed his taste by laying the foundations of a city amid the finest scenery in Europe.

After the death of Edwin it was unsafe for his widow to remain in Northumbria, and as Paulinus had been in her suite ever since she came into the North, it was clearly his duty now to take measures for her protection. He found a ship on which he placed the queen and her family, and with the assistance of Bassus, one of Edwin's warriors, the party reached the shores of Kent. Here there was a hearty welcome for them from archbishop Honorius and king Eadbald, the brother of Ethelburga.[s]

The fugitives carried away with them the treasures of king Edwin, and among them were a cross and chalice of gold which had been used at the celebrations on the altar. Beda tells us that they were preserved in his day in the church of Canterbury.[t] Paulinus also took with him his pall; and more than a century elapsed before York was again an archiepiscopal see.[u] One missionary there was who remained behind in the deserted kingdom at the bidding of his leader, and that was James the deacon, who had been the companion of Paulinus during his residence in the North. He resided for some time at Akebargh, James' town, near Catterick in Deira, and was very diligent in teaching and baptizing. But he was especially famous for his great skill in singing and his fondness for the Gregorian tones, which he taught as well as chanted. He is supposed to be buried in the churchyard of Hauxwell, and to be commemorated by an ancient cross.[v]

Such was the termination of the mission of Paulinus into Northumbria. A failure it undoubtedly was, but a failure for which the missionary cannot well be censured. The system that he pursued, or rather his want of system, has been severely criticized. Possibly in the outset he might appeal too strongly to the temporal advantages that would accompany Christianity;

priusquam altitudo parietis esset consummata, rex ipse impia nece occisus opus idem successori suo Oswaldo perficiendum reliquit." Alcuin (Gale, i., 707, 8) gives the following account of Oswald's church building.

"Extruit ecclesias donisque exornat opimis,
Vasa ministeriis præstans pretiosa sacratis
Argento gemmis aras vestivit et auro,
Serica parietibus tendens velamina sacris,
Auri blateolis pulcre distincta coronis,
Sanctaque suspendit varias per tecta lucernas."

[r] There is an account of St. Edwin, king and martyr, in Capgrave's Nova Legenda, 116—20.

[s] Beda, ii., 20. Saxon Chron., 35. Roger of Wendover, i., 81. Hist. Mon. S. Aug. Cantuar., 173. Angl. Sacra, i., 155. Higden, apud Gale, i., 207. Rad. de Diceto, col. 438. Bromton, col. 784. Stubbs, col. 1688. Baronii Annales, viii., 328. Mabillon, Ann. Ben., i., 360.

[t] Beda, ii., 20. Bromton, col. 784. Roger of Wendover, i., 81.

[u] Beda, ii., 20. Hist. Mon. S. Aug. Cant., 182. Higden, apud Gale, i., 207.

[v] Beda, ii., 16, 20; iii., 26; iv., 2. Bromton, col. 785. Arch. Æl., n. s., i., 185. Possibly the word Hawkswell is Jake's-well, just as Akebargh is Jake's-bargh. W. H. D. L.

but was it wrong to make use of an argument which was innocent in itself, and would have great weight with the people of the North? The power to discover this approach to their hearts, and to avail himself of it, tends to shew that Paulinus possessed discernment as well as tact. When royal favour at last smiled upon him, and a kingdom more than 300 miles in length became his field of labour, did he neglect his work? The evidence of history and the whisper of tradition still tell us that he was not "an unprofitable servant." It is idle to suppose that a man, with few fellow-labourers and an immense diocese filled with heathen, could in six years mature what we call "organization." That comes after the rougher work has been done. Before there is any arrangement there must be something to arrange. The word must be first heard and the listeners received into the fold, and then "organization" follows. Paulinus was no sluggard in preaching and baptizing. But when the network of a great religious system might have been advantageously woven, he was, unfortunately, removed. He was no recreant to his duty in following his widowed mistress. Had it not been for her he never would have reached Northumbria at all, and now he was bound to protect her by the most solemn obligations that loyalty and gratitude could suggest. But why did he not return, it may be asked, when Oswald became king? It must be remembered that it was some time before the influence of Oswald extended into Deira. Paulinus was becoming an old man, and would he be wise in returning to a district where security, perhaps, was not firmly re-established? He would be less able to work than before, and in addition to this, was not the necessity for his return removed to a great extent by the exertions of Aidan and the monks of Lindisfarne? We must remember, also, that James the deacon was still his deputy in Northumbria. Paulinus, however, was not idle after he left the North, and he never shrank from the hard path of duty. His position in the South was, indeed, a humbler one, but, as Fuller charmingly observes, "he minded not whether he went up or down hill, whilest he went on strait in his calling to glorifie God and edifie others; sensible of no disgrace, when degrading himself from a great archbishop to become a poor bishop. Such betray much pride and peevishness, who, outed of eminent places, will rather be nothing in the church, then anything lesse then what they have been before."[w]

The bishopric to which the quaint historian alludes was that of Rochester, which Paulinus accepted at the request of Honorius and Eadbald.[x] We know little, henceforward, of his mis-

[w] Fuller's Ch. Hist., book ii., 77. Cf. Wm. of Malmesbury, apud Savile, 132; and Harpsfeld, Hist. Angl., 67.

[x] Beda, ii., 20. Saxon Chron., 35.

sionary work. He was a great benefactor to the monastery of Glastonbury, rebuilding the church and covering it with lead, and we are told that he lived some time within the walls of that ancient house.[y] He died on the 10th of October, 644,[z] and was interred in the secretarium or chapter house of the church of St. Andrew at Rochester which king Ethelbert had built.[a] He was commemorated by the following epitaph.

"Siste gradum, clama, qui perlegis hoc epigramma,
Paulinum plora quem subtraxit brevis hora
Nobis per funus: de presulibus fuit unus,
Prudens, veredicus, constans et firmus amicus.
Anni sunt rati Domini super astra regentis
Quadraginta dati quatuor cum sex quoque centis."[b]

The name of Paulinus was placed in the calendar after his decease, and he became the great patron saint of Rochester.[c] Archbishop Lanfranc translated his remains, and deposited them in a silver shrine which he presented to the church, giving at the same time a cross to hang over the feretory.[d] Among the relics in the minster of York were a few of his bones and two teeth.[e] The monks of Durham wrote his name in golden letters in their Liber Vitæ.[f] He had never been a benefactor of theirs, for in Beda's day and long after it, there was "nulla cognitio Dunelmi,"[g] but they gratefully commended him to God as one of the earliest Christianizers of the North.

Roger of Wendover, i., 81. Hist. Mon. S. Aug. Cantuar., 173. Rad. de Diceto, col. 438. Stubbs, col. 1688. Reg. Roffense, 4. Dugd. Mon., i., 152. Weever's Funerall Mon[ts.] 310. Mabillon, Ann. Ben., i., 360. Gaimar, l'estorie des Engles, apud Mon. Hist. Brit., 779, says,

"Eadbald li reis bien les recuilli,
Mult honora Paulins e joi.
Quant arcevesque ne pot estre,
Evesque en fit a Roucestre."

[y] Wm. of Malmesbury, apud Gale, i., 300. Dugd. Mon., i., 3.

[z] Saxon Chron., 38. Flor. Wigorn., 237. Anglia Sacra, i., 154, 341. Asserii Ann., apud Gale, i., 144. Hist. S. August. Cant., 182. Roger of Wendover, i., 87, gives the date 646. Hermanni Contracti Chron., apud Canisii Lect. Ant., iii., 234. Baronii Ann., viii., 365. Mabillon Ann. Ben., i. 388.

[a] Angl. Sacra, i., 154. Lell. Coll., iv., 81. Reg. Roffense, 22.

[b] Weever's Funerall Mon[ts.] 310, 11; and Dugd. Mon., i., 152, from a metrical chron. Archiep. Ebor. inter MSS. Cotton. Chron. S. Aug. Cantuar., 182.

[c] Malmesbury, apud Savile, 132. Reg. Roffense, 33. Acta SS, sub. Oct. 10. Capgrave's Nova Legenda SS., 264-5.

[d] Reg. Roffense, 126.

[e] Fabric rolls of York minster, ed. Surtees Soc., 151.

[f] Publ. by Surtees Soc., p. 7.

[g] Flor. Wigorn., 368.

Ceadda, or Chadd, for I shall give him the name by which he is generally known, was one of those holy and apostolic men of whom the early church had so much reason to be proud. He was, probably, a native of Northumbria,[h] and was the youngest of four brothers,[i] Cedd, Cynibill and Cælin, all of whom were priests,[j] the first of them being the bishop of the East Saxons whom he converted to the Christian faith.

Chadd first became acquainted with the monastic life in Ireland.[k] He was, subsequently, an inmate of the monastery at Lindisfarne, and was one of the twelve pupils under the guidance and instruction of the venerable Aidan.[l] He was educated, therefore, in the tenets of the Scottish school which had been brought to that place from Iona.

About the middle of the seventh century, bishop Cedd, by the permission of Ethelward, king of Deira, founded the monastery of Lastingham near Kirkbymoorside, in accordance with the Scottish rule.[m] The remains of that little sanctuary may still be seen. They are standing on the slopes of a long hill that looks towards the North, and the heather creeps up towards its foot as if it were envious of the bright green turf that lies in the hollow below the church. Solitary is the village now, and solitary it must have been at all times. In that little shrine are resting the bones of the evangelizer of the East Saxons, and to the cell which once stood near it came the venerable Beda to learn from the brethren of the house how their two first abbats, Cedd and his brother Chadd, had lived and died.[n]

In the year 664 Cedd[o] went to his rest at Lastingham, having previously commended his infant monastery to the charge of his brother Chadd, who succeeded him as abbat.[p] Of Chadd's rule at Lastingham there is very little known. Beda tells us

[h] Beda, iii., 23, speaks of Cedd's custom "suam, id est Nordanhymbrorum, provinciam revisere," from which Dr. Smith infers, and reasonably enough, that it was his patria.

[i] Bollandists, Acta SS., March 2, where there is a short account of Chadd compiled principally from Beda. Cf. Lel. de Script. Brit., i., 78.

[j] Beda, iii., 23.

[k] Beda, iv., 4. Eddii vita S. Wilfr., apud Gale i., 58. Flor. Wigorn., 246. Higden, apud Gale, i., 186.

[l] Beda, iii., 28. Symeonis Hist. Eccl. Dunelm., 29. Bromton, col. 788. Mabillon, Ann. Ben., i., 557.

[m] Beda, iii., 23. Flor. Wigorn., 239.

[n] Beda, pref. to history. Cf. ibid., iii., 23.

[o] The names of the two brothers are frequently confused, especially by Hen. of Huntingdon and Bromton. Fuller (Ch. Hist., bk. ii., 83) quaintly observes "though it be pleasant for brethren to live together in unity; yet it is not fit by errour that they should be jumbled together in confusion."

[p] Beda, iii., 23. Flor. Wigorn., 244, Bromton (col. 789) says, that Cedd died "tempore mortalitatis," and probably, therefore, of the great plague, and Henry of Huntingdon (Savile 190 *a*) in addition to this makes the incorrect statement "cui successit in episcopatu frater ejus Ceadda." Dugd. Mon., i., 342.

how a party of thirty brethren became the inmates of that house, whilst he was there, out of love to their old master, Cedd, who had placed them in a monastery in his diocese. The period of their sojourn at Lastingham was but short, as the whole party, with the exception of a little boy, was cut off by a pestilence.[q]

The year 664 witnessed the great struggle between the Roman and the Scottish parties, and Chadd, doubtless, would be deeply interested in the controversy and its result. He would little think, however, that it would effect so great a change in his own life and fortunes. The decision of the royal president of the council of Streonshal gave such offence to bishop Colman and the Scottish monks, that that prelate, accompanied by a number of his adherents, retired from Northumbria. This was probably an unexpected triumph to the Roman party, which were strong enough, soon afterwards, to advance their leader, Wilfrid, to the northern primacy. Wilfrid refused to be consecrated by the British bishops, and on that account, by the permission of Alchfrid, the prince-regent of Deira, he went abroad to receive that rite in France. During his absence the Scottish party were not idle. They gained the ear of Oswy, the king of Northumbria. They could not forget the injury that Wilfrid had done to them at Streonshal, and the insult that he was now offering to the native prelacy by seeking consecration in France. They would endeavour to arouse suspicions in Oswy's mind against his son, Alchfrid, who was only his deputy in Deira. They commented severely upon the injury that Northumbria was sustaining by Wilfrid's prolonged and unaccountable absence.[r] Oswy, who, in all probability, had never expected that Colman would desert his see, was influenced by them. He prevailed upon the humble-minded Chadd to leave his cell at Lastingham and to become bishop of his province.[s] With great adroitness he placed the seat of Chadd's episcopate, not at Lindisfarne or Hexham, but at York. Thus there was no room for Wilfrid. Alchfrid could not introduce a second bishop into Deira, and with Bernicia he had nothing to do.[t]

Chadd was thus placed in a position for which, however alien to his disposition, his piety and humility peculiarly fitted him. His appointment would be regarded as a party triumph; for although Cedd, before he died, renounced the Scottish

[q] Beda, iii., 23.

[r] Eadmer, Vita Wilfridi, apud Acta SS. ord. S. B. sæc. tert., i., 203. Ric. of Hexham, col. 294. Fuller's Ch. Hist., bk. ii., 86. Wright (Biog. Lit., i., 173) says that Wilfrid was abroad for three years.

[s] Stubbs, col. 1689. Fridegodus, Vita S. Wilfr., apud Acta SS. ord. S. B. sæc. tert., i., 179.

[t] Beda, iii. 25, 27.

mode of observing Easter,[u] we are told that Chadd did not relinquish it.[v] At the request of Oswy, the bishop-elect went to seek for consecration at the hands of Deusdedit, but on his arrival in Kent he found that that prelate was in the tomb. What was to be done? Wina bishop of Winchester was at that time the only prelate in England who had been consecrated according to the Roman ritual, and to him Chadd went.[w] Wina called in to his assistance two of the British bishops who still adhered to their old method of observing Easter, and the ceremony took place. This was the first occasion on which British and Roman bishops were associated together. I cannot think that there would have been any union even at this period, if the Welsh bishops had not thought that by their assistance they were checking the dreaded and impetuous Wilfrid. In Chadd they knew that they had a brother, and their presence at his consecration was at the same time a tribute of respect to the simplicity of his character and the purity of his life.

Chadd was now bishop of York, and the spiritual ruler of Northumbria, and he was not unequal to the requirements of that high office. He had none of the restless energy and fiery zeal of Wilfrid, but he surpassed him in all those gentler virtues which should bud and blossom in the true Christian's heart. More congenial to his quiet and retiring disposition would have been the purple heaths and the silent woods of Lastingham, but his was a spirit capable of adapting itself to any position, busy or secluded, to which the path of duty guided it. Every ancient writer speaks of Chadd with reverence and affection. Gentle he was, and amiable, illustrating by his blameless life the holy rule that he taught others to abide by. The Scriptures were his constant study and his guide. In his management of his diocese, the lives of his old master Aidan and his brother Cedd were his exemplar. There was no place that he did not visit on his missionary journeys. If he passed through the gateway of the hall he did not despise the hovel of the serf,

[u] Beda, iii., 26. Flor. Wigorn., 242.

[v] Beda, iii., 28. Eddius, Vita S. Wilfr., apud Gale, i., 58. Mabillon, Ann. Ben., i., 478, says, that Oswy summoned Chadd out of Ireland, and Colgan, on that account I suppose, makes Chadd an Irish saint. Trithemius calls Chadd a Benedictine! (Acta, SS., Bollandists, Mar. 2).

[w] Asser (Gale i. 146) says that Chadd was consecrated in 654. The usual date is 664, and it is assigned by the following authorities, Beda, iii., 28; Saxon Chron., 48; Roger of Wendover, i., 98; Flor. Wigorn., 244; Henr. of Huntingdon, apud Savile, 191, *b*; Ric. of Hexham, col. 293; Bromton, ibid., 789; Gervase, col. 1636; Stubbs, ibid., 1689; Chron. S. Crucis, apud Angl. Sac., i., 155. Rad. de Diceto (col. 439) places the consecration in 665, and it must be remembered that Agilbert, by whom Wilfrid was made a bishop, was not promoted to the see of Paris until 665 (Mabillon, Ann. Ben., i., 478). Cf. Hist. Mon. S. Aug. Cantuar., 197; and Eadmer, Vita S. Wilfr., apud Acta SS. ord. S. B., sæc. tert., i., 203.

travelling always on foot from place to place like the holy men of old.[x]

It must have been very galling to Wilfrid on his return from France to find himself deprived of his expected see, and one of the Scottish party in his room. It was useless to make any opposition, and he shewed his discretion by remaining quiet in his monastery at Ripon, exercising his episcopal functions in the pastorless district of Kent, and elsewhere, whenever his services were required.[y] In 669 Theodore came to England as metropolitan, and was soon actively engaged in measures of reform. He paid especial attention to the episcopate, and he would soon come into contact with Chadd.[z] Chadd, it must be remembered, had no pall, he was only bishop of York; so that the rule laid down by Gregory about the independence of the two metropolitan sees was not now in force, and Theodore knew that well. Indeed, from the power that he seems to have exercised in the North I have actually found him invested with the title of archbishop of York,[a] an honour to which he had no claim. Chadd and Theodore, the Briton and the Greek, meet face to face, and the contrast is a striking one. Both were men of piety and goodness, but the respect of Theodore for Chadd would be lessened by the idea that he had taken possession of Wilfrid's see, and that he had been consecrated in an irregular manner.[b] He hesitated not to tell Chadd what he thought, and possibly, with some asperity. The reply that Chadd made, "humillima voce," was characteristic of the man. "If," said he, "I have not been consecrated in due form, I willingly resign my office; I never at any time deemed myself worthy of it, but at my monarch's bidding I accepted it, unworthy as I was, for it was my duty to obey him."[c] Any latent pique that there was against the speaker in Theodore's mind, must have been driven away by this reply. "The soft answer turneth away wrath." He answered, that he ought not to resign his see,[d] but Chadd's determination was made. Peace and quiet had been the object of his life, and he would seek them now. He voluntarily gave up his bishopric in favour of Wilfrid,[e] and returned with pleasure to his old home at Lastingham.[f]

It has been said that Chadd was removed from his see,[g] but

[x] Beda, iii., 28. Hist. Mon. S. Aug. Cantuar., 197. Gervase, col. 1637. Mabillon, Ann. Ben., i., 557.

[y] Beda, iv., 2. Eddius, apud Gale, i., 58. Bromton, col. 789.

[z] Beda, iv., 2. Eddius, 58, 59.

[a] Vita S. Cuthberti, apud X Scr., 67, 70.

[b] Beda, iv., 2. Eddius, apud Gale, i., 59.

[c] Beda, iv., 2. Rad. de Diceto, col. 439; Bromton, col. 789.

[d] Beda, iv., 2.

[e] Eddius, apud Gale, i., 59.

[f] Beda, iv., 3. Flor. Wigorn., 244. Eadmer, apud Acta SS. ord. S. B. sæc. tert., i., 205. Ric. of Hexham, col. 293; Stubbs, col. 1689. Anglia Sacra, i., 426.

[g] Some writers say that Theodore

the whole of Theodore's conduct towards him seems to contradict this assertion, and he had not the power to displace him without the consent of Oswy, even if he had had the wish. It would be equally unfair to charge Wilfrid with intrigue because he stepped into Chadd's place. It was only proper that he should succeed him. A man to whom a bishopric had been promised, and who, when he had lost it, had laboured patiently for three years in another and a humbler vineyard, deserved to be thus rewarded. The meekness of Chadd induced him to give way, and is he to be blamed for it?

This change took place in 669,[h] and Chadd returned to Lastingham. His days, however, were not to end in that secluded monastery. Jarumnan, the bishop of Mercia, died about this time, and Wulfhere, the king of the province, requested Theodore, to whom he was greatly attached, to fill up the vacant see. Theodore, unwilling to consecrate a new bishop, named Chadd,[i] whom he had never forgotten, to the king, and he with the assistance of Oswy and the archbishop induced the humble-minded recluse to accept the proffered honour.[j] It was then, in all probability, that yielding to the solicitations of Theodore, Chadd was re-ordained "per omnes gradus ecclesiasticos."[k] The propriety of the step may be questioned, but it shews how anxious Chadd was for peace and unity.

If the old traditions of the abbey of Peterbrough are true, there was a connection between Wulfhere and Chadd, or his brother Cedd, which easily accounts for Wulfhere's wish to make Chadd the bishop of the Mercians. The legend says that he was converted by him.[l] The king had two sons, Wulfade and Rufine. Wulfade was a mighty hunter, and was pursuing

removed Chadd, *i.e.*, Eddius, 59. Fridegodus, apud Acta SS. ord. S. B. sæc. tert., i., 180. Roger of Wendover, i., 99. Wm. of Malmesbury, apud Savile, 147, *b*; Ric. of Hexham, col. 293, and Anglia Sacra, i., 65. Eddius, however, in another place, says that Wilfrid's appointment was made with Chadd's *consent*. Cf. Mabillon, Ann. Ben., i., 495.

[h] Chadd is said to have been bishop of York for three years. Symeon de Arch. Ebor., col. 78. Stubbs, col. 1689. Rites of Durham, publ. by Surtees Soc., 43.

[i] Beda, iv., 3. Eddius, 59. Hen. of Huntingdon, apud Savile, 191, *b*. Bromton, col. 789-90. Eddius says that Wulfhere promoted Chadd to Lichfield at the request of Wilfrid. Malmesbury (Savile, 148, *b*) says that Wilfrid aided Chadd to Lichfield, "suffragio suo," alluding probably to some council.

[j] Beda, iv., 3. Eddius, 59. Eadmer, ut supra, 205. Bromton, col. 789-90. Gervasius, col. 1638. Lyfe of Saynt Werburge, 21.

"To graunt them a bysshop of holy lyvynge,
To governe the people by spyrytuall techynge,
To shewe to his subjectes the ensample of vertu,
And to preche and teche the fayth of Chryst Jhesu."

[k] Chadd's re-ordination, or perhaps, the completion of his previous consecration, is alluded to in Beda, iv., 2. Eddius, apud Gale, i., 59. Flor. Wigorn., 245. Gervase, col. 1638.

[l] Appendix to Smith's Beda, 745. Gunton's Church of Peterbro', 104, etc. Lel. Coll., i., 1, 2. Fuller's Ch. Hist., book ii., 84. Gunton (2, 3) says that Wulfhere was converted by Finan. Lyfe of Saynt Werburge, 40-6. I say nothing of the story of Chadd hanging his garment on a sunbeam!

a stag one day when it led him past the cell in which Chadd was living the life of a hermit. The story is a beautiful one, and it was told in nine of the old windows in the west cloister at Peterbrough.[m]

"The hart brought Wulfade to a well
That was besyde Seynt Chaddy's cell.

"Wulfade askyd of Seynt Chad,
Where is the hart that me hath lad?

"The hart that hither thee hath brought
Is sent by Christ that thee hath bought.

"Wulfade prayd Chad that ghostly leech
The faith of Christ him for to teach.

"Seynt Chad teacheth Wulfade the feyth
And words of baptism over him seyth.

"Seynt Chad devoutly to mass him dight,
And hoseled Wulfade Christy's knight."

Wulfade induces his brother Rufine to be baptized, and the end is that the brothers were surprised by their father in Chadd's cell and were killed by him. Remorse, however, followed, and the penitent sire adopted the faith of his murdered children, at the instance of Ermenilda his queen.

"Wulfere contrite hyed him to Chad
As Ermenyld him counselled had.

"Chad bade Wulfere for his sin
Abbeys to build his realm within.

"Wulfere endued with high devotion
The abbey of Brough with great possession."

I mention this story merely as a legend, but it is too picturesque to be discarded. It is quite possible that there are in it some shadows of the truth. It is not known at what period of his life Wulfhere became a Christian. Chadd may, perhaps, have lived a solitary life in Mercia, and may have converted its monarch. At all events, when he became bishop at Lichfield, he had a fast friend in Wulfhere, who gave him a piece of ground, large enough to maintain fifty families, on which he was to erect a monastery at a place called Ad Barue.[n]

The seat of the bishopric of Mercia was at Lichfield, and Chadd had an immense diocese extending over a great portion of

[m] Destroyed in 1603. Cf. Gunton, 337-8.

[n] Beda, iv., 3. Flor. Wigorn., 246. Bromton, apud X., Scr. col. 790. Mabillon Ann. Ben., i., 557. Dr. Smith, the learned editor of Beda, thinks that Ad Barue may be Barton on Humber. It is, rather, Barrow.

the Midland counties.[o] He ruled over it for two years and a half,[p] and illuminated it with those virtues which distinguished him in the North.[q] His good deeds and his holy life are not yet forgotten. His journeyings in his diocese were all made on foot, and it was with difficulty that archbishop Theodore, who was struck by his simple piety, prevailed upon him to ride, and helped him to mount his horse with his own hands.[r] He might well be proud of such a suffragan as Chadd.

The story of Chadd's end is given by Beda[s] with all that power of description for which he is so remarkable. He lived, the historian tells us, near his church at Lichfield, and there were with him seven brethren, with whom, when their labours were over, he would read and pray. In addition to these seven there was a monk of the name of Ouini.[t] He had been in old days one of the suite of the queen in the court of East Anglia, and having given up all for God when his fortunes were at their height, had gone in the dress of a humble labourer to live with Chadd at Lastingham. Thenceforward there was between him and his master a bond of union that was knit together by common feeling and mutual regard. One day at the end of February, whilst the brethren were at their devotions in the church, and Chadd was in his cell at prayer, Ouini was away from them. Suddenly he heard the sweet voices of a celestial choir "descending as from heaven," and singing as they came. Jubilee there was there, and not a note of sadness. His eye could discern nothing whilst his ear was drinking in the melody. The band seemed to hover around the little oratory in which Chadd was praying; it entered in, and, after a while, pouring forth a still more glorious burst of music, it passed away as it came, and the strain

> "Then seemed to go right up to heaven and die among the stars."

As Ouini was musing anxiously on what he had heard, the window of the little cell was opened, and his master summoned him with his accustomed signal. "Haste," he said, "to the church, and call to me my seven brethren, and come with them

[o] The title given to him was, "Merciorum et Lindisfarorum episcopus;" Lindisfarorum referring to Lindsey. Beda, iv., 3. Flor. Wigorn., 246. Gervase, col. 1638.

[p] Beda, iv., 3. Anglia Sacra, i., 425-6. Stubbs, col. 1690.

[q] Beda, iv., 3.

[r] Beda, iv., 3. Gervase, col. 1638.

[s] Beda, iv., 3. Beda's affection and veneration for Chadd's memory seem to have been very great. He records several traits in the life of the saint which are omitted here.

[t] In Ely cathedral is a portion of a cross which was found in the adjacent village of Hadenham, bearing the following inscription, "+. Lucem tuam Ovino da, Deus, et requiem. Amen." It is supposed that this was the friend of Chadd. Ouini was commemorated in the Benedictine Martyrology on March 11. Cf. Bentham's Ely, 50, 51.

thyself." And when they came, he bade them live together in love and holiness, and told them that he should soon leave them. "The sweet stranger that has visited our brethren has come to me to-day, and I have had my summons. Go, bid the brethren in the church commend me to the Lord, and let them never forget that they must die themselves." Hallowed by his blessing and sad at heart they went upon their errand, but Ouini returned, and prostrating himself at his master's feet, begged of him imploringly, "Tell me, father, tell me, if I may ask, what melody that was which I heard." "Heardest thou that?" said Chadd to him. "I charge thee in the Lord's name to speak of that to no one before I die. Thou didst hear the voices of the angels bidding me to those joys of heaven that I have loved and longed for always. In seven days they shall be mine, for they shall then come for me."

> "So now I think my time is near. I trust it is. I know
> The blessed music went that way my soul will have to go."

Seven days after this prophetic announcement, on the 2nd of March, 672,[u] he was taken to his rest; and was it a wonder, says Beda, "si diem mortis, vel potius diem Domini lætus aspexit, quem semper usque dum veniret, sollicitus curavit."[v] A life like his, hallowed by the practice of every virtue, humble, prayerful, and self-denying, had generated that perfect love of God by which fear is driven out.

> "With as much zeal, devotion, pietie,
> He always liv'd, as other saints do die."

And when his summons came, as Eddius beautifully observes, "tempore opportuno in viam patrum exegit, expectans diem Domini in judicio venturo, ut credidimus sibi mitissimum, sicut dignum est."[w]

They buried him at Lichfield, near the church of St. Mary,[x] by the waterside;[y] and when a fairer temple, dedicated to St. Peter, was erected, they enshrined his remains within it in a feretory of wood. Miraculous powers are said to have belonged to them even in Beda's days,[z] and in after ages the renown of Lichfield and its wonder-working shrine was very widely spread.[a] A place was found for Chadd in the calendar, and his day is the 2nd of March.[b] In the Sarum and Aberdeen breviaries there was an office appropriated to him,[c] and his life was

[u] Beda, iv., 3. Flor. Wigorn., 246. Peterbro' Chron., 2.

[v] Beda, iv., 3.

[w] Eddius, apud Gale, i., 59.

[x] Beda, iv., 3.

[y] Hickesii Dissert. Ep., 118. Lel. Coll., iv., 80.

[z] Beda, iv., 3.

[a] Hen. Huntingdon, apud Savile, 191, b. Bromton, col. 790.

[b] Acta SS., Bollandists, Mar. 2, where there is a short life of Chadd compiled principally from Beda.

[c] Acta SS.

inserted in the *Nova Legenda*.[d] Proud of his having been brought up at Lindisfarne, the monks of Durham inscribed his name in golden letters in the *Liber Vitæ* of their church;[e] and in one of the windows in the Galilee of their cathedral was Chadd's portraiture "in fyne coulored glass, as he was accustomed to say masse, with his myter on his head, and his crosier staffe in his lefte hand exquisitelie shewed."[f] At Lichfield a text or evangelistarium, said to have been Chadd's, is still preserved.[g]

Wilfrid, a very great name in the ecclesiastical annals of the North of England. He was, I believe, a native of Northumbria, and his parents are said to have been persons of some consequence and position.[h] I pass by the marvels that are said to have attended his birth, which occurred, according to Eadmer, in 634, but probably, a little earlier. When he was thirteen years of age he was precocious enough to wish to desert his home, and to devote himself to God's service. The mainspring of this desire was probably the harshness of his step-mother, who was not slow to encourage him in his design. She gave him and his companions everything with which boys would be delighted, arms, horses, and brave attire, all that would set off a comely youth, and produce a favourable impression at the court, for thither would each aspirant after a name bend his steps. Eanfleda was then the queen of Northumbria, and to her notice was Wilfrid introduced. He soon won her favour, for even at that early period of his life Wilfrid seems to have been a courtier. Cudda, an aged and faithful member of the royal household, retired to Lindisfarne to spend the remainder of his days, and with him the youth was sent. In that secluded monastery the boy became a favourite

"Incensæ pietatis ardor
Prodidit sese, micuitque primo
Flore juventæ."

He was a zealous and an attentive student. He committed to memory the whole of the Psalms according to Jerome's ver-

[d] Capgrave, 58, 59.

[e] Publ. by Surtees Society, p. 7.

[f] The Rites of Durham, publ. by Surtees Society, p. 43.

[g] Nichol's Literary Anecdotes, i., 86. Among the MSS. of Fr. Junius in the Bodleian library, 5136, is a Saxon Homily, "In natale S. Ceaddæ Episc." (Smith's Cat.)

[h] Eddii Vita S. Wilfr., apud Gale, i., 44. Wm. of Malmesbury, apud Savile, 147, *b*. Eadmer, Vita S. Wilfr., apud Acta ord. S. B., iii., sæc. i., 198.

sion, together with several other books, and he won the hearts of all by his docility and gentleness.[i]

Years passed away, and Wilfrid was still at Lindisfarne, but a commanding spirit such as he possessed could not brook the idea of a life-long exclusion in that solitary island. Ambition was a stranger to those simple hearts that beat around him, but Wilfrid was longing to see more of that world which the holy brotherhood had renounced. He had mastered himself, and now he would fain master others. Far away across the angry seas that surrounded him, and beneath softer skies, there was a city of which he would often hear, and a mind like his would never be wearied with the recital of its present and departed glories.

> "The city, that by temperance, fortitude,
> And love of glory, towered above the clouds,
> Then fell—but, falling, kept the highest seat,
> And in her loneliness, her pomp of woe,
> Still o'er the mind maintains, from age to age,
> Her empire undiminished."

Everywhere the young scholar would hear with rapture of the light that had radiated in all ages from the eternal city. Oh! that he could, visit the limina Apostolorum, and behold the hallowed shrines of which such great things were spoken! To Rome, therefore, he resolved, if possible, to go.[j]

His royal patroness, Eanfleda, encouraged him in his design, glad, perhaps, to rescue her favourite from the hands of the Scottish monks. She sent him to her kinsman, Erconbert, king of Kent, who gave the youth a kindly welcome, and recommended him to tarry at his court till he could find companions for his journey. During his stay in Kent he neutralized the effect of what he had been taught at Lindisfarne by learning the Psalms after the fifth edition of the Roman use. Wearied at length with the delay, he set sail from England in 652. He went with a single companion, Benedict Baducing, who is better known by the name of Benedict Biscop.[k]

Lyons was the first place at which the pilgrims halted. A prelate of the name of Dalfinus[l] is said to have occupied at that time the chair of Irenæus, and in him Wilfrid found a most sincere friend. Dalfinus did all he could to induce his guest to

[i] My authorities for this paragraph are Eddius, ut supra, and Wm. of Malmesbury, Stubbs, col. 1690, Eadmer, ut supra, 198; and Fridegodus, Vita S. Wilfr., apud Acta SS. ord. S. B., iii., sæc., i., 172.

[j] Eddius, 41. Beda, v., 19. Eadmer, 198. Fridegodus, 172. William of Malmesbury, apud Savile, 148.

[k] Beda, v., 19. Eddius, 44-5. Fridegodus, 173, who says that he was in Kent "triquadro anno." Eadmer, 199. Stubbs, 1690, Malmesbury, 148.

[l] Mabillon observes that no such prelate as Dalfinus occurs in the Fasti of Lyons, and he conjectures, probably enough, that the bishop here mentioned was Annemundus. Dalfinus' comes was the brother of Annemundus, and hence the error. Act. Ben. i., 443.

remain with him; he offered to adopt him as his son—to marry him to his niece[m]—to make him governor over a part of Gaul—but it was all in vain. Wilfrid's face was set towards Rome; and to Rome, after a long but necessary delay, did he make his way.[n]

We can well imagine the enthusiasm with which the pilgrims would gaze upon the eternal city. An ardent mind, such as Wilfrid possessed, might indeed think with the poet,

"I am in Rome! Oft as the morning ray
Visits these eyes, waking at once I cry,
Whence this excess of joy? What has befallen me?
And from within a thrilling voice replies,
Thou art in Rome! A thousand busy thoughts
Rush on my mind, a thousand images;
And I spring up as girt to run a race."

The piety and earnestness of Wilfrid soon attracted the attention of an archdeacon, of the name of Boniface, who found in the youthful Saxon a ready and intelligent scholar. He taught him the rules and customs of the Roman ritual, and shewed him the correct mode of observing Easter.[o] He explained thoroughly to him the four gospels, and, pleased with his pupil, he introduced him to the pope, who laid his hand upon the young scholar's head and blessed him.[p] Wilfrid's attachment to the Scottish system would be on the wane when he left Rome for Lyons, and on his arrival in that city he received the tonsure, after the Roman fashion, from Dalfinus, who completed the conversion which Boniface had begun.[q] Wilfrid remained with the good prelate for three years,[r] and would in all probability have been his heir, had not his patron lost his life in a persecution raised by Baldhild, the widow of Clovis II.[s] The church of Lyons may well glory in its martyrs. Dalfinus was added to the noble list, and Wilfrid was all but suffering with him. "Who is that fair youth that is making himself ready for death?" was the question of the murderers. "A Saxon from Britain," was the reply, and then came the unexpected rejoinder, "Let him go, and touch him not."[t] There was still a great work for the youthful confessor to perform!

In 658, after an absence of five years, Wilfrid returned to

[m] A son of Wilfrid is mentioned by Eddius and Frithegode, but he was only an adopted child (61, 85.)

[n] Beda, v., 19. Eddius, 45. Eadmer, 199. Fridegodus, 173. Malmesbury, 148.

[o] Beda, v., 19. Eddius, 45. Eadmer, 200. Stubbs, col. 1690. Malmesbury, 148.

[p] Eddius, 45-6. Fridegodus, 174. Eadmer, 200. Malmesbury, 148.

[q] Beda, iii., 25. Eddius, 46.

[r] Eddius, 46. Stubbs, col. 1690.

[s] There is a difficulty here, as Bathildis was a good Christian; other MSS. read Brunichildis. Cf. Mabillon, Ann. Ben. i., 443.

[t] Beda, v., 19. Eddius, 46. Eadmer, 200. Fridegodus, 175.

England. Great changes had taken place whilst he was abroad. In Northumbria Alcfrid was now, under his father Oswy, the ruler of Deira. His friend, Coenwal, king of the West Saxons, had persuaded him to adopt the views of the Roman party,[u] and it was with no little joy, therefore, that Alcfrid heard of the return of Wilfrid. What an opportunity for the dissemination of the opinions which he had adopted! He begged Wilfrid to come to him, and the missionary was ready enough to obey. Alcfrid did everything to induce him to reside permanently within his kingdom. He became, as it were, his scholar.[v] He gave him lands in East Stanford,[w] and, soon after, the monastery of Ripon. Over this house Wilfrid was abbat, and introduced within its walls the Benedictine rule,[x] the Scottish monks retiring at the accession of their new superior, rather than give up their views.[y] Wilfrid directed the establishment for at least five years, at the close of which period he was ordained a priest by Agilbert the French bishop of the West Saxons, at the request of Alcfrid, in the monastery of Ripon.[z]

This event seems to have occurred in 664, a year in which great changes took place in the Northumbrian church. The painful contrast between the Scottish and the Roman party was becoming every day more discernible, especially in the observance of Easter. In the Northumbrian court there was, on this point, a most annoying discord. King Oswy, who had been brought up and baptized by the Scottish monks, whose language he also spoke, observed their method of keeping the great festival, but Eanfleda his queen, with her suite and Romanus her chaplain, followed the Roman rule. Thus, in point of fact, the festival might be celebrated twice in the same year in the same court, and whilst the one party was full of joy at the arrival of the anniversary of the resurrection, the other might be still observing the fasting and the humiliation of the solemn period that preceded it. Something clearly ought to be done to remedy the scandal and the discrepancy. The Italian party was gaining strength, and resolved to suppress the evil against which it contended. It had among its supporters the queen and Alcfrid, the regent of Deira, who was under the influence of Wilfrid. Agilbert was ready to give his assistance, for he had been dis-

[u] Eddius, 46.

[v] Beda, iii., 25. Eddius, 46. Eadmer and Fr., ut supra, Roger of Wendover, i., 96.

[w] Beda, v., 19, who gives the date 661. Eddius, 47. Wright, Biog. Lit., i., 170. Dr. Haigh thinks that the place is Stamford, co. Lincoln. Cf. Arch. Æl. *n. s.*, i., 161.

[x] Beda, iii., 28; iv., 11. Hist. Mon. S. Aug. Cant., 198-9. Preface to Fridegode's life of Wilfrid, apud Acta SS. ord. S. B., iii. sæc., i., 170.

[y] Beda, iii., 25. Gervasius, apud X Scr., col. 1636. Roger of Wendover, i., 96, gives a rather different account.

[z] Beda, iii., 25. Eadmer, 201. Fridegodus, 176. Wendover, i., 97. Stubbs, col. 1690.

placed for a while from his see by a Scottish bishop. King Oswy is induced to summon together a council at Streonshal to settle, if possible, the points in dispute, and to come to some unity in practice.

On the one side was Colman the Northumbrian bishop, with his Scottish clergy, the abbess Hilda and bishop Cedd; on the other, were Agilbert and his priest Agatho, Wilfrid, James the deacon, the fellow-worker of Paulinus, and Romanus. Cedd acted as interpreter between the two parties, as they spoke different languages.

The arguments made use of and their result are so well known that it is unnecessary to repeat them here. Colman grounded the practice of his party in keeping Easter, on the authority of St. John the Divine and Columba. Wilfrid, the spokesman of the other side, claimed the countenance of St. Peter. Peter, as Wilfrid asserted, was the rock upon which Christ had built his church, and to him had been given the keys of heaven. The argument was a fallacious one, but Oswy was unable or unwilling to see its defects. "Is it true," he said to Colman, "that our Lord said that to Peter?" Colman could but assent: and then the monarch resumed, "Can you shew that any such authority was given to Columba?" He could not say that. "Do you then both agree that Peter received the keys from our Lord?" They assented. "If it be so," said Oswy, "I cannot gainsay the power of him that keeps the keys, 'for fear (as he said) lest coming to heaven-gate, St. Peter should deny him a cast of his office, and refuse to let him into happiness.'"[a] The reply, seemingly given half in earnest half in jest, pleased the bystanders, and Colman, to his great disappointment, found himself the loser, it having been arranged at the commencement of the sitting, that the defeated party should alter its practice. The tone of levity which the king had assumed would be more galling, perhaps, to Colman than the adverse decision, and he took a step which in more sober moments he would, probably, regret. He practically contemned the decision of the monarch by which he had promised to abide, and, deserting his diocese, retired eventually with his monks to Ireland.[b]

Wilfrid's victory was thus complete; indeed, it would be far greater than either he or Alcfrid could have possibly anticipated. The field was now their own. A person of the name of Tuda was appointed to succeed Colman, but he occupied the

[a] Fuller's Church History, book ii., 85.

[b] An account of the whole conference is given in Beda, iii., 25. Eddius, 56. Eadmer, 201, 2. Fridegodus, 176, 7. Flor. Wigorn., 242. Spelmanni Conc., 145, etc. Stubbs, 1690. Wendover, i., 97, 8.

see for a very short time, and his death caused another vacancy. These changes were dangerous, and the Roman party would feel the necessity of vigorous and instantaneous action. They must have a bishop who would press forward their views with promptitude and energy. Wilfrid had won for them the victory at Streonshal; who was more worthy to be the new bishop? It was Wilfrid that they chose.[c] Eddius tells us that he was unwilling to accept the office; but his scruples, which are perhaps magnified, were overcome. He objected, however, to be consecrated by any of the native bishops, whom he regarded as schismatics; and he requested permission to receive that rite in France. The royal assent was obtained, and Alcfrid sent his favourite across the seas to his old friend Agilbert, who was then at Paris.[d] Wilfrid was consecrated at Compiegne. There was at the ceremony all that pomp and show of which he was so fond. Twelve bishops were present on that occasion, and they carried their new brother, with hymns and joyous music, in a golden chair.

These things were done in 665,[e] when Wilfrid was about thirty years of age. Everything that he had hitherto taken in hand had prospered. His most ardent aspirations were being realized. His party was victorious, and he was at its head. If strength of intellect and strength of hand could stamp the Benedictine rule on England, he was the man to do it. Little, however, did he think, when he set sail for England, that the cloud was even then gathering over his head which was to darken the remainder of his life.

His disasters began as soon as he left France. He was caught by a tempest in the Channel, and was dashed upon the coast of Sussex. The savage wreckers rushed to the stranded vessel. A struggle took place in which the priest of the pagan plunderers was slain. Exasperated at this, they assailed the voyagers, who, after four contests in which they sustained some loss, made good their retreat to the ship, which was set afloat by the returning tide. A fair wind carried them, at length, into the port of Sandwich.[f] After he had landed, Wilfrid would soon learn that he had suffered a worse shipwreck than that from which he had just escaped. The see of York was lost to

[c] Eddius, 56. Fridegodus, 178. Ric. of Hexham, col. 293.

[d] Beda, iii., 27; v., 19. Eddius, 57. Eadmer, 202-3. Fridegodus, 178. Wendover, i., 98. Flor. Wigorn., 243. Ric. Hexham, col. 293. Rad. Diceto, col. 439. Bromton, col. 789. Gervase, col. 1636. Stubbs, col. 1690. Hen. Huntingdon, apud Savile, 191, *a. b.* Hist. Mon. S. Aug. Cantuar., 193.

[e] Asser (Gale i., 146) makes the date 654, a manifest error. The Saxon Chron. (48) places it in 664. Rad. de Diceto (439) in 665, and the event could not have occurred earlier, as Agilbert became bishop of Paris in that year. Cf. Mabillon, Ann. Ben., i., 478. The Peterbro' Chron. (2) puts it in 664.

[f] Eddius, 58. Eadmer, 203. Fridegodus, 178-9.

him. His long absence[g] had aroused the Scottish party, and it had gained the ear of Oswy. Alcfrid was either dead[h] or unable to assist his old favourite; the Culdees were again paramount, and the holy Chadd was now the bishop of Northumbria.

Wilfrid must have been deeply mortified when he heard of this news, but he shewed his good sense by shaping himself, with all resignation, to his altered fortunes. The character of Wilfrid was always most noble in adversity. He is said to have retired to his monastery at Ripon, of which he was still the abbat.

"Spe meliore manet latebris contectus in illis"[i]

is the assertion of his poetical biographer, but I can scarcely believe that he would seek a permanent abode in the province of his successful rival. The greater part of his time seems to have been spent in Kent and Mercia, where he exercised his episcopal functions without let or hindrance,[j] and won the good opinion of all by his piety and zeal.[k]

Thus was Wilfrid employed till Theodore arrived in England, in 669, and through his means, as has been previously shewn, that active prelate was reinstated in the see of York.[l] He was now in the position which he had so long coveted, and who could have a nobler or a more responsible charge? Oswy had extended his kingdom far into Scotland, and the whole of his vast realm was under Wilfrid's spiritual superintendence.[m] He was not unequal to the duties of his high office. Earnest and energetic he seems to have been at all times, and his efforts were crowned with signal success. Firmly and boldly did he moderate his churches, introducing, wherever he could, the Benedictine rule, or something like it, and multiplying in every direction the clergy and the shrines. He journeyed through his diocese, preaching and baptizing. It was a common thing for the presidents of religious houses to make him their heir. Many were the gifts that he received for sacred purposes, and the nobles generally shewed their confidence by entrusting to

[g] Fridegodus, 179. Ric. of Hexham, col. 294.

[h] Cf. Arch. Æl., *n. s.*, vol. i., a paper by Dr. Haigh, who considers the cross at Bewcastle to be the monument of Alcfrid, and that he died in 664. He says that the words "Wilfrid preaster" occur on the stone, shewing, as Dr. Haigh thinks, that Alcfrid died before Wilfrid was a bishop. I am inclined to doubt all this.

[i] Fridegodus, 179. Eddius, 58.

[j] Beda, iv., 2. Eddius, 58. Eadmer, 204. Fridegodus, 179-80. Stubbs, col. 1690.

[k] Beda, iii., 28. Eddius, 58. Ric. of Hexham, col. 293. Gervasius, col. 1636. Henr. Huntingdon, apud Savile, 191, *b*. Hist. Mon. S. Aug. Cant., 198.

[l] *Cf. Chadd.* Flor. Wigorn., 204. Eddius, 59. Simeon, col. 78. Bromton, col. 790. Gervasius, 1636. Stubbs, 1690. Fridegodus, 180.

[m] Beda, iv., 3. Symeon, Hist. Eccl. Dunelm., 44. Gervase, col. 1638. Stubbs, col. 1690.

him the education of their children.[n] The influence of the Scottish party began quickly to disappear. Many gave in their adhesion to the new rule, and those who saw that there was no chance of their own return to power, retired to those districts where Columba was not yet forgotten.[o]

Temperate and sparing as Wilfrid seems to have been in his personal expenditure,[p] he was well aware of the importance of outward forms and beautiful sights and sounds in religious worship. He was wise enough to know what a powerful auxiliary to deep fervour and holiness is to be found in a highly ornamented temple. It was not for nothing that he had visited the eternal city, and gazed with rapture upon those glorious shrines that were even then there! What a contrast to the humble edifice of wood and reeds in which he had prayed at Lindisfarne! Now, happily, he was in a position to raise the religious tone of his diocese by improving and decorating its churches. With the assistance of Eddius and Æona he taught the Christian worshipper that simple and yet exalting music with which the name of Gregory is immortally connected. The temples, also, in which were heard the voices of the sweet singers, were made more worthy of the chants with which they now resounded. Masons, glaziers, and limners, the ministers of civilization as well as art, were always in the train of Wilfrid.[q] At Hexham, on "the silver Tyne,"[r] arose at his bidding that beautiful shrine, which the Scot afterwards despoiled,[s] the "pulcherrimæ habitationes" of which even Alcuin could speak,[t] and which justified the boast of Eddius and Hexham's learned prior, that their peer did not exist on this side of the Alps.[u] At York, also, the great renovator was not idle. The church that Edwin and Oswald had erected was greatly in decay, and it grieved the energetic Wilfrid to see the Lord's house thus desolate and forlorn. A new roof of lead was put upon the minster. Glass was placed in the windows, for the first time, so that the birds could no longer fly in and out, and defile the sanctuary within. The walls were covered with plaster, the altar was decorated with appropriate furniture, and means were found to keep the temple continually in repair, and to maintain its ministers.[v] But it was on Ripon that Wilfrid's choicest gifts

[n] Eddius, 62. Eadmer, 207.
[o] Beda, iii., 28. [p] Eddius, 62.
[q] Beda, iv., 2. Eddius, 58.
[r] Were Cowley living now, he would alter his epithet.
[s] Chron. de Lanercost, 174-5.
[t] Alcuini Opera, i., 196. Canisii Lect. Ant., ii., 405.
[u] The site was given by Etheldreda (Lel. Coll., iv., 108). The author of the Mirac. S. Wilfr., apud Acta SS. ord. S. B., sæc. tert., i., 230, says that Wilfrid merely restored an old church, "ab antiquissimis fundata regibus." Cf. Eddius, 62; Eadmer, 208; Fridegodus, 183; Ric. of Hexham, col. 289-94.
[v] Eddius, 59. "Basilicæ oratorii Dei, officia semiruta lapidea eminebant.

were showered, for no place was dearer to his heart than that little monastery which he had ruled in prosperity and adversity. Eddius speaks with rapture of the shrine that Ripon now beheld, and with which he himself was so intimately connected.[w] Of polished stone, it was with its pillars and its porches, a copy, no doubt, of some temple in that famous city that Wilfrid had longed to visit amid the solitude of Lindisfarne. Would that we could see the precious text that, among other splendid gifts, he bestowed upon his favourite church, written in golden letters upon purple vellum, and enclosed in a jewelled case![x] And when all things were completed, the founder resolved that the new shrine should be solemnly set apart for God, and that the feast of the dedication should be observed as in the days of old. You might see at that time all the pomp and circumstance that befitted so high a ceremony, and which Wilfrid was so fond of manifesting and educing. King Ecgfrid and his brother Alwin came, with the princes and nobles of Northumbria, the abbats and the various officers who bare rule both in church and state. In the presence of that great concourse did Wilfrid dedicate the church and the altar, vesting it[y] with precious coverings of purple and of gold. And then, after the celebration of the eucharist, the consecrator turned himself to the worshippers, and, like the great Eastern potentate, declared what great things had been done for God. All the gifts that princes and holy men had made on that day to the church did he recite; and then, purposely no doubt, he enumerated, as far as he could, the possessions of the British priesthood which had passed into other hands when the Saxons had come in. The lesson which he meant to teach would be obvious to all. "Follow the example that has been this day set you. Give back to us the rightful

Nam culmina antiquata tecti distillantia, fenestræque apertæ, avibus nidificantibus intro et foras volitantibus, et parietes incultæ, omni spurcitia imbrium et avium, horribiles manebant—Primum culmina corrupta tecti renovans, artificiose plumbo puro tegens, per fenestras introitum avium et imbrium vitro prohibuit, per quod tamen intro lumen radiebat. Parietes quoque lavans, super nivem dealbavit." Cf. Eadmer, 205. Lel. Coll., iii., 258. The description of Fridegodus is new (180)—

"Ecclesiæ vero fundamina cassa vetustæ,
Culmina dissuto violabant trabe palumbes.
Humida contrito stillabant assere tecta:
Livida nudato suggrundia pariete passa
Imbricibus nullis: pluviæ quacumque vagantur.
Pendula disscissis fluitant laquearia tignis,
Fornice marcebant cataractæ dilapidato.
His ita contuitis, exhorruit ilicet alti
Viribus ingenii reparare peribula templi,
Incumbunt fessi vasto sudore latomi,
Nec minus approperant opicizi emblemata proni
Arcus incultos hyalino claudere velo.
Pondus et informes atlantes ferre priores
Jussit et expletum: lymphis perfunditur absis,
Albanturque suis lustrata altaria peplis."

[w] Eddius, 59, 60. Alcuin, apud Gale, i., 714. Lel. Coll., i., 54. Mabillon, Ann. Ben., i., 495.

[x] Eddius, 60. Lel. Coll., iv., 110-11, where there is an extract from a life of Wilfrid by Peter de Blois, once in the vestry at Ripon.

[y] "Altare cum *basibus* suis Domino dedicantes." The word *basibus* has occasioned some little difficulty. It is clearly an error for *vasibus*.

possessions of our church, and thus we will employ them." The striking ceremony was over, and it was followed by a banquet for all comers which lasted for three days and three nights.[z]

Wilfrid was now at the height of his prosperity. By the commonalty he was regarded with a kind of adoration. The simple natives would gaze with astonishment upon the tokens, everywhere evident, of his wealth and popularity, the numerous monasteries that he had erected and endowed, the splendour and length of his train when he rode abroad, dressed and armed as if it had been the escort of a king.[a] But there was a Nemesis amid all this prosperity which a little discretion on the part of Wilfrid might easily have appeased. Shrewd and mischievous observers were not wanting who would point out to the monarch of Northumbria the increasing influence of the prelate, greater than any subject ought to possess; they would whisper in his ear that Wilfrid's pomp and magnificence was alien altogether from that humility which was the true master-chord of the religion he professed, and alien, also, from the simple lives of men like Aidan and Chadd, whom he apparently despised. Those who affect greatness are liable to the evils that attend it.

'Ω πλοῦτε καὶ τυράννι καὶ τέχνη τέχνης
Ὑπερφέρουσα τῷ πολυζήλῳ βίῳ,
Ὅσος παρ' ὑμῖν ὁ φθόνος φυλάσσεται.

The arrow was shot against Wilfrid, and there were many that watched its flight.

Ecgfrid was the son of Wilfrid's old patron Oswy,[b] and he seems to have inherited for a while the affection of his father and brother for their favourite prelate. This kindly feeling, however, only lasted for a time. The first consort of Ecgfrid was the princess Etheldreda, the great patron-saint of Ely, and she made and observed a foolish vow of perpetual virginity. Wilfrid had over her, as he had over every one, a very great influence, and Ecgfrid sought his aid in endeavouring to alter the resolution of his wife, promising him almost anything if he could succeed. It was to no purpose. If Wilfrid tried to dissuade her from her resolve he was unsuccessful; but from the record of the circumstances which Beda gives I cannot but think that he applauded her resolution, and, in the end, after a twelve years' union with Ecgfrid, he permitted her to take the veil in the nunnery of Coldingham.[c] The king could not fail to regard

[z] Eddius, 60. Fridegodus, 180-1. Lel. Coll., iv., 109, 495. Cf. a valuable paper by Mr. Walbran for the Yorkshire Architectural Society. [a] Eddius, 63.

[b] Wilfrid obtained a great influence over Oswy before his death. The monarch made a vow to go with him to Rome to end his days, if he recovered from the illness that killed him. Beda, iv., 5.

[c] The authorities of this paragraph are Beda, iv., 19. Eadmer, 208. Wen-

Wilfrid as Balak did Balaam, "I called thee to curse mine enemies, and behold, thou hast altogether blessed them. I thought to promote thee to great honour, but the Lord hath kept thee back from honour."

The ill-matched couple were divorced, and Ecgfrid took for his second wife a daughter of the king of Wessex. She is said to have been a woman of a hasty and impetuous disposition, and there soon sprang up an implacable feud between her and Wilfrid.[d]

> "Quæ tantum accenderit ignem
> Causa latet—"

What the cause of that enmity was it is impossible to say, but bitter words must have been spoken, and bitter feelings generated, if we may judge from the result. A little of Chadd's gentleness might have prevented all this acrimony and contention, but Wilfrid had a very different disposition. Nine years had elapsed since he had stepped into Chadd's place; now the same hand that placed him in it was to make him a wanderer and an exile, seeking for justice at the hands of a foreign potentate, and finding his decree, after all his trouble, to be but a *brutum fulmen*.

When this quarrel was at its height in the Northumbrian court, archbishop Theodore was busily engaged with his measures of reform. Much there was for him to do, and, aged though he was, he did not shrink from the undertaking. One point to which he especially directed his attention was the subdivision of the English dioceses, for, undoubtedly, they were far too large to be managed efficiently by any one man. He began with the province of Mercia, and then he would look, naturally enough, to Northumbria. How to proceed in this case was a matter of some difficulty. It was undoubtedly to the interest of the southern metropolitan to have as many suffragans as possible, and it was equally desirable to keep the bishop or bishops of Northumbria subject to the same authority; but how was this to be effected?[e] To make several bishoprics in Northumbria would add materially to his own power. He

dover, i., 106. Hist. Eliensis, apud Gale, i., 510—apud Angl. Sac., i., 598. Ric. of Hexham, col. 294. Capgrave's Nova Legenda, fol. cxli. Wilfrid made her abbess of Ely, and was of great use in aiding her in arranging her convent and securing its privileges. Cf. Vita S. Etheldredæ, apud Acta SS. ord. S. B., sæc. ii., 747-57. Bromton, col. 791, and Bentham's Ely, 24, 57. In the "Lyfe of Saynt Werburge" (72) it is said that Etheldreda

> "Was reverently receyved into relygyon,
> And after the yere of her probacyon
> Professed there was by bysshop Wylfryde;
> Where all worldly honours she set on syde."

[d] Eddius, 63. Eadmer, 208. Fridegodus, 183-4. Hist. Eliensis, apud Angl. Sacr., i., 598. Simeon, col. 78. Ric. of Hexham, col. 294. Stubbs, col. 1691.

[e] Eddius, 63. Oudinus de Script. Eccl., i., 1661-2.

might subdivide that kingdom in virtue of the legantine authority, but this was rather a bold step to take. He might presume upon the absence of the pall at York, for Wilfrid had never received it, and consider Wilfrid as a suffragan of his own, but to do as he wished, and to intrude within Northumbria, he would require the consent of the king. And just at the time when that consent was needed it was voluntarily offered. The queen had made her husband Wilfrid's enemy, and the feud was then raging, and Theodore, who was watching his opportunity, rejoiced to find himself invited into Northumbria by its sovereign.

He went, and the king and he, without consulting Wilfrid, proceeded to subdivide the diocese of Northumbria. The plan, as it was finally arranged, in addition to York, placed a bishop at Lindisfarne, Hexham, and Whitherne.[f] There is nothing to be said against the policy of extending the episcopate, indeed there is nothing to shew that Wilfrid was in this instance averse to it, but the change was effected in a manner which is liable to grave censure. Decency, to say nothing of law and justice, ought to have suggested to Theodore and Ecgfrid the propriety of consulting Wilfrid on a step in which he was especially concerned. It was not to be expected that Wilfrid would submit to such treatment. He went to the two dividers, and demanded of them what he had done to be thus plundered. "We have no fault to find with thee," was the reply, "but we cannot alter what we have done." Disappointed in this manner of the justice that he had demanded, the indignant prelate turned to his last resource; he made an appeal, which was then for the first time heard before an English sovereign—"appellatus est ad Cæsarem"—he referred his cause to the decision of the pope.[g]

There is a fascinating account of his adventures on the way. It reminds us, strikingly, of the *Odyssey*, and of the varied fortunes of one, who, like Wilfrid, was a visitor at strange

[f] In the first instance, Eata was placed at Hexham and Eadhaed in Lindsey, which was annexed to Northumbria by Ecgfrid. (Saxon Chron., 54, says that Bosa and Eata were first appointed.) After Wilfrid went abroad Eata seems to have had the charge, for a while, of the whole of Northumbria, except Lindsey, and on that account I find him called archbishop of York (Vita S. Eatæ, Biogr. Misc., Surtees Soc., 125. Walbran on the Saxon Church of Ripon, 96 *d.*) Bosa was soon made bishop of York, and in 680 or 681 Eata was translated to Lindisfarne, Trumbert succeeding him at Hexham. Trumwin, also, was placed over the Picts, and Eadhaed, Lindsey being lost to Northumbria, became bishop of Ripon. Cf. Beda, iv., 12. Fridegodus, 184. Wendover, i., 104. Hist. Mon. S. Aug. Cant., 275. Symeon, Hist. Eccl. Dunelm., 44. Ric. of Hexham, col. 294.

[g] Beda, v., 19. Saxon Chron., 61. Eddius, 63. Eadmer, 209. Fridegodus, 184. Simeon, col. 78. Ric. of Hexham, col. 294. Diceto, col. 440. Bromton, col. 792-3. Gervasius, 1638. Stubbs, 1691. Malmesbury, apud Savile, 10, *b.* Hen. Huntingdon, ib., 191, *b.* Symeon, Hist. Eccl. Dunelm, 44. Chron. S. Crucis, apud Angl. Sacr., i., 155.

courts, and could adapt himself, with equal readiness, to the inhabitants of the wild lands on which he was driven with his companions by the stormy waters. Both possessed unto the end

> "One equal temper of heroic hearts,
> Made weak by time and fate, but strong in will
> To strive, to seek, to find, and not to yield."

Wilfrid left the shores of England in 678,[h] with a large train, regretted deeply by the thousands of monks whom he had left behind him in Northumbria. But, even now, the hatred of his enemies, changing, perhaps, into that fear which is more diabolical than hatred, concerted measures for his overthrow. A message had been sent to Theodoric, king of Neustria, desiring him to detain Wilfrid on his journey, and he, with the assistance of Ebruin, his chief minister, prepared to arrest the exile. He escaped from them in a very singular manner. By a most extraordinary coincidence Wilfrid or Winfrid, bishop of Lichfield, was wandering at that time in Neustria. Deceived by the remarkable similarity of name, Ebruin seized upon him and his companions, and most cruelly were they used. Wilfrid, however, escaped from one peril to fall into another. A contrary wind drove him out of his course, and he landed among the savage tribes upon the shores of Friesland.[i] And here, with that noble and energetic spirit of devotion, to which his own interests were at all times subordinated, he remained till he had taught the heathen natives and their monarch, Adalgisus, the rudiments of the true faith. It was the first time that the saving word had been preached upon the shores of the northern seas. Fuller has beautifully remarked that "as nightingales sing the sweetest when farthest from their nests, so this Wilfride was most diligent in God's service when at the greatest distance from his own home."[j] There was nothing in such a country to tempt ambition or elicit pride. The love of self could never have induced a man like Wilfrid to sojourn in a district like that, and, to his credit be it spoken, at every period of his life when he was required to surrender personal considerations to the cause of God that sacrifice was willingly made. The princes and the people were baptized by thousands, and they shewed

[h] Saxon Chron., 54. Asser, apud Gale, i., 146. Flor. Wigorn. (251) makes the date 677.

[i] Beda, v., 9. Eddius, 64. Eadmer, 210. Fridegodus, 185. Alcuin, de Pont. Ebor., apud Gale, i., 713. Wendover, i., 105. Flor. Wigorn., 252. Diceto, col. 440. Stubbs, col. 1691. Chron. Petrob., 3. Mabillon, Acta SS. ord. S. B. sæc. iii., i., 603, prolog. in vitam S. Willibrodi. Mabillon, Ann. Ben., i., 540, who says that Wilfrid, knowing the designs of his enemies, sailed voluntarily to Friesland. Willib. Bosschaert de primis veteris Frisiæ Apostolis, ed. 1650, and Batavia Sacra, ed. 1714, p. 24, where there is a short life of Wilfrid drawn up from the Acta SS., etc.

[j] Church History, book ii., 88.

their gratitude to their converter by rejecting with scorn the proffered bribes of Ebruin,[k] who was striving to remedy his error which he had at length discovered.

In the beginning of the spring Wilfrid proceeded on his journey, finding friends at every halting-place. Dagobert, a French prince, had not forgotten the hospitable reception that Wilfrid had once given him in England, when he was an exile, and, recollecting that kindness, he gave the wanderer a most hearty welcome.[l] Having failed to induce Wilfrid to take up his abode in France by offering him the see of Strasburg, he sent him on, with rich presents and bishop Deodatus for his guide, to Berchtar the monarch of the Lombards, who had refused to be a party to the evil designs of Ebruin and Theodoric. From that court the pilgrims passed onwards to the eternal city.[m]

Five and twenty years had elapsed since the humble scholar from Lindisfarne journeyed into that city of which such great things were told him. At that time he was unknown to every one when he entered it, but now he was escorted on his way by kings and princes, and the father of the Christian faithful was expecting the arrival of one of the greatest of the bishops.

> "Quas ego te terras et quanta per æquora vectum
> Accipio, quantis jactatum, nate, periclis!"

The story of Wilfrid's sufferings and labours was known in Rome long before he was there to tell it. Cöenwald, the messenger of Theodore, had arrived before him, but Agatho and his bishops had turned a deaf ear to his tale. An appeal, the first appeal, from an English bishop to the court of Rome was an event of no slight importance. It gave the pope an opportunity of setting the seal of his authority upon the British church in what appeared to be a just cause. The decision of the synod was unanimously in favour of Wilfrid. He sat among the bishops who were deliberating against the Monothelites as the representative of his church,[n] and, flattered and honoured by all, he crossed the seas in triumph, bearing with him the papal mandate which authorized the restitution of his see, and hurled against the gainsayers of that bull all the terrors that the court of Rome could wield.[o]

Wilfrid reached Northumbria, little dreaming, perhaps, of the reception that awaited him. His respect for the authority of Rome was so great that he imagined, no doubt, that every

[k] Eddius, 64. Eadmer, 210. Fridegodus, 185.

[l] Eddius, 65. Eadmer, 211. Fr., 186.

[m] Eddius, 65. Eadmer, 211. Fr., 186. Gaimar, l'Estorie des Engles, apud Mon. Hist. Brit., 782.

[n] Beda, v., 19. Wendover, i., 105.

[o] Eddius, 66-8. Eadmer, 212. Frid., 187. Flor. Wigorn., 252. Diceto, col. 441. Bromton, 793. Stubbs, 1691. Labbe, Concilia vi., col. 582. Spelmanni Conc., 160.

one would give way to it. In this he committed an egregious mistake. The independence of the Saxon church was at that time very strongly marked, and Theodore, himself an emissary from Rome, was most active in maintaining it. But among the native princes the idea of submitting to any foreign jurisdiction had never once been mooted. Wilfrid's bulls and letters were treated with derision by the Northumbrian court. Ecgfrid regarded him merely as a rebellious subject. He was cast immediately into prison. His bulls were taken away from him. The reliquary that he had brought from Rome became the plaything of the queen. Nine months elapsed before the prisoner regained his liberty at the intercession of the abbess Ebba, the king's aunt, and then he was banished from that kingdom with which his name will be immortally connected. Wherever he went the hate of Ecgfrid pursued him. He paused for a while in Mercia with prince Berthwald, but king Ethelred, to serve Ecgfrid, compelled him to depart. The queen of Wessex was the sister of Ermenburga of Northumbria, so there was no sanctuary for him there. It was at length the high privilege of a heathen province to give an asylum to a bishop whom every Christian kingdom had rejected.[p]

It was in Sussex, in 681, that Wilfrid found a sanctuary at last.[q] He little thought, when on his return from his first journey he escaped with difficulty from the wild wreckers on that coast, that in after years he would find in that country a peaceful resting-place. Ethelwalch, the sovereign, and his queen had been baptized at the instigation of Wulfhere king of Mercia, and there was a little monastery at Bosham which Dicul, a Scot, had founded. It had but five or six inmates, and neither they, nor the king and queen, had made any converts to the faith which they professed. The adjacent kingdom of Kent had been the first to welcome the message of Augustine, and the light that shone there had radiated to the farthest extremities of England. How strange that Sussex should have been still in darkness! As Fuller truly observes, "herein it was verified, 'Many that are first shall be last, and the last first.' Yea the Spirit 'which bloweth where it listeth,' observes no visible rules of motion; but sometimes taking no notice of those in the middle, reacheth to them that are farthest off."[r]

The more difficult the task was, the more eager was the great heart of Wilfrid to accomplish it. He threw himself into

[p] Eddius, 71-2. Eadmer, 213-15. Fridegodus, 189. Lel. Coll., iv., 109.

[q] Eddius, 72. Eadmer, 216-17. Fridegodus, 191. Beda, iv., 13; v., 19. Alcuin de Pont. Eccl. Ebor.; apud Gale, i., 713. Wendover, i., 105. Flor. Wigorn., 252. Diceto, col. 441. Stubbs, col. 1691. Huntingdon, apud Savile, 191, *b*. Spelmanni Concilia, 178.

[r] Church History, bk. ii., 88.

the evangelization of Sussex with the energy of an apostle. The inhabitants of the district were not only heathens, but it seems that they were ignorant of all those arts in which savage tribes are generally adepts. When Wilfrid came among them the land was being desolated by a famine. It was by no means an unusual thing to see the emaciated natives assemble in parties of forty or fifty, and, hopeless for the future, grasp hold of each other's hands, and throw themselves from the cliffs to end their miseries in the sea. At this conjuncture Wilfrid happily arrived. He taught the half-starved sufferers how to fish and provide for themselves, endeavouring

> "By slow prudence to make mild
> A rugged people, and thro' soft degrees
> Subdue them to the useful and the good."

Civilization was thus the herald as well as the companion of religion. Gratitude to their benefactor winged his words to the hearts of the natives, and they adopted the faith which he preached to them. On the day of their baptism the windows of heaven were again opened, and the rain descended upon the long barren ground.[s]

Grateful for the services that Wilfrid had rendered to himself and his subjects, Ethelwalch give him a piece of land at Selsea.[t] This was the beginning of an ecclesiastical foundation which was afterwards removed to Chichester. At Selsea Wilfrid immediately erected a monastery, over which he presided for five years, exercising at the same time his episcopal functions in the adjacent country, and giving the natives a practical lesson on the vice of slavery.[u] In 686 he again reaped the benefit of the courtesy which he had at all times shewn to fugitives and exiles. When Cadwalla, a scion of the royal house of Wessex, was in banishment, Wilfrid had been his friend, and now, when the tide had at length turned in his fortunes, Cadwalla was not forgetful of his former benefactor. By force of arms he took possession of Wessex, Kent and Sussex. He then gave to Wilfrid the bishopric of Wessex and a fourth part of the Isle of Wight, which the energetic prelate brought over to the Christian faith.[v] But the greatest victory of all was the conversion of Cadwalla. The conqueror was a pagan till he became firmly seated on his throne, and then, through policy as well as conviction, he re-

[s] Beda, iv., 3. Eadmer, 217. Bromton, col. 798. Huntingdon, apud Savile, 191, *b*.

[t] Beda, iv., 13. Eddius, 72. Eadmer, 217. Hist. Mon. S. Aug. Cant., 198. Stubbs, col. 1691. Lel. Coll., iv., 70.

[u] Beda, iv., 13.

[v] The credit of evangelizing the island is, perhaps, to be shared with Wilfrid, bishop of the Mercians, and Eoppa. Cf. Beda, iv., 13, 16; v. 19. Saxon Chron., 47. Eadmer, 217. Wendover, i., 105. Flor. Wigorn., 256. Hen. Huntingdon, 192. Stubbs, col. 1691.

solved to embrace that faith which the majority of his subjects professed, and of which Wilfrid was the preacher. He determined that the pope should baptize him. And to shew that he was impelled by no sordid or common impulse, the youthful monarch, in the very flush of greatness, had the courage to throw aside his sceptre, and to prepare himself in the seclusion of a monastery for that solemn rite of which he was so soon to be the recipient.[w]

There was one person who would observe the progress of Wilfrid with the greatest interest, and that was Theodore. He could not but be struck by the energy and success of his exiled brother. He was too good a man himself to allow any personal feelings to prevent him from admiring so much industry and self-denial. And then, doubtless, a self-accusing thought would flit across his mind that it was through his means that Wilfrid had been excluded from a larger sphere of duty, where he might have done, if that were possible, a still greater work for God. There had been, in all probability, no intercourse between the two since that memorable scene in the halls of Ecgfrid. Were they to "go down to the grave in silence," without an attempt at reconciliation, or a single word of kindness and forgiveness? Theodore was approaching the patriarchal age of ninety, and Wilfrid's climacteric year was rapidly coming on,

"Lenit albescens animos capillus."

A reconciliation was happily effected,[x] Theodore making the first advances. He was not deterred by the peevishness of age from acknowledging his error, and Wilfrid, with his heart softened by adversity, was able to forgive. Theodore now shewed the sincerity of his regret by many acts of kindness. He would fain have nominated his old foe to be his successor in his see, but Wilfrid's thoughts were centred in his own kingdom in the North, and, courteously declining the proffered gift, he begged to be reconciled with the sovereigns who ought to have been his friends. None can better value the blessings of peace than those who have been scathed and seared by discord. Theodore's good offices were immediately at Wilfrid's services. He restored him to the favour of Ethelred, king of Mercia, whose kingdom, through Ecgfrid's interests, had been closed to him, and that monarch gave him lands and monasteries, and permitted him to act as a bishop within his province. But Theodore did still more for him. He wrote in his behalf to Aldfrid, an ille-

[w] Beda, v., 7. Eddius, 72-3. Eadmer, 217. Fridegodus, 191-2. Wendover, i., 115. Bromton, col. 799. Hen. Huntingdon, 193. Baronii, Ann., viii., 594. Smith's Flores Eccl. Hist., 126, a very badly arranged and badly written work.

[x] Eddius, 73. Eadmer, 218.

gitimate son of Oswy, who had recently succeeded his brother Ecgfrid on the Northumbrian throne. Aldfrid invited Wilfrid to return into the North. The sees of Lindisfarne and Hexham were at that time vacant, and they were given to Wilfrid, who left them soon afterwards for his old bishopric of York, Bosa, probably, surrendering the charge to which he subsequently returned.[y]

All these things were done in 686, and Wilfrid was thus restored to his dignities and honours, and for five years did he enjoy them.[z] But there was to be no rest for him even now. Affliction, alas! had taught him only a temporary lesson. An insane love of change lured him, a second time, to his fall. What injury has been done to the progress of true religion by men who have been thus minded. The conduct of Wilfrid on this occasion was inexcusable. He ought to have been well acquainted by this time with the feelings of the native princes of Northumbria, and yet he adopted a course of conduct which would be sure to outrage them. The highest spiritual victories have been won by men of a gentler and a more forbearing temperament. He had been but five years in his old diocese when he kindled, for the second time, the flame of contention. He was again shipwrecked by making an attempt to undo everything that had been effected during his absence. He wished to recover for the church of York its privileges and possessions, of which it is obscurely said by Eddius it had been deprived. He was desirous of obliterating the see of Ripon, which he would look upon with a jealous eye from its vicinity to York. He was eager, also, to abrogate the constitutions and decrees of his old rival Theodore, made whilst the two prelates were enemies, by which the Northumbrian province had been moderated for some years. King Aldfrid, who was a man of learning and discretion, would not assent to the wishes of Wilfrid, and the disappointed prelate, who wanted the patient endurance of Paulinus and the gentleness of Chadd, determined to have his own way or nothing. He retired to the Mercian court, where he acted as a bishop, and consecrated Ætla and Suidbert of Friesland.[a]

Actuated by a sincere wish to make peace among his divided churches, Aldfrid, with Berthwald, who was now the Southern primate, and the greater part of the English bishops, met in a

[y] Beda, iv., 29. Eddius, 74. Eadmer, 219. Fridegodus, 193. Flor. Wigorn., 256. Simeon, Hist. Eccl. Dunelm., 60. Ric. of Hexham, col. 295. Diceto, col. 441. Stubbs, col. 1691. Chron. S. Crucis, apud Angl. Sacr., i., 156. Chron. Petrib., 3. [z] Beda, v., 19.

[a] Wilfrid became bishop "Mediterraneorum Anglorum," and Leicester was, probably, the place at which he resided. Beda, v., 11. Eddius, 75. Eadmer, 220. Fridegodus, 193. Flor. Wigorn., 258. Ric. of Hexham, col. 296. Diceto, col. 441. Chron. S. Crucis, apud Angl. Sacr., i., 157. Acta SS. ord. S. B., sæc. tert., i., 242.

great synod at Edwine's path. Wilfrid, also, was there by the desire of the council, and after a long debate it was resolved to perpetuate the regulations of Theodore. Wilfrid professed his readiness to obey the decrees of the synod so long as they were in consonance with the canons; but he boldly, and most injudiciously, asked the deliberators how they could venture to prefer the judgment of Theodore to that of Agatho, Benedict and Sergius. After consulting for a while in private, they endeavoured to persuade him to resign all his offices into the hands of Berthwald, in the hope, as they seemed to imply, of having some compromise effected, but perhaps, as Eddius asserts, to deprive him of everything, and to say that he had given it up. This was a strong step to take, and one which shewed how little confidence they had in Wilfrid. A friend, however, had warned him of their design, and he met their request with the reply that he would bow to the decision of the archbishop, so long as it was not opposed to the rules of the holy fathers. Annoyed at Wilfrid's pertinacity, they began to threaten him, saying, in the end, that he should be deprived of everything save the monastery of Ripon, and that he should not be allowed to go beyond its precincts without the permission of the king. Wilfrid, upon this, broke out into an indignant expostulation, which would have come with better taste from other lips. "Was it for this that he had laboured as a bishop for nearly forty years? Was it for this that he had torn the Scottish system up by the roots, teaching the Northumbrians the correct mode of calculating Easter, and giving them the proper tonsure, the Benedictine rule, and the knowledge of chanting? And, after all this, forsooth, he was to be entrapped into putting his name to a decree which was meant to be his ruin!" Full of indignation he made his appeal, for the second time, to the court of Rome. The archbishop and the king were disposed to throw him into prison for this, but the other members of the synod reminded them that as Wilfrid had come among them with a safe conduct he could not honourably be detained. He was permitted, therefore, to depart, and he returned to the court of Mercia, and Ethelred kindly promised to do nothing to his prejudice till the question in dispute had been arranged at Rome.[b]

To Rome, therefore, did Wilfrid journey when he was above threescore years old. Age, however, could not tame that intrepid spirit. The church, which he had done so much to serve, drove him out of her communion, but he looked for justice at other hands. There were still some at Rome who recollected

[b] Eddius, 75-7. Eadmer, 220-1. Labbe, Concilia, vi., col. 1382-6. Spelmanni Concilia, 200. Fridegodus, 195. Wendover, i., 117. Stubbs, col. 1691. Chron. Petrib., 4 (in 691).

him when he came there with a splendid retinue and backed by the support of kings. Now, he was in a far humbler guise, but the papal court could not but shew their gratitude to so valuable a servant. His accusers had anticipated his arrival, but their tale was disregarded. Wilfrid was absolved from all blame, and the pope, John VI., wrote an admonitory letter in his behalf to Ethelred and Aldfrid. At Rome Wilfrid must have spent many years. Fain would the aged prelate have ended his days in the holy city which he had visited in joy and sorrow. Christian heroes had consecrated it for ever; men of spiritual prowess who had passed through the fire of persecution before they had won the victory. Glorious shrines were covering the places which had been watered with their blood; and there would Wilfrid, who had passed under the share himself, have been a watcher and a suppliant, willing to copy their death as he had imitated their life, and to pass away, like them, into the presence of the Ineffable One. His bones, however, were to rest in the country of his fathers. The pope and his council desired him to return to England to claim that justice to which he was entitled. He set his face once more towards England in 703 or 704, when he was seventy years of age. The journey was a tedious one, for the old man could not travel rapidly. A very dangerous illness, a shadow of the end, assailed him by the way at Meaux, and his life was with difficulty saved. Acca, one of his companions, who in after years became bishop of Hexham, had a marvellous tale how the archangel Michael shewed himself to his sick master, and told him that the same mercy should be vouchsafed to him that was granted to Hezekiah, and that four years should be added to his life.[c]

When Wilfrid arrived in England he had an interview with archbishop Berthwald. He was a gentle and a conciliatory prelate, and there was soon peace and amity between them. The letter that Wilfrid had brought to him from the pope could not fail to influence him, and he promised to exert his influence to abrogate the decision of the synod. From Berthwald Wilfrid passed on to the Mercian court, where he found that his old patron Ethelred had become a monk at Bardney. At the suggestion of the new sovereign, Wilfrid sent two messengers to Aldfrid to request permission to visit his kingdom, and to bring with him the letters from the pope. The monarch of Northumbria was obdurate. Not one word in any decree would he alter in obedience to a papal mandate, and he refused, henceforward, to listen to the request of Wilfrid. Aldfrid died shortly

[c] Beda, v., 19, 20. Eddius, 79—83. Eadmer, 222-3. Ric. of Hexham, col. 297. Fridegodus, 195.

afterwards, and the partizans of Wilfrid assert that he shewed his penitence on his death-bed. The throne of Northumbria was now occupied by Eadulf, and to him, also, did Wilfrid, still longing for his old charge, send his messengers. His hopes, however, were dashed to the ground by the harsh response that if he and his friends tarried for six days within his kingdom, they should lose their lives for their disobedience. With this answer Wilfrid would be sorely disappointed, for, expecting a kindly welcome, he had visited his old monastery at Ripon. Two months after this everything was reversed. Eadulf was banished, and Osred, the youthful son of Aldfrid, was on the throne of Northumbria, with Wilfrid for his friend.[d]

The case of Wilfrid would soon force itself upon the consideration of the young monarch and his council, and a great synod was assembled on the banks of the river Nidd[e] to adjudicate upon it. Osred was there accompanied by the three bishops of the province (Bosa, John, and Eadfrith) and the abbess Elfleda. Archbishop Berthwald was also present with the thanes and princes of Northumbria, and Wilfrid was by his side. Berthwald began by reading over the letters of the pope. Very few of the auditors would be acquainted with the language in which they were written, and the archbishop was requested to interpret them. In reply, he said how difficult it would be to do that with exactness, and professed his readiness to give a brief summary of their contents. He had thus an opportunity of softening down, or omitting, all the harsher portions of the letters, which, if properly understood, would have frustrated altogether his sincere wishes for peace. The epistles, as he said, desired that all the ecclesiastics of the province should be reconciled with Wilfrid. The bishops were either to restore to him his churches, or to shew cause to the contrary in the Roman court, and excommunication was to be the punishment of their disobedience. The voices of the three interested prelates were at once raised against this decree. They brought forward, on the other side, the solemn decisions of Ecgfrid and Aldfrid, alleging that they could not be altered: they quoted, also, against the archbishop, not only the example of Theodore, a prelate sent from Rome, but his own words on a previous occasion. This was the crisis of the conference, for not only did the law seem to be against Wilfrid, but Berthwald was, as it were, convicted of inconsistency. The abbess Elfleda now asserted that Aldfrid, on his death-bed, had regretted his treatment of Wilfrid, and that he had promised, if his life were spared, to rescind his decree against him and the papal au-

[d] Beda, v., 19. Eddius, 84-5. Eadmer, 223.

[e] Eddius, 85-6. Wendover, i., 118. Labbe, Concilia, vi., col. 1389. Spelmanni Conc., 203.

thority; and Berchtfrid, the confidential minister of Aldfrid and his son, mentioned a vow that his late master had made at Bebbanburg, when that fortress was besieged, by which he pledged himself to restore Wilfrid, should he be victorious; and he said, authoritatively, "It is the will of the king and his council that the wishes of Aldfrid should, in every respect, be adhered to." It was evidently the desire of the powers that be that Wilfrid should return. The bishops could not fail to see this, and they retired to hold a consultation by themselves. After a long deliberation, in which Berthwald and Elfleda took a part, a compromise was effected. Wilfrid was not, indeed, restored to York, but Ripon and Hexham were given up to him, and the prelates, glad, no doubt, that there was concord and amity at last, gave each other the kiss of peace.[f]

For the second time did Wilfrid become bishop of Hexham. Many years had passed away since the sainted Etheldreda gave him that little portion of ground by the waters of the Tyne, on which he raised the fair shrine which Eddius describes, and to that temple did the aged prelate at length return. Once he would never have submitted to the compromise that gave Hexham to him again, but age and trouble had robbed him of his old fire. Peace he would now seek, for he had had enough of the storms of life. That place of rest was to be his soon, where he would never hear their sound. The shadows of death were already darkening around him. He was attacked by the same complaint which had nearly carried him off as he returned from Rome, but the prayers that the faithful put up for him were heard, and the end was not yet. The sickness, however, was not without its admonitory lesson. The aged prelate in the presence of several of the brethren of the monastery of Ripon, which was a private possession of his own, appointed his kinsman, Tathbercht, the ruler of that house, and made the following disposition of his worldly estate. He divided it into four portions. One share was bestowed upon the churches of the Virgin and St. Paul at Rome, the city to which he had never appealed in vain. Another was given to the poor. A third was bequeathed to the rulers of his two religious houses at Ripon and Hexham, for the benefit of their monasteries. With the remaining share he rewarded the companions of his sufferings and triumphs,

"Fortes pejoraque passi
Mecum sæpe viri."

And then, when this necessary duty was dispatched, did he tell

[f] Beda, v., 19. Eddius, 85-6. Eadmer, 224. Hist. Mon. S. Aug. Cant., 280. Diceto, col. 442. Ric. of Hexham, col. 296. Stubbs, col. 1691. Mabillon, Ann. Ben., ii., 14-15. Baronii Ann., viii., 652-3.

his admiring audience that he had another journey yet to make before he traversed the valley of the shadow. Two abbats had arrived to bid him to the Mercian court, for Coelred, the successor of the faithful Ethelred, begged him to inspect and put in order the monasteries within his kingdom. And he would go. Even when the hand of death was chilling him, that undecaying spirit was still ardent when there was any good work to be done for God. The scene among the monks of Ripon reminds us strongly of St. Paul's last interview with the Ephesian elders. Wilfrid spoke, indeed, of the possibility of his return, but could they expect that? He told them also of another more probable contingency to which their hearts would sorrowfully assent. They threw themselves at his feet, and amid their prayers and tears he commended them to the Lord. They never looked upon that face again.[g]

To Mercia he journeyed, and set everything in order as the monarch wished. The exertion was too great for his aged frame. He fell sick in the monastery of Oundle, which he had himself established, and there, on the 12th of October,[h] 709, did he pass into his rest.[i] His "life was like an April-day, often interchangeably fair and foul; and after many alterations, he set fair in full lustre at last."[j] For seventy-six years had Wilfrid been a Christian soldier, but he was at length released. The final struggle is over; the victory complete; and as the mourners were gazing upon that face now so motionless and still, they fancied that there was around them the sound of rustling wings. Could it have been the spirits who were bearing away their new brother on his homeward journey? Do they now come for him, and, as Daniel Heinsius beautifully says:—

> "Circumque voluti
> Concentus edunt varios, æternaque fundunt
> Murmura, sed sensus non admittentia nostros?"

A very great man passed away that day, for, in many respects, we may consider Wilfrid as the star of the Anglo-Saxon church. It is not often that we meet with such a combination of intellect and energy. He lived in an age when a master-hand was needed, when church reform was especially required. The system of the Culdees was not calculated to make any permanent impression. It wanted discipline and

[g] Eddius, 87. Eadmer, 224-5.

[h] Mabillon, Ann. Ben., ii., 24, makes 8th kal. May the day of his death. Wendover is in error as to the date. Cf. i., 118, 130.

[i] Beda, v., 19. Eddius, 78. Saxon Chron., 61. Eadmer, 225. Wendover, i., 118. Ric. of Hexham, col. 296. Bromton, col. 794. Stubbs, col. 1692. Hen. Huntingdon, 193, b. Chron. Petrib., 5. Hist. Cænob. Burgensis, apud Sparke, 13.

[j] Fuller's Church History, bk. ii., 94.

authority to direct it. The vigorous intellect of Wilfrid at once detected its defects, and, with the laudable ambition of a man who is conscious of his own powers, he strove to remedy them. It required no little boldness and skill to influence the mind of Oswy, and to pull down the supremacy of Colman and his monks. But Wilfrid did all this, and effected a reform without which Theodore could have done little, and to which Dunstan and Oswald, in after years, were greatly indebted for their success. But Wilfrid had not only a destructive genius, but he evinced at the same time great constructive and administrative ability. He built up the Benedictine rule upon the ruins of the system of Columba. He brought it in in all its comprehensiveness, and set every part of its delicate and varied machinery in motion—its discipline—its ritual—its accompanying graces of architecture and music were all of them attended to. Hexham and Ripon are two only of the many monasteries of which he was himself the founder. It is no slight honour to have aided the establishment of such abbeys as Ely,[k] as Evesham[l] and Medhamstead.[m] In doing all this, however, he had no little opposition to contend with. The reformer has always troubles in his path, and Wilfrid, also, experienced them. And in meeting them he exhibited the defects in his character. He wanted temper and he wanted judgment. I cannot blame him, as many do, for appealing to the court of Rome, for it was natural enough that he should regard Rome as the head of that mission to England which she had herself so recently established. Rome had, at that time, as much right to moderate the ecclesiastics in England, as we have in these days to give our own ritual and discipline and bishops to heathen territories abroad. And when justice was denied to him at home, to what other arbitrator could he refer his cause? Wilfrid's error was not so much in making these appeals as in the manner in which he made them. He would make no allowance for the feelings and opinions of his opponents. His quick mind could detect what others could not see, and he had not the patience to wait till their powers of vision and apprehension became stronger. He thus stumbled where others, with half his intellect, would have succeeded. You may be conscious of your inferiority yourself, but it is by no means pleasant to be taunted with it by another. Wilfrid was in this way continually offending national pride,

[k] See page 65.

[l] Mabillon, Acta SS. ord. S. B., Vita S. Egwini Ep. Wigorn., 170.

[m] It is possible that another Wilfrid was concerned with Medhamstead or Peterbro'. Saxon Chron., 42, 46, 50, 53. Hist. Cœnobii Burgensis, apud Sparke, 12. Labbe, Concilia, vi., col. 576. Spelmanni Concilia, 181. Lel. Coll., i., 5. Gunton's Peterbro', 128. Wright's Biogr. Lit., i., 170. Archæol. Æl., *n.s.*, i., 163.

and provoking contention and dislike. And there is the less excuse for him when we consider the extraordinary influence that he could exert, his winning demeanour and address, and his marvellous powers of fascination. Any one thus highly endowed ought to manifest a little forbearance and consideration for his less gifted brethren. Glorious indeed is the picture of Wilfrid in his prosperity, basking in the smiles of courts, and scattering his treasures with no sparing hand, but, if he had thus lived and thus died, we should never have known him as the evangelizer of Sussex and the apostle of the Frisians. The landscape that is garish beneath the meridian sun, is fairer far beneath the shadows of the cloud, and lovelier still under the cool soft lights of evening. When Wilfrid was in exile, and advanced in years, we may all admire him. We never think of the hasty temper and the imperfect judgment, when we see how his proud spirit could humble itself to suit his altered fortunes, and how, when age and sorrow lay heavily upon him, he could devote himself with unconquerable ardour to the great cause of God. That must have been an honest and a noble heart that could thus forget the troubles that afflicted it, and burn, at such times, oblivious altogether of its own sufferings, with greater love and sympathy for others. These, surely, are some of the signs and the tokens of a Christian hero.

The aged prelate was not laid in the grave in his monastery at Oundle. His heart, amid its feeble throbbings, still trembled, like the magnet, towards its beloved North, and they carried his remains, at his own request, to his old home at Ripon.[n] He was entombed, by the south side of the altar,[o] with all the honours of the dead.

Forty years had passed away since Wilfrid stood before that holy place and consecrated it to God. Little thought he at that solemn festival that his own name would be connected with that work for perpetual generations. That abbey became one of the three great churches in Yorkshire, and it was famous throughout England. The privilege of sanctuary and the right of using the ordeal were among the honours conferred upon it by Athelstan.[p] The power of working miracles, which is said to have belonged

[n] Beda, v., 19. Saxon Chron., 61. Eddius, 88. Eadmer, 225. Flor. Wigorn., 264. Chron. S. Crucis, apud Angl. Sacr., i., 157. Ric. of Hexham, col. 296. Hickesii, Dissert. Epist., 118. Mabillon, Ann. Ben., ii., 24.

[o] Beda, v., 19. Wendover, i., 118. The remains were afterwards translated by archbishop Grey (Walbran's Church of Ripon, 96). "After the extension of the old presbytery," says Mr. Walbran, "the shrine of St. Wilfrid was removed to the eastern extremity of the north side of the choir, where Leland saw it shortly before the Reformation under the arch by the high altar." Cf. Lel. Itin., viii., 21-2. "reliquiæ ejus sub arcu prope magnum altare nunc sublatæ."

[p] Lel. Coll., iv., 10, ex libro Petri Blesensis.

to Wilfrid in his life-time, added in after years to the glories of his shrine. His seal was a sovereign specific for the murrain.[q] His banner went out frequently, as a talisman, to the wars. Many churches were dedicated to God in his name, and there are few cathedrals that did not possess an altar and a chantry of St. Wilfrid. At Durham, in the beautiful Galilee that bishop Pudsey erected, there was a figure of the saint in a window "in fyne coulored glasse, as he was accustomed to say masse, with his myter on his head, and his crosier staffe in his lefte hand." Under his feet was an inscription which recorded his titles, among which the monks of Durham would read with no little pride "uno anno rexit episcopatum Lindisfarnensem."[r] Among the relics in the minster of York, there was one of Wilfrid's arms, set in silver, and two texts, or evangelisteria, which had belonged to him. In the side of one of them there was a crucifix inserted, and both were richly decorated with gold and silver.[s]

There used to be some little controversy with reference to the final resting-place of the remains of Wilfrid. Fuller observes "as he had been a great traveller, when living, so his bones took one journey after his death."[t] It is said that they were removed to Canterbury. One chronicler gives to Dunstan the credit of translating them,[u] but Frithegode asserts that Odo removed them, having found the shrine most grievously neglected when he visited the church.[v] Lanfranc, in after years, deposited them in a splendid shrine.[w] The Northerns, however, allege that the remains of Wilfrid II., and not those of his predecessor, were removed into the South.[x] Several passages[y] are brought forward to shew that the bones of the saint were preserved at Ripon, especially an indulgence of archbishop Grey, in which it is stated that they were then perfect, and that they were exhibited to the worshipping beholders. It may be said with truth that another skeleton might easily be substituted for that of Wilfrid, and that the passages which speak of the bones and

[q] Hist. Dunelm. Scr. Tres., publ. Surtees Soc., Appx., 440.

[r] Rites of Durham, publ. by Surtees Society, 42. Wilfrid's name was inscribed in golden letters in the Durham Liber Vitæ (7).

[s] Fabric Rolls of York Minster, publ. by Surtees Society, 221-3. Hist. Mon. de Abingdon, ii., 47.

[t] Church History, book ii., 94.

[u] Lel. Coll., i., 216.

[v] Eadmer, 227. Diceto, col. 455. Eadmer tells a similar story of archbishop Oswald, and I cannot help thinking that Oswald and Odo have been confused. Eadmer says that Oswald carried to Worcester the bones of Wilfrid junior, whom, however, he calls a saint!

[w] Eadmer, 227.

[x] A point of some importance in the contest for precedence between York and Canterbury, cf. Eadmer, 226-7. Anglia Sacra, i., 66, ii., 50, 206. Gervasius, col. 1291 and 1301. Bromton, col. 863. Higden, apud Gale, i., 266. Malmesbury, apud Savile, 153.

[y] Lel. Coll., i., 10, iv., 80. John of Hexham, col. 273.

body of the Saint do not prove that they were *really* his. One of his arms, it must be remembered, was in the treasury of York at the dissolution.

The epitaph that was written for Wilfrid, and which was set up over his shrine at Ripon, is recorded by Beda.[z] It consists of twenty hexameter lines mentioning his good works, and setting them forth for the imitation of posterity.

> "Wilfridus hic magnus requiescit corpore præsul,
> Hanc Domino qui aulam ductus pietatis amore
> Fecit, et eximio sacravit nomine Petri,
> Cui claves cæli Christus dedit arbiter orbis;
> Atque auro ac Tyrio devotus vestiit ostro.
> Quin etiam sublime crucis radiante metallo,
> Hic posuit trophæum, necnon et quattuor auro
> Scribi Evangelii præcepit in ordine libros;
> Ac thecam e rutilo his condignam condidit auro:
> Paschalis qui etiam sollemnia tempora cursus
> Catholici ad justum correxit dogma canonis,
> Quem statuere patres, dubioque errore remoto
> Certa suæ genti ostendit moderamina ritus:
> Inque locis istis monachorum examina crebra
> Colligit, ac monitis cavit quæ regula patrum
> Sedulus instituit: multisque domique forisque
> Jactatus nimium per tempora longa periclis,
> Quindecies ternos postquam egit episcopus annos,
> Transiit, et gaudens cælestia regna petivit.
> Dona, Jesu, ut grex pastoris calle sequatur."

The name of Wilfrid was duly entered on the calendar. His feast was appointed to be observed on the 12th of February, and that of his translation on the 24th of April. His depositio or burial was commemorated on October 12th.[a]

Several works have been ascribed to the pen of Wilfrid, but, apparently, on very questionable authority. Amongst them were the following:—"De Celebratione Paschæ, lib. i. Pro Clericorum Tonsura, lib. i. Edicta Pharensis Synodi, lib. i. Epistolæ, ad Diversos, lib. i."[b]

Few persons have had more biographers than Wilfrid, but hardly any of these seem to have taken a fair and impartial view of his life. Beda, who could have thrown a great deal of light upon his character, is so sparing of information and praise, that I cannot but think that Wilfrid was no favourite of his. In Beda's account of the treatment of Chadd there are one or two most remarkable omissions. We are obliged, therefore, to seek for information in the laudatory and highly-coloured works of Wilfrid's friends or partizans. Modern writers, for the most

[z] v., 19. Eadmer, 228. Flor. Wigorn., 264. Higden, apud Gale, i., 245. Diceto, col. 442. Lel. Coll., ii., 592, ex Ann. Eliens., with some variations.

[a] The obituary of the church of Durham fixes it on 3rd Oct. Cf. Lib. Vitæ, publ. by Surtees Society, 146.

[b] Balæus de Script. Brit., cent., i., 86.

part, have treated the subject with so much ignorance and party-spirit, that no reliance can be placed upon what they say.

The first biographer, in time and reputation, is Ædde, or Eddius Stephanus, as he is called, the chaplain of Wilfrid, and the great teacher of the Gregorian music. His narrative was drawn up at the request of Acca and Tathbercht. It abounds with valuable information, and it is one of the most curious pieces of biography that we possess. It is, of course, very highly coloured, but there are many minute touches which bear upon them the impress of truth and affection. The work has been twice printed: by Mabillon, in his great work on the Saints of the Benedictine order, and by Dean Gale, in his valuable collection of English historians.[c]

The next in order is Fridegodus, a monk of Dover, who wrote a life of St. Wilfrid, at the request of Odo, archbishop of Canterbury, in hexameter verse. Odo carried Wilfrid's remains to Canterbury, and Fridegodus became his bard. His poem is a metrical version of the work of Eddius, given in striking but uncouth language, and full of Græcisms. It is printed by Mabillon.[d] Oudinus thinks that Fridegodus was the author of the poem, De Sanctis et Pontificibus ecclesiæ Ebor., which seems to be properly ascribed to Alcuin by Dean Gale. Mabillon, however, regarded the question as an open one.

Odo, archbishop of Canterbury, is said to have written a life of Wilfrid in heroic verse.[e] Some suppose that it is to be identified with the poem of Fridegodus, but Mabillon observes that the specimen of it cited by Eadmer belongs to a different work. Odo's poem is not known to be in existence. A letter of his referring to it is printed in the Anglia Sacra.[f]

[c] Printed by Mabillon, in Acta SS. ord. S. B., sæc. iv., i., 670—722, from a MS. in the Cottonian library, which was copied for him by Dean Gale. Gale gives it himself in his XV. Scr., vol. i., 40—90, with additions, etc., from a MS. at Salisbury. The MS. which both authors made use of is in the Cottonian Library, Vespasian, D. vi., but the learned Dean had one of his own (Smith's Cat[e]). In the same collection, in Titus, A. 19, there is a short treatise of two folios, "De Ortu et Vita S. Wilfridi." See Beda, iv., 2. Oudinus, de Script. Eccl., i., col. 1672. Vossius de Hist. Latinis, 278. Cave, Hist. Lit., 480. Tanner, Bibl. Angl., 774. Pitseus, 119-21. Wright, Bibl. Lit., 229. Lel., Script., 103. There was a copy of the life, by Eddius, in the library at Glastonbury (Lel. Coll., iv., 154). There was another among the MSS. of Henry Jones, rector of Sunningwell, Berks (Smith's Cat[e]).

[d] Acta SS. ord. S. B., tert. sæc., i., 171-96; sæc. iv., i., 722-6. Ex. MS. codice bibl. Corbeiensis in Gallia. There is an interesting account of Fridegode in Oudinus, ii., col. 467. See Wm. Malmesbury, apud Savile, 200. Bale, de Script. Brit., cent. ii., 32. Vossius, 346. Mabillon, Ann. Ben., ii., 24. Wright, 433.

[e] There was a copy of it in the library at Glastonbury (Lel. Coll., iv., 154). Cf. Mabillon, Acta SS. ord. S. B., sæc. tert., i., 169.

[f] ii., 50. A most pompous and affected piece of Latinity. Wharton regards it as the preface to the life by Fridegode, but, apparently, without just cause.

Eadmer, the chaplain of archbishop Anselm, drew up another life of Wilfrid, founded upon the narratives of preceding writers, and giving only some new miracles. Anselm translated the remains of Wilfrid, and, probably, desired his chaplain to record the merits of a Saint who was now connected with his church. Eadmer's work has been printed by Mabillon, and by the Bollandists in their Acta Sanctorum.[g]

Leland gives extracts from a life of Wilfrid, by Peter de Blois, archdeacon of Bath, which he found in the vestry at Ripon. This was dedicated to Geoffrey, archbishop of York.[h] Gerald Cambrensis, also, wrote verses "in porticu eccl. S. Mariæ ab Wilfrido episcopo constructa."[i] There is some account of Wilfrid, and much novel information about Hexham, which is unknown to our Northern historians, in the treatise on the Saints of the church of Hexham, and their miracles, which was drawn up in the middle of the twelfth century by a canon of that house.[j]

Bosa was one of the five bishops who were educated at Streonshal under the abbess Hilda.[k] Of his history there is very little known. When Wilfrid lost his see in 678, Bosa was one of the persons among whom his vast diocese was divided, and he received for his share the province of Deira, the seat of his episcopate being placed at York.[l] He was consecrated by Theodore.[m] In 685 we find him witnessing a grant of king Ecgfrid,[n] but this charter is generally supposed to be a forgery. There is some doubt as to the length of Bosa's tenure of the

[g] Acta SS. ord. S. B., sæc. tert., i., 196-228. Acta SS., 24 Apr. From a MS. in the Cottonian library. See Oudinus, ii., 1072, and seqq.

[h] Lel. Coll., iv. 109.

[i] Ibid., iii., 114.

[j] Printed from a MS. in the Bodleian library, by Mabillon, Acta. SS. ord. S. B., sæc. tert., i., 228-46. Other notices of Wilfrid may be found in Capgrave's Legenda Nova, 300-7. Harpsfeld, 94-6, etc. Bp. Smith's Flores Hist. Eccl., 117-18. Lel. de Script. Brit., i., 103. In Benet Coll., Cambr., is a "Vita Wilfredi" (Smith's Cat[e]). At Winchester there is a MS. intituled, "Revelatio Wilfredi, arch. Ebor." (Ibid.)

[k] Beda, iv., 23. Flor. Wigorn., 251. Wendover, i., 107. Vita S. Begæ, 57. Leland (De Script. Brit., i., 92) says that Hilda procured his elevation to the see of York.

[l] Beda, iv., 12. Saxon Chron., 54. Wendover, i., 104. Flor. Wigorn., 252. Symeon, Hist. Eccl. Dunelm., 46-7. Asser, apud Gale, i., 146. Huntingdon, apud Savile, 191 b. Diceto, col. 440. Bromton, ibid., 792.

[m] Beda, iv., 12. Flor. Wigorn., 252. Vita S. Eatæ inter Biogr., Miscell., publ. by Surtees Soc., 123. Huntingdon, apud Savile, 191 b. Diceto, col. 440. Bromton, ibid., 793. Gervasius, ibid., 1638.

[n] Lel. Coll., ii., 517. Trithemius de Viris illustr. ord. S. B., lib. iv., cap. 64. App[x] to Smith's Beda, 782. Bosa witnesses a charter of Ecgfrid in 685 (Codex Dipl., i., 29).

see of York. It seems probable that he lost his position on Wilfrid's return in 686 or 687,[o] but he regained it in the course of two or three years, and held it until his death, which occurred in 705.[p] The mandate of pope John which required him to meet Wilfrid, and come to some arrangement about the see of York, was therefore useless.[q] The little that we know of Bosa is very much to his credit. He was the instructor of Acca, who became bishop of Hexham.[r] In the life of Eata, Bosa is spoken of as "sanctus et Deo amabilis vir."[s] Symeon calls him "sanctissimus et Deo dilectus;"[t] and Florence of Worcester tells us that he was a person "multæ sanctitatis et humilitatis."[u] Alcuin also bestows upon him no ordinary praise. A short extract from his panegyric will suffice:—

> "Præfuit ecclesiæ venerandus Bosa sacerdos,
> Condignus gradui meritis nunc temporis alto,
> Vir monachus, præsul, doctor moderatus honestus,
> Quem divina sacris virtutum gratia sertis
> Compserat, et multis fecit fulgescere donis."[v]

Bosa occurs in the calendar as a bishop and confessor. The day set apart for him is Jan. 13.[w]

John, or, as he is generally called, **St. John of Beverley**, is said to have been the son of noble parents,[x] and to have been born at Harpham[y] in the East Riding of Yorkshire. In his youth he was entrusted to the care of archbishop Theodore,[z] who educated him, and gave to him his name of John.[a] Subsequently he became one of the pupils of Hilda, the abbess of

[o] Eddius, apud Gale, i., 85-6. Eadmer, apud Acta SS. ord. S. B., sæc. tert., i., 219. Fridegodus, ibid., 193.

[p] Dr. Smith, the learned editor of Beda, fixes the date of his death in 687, having been misled by Wharton in the Angl. Sacra, i., 695. The error is corrected in the app[x] (p. 759), by the editor's accomplished son. The editor of Beda, in the Mon. Hist. Brit., 233, makes a similar blunder. Florence (255) says that he died in 708. The mandate of pope John shews that he was alive in 703 or 4. Stubbs, Reg. Sacrum Angl., 4.

[q] Eddius, apud Gale, i., 82.

[r] Beda, v., 20. Mirac. S. Wilfr., apud Acta SS. ord. S. B., sæc. tert., i., 211. Symeon, col. 102. Ric. of Hexham, ibid., col. 297.

[s] Misc. Biogr., publ. by Surtees Soc., 123.

[t] X. Scr., col. 102, quoting Beda, v., 20.

[u] Chron., 255.

[v] De SS. et Pont. Eccl. Ebor., apud Gale, i., 718.

[w] Acta SS., Bollandists, where there is an uninteresting life of Bosa compiled from Beda, etc. Another day is assigned to him. Harpsfeld, 147.

[x] Stubbs, col. 1692.

[y] Lel. Coll., iv., 100. Acta SS., mense Maio.

[z] Stubbs, ut supra. Bromton, ibid., col. 794.

[a] Stubbs, col. 1692.

Streonshal,[b] "a circumstance," as Fuller observes, "which soundeth something to her honour and nothing to his disgrace, seeing eloquent Apollos himself learned the primar of his Christianity partly from Priscilla."[c] He is claimed, also, by the university of Oxford as her first master of arts.[d] We may conclude, therefore, that he was a person of more than ordinary learning.

"His light," as his biographer Folcard observes, "was not hid under a bushel." He soon began to preach the Gospel to the people. He arrested their attention by his eloquence and learning; and his holy life winged his words to their hearts. At the same time he did not neglect his own scholastic studies. Like every person of consequence and ability, he was the centre of a circle of pupils who came to him for instruction. He was an excellent expounder of the Scriptures, and was well versed in history and other subjects.[e] Among those who profited by his teaching was the venerable Beda, whom he afterwards ordained.[f] It was no slight honour to have been the master of such a scholar, and it was, probably, from John that Beda derived that taste for historical pursuits which has won for him an undying reputation.

The zeal and learning of John could not fail to attract the attention of the Northumbrian court, and his connection with Theodore would be sure to contribute to his advancement. King Aldfrid was his patron,[g] and through his means, in all probability, John succeeded Eata in the see of Hexham. This appointment is enveloped in some mystery, which may, perhaps, be cleared away in the following manner. Eata died, I believe, in the autumn of 686,[h] and about the same time Wilfrid returned into Northumbria, and was allowed to take possession of the sees of Hexham and Lindisfarne, which were then vacant. We know that Wilfrid was only bishop of Lindisfarne for a year,[i] and we are told that John was consecrated bishop of Hexham on the

[b] Beda, iv., 23. Wendover, i., 107. Vita S. Begæ, 57. Folcard (Acta SS.) calls him the pupil of Elfleda, at Whitby. Stubbs (col. 1692) is also wrong in calling John's instructress Elfrida. Mabillon, Ann. Ben., i., 474, commits an error when he speaks of John as "Wicciorum Episcopus."

[c] Fuller's Worthies, *n.e.*, ii., 497.

[d] Caius de Antiq. Univ., Cant. i., 106. Acta SS., ut supra, pref. Harrison's description of Britain, 158. Twyni Antiq., Acad. Oxon, 169. Wood's Antiq. Univ. Oxon, i., 28, and Hist. Univ. Oxon., iv., 37-8. His figure, as a fellow, was in one of the windows of the chapel at Univ. Coll. Smith's Annals of Univ. Coll., 129. Fuller (Worthies, ii., 497) says of him, "I remember his picture in a window in the library at Salisbury, with an inscription under it, affirming him the first master of arts at Oxford." It has still to be proved that there was an university at Oxford at that time.

[e] Folcard, apud Acta SS. Stubbs, col. 1692.

[f] Folcard, ut supra. Triveti Annales, 262. Mabillon, Acta SS., Ord. S.B., sæc. tert., i., 536, ex vita Bedæ, per Ceolfridum. Lel. de Script. Brit., i., 116-18.

[g] Lel. Col., iv., 100. [h] Saxon Chron., 63. Reg. Sacrum Angl., 4.

[i] Beda, iv., 29. Flor. Wigorn., 256. Symeon, Hist. Eccl. Dunelm., 60.

25th August, 687.[j] It may be inferred, therefore, that Wilfrid took possession at that time of the see of York, which was ceded to him, voluntarily or involuntarily, by Bosa, and that he left the northern portion of the great diocese of Northumbria to John and Eadbert. With Hexham John was very well acquainted. For some time before he was raised to the see he had lived in an hermitage at Harneshalg or Harneshow, otherwise called Eaglesmount, on the Tyne,[k] so that the field of labour to which he was now introduced was by no means unfamiliar to him. He presided over the see for about eighteen years, but we know very little of his labours and his life. At a little village called Carnesbroc, distant a mile and a half from Hexham, on the opposite bank of the Tyne, he consecrated a church which was dedicated to St. Michael.[l] To it, especially in Lent, John was accustomed to retire to watch and pray in secret. Thither did the needy and the sick resort, and their benefactor did not neglect them. We have an account of a miracle that John is said to have worked at Carnesbroc.[m]

On the death of Bosa in 705,[n] John was translated from Hexham to York, and Alcuin, when speaking of the new prelate and his appointment, is by no means sparing of his praise.

"Interea Bosa felicia regna petente,
Accipit ecclesiæ regimen clarissimus ille
Vir pietate, fide, meritis et mente, Johannes,
Pontificalis apex, priscorum formula patrum,
Flumina doctrinæ fundens e pectore puro."[o]

[j] The Saxon Chronicle (63) is the authority for this date. Cf. ibid., 56. Dr. Smith, in his edition of Beda, v., 2, and Richard of Hexham (X Scr., col. 295), say that John became bishop of Hexham in 685; Wendover (i., 112); Flor. Wigorn. (255), and Diceto (col. 441) put the appointment a year later. Richard of Hexham (col. 295) and Folcard (Acta SS.) say that John held Hexham for a year, and they, as well as Bromton (col. 794) and other authorities, say that he went to York in 686 or 7, Bosa being then dead, whereas he was alive in 705 (cf. Reg. Sacr. Ang., 4. Lingard's Anglo-Saxon-Church, i., 144). Wm. of Malmesbury (Savile, 153); Anglia Sacra, (i., 65); and Hist. Mon. S. Aug. Cant., (279-80) say that John was driven out of Hexham to make room for Wilfrid. The Anglia Sacra says that Bosa was expelled from York also, and Malmesbury says that John went from Hexham to York, *i.e.*, from the less to the greater! Mabillon (Ann. Ben., ii., 24) is quite at fault in the chronology.

[k] Lel. Coll., iv., 100. Stubbs (col. 1692) calls the place Arneshange. Richard of Hexham (col. 291) calls it Erneshou, and Higden (apud Gale, i., 247), the oratory of St. Michael or Harneshow. Higden and Richard identify the oratory and the hermitage.

[l] Beda, v., 2. Folcard, ut supra. Lel. Coll., iv., 100. Rich. of Hexham, (col. 292) says that the church of St. Michael was begun by Wilfrid and finished by Acca. The only church at present dedicated to St. Michael in the neighbourhood of Hexham is that of Warden. There is a village bearing the name of St. John's Lee, on the opposite bank of the Tyne.

[m] Beda, v., 2. Folcard, ut supra.

[n] Saxon Chron., 56. Fl. Wigorn., 268. Symeon, col. 76. Ric. of Hexham, ibid., col. 296, who says that he was bishop of York thirty-three years.

[o] Alcuin de SS., etc., eccl. Ebor., apud Gale, i., 722, where there is an interesting life of St. John in verse.

Of the good work that John did in Yorkshire we have several pleasing memorials. I say nothing of the miraculous powers which he is said to have possessed. It is enough to watch his good example in the ordinary path of duty. With king Osred[p] he seems to have been a favourite. He joined with that monarch and his nobles, and in synod assembled they made many wise enactments for the management of the Northumbrian church.[q] John saw, also, that they were carried into effect, for he was very diligent in visiting his monasteries and attending to the poor. When he was asked to a banquet after the consecration of Burton church, he uttered the noble sentiment, "Magis episcopum decere ad monasterium redire, et Deo in suis pauperibus servire, quam per domos divitum convivari."[r] In the midst of his labours he did not neglect the solitary watches and the prayers of the recluse. His own residence in York was adjacent to the church of St. Michael the archangel, and thither he retired at stated periods to humble himself before God.[s] There would be a charm to him in that familiar name. It would remind him of the little oratory in which he had once prayed by the waters of the Tyne.

Amid the many duties that waited upon his high office John never forgot the lessons and the example of Theodore. He had always around him a little company of pupils to whom he was the Gamaliel. Beda indeed had left him, and was preparing in his solitary cell the works that we still admire, but there were others now at the feet of his old master. St. Sigga was there, and Herebald, the abbat of Tynemouth in after years, and at this time the companion as well as the pupil of John. Bercthune, another of his scholars, became abbat of Beverley, and narrated to Beda those miracles of the good bishop which the great historian has recorded. Of Wilfrid, the pupil who succeeded him in the see, I shall elsewhere speak.[t]

Bale asserts that John was the author of the following works. "Pro Luca Exponendo lib. i. Homeliæ Evangeliorum, lib. i. Ad Hyldam Abbatissam, lib. i. Ad Herebaldum Discipulum, Epist. i. Ad Andoenum et Bertinum, Epist. ii., et alia."[u]

It is with Beverley and the East Riding of Yorkshire that the name of John is especially connected.

> "—— Natale solum dulcedine captos
> Ducit, et immemores non sinit esse sui."

[p] Folcard, ut supra. Lel. Coll. iv., 100.

[q] and [r] Folcard, ut supra. I believe that this is the synod which is said to have been held at Alne in 709, and about which there is some mystery and doubt. Labbe, Concilia, vi., 1401. Spelmanni Conc., 215.

[s] Folcard. Bromton, col. 794.

[t] Folcard. Bromton, ut supra. Stubbs, col. 1693. Lel. Coll., iv., 100.

[u] Script. Brit., cent. i., 89. Bale is probably drawing, as usual, upon his imagination.

This was the charm that bound him to that district. Among the woods and lakes with which it then abounded he found a village of the name of Inderawood, which a later generation changed to Beverley, from the beavers that then sported in the waters of the Hull.[v] At that time, no doubt, it was an oasis among the wild woods in which it was embosomed. A little church was there, dedicated to the beloved disciple,[w] the namesake of the holy prelate who now gazed in rapture upon the scenery around him. Fascinated by what he saw, and a mighty impulse moving him, John became the owner of the place. He added a choir to the existing church, and converted it into a monastery. Seven priests were placed in it with as many clerks. On the south side of the church John erected an oratory, which he dedicated to St. Martin, and made into a nunnery. Neither was there any want of permanent endowments. The founder bought and appropriated to his monastery lands in Ridings, Welwick, Bilton and Patrington, and stimulated by so good an example, the nobles in the neighbourhood most generously assisted him. One gave to him North Burton, and another the manor of Walkington. Churches were erected, and the foundations of a great ecclesiastical settlement were laid, of which John had much reason to be proud.[x]

This noble work was the great effort of John's life, and it is natural enough that he should be attached to that place which he had honoured and adorned. The affections always nestle around the labour of the head and hand. Dear to John, without doubt, would be the temples that Wilfrid had erected; Lastingham would remind him of the toil and the love of Chadd, and at Streonshal he would muse with affection upon his old instructress,

> "He gathers round him, and revives at will
> Scenes in his life—that breathe enchantment still."

But none of these places or scenes would possess the charm that attracted him to Inderawood. It was his own offering to God in the country of his birth. There the aged prelate could say with Cicero, but in a far higher sense, "hic sacra, hic genus, hic majorum multa vestigia,—Quare inest nescio quid, et latet in animo et sensu meo, quo me plus hic locus fortasse delectet." There he could meet with that solitude which the court and the crowded city could never give him. There he could watch over the infant society of which he was the founder, and, at the same

[v] Lel. Coll., iv., 100.

[w] Lel. Coll., iv., 100. Sanctuar. Dunelm. and Beverlac., publ. by Surtees Soc., 98.

[x] Folcard, apud Acta SS. Gaimar, l'Estorie des Engles, apud Mon. Hist. Brit., 783. Lel. Coll., iv., 100-101. Dugdale's Mon., ii., 127.

time, endeavour to reach a higher step on the great ladder of perfection. As each succeeding winter left its mark upon his brow, he would long more and more for the quiet that he had found in his hermitage on the Tyne, and covet that rest which the busy world denied him.

> "For there the soul, released from human strife,
> Smiles at the little ills and cares of life."

The desire was irresistible. In 718 he deserted the see of York, which he had occupied since the death of Bosa, and, nominating as his successor his old pupil Wilfrid, he retired to spend his days among the solitude of Inderawood.[y] Bercthune, a beloved scholar, was the abbat of the monastery, and by him he was affectionately welcomed.[z] For four years was the aged prelate an inmate within those walls, and then his prayers and his watchings were concluded. On the seventh day of May, 721, he was called away to his rest.[a]

He was buried in St. Peter's porch,[b] within the church that he loved so well,[c] and from which he is called to this day St. John of Beverley. His remains, like those of St. Chadd, were deposited in a feretory of wood, which was beautifully carved.[d] In 1037 he was solemnly canonized at Rome by Benedict IX., and in that year archbishop Alfric removed his bones, and deposited them in a precious shrine which was radiant with gold, and silver, and jewels.[e] The care of the pious archbishop was fruitless, for the shrine was, probably, destroyed or lost in the fire by which the church of Beverley was consumed in September, 1187. Five years after this John's remains were discovered, and deposited in another place. In 1664, whilst a grave was being dug, the ashes of the Saint were found in a case of

[y] Saxon Chron., 56. Flor. Wigorn., 272. Beda, v., 6. Alcuin de SS., etc., apud Gale, i., 724. Folcard, apud Acta SS. Symeon, col. 76. Ric. of Hexham, ibid., 296.

[z] Bromton, col. 794.

[a] Beda, v., 6. Saxon Chron., 63, having been a bishop thirty-three years, eight months, and thirteen days. Wendover, i., 135. Folcard, apud Acta SS. Liber Vitæ Dunelm., ed. Surtees Soc., 143, in which St. John's name is entered in golden letters (7). Higden, apud Gale, i., 247. Stubbs, col. 1693. Bromton, col. 794, who says that he was bishop of York twenty-three years. Chron. Petrib (5) says he died in 722. Lel. Coll., iv., 101. Gaimar, l'Estorie des Engles, apud Mon. Hist. Brit., 785, says of him,

> "Li bons Johans idonc transi,
> Celui ki gist a Beverli."

[b] Folcard, apud Acta SS., says that he was buried "in porticu S. Joh. Evang."

[c] Beda, v., 6. Saxon Chron., 63. Folcard, ut supra. Higden, apud Gale, i., 247. Ric. of Hexham, col. 296. Hickesii Dissert. Ep., 118. Stubbs, col. 1693. Lel. Coll., iv., 34, 80. Dugdale's Mon., ii., 166. Capgrave and others are wrong when they say that John was buried at Sarum. Cf. Twyni Antiq. Acad. Oxon., 169.

[d] Stubbs, ut supra, col. 1700.

[e] Stubbs, ut supra. Lel. Coll., iv., 102.

lead, and were re-interred by the order of the archbishop of the day.[f] They were again brought to light in 1736.[g]

Very great was the sanctity of that shrine in the days of old; many pilgrimages were made to it, and many miracles are said to have been wrought through the agency of St. John.[h] With the exception of Cuthbert of Durham, no Northern Saint was regarded with more veneration than St. John of Beverley. Mysterious virtues are said to have proceeded from his shrine, and a holy oil to have flowed from his tomb.[i] The fame of Beverley and its Saint attracted the attention of king Athelstan, who, like David of Scotland, was "ane soir sanct for the crown." When he was on his way to Scotland he is said to have gone to Beverley to obtain the assistance of St. John, promising his church many privileges and gifts if he were successful, and leaving behind him his "cultellum" as a pledge that he would redeem.[j]

> "He went to Beverlay
> And praied to the bishop Jon in fertre wher he lay,
> That he wild bede his bone, untille the Trinite,
> And he suld gyve his kirke franchise and fe,
> To haf and to holde als he was kyng leall."[k]

The monarch carried with him into Scotland the banner of St. John, and success attended him. I pass over the marvellous story of the sword, which reminds us of the adventure of king Arthur. On his return to England the victor did not forget his promise. He founded at Beverley a college of secular canons, adding to the old endowment divers lands in Lockington and Brandesburton.[l] He gave it, also, among other rights, the privilege of sanctuary, which the church of Beverley enjoyed until

[f] Dugdale's Vis[n] of Yks., ed. Surtees Soc., 22, where a long account of the discovery is given. Thoresby's Diary, ii., 434. Anth. a Wood's Life, ed. Bliss., 140. Camden's Brittannia, n. e., iii., 325. Poulson's Beverlac, 666.

[g] Poulson's Beverlac, 681.

[h] Beda, v., 2-6. Alcuin de SS. Ebor., apud Gale, i., 723-4. Wendover, i., 135. Folcard, Liber Vitæ, ed. Surtees Soc., 143. Hist. Mon. S. Aug. Cant., 280. Scala Chronica, 6, 210. Ric. of Hexham, col. 291-2. Bromton, col. 794. Stubbs, col. 1692-3. Lel. Coll., iv., 100, etc. Capgrave's Nova Legenda SS., 189-91.

[i] On June 14, 1443, Archbishop Kempe granted an indulgence of 100 days to those who visit the tomb, "which is now very famous, especially for the very healthful supply of sweet oil which is now observed to gush from the tomb more largely and abundantly than usual, for the healing of all faithful worshippers." The monks of Meaux had some of this oil in an ampul. (Poulson's Holderness, ii., 313). Capgrave's Nova Legenda. Harpsfeld, Hist. Angl., 147-8, where there is a short account of St. John. Twyni Antiq. Acad. Oxon., 170.

[j] Folcard, apud Acta SS. Sanctuar. Dunelm. et Beverlac., ed. Surtees Soc., 98. Triveti Annales, 321. Ailred, col. 356-7. Bromton, col. 838. Cart. Domus S. Leon. Ebor., MS., Cotton., Nero D., iii., 5 *a*. Higden, apud Gale, i., 262. Lel. Coll., iv., 100-101. Rymer's Fœdera, i., 771-2.

[k] Peter Langtoft's Chron., 29. Chron. Petrib., 28. In 938.

[l] Acta SS. Lel. Coll., iv., 101-2.

the Reformation.[m] The words in which these grants were made have been handed down by tradition:—

"Als fre make I thee
As hert may thenk
Or eghe may see."

I find them mentioned in a confirmation of the privileges of the church which was made by Henry IV.,[n] and you may still see them on a tablet in Beverley minster under a portrait of Athelstan, which it is unnecessary to describe. The canons would be glad to preserve a memorial of the monarch who regarded St. John "as his tutelar Saint,"[o] and the piety of Athelstan was duly recited in the legend.[p]

The example of Athelstan was copied by other kings who were glad to honour the Saint, and to confirm the chartered privileges of his town. Edward the Confessor was a benefactor to the minster. William the Conqueror and Stephen were prevented, it is said, by miraculous interference, from plundering its lands, and William became its patron.[q] John visited the town and added to its privileges, but not without a befitting consideration for his generosity.[r] Edward I. carried with him the banner of the Saint, as a talisman, to the wars in Scotland, and made his offerings at the tomb at Beverley on more occasions than one.[s] Henry IV. came to Beverley and confirmed its privileges,[t] but it was his son, Henry V., who paid the greatest honour to St. John. The victory of Agincourt was won on the 25th of October, the day on which the translation of the remains of the Saint was commemorated, and the monarch attributed his success to St. John's intercession.[u] He shewed his gratitude by making a pilgrimage to the shrine with his queen.[v] But he did more than this. It was probably at the desire of Henry that archbishop Chicheley wrote, on Dec. 16, 1416, to the bishop of London, requesting that in consequence of the great victory, the day of St. John's burial, *i. e.*, the 7th of May, should be observed with due state and ceremony, "cum regimine chori, ad modum festi unius confessoris et pontificis."

[m] Folcard. Lel. Coll., iv., 101. The register of the sanctuary has been published by the Surtees Society.

[n] Fædera, viii., 369. Codex Dipl., ii., 186.

[o] Weever's Funerall Monuments, 181. Sanctuar Bev., ed. Surtees Soc., 98.

[p] Triveti, Ann., 321. Lel. Coll., iii., 4. Capgrave's Nova Legenda.

[q] Acta SS. Lel. Coll., iv., 102-3.

[r] Poulson's Beverlac, 63, 537.

[s] Liber Garderobæ, 27. The king made his offerings at the tomb, "ubi S. Joh. *primo* sepeliebatur." Triveti, Ann., 321. Langtoft, ii., 303.

"Befor Saynt Jon he woke a nyght or he
thein nam."

[t] Fædera, viii., 369.

[u] Fædera, ix., 421. Sir Harris Nicolas' acc^t of Agincourt, 176. Dugd., Mon., ii., 166.

[v] Poulson's Beverlac, 595.

The honours of Oct. 25 were shared with SS. Crispin and Crispinian.[w]

A life of St. John has been written more than once. His principal biographer was Folcard, a monk of Canterbury, who wrote his work in the eleventh century at the request of Aldred, archbishop of York, to whom he dedicated his book.[x] It is printed *in extenso* by the Bollandists in their Acta SS., under the 7th of May; and it may also be found, in an abridged form, with another short life by a nameless author, in the great work of Mabillon.[y] The narrative of Folcard is meagre and uninteresting, and is evidently the production of a person who knew little of his subject. Subjoined to Folcard's life is a collection of the miracles ascribed to St. John, some of which were written down by William Kecel, a clerk of Beverley. I believe him to be identical with Asketyll, who is said to have compiled a life of St. John.[z] Leland, in his Collectanea, gives extracts from two lives of St. John.[a] The first is that by Folcard. The latter, which is by an anonymous author, is divided into three parts, and contains much interesting information. There is a brief account of him in Capgrave's Nova Legenda SS.[b]

Wilfrid II., or Junior, as he is called, to distinguish him from his illustrious namesake. He was a favourite pupil of John, who resigned the bishopric of York in his favour, when old age had rendered him unequal to the duties of the office.[c]

[w] Fœdera, ix., 421. Dugd., Mon., ii., 166. Preface to Folcard's life in Acta SS. Lyndewode's Provinciale, fol. 57, ed. 1501, and more at length in the app[x] to the ed. of 1679, p. 70.

[x] The transcript which the Bollandists used, was sent from England by a person of the name of Leander Prichart. Other copies of the MS. are in England, *viz.*, inter MSS. Cotton., Faustina B., iv., 156-78. Otho, C. 16, and MS. Harl., 560. A copy was recently sold at the dispersion of the Savile MSS. for £81, a very large sum when we remember the uninteresting character of the MS., and that it is already in print. Leland saw a copy in the library of St. Mary's, York (Coll., iv., 37). There is another among the Parker MSS., A. 11 (Cat[e]). See Vossius de Historicis Latinis, 377. Oudinus de Script. Eccl., ii., 707. Leland. de Script. Brit., i., 78, under the uncouth name of Joannes Fibroleganus. Wright's Biogr. Lit., i., 231.

[z] Vossius de Hist. Latinis, 514.

[y] Acta SS. ord. S. Ben., ed. 1734, sæc. iii., i., 410-13.

[a] Lel. Coll., iv., 99-104.

[b] Fol., 189-91, ed. 1516. A short acc[t] in Smith's Flores Hist. Eccl., 118. Pitseus, 122. My friend, Mr. Stubbs, informs me that there are some extracts from an unpublished life of St. John among the Wharton MSS., in the library at Lambeth.

[c] Beda, v., 6. Alcuin de Pont. Ebor., apud Gale, i., 724. Saxon Chron., 56. Flor. Wigorn., 272. Folcardi, Vita S. Joh., apud Acta SS., mense Maio. Symeon, col. 78. Stubbs, col. 1694, who calls him St. John's chaplain. Higden, apud Gale, i., 247. Mabillon. Ann. Ben., i., 474, where he is said to have been one of Hilda's pupils. Ibid., ii., 50. Harpsfeld, 148.

Before this Wilfrid had been the vice-dominus, or abbas, of the monastery at York, the bishop himself being the dominus or ruler. Wilfrid gave to the church of York several noble gifts, furnishing the altar with sacred vessels, and covering it and the crosses with plates of silver gilt. He was munificent, also, to other churches, and he seems to have attended diligently to his episcopal duties.[d] Wilfrid is said to have sanctioned the accusation that was brought against Beda, of promulgating heretical opinions in his treatise, *De sex ætatibus mundi*, and the historian made against him the counter-charge of indulging to excess in the luxuries of the table.[e] The words of Alcuin are probably corroborative of the testimony of Beda, when he says,

> "Hos mentes dapibus, illos sed carnis alebat:
> Hos fovet ætheriis, illos carnalibus auget."[f]

The poet, however, speaks in laudatory terms of Wilfrid's energy and goodness. There is some difference of opinion among the historians as to the year in which he vacated the see, but the difficulty is removed by the following passage, which some modern writers have overlooked.

> "At sua facta bonus postquam compleverat ille
> Pastor in ecclesiis, specialia septa petivit,
> Quo servire Deo tota jam mente vacaret:
> Contemplativæ seseque per omnia vitæ
> Dans, mundi varias curasque reliquit inanes."[g]

It thus appears that Wilfrid followed the example of his old master, John, and devoted the last portion of his life to solitude and prayer. He took this step in 732,[h] the year in which he is said to have died, but the closing scene was deferred until the 29th of April, 744[i] or 745.[j] What the "specialia septa" were to which he retired it is impossible to say. The dignitaries of York, in after times, asserted that he was interred at Ripon, and that archbishop Odo carried away his remains, and not those of his more illustrious namesake, from that church to Canterbury.[k]

[d] Alcuin, apud Gale, i., 724.

[e] Bedæ Epist. ad Ecgbertum, ed. Smith, 306. Vita S. Bedæ, inter Acta SS. ord. S. B., sæc. tert., i., 548. App^x to Smith's Beda, 802.

[f] Alcuin, apud Gale, i., 725.

[g] Ibid. Smith's Beda, 315.

[h] The year in which Egbert came to the see. Hoveden (Savile, 231) says that Wilfrid died in that year, and he is followed by Mr. Stubbs in his Reg. Sacr. Angl. Symeon (col. 78) says that Wilfrid was bishop for fifteen years. Hen. of Huntingdon (Savile, 195 *b*) says for ten. Cf. Procem. ad op. Alcuini, ed. 1777, vol. i., xvi.

[i] Saxon Chron., 67, he having been bishop of York thirty winters. Flor. Wigorn., 272. Higden, apud Gale, i., 249. Mabillon (Ann. Ben., ii., 24) puts the depositio of S. Wilfr. (*i.e.*, jun.) on 8 kal. June. Wendover, i., 145, makes Wilfrid die in 743.

[j] Symeon, col. 104. Chron. de Mailros, 4. Addit. ad Bedam, ed. Smith, 224.

[k] Anglia Sacra, i., 66. Hist. Mon. S. Aug. Cant., 281. Malmesbury de Pont., apud Savile, 153.

Eadmer, however, maintains that his bones were carried away from Ripon to Worcester by the celebrated Oswald.[l]

Egbert was the son of Eata, and a member of the royal family of Northumbria. He was first cousin to king Ceolwulf, the "most glorious Ceolwulf," to whom Beda dedicates his history.[m]

> "Regali stirpe creatus,
> Nobilium coram seclo radice parentum."[n]

The youthful noble was sent by his father to a monastery to receive his education. After awhile he went to Rome, with his brother Ecgred, to extend and complete his studies, and there he was admitted into deacon's orders. His brother having died at Rome, Egbert returned into Northumbria.[o]

In 732 Wilfrid resigned the bishopric of York, and Egbert was appointed by Ceolwulf to succeed him.[p] The selection was an excellent one. By his learning Egbert was peculiarly fitted for that high office, and his noble blood would add greatly to his influence with the court and people. Soon after he was raised to the see of York, Beda, who was now drawing towards the close of his pilgrimage, wrote a long letter to him filled with sensible advice as to the management of his diocese. It gives us an admirable picture of what, in the opinion of the writer, were the duties of a Christian bishop, and sets vividly before us the condition of the Northern church.

In the first place, the great historian recommends Egbert to illustrate personal teaching by personal holiness; to give to study and contemplation the hours that many waste in idle conversation, and to eschew the society of useless and worldly companions. He then advises him to ordain a larger number of priests to teach and administer the sacraments in the villages,

[l] Anglia Sacra, ii., 206. The inscription stated that they were the bones of *St.* Wilfrid. Wilfrid II. was never canonized. The evidence is most conflicting, and "adhuc sub judice lis est."

[m] Saxon Chron., 66. Symeon, Hist. Eccl. Dunelm., 83, 84.

[n] Alcuin de SS. Eccl. Ebor., apud Gale, i., 725.

[o] Symeon, Hist. Eccl. Dunelm., 83. "A patre Eata in monasterium traditus est." Dr. Smith, in a note to his edition of Beda, 312, commits an error, with regard to this passage. He makes Eata the bishop and not the prince. Mabillon (Ann. Ben., ii., 94) falls into the same mistake, and so does Mr. Wright (Biogr. Brit. Lit., i., 297).

[p] See *Wilfrid's life.* The Saxon Chron. makes the date 734 (66). Flor. Wigorn. puts it in 744, "archiepiscopatus insigni sublimatus" (272). Cf. Baronii Ann., ix., 110. Wendover (i., 144) makes the date 743. Addit. ad Bedam (Smith, 223) make the date 732.

and also to translate the Creed and the Lord's Prayer out of the Latin into the Saxon tongue, as well for the use of the listeners as for those who officiate in the churches. Beda, in the next place, expresses his wish that the episcopate should be extended. There are many places, he says, among the woods and hills of Northumbria, that a bishop has never visited for years, although all are regularly taxed for his support. This disinclination for subdivision was to be ascribed to the pride and avarice of the prelates themselves. Against the evils which necessarily resulted from such a system, there was an adequate remedy in the injunction of the pious and forecasting Gregory that there should be twelve bishops in the Northern province, and Beda begs his friend to secure for himself the pall, and to obtain the permission of king Ceonwulf to carry this recommendation into effect. Several of the larger monasteries could be converted with advantage into the residence of a bishop. From this point Beda passes on to the corruptions with which these religious institutions were filled, and the urgent necessity for reform. They were hotbeds of the grossest vice; no rule or discipline was observed in them, and luxury and excess, of every kind, were rife within their walls. Ever since the days of Aldfrid it had been the common practice, not only of persons of distinction, but of officers of the court, to obtain grants of land for the purpose of founding a monastery; and, when it was established, and freed, in this way, from secular jurisdiction, it was merely converted into the residence of the founder with his family and friends, who had nothing of religion but the cloak. The whole diocese, as Beda said, was full of disorder and corruption, and it would require all the determination and skill of a bold reformer to suppress them.[q] The existence of several of these evils in the Northern province is mentioned with regret in a letter that was addressed to Egbert by the pious and energetic Boniface.[r]

These warnings and suggestions were not lost upon Egbert. His first endeavour was to obtain the pall, which was given to him by Gregory III. at Rome, in 735. He thus became the second archbishop of York. More than a century had elapsed since Paulinus fled into Kent, carrying his pall with him, and no one since that time had sought for the lost honour, a neglect which was made, in after years, a strong argument for the pre-

[q] Bedæ, Epist. ad Ecgberctum antistitem., ed. Smith, 305-12. Mabillon, Ann. Ben., ii., 97-8. Acta SS. ord. S. B., sæc. tert., i., 548-9.

[r] Bonifacii Epist., apud Bibl. Max. Patrum, xiii., 73, 106. Baronii Ann., ix., 110. Mabillon, Ann. Ben., ii., 101. Spelmanni Conc., 232, 237. In MS. Cotton., Vesp. A., xiv., among many of Alcuin's letters, is said to be one from Paul the First, "ad Ethberktum Archiepiscopum et Eadberhtum filium regis." Cf. Wilkins' Concilia, i., 144.

cedence of Canterbury, when the famous controversy arose between the two metropolitan sees.[s] When Egbert thus became archbishop he stepped at once into a commanding position, and every bishop in the Northern province was made his suffragan. In 738 his hands were still farther strengthened. In that year his brother Eadbert mounted the Northumbrian throne, and the protection of the state was thereby assured to the archbishop. He could now act with authority and decision. It is impossible to say to what extent he carried out the reforms which Beda and Boniface recommended, but, at all events, it is certain that he was diligent in his duties.[t] The books that he wrote shew that he had the interests of his diocese at heart, and if he took so much pains to commit to writing a system of discipline and ecclesiastical rule, we may safely infer that he would do his best to see that they were properly observed. All the works of Egbert seem to presuppose the existence of a regular clerical organization, and as he occupied the throne of Paulinus, with such commanding influence, for above thirty years, he would have time enough to see the system in full play. Alcuin acquaints us with his piety and energy.[u] He is said to have been the first prelate who possessed a mint at York.[v] He paid great attention to the services and music of his church, introducing the observance of the hours. He was, also, a benefactor to the fabric of the minster, bestowing upon his cathedral the choice work of the jeweller and the goldsmith, and giving to it figured curtains of silk of foreign workmanship.[w] He was, in all probability, the first introducer of the parochial system into the North. His works were of great repute in the Anglo-Saxon church. They comprise a Pontifical,[x] or a series of special offices for the use of a bishop, a volume of Excerptiones, or extracts from the Fathers and canons on matters of discipline,[y] a Dialogue

[s] Saxon Chron., 66. Addit. ad Bedam, ed. Smith, 224. Chron. de Mailros, 3. Wendover, i., 145 (in 745) Symeon, col. 100. Stubbs, col. 1697. Chron., J. Wallingford, apud Gale, i., 529. Higden, ibid., i., 249. Hoveden, apud Savile, 230, *b*.—"Cæteri episcopi inter Paulinum et Egbertum nichil altius quam simplicis episcopi vocabulo anhelarunt." Anglia Sacra, i., 66. Hist. Mon. S. Aug. Cant., 281. Bonifacii Epist., apud Bibl. Max. Patrum, xiii., 73. Malmesbury, apud Savile, 12 *b*., 153.

[t] Alcuin, apud Gale, i., 723. Addit. ad Pœnitentiale Egberti, in Laws, etc., of England, ii., 233-5.

[u] Alcuin de SS. Ebor., apud Gale, i., 725. Hist. Mon. S. Aug. Cant., 281.

[v] Davies on the York Mint, 3.

[w] Alcuin, apud Gale, i., 725.

[x] Published for the first time by the Surtees Society, from a MS. in the Imperial Library at Paris, which formerly belonged to the church of Evreux. It has been reprinted by the monks of Solesmes (Sarthe) in their Spicilegium. There are some extracts from it in Martene de Ant. Eccl. Rit., t. ii., lib. ii., c. xiii. The peculiarities of the Pontifical are pointed out in Mr. Maskell's Monumenta Ritualia.

[y] Printed entire in Thorpe's Ancient Laws and Institutes of England, ii., 326-42, and, partially, in Wilkins' Concilia, i., 101-12. Labbe, Conc., vi.,

de Ecclesiastica Institutione;[z] a Confessionale[a] and a Pænitentiale,[b] the two latter works being in the native as well as in the Latin tongue, and for an obvious reason. Other treatises are also ascribed to him.[c] Egbert seems to have studied deeply, and to have borrowed much from the writings of his predecessors, especially from those of Theodore. Everything that he has done shews that he was a rigid disciplinarian. Some of his rules are severe to an excess, some of his penances are frightful. His ideal of a faithful Christian must have been something far too high to be attained by frail erring man. And yet we cannot doubt his sincerity and earnestness. A person who would commit to writing such minute directions for moral conduct and mental control was a man of more than ordinary powers. That heart must indeed have been crucified itself before it could thus teach others how to crucify the world. The enemy of all must have been battered down by long vigils and tears in the closet and in the desert. And having won the victory at length, that heart could shew others, yea, all, how to strive and conquer. An ennobled purity seems to envelop it; it reposes in the still light of holiness, but it is the brightness that surrounds an angel.

There are other reasons, besides his literary labours, which entitle Egbert to the gratitude of posterity. He is said to have been the founder of the celebrated school of York and of the library connected with it.[d] There was no nobler place of education at that time in England. The renown of the scholars and their master was mentioned with delight among the Paladins

col. 1586—1604. Spelman's Conc., 258-80. There is a manuscript in MSS. Harl., 438; another, once belonging to the church of Worcester, in the library of C. C. C., Cambridge. Cf. Wanley, ii., 109. Mabillon, Ann. Ben., ii., 210-11. Oudinus, i., 1796.

[z] Ancient Laws and Institutes of England, ii., 87-96. Bedæ, Ep. Labbe, Concilia, vi., col. 1604-11. Wilkins, i., 82-6. Leland found a copy in MS. in the library at Sarum (Itin., iii., 92). There is one in MS. in MSS. Cotton., Vitellius, A, xii. See Oudinus, i., 1796. Lel. de Script. Brit., i., 114.

[a] Ancient Laws and Institutes of England, ii., 128-69. There is a copy in MS. in MSS. Harl., 438. See Oudinus.

[b] Ancient Laws and Institutes of England, ii., 170—239. Extracts from it, sub nomine Bedæ, in Labbe, vi., col. 1611-19, and Spelman, 281-8. Wilkins, i., 113-44. There is a MS. of it in the library of C. C. C., Cambridge. Cf. Wanley, ii., 109. Leland found another in the library at Sarum (Itin., iii. 92). See Oudinus, ut supra, and Leland, De Script. Brit., i., 114, and Wright, 305. Fuller (Ch. Hist., bk. ii., 101) is anything but complimentary about the tendency of these works.

[c] Sc. "Eruditiones Discipulorum, lib. i. Homeliæ et Lectiones, lib. i. Ad Ecclesiarum Pastores, lib. i. Ad Zachariam pro Pallio, epist. i. Ad Eadbertum fratrem, regem, epist. i. Ad Atinium diaconum, epist. plures, etc. (Bale, Script. Brit., cent. ii., 109.) Pitseus, 153-4; a most inaccurate writer.

[d] Higden, apud Gale, i., 249. Lel. Coll., iii., 259. Alcuini Op., ed., 1777, procem. to vol. i., xvi. Baronius, ix., 338. Smithi Flores Hist. Eccl., 153. There is a long account of Egbert's literary labours in Oudinus, i., 1796. Cave, Hist. Lit., 486. Cf. Harpsfeld, 148. Lel. Script. Brit., i., 114.

of Charlemagne.[e] Beda, in his cell of Jarrow, rejoiced to hear of the good work which was being done at York, and longed to throw aside the infirmities of age, that he might pay another visit to his illustrious diocesan.[f] From all parts of Europe youths of noble birth found their way to the seat of the Northern primacy to be taught by the prince-bishop.[g] Egbert himself was the moderator of the school, and Albert was the vice-dominus or abbas, the former giving lessons in divinity, the latter in grammar and in the arts and sciences.[h] The reputation of one of Egbert's scholars is enough to rescue his name from oblivion. It was no slight honour to have cultivated the tastes and fostered the genius of Alcuin.[i]

In the life of Alcuin there is an interesting description of the daily work of his master in the monastery of York whenever his attention was not distracted by weightier and more important matters. The cares of his diocese would occupy of course the first place. "As soon as he was at leisure in the morning he sent for some of the young clerks, and sitting on his couch taught them successively till noon, at which time he retired to his private chapel and celebrated mass. After dinner, at which he ate sparingly, he amused himself with hearing his pupils discuss literary questions in his presence. In the evening he recited with them the service of complin, and then calling them in order, he gave his blessing to each as they knelt in succession at his feet."[j]

The pen of Alcuin was not dipped in gall when he spoke of his instructor. The verse may haply be uncouth, but it cannot conceal the affection of the writer.[k] He tells us of the learning of Egbert, of the suavity of his manner, of his gentleness and goodness. Stern he could be where a rebuke was merited, and yet who was more loving or beloved? Alcuin could descend from the height to which his own surpassing genius had raised him, and speak of his old teacher with the affectionate humility of a child. That is no slight tie which binds the scholar to his master. It will be long before I forget mine, although those once observant eyes are closed, and that well-remembered voice is still.

Towards the close of his life Egbert seems to have resigned

[e] Hist. Mon. S. Aug. Cantuar., 281. Malmesbury, apud Savile, 12, *b*. Higden, apud Gale, i., 250. Lel. Coll., iii., 259.

[f] Bedæ Epist. ad Egbertum, ed. Smith, 305.

[g] Vita Alcuini, procem. ad Op., ed., 1777, i., lxi.

[h] Lorenz, Life of Alcuin, 9.

[i] Vita Alcuini, procem. ad Op., ed., 1777, i., lxi.-iii. Mabillon, Acta SS. Ord. S. B., sæc. iv., 148. Lel. Coll., iii., 259. Baronii Ann., ix., 338. Lel. de Script. Brit., i., 121.

[j] Lingard, i., 98. Vita Alcuini, apud Acta SS. ord S. B. sæc. iv., i., 149.

[k] Alcuin, ap. Gale, i., 725. Malmesbury, apud Savile, 12, *b*. Mabillon, Ann. Ben., ii., 94.

the management of his school to Albert and Alcuin.[l] It could be in no better hands. He himself had weightier matters to attend to now. Tranquil must have been his life within the walls of his monastery at York, happier far than if he had tarried in his father's court. And now, when the heat of the day was over, there was the contemplation of the future left to him; there was also the remembrance of the past, and to him in his declining years there would be pleasure in the retrospect. "Est enim quiete, et pure, et eleganter actæ ætatis placida ac lenis senectus." Whilst the aged prelate was watching in his cloister, his brother Eadbert was on the Northumbrian throne, and amid the cares of royalty he would envy the peacefulness of that life which the archbishop had adopted. He would see him resigning his scholastic duties to prepare himself for a very different scene; and then the monarch would muse upon those startling thoughts which a later poet so beautifully moulded into verse.

> "The glories of our birth and state
> Are shadows, not substantial things;
> There is no armour against fate;
> Death lays his icy hand on kings:
> Sceptre and crown
> Must tumble down,
> And in the dust be equal made
> With the poor humble scythe and spade."

Was he ready for the change which even he was to expect? He voluntarily laid aside his honours, and, taking the tonsure like his uncle Ceonwulf, entered his brother's monastery in 757. to spend with him in quietude and prayer the remainder of his days.[m] It was a sight worthy of an exalted age. The remnant of their earthly lives was devoted to Him "who seeth in secret," and ere long they passed into His presence. The archbishop was summoned first, on the 19th November, 766, having been the ruler over his see for thirty-four winters.[n] His brother followed him on the 19th August, 768.[o] They were laid side by side in one of the porches or chapels in the cathedral of York.[p]

[l] Alcuini opera, ed., 1777., proœm. to vol. i., xxii. Lorenz, Life of Alcuin, 10. Malmesbury de Pont., apud Savile, 153, *b*.

[m] Saxon Chron., 72, Wendover, i., 149. Wallingford's Chron., apud Gale, i., 529. Chron. Petrib., 7. Baronii Ann., ix., 119.

[n] Some writers say that he was bishop thirty-six winters. Sax. Chron., 74. Flor. Wigorn. (276) gives the 14 Cal. as the day of his death. Symeon, col. 106. Chron. de Mailros, 7. Hen. of Huntingdon, apud Savile, 196, *b*. Hoveden, ibid., 231, *b*. Chron. Petrib., 8. Symeon, Hist. Eccl. Dunelm., 84, where he is said to have been bishop thirty-two years. Mabillon, Ann. Ben., ii., 210-11. Wendover, i., 151, says that Egbert died in 767, and that Eanbald succeeded him. Addit. ad Bedam, ed. Smith, 224, make the date 766.

[o] Saxon Chron., 74.

[p] Alcuin, apud Gale, i., 725. Saxon Chron., 66. Malmesbury, apud Savile, 153. Symeon, Hist. Eccl. Dunelm., 83.

Fuller, therefore, is slightly incorrect when he says, "In that age the greatest princes and prelates their corpses came no nearer than the church-porch; though in after ages the bodies of meaner persons were admitted into the church, and buried therein."[q] I cannot but call to mind the directions which good bishop Hall gave in his last will to his executors, "My body," he says, "I leave to be interred without any funeral pomp, with this only monition, that I do not hold God's house a meet repository for the dead bodies of the greatest saints."[r]

Albert, who succeeded Egbert in the archbishopric, was the son of parents of influence and rank.[s] He was educated in the monastery of York, where he was soon regarded as a youth of no ordinary ability. Egbert the prince-bishop was his kinsman, and the ties of blood, which at that time were valued and regarded, would link the two together; but they had another bond of union, a far nobler one than the accident of birth,—in the fascinating tastes which they both cultivated and enjoyed. With what pleasure and affection would the prelate look down upon the youthful scholar! How delightful to watch the spreading of those radiant fires of genius which he had himself enkindled![t] He marked Albert out for a career of usefulness and distinction. He raised him in course of time to the priesthood. He associated him with himself in the charge of his pupils, making him the master of the schools, and also the *defensor cleri*. It is not exactly known what were the duties of this officer. In all probability he was the abbas or vice-dominus, who has been already mentioned, and, therefore, the superintendent of the clergy within the walls of the monastery, if not beyond them.

Lel. Coll., iii., 259. Gaimar, l'Estorie des Engles, apud Mon. Hist. Brit., 785.

> "Ecberith Eatinc out nun son frere;
> Arcevesque ert, e gentil ere.
> Ambedeus gisent, pres a pres,
> A Everwich, a portices."

[q] Church History, book ii., 101.

[r] Winstanley's Worthies, 358.

[s] For this memoir the poem of Alcuin de SS. et Pontificibus Ebor. is the chief authority (Gale, i., 727, etc.)

Albert's name is variously spelt. I find him called Æthelbert, Adalbert, Edbert and Albert, alias Cœna. Saxon Chron., 74. Fl. Wigorn., 276. Liber Vitæ Eccl. Dunelm., 7. Huntingdon, apud Savile, 196 *b*. Symeon, De Arch. Ebor., col. 78. Stubbs, ibid., 1697. Mabillon, Ann. Ben., ii., 211, 212.

Albert's name is not inserted among the archbishops of York by Malmesbury, nor is it in the Hist. Mon. S. Aug. Cantuar. Hen. Huntingdon inserts his name and then contradicts himself.

Albert consecrated Frithwald bp. of Hexham at York, and Ethelbert to the same see in 776. Saxon Chron., 73, 76. Huntingdon, apud Savile, 191 *b*.

[t] "Pontificique comes Ecgbert conjunctus adhæsit,
Cui quoque sanguineo fuerat jam jure propinquus."

The renown of the school of York was spread at this time through the greater part of Europe. Egbert had built it up, and it was a triumph to the genius of Albert to be able to increase it. It was a noble work that these two illustrious scholars were then doing. Egbert, indeed, when Albert became his assistant, merely gave instruction in the New Testament, but Albert explained the Old Testament, and gave lessons generally in the arts and sciences. He led his numerous scholars into a wide field of learning—grammar, rhetoric, law, poetry, astronomy and natural philosophy. And not only was he the master of such stores of erudition, but he had the happy power of imparting them to others. He was able at the same time to communicate and evoke. Wherever there was the slightest ray of genius, however tremulous and feeble, he could detect and strengthen it. His pupils, also, could love their instructor whilst they admired his learning. Fascinating he was and affectionate, with a winning kindliness of manner that entwined itself around the hearts of all. There have been many like him since who have sacrificed their very lives for others, and for the sacred cause that they have striven to advance. The busy world has too often marked them only to censure the modest tastes that shrunk from its follies, and to sneer at a disposition which it could neither appreciate nor understand. Neglected or unobserved, those teachers of the young, the thinker and the scholar, have gone down to their graves in silence, living only in the hearts of those who have drunk in from their lips the lesson of their lives. There is a day coming on which men of genius and learning shall emerge from the darkness in which posterity has buried them, to witness a strange cancelling of opinions and reversing of degrees. How often in this world has the fame of a great man been rescued from oblivion by an accident or a chance! If there had been no Alcuin, we should have known, perhaps, nothing of the toil and work of Albert!

Alcuin was without doubt the greatest scholar of his age, and one of the brightest stars in the Anglo-Saxon church. He was a native of York, and a pupil in the school of Egbert. We have already seen how he loved and venerated his master. To Albert he was bound by the closest ties of affectionate regard. He was his companion and his friend as well as his pupil. Alcuin became an assistant in the school,[u] and subsequently, when elevated to the see, Albert appointed him one of the canons of the minster, and raised him to the honourable and arduous office of *magister scholarum*. In that position Alcuin won for himself an undying name. The learning and the character of such men

[u] Appointed by Egbert. Alcuini Op., 1777, vol. i., procem., xxii.

as Sigulf, Eanbald, St. Liudger and Fridugisus confer immortal honour on Alcuin and York.[v]

Not only did Albert devote his energies to the school-room, but it was his ambition to leave behind him a splendid collection of books for the benefit of his college. There were some there already which Egbert had collected, but Albert may be called the founder of that library, although his predecessor had begun it.[w] He was anxious that the fruits of his zeal should survive to generations yet unborn, long after his own lips were silent. Books, as he well knew, were

"The only men that speak aloud for future times to hear."

And he resolved to leave behind him a noble library for the benefit of posterity. This would ensure to the North of England a continuance of the school for which York was now so famous, for wherever there was a library there would be students, and wherever there was learning the light of religion would never be extinguished. To gather books together in that illiterate age was a noble enterprize, but Albert was not appalled by the difficulty of the undertaking. He threw himself into it with all the ardour of a bibliomaniac. The English collections could not allay his thirst for literature. More than once did he cross the seas with Alcuin for his companion,[x] never caring for the perils with which the traveller was beset, if only he could secure some of the precious tomes that he saw for his library at home. Italy was one of the countries that he visited, and he wandered among its monasteries and shrines on the same ground which, in a later age, tempted the author of the *Philobiblon* to desert his monarch and his see. The treasures which fascinated Poggio and Petrarch were as yet unknown, and there were no Medici to patronize and commend. Albert had a welcome everywhere, for his reputation had preceded him. Fain would they have detained him in Italy to scatter there the rich seeds of learning which were springing up in England, but he would not desert his scholars and his school. He came back to York bringing with him the treasures that he had collected. Alcuin speaks with rapture of these precious volumes in a well-known passage which, although often quoted, must not be omitted here. It describes the contents of the library at York, which he calls in another place the

[v] Alcuini Op., i., procem., xxii. Ibid., lxiii., Sigulf is called "custos Heboricæ civitatis ecclesiæ." He goes to Rome "ad eccles. ordinem discendum—et causa cantus." Vita S. Liudgeri, apud Mabillon, Acta SS. ord. S. B. sæc. iv., i., 37, and Vita B. Alcuini, ibid., 150, 2. Ann. Ben., ii., 186, etc. Alcuin, et son Influence Litteraire, etc., par Fr. Monnier, 10.

[w] On the table of benefactors in the minster Albert is called "Quartus fundator. Primus bibliothecam condidit." Gent, 61.

[x] Alcuini Op., i., procem., xvi., 287. Lorenz' Life of Alcuin, 9, 10.

flowers of Britain.[y] It will be seen that the authors of the ancient world were very fairly represented in that collection.

> "Illic invenies veterum vestigia Patrum,
> Quidquid habet pro se Latio Romanus in orbe,
> Græcia vel quidquid transmisit clara Latinis:
> Hebraicus vel quod populus bibit imbre superno,
> Africa lucifluo vel quidquid lumine sparsit.
> Quod pater Hieronymus, quod sensit Hilarius, atque
> Ambrosius præsul, simul Augustinus, et ipse
> Sanctus Athanasius, quod Orosius edit avitus:
> Quidquid Gregorius summus docet, et Leo papa;
> Basilius quidquid, Fulgentius, atque coruscant
> Cassiodorus item, Chrysostomus atque Johannes.
> Quidquid et Althelmus docuit, quid Beda magister,
> Quæ Victorinus scripsere, Boetius, atque
> Historici veteres, Pompeius, Plinius, ipse
> Acer Aristoteles, rhetor quoque Tullius ingens.
> Quid quoque Sedulius, vel quid canit ipse Juvencus,
> Alcuinus et Clemens, Prosper, Paulinus, Arator,
> Quid Fortunatus, vel quid Lactantius edunt.
> Quæ Maro Virgilius, Statius, Lucanus et auctor
> Artis Grammaticæ, vel quid scripsere magistri.
> Quid Probus atque Focas, Donatus, Priscianusve,
> Servius, Enticius, Pompeius, Comminianus.
> Invenies alios perplures."

We may picture to ourselves the life of Albert and his pupils in the monastery of York when these heroes of past ages were their companions. Horace was not there, nor the lighter writers of antiquity. They listened not to the melodious numbers and the glorious poetry of Greece, but they could open the pages of the historian, and read for themselves the thrilling legend, and the exploits of the warriors and statesmen of that mighty city, which, rising even when it fell, had become the abode of the greatest bishop in the West. Here they could drink in the persuasive arguments and the glowing eloquence of the standard-bearers of their own church, men of prowess and renown, who, whilst they lived on earth, were fit already for the society of angels. Here, before them, was the story of their sufferings and their victories, the sighings and the vigils of the recluse, the fiery trials which the martyrs met and scorned, the ecstasies of the enraptured devotee, the heaven-born words that had flowed from the lips of the departing saint, when the light of another world was already beaming upon his face. The heart of the youthful Saxon would burn within him when his master told him of the triumphs of faith that had been achieved, and of the glories that he could himself secure. With delight he would hear how many of these holy men had lived and died in

[y] Malmesbury, De Gestis Pont., apud Savile, 153. Alcuini Op., i., 53.

the seclusion of a monastery, working as he worked, and he would study to be like them. The remembrance of this would be with the pupil in the class-room and the dormitory; it would make his eye grow brighter when it rested upon the sacred page; it would guide his hand when it wrote down the words by which he was enthralled; it would nerve him for his daily occupations, and sanctify them all. What a happy life was his when the silence of the study was broken only by the summons to the house of God, where the voice of prayer and praise chimed in with those secret aspirations which it strengthened and ennobled! Monotonous it may seem, but it was not wearisome. A holy light illumined it, unchanging and serene as that heaven from which it came.

The highest honour in the North awaited Albert. At the death of archbishop Egbert in 766 Albert was appointed his successor, in compliance with the wishes of the people. He was consecrated, together with Alchmund, bishop of Hexham, on the 24th of April, 767.[z] In 773 pope Adrian sent to him the pall.[a] The great scholar was an excellent archbishop. He was a strict disciplinarian, as we might expect, and a terror to evil-doers, but a true follower of the Good Shepherd in his affection for his flock. It is such a leader that the sheep love to follow to the still waters and the pleasant fields. And they who had known him in the lowlier position which he had previously adorned were conscious of no alteration in his manner or disposition. The pomps and luxuries of the court could not ensnare or dazzle him; the old simplicity of his habits and his kindliness of heart were still unchanged.

To his church at York Albert was a great benefactor, for he was a man with splendid tastes, and personal frugality had not led him to neglect the decoration of God's house. In 741 the minster had been greatly injured by a fire,[b] and it was reserved for Albert to erect what was really a new temple. His first care was bestowed upon the *sanctum sanctorum*, the little chapel in which Paulinus had baptized Edwin.[c] The great altar

[z] Symeon, col. 107. Chron. de Mailros, 7. Hoveden, apud Savile, 231 *b*. The Saxon Chron. says 766.

[a] Symeon, De Archiep. Ebor., 78. De Gestis, col. 107. Stubbs, col. 1697. Chron de Mailros, 8. Hoveden, apud Savile, 231 *b*.

[b] Hoveden, apud Savile, 231. "Monasterium in Eboraca civitate succensum est nono. Cal. Maii, feria prima, 741."

[c] Cf. Willis' Architectural History of York Minster, 4-5. Browne's York Minster, i., 3, 4. Fabric Rolls, ed. Surtees Soc., pref., ix. Gent's York, 61. Bentham's Ely, 25-6. Mr. Willis is of opinion that Albert built two churches, the one, with the altar at which Edwin was baptized, was the minster, the other with the thirty altars, a different building. It seems to me that they were the same (pref. ix.), and Edwin's chapel was probably renovated, *in the first instance*, that it might be used for service whilst the minster was being erected.

in it he renovated and dedicated to St. Paul, and he made another near it. All the sacred vessels and crucifixes were of silver or gold, and were inlaid with precious stones. Around this little shrine Albert began and completed a new church, a good work that won for him the title of one of the founders of the minster.[d] Alcuin and Eanbald were the superintendents of the work, which remained uninjured until the Norman Conquest. It contained as many as thirty altars, and was probably of that Byzantine style of architecture which was then so prevalent abroad.

The lamp of life was now flickering out; the days of Albert were drawing towards their close. Rich in good works and active piety as they had been, the aged prelate, when he looked back upon the past, could only see that it was full of opportunities neglected or misused, of numberless shortcomings. He would sigh to himself,-

> "O quid solutis est beatius curis
> Quum mens onus reponit!"

And he resolved to tear himself from that world by which he had been enthralled. He would follow the example of John and Wilfrid; and the remainder of his days should be dedicated to God. Like the aged Jacob, he called around him his spiritual children. Eanbald, a beloved pupil, he nominated his coadjutor in the see, and consecrated him to that high office.[e] To the faithful Alcuin he gave up the school on which so much of his energies had been spent, and the care of the library that they had collected, and then he entered upon his solitary watch, to atone, as far as he could, for the offences of the past.

Two years and two months were spent in this retirement.[f] Ten days before his eyes were closed in death, he was permitted to witness the completion of the church that he had begun, and to join Eanbald in dedicating it to God. He retired to his cell to die. The affectionate Alcuin was a witness of his end, and among the last words that Albert uttered was a desire that his friend should cross the seas, and pay a visit to France and

[d] This title is given to Albert on the board preserved in the minster, which is of the age of Dean Gale, who was thoroughly conversant with the history of the cathedral. Gent (p. 61) gives a copy of it in his account of York.

Alcuin's description of Albert's church is too curious and valuable to be omitted:—

> "Ast nova basilicæ miræ structura diebus
> Præsulis hujus erat jam cæpta, peracta, sacrata.
> Hæc nimis alta domus solidis suffulta columnis,
> Suppositæ quæ stant curvatis arcubus, intus
> Emicat egregiis laquearibus atque fenestris,
> Pulchraque porticibus fulget circumdata multis,
> Plurima diversis retinens solaria tectis,
> Quæ triginta tenet variis ornatibus aras."

[e] Chron. de Mailros, 8. Hoveden, apud Savile, 232 *a*.

[f] Symeon, De Archiep. Ebor., col. 78. Stubbs, col. 1697. Mabillon, Ann. Ben., ii., 255.

Rome.[g] Albert was taken to his rest at York[h] on the 8th of November, 781 or 782,[i] at the sixth hour of the day. A noble procession of laymen and ecclesiastics accompanied him to his burial, all full of grief for the patron whom they had lost, yet with that sorrow there would be the conviction in every mind that the great scholar was at rest, and each would share in the thought which Alcuin has thus expressed:—

> "Jam cui Christus, amor, potus, cibus, omnia Christus;
> Vita, fides, sensus, spes, lux, via, gloria, virtus."

Eanbald I. was the pupil and the successor of Albert. The greater part of his life had, in all probability, been spent in the monastery of York, and there he had made himself acquainted with the stores of learning that Egbert and Albert could impart. From a student he became a teacher, and, with the famous Alcuin, he shared the affections of Albert. Eanbald was probably the vice-dominus of the monastery, and when the good bishop in his declining years threw aside the cares of his high office, he made Eanbald his coadjutor, thereby nominating him as his successor. Eanbald had already evinced his aptitude for business by taking the charge, with Alcuin, of the rebuilding of the minster. It was his high privilege to join his aged benefactor, Albert, in dedicating it anew to God. He was then in a more exalted position than he had occupied when the work began. The mitre was upon the brows of the architect.[j]

Eanbald took the place of Albert in 782, and the first care of Alfwold, king of Northumbria, was to provide him with the pall.[k] Alcuin himself, at the request of his friend, went to Rome to bring it.[l]

> "I tamen, pro me, tu, cui licet, aspice Romam,"

and on his return Eanbald was solemnly confirmed in his office.

[g] Alcuini Op., i. Vita in procem., lxiii.

[h] Saxon Chron., 77. Huntingdon (196 b) and Hoveden (235), by a mistake, say that he died at Chester.

[i] Saxon Chron., 77. Chron. de Mailros, 8, and Symeon, De Gestis, col. 108, make the date 780. Fl. Wigorn., 278, and Chron. Petrib., 9, say 781. Mabillon, Acta SS. ord. S. B., sæc. iv., i., 152. Alcuini, Op., i., Vita Alc., procem., lxiii.

[j] Alcuin, De Pont. Eccl. Ebor., apud Gale, i., 730. Symeon, De Gestis, col. 107. Malmesbury (Savile, 153 a) makes *one* Eanbald and not two, missing out Albert; so does Wendover, i., 151.

[k] Saxon Chron., 77. Chron. Mailros, 9. Huntingdon, apud Savile, 197. Hoveden, ibid., *235 b. Symeon, De Gestis, col. 108. Bromton, col. 797. Stubbs, col. 1697. Labbe, Bibl., i., 323.

[l] Mabillon, Acta SS. ord. S. B., sæc. iv., i., 152. Vita Alc., procem., Op. i., lxiv. Recueil des Historiens des Gaules, v., 445.

Between the two scholars there existed the closest intimacy and regard. They worked and taught together. Eanbald, like his master and his namesake, lives for us in the light of Alcuin!

The state of Northumbria during the archiepiscopate of Eanbald was anything but favourable to the progress of Christian teaching. The country was full of violence and bloodshed. Alfwold ascended the throne at the expulsion of king Ethelred, and was murdered after a short but useful reign by one of his own captains. Within a twelvemonth his successor and nephew, Osred, died a violent death. Tempted by the chances of success, amid the general confusion, the exile Ethelred seized his old kingdom, and, after wreaking a futile vengeance upon his enemies, fell a victim soon after to a conspiracy among his own nobles. To add to the general dismay, the Danes broke in upon the divided and unhappy country. They desolated that sacred shrine which Aidan reared at Lindisfarne, and in which Wilfrid and Cuthbert had watched and prayed. Those holy men would think in their day that no foeman would ever reach that little temple which cliff and wave had made into a sanctuary, but the sea-kings cared neither for rock nor storm. The startled inmates were slaughtered at their altars. In the succeeding century they deserted their insecure abode, and, after many wanderings, found a resting-place at last, yea, another Salem with its holy hill, beside the waters of the Wear.

All this trouble and confusion must have materially crippled the Northumbrian church. What satisfactory progress would it now make? The labours of the school of York went on, although there were, probably, fewer pupils. The great library was used and treasured, and there would always be scholars when Alcuin was the master. That illustrious teacher, however, was at this time very frequently abroad. The royal court of France had for him far greater charms than the devastated kingdom of Northumbria. Peace he found there and security, a noble patron, the most accomplished court in Europe, and the society of men of letters and intelligence. Can we wonder that in 790, troubled by the confusion around him, he deserted York for France? Six years after this, in a letter to king Offa, he says that it had been his wish to return, had the violence of the pagans not deterred him from making the attempt.[m] But although he was thus absent, he was still present in heart and spirit with Eanbald and his old associates at York. He corresponded with them, and strove to mitigate the disasters that appalled them. He rebuked Ethelred and his nobles, and gave them good advice which they forgot.[n] He reminded the brethren

[m] Alc., Op., i., 57. [n] Ibid., i., 17, 20.

at Hexham and their bishop of the light of Christian excellence that had illumined their beautiful shrine, and bade them recollect and cherish it.[o] He begged the inmates of the monasteries of Wearmouth and Jarrow to call to mind the spiritual renown of Beda, Benedict and Ceolfrid, and exhorted them to patience and endurance.[p] He consoled the monks of Lindisfarne for their sufferings and affliction.[q] To the brethren at York he speaks in terms of the most affectionate regard.[r] He praises them for their constancy and zeal in a manner which shews that they had not yet fallen, in spite of all their troubles, from their first estate. He gives them advice in a tone that expresses his firm conviction that they would adopt it. He yearns towards them with sympathy and kindness: "You," he says, "are ever in my heart. I pray for you first of all. Oh, for the love of God, cherish with heart and tongue your son Alcuin! Oh, remember me, fathers and brothers mine, who are all most dear to me. I am yours in life or death. And haply it may be mercifully allowed that my body, in its old age, may repose with you who nurtured it in its youth. But if another resting-place shall be mine, yet, if God will, there shall be rest for my soul, wherever it may be, through your holy prayers. I trust in you. For—we believe that the souls of our brotherhood are to be gathered into the same abode of bliss. Although a difference in merit shall necessitate a difference in reward, still the nature of eternity is such, that all must be happy who enjoy it. And like as there is one sun that shines on all, a sun that all see alike, whether they are near or distant, so a never-ending bliss shall be given to all the righteous in God's kingdom, although the height of their excellence may crown some with a greater glory. Oh, most beloved brethren, make yourselves ready to attain to that glory with the fullest intention both of will and deed."[s] These are indeed the aspirations of a poet and a saint! His bones were not laid where he wished, in the city of his birth. They are resting in the country of his adoption.

There is little more to be said about Eanbald. His lot was cast in troublous times. He would look, however, upon the last public act of his life as a sign and promise of peace to his distracted diocese. This was the coronation of Eardulf, on whose hand he placed the Northumbrian crown on the 25th of June,

[o] Alc., Op., i., 196.

[p] Ibid., i., 21, 80, etc.

[q] Ibid., i., 11.

[r] In a letter to Ethelred (i., 20) Alcuin mentions a singular portent that occurred in the church of York shortly before the arrival of the Danes. "Quid significat pluvia sanguinis quam in quadragesimali tempore in Heboraca civitate, quæ est caput totius regni, in ecclesia Beati Petri principis Apostolorum, vidimus, de borealibus domus, sereno aere, de summo tecti minaciter cadere? Nonne potest putari a borealibus partibus venire super terram sanguinem?"

[s] Alc., Op., i., 8, 9.

796, the bishops of Whithern, Lindisfarne and Hexham assisting him.[t] On the 10th of August Eanbald died at the monastery of Etlete or Edete.[u] They bore his remains to York with a noble procession, and interred them in St. Peter's minster.[v]

Eanbald II. was consecrated bishop of York in a monastery called Sochasburg, on Sunday, the 14th or 15th of August, A.D. 796. Ethelbert, Higbald and Badulf were the officiating prelates.[w] On the 8th of September in the following year, being the festival of the nativity of the Virgin, Eanbald was solemnly confirmed in the archbishopric, having received the pall from Rome[x] which qualified him for that high position.

Eanbald was one of the presbyters of his predecessor,[y] and a very favourite pupil of Alcuin. That illustrious scholar was in France when Eanbald I. died, and he was summoned thence to York, as one of the fratres of that church, to proceed to the election of a new president. The choice, in all probability, would have fallen upon himself. Unwilling to desert the French court and schools, and to venture into a divided and unhappy country, Alcuin gave up all idea of journeying again to England, and he had the satisfaction of hearing that his pupil Eanbald had been raised to an honour which had been within his own reach.[z]

Between Eanbald and his old master there was maintained the most affectionate intercourse. Alcuin addressed him under the friendly title of Symeon.[a] He held him up as a pattern to the recreant Osulf.[b] He spoke in his praise to Charlemagne, and the "præfulgidus" David honoured him with an epistle. He sent him a ship's load of metal to be used in the bell-tower of

[t] Saxon Chron., 81—the date made 795. Huntingdon, apud Savile, 197 *a*. Hoveden, 23.

[u] Stubbs, 1697, calls this place Aclete. Where is it? It may be Yokefleet, in Yorkshire. May it not rather be Aycliffe, in the county of Durham, where there are some early Saxon crosses? There were ecclesiastical meetings at Acle, whilst Eanbald was archbishop (Saxon Chron., 79; Ric. Hexham, col. 298. Huntingdon, 196 *b*). Symeon (De Gestis, col. 138) speaks of a place called Aclea in the South, and calls it "campus quercus."

[v] Saxon Chron., 82. Chron. de Mailros, 12. Symeon, De Gestis, col. 114. Hoveden, 233.

[w] Saxon Chron., 82. Chron. de Mailros, 12. Symeon, De Gestis, col. 114. Stubbs, col. 1697. Hoveden, apud Savile, 233.

[x] Saxon Chron., 83. Symeon, etc., ut supra. [y] Labbe, Bibl., i., 323. Stubbs, col. 1697.

[z] Alcuini Op., i., 62-3. Malmesbury, apud Savile, 153. "Dignité réservée à Alcuin, s'il eût voulu rester dans sa patrie." Monnier, Vie d'Alcuin, 11.

[a] Alc. Op., i., 230-1, etc.

[b] Vita Alc., procem. ad Op., i., xxiv., and Op., i., 217.

his church.[c] When the lawlessness of the times had originated a general declension in manners and morals in Northumbria, especially in the monasteries, Alcuin wrote to Eanbald one of his most useful and remarkable letters of advice. It is easy to see from the tone of the epistle that the prelate had been the writer's pupil. It recommends the archbishop to be a rigid disciplinarian, to attend to the rules and customs of the Roman church, to bestow especial care upon the management of his school. It lays down many rules for Eanbald's instruction as to his own deportment, and the governing of his churches and clergy,[d] and contains many sound and practical suggestions. There is, unfortunately, an absence of any specific information as to the state of the Northern archiepiscopate. The writer speaks of what ought to be done, and not of what had been done, and he leaves the general impression that there was great room for improvement in the management and discipline of the vast diocese of Northumbria.[e]

As far as can be ascertained, Eanbald appears to have been an active prelate. He did his best to recover for Ethelard of Canterbury, at the request of Alcuin, the portion of his diocese which had been taken away from it by Offa.[f] He presided in A.D. 798 over a synod at Pinchenheale, at which, according to Symeon, some wise and judicious enactments were made relating to the ecclesiastical courts and the observance of Easter.[g] There is no evidence to shew that he was the author of a book of synodical decrees.[h] If he was, the fact is a slight proof of the assertion that he introduced into the church of York the Roman ritual. Eanbald enjoyed the privilege of coining money.[i]

There is one portion of Eanbald's life which is involved in some mystery,—his connection with Eardulf, the Northumbrian king. Before the close of Alcuin's life we find the archbishop reprehended by his old instructor for placing himself in opposition to his sovereign. He protected the lands and persons of the enemies of Eardulf, adding to his own territories, and maintaining a greater number of military retainers than any of his predecessors, to the discredit of his office and the overburdening of the monasteries at which he chanced to be a guest. With regard to the first charge, Eanbald pleaded the dictates of Chris-

[c] Alc. Op., i., 231. "Ut domuscula cloccarum stagno tegatur."

[d] One of the offences of the Northumbrian clergy at this time was fox-hunting!

[e] Canisii Lect. Antiquæ, ii., 450. Alc. Op., i., 63, etc.

[f] Alc., Op., i., 80, 233-4, etc. Malmesbury De Pont., apud Savile, 153 *b*. Hist. Mon. S. Aug. Cantuar., 281. Wendover, i., 167.

[g] Chron. de Mailros, 13. Symeon, De Gestis, col. 114. Stubbs, col. 1697. Labbe, Conc., vii., col. 1148. Spelmanni Conc., 316.

[h] Pitseus, 164-5. Tanner, Bibl. Brit., 248.

[i] Davies on the York mint, 7.

tian charity as his excuse, and it was not a bad one. With regard to the number of his followers, he might have said with justice that it was necessitated by the turbulence of the times. But we hear of the archbishop again in connection with the same matter.[j] In A.D. 808, when Eardulf was deposed, Eanbald was concerned in the negotiations that preceded his restoration by Charlemagne, and we are told that the archbishop and king Kenulf were suspected by pope Leo of unfair dealing in that affair.[k] It was probably his past regard for the city of York in the time of Alcuin that induced Charlemagne to become a peace-maker in Northumbria.

Eanbald is said to have died in 812, in the reign of Eanred;[l] there is, however, some uncertainty about the exact date.

Wulfsy was the successor of Eanbald. The date that has been generally fixed for his consecration is 812. Symeon tells us that he became archbishop in the reign of Eanred, who came to the throne of Northumbria in 810. Of the official acts of Wulfsy there is little known, and the history of the North at that period is involved in equal obscurity. In the Cottonian library there is a letter addressed to Wulfsy, by Egred, bishop of Lindisfarne, about an alleged miracle.[m] Wendover says that Wulfsy died in 831.[n]

Wigmund became archbishop whilst Eanred was king of Northumbria, about the year 837. This may be inferred from the statement of Symeon, who says that Wulfere died in 900, having been bishop forty-seven years, and that Wigmund, his predecessor, held the see for sixteen years. Some coins of this prelate, issued from the York mint, are in existence.[o]

There are one or two interesting allusions to the church of York at this period among the letters of Lupus, the well-known abbat of Ferrieres, which have been printed by Baluz.[p]

[j] Alc., Op. i.— Cf. Lingard, Anglo-Saxon Church, i., 126.

[k] Mabillon, Ann. Ben., ii., 383. Recueil des Historiens des Gaules, v., 602.

[l] Symeon, De Gestis, col. 78.

[m] Lel. Coll., ii., 298. MS. Cotton, Tib. A., 15.

[n] Labbe, Bibl., i., 323. Stubbs, col. 1698. Wendover, i., 176. Liber Vitæ Dunelm., 7, where he is called Uulfsige. Malmesbury, De Pont. (Savile, 153 b) calls him Wilfrid.

[o] Symeon, De Arch. Ebor., col. 78. Stubbs, col. 1698. Wendover, i., 183. Liber Vitæ Dunelm., 7, where he is called Wimund. Davies on the York mint, 7. On the stycas the archbishop's name is Vigmund.

[p] Lupi Epist., ed. Baluz, ed. 1710, 103-4. Mabillon, Ann. Ben., ii., 684. He makes the date of the letters 849.

One epistle is addressed to Guigmund, bishop of York, and to the congregation under him. It informs them that the writer had recovered a cell that he had lost, and expresses a wish for the renewal of friendly intercourse between the two houses.

There is another letter addressed by the same dignitary to Altsig, the abbas (or vice-dominus) of the church of York, repeating the request that he had made to Guigmund.

These letters are valuable in several respects. They shew that there was a friendly feeling at that time between the monastery of York and the society of Lupus, and that the communication between Northern and foreign houses, which existed to so great an extent in the preceding century, was still kept up. They tell us, moreover, that the monastery of York was under the same government that was described, sixty years before, in the writings of Alcuin, and that the famous library was still in existence, inasmuch as Lupus solicits the loan of a manuscript of Quintilian, one of the Questions of St. Jerome on the Old and New Testament, with a similar work by Beda.

Wulfere is said to have succeeded Wigmund in 854, in which year he received the pall, and thereby became archbishop of the Northumbrians.[p]

The kingdom of Northumbria during the latter half of this century was in the most lamentable condition. It was torn in pieces by internal dissensions, and the incursions of the Danes were very numerous and appalling. The sufferings of the famous Regnar Lodbrog on his bed of snakes were bitterly avenged. The sea-kings covered the ocean with their fleets, and fire and blood marked their track through the desolated country. Nearly all the Northern monasteries were destroyed by them. What progress could Christianity make? The preacher could scarcely save his own life.[q]

In 872 the Northumbrians expelled Egbert their king, who had been appointed by the Danes, and Wulfere is said to have gone into exile at the same time.[r] They are said to have gone to the court of Burhed, the monarch of the Mercians.[s] The

[p] Chron. de Mailros, 18. Symeon, De Gestis, col. 121, 139. Stubbs, col. 1698. Liber Vitæ Dunelm., 7. Hoveden, apud Savile, 232 *a*. Wendover, i., 183. Labbe, Bibl., i., 323.

[q] Mabillon, Ann. Ben., iii., 169. Hoveden, 232 *b*. Asser, apud Gale, i., 159, where it is said of the city of York, "Non tunc adhuc illa civitas firmos et stabilitos muros illis temporibus habebat."

[r] Symeon, De Gestis, col. 145. Hoveden, 233 *b*. Symeon, Hist. Eccl. Dunelm, 95. In 870.

[s] Wendover, i., 206.

following year witnessed the death of Egbert, and the restoration of the archbishop.[t] But this was not the only trouble that Wulfere is said to have experienced. At another period of his life, probably in 867, when York was captured by the Danes, Wulfere made his escape and got himself away to Addingham in Wharfdale. He is said to have stayed there for seven years.[u] If this was the case, we are involved in a chronological difficulty. Possibly the year that Wulfere spent in exile in 872 may form a part of the seven? In the chronicle of Melrose it is asserted that that prelate returned to York at the death of Egbert, by whom he was driven out.[v] Egbert, it will be remembered, was supported by Danish influence, which Wulfere would, in all probability, despise. It is reasonable enough to conjecture that Wulfere fled from the Danes in 867, and that he returned at the decease of Egbert in 873 "when he heard that Herod was dead." This will do away with the chronological difficulties which this paragraph presents.

There is much uncertainty as to the period of Wulfere's death. Symeon says in one place that he died in 892; in another that he lived eight years longer, thus making him preside over the Northumbrian archiepiscopate for the long period of forty-seven years.[w] Hoveden places his death in 890.[x]

Ethelbald succeeded Wulfere. He witnessed a charter which was made in the year 895. It has been generally said that he was consecrated in 900, receiving the pall four years afterwards. There is nothing whatever known of him.[y]

---

[t] Wendover, i., 207. Symeon, De Gestis, col. 145.

[u] Symeon, De Arch. Ebor., col. 78. Stubbs, col. 1698. Asser, (Gale, i., 172) under the year 893, says, "Eodem anno capta est civitas Ebroacensis a Nordmannis, sed episcopus, Sebar nomine, Deo auctore, evasit." This is Evreux, not York.

[v] Chron. de Mailros, 20. Stubbs, col. 1698, seems to countenance this view.

[w] Symeon, De Gestis, col. 133 and 150, and Chron. de Mailros, 24, make Wulfere die in 892. Symeon, De Arch. Ebor., col. 78, says in 900, "anno xlvii. episcopatus." Stubbs, col. 1698.

[x] Apud Savile, 241 *b*.

[y] Codex Diplom., ii., 126. Chron. de Mailros, 25. Symeon, De Arch. Ebor., col. 79;—De Gestis, col. 133, 151. Labbe, Bibl., i., 323. Liber Vitæ Dunelm., 7. Stubbs, col. 1698, says that Ethelbald received the pall four years after his consecration, "regnante Edwardo seniore, Elfredi regis filio." Hoveden (Savile, 241 *b*) dates his consecration in 898. Malmesbury, Savile, 153 *b*.

Redewald, Rodewald, or **Lotheward,** followed after Ethelbald, but the year of his consecration has not been ascertained. I find him witnessing charters between 928 and 930, but there is nothing to throw any light upon his acts and deeds.[c]

Wulstan occurs as archbishop of York as early as 931; in which year we find him witnessing a charter which has been printed by Mr. Kemble.[a]

Wulstan is said to have been raised to the see by the famous Athelstan.[b] That monarch was the first of the English kings who reduced Northumbria to subjection, and a considerable portion of his reign seems to have been spent in the North of England. Athelstan's affection for Christianity was very strongly marked. To the church of Beverley, at the instigation of Wulstan, and in gratitude to St. John, he granted several noble privileges and possessions. To the minsters of York and Ripon he was equally munificent. His generosity would, to a certain extent, be prompted by the wish to conciliate the good opinion of his new subjects, and, in the dispensing of it, he would, in all probability, be guided by the advice and suggestions of Wulstan.

After the death of Athelstan Wulstan appears in a new character. He comes before us as a diplomatist and a soldier. Gratitude to his benefactor Athelstan ought to have strengthened his loyalty to his successor, but we find the archbishop intriguing with the Danes, and joining the Northumbrians in renouncing their allegiance to Edmund. In the first instance, indeed, he had shewn himself a peacemaker, as, in conjunction with Odo of Canterbury, he interposed his authority, and prevented a

[c] Symeon, De Arch. Ebor., col. 79. Stubbs, col. 1698. Malmesbury, apud Savile, 153 *b*. Codex Diplom., ii., 163-4.

[a] Codex Diplom., ii., 168. In the same collection there are other deeds to which Wulstan was a witness. There are some in the Hist. Mon. de Abingdon, i., 66, etc. One of the titles assumed by the archbishop was, "Wulfsanus archons servitutis officio mancipatus, Eboracæ civitatis archiepiscopus."

[b] Sanctuar. Dunelm. et Beverlac., ed. Surtees Soc., 98. Stubbs, col. 1698, where it is said that the king gave at that time the whole of Amounderness to York. Symeon, de Arch. Ebor., col. 79. Polydore Vergil, 114. Smithi Flores Hist. Eccl. Angl., 191. Leland (Coll., iii., 8) mentions the following story:—

"In the time of king Athelstan, when the king lay in his tentes beside York, the king of Scottes faynid himself to be a mynstrelle, and harped before king Athelstane, only to espy his ordinannce and his people. The same night he cam to the host and slew Targe, archebishop of York, and al the people in his ward."

combat between Edmund and the Northumbrians near Lincoln.[c] This was in 941, but, soon afterwards, Wulstan allied himself with Anlaf the Dane, forgetting how the father of his youthful patron had but a year or two before swept away or desolated more than one Christian establishment in his diocese.[d] Anlaf was subsequently baptized,—a fact which seems to account for the conduct of the archbishop; but the ministers of the church ought to pause, under any circumstances, before they throw their influence into the scale of violence and bloodshed.

The sympathies of Wulstan seem to have been henceforward on the side of the Danes. In 943 he was with Anlaf when he stormed Leicester, and when that city was besieged by Edmund, the prelate and the prince with difficulty made their escape by night.[e] A treaty was soon after made, and there was a hollow peace, which lasted for a few years. In 946 Edmund was assassinated, and was succeeded by his brother Edred. Wulstan, with the Northumbrian magnates, took the oath of allegiance to him at a place called Taddenscliffe;[f] this concession having been brought about, according to Ingulph, by the good offices of Turketyl, the archbishop's cousin, who was at that time the king's chancellor, and afterwards the abbat of Croyland.[g] As a thank-offering, in all probability, for this reconciliation, Edred is said to have given two silver images to the church of York.[h] The gift, to say the least, was a premature one. The sympathies of the Northumbrians in favour of a Danish line of monarchs soon overpowered their loyalty. In 947 the archbishop and his compatriots broke out into open rebellion, and made Eric, a Northman, the son of Harold Harfager, their king.[i] This treachery necessitated a hostile invasion of Northumbria by Edred, in which, among other disasters, the monastery of Ripon was destroyed.[j] The wayward people then sought and obtained a reconciliation with Edred, and made specious promises that were speedily to be broken. The homage of the Northumbrians for the next few years was given alternately to

[c] Chron. de Mailros, 29. Symeon, De Gestis, col. 134. Hoveden, apud Savile, 242 *b*. Wendover, i., 251.

[d] Symeon, De Gestis, col. 134. Wendover, i., 251. Hoveden, apud Savile, 242 *b*.

[e] Saxon Chron., 147.

[f] Saxon Chron., 148, in 947. Fl. Wigorn., 352. Symeon, De Gestis, col. 156, in 949. Wendover, i., 253. Hoveden, apud Savile, 243.

[g] Ingulph, apud Gale, iii., 31. Mabillon, Acta SS. Ord. S. B., sæc. v., 496. Turketyl was the son of Cilward, Wulstan's uncle. He is said to have held with the chancellorship, "pinguissimam præbendam in eccl. Ebor;" a statement which throws discredit upon the authenticity of Ingulph's Chronicle, as there were no præbendæ at York at this time. There were but seven canons, who seem to have lived upon a *common* fund. Ingulph is not to be relied upon.

[h] Symeon, De Gestis, col. 156.

[i] Saxon Chron., 148. Symeon, *ut supra*. Ethelwardi Chron., apud Mon. Hist. Brit., 520. Aluredus Beverlac., 111.

[j] Wendover, i., 255.

Eric and Anlaf. In all these convulsions Wulstan must have played a conspicuous part, and it was the fear of his influence and his treachery that induced Edred, in 952, to throw him into prison at Jedburgh.[k] The nominal reason for his incarceration, according to Wendover, was his putting to death many of the citizens of Thetford in revenge for their having unjustly killed the abbat Aldelm.[l] Wulstan was in restraint for a short time,[m] and then the king, out of respect to his office, allowed him to resume his episcopal functions at Dorchester.[n] Malmesbury, however, informs us that the prelate scornfully rejected the proffered pardon, and died soon afterwards, probably of disappointment and baffled pride.[o] We hear nothing more of Wulstan, as the hopes of the Danish party were destroyed by the death of Eric and the banishment of Anlaf. He died at Oundle on the 26th of December, 955, and he was there interred.[p] At the same place the light of life had deserted his famous predecessor Wilfrid, but the greatness of the apostle of the Frisians demanded a nobler sepulchre than was accorded to his spiritual descendant. Both had been tossed about by the waters of affliction, but they exalted the one whilst they overwhelmed the other. The one was only a scheming politician, the other was a confessor and a Saint.

Oskytel, the successor of Wulstan, was a kinsman of Turketyl, the celebrated abbat of Croyland,[q] and a friend and coadjutor of St. Dunstan. In 950 he was made bishop of Dorchester,[r]

[k] Withabury or Juthanbury. Saxon Chron., 149, makes the date 952. Fl. Wigorn., 353. Chron. de Mailros, 31. Symeon, De Gestis, col. 156. Malmesbury, De Gestis, apud Savile, 153 *b*. Hoveden, ibid., 243. Ingulph (Gale, iii., 41). Chron. Petrib., 29, giving the date 949.

[l] Wendover, i., 256.

[m] The chronology is much confused. Ingulph, Gale, iii., 41, says that Wulstan was released in 948. In Hist. Mon. de Abingdon, he appears as a witness to charters granted in 951, 2, 3. He could only have been in prison for a short time.

[n] Saxon Chron., 149. Fl. Wigorn., 353. Chron. de Mailros, 31. Symeon, De Gestis, col. 154. Wendover, i., 256. Hoveden, 243. Wulstan was not made bishop of Dorchester, as some say, but merely resumed his episcopal functions *at* that place.

[o] De Pont., apud Savile, 153 *b*. The passage is obscure, "Datam veniam indignatus vitam e vestigio exierit."

[p] Saxon Chron., 150. Fl. Wigorn., 354. Chron. de Mailros, 31. Symeon, De Gestis, col. 157. Stubbs, col. 1699. Hoveden, apud Savile, 244. Wulstan witnessed a charter in 956. Codex Diplom., ii., 331.

[q] Saxon Chron., 158. Ingulph, apud Gale, iii., 41. Turketyl is said to have been a canon of York. Oskytel is probably the person mentioned in the Hist. Eliensis, apud Gale, i., 482. Ord. Vitalis, apud Duchesne, 541.

[r] Saxon Chron., 158. Vita S. Oswaldi, apud Angl. Sacr., ii., 197. Stubbs' Episcopal Succession, 15.

from which post, in 956, he was translated to the see of York,[s] with the consent of king Edward and his council.[t] He made a journey to Rome to procure the pall, his kinsman and successor, the well-known Oswald, being his companion across the channel.[u]

There is but little known of Oskytel's career at York or elsewhere. He was a man of piety and learning.[v] To Oswald he was extremely kind. He aided him in his distress after the decease of his uncle Odo, and, subsequently, he sent for him to Fleury to request his aid in making reforms in his diocese,—a good work which Oswald was ready enough to assist in.[w] Oskytel was, therefore, a coadjutor of Dunstan in his endeavours to introduce the Benedictine rule. How far he was successful it is impossible to say, but the number of charters to which he appears as a witness shews that he was frequently absent from his see.[x] In 968 he consecrated Elfsig to the bishopric of Chester.[y] He joined with archbishop Dunstan in confirming the privileges of Croyland,[z] and his intimacy with Turketyl led him to shew much kindness to that monastery.[a]

Oskytel died at Thame on Allhallow-mass night (Nov. 1), 972.[b] The event evoked much sorrow and regret.[c] Turketyl, his friend and kinsman, carried his remains to Bedford, where he was the abbat, and there the archbishop was interred.[d]

Sir Simonds D'Ewes had in his library an account of the lands that belonged to Oskytel, in right of his archbishopric, written in Saxon.[e]

---

[s] Fl. Wigorn., 354. Chron. de Mailros, 31. Symeon, De Gestis, col. 157. De Archiep. Ebor., col. 79. Stubbs (1699) says that he was sixteen years at York, and Wendover (i., 256), asserts that he became archbishop in 954.

[t] Saxon Chron., 158. Symeon, De Gestis, col. 157.

[u] Eadmer, Vita S. Oswaldi, apud Angl. Sacr., ii., 197. Hist. Rames., apud Gale, i., 392.

[v] Wendover, i., 256. Smithi Flores Hist. Eccl., 202.

[w] Ang. Sacr., ii., 197. Servatus, prior of Worcester, speaks of Oskytel in a way that seems to imply that he was only a learner, "Erat enim rudis adhuc in castris Domini, novitas ei extranea, novorum traditio aliena" (MS. at Durham, fol. 10).

[x] Oskytel subscribes himself as "Oscytel Eboracensis basilicæ primas insegnis." Hist. Mon. Abingdon, vol. i., 261, and many other places. Codex Diplom., ii., 374, etc.

[y] Symeon, Hist. Eccl. Dunelm., 138.

[z] Ingulph, apud Gale, iii., 44. Dugd. Mon., ii., 116.

[a] Savile, 501. Mabillon, Acta SS. ord. S. B., sæc. v., 505.

[b] Saxon Chron., 158. Higden, apud Gale, i., 267. Fl. Wigorn., 354. Chron. Mailros, 33, and Symeon, De Gestis, (col. 159).

[c] Angl. Sacr., ii., 203.

[d] Saxon Chron., 158.

[e] Wanley, 306.

Ethelwold is said by two chroniclers to have succeeded Oskytel, and his name appears on the old lists at York. We are told that he resigned his see, preferring a quiet life.[f] This is all that we know about him. He must not be confused with "the father of monks," Ethelwold, the benevolent bishop of Winchester.

Oswald was the son of Danish parents of high rank and consequence. His father was a great favourite of king Athelstan. His uncle, Odo, presided over the see of Canterbury, and to another archbishop, Oskytel of York, he was related by the ties of blood.[g]

The youth was gifted by nature with a noble bearing. His manners were fascinating and attractive, and there was every prospect of success in the path to greatness. But even in those early years, from which holy thoughts and aspirations are too frequently excluded, the boy was nursing a high and a determined spirit. The sports of other children had for him no charm. The honour of his family should suffer nothing in his hands, but could it not be enhanced, he thought, if he became the servant of the King of heaven? Frithegode, the poetical biographer of Wilfrid,[h] was his instructor, and placed before the youth the authors of antiquity, but it was upon the page of the Divine story that Oswald loved especially to dwell. His ardent spirit burned within him at the glorious recital. Dane although he was, he could there observe a wisdom deeper and more sublime than the greatest Northmen could have imagined. There were poetry and adventure grander and more vivid than those of the most impassioned sagas. And then Frithegode would tell him what great men, in later days, had learned out of that book the lesson of their lives. He would hear of Benedict and his noble rule—of Augustine and his spiritual triumphs—how Beda

[f] Symeon, De Arch. Ebor., col. 79. Stubbs, col. 1699. Mr. Stubbs omits his name altogether.

[g] Eadmer, Vita S. Osw., apud Angl. Sacr., ii., 192-3, compared with MS. Cotton, Nero, E. i., and the life by Servatus, prior of Worcester, in the library of the dean and chapter of Durham, B. iv., 39, B. Chron. de Mailros, 33. Hist. Ramesiensis, apud Gale, i., 391.

Oswald had two brothers, Osulf and Athelstan, and a nephew, Elfwin. (Cf. Thomas' Worcester, 41-7.) Oswald, another nephew, was a monk at Ramsey (Hist. Rames., 430), and an author (Pitseus, 181. Bale, cent. ii., 150). A grammarian of the name of Constantine, according to Leland, wrote a poem in Latin Elegiacs, which he addressed to archbishop Oswald in commendation of his learned nephew.

[h] Eadmer, 193. Hist. Rames., 391. Mabillon, Ann. Ben., iii., 541.

toiled and died—how Wilfrid worked and suffered for the cause of God. There was his uncle Odo with the pall of primacy upon his shoulders. Why should not he follow in the steps of those who had done great things for God? The die was cast, and the boy's resolution was firmly taken.

He was sent by his uncle to Winchester, and there he became, in the first instance, an ordinary canon, and, afterwards, the superior or dean.[i] The glories of Winchester had not yet arisen. The ecclesiastics there were merely secular canons. They were married men, and their lives were anything but what they ought to have been.[j] The evil was too firmly seated to be remedied by a youthful superior, and Oswald was too conscientious to be a silent spectator of what he could not cure. He went in sorrow to archbishop Odo[k] and acquainted him with his difficulties and scruples. He told him how unprofitable to himself and others had been his life at Winchester. He was disgusted with the pride and avarice of his brethren. Their praises sickened him. He was resolved to attach himself to a religious order and become a monk. He would seek for the repose, which he had not yet found, within the walls of Fleury, and learn the rule of Benedict at the resting-place of its holy founder by the waters of the Loire.

Odo was overjoyed at his nephew's determination, and sent him on his way with commendatory letters, and blessings, and advice. He had passed some time at Fleury himself, and the toilsome honours of age had not banished from his recollection that sacred shrine. The youthful scholar was received within the same walls, and professed himself a monk. The same ardent longing that led Wilfrid to the eternal city from the solitudes of Lindisfarne, directed the steps of Oswald to the "Queen of Monasteries." The noble stranger was received with open arms by the abbat and his brethren. They watched with affectionate admiration the zeal of the youthful devotee. They had grown grey themselves in the path of duty, but when they looked at Oswald they were not ashamed to confess that they could still take a lesson from one so much younger than themselves.

[i] Elected dean "concanonicorum conciliante suffragio." MS. Dunelm., fol. 7.

[j] The following account of Oswald's life at Winchester is taken from the MS. in the Cottonian library. "Erat enim valde inclitus in omnibus operibus suis, amabilis et affabilis omnibus amicis suis. Fulgebat cotidie in sericis vestibus, et epulabatur per singulos soles splendide, cui suppeditabant gazæ terrestres, nec vero honores quos servavit Christo non sibi, sicut postea rei probavit eventus. In diebus illis non monastici viri ipsius sanctæ institutionis regulæ erant in regione Anglorum, sed erant religiosi et dignissimi clerici, qui tamen thesauros suos quos avidis adquirebant cordibus non ad ecclesiæ honorem sed suis dare solebant uxoribus."

[k] Eadmer, 193-4. Hist. Rames., 391.

Docility there was in him, and a gentle manner far beyond his years. He would watch and pray in secret over the requirements of his high calling. He mastered all that the brethren could teach him, moving quietly among them with a happy countenance. Several years[l] passed away, and he was still at Fleury. He had taken upon himself all the orders of the church. He was now a priest, and his highest aspiration was that he might pass away to his rest within those walls where he had learned the lesson, that there is joy and pleasure even in the cloistered cell.

Odo was delighted when he heard what his nephew had done at Fleury, how he had answered, and more than answered, his warmest wishes and desires. His own day of life was closing, and, before it ended, he was eager to see again his kinsman, of whom he was so proud. He besought him to return to England, to aid him in his diocese, to visit him once more. The summons was not one that an affectionate heart could refuse. The brethren would fain have detained Oswald, and wept at his departure, but he hastened across the channel. With all his speed he was too late. The primacy was vacant before he reached the shores of England. The death of his uncle caused him the most poignant affliction. He went to Canterbury, but the sight of the place awakened many bitter memories. His patron, his dearest kinsman, was lost to him. Whither should he now turn?[m]

Oskytel, another relation, had just become the head of the Northern province. He welcomes Oswald with open arms. The prelate sets out for Rome to secure for himself the pall, and his kinsman accompanies him. Oswald, however, was unable to pass by the walls of Fleury. He left the train of Oskytel, and turned aside to his favourite abode. The inmates welcomed him with joy; and he returned with a happy heart to his old path of duty.

Whilst he was at Fleury the archbishop returned to England, but in the management of his vast diocese he soon missed the energy and experience of his kinsman. He entreated him to desert the Loire for the Ouse, and to revive within his province a stricter form of discipline; and Oswald, nothing loth, accepted his invitation.[n] The English monasteries were at that time in

[l] Mabillon, Ann. Ben., iii., 541, says that Oswald went to Fleury circa 959. It was probably earlier than this. Recueil des Historiens des Gaules, viii., 307. Mabillon, Acta SS. ord. S. B., sæc. vi., i., 36.

[m] Eadmer, 194-6. Hist. Rames., 391. Malmesbury, apud Savile, 153 *b*. Odo died in 961.

[n] Eadmer, 197. Hist. Rames., 392. "velut Joseph uterinum Benjamin, cepit eum amplexibus fovere; quem secum retinuit plurimis diebus, commendans ipsum omnibus amicis suis, presertim Dunstano" (MSS. Cotton, Nero E., i., 6, *a. b.*) "In omni man-

great need of a reformer. They were filled, principally, with secular canons who observed no discipline, and were guided, for the most part, by no religious rule. Time and neglect had all but obliterated the lessons of Theodore and Wilfrid. A master-spirit, however, was now arising, who was bold enough to correct the evil and to enforce, as far as he could, the great system of which Benedict was the author. Dunstan was now sitting in the chair of Odo. That energetic man had heard of the fame of the monk of Fleury. Who would be more able to assist him in his projects of reform? They met, and the most affectionate intercourse ensued. As a proof of his esteem, and that Oswald might have a larger sphere of usefulness, Dunstan prevailed upon king Edgar to advance his friend in the year 961 to the bishopric of Worcester, which he had himself recently vacated.[o]

Oswald was a most energetic prelate. The main object of his endeavours was the revival of the ancient order and discipline of the church, which had been too long neglected, and he saw no other method of bringing this about except by the re-introduction of the Benedictine rule and the suppression of the houses of secular canons. In these designs he had two able coadjutors in the archbishop and Ethelwold of Winchester, the triple light, as the historian calls them, which scattered the darkness from off the face of England.[p] The position of Dunstan gave him the greatest amount of influence, especially with the king, but Oswald was in reality the designer and chief mover in the reformation. The sovereign was induced to pass a decree at a council of the church, ordering the expulsion of the married clergy, and the name of 'Oswald's law' which was given to it, points to the bishop of Worcester as its originator.[q] That prelate had already established a little colony of twelve monks from Fleury at a place called Westbury, under the charge of Germanus, and the sight of that house was so gratifying to the king that he directed more than forty monasteries to be constructed after the same model.[r] As soon as the "law" was passed, Oswald expelled the secular canons from seven churches

suetudine susceptus, mansitabat a latere ejus in magnificentia dies non paucos" (Servatus., 10).

[o] Eadmer, 198. Flor. Wigorn., 356. Hist. Rames., 392-3. Chron. de Mailros, 32. Wendover, i., 260. Symeon, De Gestis, col. 158. Hoveden, apud Savile, 244. Chron. Petrib., 30, where the date 960 is given. Dunstan was the consecrator.

[p] Malmesbury, apud Savile, 31 *b.*, Eadmer, Hist. Novorum, apud Anselmi Op., 28. Turketyl of Croyland was a great friend of the three (Ord. Vitalis, apud Duchesne, 541). Polydore Vergil, 119.

[q] Eadmer, 200. Hist. Rames., 393. Labbe Conc., ix., 696-9. Spelman, 476. Wilkins, i., 239, 246-9. The circumstance was recorded in the windows at Worcester. (Thomas, 16, 31.)

[r] MSS. Cotton, Nero E. i., 7 *b*.

in his diocese, putting monks in their room, Pershore and Winchcombe being, probably, two of the places in which the change was made.[s] But the career of the reformer was beset with many difficulties. He was powerful enough to remodel the monasteries of Ely and St. Albans;[t] nay, one chronicler goes so far as to say that he had a controlling power over all the religious houses in England,[u] but he was foiled within his own diocese, where the secular canons had great influence. He could do little with his own church at Worcester. He endeavoured to lessen the authority of the canons, and granted leases of their property.[v] He built, also, by Dunstan's advice, a rival church in the cemetery of that belonging to his opponents. In it he was accustomed to officiate himself, and by his personal demeanor and holy life, accompanied by a little justifiable adroitness, the new sanctuary became gradually thronged with worshippers, and was regarded as the principal temple in the diocese. The secular canons were slowly but surely pushed out of their places.[w]

The year 972 witnessed the end of Oskytel of York, and Dunstan seems to have been exceedingly desirous that the Northern primacy should fall into the hands of some one who would uphold the Benedictine rule. The struggle between the two religious parties was at its height, and York, as Dunstan felt, could not be safely given up. Who was so well qualified to moderate the vacant see as Oswald, who had worked in the province under his kinsman Oskytel? He induced Edgar to offer it for his acceptance, and, after some hesitation, Oswald was prevailed upon to take it.[x] But that the good work which was going on in the diocese of Worcester should neither be prevented nor retarded, the new occupant of the chair of Paulinus was allowed, at Dunstan's suggestion, to retain *in commendam* the ecclesiastical superintendence of his bishopric in the South.[y] It was quite impossible, as was proved by the

[s] Eadmer, 200. Baronii Ann., x., 937.

[t] Eadmer, 201.

[u] Ord. Vitalis, apud Duchesne, 517. "Quia multiplici tam sagacitate quam bonitate pollebat, omnibus Angliæ cœnobiis præpositus erat."

[v] Thomas's Bishops of Worcester, 40, etc. Oswald justified this practice to the king. Codex, Diplom., i., pref. xxxv. In that valuable work, vol. iii., there are many of these grants.

[w] "Non vi pulsis sed arte circumventis" (Malmesbury, apud Savile, 153 *b*). Eadmer, 202-3. Fl. Wigorn., 359. Chron. Mailros, 33. Other writers seem to say that more or less force was used. Wendover, i., 262. Hoveden, 244 *b*. Symeon, De Gestis, col. 155. Chron. Petrib., 31. Higden, apud Gale, i., 267. This seems to have taken place in 969.

[x] Symeon, De Gestis, col. 159. Labbe, Bibl., i., 323. Chron. de Mailros, 33. Hoveden, apud Savile, 244 *b*. Higden, apud Gale, i., 217. Several writers make the year 971. Fl. Wigorn., 359. Eadmer, 203. Wendover, i., 268. Symeon and Hoveden. Stubbs, col. 1699. Servatus, fol. 14.

[y] Eadmer, 204. Rad. de Diceto, col.

result, for any one to do justice to such a charge, and nothing but a very cogent reason ought to have suggested even the temporary union of two dioceses which were so far apart.

Immediately after his acceptance of the Northern see, Oswald set out for Rome and obtained the pall at the hands of John the pope.[z] On his return to England he was solemnly installed at York. A biographer of the archbishop gives us an interesting account of the city at that early period.[a] The walls and the magnificent buildings were greatly in decay, which had been accelerated no doubt by the neglect of its inhabitants and the assaults of invaders. From a strong military position it was being gradually changed into the mart for commerce, which was its glory in the middle ages. The wealth of the city, even then, was in its shops and warehouses. It was thronged with Danish merchants. The adult population was at least thirty thousand. All this seems to shew that the accounts of the great mischief which the Danes did to York has been exaggerated. They seem to have occupied the city and not to have spoiled or destroyed it. Oswald, who was a Dane himself, would be welcomed by the inhabitants. The ceremonial at his installation was a magnificent one. When his devotions in the church were over, he went to his own hall which was sprinkled with holy water. He then distributed the *panis benedictus* with his hands in the shape of a cross, according to ancient custom. The banquet then began.[b] After this the chroniclers are silent, and we know next to nothing of what Oswald did at York, although he presided over that see for twenty years. There was no Northern writer to speak of what he effected in Northumbria. One biographer records a visit which the archbishop paid to Ripon, where he discovered the remains of Wilfrid and the early abbats of that place. He placed the bones of that great prelate in a feretory and carried them, as Eadmer says, to Worcester.[c] The same writer, in another work, has told us that Odo had previously removed the bones of the Northern worthy

456, says that the two sees were held together because the Danes had wasted Northumbria.

[z] Some writers say pope Stephen. Eadmer, 204. Chron. de Mailros, 33. Symeon, De Arch. Ebor., col. 79. Stubbs, col. 1699. Fl. Wigorn., 359. The pope was John XIII. Cf. L'art de vérifier les Dates, i., 272, ed. 1783.

[a] This new and most valuable information is taken from MSS. Cotton, Nero, E. i., 15 *b*. "Est civitas Eboraca metropolis totius gentis Northanimbrorum, quæ quondam erat nobiliter edificata et firmiter muris constructa, quæ nunc dimissa vetustate; quæ tamen gaudet de multitudine populorum, non minus virorum ac mulierum, exceptis parvulis et pubetinis, quam xxx milia in eadem civitate numerati sunt, quæ inediciabiliter repleta et mercatorum gazis locupleta qui undique adveniunt, maxime ex Danorum gente."

[b] MS. Cotton, Nero, E. i., 16.

[c] Eadmer, 205-6. He says that the resting-place of these good men was revealed to Oswald in a dream. The Cottonian MS. omits this.

to Canterbury, and he speaks of this Wilfrid as if he were the second bishop of that name, forgetting entirely that that prelate was never canonized. The whole story must be looked upon with suspicion.

We hear a good deal of Oswald's reforms in the South, but there is little to shew us that he made any change in the Northern monasteries. From this want of evidence it has been inferred by some that the Benedictine rule was already in existence in the North, and that there was nothing for him to reform. With this opinion I cannot agree.[d] I do not believe that the Benedictine rule was ever firmly established in the North till after the Conquest. The minster at York was never occupied by monks. The observance of order and discipline may have been pressed upon the canons, and it may, perhaps, have been partially attended to under a diligent archbishop, but they never became monks, in the proper sense of that word. They lived upon a common fund and had a common dormitory and refectory, from which it may be inferred that they were unmarried, but they were never Benedictines. Had they been so, the minute instructions which Alcuin wrote to the brethren at York would have been unnecessary; and within thirty years after the death of Oswald the canons rejected a strict archbishop, and they were thence called *"osores monachorum."*[e] If the Benedictine influence had been strong in Northumbria the bones of Wilfrid would never have been removed into the South, assuming that they were actually taken away. I believe that Oswald accepted the see of York, not with the certainty of being able to carry out his reforms in that province, but to keep some religious opponent out of the position. To attend adequately to the two dioceses was impossible. The whole of the North was seamed and scarred by the sanguinary warfare of the native princes in years gone by, and the incursions of the Danes. How could Oswald work there? There were troubles enough in his old diocese of Worcester. The duke of Mercia was taking the part of the secular canons, and he was to be withstood. He would carry the day if the archbishop remained in

[d] In the Cottonian MS. is the following remarkable passage, "De loco in quo ejus pontificalis cathedra posita est, quid referam, quidque dicam? Nonne in eo in quo quondam mansitabant diacones et struciones(*sic*) fecit Deo servire monachos? Edificavit novæ Hierosolimæ portas, construxit ipsius cœnobii nova fundamenta quæ ad perfeccionem perfecit, et cum simplicitate cordis Deo optulit."

This comes immediately after the account of the visit to Ripon, and probably refers to that church or to that of Worcester. The writer, it will be observed, speaks with doubt and uncertainty, and knew little or nothing about Northern affairs. Ripon had been, in the first instance, a Benedictine house, and had been recently destroyed by the Danes.

[e] This title is given to them by Leland. See the beginning of the life of Alfric, p. 134.

Northumbria. It was wiser to strengthen the house which he had erected in the South, than to try to erect another in the North with its foundations on the sand.

The number of charters in existence which were granted by Oswald in connection with the see of Worcester, shews how permanent was his continuance in that diocese.[f] But he had many other avocations, and during the reign of Edgar he seems to have occupied a very important position in the state. He was a witness to the charter of privileges granted to the abbey of Peterborough by king Edgar; he was present when the same monarch re-founded the ancient monastery at Glastonbury.[g] He took an active part in the coronation of Edgar, Edward, and Ethelred.[h] But when the sceptre fell from the grasp of Edgar, a series of troubles began which embittered the remainder of Oswald's life. The power of the secular canons revived under the influence of Elfhere of Mercia; his favourite monks were neglected or expelled, and the plans upon which the best of his energies and intellect had been spent were scattered to the winds.[i] This was a cruel issue for a life full of honest purposes and self-sacrificing devotion.

There was one place, however, where Oswald was not forgotten, and which he watched and tended in prosperity and adversity, and that was the monastery of Ramsey. There it was that he had prevailed upon the pious Alwine to erect a shrine to God, and he had himself assisted him. Lonely that place was before that temple was erected, girt with stagnant pools, and covered with reeds and brushwood that love the water; but even there three holy men had fixed their abode, and the voice of praise was heard among the rushes as they trembled in the wind and startled the bittern from its resting-place. The walls of a church were raised upon that island, for such it then was; a colony of monks soon nestled within them, fostered and endowed by the offerings of the faithful. As years passed on there was a shrinking in the treacherous fen; two towers fell to the ground; the pillars and arches cracked and terrified the trembling inmates. A nobler shrine was now reared upon the old foundations, and one of the last acts of Oswald's life was its

[f] Codex Diplom., ii., 383, etc. Hist. Mon. de Abingdon, i., *var. loc.* There are also charters granted or witnessed by Oswald in Wanley, 199, 200, etc. MSS. Cotton, Vesp. A. v. Appendix to Smith's edition of Beda, 773-4, 8. Hickes' Dissert. Ep., 70. Wilkins, i., 258.

[g] Saxon Chron., 156. Malmesbury, apud Gale, i., 321. Hist. Cœnobii Burg. (Sparke), 19. Labbe, Conc., ix., 704. Spelman, Conc., 483. Dugd. Mon., i., 51.

[h] Chron. de Mailros, 33, 35. Fl. Wigorn., 359, 362. Ingulph, apud Gale, iii., 54. Wendover, i., 265-7. Hoveden, 244-5. Symeon, De Gestis, col. 159-60. Diceto, col. 457-9. Gervase, col. 1647. Stubbs, col. 1699.

[i] MSS. Cotton, Nero, E. i., 12 *b*. Mabillon, Ann. Ben., iii., 638.

consecration. This was in November, 991. It must have been a touching and a melancholy sight. The archbishop and his friend Alwine met there for the last time. The aged prelate was bowed down with years, and sorrow had sets its mark upon his brow; and all felt within themselves, as they gazed upon his face, that the light of this earthly sun would not long illumine it. "I am going hence," he said, in that strangely prophetic tone which the world-worn saint can use, "I must leave you all soon; may Christ make us all one in paradise."[j]

These were his last words; and with tears and blessings he returned to Worcester to prepare himself for the end. The summons, however, was not given for awhile. The winter came and was passing away with its snows and showers. It was now the holy season of Lent. In addition to his many acts of piety and devotion it was the custom of the aged prelate at that sacred time to wash day by day the feet of twelve poor persons, kissing and wiping them with a towel after the example of the Magdalene and her Lord. One day the brethren found him standing beneath the open canopy of heaven and gazing, with silent prayer upon his lips, on the skies above him. "I am looking," was his answer to an enquiry, "on the way that I am to take. Oh, my children, let me have a little foretaste of the joys that are to be mine. The morrow shall not pass before I see that eternal rest for which I have laboured until now." He spoke and re-entered the little oratory that he had left, but his eye was still bright, and there was no symptom nor shadow of the end that was so near.

The morrow came with its customary work, and the holy eucharist was given to him, for he desired it. The twelve poor people came to him according to their wont. He tottered as he stooped to them, but he would stoop. He washed their feet and kissed them as of old. It was done, and the verses of the psalm—"*Oculi mei semper ad Dominum*"—mine eyes are ever waiting upon the Lord—were over, and he was in the midst of them. When he came to the doxology they bowed in suppliant obeisance. "*Gloria Patri et Filio et Spiritui Sancto*"[k] was what he said. There was a pause. He spoke no longer to earthly ears, and yet, perchance, that sentence was completed in another state and in a more exalted presence.[l]

The day of his departure was the 28th of February, 992.[m]

[j] Eadmer, 207-8. Hist. Rames., apud Gale, i., 395. Chron. de Mailros, 38. Fl. Wigorn., 365. Chron. Petrib., 31, 5. Hoveden, col. 245 *b*. Symeon, De Gestis, col. 162. Stubbs, col. 1699.

[k] The venerable Beda departed with the same words upon his lips.

[l] Eadmer, 208-9. Chron. de Mailros, 38. Hoveden, apud Savile, 245 *b*. Higden, apud Gale, i., 267. Mabillon, Ann. Ben., iv., 81. Baronii Ann., x., 1024-5.

[m] Saxon Chron., 168. Eadmer, 210. Hist. Rames., 426. Wendover, i., 271.

They laid his bones in his own church at Worcester,[n] and his successor, Adulph, placed them honourably in a scrinium or feretory.[o] Miracles are said to have been wrought there, and a halo of sanctity hung around the memory of Oswald.[p] He was entered on the calendar. Two of that name were enshrined in that sacred page. The one was the holy prelate of whom we are now speaking; the other was the good king of Northumbria who earned for himself a crown of martyrdom on the battle-field. The former sleeps in the church that he erected; the mutilated head of the latter was laid, where it still reposes, on the breast of St. Cuthbert in his tomb at Durham.

The portiphor of St. Oswald is still preserved in the library at C. C. C. Cambridge.[q] His infula or stole of purple and gold, set with gems and of radiant beauty, was treasured in the minster at Beverley in the time of Stubbs. This was probably the stole which Adulph found in his tomb at Worcester.[r]

Oswald is said to have been the author of several works which are now lost. They were, a Collection of Letters to his uncle Odo; a work inscribed to his friend Abbo, commencing with the words *Præscientia Dei monachus;* a treatise, *Ad Sanctos,* composed whilst he was at Fleury, and beginning *Oswaldus, supplex monachus;* and *Statuta Synodalia,* in one book.[s]

Oswald, himself, has had several biographers. The first in age and importance, is an unknown monk of Ramsey, whose work is now in the British Museum.[t] It is a MS. of the noblest kind, written certainly within twenty or thirty years

Symeon, Higden, Fl., Stubbs, Hoveden, Chron. Petrib., and Mailros, *ut supra.*

[n] Symeon, Higden, Flor., Wendover and Eadmer, *ut supra.* Lel. Coll., iv., 81, 160. Hickes, Dissert. Ep., 120. Mabillon, Ann. Ben., iv., 81.

[o] Servatus, fol. 21. Chron. de Mailros, 40. Diceto, col. 461. Dr. Thomas, in his history of Worcester (61), gives an engraving of a tomb attributed to Oswald, the work of a later age. I have, unfortunately, been unable to examine a copy of Hemming's Chronicle of Worcester. Dr. Thomas, however, has made great use of it.

[p] Eadmer, 209.

[q] Among the Parker MSS., K. 10 (Catalogue, pr. in 1722. Wanley, 110. Smith's Cat. of MSS). The book formerly belonged to the church of Worcester.

[r] Stubbs, col. 1699. Servatus, fol. 21. Mabillon, Ann. Ben., iv., 81.

[s] Bale, cent. ii., 141. Pitseus, 180. Tanner, Bibl. Brit., 560. Wright, Biogr. Lit., i., 467.

[t] One of the finest MSS. that I ever saw. It is entituled, "Vitæ et Passiones Sanctorum," and is written, in various hands, by a very bold scribe upon the finest vellum. It is of the folio size, and the caligraphy is excellent. The class mark is Nero, E. i. The life of Oswald is written in double column, and occupies twenty-one folios. On the first leaf is a note in the hand of the celebrated archbishop Ussher, suggesting that Elfric was the author. The writer, however, disproves this by saying (15 *a*) whilst speaking of a miracle, "Est hujus rei testis Elfricus archiepiscopus civitatis Cantiæ. Sunt alii quam plurimi conspicui viri (qui dicant) quod vera sunt quæ dicimus."

The following passage shews that the author was a monk at Ramsey or Worcester, "Nobis autem præposuit Æthelnothum, et illis, qui sub eo erant in civitate, anteposuit Wynsinum, qui erat nostri cenobii gimnasio eruditus."

after the decease of Oswald, and full justice has not yet been done to it. The style is occasionally inflated and diffuse, but the life contains some novel and valuable information.

There is another life of the archbishop by Eadmer, the biographer of Wilfrid, which is printed in the Anglia Sacra.[u] This is merely an abstract, at times carelessly and clumsily done, of the earlier account by the monk of Ramsey. There is an abridgment of the life by Eadmer among the Lansdowne MSS.[v] in the British Museum, which forms the text, I believe, that is adopted by Mabillon.[w]

Servatus, who was prior of Worcester in the twelfth century, drew up an account of Oswald. There is a copy of this MS., which is generally believed to be lost, in the valuable library of the dean and chapter of Durham. It is founded upon the earlier biographies, especially upon that of Eadmer, and makes use very frequently of the same sentences and words. It is evidently a compilation for the use of the church of Worcester, with additions to the previously received accounts; one, in particular, describes the translation of Oswald's remains by Adulph.[x]

Alfric of Canterbury and Folcard, the biographer of St. John of Beverley, are said to have described the acts and deeds of Oswald, but their works are not known to be in existence.[y] There is much interesting information about Oswald in the history of Ramsey abbey, which has been published by dean Gale.[z] The chroniclers of that house had good reason to remember and commemorate him.

[u] Anglia Sacra, ii., 191. Cf. præfat. ad eandem, xiv.

[v] No. ccccxxxvi., 76-81. Among other lives of the Saints written in the fifteenth century. The book once belonged to Ramsey abbey.

[w] Acta SS. ord. S. B., sæc. v., 728.

[x] A most beautiful MS. of the twelfth century, in small folio. The class mark is B. iv., 39 B. The volume, also, contains the life of St. Wulstan, and probably belonged at one time to the church of Worcester. It has been at Durham for many centuries, as is evident by the following inscription upon a fly-leaf, "Iste liber assingnatur communi almariolo Dunelm. ex procuratione domini Johannis de Rypon monachi et medici."

[y] Ord. Vitalis, lib. ii. Oudinus ii., 1076. There are lives and notices of Oswald in Acta SS. Feb., vol. iii., 753-56. (Taken from Eadmer). Mabillon, Acta SS. ord. S. B., sæc. v., where there are three lives, one abridged from Eadmer, another extracted from the Ramsey chronicle, and the third, a compilation from Capgrave and the Bollandists. There is a life in Capgrave's Nova Legenda, ccli., etc.

[z] Other works relating to Oswald are in existence which I have not seen, but it is not probable that they contain anything new, *e.g.* "Vita S. Oswaldi archiepiscopi, ejusdemque miracula" (MSS. Bodl. F. 6, 2430, 15) and "Miracula S. Oswaldi Ebor. archiepiscopi" (Benét Coll. Cambr.)

In the old library of the monks of Peterbro' were "Versus magistri Henrici de vita S. Oswaldi" (Gunton's Peterbro, 205). In MSS. Bodl., 3886, is a tract "De Vita et miraculis S. Oswaldi," given by Thomas Lord Fairfax; and there is a similar life in the library of St. John's Coll. Oxford (Smith's Cat.) These may, perhaps, refer to king Oswald, and not to the archbishop.

Adulph, the abbat of the monastery of St. Peter at Burgh, was the successor of Oswald. The retreat, of which he was the president, was founded three centuries before his time by Wulfere of Mercia. It was then known by the name of Medeshamstead, and had a munificent endowment. The Danes at length laid it in the dust, and it was the privilege of Ethelwold of Winchester, in the latter part of the tenth century, to prevail upon his royal master, Edgar, to restore it. The inmates were henceforward to observe a new rule, and the place received at the same time a new name. It was called the burgh or town of St. Peter, a title that still survives to us in the modern Peterborough.

The history of Adulph and his connection with Burgh is a remarkable one. Like others of his day, he held a high position at court, and was chancellor to king Edgar. A domestic affliction is said to have opened his eyes to the vanity of earthly honours, and to have changed the whole current of his life. He had an only son who was unhappily overlaid by his parents as he slept between them. The distressed father was appalled at this involuntary crime, and was about to cross the seas to seek for absolution at Rome, when bishop Ethelwold told him that he could best atone for what had occurred by deeds of mercy and charity at home. The old abbey of Medeshamstead was in ruins: Croyland had already arisen in beauty through the care of Turketyl; there was an example for him to copy and a field to work upon. The resolution of the nobleman was soon taken. He went to Medeshamstead, and there, in the presence of the monarch and his court, devoted his worldly substance to the restoration of that ruined temple. He resigned his office, and assuming the dress of a Benedictine, gave up the remainder of his days to unlearn the ways of the world that he had renounced.[a]

Adulph could not have been long at Burgh before he was raised by Ethelwold to the post of abbat of that monastery.[b] Who was more worthy of that honour? To his munificence and energy was due the restoration of that shrine, and he had set an example which the monarch and his nobles had been glad to follow.[c] A church of rare beauty had arisen in that

[a] Hist. Cœnobii Burg., apud Sparke, 18. Chron. Petrib., 35. Lel. Coll., i., 6, 7. Gunton's Peterbro', 10-11. The metrical hist. of Peterbro' in Sparke, 247, which begins thus:—

"Un chaunceler avoit le rei, Adulf lapell;
Cil en out un petit fiz, qu'il tant amat."

[b] Ingulph, apud Savile, 502 *b*. Vita S. Ethelwoldi, apud Mabillon, Acta SS. ord. S. B., sæc. v., 616. Hist. Mon. de Abingdon, ii., 262.

[c] Hist. Cœnob. Burg., 18. Adulph's gift to the church when he became a monk was a remarkable one, "plenam hastam armillis extra argentum et variis ornamentis."

wild country. The brakes and forests were cleared away, the fens were drained, and moss and moor at length owned the supremacy of man.[d] Good work like this cannot be too highly praised, and, unfortunately, we know too little of its author. We are told that Adulph was present at the consecration of Ramsey abbey,[e] and, in the year 975, he and the abbat of Thorney committed their friend Turketyl to the tomb.[f] For the next seventeen years his energies seem to have been quietly and unostentatiously devoted to the interests of his monastery.

In 992 the death of Oswald vacated the sees of York and Worcester, and the abbat of Burgh was appointed his successor by the common voice.[g] He held both these arduous and honourable posts for the same reason, in all probability, that had united them in the person of his predecessor. We know little of his episcopal career. He did not, as it is said, make his obedience to Canterbury.[h] The prelate who did so was Adulph a bishop of Lindsey. Like Oswald, he was a great friend and benefactor to Fleury.[i] We find him making and witnessing a few grants,[j] and we hear nothing more of him. But who can say that that life was fruitless and those years misspent about which the chroniclers are mute? Out of that silence there seems to come the sound of a far more approving voice which whispers to us of the good deeds of one "whose praise is not of man but of God."

There was, however, one great scene at Worcester in which Adulph took a part, the translation of the remains of Oswald to a more befitting resting-place. This was done on the 15th of April, 1002. King Ethelred was there with a long array of bishops and holy men, and the ceremonial must have been a magnificent one.[k] Six weeks after this, on the 5th of June,[l]

[d] Saxon Chron., 156. Lel. Coll., i., 6, 7. Gunton, 9-10, 248-9.

[e] Gunton, 11.

[f] Ingulph, apud Savile, 505.

[g] Saxon Chron., 169. Chron. Mailros, 38. Anglia Sacra, i., 473. Symeon, De Gestis, col. 162. "Omnium consensu, vel voluntate regis et episcoporum, cleri et populorum" (Hist. Cœnobii Burg., 31). In 995 he signs a charter as "electus in episc. Ebor." (Hist. Mon. de Abingdon, i., 391) Was he at that time without the pall?

[h] Anglia Sacra, i., 78. Textus Roffensis, 248.

[i] Malmesbury, apud Savile, 154.

[j] Codex Diplom., iii., 280, 295, etc. Hist. Mon. de Abingdon, i., 365, etc. Thomas' Worcester, 56.

[k] Fl. Wigorn., 370. Chron. de Mailros, 40. Chron. Petrib., 38. Wendover, i., 276. Hoveden, apud Savile, 246. Symeon, col. 164. Diceto, col. 461. Stubbs, col. 1699. There is a rather long account of the ceremony in the life of Oswald by Servatus (MSS. Dunelm., B. iv., 39, B., 21). The author speaks of Adulph as "vir habitu monachus et mandatorum Domini eximius executor."

[l] Ann. Wigorn. (apud Angl. Sacr., i., 473) make him die on May 6th; so do Fl. Wigorn. (370) and Symeon (col. 165.) A Worcester obituary says that he died on June 4 (Wharton i., 473.) The Peterbro' Obituary, on June 5 (ibid.), the day on which his depositio was commemorated in that church

Adulph's own body was laid in the grave in the same church in which his predecessor was sleeping, whose holy life he had made the model for his own.

Wulstan II. was raised to the archiepiscopate of York and the see of Worcester on the death of Adulph.[m] Of his previous history there is little known. He is said to have been a monk and an abbat.[n] His family was an honourable one; many of his kinsmen were persons of consequence, and his sister's son Brihteage became bishop of Worcester.[o]

Like most of the prelates of his time Wulstan was a courtier, and he is said to have been an especial favourite of Ethelred, Edmund, and Canute. I find him witnessing at York the gift of Darlington which Ethelred made to St Cuthbert,[p] and he was present in 1004 when the same monarch confirmed the foundation of Burton abbey.[q] About 1006 he was at the council at Eynsham in Oxfordshire, when thirty-two canons were enacted for the direction of the church and state, with a special reference to the ravages of the Danes.[r] In 1018 he witnessed king Canute's grant of privileges to Canterbury.[s] In 1020 he was with the same sovereign at the dedication of his church at Assington.[t] In the same year he consecrated archbishop Ethelnoth, and one of his own suffragans, Edmund, bishop of Durham.[u] He was a kind benefactor to the church of Ely, and was a man of consequence and repute both in the church and the court.

The character of Wulstan has been very severely assailed. William of Malmesbury attacks him for holding two sees at one

(Dugd., Mon. i., 362.) A Lambeth Calendar makes the date June 5 (Gunton, 248, 9.) The Peterbro' Chron. says, wrongly, that he died in 1003 (38). Cf. Saxon Chron., 176. Chron. Mailros, 40. Hoveden, 246. Symeon, col. 165. Stubbs, col. 1699.

[m] In 1002 or 1003, Fl. Wigorn., 370. Chron. de Mailros, 40. Symeon, De Gestis, col. 165. Wendover, i., 276.

[n] Fl. and Symeon, *ut supra*. Diceto, col. 461. Hoveden, apud Savile, 246 *b*. Ann. Wigorn., apud Angl. Sacr., i., 473. Hist. Eliens., apud Gale, i., 506, where it is said that he was a monk.

[o] Fl. Wigorn., 397. Hoveden, 251. Hist. Eliens., 506. Symeon, col. 178. In the Hist. Eliens. (Gale, i., 506) it is said of Wulstan, "Secto matris utero in hanc lucem productus fuerat et vaccæ uberibus proximorum industria educatus." The same thing was said of archbishops Kinsius and Frewen!

[p] Symeon, Hist. Dunelm., 149.

[q] Ann. Burton, apud Gale, iii., 246.

[r] Spelmanni Conc., 510.

[s] Ibid. There are other grants witnessed or made by him in Codex Diplom., iii., 330, etc.; iv., 1, etc. Chron. de Abingdon, i., 380, etc. Smith's App[x] to Beda, 778-9. Hist. Eliensis, apud Gale, i., 522-3. Dugd., Mon., i., 51. Wanley, 300, etc.

[t] Saxon Chron., 202. Fl. Wigorn., 392. Hoveden, 250, *b*. Symeon, col. 177. Diceto, col. 467. Stubbs, col. 1700. Hist. Eliens., apud Gale, i., 506.

[u] Saxon Chron., 202. Symeon, Hist. Dunelm., 156.

time,[v] whilst he never censures Oswald and Adulph who did the same thing. "Bigamy of bishops," says Fuller, "goes by favour, and it is condemnable in one what is commendable in another."[w] The Worcester historians are more severe than Malmesbury. Abuse is recklessly showered upon Wulstan. He is called a plunderer and a robber.[x] They charged him with taking away some of the lands of the see of Worcester and appropriating them to that of York. Dr. Thomas, however, a more recent chronicler of the church of Worcester,[y] takes a juster view. He says that, in all probability, the estates of the two bishoprics had become so mixed together that it was extremely difficult to separate them, and that, therefore, it is unfair to attribute to design what may merely have been the result of accident. It was intended also, I believe, at this time that the two sees should be always united. This scheme seems to have had its origin, as I have already stated, in the policy of Dunstan and Oswald; but afterwards when Northumbria was ravaged by the Danes, the possession of the Southern bishopric was found to be necessary for the maintenance of the Northern primate. It was on this ground that Edward the Confessor subsequently decided in favour of their union.[z] The archbishops of Canterbury would not be likely to oppose it, as the primate of the North would thus be placed in the position of a suffragan to the successors of Augustine.

Wulstan is very honourably connected with Anglo-Saxon literature. It is generally believed that he was the author of the Homilies, to which the name of Lupus Episcopus is affixed.[a] All of them are still unpublished, with the exception of one which is a striking address to his countrymen on the Danish invasion.[b] It was written in the year 1012, and exhibits a fearful picture of the vice and lawlessness of the age. Wulstan was also the author of an Encyclical Letter to the inhabitants of his

[v] De Gestis Pont., apud Savile, 154. He says that Wulstan ought not to have held Worcester, because he differed from his two predecessors, "sanctitate et habitu." He was, however, a monk, and we can form an opinion now, as well as Malmesbury, as to his sanctitas.

[w] Church History, book ii., 130.

[x] *Improbus* was the epithet generally applied to him. Thomas' Worcester, 57.

[y] Hist. Worcester, 57.

[z] Thomas' Worcester, app[x], i.

[a] Wanley (140) made this discovery. These Homilies are among the Parker MSS. at C. C. C., Cambridge (Smith's Cat.) There are some of them in MSS. Cotton, Nero, A. i.; and others, called "concionunculæ," in Tiberius, A. iii. There is a transcript of five made by Fr. Junius, with collations, in MSS. Bodl., 5213 (Smith's Cat.) See Oudinus, ii., 501. There is a list of these Homilies and much interesting information about them in Wanley, 27—30, 140-3.

[b] This is in MS. in C. C. C., Cambr. (Smith's Cat.), and a copy by Junius in MSS. Bodl., 5213. It is printed in Hickes' Dissert. Ep., 99—106, edited by W. Elstob. A separate edition in folio was published at Oxford in 1701, "Sermo Lupi Episcopi, Saxonice. Latinam interpretationem notasque adjecit Gulielmus Elstob."

diocese,[c] and he is said to have been the promulgator of a code of rules which are called the Laws of the Northumbrian priests.[d] We are indebted to him, besides, for two Pastoral Letters which Alfric Bata translated, at his suggestion, into Anglo-Saxon from the Latin in which they were originally composed.[e] Wulstan, therefore, in spite of what has been said against him, was a man of piety and learning. He dared to be a censor at a time when it was dangerous to rebuke. He was not ashamed of literature when there were few to cultivate or appreciate it. Haymo studied under his care at York;[f] Alfric Bata assisted him in his literary labours; and Alfric of Canterbury, another scholar, remembered him affectionately in his will.[g]

There is a curious story connected with Wulstan's end. He had come to the monastery of Ely, a place to which he was much attached, and the brethren welcomed him to their abode with a reverent procession. The archbishop placed himself at its head, and as he was moving up the church the staff, on which he was leaning, sank deep into the ground. "Here shall be my resting-place,"[h] he said; and so it was.[i] He died at York on the 28th of May, 1023,[j] desiring again, before his eyes were closed, that his bones should be removed to Ely. They laid him in the ground at the appointed place, and miracles are said to have borne witness to the sanctity of the archbishop. When the monks of Ely restored their cathedral they were obliged to disturb his remains, and they were laid for a while in the cemetery of the brotherhood before they found a resting-place in the renovated choir. The body had returned to its kindred

[c] In MS. at Corpus, Cambridge. There is a copy of it by Junius in MSS. Bodl., 5150, collated with MSS. Cotton, Tiberius, A. iii. (Smith's Cat.) Cf. Wanley, 85, 137.

[d] There is a copy of this in MS. at Corpus. The Laws have been printed in Labbe, Conc., ix., col. 495; in Laws and Institutes of England, ii., 290—303, and in Wilkins, i., 218-21, where they are put among documents of the tenth century. Wilkins' Anglo-Saxon Laws, 98-102.

[e] Oudinus, ii., col. 494. In MS. at Corpus, and in MSS. Harl., 438, and elsewhere. Published in Laws and Institutes of England, ii., 364-89, and in Wilkins' Anglo-Saxon Laws, 161—172.

[f] Tanner, Bibl. Brit. Pitseus, 181.

[g] "And he becwœth Uulfstane ærcebiscope ane sweor-rode (a cross for the neck), and anne ring and anne psaltere" (Hist. Mon. de Abingdon, i., 416). Hickes, Dissert. Epist., 62. Codex Diplom., iii., 352.

[h] Hist. Eliens., apud Gale, i., 606. Diceto, col. 467. The legend of St. Wulstan thrusting his staff into the stone will be remembered.

[i] Leland (Coll., i., 13) says that he died at Ely, and expressed a wish to be interred at Peterbro'. He was buried at Ely. Fl. Wigorn., 393. Hoveden, 250, *b*. Ann. Wigorn., apud Angl. Sacr., i., 473. Symeon, col. 177. Diceto, col. 467. Stubbs, col. 1700. In the Hist. Cœnob. Burg. (45), it is said that Wulstan had given to Peterbro' "se et omnia sua. Sed cum isset ad visitanda Sanctorum loca, et venisset ad Ely, ibi infirmatus est et mortuus et sepultus."

[j] Saxon Chron., 203. Fl. Wigorn., 393. Ann. Wigorn., apud Angl. Sacr., i., 473. Chron. de Mailros, 45. Symeon, col. 177. Stubbs, col. 1700. Hoveden (Savile, 250, *b*), says that he died on the 29th. Chron. of Winchester, ed. Stevenson, 390.

dust when the grave was opened, but the vestments were undecayed. The dress of the prelate was complete, and the wondering monks beheld the pall with its golden pins.[k]

Alfric, surnamed Putta or Puttoc, was the next archbishop of York.[l] At the time of his appointment he was provost of the church of Winchester, one of the most important positions in England. He was consecrated at Canterbury by archbishop Egelnoth in 1023,[m] and received the pall at the hands of pope John at Rome on the 12th of November, 1026.[n] The see of Worcester, in this instance, did not accompany the Northern primacy, as Leofsi seems to have occupied it since about 1016, acting probably as a suffragan to Wulstan during his life.[o]

Alfric was closely connected with the court, and for many years took a prominent part in public affairs. In 1026 or 1027, when Canute, eager to atone for the offences which had raised him to the throne, went as a pilgrim to Rome for absolution, he wrote a letter to the two archbishops acquainting them and his subjects with his design, and he addressed another to them on his return.[p] In all probability the two prelates had recommended that journey, and speaking to the monarch of the crimes of his earlier years had said to him,

> "For, save alone
> The hand of Christ's high vicar upon earth,
> A hurt so heinous what may heal?"

Not long after he came back the king was called away from the kingdoms that he had won before a higher Sovereign, and Alfric assisted his brother of Canterbury in placing the crown upon the head of Harold Harefoot.[q] In 1039 the throne was again vacant, and Hardicanute took up the sceptre to which he

[k] Hist. Eliens., 507. Bentham's Ely, 86, 91.

[l] Puttoc (Fl. Wigorn., 393). Putta (Chron. Mailros, 45). Puttoc signifies a kite, and the name, probably, is an unpleasant allusion to some of Alfric's cruel acts. I am indebted to archdeacon Churton for this suggestion.

It was at this vacancy, probably, that Egelric (afterwards bishop of Durham) was chosen archbishop, but was rejected by the canons, "quia pæne naturale est eis semper invidere monachis; quia monachus erat, noluerunt pati eum archiepiscopum esse" (Hist. Cœnob. Burg., apud Sparke, 45).

[m] Saxon Chron., 203. Fl. Wigorn., 393. Chron. de Mailros, 46. Hoveden, apud Savile, 250 *b*. Symeon, col. 177. Diceto, col. 468.

[n] Saxon Chron., 205. Stubbs, col. 1700. Flor., etc., *ut supra*.

[o] Lel. Col., iii. 259. Thomas' Worcester, 60.

[p] Wendover, i., 298. Flor. Wigorn., 394. Ingulph, apud Gale, iii. 59. Malmesbury, De Gestis Regum, apud Savile, 41 *b*.

[q] Gervase, col. 1651.

had been previously entitled. One of the first public acts of the new king was the manifestation of a miserable and unfeeling spite against his predecessor, which Alfric, unfortunately for his own character, is said to have suggested as well as to have carried out. The body of Harold was torn from its grave, and was cast, without its head, into the Thames, to shew that he had been monarch by a false title.[r] In 1040 the archbishop appears as an informer. He accused earl Godwin, and Living, bishop of Worcester, of being implicated in the murder of Alfred, the half-brother of the king. The earl was too powerful to be assailed, but the prelate was driven away from his see, which became the prize of the archbishop. Whilst he was in possession of Worcester he had an opportunity of giving a blow to the people of that city which they would long remember, and which was prompted, it is said, by the angry disappointment that he felt at their not choosing him originally as their bishop. One of the unpopular taxes of the day was being collected, and the people arose against the king's servants who were gathering it in, and two of them were slain. Upon that the archbishop is said to have advised his master to plunder and burn the city as a punishment for the offence.[s] His advice was adopted, and Alfric is said to have been the chief agent in perpetrating the crime. In the following year Alfric gave up the bishopric, and permitted Living to return.[t] All this does not place the archbishop before us in a favourable light. The example of his old master, Canute, might have taught him a very different lesson, to say nothing of the words of a still greater Sovereign which he professed especially to follow. In 1043, Alfric assisted at the coronation of Edward the Confessor.[u] We find his name appended to numerous deeds, especially to one which Canute made to the monks of Croyland.[v]

There is some good to be set against the evil. I cannot indeed attribute to Alfric the works that were composed by a writer of that name.[w] The head and the hand which prompted

[r] Malmesbury, De Gestis Pont. (Savile, 154), brings this accusation against Alfric. Other writers do not allude to it, *e.g.*, Fl. Wigorn., 401. Malmesbury, De Reg., 43. Hoveden, 251 *b*. Symeon, col. 180. Diceto, col. 474. Bromton, col. 933. Higden, apud Gale, i., 276. Lel. Col., iii., 259. The chief argument brought forward to shew that this Alfric was not the writer, is his political character, and he is condemned on the sole testimony of Malmesbury. The point seems to be yet an open one, but I leave it as I found it.

[s] Fl. Wigorn., 402. Wendover, i., 303. Hoveden, Symeon, and Leland, *ut supra*.

[t] Symeon, col. 180.

[u] Fl. Wigorn., 404. Chron. Mailros, 48. Chron., Petrib., 46. Alured Bev., 119. Wendover, i, 306. Symeon, col. 181. Diceto, col. 474. Bromton, col. 936. Stubbs, col. 1700. Ailred, col. 366 and 375. Gervase, col. 1651.

[v] Dugd. Mon., ii., 118. Hist. Mon. de Abingdon, i., 54, 438, etc. Codex Diplom., iv., 22, etc.

[w] As there were several persons of

them were animated by a nobler and a more Christian spirit. But there are still some acts of charity and generosity which will buoy up the archbishop's memory. He was a noble benefactor to Beverley and Peterborough. On the 25th of October, 1037, he took up the remains of his predecessor, St. John, and translated them to a new shrine with a gorgeous ceremonial. John had been canonized in the same year, probably at Alfric's request. The bones were placed in a rich case, bright with gold and silver and precious stones, which was deposited in a feretory of cunning workmanship and marvellous design. In the same church he established a sacrist, a chancellor and a precentor, and added to the endowments by purchasing and presenting lands in Middleton, Fridaythorpe, and Holm. He also obtained from Edward the Confessor a grant of three annual fairs to be held in Beverley.[x] To the abbey of Peterborough he was also most munificent. He bestowed upon it some precious vestments and plate. Their end was an unfortunate one. About the year 1100 some Flemish and French thieves broke into that famous monastery and stole a large cross, which stood upon the altar, set with gems, two chalices with their patens, and two candlesticks, all of pure gold, which had been given by archbishop Alfric. The robbers were subsequently captured, but their booty came into the possession of the king.[y]

Alfric died at Southwell on the 22nd of January, 1050,[z] and was interred at Peterborough,[a] that nursery and resting-place of Saints and prelates to which York owes so much. Gunton, the historian of Peterborough, who wrote in the seventeenth century, mentions a discovery which revealed the tomb of the archbishop. "On the north side of the choir in the cathedral, in two hollow places in the wall, were found two chests of about three foot long a piece, in each of which were the bones of a man, and of whom appeared by a plate of lead in each chest,

the name of Alfric living about the same time, it is not easy to discover which of them was the grammarian. The learned Henry Wharton wished to shew that he was our archbishop, and wrote a dissertation to prove it (Dissertatio utrum Elfricus Grammaticus?) which he printed in his Anglia Sacra, i., 125. The other side, on behalf of Alfric of Canterbury, was taken up, apparently with success, in the following work, "Edwardi-Rowei Moresi de Ælfrico, Dorobernensi archiepiscopo, commentarius: edidit Grimus Johannes Thorkelin, 4to. London, 1789." Cf. Wright, 480. Oudinus, ii., col. 489, etc. Cave, 588-9.

[x] Stubbs, col. 1700. Lel. Coll., iv., 102.

[y] "Dedit cum corpore suo albam de purpura cum optimis aurifriciis paratam et duas cappas optimas, et stolas, et dalmaticam albam, et altare cum reliquiis optime cum auro paratum, tria pallia et baculum suum," etc. (Hist. Cœnob. Burg., 45). Lel. Coll., i., 12, 15.

[z] Saxon Chron., 224, "A very venerable man, and wise."

[a] Ibid. Fl. Wigorn., 410. Chron. Mailros, 49. Chron. Petrib., 48. Hoveden, 251, *b.* Ingulph, apud Gale, iii., 64. Symeon, col. 184. Diceto, col. 475. Stubbs, col. 1700.

whereon the name of the person was engraven. In the one was Elfricus, on the other Kynsius; both which had been archbishops of York, and, being dead, their bodies were interred in the monastery of Peterborough, where formerly they had been monks."[c]

Kinsius, the next archbishop,[d] began his religious career as a monk at Peterborough.[e] In course of time he became the chaplain of Edward the Confessor, and when the see of York was vacant by the death of Alfric, Kinsius was advanced to that honourable post,[f] after it had been retained for some time in the king's hands.[g] In 1055 he journeyed to Rome, and obtained the pall from pope Victor.[h] Kinsius was at York for a very short period. His name is appended to a few charters.[i] In 1059 I find him witnessing a grant which his royal master made to the abbey of St. Denys, near Paris,[j] and, in the same year, he was acting the part of a peacemaker together with Egelwin, bishop of Durham, and Earl Tosti, in preventing a war with Scotland, by prevailing upon king Malcolm to make some timely concessions.[k] On the 22nd of December, 1060, the archbishop ended his days at York, having in the earlier part of that year consecrated the abbey at Waltham.[l] They carried him to Peterborough, and laid him honourably in the monastery in which his earlier years had been spent, and where he wished to be interred.[m] His resting-place was in the choir, close to the high altar, on the north side.[n]

The historian of Peterborough speaks in high terms of the

[c] Gunton's Peterbro', 98.

[d] The Saxon name of this prelate is Kynesige. Stubbs (col. 1700) mentions the singular circumstance, "quod non natus sed de ventre matris cæsus fuit."

[e] Ingulph, apud Gale, iii., 66. Chron. Petrib., 48. Hist. Cœnob. Burg., apud Sparke, 45.

[f] Fl. Wigorn., 410. Chron. de Mailros, 49. Wendover, i., 308. Symeon, De Gestis, col. 184. Hoveden, apud Savile, 253.

[g] Bromton, col. 943. [h] Ibid., 243.

[i] Codex Diplom., iv., 140, etc.

[j] Histoire de l'Abbaye de St. Denys, 126, & l'appendix, 85.

[k] Symeon, De Gestis, col. 190.

[l] Chron. de Waltham, ed. Stubbs, 18.

[m] Saxon Chron., 250. Fl. Wigorn., 421. Chron. de Mailros, 54. Symeon, De Gestis, col. 190. Ingulph, apud Gale, iii., 66. Hoveden, apud Savile, 255. The Peterbro' Chron. (32), says that he died at Peterbro', and Dugdale (Mon. i., 363), says that his depositio was observed in that monastery, on Dec. 20.

[n] "Jacet tumulatus in scrinio juxta magnum altare in parte boriali" (Chron. Petrib., 52. Gunton (History of Peterbro', 98), says, "For Kynsius, I have heard my father, who was well read in the antiquities of this church, say, that the marble monument, now lying on the north side of the quire, was his. It bears the portraicture of a shaven monk lying on the top."

piety of the archbishop's life. Whilst there was a lavish expenditure among his clerks and household, Kinsius himself was as abstinent as a hermit. He lived upon the coarsest fare. During Lent it was his wont to journey from village to village, preaching and bestowing alms, frequently with bared feet, and making no use of a litter or a horse. To avoid ostentation and vain glory, he travelled generally by night.[o] Such, doubtless, were the traditions in the monastery at Peterborough, and they are pleasing reminiscences.

Kinsius was a great benefactor to the Church. He built a large tower of stone at Beverley, and hung in it two bells, bestowing also upon the minster divers books and ornaments. He gave other bells to the churches of Southwell and Stow.[p] To the abbey of Peterborough he gave, with his body, the vill of Tinwell, a text or copy of the Gospels decorated with gold, and jewels and treasures to the value of £300. These were lost afterwards to the house through the cupidity of queen Edgith.[q]

Aldred, the last of the Saxon archbishops of York, was a person of extraordinary energy and influence. He was brought up in the famous monastery of Winchester, which had so recently furnished a primate to the Northern province in the person of Alfric. After a while he was appointed abbat of Tavistock.[r] That house had been recently endowed and renovated by bishop Living of Worcester, and, in 1046, after a life remarkable for its strange vicissitudes of fortune, that prelate was laid in the tomb by the monks of Tavistock, who had great reason to remember him. Their abbat, Aldred, became his successor in his bishopric.[s]

In this position Aldred had a wide scope for the exercise of his varied and extraordinary powers. There was in him much restless energy and versatility of talent. He could take up arms, were it required, and attack the marauders on the Welsh marches; he could toil at another time for the rule of Benedict, and establish new houses of monks to observe it, but he was more at home in the palace than in the convent. He was pro-

[o] Hist. Cœnobii Burgensis, apud Sparke, 45.

[p] Stubbs, col. 1700. Lel. Coll., iv., 102.

[q] Hist. Cœnobii Burg., 45. Lel. Coll., i., 12-13. Tinwell was "de patrimonio suo."

[r] Hoveden, apud Savile, 252. Stubbs, col. 1700. Rudborne, apud Angl. Sacr., i., 240.

[s] Saxon Chron., 216. Symeon, col. 182. Diceto, col. 475. Aldred, however, makes his subscription as a bishop before this. Possibly he had acted as coadjutor to Living.

bably indebted to bishop Living, a friend of Edward the Confessor, for his introduction to state affairs, in which he played so conspicuous a part. With that monarch, who was easily subjected to ecclesiastical influence, Aldred was a great favourite, and he served him loyally and well. His first achievement as a statesman was the effecting a reconciliation between the king and Sweyn, the son of Godwin, who had recently murdered his cousin Biorn.[t] In 1049 he and Herman bishop of Sherburn went as the royal ambassadors to Rome, and they prevailed upon the pope to absolve their master from the vow which he had formerly made of going on a pilgrimage to that city.[u] To the circumstance of Edward's staying in his own kingdom we owe the re-foundation of the stately abbey of Westminster, in which he sleeps.[v] Soon after this we hear of Aldred as the commander of an expeditionary force which the king sent forth to secure earl Godwin and his restless sons, but they had escaped before it arrived.[w] Shortly afterwards Aldred was very roughly handled by Griffin, a Welsh prince, when he was leading his men against a band of Irish pirates in the neighbourhood of the Wye.[x] In 1054 he was honoured by the king with a commission of great national importance. This was an embassy to Germany, to the emperor Henry III., who was then residing at Cologne. Aldred, who was treated with the utmost courtesy, was in that famous city for a whole year as the guest of the archbishop, and, with his assistance, he prevailed upon the emperor to allow his nephew by marriage, the son of Edmund Ironside, to return to England with his family.[y] The English monarch was wishful that he should succeed him on the throne. The hand of death, however, was laid upon the future monarch, and the crown of his uncle, which was intended for him, was afterwards placed by Aldred upon the brows of Harold.[z] To Edward the bishop seems to have attached himself with the pliant readiness of a courtier. In 1058 he crossed the seas

[t] Fl. Wigorn., 409. Hoveden, 252 *b*. Symeon, col. 184. Stubbs, col. 1701. Knyghton, col. 2331.

[u] Saxon Chron., 223. Chron. de Mailros, 49, where the date 1050 is given. Symeon and Stubbs, *ut supra*. Lives of Edw. the Confessor, ed. Luard, 70, where Aldred is prematurely called archbp. of York.

[v] Ailredus, Vita Edw. Conf., col. 385. Spelm. Conc., 635. Wilkins, Conc., i., 316. Mabillon, Ann. Ben., iv., 610, 672.

[w] Saxon Chron., 229.

[x] Flor. Wigorn. Thomas' Worcester, 67.

[y] Saxon Chron., 243. Fl. Wigorn., 416. Chron. Mailros, 51. Higden, apud Gale, i., 280. Symeon, col. 187. Ailred, col. 366, 381. Bromton, col. 945. Stubbs, col. 1701. Knyghton, col. 2333. Wendover (i., 314) makes the date of this mission 1057. Anglia Sacra, ii., 249. The emperor gave him a Sacramentarium and a Psalter, about which there is a curious story.

[z] Fl. Wigorn., 427. Symeon, col. 193. Diceto, col. 479. Bromton, col. 958. Stubbs, col. 1702. Knyghton, col. 2339. Higden, apud Gale, i., 284. Hist. Eliens., ibid., 515. Hoveden, apud Savile, 256. Ingulph, ibid., 511. Hist. Mon. de Abingdon, i., 489.

again on a very different progress—a pilgrimage to Jerusalem.[a] The enterprize itself, and the way in which it was carried out, are indicative of the character of the man. The Bedouins of the desert had never gazed upon an English bishop before. The pomp and dignity on which they looked ill beseemed a disciple of the poor carpenter of Nazareth. The illustrious pilgrim stood upon those holy hills, on which, in after years, the noble-hearted Godfrey was content to watch and weep. He offered a precious chalice at the sacred tomb in which there was once laid, for a few memorable hours, the corpse of one who stinted not to any the riches of His grace, whilst He knew not Himself where to lay His head.

Whilst Aldred was actively engaged in the service of the state, he was not oblivious of his higher calling. In 1055 the charge of the see of Wilton was entrusted to him, which Herman had resigned, and he held it until 1058, when he restored it to that prelate, who was at length willing to receive it.[b] In 1056 prince Griffin, the restless leader of the Welsh, broke into the English territory, and slew the bishop of Hereford and his clerks at Glastbrig. The vacant see was committed to the charge of Aldred, who held it, *in commendam*, with that of Worcester, and his first business was to effect a reconciliation between Griffin and the king.[c] About the same time he had a munificent benefactress to Worcester in Godiva,[d] the fair lady of Coventry,—the same who

——— "took the tax away,
And built herself an everlasting name."

In 1058 Aldred dedicated the abbey church of Gloucester, which he had himself erected, and made the holy Wulstan the abbat.[e] The rule of Benedict was observed there, for Aldred, although a courtier, was a disciplinarian, and came back from Germany with larger views on ecclesiastical matters, and a strong resolution to enforce them, which he did also in the North.[f]

At Christmas, 1060, the death of Kinsius vacated the see of York, and Aldred succeeded him,[g] resigning the bishopric of

[a] Saxon Chron., 249. Chron. de Mailros, 53. Chron. Petrib., 52. Anglia Sacra, i., 474. Symeon, col. 190. Stubbs, col. 1701.

[b] Symeon, col. 189. Bromton, col. 946. Stubbs, col. 1701. Knyghton, col. 2335. Higden, apud Gale, i., 281.

[c] Saxon Chron., 247. Fl. Wigorn., 418. Symeon, col. 189. Stubbs, col. 1701. Hoveden, apud Savile, 254, *b*.

[d] Wendover, i., 315. Symeon, col. 189. Ailred, col. 389. Knyghton, col. 2334.

[e] Saxon Chron., 249. Symeon, col. 189. Diceto, col. 477. Stubbs, col. 1701. Hoveden, 255. Lel. Coll., i., 28; iii., 262. Dugd. Mon., i., 531. Mabillon, Ann. Ben., iv., 583.

[f] Stubbs, col. 1701.

[g] Wendover, i., 318. Symeon, col. 190. Diceto, col. 478. Malmesbury (Savile, 154), says that Aldred bought

Hereford,[h] but retaining that of Worcester. In the following year he went to Rome for the pall. Earl Tosti, one of the most illustrious subjects in England, was his companion. The honour was not obtained, for the pope was indignant at the proposed tenure of the two sees by one person, and that his licence had not been solicited for Aldred's promotion. He also charged the petitioner with simony and want of learning. He deprived him of all his honours, and the degraded prelate quitted the eternal city in disgrace. Other misfortunes were awaiting him. The bishop and his friends had gone about a day's journey from Rome on their way homewards when they fell into the clutches of a party of brigands, who maltreated the travellers, and stripped them of everything they possessed. In a happy moment the thought occurred to the despoiled prelate that he would return to Rome as he was, and make a last appeal, *in forma pauperis*, to the mercy of Christ's vicar. It was successful. After Aldred had promised to resign the see of Worcester, the archbishopric was confirmed to him, together with the honour of the pall. The conversion of the pope was caused, in all probability, by what earl Tosti said to him. The rage of the stalwart Saxon was excessive at the insult and the robbery. It boiled over in language seldom heard at the papal court. "What distant nation," he said, "would heed the excommunication of the pope, if villains at home despised it? Why should he trample on suppliants, and leave the bandits to themselves? If the goods which they had lost were not restored by him who should have taken care that no one touched them, the king of England would repay them out of the Peter-pence when they crossed the seas." The words are worthy of a son of the patriotic Godwin.[i]

As soon as Aldred arrived in England he vacated the see of Worcester, and Wulstan was his successor, whom he consecrated at York, Stigand of Canterbury being under suspension.[j] The king, however, subsequently made Wulstan of Worcester a suffragan of York,[k] and Aldred, in consequence of the poverty of

his way to the archbishopric. Malmesbury has scarcely one good word for Aldred.

[h] Wendover and Symeon, *ut supra.* Bromton, col. 952. Stubbs, col. 1701. Hoveden, 255. Ingulph, apud Gale, iii., 66.

[i] Saxon Chron., 250. Fl. Wigorn., 421. Symeon, col. 190. Diceto, col. 478. Bromton, col. 952. Stubbs, col. 1701. Knyghton, col. 2336. Malmesbury, apud Savile, 154. Hoveden, ibid., 255. Higden, apud Gale, i., 282. Wendover, i., 318. Vita S. Wulstani, apud Angl. Sacr., ii., 251. MSS. Lansd., ccccii., 29. Baronii Ann., xi., 337.

[j] Vita S. Wulstani, apud Angl. Sacr., ii., 250-1. Chron. de Mailros, 50. Symeon, col. 191. Diceto, col. 478. Bromton, col. 952. Knyghton, col. 2336. Hoveden, 255, *b.* Wendover, i., 318. Anglia Sacra, 474, 541. Fl. Wigorn. (424) says that at the time of consecration Aldred professed before the king to claim no subjection from Wulstan. Knyghton, col. 2367.

[k] In 1062, Edward the Confessor made a grant to Aldred of the church

the Northern province, which had not yet recovered from the incursions of the Danes, appropriated to it twelve of the manors belonging to his late bishopric in the South.[l] For this act, which may be justified, the Worcester historians have not been sparing of their censure, but they seem to forget that, even after his departure into the North, Aldred was a noble benefactor to the church of which he had been deprived.[m] Meanness was not an element in his character. He scattered abroad his treasures with the liberality of a prince. The York historian is trumpet-tongued in his praise, and well he might be. Aldred was a great builder and endower. He established stalls at Southwell, now for the first time rising into importance,[n] and at York, according to Leland, he finished a refectory and a dormitory in the Bedern. He completed, also, a similar suite of rooms at Beverley which his predecessors had begun.[o] To the minster in that place he was an especial benefactor. He added to it a presbytery, and rebuilt the whole of the old church towards the west as far as the great tower of Kinsius. He decorated the roof with glowing colours, till it looked like another heaven. He made a pulpit of Teutonic work of marvellous construction, and rich in costly metals and ingenious devices.[p] He directed the pen of Folcard to describe the virtues of St. John.[q] The privileges of the sanctuary were extended by him, and he procured for the town the grant of an annual fair. He prevailed upon king Edward to give to the church the lordship of Leven, and he converted the seven canonries into prebends, adding an eighth to the number, and giving them fixed endowments and subsidiary vicars.[r]

Whilst Aldred was thus generous and active, he was not without his share of troubles. The state of the North was anything but satisfactory. The intrigues of his old friend, earl Tosti, filled that part of England with tumult and dismay. In 1066, after Harold had been crowned by Aldred, these disorders were multiplied. Tosti broke into Yorkshire to win for himself

of Worcester on account of the desolate condition of the see of York. The bishop was to be his vicar or deputy. This was evidently a personal favour to Aldred, and not a grant in perpetuity to his church. The deed is in Thomas' Worcester, App^x, i.

[l] Symeon, col. 190-1, 202. Bromton, col. 952. Stubbs, 1702. They were restored by Thomas. The Worcester historians, on this account, are extremely violent against Aldred.

[m] Thomas's Worcester, 72. Anglia Sacra, i., 474.

[n] Stubbs, col. 1704, 13. The History of Southwell (276) seems to take it for granted that Aldred was buried there.

[o] Lel. Coll., iv., 102-3. Stubbs speaks only of a refectory at York.

[p] Stubbs, 1704. Lel. Col., iv., 102-3.

[q] Folcard de Vita S. Joan. Bev., apud Acta SS., mense Maio. In the dedication to the archbishop Folcard speaks of Aldred as "Lucerna ardens et lucens in caliginoso loco, Anglorum archipræsul."

[r] Stubbs and Lel., *ut supra.*

a kingdom, and brought with him the king of Norway, the famous Harold Hardrada, with a vast host of followers. They were met in the fields of Water-Fulford, in front of the present palace of the archbishops of York at Bishopthorpe, by the earls Edwin and Morkere, but the invaders carried the day, and there was a vast slaughter of ecclesiastics as well as soldiers, for the feelings of the clergy and their spiritual head were with Harold and the Saxons. Harold himself arrived a few days after this, and the rebels were completely vanquished in a battle near Stamford-bridge. Tosti, the brother of the victor, was slain in spite of his great personal bravery. Hardrada never returned to his home in the wild North. The treasures which he had won in the far East were lost to him. The famous Landeyda was taken on the field, and the conqueror Harold, overjoyed at his success, went to celebrate his triumph in high state at York.

There soon came to him in that city the tidings of another advent which silenced at once the revel and the song. William the Norman had arrived in England. The spoils of the Norsemen were left behind in the charge of archbishop Aldred, and Harold hastened into the South with all the strength that he could gather together to oppose the new invader. The results of that disastrous field are too well known to be repeated. The independence of the Saxon church, the freedom of a noble people, the glories of the house of Godwin, were obliterated, when the bravest of the Anglo-Saxon princes died at Hastings.[s]

The position of Aldred was now a perilous one, but he was fully equal to the emergency. His connection with Harold was well known. He was still holding the spoils which had been won at Stamford-bridge. Would the Saxon primate throw himself and the church into the arms of the victorious invaders? He could not surrender his patriotism at once, however necessity might demand the sacrifice. We are told that it was the wish of the archbishop and the chief men of London to place the crown upon the head of Edgar Atheling,[t] the grandson of Edmund Ironside, for whose family he had toiled and laboured in the days of Edward the Confessor. But the scheme was impracticable, and the temper of the Norman conqueror would brook no doubt or delay. Aldred's opposition might destroy the Anglo-Saxon church, of which he was the spokesman and the chief ornament. He was not ready to precipitate such an end as that. With the good judgment which seems to have

[s] Saxon Chron., 260-3. Symeon, col. 194. Ailred, col. 404. Diceto, col. 479. Bromton, col. 958. Knyghton, col. 2339. Wendover, i., 327. Hoveden, 257. Master Wace, his Chronicle, 134-5. Gaimar, ed. Petrie, 827.

[t] Saxon Chron., 263. Fl. Wigorn., 430. Symeon, col. 195. Diceto, col. 480. Bromton, col. 961. Knyghton, col. 2343. Hoveden, apud Savile, 257 b.

guided him at every crisis the archbishop gave way.[u] He met the conqueror at Berkhamstead, on his way to London, and took the oaths of allegiance.[v] But he did more than this. On mid-winter day, 1066, in the absence of Stigand of Canterbury, who was not permitted to officiate, Aldred crowned the new monarch in the abbey church at Westminster.[w]

> "This noble duc Wyllam hym let crownyng kyng,
> At London, a myde wynter day, noblyche thorw alle thyng,
> Of erchebyssop of Euerwyk, Aldred was hys name."[x]

But, before the prelate would celebrate that rite he made the conqueror pledge his word, in the most solemn manner, that he would reverence the laws, and pay due respect to the rights and liberties of the church.[y] Vain hope! In a few years the old Saxon fabric was rent in pieces, and a new race of bishops occupied the churches which had been reared by the piety of the native princes and the now despised nobles.

William kept his word to Aldred as far as he was able to observe a promise. He was wise enough to conciliate the favour of so influential a prelate; and Aldred, also, saw the necessity of being a courtier. He was frequently with the king.[z] In 1068 he consecrated the countess Matilda, queen.[a] Aldred was treated by the monarch with uniform respect, and, in the end, he and the bishops of Worcester and Rochester were the only native prelates who were allowed to retain their sees.[b] The archbishop, however, was indebted for the respect which was shewn him to his own firmness and independence. He was a fearless champion of the rights of the church. On one occasion when Urse, the sheriff of Worcester, had infringed upon the sanctuary of the canons by building a castle or residence on the south side of their church, Aldred excommunicated him, and laid his pos-

[u] Hemingford, apud Gale, ii., 437. Wm. Neubrig., i., 15. Bromton, col. 962.

[v] Saxon Chron., 264. Hoveden, 258. Symeon, col. 195. Diceto, col. 480.

[w] Saxon Chron., 264. Fl. Wigorn., 431. Chron. Mailros, 55. Chron. Petrib., 54. Ord. Vitalis, apud Duchesne, 503. Alured. Bev., 127. Symeon, col. 195. Diceto, col. 480. Bromton, col. 962. Stubbs, col. 1702. Knyghton, col. 2343. Malmesbury, apud Savile, 58. Huntingdon, ibid., 211. Hoveden, ibid., 258. Hist. Eliens., apud Gale, i., 515. Wendover, i., 333. Matthew Paris, 4. Rudborne, apud Wharton, i., 248.

[x] Robert of Gloucester, ii., 367.

[y] Hoveden, Symeon, Stubbs, Alured. Bev., *ut supra*. Malmesbury, 154 *b*. Huntingdon, 210 *b*. Gesta Willelmi ducis, apud Recueil des Historiens des Gaules et de la France, xi., 100.

[z] Maseres, 166. I find him witnessing royal charters. Gunton's Peterbro', 141-2. Histoire de l'abbaye de St. Denys, appendix, p. 88. Smith's Beda, app^{x}, 782. Hist. Mon. de Abingdon, i., 454, etc. Wanley, 299, etc. There are many deeds witnessed by him in Kemble's Codex Diplom., vol. iv.

[a] Saxon Chron., 268. Maseres, 212. Hoveden, 258. Symeon, col. 197. Diceto, col. 482. Bromton, col. 953. Stubbs, col. 1702. Knyghton, col. 2344.

[b] Hist. Mon. de Abingdon, i., 490. Mapes, De Nugis Curialium, 224.

terity under a curse which is said to have been marvellously fulfilled.[c] On another occasion, at York, some of his own carts, whilst on their way to his farms, were seized by the king's officers, and all compensation and justice were contemptuously refused. The indignant archbishop hastened up to London with that decision and energy which he could always exhibit. The king was in the abbey of Westminster when he found him. Aldred refused him the customary salutation, and stood fearlessly before him with his pastoral staff in his hand. "Did not I give thee the crown and bless thee," he said, "when thou camest from another country, and didst win this kingdom which the just vengeance of the Lord surrendered to the destroyer? Now thou hast broken the oath that thou didst take, and thou shalt have a curse, and not a blessing." Stricken with a terror which he rarely felt, the monarch threw himself at Aldred's feet, deprecating the expected malediction. It came not. The story of the wrong was told; justice was at once done; and the benediction flowed from the lips of the intrepid prelate which had been opened to condemn.[d]

The lesson, however, was only partially remembered, and Aldred must have watched with sorrow and dismay the progress of the king. A conqueror is too frequently the servant of his followers, and so it was with William. He, as Fuller says, soon began to make "the Normans his darlings, and the English his drudges."[e] From church and state old faces gradually disappeared. Discontent increased to be repressed by force. There was soon an iron domination. In 1069, the two sons of Sweyn king of Denmark, Harold and Canute, landed in the Humber to make an attempt on England.[f] The whole North welcomed them with open arms. Aldred had striven to make peace, and there was no peace. All his endeavours had been fruitless. His labours were unrequited, and those for whom he had toiled —the country and the church which he had loved so well—were on the brink of ruin. The heart of the afflicted patriot was broken, and his last prayer was that he might be spared the sight of the misery which he anticipated. He died on the 11th of September, 1069, the day of SS. Protus and Hyacinthus, and his remains were interred in the minster at York.[g]

[c] Malmesbury, apud Savile, 154 *b*. Thomas' Worcester, 72. The curse took the form of a rhyme.

"Hightest thou Urse?
Have thou God's curse!"

[d] Stubbs, col. 1703-4. Malmesbury, 154 *b*, tells the story in a slightly different form. Wm. Neubrig, i., 16. Baronii, Ann., xi., 492.

[e] Church History, book iii., 2.

[f] Symeon, col. 198. Hoveden, 258 *b*.

[g] Saxon Chron., 270. Fl. Wigorn., 433. Chron. de Mailros, 55. Alured. Bev., 128. Hoveden, apud Savile, 258 *b*. Thos. Wikes, apud Gale, ii., 22. Symeon, col. 198. Diceto, col. 482. Bromton, col. 965. Stubbs, col. 1708. Knyghton, col. 2344.

Aldred was indeed removed "from the evil to come." In a later age, the ruin that he saw around him and the desecration of God's house hastened the end of bishop Hall, and, as his panegyrist Duport observes,

"Pati hæc nescius hinc abivit ultro."

Aldred was happily delivered from that sight. Within a little while after his decease the city of York, captured and re-captured, was in ashes; the minster with its treasures—its muniments, and the glorious library which had been the pride of Saxon England—all were surrendered to the flames. The archiepiscopal lands were wasted.[h] Beverley was the only place in Yorkshire that escaped.[i] The vengeance of the conqueror suffered scarcely a single homestead to remain between the Humber and the Tees. The last of the Saxon primates of York was scarcely laid in the tomb before the church in which he rested was sacked and burned.[j]

Thomas of Bayeux,[k] was the successor of Aldred, and with him there commences a new dynasty of archbishops. He was born at Bayeux, a little town in Normandy. The names of his parents were Osbert and Muriel.[l] His father was a priest,[m] and Sampson, afterwards bishop of Worcester, was his brother.[n] From his earliest years Thomas was distinguished for the elegance of his taste and his ardour in the pursuit of literary distinction. The schools in his own country were insufficient to satisfy his cravings after knowledge, and he sought for additional supplies in Germany and Spain. When he returned to Bayeux, his learning attracted the attention and gained for him the intimacy of Odo the bishop of that place, who was a brother of the Conqueror of England and a person of commanding influence. Odo is said to have taken Thomas and Sampson under his protection, and to have sent them to study at Liege and other places. Thomas became the favourite of the

[h] Ellis' Introduction to Domesday, i., 319.

[i] Miracles of St. John of Beverley, apud Acta SS., mense Maio, 174.

[j] A vivid account in Symeon, col. 199. Saxon Chron., 271. Bromton, col. 966. Knyghton, col. 2344. Wendover, i., 337. Symeon, Hist. Eccl. Dunelm., 183. Hoveden, apud Savile, 258 *b*. Malmesbury, ibid., 154 *b*. Ord. Vitalis, apud Duchesne, 515.

[k] He is also called Thomas Major, and Thomas the Norman.

[l] Liber Vitæ Dunelm., ed. Surtees Soc., 139-40.

[m] Bromton, col. 969.

[n] Ric. of Hexham, col. 303, says that Thomas was "ex nobilissima prosapia oriundus, vir magnificus."

prelate, and was made the treasurer of the church of Bayeux. When Odo crossed the channel to visit his royal brother Thomas accompanied him, and had soon the honour of becoming one of the king's chaplains.[o]

In the year 1070 William shewed his regard for Thomas by raising him to the see of York. This was done at Windsor at the feast of Pentecost.[p] A difficulty at once arose about his consecration. In the ordinary course of things that ceremony ought to have been performed by the archbishop of Canterbury, but at this time there was no Southern primate, and, in the North, the see of York, by an accident, had not a sufficient number of suffragans to officiate.[q] Thomas therefore, most provokingly, was obliged to wait until Lanfranc was made archbishop in the month of August. He then went to him to be consecrated. This Lanfranc refused to do unless he would first profess obedience and subjection to Canterbury. Thomas at once refused, and stated his case to the king, who sent him back to Lanfranc with an order that the rite should be performed without the condition. That prelate then went to William, and defended the course which he had adopted. He said that it was necessary for the safety of the country that England should have one primate as well as one sovereign. An archbishop of York might easily side with some of the foreigners who visited his diocese, and set up a new monarch, thus splitting the kingdom into two.[r] The argument was a plausible one, and had its due weight with the Norman courtiers, who forgot that Thomas was one of their own countrymen, and that there was no reason to doubt his loyalty. It convinced the king, who tried in vain to alter the determination of Thomas. What soft words were unable to produce, threats at last effected. William told him that if he persisted he would bring down upon himself his heaviest displeasure, and that all his kindred should be banished from Normandy and England. After this, Thomas went to

[o] Stubbs, col. 1705. Ord. Vitalis, apud Duchesne, 516, 665. Dugd., Bar., i., 24. Thomas' Worcester, 103.

[p] Fl. Wigorn, 435. Chron. Petrib., 55. Hoveden, 259 *b*. Symeon, col. 202. Diceto, col. 483. Bromton, col. 968. Stubbs, col. 1706. Knyghton, col. 2345.

[q] Stubbs, 1706. The information which this writer gives is derived from the life of Thomas by Hugh Sotevagina, the precentor and archdeacon of York, which is preserved in the Registrum Magnum Album in the office of the dean and chapter of York. Full use has been made of it, especially in this account of the controversy with Lanfranc.

[r] "Porro utile esse ad regni integritatem et firmitatem conservandam, ut Britannia tota uni quasi primati subderetur. Alioquin contingere posse vel suo vel successorum tempore ut de Dacis seu Norensibus sivi Scotis qui Eboracum navigio venientes regnum infestare solebant, unus ab Eboracensi archiepiscopo et a provinciæ illius indigenis mobilibus et perfidis rex crearetur, et sic regnum turbatum scinderetur" (Hugh). Möhler, in his Life of Anselm (ed. 1842, pp. 112-13) commends this policy.

Canterbury prepared to submit. "Wilt thou be subject to the church of Canterbury, to me and my successors?" was Lanfranc's question. "To thee," was the reply, "but not to thy successors."[s] The tears rushed from the eyes of the petitioner, when he thus spoke, and no farther would he go. Lanfranc was not too exacting, and the wished-for consecration took place.[t]

This occurred in 1070, and in the following year Thomas and Lanfranc went to Rome together to obtain the pall. Remigius, the bishop of Dorchester, accompanied them.[u] The three prelates excited the admiration of the Romans by their ready wit, their munificence and their learning.[v] Whilst they were in that great city Thomas mooted before the pope the question of the subjection of his church to Canterbury. He raised at the same time another point of interest. He claimed for his successors the supremacy over the sees of Dorchester (Lincoln), Worcester, and Lichfield. The connection between York and Worcester has been already mentioned. The other two places were in the old province of Mercia, and had, therefore, been occasionally dependent upon Northumbria. Lanfranc was taken by surprise, but he soon recovered himself. He met the first part of Thomas's claim by the somewhat unfair assertion that Gregory wished York to be the equal of London, but *not* of Canterbury, which had become the seat of the primacy. Lanfranc then made a terrible counterstroke, and turned the tables most completely upon Thomas and Remigius. He charged them with being uncanonically elected; Thomas, because he was the son of a priest, and Remigius, for having been guilty of simony. Alexander, who was a great admirer of Lanfranc, decided against them, and took from each his pastoral staff and ring. These he subsequently restored at the request of Lanfranc, who had no wish to injure his companions. Upon the main point in the dispute, the question of subjection, Alexander very cautiously refrained from expressing an opinion, but he referred the settlement of it to a national synod in England. The controversy about Worcester was to be terminated by the decision of Lanfranc himself.[w] The three

[s] Lanfranci Opp., ed. 1648, 11-12. Bromton, col. 969. Stubbs, col. 1706.

[t] Fl. Wigorn., 435. Chron. Mailros, 56. Malmesbury, apud Savile, 117. Symeon, col. 203. Diceto, col. 483. Bromton, col. 969. Gervase, col. 1653. Knyghton, col. 2343. Baronii Ann., ix., 512. The Saxon Chron. (273), says that he was consecrated on his return from Rome after making the profession. There is a long account of the controversy between York and Canterbury, on the question of the profession, in the Anglia Sacra, i., 65-77.

[u] Chron. Mailros, 56. Fl. Wigorn., 437. Hoveden, 260. Symeon, col. 203. Diceto, col. 483. Knyghton, 2348. MSS. Lansdowne, 402, col. 29.

[v] Ord. Vitalis, apud Duchesne, 248.

[w] Eadmer, Hist. Nov., apud Anselmi Opp., 30. Diceto, col. 484. Bromton, col. 970.

prelates now returned to England, having halted for a while at Evreux, where they were the guests of Gislebert, the bishop of that place.[x]

When they arrived in England, a synod was held in the presence of the king, at which the controversy between Canterbury and York was thoroughly considered. The result was favourable to Lanfranc and his church. That prelate, who had far more eloquence and ready wit than his opponent, drew up his case in the most elaborate manner, and the listeners took his part. The Humber was made the Southern boundary of the diocese of York. The Northern archbishops were to swear allegiance to Canterbury, and to appear with their suffragans at all the councils, etc., within that province to which they should be bidden. By a subsequent order, made in 1075, they were to sit at the right hand of the primate.[y] The archbishops of Canterbury were to be consecrated at home by their brethren from the North, who were to come to the same place to receive the same rite. All this was against Thomas and his see; indeed, he seems to have made but little opposition. He was spared, however, at the king's request, the shame of taking the oath of obedience. He simply made his profession in writing, and nothing farther seems to have been required of him.[z] Lanfranc was overjoyed at his success. He announced it to the pope in a lengthy and jubilant epistle.[a] It was communicated, also, to a friend of his at Rome who was rapidly rising into importance, the energetic and fearless Hildebrand.[b]

The controversy between York and Worcester must next be considered. The relations between the two sees were of a most peculiar kind. Oswald and his two immediate successors held the Southern diocese conjointly with that of York, partly no doubt for influence, and partly to eke out their archiepiscopal income. Edward the Confessor made a grant of the see of Worcester to Aldred for his life, with power to nominate a deputy, and in right of his authority over that diocese Aldred

[x] Gallia Christiana, xi., 572.

[y] Gervase, col. 1654. Malmesbury, 66 b. Labbe, Conc., x., 347-8. Wilkins, i., 363.

[z] Lanfranci Opp., 12, 301. Eadmer, Hist. Nov., apud Anselmi Opp., 30. Mabillon, Acta SS. ord. S. B., sæc. vi., ii., 651. Anglia Sacra, i., 1, 5, 253. Malmesbury, apud Savile, 65-6, 111, 118. Diceto, col. 484-5. Bromton, col. 970-2. Gervase, col. 1653. Knyghton, col. 2348-9. Mat. Paris, 6-7. Capgrave, 130. Baronii Ann., xi., 522. Labbe, Conc., ix., 1211.

[a] Labbe, Conc., ix., col. 1213. Wilkins, i., 326.

In Stubbs (1706-7), a letter from Urban II. to Thomas is alluded to, referring to the profession. It is given at length by Hugh the Chantor. The pope rebukes Thomas severely for making the profession contrary to Gregory's decree, and orders him to explain his conduct either to himself or to his legate. He speaks as if the profession had only recently been made, and he had just heard of it. There is a chronological difficulty in this, as Urban did not become pope till 1088.

[b] Lanfranci Opp. 304.

took away from it twelve vills, and appropriated them to York. As that archbishop had only a life-interest in the see, it is clear that these estates ought to have been restored at his decease. When he died, however, they passed with his other estates into the hands of the king. Wulstan, the bishop of Worcester, was not disposed to give them up. He desired that they should be restored at the council of Winchester at Easter, 1070, but as the archbishopric of York was then vacant, the consideration of the question was deferred.[c] It will be remembered, that when Thomas went to Rome for the pall, he claimed the bishop of Worcester as a suffragan. This question was left by the pope to the determination of Lanfranc. It was settled in a synod which was held in 1072. Odo, bishop of Bayeux, was on the side of Thomas, but Lanfranc decided against him. The twelve vills were to be given up, and Worcester was for the future to be subordinated to Canterbury, and not to York.[d] In this judgment, Thomas seems to have quietly acquiesced. Wulstan and he became friends, and he requested him to pay him a visit in the North.[e]

We now come to the dispute between Thomas and Remigius with reference to Lindsey. It will be recollected that Paulinus and Blecca erected the first church in that district, and that Sidnacester, or Stow, was under the especial care of the archbishops of York, who claimed and seem to have exercised the right of controlling the spiritual affairs of that part of England previous to the Conquest. In 1067, Remigius, a Norman, was advanced to the see of Dorchester. He seems to have been soon dissatisfied with the seat of the episcopate, and was desirous of transferring it to Lincoln. This project would meet with the strenuous opposition of the archbishops of York. In 1071, when Thomas and Lanfranc went to Rome Remigius accompanied them, and the question about Lindsey was mooted. Alexander referred it to the decision of a synod at home. Among the decrees of that assembly, which was held in 1072, there is no special reference to Lindsey, but the resolution that the Humber should be the boundary of the diocese of York on the South was practically a settlement of the controversy. Thomas, however, by no means regarded it in that light. About

[c] Mat. Paris, 17. Hoveden, 259 b. Symeon, col. 202. Diceto, col. 483. Bromton, col. 968. Stubbs, col. 1709, who says that Thomas enjoyed the twelve vills for a while of the king's gift, but that William afterwards took them away "molimine Lanfranci."

[d] Vita S. Wulstani, apud Angl. Sacr., ii., 255. Flor. Wigorn., 437. Symeon, col. 203. Diceto, col. 483. Bromton, col. 976. Hoveden, 260. Mat. Paris, 18. Baronii Ann., xi., 532. Labbe, Conc. ix., col. 1204. The date of this synod is variously given between 1070 and 1072.

[e] Malmesbury, apud Savile, 66 b. Wendover, i., 374.

1078 Remigius had his see formally transferred to Lincoln, and began to erect a cathedral on that "sovereign hill." It was finished in 1092, but Thomas refused to dedicate it. Upon this Remigius sought the assistance of the king, and with the aid, as it is said, of a bribe, prevailed upon him to summon a large number of the English bishops to officiate on the occasion. This arrangement, however, was broken through. The time was fixed, but two days before the ceremony was to take place Remigius died. Robert Bloet, the chancellor of England, was his successor. Thomas refused to consecrate him, and when in the following year he performed that rite for Anselm, the new archbishop of Canterbury, he forbade him to lay his hands on Bloet. Thomas had no objection to his being made bishop of Dorchester, but not of Lincoln, because he claimed that place and a great part of Lindsey for his own see. Bloet was standing by when Thomas spoke to Anselm, and he took a surer course than argument to gain his end. He is said to have paid a large sum of money to William Rufus to enable him to carry his point.[f] The king, in spite of the strenuous opposition of Thomas, brought the dispute to a termination. Lincoln and Lindsey were taken away from York, and were transferred to Canterbury, and, in their room, the Northern primate received the abbey of Selby and the monastery of St. Oswald at Gloucester.[g]

[f] Various sums are stated by the chroniclers, from £500 to £5000.

[g] There is an account of this controversy in Fl. Wigorn., 458. Symeon, col. 217. Diceto, col. 490. Bromton, col. 983, 988. Stubbs, col. 1711. Knyghton, col. 2364. Malmesbury, apud Savile, 165 *b*. Huntingdon, ibid., 213. Hoveden, 265 *b*. Mat. Paris, 13-15. Vita S. Remigii, apud Mabillon Acta SS. ord. S.B., sæc. vi., ii., 766, and Anglia Sacra, ii., 410, etc. Dugd. Mon., vi., 1269-70.

William's deed arranging the dispute is in Dugdale's Mon., vii., 1177. The confirmation by pope Paschal is in the Reg. Magnum Album at York, fol. 42. The king's charter is so curious that I give it *in extenso*. It is taken from the Register of Archbishop Greenfield, i., 45.

"Carta Regis Willelmi.

"In nomine Patris et Filii, et Spiritus Sancti, amen. Summi Patris fuit consilium ut sanctam civitatem suam, celestem scilicet Jerusalem, quæ superbia diaboli divisa erat, morte dilectissimi Filii Sui intercedente, redintegretur, et per redempcionem generis humani angelica dampna reparet; hac consideracione, ego Willelmus Dei gratia rex Anglorum, Willelmi regis filius qui Edwardo regi hereditario jure successit, videns ecclesiam Anglorum ex parte divisam et discordantem, resartire concupimus quod male scissum fuerat, et ad unitatem veræ caritatis revocare quod diu indiscussum sub discordia manserat. Redemi igitur de meis propriis possessionibus calumpniam quam habet Eboracensis ecclesia et Thomas ejusdem ecclesiæ archiepiscopus super Lincolnia et super Lindissim et super mansiones Stou et Ludam, et dedi pro eis ecclesiæ Sancti Petri Eboracensis jure perpetuo possidendas abbaciam Sancti Germani de Saleby et ecclesiam Sancti Oswaldi de Gloecestria, cum omnibus ad eas jure pertinentibus, et ita dedi archiepiscopo Thomæ et successoribus ejus abbaciam Sancti Germani, sicut archiepiscopus Cantuariensis habet episcopatum Rofensem. Et propter hæc predicta beneficia benigne dimisit et gratanter Thomas archiepiscopus in eternum, consenciente clero ejus, pre-

It may perhaps be thought from what has been said that Thomas had an angry and a contentious spirit. It was not so. Those were days in which great changes were being effected in the English church; new landmarks were being laid down, and it was necessary for every prelate to be on the alert in the defence of his diocese. Violence and encroachment were too frequently triumphant. If Thomas had been better acquainted with English precedents and customs he would probably have been more successful than he was. He tried boldly and honestly to do his duty, and he cannot be blamed for doing so. When he was defeated he cherished no ill-will against his opponents. Wulstan and he became good friends, and it was the same with Lanfranc. Thomas had promised to obey him as long as he lived, and he kept his word. They corresponded together. Thomas requested his brother-archbishop to allow two of his suffragans to consecrate for him a bishop of the Orkneys, and it was done. In 1075 he was present at the council at London:[h] in 1089 he was at Canterbury when the remains of Lanfranc were laid in the tomb.[i] He would fully appreciate the virtues and the learning of that great and good man.

The see of Canterbury was vacant after the death of Lanfranc for several years, and during this time Thomas officiated in the Southern province when his services were required. He consecrated the bishops of Norwich, Chichester, and Bangor.[j] In 1093 he was requested to do the same thing for Anselm, the archbishop-elect. Thomas went up from York, accompanied by the dean and the dignitaries of his cathedral, and there was a goodly array of bishops to join in the imposing ceremonial. The officiating prelates were in their robes, and Anselm's petition was read, in which he solicited consecration as primate of *all* England. This was too much for Thomas, who had subjected himself to Lanfranc during his life, but not to his successors. He was now free to act as he chose. He retired to the vestry with the officers of his own cathedral, and began to unrobe himself. The Southern bishops were excited and alarmed; they followed the Northern primate, and Walkeline of Winchester threw himself at his feet and implored him to return. He would not. "There are two metropolitans in Britain," he said, "and one of them can only be master at the expense of the other. I shall consecrate no one to rule unjustly over myself." Thomas was at length the master of the

dictam calumpniam, in presencia mea et episcoporum et procerum meorum, mihi et Roberto episcopo Lyncoln et successoribus ejus. Hujus autem calumpniæ redempcionem feci ego gratia ejusdem Roberti episcopi quia cancellarius meus extiterat."

[h] Lanfranci Opp., 305-6. Vita ejusdem, ibid., 13-14. Wilkins, i., 362.

[i] Gervase, col. 1655. Wilkins, i., 369.

[j] Stubbs, col. 1707.

position, and he knew it. This was the counter-stroke of the scene in the synod of 1072. The bishops were very urgent and importunate: they promised largely. The petition was altered, and the words, *metropolitan of Canterbury*, were substituted for *primate of England*, and then the prelates returned into the church, and the ceremony was completed.[k] The advantage which the see of Canterbury had gained twenty years before was now lost. Anselm, indeed, did not give the question up, but, in all probability, the troubles in which he was involved and his unpopularity with the king caused the matter to be shelved.

When William Rufus was killed Anselm was in exile, and it devolved, therefore, upon Thomas, according to ancient custom, to crown the new king. Thomas was at Ripon when the news was brought to him, and he hastened up to London to perform his office. He was too late, for Henry, fearful of delay, had availed himself of the services of some of the Southern bishops. Thomas was greatly annoyed, but the king and the prelates acquainted him with the reason for the haste, and begged him to overlook what had been done. He was easily appeased, and having paid his homage to the new sovereign, the weak and aged archbishop was allowed to return into the North to die.[l] I must now speak of his good works in the diocese of York.

I have elsewhere alluded to the wretched state of the North at the death of Aldred. All the fury of the Conqueror and his opponents had fallen upon it, and the result was indeed appalling. There was scarcely a village or a homestead between the Tees and York which escaped from the fire or the plunderers. To add to the horrors of the time, a famine slew the greater part of those whom the sword had spared.[m] It was when all this wretchedness was at its height that Thomas reached the diocese of which he was to be the spiritual head. The prospect was not a pleasant one. The bishopric of Durham was vacant, and the head of that see was his only suffragan in England. Upon the Scottish prelates no reliance could at any time be

[k] Eadmer, Hist. Nov., apud Anselmi Opp., 37. Symeon, col. 219. Diceto, col. 491. Gervase, col. 1658. Stubbs, col. 1707. Wendover, i., 365. Hoveden, 266.

Sir Thomas Grey also says, "En le temps William le Conquerour comensa le debate entre lez ercevesques de Cantorbirs et Euerwik pur le porter de lour croitz en autry dyocys" (Scala Chron., 2).

[l] This fact is mentioned for the first time by Hugh the Chantor. The chroniclers give a different account. Malmesbury and several others say that Thomas crowned Henry. The chronicle of Peterbro' informs us that Maurice, bishop of London, consecrated the king, but that he was crowned by Thomas (69). Walsingham, in his Upodigma Neustriæ (Camden, 443), says that both officiated.

[m] There is a sad account in Symeon, col. 199, and Stubbs, col. 1708.

placed. There was no one to consecrate him when he was elected to the archbishopric! The greater part of the monasteries also had been destroyed or injured, and Durham and Beverley were almost the only two which had escaped. The light of religion in the North had been almost quenched! But Thomas was an energetic man, and he was not to be easily appalled. With the Norman love of labour and organization, he set himself manfully to work to reconstruct and restore. He began very properly with the principal city in his province. The minster at York had been gutted and set on fire, although many of the old walls were probably still standing; the ornaments and furniture had of course disappeared, and the muniments and library had been given to the flames. Thomas rebuilt and renovated the cathedral as far as he could, putting on a new roof, and procuring new service-books and decorations.[n] He restored the old endowments, and added others in the shape of estates and churches to such an extent that Malmesbury charges him with impoverishing his see;[o] he contributed from his private purse towards the necessities of the minster and its inmates, and repaired the dormitory and refectory; he made still greater changes in the constitution of the cathedral,—he completely remodelled it. Up to this time the number of the canons had only been seven,—the old Culdee number, and those at York still retained that peculiar name. Of these, one had been the *abbas* or superior, another the *magister scholarum*,[p] and a third the *custos civitatis*. They had all lived together upon a common fund. Of these seven three only were at York when Thomas arrived; the rest were either dead or in some other place. The survivors were now recalled and reinstated under a different *régime*, although they were still seculars. A dean took the place of the *abbas*, the *magister scholarum* became the chancellor, and the treasurer was the

[n] There is some doubt as to the extent of these restorations. "Perpulcram ecclesiam construxit, clericos multipliciter ditavit" (Bromton, col. 969. Knyghton, col. 2345). "Ecclesiam a fundamentis inchoatam consummavit" (Malmesbury, 155 *b*). "Ecclesiæ recoopertæ, et juxta possibilitatem suam restructæ, canonicos restituit" (Stubbs, col. 1708). See "The Architectural History of York Cathedral," by Professor Willis, pp. 14-15. Mr. Willis is of opinion that Thomas first renovated the Saxon church, and afterwards erected a new cathedral, or, at all events, the greater part of one. Cf. Lel. Coll., ii., 337.

In 1075 an invading Danish force went to York, broke into St. Peter's minster, and took away much treasure (Saxon Chron., 282).

[o] Malmesbury, apud Savile, 155 *b*.

[p] This office seems to have fallen into desuetude, and was revived by Thomas before he proceeded to re-arrange the minster. Stubbs, whilst describing the creation of the dean, treasurer, and precentor, says that Thomas "magistrum scolarum antea statuerat."

I hope to speak at greater length about the origin and duties of these officers in my account of the dignitaries of the cathedral.

custos civitatis: a chantor or precentor was added, and the number of the canons was increased. The diocese was mapped out, and placed under the charge of archdeacons. Those officers, indeed, had been for some time in existence, as they are mentioned in the Laws of the Northumbrian Priests, but their duties and their districts seem to have been at this time properly defined. The common property of the minster was also broken up and divided, and to each office there was assigned a separate endowment. This was done to allow each canon to attend to and improve his own allotted portion, and due provision was at the same time made for any other stalls which might subsequently be established.[q] Thomas was also a benefactor to the minster in another way. He prevailed upon the Conqueror to increase the endowments of the hospital of St. Peter, which was better known in after years as that of St. Leonard.[r]

There were at this time three other collegiate churches within the diocese of York,—Beverley, Southwell, and Ripon, all of which were held by secular canons. All the three had been remodelled within the last century, but so firmly rooted in the North had the secular system become that in each instance it was perpetuated. Aldred was the first person who placed prebendaries at Southwell, and he is said to have established them at Ripon.[s] Alfric made alterations in the constitution of the church of Beverley as it had been arranged by Athelstan. He found there seven canons and seven clerks; he added to them an eighth canon, a precentor, a chancellor, and a sacrist. This was the state of things at Beverley when Thomas came into the North. In course of time some complaints reached his ears about the management of the property of that church, and he met the difficulty by appointing a provost. The first officer who bore that title was his own nephew and namesake, who was afterwards archbishop.[t]

The monastic system in the North was at this time literally extinct. The Danes had done their work well, and many of the

[q] Stubbs, col. 1708-9.

[r] MSS., Cotton, Nero, D iii., 5 *a*. St. Leonard's Chartulary, a magnificent book. The writer fixes this grant at Pentecost, 1069,—a manifest error.

The archiepiscopal seal of Thomas (not the matrix) is in existence. After him the series is nearly complete, and may be found among the archives of the dean and chapter of Durham.

[s] I have nowhere seen the authority for this statement, which has been frequently made. There were canons at Ripon at the time of the Domesday. Thomas is supposed to have begun the new minster at Ripon (Walbran's Ripon, 31). In Leland (Coll., ii., 337) it is said that Aldred founded stalls at Ripon, York, and Beverley.

[t] Lel. Coll., iv., 103. Dugd. Mon., vi., 1308. Scaum's Beverlac, 522. Oliver's Beverley, 385. This appointment was too good a one to verify the old saying with regard to bishops, "Filios Deus abstulit, Sathanas dedit nepotes!"

early religious houses had totally disappeared; others were to be recognized only by charred beams and tottering walls. The seculars were the masters everywhere, and they were few in number and poorly endowed. Durham was the only place where any semblance of discipline was retained, and yet that famous monastery was at that time in the hands of secular canons, who, save in one point, had abandoned altogether the Benedictine rule. This was the state of things in the North when, in 1074, three wandering Benedictines from Winchcombe and Evesham made a pilgrimage into that district to visit the holy shrines of which they had read in the history of Beda: a single ass carried everything that they possessed. A change had come over the country since the days of the great chronicler. Jarrow and Wearmouth were in ruins, and there were none to tell them there of Benedict or Beda; Whitby and Lastingham were neglected and destroyed. It is to those three faithful and energetic men that the North of England is indebted for the re-establishment of monasticism. They took up their abode at Monkchester, or Newcastle-upon-Tyne, and, after many adventures, became at last the founders, as we may call them, of three famous Benedictine houses,—Durham, Whitby, and St. Mary's, York.[u] With each of these establishments archbishop Thomas was more or less concerned. Whitby and St. Mary's were in the diocese of York, and the monks could not be located there without his support and consent. He looked indeed on St. Mary's for some time with a jealous eye, perhaps on account of its propinquity to his own minster,[v] but he subsequently became its friend. He was intimately connected with the church of Durham and its bishops. He consecrated St. Carileph and Flambard, and administered the last offices to the former.[w] He must have observed with pleasure the activity and the munificence of St. Carileph when he replaced the secular canons of Durham by a colony of Benedictines, and reared a noble cathedral upon that grey rock which overhangs the Wear. He permitted the monks of that place to possess their lands in Yorkshire free from any payment or ecclesiastical exaction.[x] There is a curious story connected

[u] Symeon, col. 199, 206, 210. Hist. Eccl. Dunelm., 198, etc. Bromton, col. 973. Malmesbury, apud Savile, 154 *b*. Mabillon, Ann. Ben., v., 84, 257. Lel. Coll., ii., 382. Drake's Eboracum, 578-9, ex Hist. Fundationis S.M. Ebor.

When Selby abbey was founded "per totam Eboraci-Siriam, excepta Dunelmensi congregatione, nec monachus nec monachorum locus aliquis in illis diebus facile valuit reperiri" (Hist. Mon. Seleb., apud Labbe, Nov. Bibl., i., 601). Thomas was a benefactor to Selby.

[v] Drake, *ut supra*, 579.

[w] Fl. Wigorn, 446. Symeon, col. 224. Stubbs, col. 1709. Hoveden, 263, 268. Symeon, Hist. Eccl. Dunelm., 218, 245, 255. Lel. Coll., ii., 384. Carileph had been connected with Bayeux.

[x] Hist. Dunelm. Scr. Tres, ed. Surtees Soc., appendix, xi.

with his charter of exemption. The archbishop had been ill for two years, and was a martyr to attacks of fever. "Physicians were in vain." A vision warned him to seek for relief in Durham, at St. Cuthbert's tomb. He went and passed the night there in great distress and pain, as might reasonably be expected. Weariness at last brought on sleep, and the slumberer beheld the saint standing by him: he ran his hand over his limbs, and the torture went away. But before the healer departed he must have his fee: he desired the prostrate archbishop to manifest his gratitude by granting to his favourite place and see the immunities which were afterwards bestowed. Thomas, in an encyclical letter, narrated his sufferings and his cure.[y]

Thomas seems to have vindicated and exercised his right to be the head of the Scottish bishops. The ecclesiastical superintendence of that country was entrusted to him at the council in 1072. He consecrated Ralph bishop of the Orkneys. Foderoch, the bishop of St. Andrews, came to him at the bidding of Malcolm and his queen in the character of a penitent. He had been consecrated at home, but he acknowledged his offence, and made his profession of obedience to Thomas. He is said to have acted as a suffragan within the province of York.[z] These names, it must be observed, do not appear in the fasti of the Scottish Church. There must either be some forgery in this matter by the York historians, or a suppression of the truth by the Scottish chroniclers.

Thomas died at York on the 18th of November, 1100,[a] having been archbishop for about thirty years. He had been infirm for some time before his death, and he must have been an old man. He was buried at York, and was interred in the minster near his predecessor Aldred. The following epitaph commemorated him :—

> "Orba pio, viduata bono pastore patrono
> Urbs Eboraca dolet, vix habitura parem.
> Qualia vix uni persona, scientia, vita,
> Contigerit, Thomæ nobilis, alta, bona.
> Canicies, hilaris facies, statura venusta,
> Angelici vultus splendor et instar erat.
> Hic numero atque modo doctrinæ seu probitatis
> Clericus omnis erat ut magis omnis homo.
> Hæc domus et clerus sub tanto presule felix,
> Pene quod est et habet, muneris omne sui est.
> Octavis Sancti Martini transiit ille,
> Qui pietate Dei sit comes in requie.[b]

[y] Ibid. Hoveden, apud Savile, 263 b.

[z] Stubbs, col. 1709.

[a] Saxon Chron., 321. Symeon, col. 226. Chron. Mailros, 62. Fl. Wigorn., 472. Chron. Petrib., 70. Ann. de Margan, apud Gale, ii., 3. Hoveden, 268 b. Mat. Paris, 47. Stubbs, col. 1709, who says that he died at Ripon "Octavis S. Martini."

[b] Hugh the Chantor. Stubbs, col. 1709, has several variations.

These words are highly eulogistic, but the see of York owes a deep debt of gratitude to archbishop Thomas. I can see him even now as Malmesbury describes him in his later years—the graceful figure retaining even then the spring and energy of youth; the noble presence, and the courteous bearing which captivated all; the handsome florid countenance, and his hair as white as the down upon a swan. No one could impugn the purity and correctness of his life.[c] As to his learning and ability the chroniclers are for once unanimous. He brought with him into England the literary stores of three countries.[d] It was his delight to have his clergy around him to read with them and to argue. But music was his master-passion. He knew it thoroughly, and was a composer as well as a singer. He could play upon the organ, and was acquainted with its construction. If he chanced to hear any light or trivial air, he would parody it, as it were, with marvellous—may I say unfortunate—facility into a hymn. He made chants and services,[e] eschewing especially all soft and effeminate music.[f] One specimen only of his powers as a versifier has been handed down to us, an elegy upon the death of William the Conqueror.[g] As the theme was an unfavourable one the effusion must be read with some little indulgence.

> "Qui rexit rigidos Normannos atque Britannos,
> Audacter vicit, fortiter obtinuit,
> Et Cenomanenses virtute cöercuit enses,
> Imperiique suis legibus applicuit,
> Rex magnus parva jacet hic Gulielmus in urna,
> Sufficit et magno parva domus domino.
> Ter septem gradibus se volverat atque duobus
> Virginis in gremio Phœbus, et hic obiit."

Gerard, bishop of Hereford, was translated to the archbishopric of York at the feast of the Epiphany, 1101.[h] He was the nephew of Walkeline, the Norman bishop of Winchester, and of Symeon, abbat of Ely; and he was, therefore, a distant

[c] Malmesbury, 156 *b*.

[d] Vita S. Wulstani, apud Angl. Sac., ii., 255. Ric. of Hexham, col. 303. Stubbs, col. 1705. Rob., de Monte, ed. Stevenson, 680. Huntingdon, 216 *b*.

[e] Bromton, col. 968. Knyghton, col. 2345.

[f] Malmesbury, apud Savile, 155 *b*.

[g] Ord. Vitalis, apud Duchesne, 663. Wm. Neubr., ed. Hearne, appendix 684-5, where this and two other epitaphs are given.

[h] Hugh the Chantor, who wrote a life of Gerard, which is in the Reg. Magnum Album at York. Chron. Mailros, 62, in 1100. Symeon, col. 226. Diceto, col. 499. Bromton, col. 999. Cottoni Chron., 412. Hoveden, 268 *b*. Mat. Paris, 47.

connection of the Conqueror.[i] We first hear of Gerard as the chantor or precentor of the church at Rouen.[j] He next became one of the chaplains of William Rufus, and in that capacity he was sent by the king to Rome to make enquiries for him about the relative merits of the two rival popes.[k] It is also said that he was chancellor to William I. and II.[l] Gerard was consecrated to the see of Hereford at London, in June 1096,[m] by the two archbishops, having been raised to the priesthood at Lambeth on the preceding day.[n] In 1100 he was present at the consecration of the new church at Gloucester,[o] and soon after this he is said to have officiated at the coronation of queen Matilda.[p] In 1101 he was translated to York. Walter Mapes tells a curious story to account for his removal from Hereford. He says that Gerard crowned Henry I., who, as a reward for his services, promised him the first vacant archbishopric. On the death of Thomas the king repented of what he had undertaken, and endeavoured to keep Gerard at Hereford, being willing to confer upon that see an income equal to that of York and Canterbury, and a position as important as that of the bishop of Durham. Gerard, however, would have nothing to do with this arrangement, and held the monarch to his word.[q] I do not set any value upon the story, but it is necessary to mention it.

When Gerard was translated to York the old question of subjection was again opened out. Anselm demanded his profession, but he refused to make it. He had desired Anselm to give him letters to the pope to enable him to obtain the pall, but he was told that they should be given upon one condition, that he should either make his profession at once or on his return from Rome. Gerard was ready with his reply. "When he came back he would do what was just and right," and thereupon he crossed the seas.[r] He carried with him, also, a missive from the king to Paschal, begging him to bestow the pall upon the bearer.[s] Gerard, however, had another errand to the eternal city. He went there as ambassador from the king of England.[t]

[i] Ord. Vitalis, apud Duchesne, 764. Malmesbury, apud Savile, 155 *b*. Anglia Sacra, i., 611.

[j] Chron. Rob., de Monte, ed. Stevenson, 680.

[k] Eadmer, Hist. Nov., apud Anselmi Opp., ed. 1721, 44.

[l] Hugh the Chantor. Stubbs, col. 1710, Lel. Coll., ii., 337. Perhaps *cancellarius* is a clerical error for *capellanus*. The name of Gerard appears in no list of the chancellors that I have seen.

[m] Fl. Wigorn. says on June 15. Stubbs, Reg. Sacr. Angl., 24.

[n] Eadmer, Hist. Nov., 45.

[o] Symeon, col. 225.

[p] Recueil des Historiens des Gaules, xii., 679. Symeon (col. 226) says that Anselm crowned and consecrated her.

[q] De Nugis Curialium, 224. Symeon (225) says that Maurice, bishop of London, crowned Henry. Gerard, however, was present (Wendover, i., 488.)

[r] Stubbs, col. 1710.

[s] Bromton, col. 999.

[t] Eadmer, *ut supra*, 61. Malmesbury, 92 *b*, 127 *b*, 155 *b*. Malmesbury

The dispute between Anselm and Henry as to the right of investiture was running high, and the king was desirous of having the pope on his side. Paschal was too adroit a politician to take any decided part in such a controversy. Gerard obtained the pall, and was flattered and caressed. His learning was commended; his advice was sought for,[u] whilst the king's ambassadors, as well as those of Anselm, returned to England with the firm conviction that the pope was their friend.[v]

The true state of things would soon be discovered, and some little coolness between Anselm and Gerard would probably ensue. The relative position of the two prelates was a very critical one. They took different sides in the church politics of the day, and it must have been very difficult to avoid a collision. We find them, however, associated together in a great council held at Westminster in September 1102, at which many ordinances were made relating to ecclesiastical discipline, but particularly to the marriage of the clergy.[w] Even at that meeting there was a little manifestation of angry feeling. A seat had been placed for Gerard below that of his brother of Canterbury. He kicked it over and ordered it to be replaced on a level with that of Anselm, invoking the wrath of God upon the perpetrator of that injury to his see.[x]

In the following year the quarrel between the king and Anselm was at its height, and Gerard was made a party in it. Three bishops stood in need of consecration, and Anselm refused to officiate unless they received investiture from himself. This the king forbade, and requested Gerard to take the place of Anselm and act as consecrator. He was ready to do so, although his consenting manifested neither good feeling nor good taste. "Perhaps," as Fuller says, "he hoped thereby to hitch his church and degree the higher,"[y] perhaps only to oblige the king. The ceremony, however, did not take place. William Giffard, the bishop elect of Winchester, made so strenuous an opposition to the intrusion of Gerard, that the other prelates shrunk from the responsibility, and Giffard himself went abroad.[z] Anselm, also, wearied and disgusted, sought again the protection of the pope.

charges Gerard with having given to the king a false report of the pope's opinion with regard to investitures. This is probably the circumstance to which the pope alluded in a letter to Gerard, which is given by Eadmer.

[u] MSS. Lansdowne, ccccii., 27 *b*. Bromton, col. 1000. Stubbs, col. 1710.

[v] We hear of Gerard and his brother ambassadors being at Marseilles on their return in Martene, Thes. Nov. Anec., iv., 126. Eadmer, Hist. Nov., 61.

[w] Fl. Wigorn., 474. Malmesbury, apud Savile, 129 *b*. Hoveden, 269. Symeon, col. 227. Bromton, col. 1001. Gervase, col. 1660. Stubbs, col. 1710. Eadmer, Hist. Nov., 63-4. Labbe, Conc. x., 728.

[x] Stubbs, col. 1710.

[y] Church History, book iii., 20.

[z] Saxon Chron., 324. Fl. Wigorn., 475. Eadmer, 64. Malmesbury, 128.

During the next three years, which Anselm spent in exile, we know little of the archbishop of York. A letter from pope Paschal is preserved, in which he is exhorted to be on better terms with Anselm;[a] and that advice seems to have had its due weight. A portion of the correspondence that passed between the two prelates is before us; it evinces much kindly feeling, although it discloses the existence of some jealousy and bitterness.[b] Gerard joined his brother bishops in an affectionate but fruitless appeal to Anselm to return to England.[c] He wrote himself to the exiled primate, and spoke of their friendship and past intercourse. He told him how much he wished that all this should be renewed, and assured him of his kind offices with the king in his behalf.[d] It is quite possible that to Gerard's agency is to be ascribed the return of Anselm, which took place in the autumn of 1106. After this there was another chance of a feud between the two primates. Anselm required from Gerard his profession of obedience, and he was backed in this demand by a letter from the pope.[e] The king now questioned the necessity of the claim, as the profession had been made before when Gerard became bishop of Hereford. Anselm, however, was not satisfied with this; and Gerard is said to have laid his hand in that of Anselm, and to have promised to pay him the same obedience which he had rendered to him in a lower sphere.[f] It is only just to say that some doubts have been thrown upon the truth of this statement. The reconciliation, however, seems to have been complete, and Gerard assisted his brother-primate in consecrating five bishops—the greatest number that had participated in that rite, at one time, since the days of archbishop Plegmund.[g]

Gerard induced the king to give the church of Laughton to the dean and canons of York, and this was made into a prebend. He also obtained from him six other churches. Of these, he gave one, that of Snaith, to Selby Abbey. The other five, those

Hoveden, 269 *b*. Symeon, col. 228. Diceto, col. 499. Bromton, col. 999. Hemingford, apud Gale, ii., 470. Mat. Paris, 49. Chron. Petrib., 71. Möhler's Life of Anselm, ed. 1842, 100. In Baluzii Misc. Sacra, ed. Mansi, ii., 173, there is a letter from Anselm to Henry protesting against any injury being done to Giffard on account of his resistance.

[a] Anselmi Opp., 436. Diceto, col. 497.

[b] Anselmi Opp., 389, 431, 443.

[c] Eadmer, 73. Ans. Opp., 410. Wilkins, i., 384. Möhler's Life of Anselm, 104.

[d] Anselmi Opp., 436.

[e] Ibid., 413. Diceto, col. 497. Malmesbury, apud Savile, 155 *b*. Labbe, Conc., x., 647.

[f] Eadmer, 76-7. Fl. Wigorn., 479. Hoveden, 270. Symeon, col. 230. Diceto, col. 500. Gervase, col. 1659. Stubbs (1710) denies this. Cotton (Chron., 412) says that Gerard made his profession and obedience.

[g] Eadmer, 77. Malmesbury, 129 *b*. Hoveden, 270. Symeon, col. 230. Bromton, col. 1003. Chron. Petrib., 74. Gerard consecrated a bishop of Orkney (Stubbs, col. 1710).

of Driffield, Kilham, Pocklington, Pickering and Burgh, were bestowed upon his minster.[h] He seems to have been a munificent person; indeed, his successor complained that he had impoverished the see.[i] Gerard was a great disciplinarian, and acted occasionally under the advice of Anselm.[j] He is said to have been fond of correcting abuses, and on that account he secured for himself the dislike which too many are ready enough to manifest towards a conscientious and active reformer.[k]

Gerard has some pretensions to a literary reputation; indeed among his contemporaries he was famous for his eloquence and learning.[l] Hugh the Chantor is guilty, perhaps, of a little clerical adulation when he tells us he was quite able to contest the palm with Virgil in metre, and Tully in prose! The letters of Gerard, which are preserved, are well enough in their expression and Latinity, although in both respects they are inferior to those of Cicero.[m] The following specimen of his verse is the only one that I have been able to recover. It is scarcely equal to the melodious number of the Eclogues or the Georgics. But it is hardly fair to judge a poet by eight lines, two of which are not his own.

"Rex citharista David, Salomon, Paris, et Menelaus,
Occidit, liquid *(liquit?)* prodidit, introiit,
Uriam, Dariam,[n] Menelaum, Troica castra,
Ingenio, monitis turpibus, arte, dolis.
Si fortuna velit, fiet de rethore consul,
Si velit hæc eadem, fiet de consule rethor.
In precio precium nunc est, dat census honores,
Census amicitias. Pauper ubique jacet."[o]

The death of Gerard was a somewhat remarkable one. It occurred at Southwell, on his way to the court at London,[p] on the 21st of May, 1108.[q] He was suffering from a slight illness. After dinner he went to take his repose in the garden adjoining to his palace, and lay down to sleep in the open air among the grass and flowers with a cushion under his head. His clerks left him for a while at his request, and on their return their

[h] Stubbs, col. 1710. Rot. Chart., 121. Lel. Coll., ii., 337. In the Life of Thurstan, in MSS. Cotton, Titus, A, xix., 55, it is said that the churches of Pickering, Pocklington and Kilham, were given to the deanery of York, which had been previously poor, by Henry I., at the request of archbishop Thurstan.

[i] Eadmer, 80.

[j] Anselmi Opp., 386, 431.

[k] Mirac. S. Joann. Beverlac., apud Acta SS., May 2.

[l] Ibid., Wm. Neubrig., i., 25. Malmesbury, 155 *b*. Stubbs, col. 1710.

[m] One of Gerard's letters is in Ans. Opp., 436. There is one in the library at Corpus, Cambridge.

[n] The allusion here is not quite clear. Was Gerard thinking of Hiram? Perhaps of Pharaoh?

[o] MSS., Cotton, Titus D, xxiv., 61.

[p] Eadmer, 78.

[q] Saxon Chron., 331. Symeon, col. 231. Stubbs, col. 1711. Ann. de Margan, apud Gale, i., 4. Ann. Waverl., ibid., ii., 146. Rob. de Monte, ed. Stevenson, 680. Hoveden, 270. Chron. Petrib., 74.

master was dead. He had passed quietly away. His opponents asserted that this was a fitting termination of a wicked life. He had departed "unhouselled, unanealed." A few persons carried his remains to York; but, on account of the way in which he died, they were not received, it is stated, with the customary procession of the citizens and clergy. The boys pelted the bier as it passed along, and, the canons denying the corpse a resting-place within the minster, it was interred ignominiously without the walls of the cathedral.[r] It was subsequently buried within the church by his immediate successor in the see.[s] These are the things which a monkish opponent is so fond of recording. Gerard was a reformer and a successful politician, and in both these characters he would be sure to create enemies. The most upright man is not exempt from this. Gerard is arraigned by more than one chronicler for deceit and an evil life.[t] He is also charged with being addicted to curious and forbidden arts. A treatise on magic, by Julius Firmicus, is reported to have been found under his pillow in his garden at Southwell, and he is said to have been much attached to it.[u] The book was merely a work on astronomy. The same petty and vexatious spirit of ignorance which regarded Gerard as akin to a sorcerer, threw Galileo into a dungeon.

Thomas II., the namesake and the nephew of the first Norman archbishop, was the next primate of the Northern province, succeeding, as it were, by hereditary right.[v] He was a member, strange to say, of a great clerical family. His father, Sampson, became bishop of Worcester; and his brother, Richard, presided over the see of Bayeux from 1108 to 1133.[w] Thomas owed his advance in life to the care of his uncle, whom he resembled in disposition, and under whom he was brought up at York.[x] In 1092, when the minster at Beverley was reformed, Thomas was made by his uncle the first provost, and

[r] Wm. Neubrig., i., 25-6. Malmesbury, 155 *b*. MSS. Cotton, Vesp., A. ix. Harleian Misc., ix. 309.

[s] Malmesbury, ibid.

[t] Wm. Neubrig., i., 25. "Vita lubricus, in emungendis per indecoras etiam occasiones subditorum marsupiis callidus, et, ut plurimi asseverant, maleficiis etiam assuetus."

[u] Knyghton, col. 2375. Drake's Eboracum, 415.

[v] Hugh the Chantor. Stubbs, col. 1711. Knyghton, col. 2377. Hoveden, apud Savile, 270. Mat. Paris, 53.

[w] Gallia Christiana, xi., 360. Ric. of Hexham, col. 303. Malmesbury, apud Savile, 155 *b*. Stubbs, col. 1711. Tanner, Bibl. Brit., 709. Thomas's Worcester, 144; and Appendix, 4.

[x] Hugh the Chantor.

he held that office till the year 1108.[y] He was also one of the royal chaplains. The year 1108 witnessed the decease of Maurice, bishop of London, and Thomas was nominated to the vacant post. Before the appointment was completed archbishop Gerard died at Southwell. At that time, Hugh the dean, and several of the canons, of York, were at the court, and they entreated the king to give them for their new primate the bishop-elect of London. Their petition was listened to, and Thomas became archbishop of York.[z] The chapter of that city would be delighted to welcome a prelate who had been so intimately connected with their own body.

No sooner was the election of Thomas made known, than the monks of Canterbury prevailed upon Anselm to require from him the profession of obedience.[a] Thomas resolved to take the opinion of the king, and set off for London from York, where he had been already most kindly received. He had accomplished half his journey, when a messenger overtook him, urging him to be firm in terms which a long intercourse and familiarity could alone justify, and demanding that he should in no way commit or dishonour his chapter. Thomas at length reached the king, who forbade him making the profession which had been demanded; and the opinion of the court was decidedly

[y] Symeon, col. 231. Stubbs, 1711. The lists of the provosts of Beverley in Poulson and Oliver are filled with errors, many of which have their origin in the account of those officials, drawn up before the Reformation by Simon Russel.

Archbishop Thomas was the first provost. He seems to have been succeeded by another person bearing the same name, who devoted himself to the Cistercian rule at Clairvaux, but broke his pledge, much to St. Bernard's grief. The Saint tells us that he died, "Subita et horrenda morte." St. Bernard wrote to, and about him (S. Bern. Opp., ed. 1690, i., 111-15, 363-4). This Thomas was succeeded by a person of the name of Thurstan, but not the archbishop, as has generally been stated. He died in 1153 or 1154 (John of Hexham, col. 280), and was succeeded by Thomas à Becket, who seems to have been indebted for his appointment to archbishop Theobald (Becket's works, ed. Giles, i., 10). Benedict of Peterborough records a miracle wrought in behalf of Thomas de Etton, knt., who had been an opponent of Becket whilst he was provost (Bened. Petrib., Vita S. Thomæ Cant., ed. Caxton Soc., 104).

[z] Saxon Chron., 331. MSS. Lansdowne, ccccii., 20 *b*. Symeon, col. 231. Diceto, col. 500. Wendover, i., 461. Chron. Petrib., 74. Dachery, Spicilegium, iii., 506.

[a] The account of this controversy is taken from several sources. The chief authority is the life of Thomas, by Hugh Sotevagina, the chantor and archdeacon of York, which supplies some fresh information. See, also, Stubbs, col. 1711-13. Anselmi Opp., 420-1, 448-50. (Several of these letters are not in their proper chronological order). Eadmer, Hist. Nov., ibid., 79-83. Diceto, col. 500-1. Gervase, col. 1660. Malmesbury, apud Savile, 156. Labbe, Conc., x., 758-61. Wilkins, i., 388-92. Ivonis Carnotensis Epp., ed. 1610, 790. Jo. Saresber., Opp., v., 346, etc. Anglia Sacra, ii., 172.

In 1108 there is said to have been a meeting of the clergy, at which Anselm and Thomas were present. Some enactments were passed at it about the archdeacons and the clergy (Symeon, col. 231. Hoveden, 270 *b*. Labbe, Conc., x., 756).

in his favour. In the meantime Anselm was not idle. He tried to gain the king's ear, but in vain. He then sent Herbert, bishop of Norwich, to Thomas, to propose that the profession should be dispensed with, if he would only recognize the primacy of Anselm. Thomas, however, relied on the king's support, and declined to do so. Anselm now began to act with promptitude and energy, and it was time. Turgot of Durham, the bishop-elect of St. Andrews, was waiting to be consecrated. Thomas, of course, could not officiate; but Ranulph Flambard, the bishop of Durham, was willing to act in his presence, with the assistance of the Scottish prelates. Anselm refused to allow the ceremony to take place. He forbade Thomas to exercise any episcopal functions. He told him that no bishop ought to be unconsecrated for more than forty days, and desired him to be at Canterbury to receive that rite on the 6th of September following; saying that if he should be disobedient he would himself step into his place in the North, and enter upon the duties which he was neglecting. Thomas wrote to Anselm in reply, and told him that he would come to Canterbury as soon as he conveniently could. At present he was in want of money, as the see had been much impoverished by his predecessor; and he was preparing also, with the king's permission, to send a messenger to the pope to procure the pall. Anselm, upon this, forbade him to seek the pall before his consecration, and desired him to be at Canterbury on the 27th of September. He wrote also to the pope, requesting him to withhold, for the present, the honour which Thomas wished to obtain. Thomas, in reply, told Anselm that he could not act against the will of his chapter; and that body, about the same time, conveyed to Anselm the opinions which they had so strongly impressed upon their spiritual head. Anselm fixed another day for the consecration of his new brother, but to no purpose. He then resolved to try the effect of mediation, and sent the bishops of London and Rochester into the North. Thomas met them at Southwell, but all their arguments and entreaties were in vain. He said that he would gladly come to Canterbury to be consecrated if the objectionable condition was given up. He was now expecting, as he told them, the return of his messenger from Normandy whom he had sent to consult the king. This alarmed Anselm when he heard of it. He wrote a letter to Sampson, bishop of Worcester, the father of Thomas, begging him to prevail upon his son to adopt better counsels. The cautious prelate returned an evasive and an unsatisfactory reply.

In the meantime, Hugh, the dean of York, and some other friends of Thomas, had arrived at the court in Normandy. Henry wrote to Anselm, desiring that the dispute should stand over till he returned to England; and the archbishop unwillingly acquiesced. The king, also, shewed his partiality towards Thomas by writing a letter, which Hugh carried with him to the pope. It contained a request that he would send over to England some competent person to settle the quarrel between the two sees, and to bring with him the pall which Thomas was unable to seek at Rome in his own person. The pope readily assented, and Ulric, a cardinal, returned with the dean. Before they could reach Normandy and the court, Anselm had passed away out of this troubled scene into the peace and stillness that are beyond it. He had been failing for some time, and, possibly, this controversy with Thomas may have embittered and disturbed the last months of the old man's life. Upon his death-bed he is said to have indited a most striking letter, in which, in the sight of the Most High, he besought Thomas to return to his allegiance to Canterbury. The curse of God was invoked upon him if that allegiance were withheld. There is something very awful in this. Surely a death-bed is a place for blessings, and not for curses. Anselm, however, was then seeking for others, and not for his own aggrandizement, what he considered to be right. He dared to vindicate it as he was passing away to one whose highest attribute is His justice. That noble heart, palsied by suffering but unvanquished, was honest and faithful unto the end.

Whilst this was going on in England, Ulric and his companions came to Henry at the Norman court, and he sent them into his own kingdom, promising to be soon with them. When he came, the great cause between Canterbury and York was mooted, and each side did their best to carry the day. It was debated at the feast of Pentecost. The result was that the king was prevailed upon by the dignitaries of the Southern province to alter his determination, and he requested the astonished and dismayed Thomas to make the required profession to Canterbury, without any prejudice to his successors or his church. He flatly refused to do so. The hot blood of the Norman prince boiled over when he heard him. He threatened to ruin him and all his kindred if he remained obstinate. Thomas was still disposed to resist. Every influence was now brought to bear upon him. Robert, comte de Meulent, whose good offices Anselm had previously requested, endeavoured to persuade the unwilling prelate. Stephen de Whitby, the abbat of St. Mary's, York, entreated him to give way. Bishop Flambard sought in vain to warp the king's mind by a proffered bribe of a thousand marks of silver to himself, and an hundred of gold to the queen, but Henry would not relent. The mediation of the cardinal was begged for; but he declined to embroil himself in a controversy which might be productive of so much danger to himself and his church. The king would not give way: would the prelate submit? At this crisis the father and brother of Thomas, fearful for their own safety and for his, went to him, and at their earnest entreaty he was induced to alter his determination. Stern necessity seems to have compelled him, and he gave up his position most sorrowfully and unwillingly. On the morrow, Sunday, the 27th of June, 1109,[b] he made his profession, and was consecrated at London by the bishop of that diocese. He obtained, however, some little compensation for his concession. The bishops of Norwich and Durham declared aloud in the church, at the king's request, that Thomas had made his submission to Canterbury in obedience solely to his royal master's wish, and not upon the merits of the controversy. Henry also gave him a kind of encyclical letter which repeated everything that the two bishops had asserted, and added, besides, that the act was in no respect to compromise the rights and privileges of the church of York and its archbishops.

Soon after this Thomas and the cardinal set out for York, where there was a noble welcome for them. In the beginning of August the pall was solemnly given to him in the minster; and when the ceremonial, together with the mass, at which Thomas officiated, were over, the new archbishop, in the presence of Ulric, consecrated Turgot of Durham, who had long been waiting for that rite, to the bishopric of St. Andrew's.[c] After a stay of three days, the cardinal, loaded with presents and thanks, set out on his journey towards the South. Thomas escorted him as far as the Trent; and, when they were about to part, the archbishop, instead of a friendly farewell, was astonished to receive a summons to Rome. Ulric told him that in making his profession to Canterbury he had broken the decree of Gregory and the canons, and that he must answer for this at Rome. Why had not the cardinal expressed the same opinion when his advice had been previously sought for, and when it ought to have been given? The entreaties, however, of Thomas and his friends induced Ulric to recal his words, and the two separated with mutual assurances of friendship and good will.[d]

The life of Thomas was too short to allow him to do much within his diocese. We find, however, that several of the Scottish prelates came to him for consecration. Turgot of St. Andrew's

[b] Fl. Wigorn., 482. Symeon, col. 232. Diceto, col. 501. Eadmer, 83. Hoveden, 270 b. Chron. Petrib., 75. Chron. Mailros, 64. Mat. Paris, 53. Labbe, Conc., x., 761.

[c] Anselmi Opp., 421. Eadmer, ibid., 79.

[d] Hugh the Chantor. Symeon (232) and Fl. Wigorn., (482) say that the pall was given on July 30. Hoveden (270 b) makes the day Aug. 1. Malmesbury, 156. Stubbs, col. 1712. Chron. Petrib., 75.

has been already spoken of, but he was more renowned for his connexion with Durham, and his literary reputation, than for anything that he did at his see in Scotland. Wimund of the Isles, Michael of Glasgow, and Ralph of Orkney, were also consecrated by Thomas, and paid to him their spiritual homage. To the two last the diocese of York was under some obligations. The bishop of Glasgow, who came to York at the desire of prince David, was on intimate terms with Thomas, and acted as a suffragan within his diocese. He died on one of his episcopal journeys, and was buried in the church of Morland in Westmerland. The history of Ralph, the bishop of Orkney, was a remarkable one. He was a native of the city of York; and because he was consecrated without the consent of prince, clergy, or people of Orkney, he was rejected by them all. He remained, therefore, in England, and acted as a suffragan to the diocesans of Durham and York. He was a great friend of archbishop Thurstan in all his vicissitudes of fortune, and represented him at the famous battle of the Standard.[e]

We find but few traces of Thomas in the domestic affairs of his diocese. Two new stalls were founded at York in his time by Roger, abbat of Whitby.[f] Thomas obtained from the king a grant of privileges to the church of Southwell, and freed the canons and their church from the claims and exactions of himself and his successors. These endowments had been made by Aldred at his own cost, but he had been unable to secure the exemptions which were now obtained.[g] The greatest work, however, which Thomas effected, was at Hexham.[h] That once famous house had fallen from its first estate. A succession of twelve bishops had worn the mitre which rested on the brows of Wilfrid, but three centuries had elapsed since the death of the last of these prelates. The church and lordship, for some time, seem to have belonged in turn to the archbishop of York and the bishop of Durham, but at the beginning of the twelfth century, they seem to have been bestowed in perpetuity upon the Northern primates. The church up to this time was under the control of a provost, the son succeeding the father in the charge for several generations. Thomas I. appointed to this office a canon of Beverley of the name of Richard de Maton, and attached it to the stall of Holme at York. Maton seems to have been non-resident, but a person of the name of Eilau, well

[e] Symeon, col. 232. Stubbs, col. 1713. Keith's Scottish bishops, *n. e.*, 7, 220, 297.

[f] Hugh, the Chantor. Stubbs, (col. 1713) makes Thomas himself the founder.

[g] Stubbs, col. 1713.

[h] Ric. of Hexham, col. 303-6. Symeon, col. 235. Stubbs, col. 1713. Mirac. S. Wilfridi, apud Acta SS. ord. S.B., sæc. iii., i., 215-16. Lel. Coll., ii., 337-8, 391. There is an interesting paper by Mr. Longstaffe, on "The hereditary sacerdotage of Hexham," in the Arch. Æl., *n. s.*, iv., 11-28.

known in the chronicles of the church of Durham, was his deputy. It was clearly wrong that a church of antiquity and renown should languish under so feeble and imperfect an administration. The abbey seems to have been used as the parish church, and, with the exception of Eilau, there are no traces at that time of any resident ecclesiastics. On the first of November, 1113, Thomas was able to introduce a new system. During his visitation of the monasteries in his diocese he had made himself acquainted with the state of Hexham. He prevailed upon the provost to resign his post into his hands, and made it thenceforward a house of regular canons under the control of a prior; Eilau, who promoted, and was anxious for, the change, being permitted to retain a life-interest in the endowments. This he subsequently resigned, and ended his days as a professed monk among the Benedictines at Durham. Ailred, the learned prior of Rievaux, was his son. The path was now clear for Thomas and his changes. He established a new *régime*. He gave to the canons, who were Augustinians by rule, four vills, a mill on the Tyne, and a fishery in that river. He bestowed upon them one hundred shillings a year for their clothing. He furnished the church with its books and ornaments, and, had his life been spared, he would have been a still greater benefactor.

In the life of bishop Eata, there is an interesting account of an adventure of Thomas at Hexham. The church of York had no saint enshrined within its walls, and the want gave much annoyance to the dignitaries of the minster. They entreated Thomas to bring away from Hexham the remains of Eata. The canons of that place were in despair as the archbishop had made up his mind to deprive them of their saint. A singular circumstance is said to have deterred him. He had come to Hexham and was asleep, when suddenly Eata himself appeared to him in a vision. Not only did he chide Thomas in the strongest language, but he gave him two blows on his shoulder with his pastoral staff!

"Bis baculo tangens humerum."

The poor archbishop was half-dead with pain and fear, and of course nothing more was done about removing the remains.[i]

One of the two learned priors of Hexham commends Thomas very highly for his kindliness of heart, his pleasant manners and countenance, his hospitality and learning.[j] Like his uncle he had a great taste for music, and he is said to have composed

[i] Biogr. Misc., ed. Surtees Soc., 124. Mabillon, Acta SS. ord. S. B., iii., sæc. i., 222.

[j] Wm. Neubrig., i., 26. Symeon, col. 236. Ric. of Hexham, col. 303. Stubbs, col. 1713. Malmesbury, 156.

some hymns, together with an *Officiarium* for the benefit of his church at York.[k] A single letter of his addressed to Anselm is preserved.[l] In his personal appearance Thomas is said to have been stout and unwieldy, and to the inertness, which so frequently results from corpulency, the York historians have ascribed the too hasty surrender of the privileges of his see to the encroachments of Canterbury.[m]

Thomas died at Beverley on the 24th of February, 1114,[n] and was interred at York near his uncle and his predecessor Aldred.[o] He had for some time been suffering from a peculiar complaint, and he might have survived it, if he had not had some conscientious scruples in applying the prescribed remedy. He felt it first when he was provost of Beverley, but he is said to have obtained some temporary relief from the aid of his predecessor St. John, whose assistance he had besought.[p] The complaint, however, returned and carried him off. It was the same which in after years terminated the life of James Rossa, the archbishop-elect of Lisbon. Thomas was still a young man when he was called away.[q]

Thurstan, a well-known name in the North of England, was the next archbishop of York. It is impossible to do full justice in a few pages to this great and noble-minded man. Like several of his predecessors, he was the son of an ecclesiastic, Auger, prebendary of Kentish Town, in the church of London.[r] Thurstan was a native of Bayeux,[s] and his brother, Audoenus, was for many years the bishop of Evreux.[t] Thurstan's sagacity and

[k] Bale, cent. xiii., 132, where he is confused with his uncle. Tanner Bibl. Brit., 709. Wright Biogr. Lit., ii., 109.

[l] Eadmer, Hist. Nov., apud Anselmi Opp., 80.

[m] Hugh the Chantor. Stubbs, col. 1712.

[n] Fl. Wigorn., 488. Hoveden, 271. Ric. of Hexham (306) makes the date Feb. 16, and Stubbs (1713) Feb. 18. Saxon Chron., 334. Chron. Petrib., 77. Chron. Mailros, 65. Wikes, apud Gale, ii., 25. Symeon, col. 236. Matt. Paris, 55.

[o] Ric. of Hexham, col. 306. Stubbs, col. 1713.

[p] Ric. of Hexham, col. 303-4.

[q] Wm. Neubr., i., 26. Stubbs, col. 1713.

[r] Newcourt, i., 169. Godwin, ed. Richardson, 668. Auger was succeeded by his son, who is called "Audoenus frater archiepiscopi."

[s] Ord. Vitalis, apud Duchesne, 858.

[t] He was born at Bayeux, and was a very learned man. He was scribe and afterwards chaplain to Henry I. He was bishop for twenty-four years, and died in 1139, having rebuilt his church which had been burnt down. He was interred at Merton, having before his death taken upon him the habit of a canon. (Gallia Christiana, xi., 573-6. Recueil des Historiens des Gaules, xii., 769. John of Hexham, col. 265.)

energy of character soon gained him a position in the world. He became a member of the household of William Rufus, and was a great favourite of his master. At the death of that monarch, Thurstan was made the chaplain and the confidential secretary of his brother, the new king.[u] He was clearly marked out for greatness, but up to this time the only clerical appointment which he enjoyed was a canonry at St. Paul's.[v]

Archbishop Thomas died in 1114, and Thurstan was nominated by the king to succeed him. This was done at Winchester on the festival of the Assumption of the Blessed Virgin.[w] The difficulties which had beset his predecessors soon forced themselves upon his consideration. Thurstan had a stouter spirit and far greater influence than those who went before him, and he was not disposed to submit to the claims of Canterbury, to which they had been obliged to succumb. He speaks about the matter to the king.[x] He tells him that it was improper that a metropolitan should make two professions of ecclesiastical subjection, one to the pope, and the other to his brother metropolitan. Supposing that a dispute arose between the king and the Southern primate, the archbishop of York, in consequence of his oath, would be obliged to obey the latter. The king, in reply to these words, told the comte de Meulent that he would not require Thurstan to make any profession to Canterbury.

Thurstan, at this time, was only a subdeacon, but in the

[u] Saxon Chron., 334. Chron. de Mailros, 65. Stubbs, 1714.

[v] His stall was the prebend Consumpta per mare, the corpus having been swallowed up by the sea before the Conquest. (Newcourt, i., 141.) When Thurstan became archbishop, the bishop of London allowed him to resign this stall. (Hugh Cantor.)

The Beverley historians made Thurstan the second provost of that church, but there is no proof that he was at all connected with the place (Poulson, 646. Oliver, 385.) Herbert de Losinga wrote a letter to a person whom he addressed as "Thurstin, monachus," who may perhaps be identical with our archbishop, recommending caution and freedom from worldly-mindedness, and beginning "tuam abhorrens hæreditatem, frater Thurstine, peregrinis delectaris divitiis, et nostra arundinea condempnens tuguria, marmoreis habitas in palatiis" (Epist. ed. Anstruther, 8vo, 1846, 58). In the same volume (217) there is also a letter from Elmer, prior of Canterbury, "ad Turstanum, archidiaconum," on religious subjects.

[w] Saxon Chron., 334. Fl. Wigorn., 488. Chron. Mailros, 65. Symeon, col. 236. Bromton, col. 1005. Hoveden, 271. Hemingford, apud Gale, ii., 472. Eadmer (Hist. Nov., 90) says that he was elected "connivente Radulfo archiepiscopo, et aliam quam rei exitus probavit, de eo habente opinionem." Rob. de Monte, 688.

[x] The narrative of the troubles and exile of Thurstan is taken from the account of his life by Hugh the Chantor, which is still unpublished. The writer was an officer in the church of York and was well acquainted with Thurstan, and tells us a good deal about him, which has been hitherto unknown. I have based my life of the archbishop upon this MS. The character of Thurstan has been judged and condemned up to this time on the testimony of the partizans of Canterbury, now *audi alteram partem*. Stubbs has taken from Hugh the greater part of his narrative, omitting much that is important (col. 1714-20). I have given references to other writers when they corroborate or differ from Hugh.

month of December he was advanced to the diaconate by his old friend and patron, William, bishop of Winchester. He then paid a visit to the North. At York he met with an honourable reception, and was solemnly enthroned in the minster by Robert, bishop of Lichfield. He went from thence to Durham, and became the guest of bishop Flambard, an unprincipled but potent statesman. He there beheld, probably for the first time, the noble cathedral which St. Carileph had begun, and within its walls he had an interview with Turgot, who had left his see of St. Andrew's to die in the monastery of St. Cuthbert, of which he had been the ornament and the head. The great scholar was stretched upon that bed which he never left alive.[y] He was delighted to see his new superior, and promised him his allegiance if he were spared to render it. Thurstan spent, after this, a few days at Hexham to supervise the good work of Thomas, and then he returned to York. As soon as the bishop of Lichfield left him he began to busy himself with the affairs of his new cure, and to meditate upon the future. The thought of the dreaded profession which he would soon be required to make induced him to seek for counsel from his chapter. They declined to give him any advice, as their past difficulties were still remembered. They told him, however, that on his side there would be custom, justice, and the decree of Gregory; on the other, the king and nearly the whole of England: no one was more conversant with the canons than himself, and it was not for them to recommend him what to do: if he declined to make the profession, and should be ejected for his contumacy, they would obey no one else. The frankness of this reply would please Thurstan, and he told them that he was unwilling to make the required profession of inferiority, and that he would go to Rome, if possible, and refer the matter to the pope. They then gladly acknowledged him as their ecclesiastical superior, although he was only in deacon's orders. They drew up letters to the pope announcing his election, and Thurstan, having selected several of the canons to accompany him, prepared himself to cross the seas. The king had been for some months in Normandy, and Thurstan wished to see him.

The archbishop of Canterbury had already desired him to come to him to be consecrated priest and prelate, and now the summons was repeated. It was declined, and Thurstan, about Christmas, 1114, reached the court in Normandy. He re-

[y] In Eadmer (90, 97-100) are letters from the king of Scotland to archbishop Ralph announcing Turgot's death, and asking his advice about his successor. Eadmer's own difficulties about this see prompted the pen of Nicholas to write the letter on the right of the see of York to the primacy of Scotland, which is printed in the Anglia Sacra, ii., 230-6.

quested permission to visit Rome, but the archbishop had anticipated his petition, and the king put his veto upon the proposed journey. The cardinal-bishop of Præneste was at that time the papal legate in France, and Henry, who scarcely knew how to act, sought for his advice. What was he to do with Thurstan, who was not a priest, and whom the primate of Canterbury would not consecrate without the profession which the other would not make? The answer of the legate was prompt and decisive. He told the king that Thurstan might easily be ordained priest by one of the suffragans at the court; when that ceremony was over, he would himself direct him to the pope, who would solve the difficulty at once by consecrating Thurstan himself, and giving him the pall. This advice was only followed in part. To the consecration at Rome Henry would not consent, but he permitted Flambard, bishop of Durham, to ordain Thurstan priest. This, according to Stubbs, was done at Bayeux in Normandy.

The year advanced, and things remained as they were. The court, however, returned to England. The delay was most annoying and wearisome to Thurstan, but this was only the beginning of his troubles. About Michaelmas there was a council at London, and the king alluded to the unfortunate dispute between Canterbury and York. The comte de Meulent and Nigel d'Albeni[e] were standing by, and Thurstan, availing himself of the opportunity, complained with justice of the great delay in his consecration. Henry advised him to take some honourable and trustworthy person, and to go and ask the archbishop to grant his often-preferred request. If any unjust demand should be made, he had the king's permission to refer the matter to the pope. Upon this Thurstan went to Ralph; Geoffrey, archbishop of Rouen, John, bishop of Lisieux, his old friend Ranulph Flambard, and many others, accompanying him. Ralph, however, refused to consecrate without the profession. Thurstan then announced his intention of appealing to Rome. "If the pope were to meet me face to face, and order me to waive my demand and consecrate you, I would not obey him," was the hasty and ill-judged reply. The party then returned to the king, and Thurstan begged earnestly to be permitted to visit the papal court. He was emboldened by what Henry had recently said, and he spoke out, "It was a sin and a crime that the matter should remain so long unsettled. The church of York was being injured; the diocese was going

[e] There is a long account of this distinguished person in L'Art de vérifier les Dates, ed. 1784, ii., part ii., 692. Nigel d'Albeni afterwards assumed the name of Mowbray, and was the progenitor of a long line of illustrious barons.

to ruin. It was hard to be an archbishop in name only without the power to act. The king would be blamed at Rome for sanctioning all this, and was that right? Would Henry allow him to go, or, at all events, to send a messenger to Rome?" The king would not move. He was too indolent to be an active partizan, and the archbishop of Canterbury reproached Thurstan in his hearing for having summoned him to Rome without the permission of the sovereign. Henry had neither the spirit nor the fairness to say that that leave had just been given.

In the meantime the letters which the chapter of York had written to the pope announcing the election of Thurstan, and deprecating any farther delay in his consecration, have been lost sight of. They were drawn up in the winter of 1114, but a whole year elapsed before they were delivered.[a] Before that time the chief pontiff must have heard of the dispute from other sources.[b] He at last received the letters of the chapter, and answered them immediately. The reply was everything that could be wished for. Paschal confirmed the choice of the chapter, and directed the archbishop of Canterbury to consecrate Thurstan without any profession and without delay. The bearer of these missives arrived in England in Lent 1116, when the king was holding a council at Salisbury. Henry had gradually been brought over to take the part of Canterbury, and a vigorous attempt was now made to bring Thurstan to submission. The king brought his influence to bear upon him. He sent the comte de Meulent, William, earl of Warren his brother-in-law, William the chamberlain, and Nigel d'Albeni to Thurstan, beseeching him, in recollection of the kindness which he had received from himself and his brother, not to break the customs of the land, and scandalize the church by withholding the profession. Thurstan made a noble and a bold reply. He acknowledged with pleasure his debt of gratitude to the king and his brother. No one shall question his loyalty or his love of order. Where is the injury to the law or the scandal to religion in his standing up for his own church, which it is his duty to protect? To defend the right is one half of the diadem of the king,—"the brightest jewel in his crown,"—and the judge ought not to

[a] Eadmer (90) speaks of Thurstan sending letters to the pope which were of no avail.

[b] Ivo, bishop of Chartres, writes to Paschal begging him to defend the see of York and to confirm Thurstan's election, "Qui, quantum ad personam pertinet, continentis est vitæ et honestæ famæ, et utilis, quantum humana conscientia de alterius vita potest judicare, sanctæ Dei ecclesiæ" (Epist., ed. 1610, 482). There is another courteous and complimentary letter from Ivo to Thurstan in the same work (375). Hildebert, bishop of Mans, writes to Thurstan contradicting the report that he wished to go to Rome to take the part of Canterbury against him (Hildeberti episc. Cenomaneus. Opp., ed. 1708, appendix, p. 1. Ivonis Carnotens. episc. Epist., 790).

make himself a partizan. Let the real originator of the scandal recollect who it was that said, "Woe to that man by whom the offence cometh." He neither can nor dare make this profession in contravention of the decrees of Gregory, Honorius, and Urban. If his predecessors rashly or by compulsion did otherwise, what is that to him? The sanctuary of God cannot be inherited. He humbly intreated the king to judge according to the right by himself and his church. The royal messengers returned and told the king what Thurstan had said. He was then in his chapel with archbishop Ralph. The hot blood of his father boiled within his veins. He sent them back to Thurstan to tell him that if he continued to refuse to make the profession, banishment and ruin should befall him and all his kindred, and that he should lose York altogether.[c] It was this threat which extorted the compliance of two of his immediate predecessors, but Thurstan was undaunted. He paused awhile, for it was a time for deliberation, and then he made the courageous reply, "It is painful indeed for me to incur the king's perpetual dislike, but it is much more painful to be a conscious offender against God and the church of Rome. I shall do neither: I shall restore to the king everything that he has given me." The words were reported to the king. How strange they must have sounded in the ears of worldly and selfish men! The archbishop would not believe that they had been spoken. The comte de Meulent, who was kindly disposed towards Thurstan, then observed that he did not understand that Thurstan had *refused* to do what was required. Let him be summoned and answer for himself. He came and repeated what he had said before. He laid his hand on that of the king and surrendered to him, as his suzerain, everything that he possessed.[d] The scene was an affecting one, and many were in tears, nay, even the king was moved. Pleasure, however, was visibly written upon the face of Ralph, who had not yet received his letter from the pope, for Thurstan had forgot to bring it with him. With a strange want of feeling he turned to the York clergy, and blamed them for depriving their head of his archbishopric by their evil counsels. They were all weeping, and the voice of Thurstan was raised at once in their behalf. He bore a noble testimony to the honesty of their motives, their

[c] Eadmer, 90, who is quoted by Symeon, col. 237. Diceto, col. 502. Bromton, col. 1006. Gervase, col. 1661. Knyghton, 2379. Hoveden, 271 *b*. Matt. Paris, 55. Chron. Petrib., 78. Wilkins, i., 393.

[d] Eadmer (90) says that he gave it up and promised never to seek for it again during his life. This is copied by Fl. Wigorn., 490. Hoveden, 271 *b*. Symeon, col. 237. Gervase, col. 1661. Bromton, col. 1006. Hemingford, apud Gale, ii., 473.—Malmesbury, 156.

learning and their excellence,[e] and declared that with their help he was still ready to maintain the right.

The news spread far and wide through the English dominions on either side of the channel. Astonishment and sorrow were uppermost in men's minds; astonishment, that so loyal and trusty a subject had been thus treated; and sorrow, that he had suffered in the cause of right and justice. The chapter of York wrote an affectionate letter to Thurstan, commending his past conduct, and exhorting him to endurance. The pope sent a sharp reproof to Ralph, and ordered him to give way, but he neglected this mandate as he had despised the other. In the meantime Thurstan entreated the king to have pity upon the diocese which should have been his, and to appoint another archbishop. Henry, however, did not do this: he felt, probably, that he had gone too far already, and nothing more was done.

Henry now paid another visit to Normandy, and Thurstan went with him. He was still treated by his master with respect. The present position of himself and his church was uppermost in his thoughts. When he had requested Henry to nominate an archbishop in his room, he had declined, with the remark that the see, in his opinion, was not vacant. What could now be done? Thurstan began to regret his recent resignation: he could not properly make it, as he thought: how could he give up to the king what he had not received from him? it was the pope who had confirmed his election; the pope ought clearly to be the arbiter. He urgently entreated Henry to allow him to go to Rome, and his friends seconded his prayers. It was all in vain.[e] The king was unmoved, and Thurstan remained at the court in what was, in point of fact, a kind of honourable restraint.[f] He could not steal away from his master, and he was afraid of exasperating him farther. Henry himself had sent the bishop of Exeter to Rome to take the advice of the pope about the question in dispute, and he now returned after a fruitless journey. He gave, however, a hint to the archbishop of Canterbury, of which that prelate at once availed himself, and the primate, at his suggestion, started at once for the papal court.

After a lapse of three months several representatives of the York chapter reached the king. That body had resolved to demand their archbishop as a matter of right and justice, and for that purpose they sent two of their archdeacons—a canon of

[e] Eadmer, 90. Chron. Mailros, 63. Symeon, col. 238. Gervase, col. 1661. Hoveden, 271 b.

[f] "Ab Anglia longa cathena retentus in Normanniam quasi sub custodia detinebatur" (Hugh).

Beverley and a monk of St. Mary's Abbey. When these persons solicited an interview, Henry sent them a message to demand why they had crossed the seas without his permission. They replied that they thought that in such a case the royal licence would be unnecessary. The king would not see them then, but fixed the day and the place for an interview. He now began to weary them with delays. They were disappointed three or four times, but at length they obtained the wished-for meeting, Flambard, bishop of Durham, and several other friends, accompanying them. They required their archbishop at the king's hands, speaking of the injury which his absence was doing to the church and diocese of York. It was at their request that Thurstan had been ordained deacon and priest; they had made him the provost of their souls, and had promised to obey him, why should they lack his superintendence? If they could not have him, whom were they to have? The pope alone could absolve them from their oath of subjection to Thurstan, and give them another archbishop.[g] There was much reason in what they said, and the king, at their most earnest request, promised to take the subject into his immediate consideration. After a conference with Thurstan they proceeded homewards. As soon as they were gone Thurstan renewed his old petition, but without effect. He was desired to wait till the archbishop of Canterbury returned. Thurstan then mentioned a report that Ralph had resolved to make a pilgrimage to Jerusalem, in which case there was little chance of his coming home. "It matters little to me," said the king, "what either of you say or do; it is my wish to hear the opinion of the pope from his own lips." Ralph at last came back vexed and disappointed with his journey, and Thurstan again made a fruitless appeal to Henry, reminding him of his past promises. The heart of the king was hardened like that of Pharaoh. Ralph had been whispering in his ear that his adversary, if he went to Rome, might perhaps be consecrated, and that was, of all things, to be prevented. Thurstan was bitterly disappointed. He would not make the king his open enemy, but how vain it was to hope for an alteration in his opinion. He began to cast in his mind what he should do. It was ignominious and unjust that he should be thus treated. He seems to have thought of leaving the court without the king's permission, and in this emergency he again sought the advice of the chapter. They entreated him, if it were possible, to retain Henry's good opinion. If his departure should be sanctioned he might take any of their body with him: in any case he might have them, but if he left the

[g] This embassy is mentioned in Eadmer, 92.

court by stealth it would be unsafe and unfair to leave them behind. William de Beverley, their last messenger to the pope, had been very closely questioned by the king. At the same time the chapter sent to Thurstan another epistle, which he was to deliver to the pope. In it they appealed to his justice and compassion. Their hopes and hearts were fixed upon him. They told him that Ralph had inveighed against the venality of the papal court, which all the world, they said, knew to be a false charge. The letter was an adroit mixture of flattery and abuse. It was conveyed, in all probability, to Paschal by some messenger of Thurstan or the chapter.

The pope's reply reached the English court in Normandy by the hands of Anselm, afterwards abbat of St. Edmund's, who was a nephew of the celebrated archbishop, and the legate to England. Paschal requested the king to restore the see of York to Thurstan and to hasten his consecration, and he took upon himself to settle any dispute which might arise.[h] He ordered Ralph to do his duty at once without the profession, which he had no right to demand; if he persisted in refusing, the suffragans of the see of York should act in his stead. This letter, however, was not given to the archbishop at the time. The decision of the royal council was unanimous in Thurstan's favour, and he was restored to his lost position.[i] It was his intention to place the pope's missive in the hands of Ralph as soon as he returned to his province, where alone he could consecrate him. In the meantime, full of joy at his good fortune, Thurstan went back to York. Several months pass away, and Ralph never comes to England. He was evidently loitering abroad to avoid the fulfilment of the papal mandate.

It was now the month of February, 1118, and there was every expectation at York that the great dispute would speedily be terminated. "There is many a slip between the cup and the lip." The unexpected news was brought of the death of Paschal, and of the accession of John Gaetano to the papal chair under the title of Gelasius II. Everything was to be begun again, and no time was to be lost, as the new pontiff was in France. A messenger was at once sent off to state the case, and enlist the sympathies of the pope, and Thurstan prepared to follow him. He must cross the seas to Normandy, and pass on to have an interview, if possible, with Gelasius. It was treason to leave the country without the permission of the king, and the utmost secresy was necessary. Thurstan and a few companions make their way to London, seemingly upon a different errand.

[h] This letter is also printed in Eadmer, 92, and Malmesbury, 156. Labbe, Conc., x., 655. Wilkins, i., 376. Ivonis Carnotens. Episc. Epistolæ, 793. Rymer's Fœdera, *n. e.*, i., 9.

[i] Eadmer, 92.

They now separate to reach the coast as they best can. A rendezvous in Normandy had been appointed. Thurstan condescended to disguise himself, and rode to Dover with his father, and got safely across : the rest of the party took ship at Hastings. The plans of the adventurers had been laid with the greatest secrecy, but still some rumours had reached the king, and Thurstan had been waiting for the rest a single night in Normandy when he was discovered. Henry demanded the reason of his coming,[j] and Thurstan, who was too honest to slur over or conceal the truth, gave him a prompt reply, "It is neither fit nor decent for myself or my church that I should remain in York an archbishop merely in name. I know too that the archbishop of Canterbury is the cause of this. He is aware that I have letters from the pope commanding him to consecrate me. By his staying here to thwart me he has deprived both York and Canterbury of its metropolitan. I have come to see the new pope, that he may release me from my sinecure, but I shall not go to him without your knowledge and consent." The king, satisfied apparently with the answer, told him that he would reply to what he had said on the morrow. Some letters from Gelasius, evoked no doubt by Thurstan's messenger, had already reached him. The pope took up the cause of York with more warmth than his predecessor. If the dispute were continued, he desired Henry to send both Ralph and Thurstan to the papal court. To the former he used the strong language of indignant reproof.

Soon after this Thurstan had an interview with Ralph, and offered to give him Paschal's letters which he had so long retained. Ralph would not receive them. Of what use are they, he cried, for that pope is dead? At last he promised to inspect them, and then to give his answer. He now began to defend his conduct. He could not, he said, consecrate Thurstan out of England, and, at present, he had no intention of returning, as he was going to see the French king. Thurstan upon this again begged Henry to allow him to meet the pope, but in vain. He might send a messenger, if he liked. Another delay now unexpectedly arose. Thurstan's messengers were with the king of France at Vercignies when they heard that Gelasius was dead, and that he had been interred at Clugny.

Guy, archbishop of Vienne, was his successor under the title of Calixtus II. He was elected to the papal chair in the beginning of February, 1119. As he had been so recently appointed, he very properly declined to proceed to the immediate consideration of appeals. He spent some time in a tour through Bur-

[j] Eadmer (93) says that Thurstan came to the king at Rouen. He forbade his journey "donec certiorem de processu papæ sententiam edisceret."

gundy and Aquitaine, and at length held a council at Narbonne. He there heard from many mouths the story of the wrongs of Thurstan. He wrote at once an angry letter to Ralph rebuking him for his pride and disobedience. The archbishop was alarmed, and wished to explain his conduct in a personal interview; but the king of France and the comte de Angers, who had warmly espoused the cause of Thurstan, refused to grant him letters of safe-conduct, or to allow him to enter their territories. Ralph, therefore, could only write a deprecatory letter. He begged not to be censured unheard. He expressed his willingness and ability to explain everything to the pope, if he were only permitted to visit him. He had not received the mandates of Paschal and Gelasius whilst they were alive; how then could he obey them? In a subsequent epistle he spoke in a somewhat humbler tone, and endeavoured to vindicate himself from the charge of pride.

It was most necessary for Thurstan's interests that he should have an interview with Calixtus, but he was retained by the king's side. Ralph was now thoroughly alarmed. He knew that the pope was offended at him, and that Thurstan had many powerful supporters. Calixtus was at no great distance, and he was terrified at the idea of his opponent reaching him. He entreated Henry to send Thurstan home to England. He, it will be imagined, was as anxious to remain. Of what use, he said, can I be in my church of York at the festival of Easter which is approaching? How can I consecrate or celebrate as I ought? The matter was deferred; but Henry expressed a wish that he should return as soon as Easter was over. Thurstan placed himself at the disposal of God and of the king.

The pope had now resolved to hold a council at Rheims; and summoned to it the prelates who bare office in France, Germany, Burgundy, and Provênce. He requested Henry to send his two archbishops, and told Ralph that he would there be obliged to answer for his disobedience. The king was perplexed. Thurstan saw by this time the folly of trusting to his promises, and resolved to leave Normandy before long, whether Henry wished it or not. He sought, for the last time, his leave to be present at the council to which he had been invited; but it was refused unless he would pledge himself not to receive consecration from the pope. Thurstan would promise nothing; and sheltered himself under a text, that never-failing resource of ecclesiastics when they were in a difficulty. He would render unto Cæsar the things that were Cæsar's, and unto God the things that were God's.[k] At this crisis the bishop of Exeter,

[k] Eadmer (94) says that Thurstan was under a strict obligation that he would not be consecrated, or do anything to the prejudice of Canterbury,

the well-known William de Warlewast, came to Henry from Calixtus, and told him that Thurstan might safely be permitted to depart, as there was no chance of his being consecrated. The king, therefore, allowed him at last to go.

Thurstan left the court with the delight which the released captive feels. He had been too long one of Pharaoh's bondsmen not to value the blessings of liberty and freedom. He was speedily at Chartres, where several of his friends were waiting for him who had promised to aid him in his flight, for which preparations had been made. They were overjoyed to find that he was not a fugitive. Four days after this the party reached the papal court at Tours. His reception was cordial in the extreme. Pope and prince seemed to vie with each other in the warmth of their praises and attentions. The sufferings which the honest-hearted English priest had borne so heroically for five long years had won the sympathy of all.[l] He met Calixtus at the celebration of the great feast of Easter in the church of St. Maurice at Tours, and for half a year he was scarcely ever from his side. The charm of manner which had fascinated the Red king, and captivated or mollified his successor was now visible to all. Thurstan played the courtier with the ease and dignity which were native to him. He was full of ready wit, with a great facility of expressing himself, and a marvellous power of adapting himself to others. No one was more ready to receive or to manifest a kindness. He became a great favourite with king Louis and his nobles. He was flattered and admired by all. And yet in those days France had children of her own who were full of piety and genius. What country has not heard of Clairvaux and its sainted founder? How many have wept and wondered at the learning and the loves of Abelard?

There would be much curiosity to know what Calixtus would do to restore Thurstan to his right. At the castle of Blois two of the York archdeacons and a scholar, who had accompanied the exile, placed his case before the pope, who promised, in kind terms, to consult with the Sacred College. They spoke to him again near Paris, some time after this, when Calixtus was leaving the church of St. Martin des Champes, and he expressed his hope that everything would be arranged at the council.

and that the pope had also made a promise to Sieffrid, the king's messenger, that he would do nothing to injure the see of Canterbury. This statement has been adopted and followed by Symeon, col. 240; and Malmesbury, 156 *b*; and, partly, by Diceto, col. 503. Bromton, col. 1008, 1014. Gervase, col. 1661. Wendover, i., 470. Chron. Petrib., 79.

[l] Eadmer (94) insinuates that he won their favour by bribes. He is followed and quoted by Diceto, col. 503. Bromton, col. 1014. Wendover, i., 470. Chron. Petrib., 79.

That assembly was held at Rheims in October, 1119. It was to begin on the Monday. On the Saturday evening the pope sent for Thurstan, and told him, to his great delight, that he should be consecrated on the morrow. The archbishop of Canterbury was not coming, and the bishops from Normandy and England had not yet arrived. Ralph, bishop of Orkney, was at Thurstan's side. He had come to Rheims two days before with one of the York archdeacons, on a visit to the exiled primate.

The scene at Rheims on Sunday, the 20th of October, 1119, must have been a magnificent one. Many a brilliant spectacle, many a stirring adventure, has that fair city witnessed. It is associated with French history from the very earliest times. The sovereigns were crowned within its walls. We think of the triumphs and the munificence of Clovis, and the most striking incident in the victorious career of the Jungfrau. We see her looking upon the city, and listening to the words of the black knight:—

> "Schau hin! Dort hebt sich Rheims mit seiner thürmon,
> Das ziel und ende deiner fahrt—die kuppel
> Der hohen kathedrale siehst du leuchten,
> Dort wirst du einziehn im triumphgepräng,
> Deinen könig krönen."

Flodoardus has described the glories of the archbishopric which dates from the close of the third century. No less than nine of the early prelates who presided over it are enshrined in the calendar. We can still read of the learning of Hincmar, of the miracles of Remigius, and his wondrous walk. In the beginning of the twelfth century Rheims was one of the greatest sees in Europe. At least fifteen councils had been held at that place; and, at the most recent, the terrors of excommunication had been thundered against the emperor Henry. On the occasion which I shall now describe, the great church of St. Mary was crowded with illustrious ecclesiastics who had come to take part in the deliberations that were to begin on the morrow. An honest and simple-hearted priest was in that throng to witness, after years of suffering and neglect, his own triumph. There would be but few there who were ignorant of Thurstan and his trials. Now he was to be rewarded. Calixtus summoned him forth, and consecrated him with his own hands before that vast assembly.[m] One voice alone was raised against that act. John,

[m] Saxon Chron., 334. Eadmer, 94. Fl. Wigorn., 494. Chron. Mailros, 66. Symeon, col. 240. John of Hexham, col. 266, who says that Thurstan was consecrated "intercedentibus cardinalibus." Diceto, col. 503. Bromton, col. 1008. Gervase, col. 1661. Knyghton, col. 2379, who censures the pope. Malmesbury, 131 *b*, 156 *b*. Hoveden, 272. Mat. Paris, 56. Ann. Waverl., apud Gale, ii., 147. Hemingford, ibid., 474. Labbe Conc., ix., 878.

archdeacon of Canterbury and the nephew of the archbishop, was the only representative of his church who was there. Undaunted by the presence in which he found himself, and careless of sympathy or aid, he arose, and, with an honest intrepidity, protested against this apparent violation of the privileges of his uncle and his see.[n] What he said was disregarded. The Italians laughed at him; and as he left the church, he heard around him several expressions of contumely and insult. Ralph, when he heard of what had occurred, wrote a long expostulatory letter to Calixtus.[o]

Late on the same day, the English and Norman bishops arrived at Rheims. Henry had desired them to oppose the consecration of Thurstan, and to send him home if he should be disposed to neglect their advice. As they neared the city they heard of what had been done. They were greatly troubled and perplexed. There were some who looked with sorrow upon the too certain consequences of Thurstan's disobedience. The bishop of Exeter, in particular, reproached himself for advising the king to permit him to leave the court. All, however, were agreed as to the folly and heinousness of the offence, and they resolved to have no communication with the culprit. On the morrow, when they went to the council, they kept aloof from him. Flambard, his own suffragan, would not sit beside him lest he should offend the king. The faithful bishop of Orkney was the only prelate who was near him. Several of his old friends, however, seem to have seen Thurstan secretly during the continuance of the council. He heard from them that he would certainly be disseised of his archiepiscopal lands. The king of England was excessively indignant when he heard what had occurred. He vowed that Thurstan should never return to his country during his own life unless he professed obedience to Canterbury.[p] He then made enquiries about the pall, but no one could say that it had been given. The pope presented it to Thurstan on the twelfth day after the conclusion of the council, and enjoined him to mention the circumstance to no one as long as he was in France. Soon after

[n] Eadmer, 94. Labbe, x., 878, where it is said that the archbishop of Lyons kept away from the council on account of what was to be done. The pope, in answer to what John said, vindicated himself from the charge of breaking his word, "Quod feci, semper salva justicia Cantuariensis ecclesiæ, si qua est, facio" (Hugh). In Martene (Thes. Anecd., iii., 884) it is said that Thurstan was at Rheims with two suffragans.

[o] Twysden, col. 1735-48, Wilkins, i., 396-404, where the letter is printed entire. Somner's Canterbury, part ii., 149.

[p] The chroniclers say, in general terms, that he was forbidden to return, *e.g.*, Saxon Chron., 340. Eadmer, 94. Symeon, col. 241. Diceto, col. 503. Bromton, col. 1008. Gervase, col. 1661. Knyghton, col. 2379. Malmesbury, 156 *b*. Mat. Paris, 56. Ann. Waverl., apud Gale, ii., 147. Hemingford, ibid., 473.

this, when they were at Beauvais, Calixtus gave him a letter to his suffragans in the North of England, in which the bishops of Durham, Orkney, and Glasgow were addressed. The pope informed them that Thurstan had been duly consecrated, and desired them to regard him as their ecclesiastical superior.

The council lasted eight days, and the pope was detained in Rheims for fifteen more, by an attack of illness. During this time Thurstan was not idle. Everything now depended upon his reconciliation with Henry; and how was it to be effected? He joined Conon, bishop of Præneste, and the other cardinals in entreating Calixtus to have an interview with the king, and to make peace, if that were possible, between France and England. He was desirous, also, that the pope should speak to the English king in his behalf. After much hesitation, Calixtus desired a conference, and mentioned a day and the place where they could meet. Henry readily assented, for the pope and he were cousins. They saw each other at a church between the castles of Chaumont and Gisors,[q] in the neighbourhood of Rouen. The king of France was at that time at Sens. On the question of peace, very little seems to have been said.[r] Both sides expressed their wishes for it, which it is easy enough to do when you have war all the while in your heart. The dispute with Thurstan was then brought forward, and the pope and cardinals urged its speedy termination. Calixtus was indignant at Ralph of Canterbury and his disobedience. He had himself consecrated Thurstan, he said, to leave the matter undecided, and he was desirous of adjudicating upon it at Rome. He implored Henry to receive Thurstan kindly, as rumours of his punishment had already reached him. Henry, after accounting for the absence of Ralph from the council on the score of ill health, assured Calixtus that he could not gratify him. He had made a vow that Thurstan should not enter England during his life-time without making the profession of obedience to Ralph, but not to his successors. Would the pope sanction and confirm this? Calixtus would not do so, and he told the king that as the profession would be unlawful, his vow was unlawful also, and that he would absolve him from it; but Henry cautiously observed that he could not act otherwise without deliberating with his council. All attempts to alter the king's determination were fruitless. It would have been undignified if Calixtus had begun to beseech. Nothing more, therefore, was said at that time, although the pope was deeply offended and annoyed.

[q] This castle was built by William Rufus, and strengthened by Henry, who frequently resided there (Wm. Gemiticensis, apud Camden, 673).

[r] There is an account of this interview in Eadmer, 94-5. Symeon, col. 241. Bromton, col. 1008. Hoveden, 272 *b*.

Before Henry went away, some overtures were made to Thurstan, and he was entreated, for the sake of peace, to yield. They were indignantly rejected.

After this meeting, Henry returned at once to England and disseised Thurstan of his archiepiscopal property, without meddling with that of his clergy. He was reconciled with difficulty to the bishop of Orkney and the archdeacon who had been at Rheims, although they protested that their presence at the council had been accidental. Hard measures were dealt out to Thurstan at home, but, abroad, he was regarded with much sympathy and compassion. The pope was severely censured for not seeing justice done to him. Calixtus assured him that he should want for nothing from the church of Rome till he was restored. The cardinals made him their friend and companion. He heard causes among them, and was with them even in their secret conclaves. They gave him money and everything that he required. They openly expressed their displeasure at his not having been fairly treated by Rome. The archbishop of Rouen spoke on that point in strong terms. When the king and queen of France met them at the abbey of Ferrière, they begged him to advance Thurstan to a bishopric or some higher office, and he consented. When Calixtus was leaving Ferrière for Sens, he made Thurstan his legate in France, Aquitaine, and Normandy. This honour would have involved a separation from his friends and the retarding of his restoration. The exile would now think,—

> "Quam fessis finem rebus ferat, unde laborum
> Tentare auxilium jubeat, quo vertere cursus."

With tears and most earnest entreaties he begged for a continuance of their good offices. They were at once promised, and from that time Thurstan was constantly in their company. They seemed to treat him with increasing kindness. At Auxerre he contracted a friendship with two great and learned scholars, cardinal Peter de Pisa, and Guy de Castro, archdeacon of Pisa, and the friend of St. Bernard,[a] better known in after-times as Celestine II. When the pope was crowned, Thurstan rode in the procession by the side of the bishop of Ostia, the most distinguished of the cardinals, and Calixtus gave him two hundred bezants of gold, the same sum which all the cardinals received. He raised, at the pope's request, the provost of Geneva to the three minor degrees of orders, preparatory to his consecration as bishop of that beautiful province. He officiated at the dedication of churches, and arranged the programme on such occasions. He was allowed to wear his pall even in the

[a] S. Bernardi Opp., ed. 1690, i., 307.

presence of the pope, a very high and unusual privilege. Every little attention seems to have been shewn to him, which would gratify an upright man and raise the spirits of an exile.[t]

Archbishop Ralph now made a last attempt to recover the ground which he had lost. Henry, at his request, sent the bishop of Exeter to the pope to see what could be done. Conon, the papal legate in France, had heard of his mission, and wrote about it to Thurstan and the cardinals. Bishop Warlewast found Calixtus at Valencia. He was an old politician, and was well acquainted with the ways of the Roman court, but now he could do nothing. The cardinals and the pope were obdurate. As a last resource, he desired Calixtus to make Thurstan render the required profession, and then to send him as his legate into England. The meaning of this was so patent that there was no chance of its being acceded to. Warlewast's bribes were of no avail, and his embassy was fruitless. He returned to Henry, having shewn some better feeling towards Thurstan before he went. The shrewd politician had probably observed some symptoms of a change. He must have witnessed the regard which all manifested towards Thurstan. Some too zealous clients of the Roman court were even desirous of molesting the ambassador on his homeward journey.

Calixtus at last resolved to act with energy and decision. He was in the neighbourhood of Rimini, the point nearest to Rome that Thurstan then reached.[u] It was resolved that the church of York should be for ever freed from the profession to Canterbury, and that to the charter of exemption the papal bull should be affixed. This, together with letters to the clergy of the diocese of York and to Henry, who was threatened with excommunication if he were contumacious, was to be conveyed to the English court by the archbishop of Tours and the bishop of Beauvais. Thurstan now made himself ready for his departure. The pope gave him his benediction, together with some relics which Thurstan had desired, and which were treasured long afterwards in the minster at York.[v] He made him a present, also, of some holy oil. "If you had asked me for my own blood," Calixtus jocularly observed, "you should not have been refused." The bishops and cardinals escorted him without the town, and bade him farewell with many tears and expressions of their affection. For half a year he had lived with them as a brother; and he was deeply grateful for their kindness. Before he started on his journey he had heard of the

[t] Eadmer (95) says with a sneer, "Thurstanus papam secutus est, sed non diu ab eo, ne præsentia ejus gravaretur, detentus."

[u] The Saxon Chron. (341) tells us that he went to Rome.

[v] Fabric Rolls of York Minster, ed. Surtees Soc., 152.

death of his old adversary, Ralph of Canterbury, and every one would now feel that the chief stumbling-block in the way of his restoration had been removed. The news, however, was premature: Ralph had been seized with the palsy, but he survived this attack for two years.[w]

Thurstan's journey resembled in some respects a triumphal progress. All along the route he was treated with courtesy and respect. Every castle was open to him, and he was welcomed everywhere by the clergy and the laity. They assured him that if their resources had not been crippled by the recent visit of the pope he should have had a far more befitting reception. Thurstan entered France, but, prudently and like a good patriot, avoided an interview with the king, who was an enemy of England. He became the guest of Adele, countess of Blois, and her son count Theobald. That high-born lady was a daughter of William the Conqueror, and was sister, therefore, to Henry I. She was delighted to receive Thurstan. He soon paid a visit to Rheims, and thanked the archbishop, who seems to have supported him to a great extent during his exile, for his kindness. At Soissons he met the legate Conon, who had always been his friend. After an affectionate greeting, Thurstan told him about the letters from the pope, and desired him to make provision for their transmission to the English court. After this he returned to the countess of Blois, and was with her several days.[x] During this time he had many conversations with her about taking the veil, and she resolved to do so. On Easter-day, 1120, he sang the high mass in the church of Coulomb, the first occasion of the kind on which he had worn his pall. Three days after this he had another interview with the legate, who informed him that the archbishop of Tours and the bishop of Beauvais were too much occupied to go on the mission to Henry: two persons of repute and learning, an abbat and a prior, would act in their stead. Thurstan now went back to the countess of Blois, and with a noble train accompanied her to the convent of Marcigny, where she professed herself a nun. She had been the wife of Stephen, count of Blois, in 1081, and had borne him six children, one of whom was Stephen, king of England. She was a woman of a masculine and intrepid spirit, with little feminine delicacy or softness.[y] Her elder son was disinherited by his father through her instrumentality.

[w] In the Anglia Sacra (i., 7) it is said that this attack disabled Ralph, and made Thurstan bolder.

[x] John of Hexham (col. 266) speaks of the influence Thurstan had over this lady.

[y] "Qua, quidem, testimonio regis Ludovici et principum totius Franciæ, nulla prudencior, nec melius composita, nec magis virilis virago ex multa retro ætate in tota Gallia extiterat" (Hugh). Ivo, bishop of Chartres, did not hesitate to rebuke her in strong language (Epist., ed. 1610, p. 322). Hildebert,

Her husband died in the East in 1102,[z] and after his decease, in conjunction with her son Theobald or Thibaut, she ruled over the lands of Blois. She died in the convent of Marcigny in 1137, having been a nun for seventeen years.[a] She went to that place in all probability at the suggestion of Thurstan, who had been present when it was consecrated by Calixtus a few months before the countess took the veil.[b] About the same time, or a little later, we hear of Thurstan joining Geoffrey, archbishop of Rouen, and attending upon Eudo, the dapifer, in his last sickness.[c]

The two ambassadors now started for the English court, and found Henry in Normandy. The letters were delivered authorizing the restoration of Thurstan, doing away with the profession, and quietly speaking of other weapons which the pope could wield if his wishes and directions should be disregarded.[d] The king's answer was, as usual, delayed. After three disappointments the messengers hinted to Henry the necessity of wise counsels, as he would be written to, in the next instance, in a very different tone. The king expressed his wish to follow the advice of the legate, with whom he had hitherto been on unfriendly terms. Conon refused to meet him, and charged him with deceit and treachery, but at last he was prevailed upon to agree to the interview, which took place at Châteaux-Landon on the Sunday after the Ascension. Thurstan, who was at Marcigny, knew what was being done, as he had a friend at court. At the king's request he came to the place of meeting, and whilst Henry and the legate were talking to each other, Thurstan was in the castle hard by. Henry told Conon that on account of his vow he could not gratify the pope's wish unless Thurstan would make the profession to Canterbury. Conon told him what Calixtus had previously said, that as the profession was wrong the vow was also unwarrantable, and that he should be, and was, released from it. After a long and a somewhat angry debate, Henry promised to reinvest Thurstan, and give him the temporalities of his see if he would not enter England for a time, and he desired the legate to assent to this. Conon refused, and there was every chance of the negotiation being broken off, when some one hinted to the king that Thurstan, perhaps, might be more compliant than

bishop of Mans, thought somewhat differently of her, especially when she took the veil (Hildeberti Epist., ed. 1708, 5—7).

[z] Triveti Ann., 4.

[a] L'Art de vérifier les Dates, ii., part ii., 615-16, ed. 1784. Recueil des Hist. des Gaules, xi., 584. In both these works the countess is said to have become a nun in 1122.

[b] Recueil des Hist. des Gaules, xii., 75. It was an ancient foundation, but the inmates now became nuns instead of canons (Mabillon, Ann. Ben., vi., 86-7).

[c] Ibid., 791.

[d] Eadmer, 101.

his friend. It was a happy suggestion. The exile was waiting eagerly for the issue, and when Conon told him what had happened, he entreated that the point might be given up. With some difficulty he induced him to cede it, and the two friends returned into the presence of the king. After many months, nay years, of anxiety and neglect, there was peace at last between the monarch and his subject. Kind words were at length spoken with mutual assurances of forgiveness and goodwill. Things were to remain as they were till Michaelmas, but Thurstan might come and go in Normandy as he pleased. A message was sent to England to announce his re-investiture. The party now proceeded into France, and Thurstan had an opportunity of exhibiting his diplomatic skill, and of returning good for evil. His influence with the legate and the chief estates of France was the chief cause of the restoration of peace with England.[e] Henry was most grateful and delighted. It was this ill-feeling between the two nations, and the peril which consequently threatened his French possessions, that had detained him so long in Normandy, and he was now eager to go home. It was Michaelmas, and the king was ready for his journey. The peacemaker would gladly have accompanied him, but he was again detained. The delay bore some good fruits to Henry and his subjects. A council was held at Beauvais in October, 1120, under the presidency of Conon. Henry was desirous that the Norman bishops should be exempted from attendance, and they stayed at home. The prelates who were at Beauvais pronounced them guilty of contempt and worthy of excommunication, which would probably have been their punishment had not Thurstan hastened to Beauvais when he heard of the danger, and mediated successfully in their behalf. Henry would now be more grateful than ever. He expressed his friendly feelings towards the legate in an interview at Gisors in the presence of the bishops of Châlons and Senlis, when he paid him the great compliment of asking him to superintend the sees and abbeys in Normandy. Conon, upon this, ventured to hope that the negotiations about Thurstan would speedily be arranged to the satisfaction of Calixtus. Henry reciprocated the wish, and promised that they should be completed. Many kind words were spoken on both sides, and Henry, conscious at last of Thurstan's value, told his bishops that he would as lief have lost five hundred marks as have been without him. The king was ready now for his homeward journey, and moved by slow stages towards the sea. He set sail from Barfleur on the 25th of November, 1120. He had previously requested Thur-

[e] Symeon, col. 242. Hoveden, 273.

stan to remain behind till Christmas, as he wished to have an interview with the bishops of the English church, and the archbishop assented.[f] William, Henry's son, followed his father in another vessel with a great company of nobles. The hand of Providence was upon Thurstan when he stayed behind. In a freak of mad folly the young prince and his friends allowed their ship to run upon a rock, and every person on board, but one, was lost. The disconsolate father was an altered man after that sad November: he was never observed to smile after his son was drowned.

"The bark that held a prince went down,
The sweeping waves rolled on;
But what was England's glorious crown
To him that wept a son?
He lived—for life may long be borne
Ere sorrow break its chain;
Why comes not death to those that mourn?
He never smiled again!"

Thurstan was with the legate at Chartres when this disaster occurred, and his heart bled for the master who in bygone days had so deeply injured him. Henry, in turn, remembered him, for he was changed for a time and softened by affliction. At Christmas he called together the archbishop of Canterbury and his suffragans, and shewed them the letters and the mandates of Calixtus. They did not dare to disobey them, and a royal messenger left England to summon Thurstan to his country.[g] He was at that time at Rouen, and he was not slow in obeying the welcome invitation. Three days before the feast of the Purification he crossed the seas and hastened to the court at Windsor. The king, the queen, and every one seemed desirous of making amends for the past. But he did not tarry there long. He hastened into the North. When he drew near to York a vast multitude was ready to receive him. Great numbers of people, on horseback and on foot, lined the road along which he was to pass. Knights and nobles, canons and monks, men and women of every grade and age, welcomed their long-lost diocesan. That Lent would not soon be forgotten in the North: nor would the delight of the listening and admiring throng be diminished when, seated in St. Peter's chair, in that noble church which Thomas the Norman had so recently adorned and renovated, on the third day after his arrival, he recited in the ears of that vast crowd of worshippers[h] the papal

[f] Hoveden, 272.

[g] Saxon Chron., 341. Symeon, col. 244. John of Hexham, col. 266-7. Bromton, col. 1014. Malmesbury, 156 *b*. Hoveden, 272. Ann. Waverl., apud Gale, ii., 148. Hemingford, ibid., 475.

[h] John of Hexham (267) says that Thurstan was enthroned on this occasion. A repetition of this ceremony would probably be necessary.

privilege with the immunities to his church of which he was so proud. To win this he had spent years of exile and disgrace,—sufferings, too, under which a craven spirit would have given way, and injuries and injustice that would have palsied any but an honest and an intrepid heart. At last he had been triumphant, and this was his reward; and even then, when he most of all required the aid of others, he was careless of himself. A poor neglected exile returning from a banishment in which he was entirely dependent on the charity of others, might surely have accepted, what others generally were at all times too ready to evoke, the generous benevolence of his compatriots and his clergy. But Thurstan would not. Instead of relieving himself, as he might very properly have done, he at once began to lighten the burdens which pressed upon his diocese.

Fain would Thurstan have spent the rest of his days in peace, studying the spiritual welfare of the North, from which he had been too long separated. There was to be more annoyance for him still. It was scarcely to be expected that the church of Canterbury would forget her defeat. Archbishop Ralph, with the cold touch of the palsy already benumbing him, began another attack. He gained the ear of Henry, who seems to have been always amenable to his influence. He told him that the monks of Canterbury had discovered several papal grants and privileges, assuring to their church the rights on which Calixtus had trenched.[i] He said that as there was one king, so there ought to be but one primate. Henry, too prone to gossip and mischief-makers, listened to what he said. In August, 1121, he sent a messenger to Thurstan to summon him to a great council which was to be held at Michaelmas. When the archbishop arrived, Henry, to his great astonishment, revived the old subject of dispute in bidding him make his profession to Canterbury. Thurstan's answer was an excellent one. "If I refused to make this profession before I was formally exempted from it by the pope, I am much less likely to submit to it now. Why does the king ask me to do this, which, if done, would bring me under an anathema?" Henry lost his temper, according to his wont, but it was to no purpose. Thurstan told him that if the papal order were recalled he would profess at once. The privilege granted by Calixtus was sent for, and tears of rage and vexation gushed from Henry's eyes as he read it. Flambard and Nigel d'Albeni, an old friend of Thurstan, were standing by in sorrowful amazement. The document was then shewn to the bishops, at the king's request, by some of Thurstan's officers, in the absence of their master.

[i] These are recited in Eadmer, 95-6.

"It is a forgery!" they cried. "It cannot be that," said one of the York clergy, "as I saw it myself come from the pope's hands; nay, there is one line of it which he wrote himself." No reply could be made to this, and the men of Canterbury were mute. Two or three days after this Ralph was seized with the attack of illness under which he ultimately sank.

Thurstan's troubles were not yet over. In 1122 there came a messenger from Rome summoning the two English archbishops to a council at the Lateran. Ralph had already gone to his account, but Thurstan received the papal mandate. It was soon whispered to the king that he had done so without the royal sanction, and Henry ordered him to be at court to explain his conduct at the next festival of the Purification, and to bring the messenger with him. This was quite impossible, as Thurstan had not the least idea where the man was gone. A council was to be held at Gloucester in February, 1123, to choose a new archbishop of Canterbury. Three days before it met, Thurstan was with the king, and little, if anything, was said about the papal letter. He went in the royal train to Gloucester. William de Corbeil was there elected, after much angry debating, to fill Augustine's chair. "Who is he?" asked the king, and then Thurstan and Adelulf, the prior of Nostell, who was afterwards the first bishop of Carlisle, spoke in high terms of his piety and learning. Thurstan himself had taken no part in the election, as he was the head of another province, and the bishops would not permit him to be present. The duty of consecrating Corbeil, according to ancient custom, now devolved upon Thurstan. The king, who was aware perhaps that there might be some difficulty in the case, asked him if he should oppose the consecration of the new archbishop by his own suffragans? He told Henry, after some deliberation, that out of regard to him he would be ready to waive his claim on this occasion, but he desired every one to know that he was ready to do his duty. He then sent Geoffrey abbat of St. Mary's York, Adelulf, prior of Nostell, and others of the York archdeacons and canons to Corbeil to give him the same intimation. The archbishop-elect was with the bishop of London when they arrived. He told them that the separation of York from Canterbury had abrogated the old custom.[j] In reply to this Thurstan's friends informed him that the assigning to each see its proper rights and privileges did not constitute division, and expressed, on the part of their master, his readiness to do his duty. The two prelates returned an evasive answer, that for the present it could

[j] Symeon (col. 248) puts the following words into Corbeil's mouth: "Si me ut primatem totius Angliæ volueris ordinare, libenter me manibus vestris inclinabo, sin autem, inconsulte contra morem antiquam nolo ordinari."

not be done. Thurstan now spoke to Henry of the pope's recent summons to the council, and asked his permission to set out. The king begged him as a favour to delay his journey till the archbishop of Canterbury could go with him to procure the pall. He undertook, also, to acquaint the pope with the cause of his absence, and promised that the bishops from Normandy, and Jeremias, archdeacon of Rouen, should remain in Rome, after the council was over, till they arrived. Corbeil and he were then requested to be at Woodstock on the first Sunday in Lent that they might start from thence to Rome. All this was done in the spring of 1123. They met at the appointed time, Corbeil in the meanwhile having taken the unwarrantable liberty of receiving consecration at the hands of the bishop of London and his own suffragans.[k] Thurstan, however, seems to have made no complaint. At Woodstock Henry requested him, through the prelates and nobles, to assist his brother, when they were at Rome, to the utmost of his power, and to make no unjust claim upon him whilst they were there. To this Thurstan assented, and the two started on their journey.[l] By an accident Thurstan reached the papal court before his fellow-traveller, and he found there many of his old friends, who were rejoiced to see him. Corbeil arrived shortly afterwards with a long train of ecclesiastics, among whom were Bernard, bishop of St. David's, and the abbats of Glastonbury and St. Edmund's.[m] He now became a suppliant for the pall. On this question there was a long debate. It was alleged that Corbeil's election and consecration had been uncanonical, and it was decided that the pall should not be given to him, but that he should be permitted to accept a bishopric. Thurstan now pleaded in his behalf; indeed, during the whole controversy he acted towards Corbeil in the most generous and honourable manner. He praised his piety and learning, and entreated the pope and the sacred college to alter their decision in consideration of his royal master and the emperor, who had furthered the suppliant's cause. After a suspense of fifteen days, through the agency of Calixtus the sentence was rescinded, out of respect to the emperor, and Corbeil received the pall. His party now turned upon Thurstan in the most ungrateful manner. As soon as the pall had been secured, the bishop of St. David's raised the old question of the profession and the primacy in a tone which he afterwards regretted. He assured Calixtus that

[k] Symeon, col. 248. Gervase, col. 1662.

[l] Fl. Wigorn., 497. Chron. Mailros, 67. Chron. Petrib., 81. Huntingdon, apud Savile, 219. Hoveden, 274. In the Saxon Chron. (247), it is said that Thurstan was reconciled to Corbeil, and swore subjection to him!

[m] Symeon, col. 248-50. Diceto, col. 604.

the recent papal grant was in direct contravention of the old privileges of the church of Canterbury. Thurstan seems to have deprecated any discussion; he observed that he was quite unprepared for anything of this kind; he had come at the present time to please the king; had he thought of himself he would have been at the recent council. Bernard was ordered to produce the privileges of which he spoke. He read them. They had a show of genuineness without the *sapor*. He was now assailed with some awkward questions. "Had these privileges the bulls appended to them?" "No; but the originals had which were at home." "Would they swear that?" After some hesitation they said that the bulls were either wasted away or lost. At this there was a general titter. "If the leaden bulls had wasted away, was it likely that the parchment was remaining?" They then hinted the possibility of the non-existence of the bulls at that early time, but this straw was plucked away from them. Bribery seems now to have taken the place of argument, and the chamberlain of the pope,—a person of great influence at Rome,—seems to have been bought over. Thurstan was asked about the muniments of the see of York, but he had none of them with him. One of his followers, however, had several copies, and the letters and decrees of Gregory, Honorius, Urban, Paschal, and Calixtus were recited. They could say nothing about the originals possessing bulls. It would, therefore, have been clearly unfair to decide the matter at present in favour of either disputant. Calixtus proposed to fix a time when the matter could be debated upon proper evidence. Thurstan was ready to agree to this arrangement, but Corbeil declined to do so without the permission of his sovereign. The two archbishops, therefore, returned home; the one with letters from the pope announcing the reception of the pall, the other with a commendatory epistle to Henry, in which Calixtus spoke in high terms of the wisdom and usefulness of his old friend. As soon as the Canterbury party reached the court in Normandy, many unkind speeches were made against Thurstan, but the slander seems to have made no impression upon Henry, if we may judge from the welcome which the archbishop of York received on his arrival. He was accompanied by abbat Anselm[n] and others, who told the king a very different story from that which he had heard. They said that Thurstan had behaved towards Corbeil in the most honourable manner, and that without his generous mediation he would

[n] Anselm was not a favourite. In 1134, when he was elected to the see of London, Thurstan wrote to the pope and told him that Anselm was more fit to lose his abbey of St. Edmund's than to gain a bishopric. He was not allowed to be consecrated (Diceto, col. 506-7).

never have received the pall. In the following September Calixtus wrote to Corbeil blaming him for his attacks on Thurstan, and entreating him to banish malice from his heart.

In 1124 Calixtus died, and was succeeded by Honorius II., who sent the cardinal of Crema as his legate into England. Corbeil now renewed his claims and complaints against Thurstan, and desired the pope to authorize his legate to bring them to an amicable adjustment. About Pentecost the two archbishops received a mandate from Honorius summoning them both to Rome. They went to the court in Normandy. Thurstan was astonished when he heard the king require him to put his churches in the position which they had occupied during the reign of his father and brother, otherwise he should regard him as a traitor and an enemy. Thurstan, with his usual address, defended himself from the charge of treason, and said that he would gladly allow his churches to remain as they were in the time of his predecessor Aldred, who had crowned the Conqueror. "No," replied Henry; "they must be in the state in which my father left them." Thurstan declined to do this, and appealed to the papal privilege as his warrant. He was now, he said, on his way to Rome, was it fair that he should be obliged to defend himself in two places against the same attack? Every effort was made by the king and his council to bring the matter to a conclusion. An offer was even made that if Thurstan would merely verbally acknowledge Corbeil as primate, committing his successors to a more humiliating form of subjection, the see of Canterbury should be dismembered, and the bishoprics of Lichfield, Bangor, and another, which is not named, should be given up to York. This scheme was to be formally proposed to the pope, and about this, as well as the other plans that were to be mentioned at Rome, the king commanded that on the part of the English prelates there should be no controversy or dispute. The most important proposition was this, that the legantine power should be secured, if possible, for Corbeil and his successors. This would give them an excellent title for superiority as the immediate representative of the pope. Of all the plans that could be devised for terminating the never-ending feud between York and Canterbury, this, perhaps, was the most sure. The cardinal of Crema had made anything but a favourable impression in England, and if the archbishop of Canterbury became the permanent legate there would be no necessity for the appointment of a foreigner.

The two archbishops visited Rome in 1125,[o] Thurstan being

[o] Ann. Waverl., apud Gale, ii., 149. The Saxon Chron. (352) and Chron. Mailros (68) make the date 1126. Symeon (254) says in 1126, with the legate; and again in 1127 by themselves, when Corbeil was made legate.

accompanied by his brother and faithful companion in trouble, Audoenus, bishop of Evreux.[p] The controversy in the presence of the pope exhibited many phases and fluctuations. Nothing, however, seems to have been done except the appointment of Corbeil as legate in England. This was done entirely in accordance with the wish of Thurstan, who, at that time, had a very favourable opinion of Corbeil. He soon had occasion, unfortunately, to regard him in a very different light. The archbishop of Canterbury owed his very election to Thurstan, but he returned him evil for good. He took the part of the Scottish bishops when they endeavoured to break away from their allegiance to York. He forbade him to bear his cross erect within his province, or to take any part in the coronation of the king.[q] When Corbeil, in virtue of his power as legate, called together a council at London, he summoned Thurstan to it, but he very properly stayed away.[r] The Southern primate complained of this to Henry, and the king told him that his past ingratitude to Thurstan had fully merited that slight. For some time there was no communication whatever between the two archbishops.

An allusion has been made to the feud between York and the Scottish bishops. This was only a continuation of the old controversy. The claims of York were nearly always questioned by the Scottish prelates long before they were for ever set aside. Ralph Nowell, bishop of Orkney, resided generally with Thurstan, as the people of Scotland and Norway[s] rejected him on account of his English consecration, in spite of the remonstrances of Honorius and Calixtus. Thurstan is said to have made Gilaldane bishop of Whitherne.[t] He also consecrated Robert, prior of Nostell, to St. Andrew's, after the death of Turgot and the intrusion of Eadmer,[u] but at the earnest request of king David he required from him no profession.[v] It was the wish of the Scottish people and king that the bishop of St. Andrew's should be the metropolitan of Scotland, and on that account they were frequently coquetting with Canterbury to

[p] In 1132 Audoenus and Thurstan dedicated the church "B. M. de casa Dei parthenonis Fontebraldensis" (Gallia Christiana, xi., 575).

[q] This occurred at Windsor at Christmas, 1126. Diceto, col. 504. Bromton, col. 1016. Gervase, col. 1664. Fl. Wigorn., 502. Chron. Petrib, 83. In 1127, Wendover, i., 476. In Dugd. Mon., vi., 1188, is a letter written by Honorius to king Henry, desiring him to allow Thurstan to bear his cross and to crown him according to ancient custom.

[r] Diceto, col. 504.

[s] In Dugd. Mon., vi., 1186, there are two letters in his behalf from popes Calixtus and Honorius addressed to kings of Norway.

[t] Stubbs, col. 1720. In Dugd. Mon., vi., 1187, there is a letter from pope Honorius to the bishop of Whitherne, ordering him to obey the Northern primate.

[u] Symeon, col. 251. The consecration was delayed for a time on account of the subjection.

[v] Dugd. Mon., vi., 1187. Although he was a canon of York (Flor. Wigorn., 506). Fordun, Scotichronicon, ed. Goodall, i., 340. Anglia Sacra, ii., 237.

obtain the emancipation of that see from York.[w] But it was in John, bishop of Glasgow, that Thurstan found his strongest and most pertinacious adversary. He is said to have been a person of piety and learning, and had been the tutor of prince David. Pope Paschal consecrated him bishop of Glasgow in 1115. He would render no submission whatever to the see of York, and the result was that Thurstan suspended him for insubordination. This was in 1122. John now went to Rome to appeal against this sentence, but, his cause having been given against him, he went off to Jerusalem, and spent several months with the patriarch, acting as his suffragan. In the following year Calixtus summoned him home, and ordered him to his diocese.[x] But still he rendered no profession of obedience, and paid no attention to any papal order. In 1125, when Thurstan and Corbeil were at Rome, John, in an unlucky hour, was there in the train of the archbishop of Canterbury. Thurstan, unwilling to lose so good an opportunity, pounced upon John before the papal court, reproaching him for his neglect of the mandates of Paschal and Calixtus,[y] his desertion of his diocese, and his disobedience to himself: he made at the same time a general complaint against all the Scottish prelates. John defended himself by saying that he was there as the ambassador of the king of Scotland. Honorius told him in a warning tone that he must not expect to be released from the obligation laid upon him by Gelasius and other popes,[z] and a day was fixed in the following Lent when John and the Scottish bishops should meet Thurstan before the papal court, and the question should be decided. Christmas came on, and the day of meeting was drawing near. Thurstan was at the court at London, and there he met with David, king of Scotland, John's old pupil, and Conan, earl of Brittany. David with some trouble induced Thurstan, as a personal favour, to beg the pope to put off the hearing of the cause for another year. This arrangement was with difficulty effected, but there is nothing to shew that John ever made the submission that was required.[a] Innocent II. followed the example of his predecessors, and ordered him, apparently in vain, to obey Thurstan.[b] In 1138, when Alberic,

[w] There are letters on this subject between Alexander king of Scotland and archbishop Ralph in Eadmer, Hist. Nov., 90, 97—100.

[x] Symeon, col. 245, 248.

[y] I have not seen these letters of Paschal. Those of Calixtus are in Dugd. Mon., vi., 1187-8. These are partly about John and partly about the Scottish bishops. Wilkins, i., 481.

[z] Stubbs, col. 1719. Hugh the Chantor, where there is a long account of the scene at Rome.

[a] Symeon (col. 252) says that in 1125 Honorius wrote to king David, saying that he had empowered his legate to settle the dispute between Thurstan and the Scottish bishops.

[b] Dugd. Mon., vi., 1187-8. In Wilkins, i., 480, is a bull of pope Innocent II. subjecting the Scottish bishops to Thurstan.

bishop of Ostia, was in England as legate, he was told that John had deserted his charge, and professed himself a monk at Tiron, and he was summoned home to answer for his conduct. John died in 1147, and was buried at Jedburgh.[c] He is said by the Scottish writers to have atoned for his wandering and restless disposition in early life by his subsequent activity in advancing the interests of his see.[d]

So much of Thurstan's life had been spent in controversy, which he could not shun, that he had but little time to take that position in the affairs of the church and state at home for which he was marked out by his genius and energy. In 1129 he was present at the council at London,[e] and in 1133 he had the honour of presiding over that which was held at Northampton.[f] In 1135 he was at the coronation of king Stephen, but he did not officiate.[g] In the same, or in the following year, Stephen was at York, and Thurstan, who had known him in another country and in an humbler sphere, would give him a hearty welcome. In 1137 there was a cloud gathering in Scotland, and Thurstan went to that country as ambassador, and had an interview with king David at Roxburgh, at which he induced that restless monarch to make a truce with England till the return of Stephen from abroad.[h] In the following year the Scottish army broke into the North, and, after sweeping the whole country before them, the invaders found themselves at Cowton moor, near Northallerton, a little after Easter. The crisis was a most serious one, but Thurstan, broken down as he was with age, was not unequal to it.[i] He was carried about on a couch or litter wherever he was required. He did everything in his power to excite the spirit of the North. He sent the priests with crosses and banners and relics through the parishes to arouse the inhabitants. He gathered together with speed

[c] John of Hexham, col. 264, 276. Ric. of Hexham, 325. Fordun, Scotichronicon, i., 449, where it is said that John, according to old custom, acted as a bishop in Cumberland. Henry I., at Thurstan's desire, made a bishop of Carlisle, and upon this John went to Tiron.

[d] Keith's Scottish Bishops, ed. 1824, 231-2.

[e] Huntingdon, apud Savile, 220. Hoveden, ibid., 274 *b*. Wendover, i., 478. Ann. Waverl., apud Gale, ii., 150. Mat. Paris, 60. Rob. de Monte, 701. Labbe, Conc., x., 910, 940. Several dates are given for this meeting.

[f] Fl. Wigorn., 519. Labbe, x., 991. Wilkins, i., 413.

[g] Opera Thomæ Becket, ed. Giles, iii., 69.

[h] John of Hexham, col. 259. Chron. Mailros, 70. Chron. Petrib., 89. Liber Vitæ ed. Surtees Soc., 59, 67.

[i] John of Hexham, col. 261-2. Ric. of Hexham, col. 320-1. Ailred, col. 338, etc. Fl. Wigorn., 524. Diceto, col. 506. Bromton, col. 1026-7. Gervase, col. 1346. Knyghton, col. 2385. Huntingdon, apud Savile, 222-3. Hoveden, 277. Triveti Ann., 6. Hemingford, apud Gale, ii., 480. Peter Langtoft, *n. e.*, 114-15. Scala Chronica, 33. Mat. Paris, 63-4. Chron. Petrib., 90. Rob. de Monte, 712. Dachery, Spicilegium, iii., 144.

and labour the great barons of the district, allaying their jealousies and fears, and an army was soon collected. The ensign which the archbishop sent with it to the scene of conflict gave to that field the name of the battle of the Standard. The mast of a ship was erected upon a car, and from it were fluttering the holy banners of the saints of York, Beverley, and Ripon. A silver pix, in which the blessed sacrament was enclosed, was fastened to the summit. A sacred influence would thus seem to hover around the little band of Yorkshiremen. Thurstan would fain have been there himself had not the barons insisted upon his absence, but his suffragan, the bishop of Orkney, the archdeacons and the clergy were on the field to bid the God of battles go forth with their compatriots to the fight, and to minister consolation to the dying. The aged prelate was thinking all the while of those whom he could not see; he was praying for them with bitter tears, and commending them and their arms to the Lord, when the welcome news arrived of the victory that had been won. He might well be satisfied with his own personal exertions in securing it, for he had certainly saved the North of England.

> "How oft has strength, the strength of heaven,
> To few triumphantly been given!
> Still do our very children boast
> Of mitred Thurstan, what a host
> He conquered!—Saw we not the plain
> (And flying shall behold again)
> Where faith was proved?—While to battle moved
> The standard on the sacred wain
> That bore it, compassed round by a bold
> Fraternity of barons old;
> And with those grey-haired champions stood,
> Under the saintly ensigns three,
> The infant heir of Mowbray's blood—
> All confident of victory!"

The province of York had good reason to remember the good deeds and the energy of Thurstan. The example which he set was worthy of all imitation, and his clergy might well regret his prolonged absence from his see. He was a man of learning, and several works have been attributed to his pen. Of these we have nothing but two or three letters. In that which is addressed to archbishop Corbeil, describing the secession from St. Mary's abbey, much kindly and devotional feeling is expressed, and the style is extremely good and pleasing.[j]

[j] Bale, cent. ii., 185, says that Thurstan wrote "De origine Fontanensis cœnobii, lib. i. De suo primatu, ad Calixtum, lib. i. Contra juniorem Anselmum, lib. i., et alia quædam." The first of these works will be mentioned afterwards. Pits, 216. Vossius, De Hist. Latinis, 413. Wright, Biogr. Lit., ii., 109. Tanner, 728. Oudinus, ii., 1122.

The personal character of Thurstan was unimpeachable.[k] He had learned in other lands the necessity of a stricter discipline than that which he saw at home, and, full of honest zeal and fervent piety, he was not afraid of practising it himself. Luxury was a stranger to his table. In his dress and demeanour he was almost an ascetic. The poor blessed him for his kindness and munificence, for they had no surer friend than Thurstan. He was frequently on his knees, and tears streamed from his eyes when he administered the eucharist. He wore sackcloth next his skin, and disciplined himself with the scourge. Men of piety and learning found in him a patron and a friend. He was affable and courteous, stern when severity was needed, and yet at all times ready to forgive. Thurstan did a great deal for his diocese, far more indeed than any of his predecessors. Pope Innocent advised him to divide the large parishes within his district, and this recommendation was most probably obeyed.[l] At his enthronization he exempted his churches from the regular charge for the *crisma*, and made the fees for burial, extreme unction, and baptism, voluntary and not necessary.[m] He made also an ordinance about the income of the canons throughout his churches, which was beneficial to themselves as well as to the minsters in which they were located.[n] Thurstan was most useful, too, and active in seeing that all the ministers and ecclesiastical corporations were properly remunerated and endowed. At York, Hexham, Ripon, Beverley, and Southwell, he was a great benefactor;[o] and in 1137 there was a fire in the minster at York, which would be sure to evoke his munificence.[p] He is also called the founder of the hospital of St. Peter, or St. Leonard, which was in connection with the cathedral. How far this title was merited is somewhat doubtful. In 1122 Henry I. kept his birthday at York; and at the request of queen Matilda, who was instigated by Thurstan, the king granted several privileges to that establishment himself, and prevailed upon his barons to add to the endowments of the house.[q] It was burned in 1137; and, soon afterwards, it was

[k] John of Hexham, col. 267. Ric. of Hexham, col. 306. Stubbs, col. 1714.

[l] Reg. Magn. Album at York, 53.

[m] Stubbs, col. 1717, from Hugh.

[n] Ibid., 1720. Thurstan's Constitution, "De debitis clericorum defunctorum," is in Wilkins, i., 412.

[o] John of Hexham, col. 267. Ric. of Hexham, col. 306-7. Walbran's Ripon, 25.

[p] Gervase (col. 1343) says that on "sec. nonas Junii 1137, apud Eboracum combusta est B. Petri ecclesia, ubi sedes est epis[s], et, extra muros, ecclesia B. M., ubi est abbatia, cum egregio hospitali quod fundavit Turstinus archiepiscopus." Lel. also, apud Coll., i., 45. The fire in the minster was probably only partial in its effects and extent.

[q] MSS. Cotton, Titus A., xix., 55. Symeon, col. 246. There is a noble chartulary of St. Leonard's among the Cottonian MSS., Nero D. iv. Some of the yearly account rolls of the hospital are also in existence.

rebuilt by Stephen on a much larger scale, and received the name which it has since borne, that of the hospital of St. Leonard.[r] At Ripon, Beverley, and Southwell, Thurstan was the founder of new prebends;[s] and he was, doubtless, the means of the establishment, in 1133, of the bishopric of Carlisle, to which his old friend Adelulf, the prior of Nostell, was appointed.[t] This was effected at the death of Ranulph Flambard, bishop of Durham, and the election of his successor, Geoffrey Rufus, whom Thurstan consecrated at York.[u] The see of Durham now subsided within the territorial boundaries which enclosed it until the Reformation. Within the last half-century it had been deprived of a great deal. It had lost Tynemouth and Hexham, Cumberland, Westmerland, and Teviotdale. The wiles and the instability of Flambard had, without doubt, been the main cause of this great dismemberment of his diocese.[v]

Thurstan is especially to be commemorated as the reviver of monasticism in the North. His intercourse with the ecclesiastics of other countries; the religious houses which he would see during his exile, exhibiting, as far as human agency could effect it, the perfection of discipline and organization, would open his eyes to the wants of his diocese at home, and make him eager to meet and remedy them. The example and the exhortations of St. Bernard, with whom he was acquainted, would strengthen and nerve his hand. The letter which he wrote about the poor Cistercians of Fountains shews that he was thoroughly saturated with the monastic principle. His knowledge of it was of a kind that long study and practice could alone impart, and it seems to me that Thurstan, together with St. Bernard and two or three others, are to be regarded as the great Church reformers of the twelfth century. It was at Thurstan's suggestion that pope Honorius confirmed the privileges of the monastery of Savigny, and he witnessed the grant of a hundred marks of silver which was made by Henry I. to the monks of Clugny,[w] to which order the archbishop was especially attached. When Thurstan arrived in the North he would find there a very small number of religious houses, one or two of which were occupied by Augustine canons, and the rest by Benedictines. A new impetus was now given to the diffusion of the monastic principle. The two existing

[r] Lel. Coll., i., 38.

[s] Dugd. Mon., vi., 1313-14. Walbran's Ripon, ed. 1858, 25. Poulson's Beverlac, 531. Fœdera, i., 10, *n. e.* Thoroton's Notts, 310. Lel. Coll., ii., 391.

[t] John of Hexham, col. 257. Hoveden, 275. Mat. Paris, 60. The foundation of the see of Carlisle was completed by king Stephen. Reg. Magn. Album, at York, 53.

[u] Hexham, *ut supra.* Symeon, Hist. Eccl. Dunelm., 261. Stubbs, col. 1720. Chron. Mailros, 69.

[v] Symeon, *ut supra,* 256, etc.

[w] Martene, Thes. Nov. Anecdot., i., 361, 382.

orders were reformed and enlarged, and the Cluniacs and Cistercians, monks of a stricter rule, were brought in. The time for their introduction and for the revival of discipline was well chosen. The Norman and the Saxon elements in the English Church were now happily blended together. Everything in religious as well as civil affairs was now settled and laid down. The great baronies and fees throughout the country were for the most part marked out. Peace and rest superinduced other and better thoughts. Many of the great knights and nobles had grievous offences to atone for. They were living upon the possessions of others—very frequently upon church property; and their lives had been stained with violence and bloodshed. The wish to make amends as well as to honour God, led them to establish monasteries where their souls might be prayed for, and to which their names, "*in perpetuam rei memoriam,*" might be honourably attached. When one leads, another soon will follow, and the erection and endowment of religious houses soon became the fashion, but like every freak and sudden feeling of that kind it was only temporary. It began with the twelfth century, and it did not outlive it. Thurstan was eminently successful in kindling this spirit of zeal in the North, for he was just the man that the feudal chieftains would most admire, although, on one occasion at least, he was ill-treated by them.[x] The energy with which he fought in his own conflicts was very much akin to theirs, for he was illustrious both in arts and arms. Between the years 1120 and 1125 six houses of Augustine canons seem to have been established in Yorkshire. Kirkham owed its origin to that great patron of religion, Walter l'Espec,[y] and Gisburgh to Robert de Brus, an ancestor of the well-known warrior, who was guided in what he did by Calixtus II. and Thurstan.[z] Bridlington, which overhangs the sea, was founded by Walter le Gant,[a] and the archbishop, who had probably directed him in his good work, was a witness to his charter of endowment. William de Meschines about the same time began to draw together the body of ecclesiastics which settled finally in the beautiful solitudes of Bolton, and Thurstan, to shew his sympathy, appropriated to them the neighbouring churches of Skipton and Kildwick.[b] The piety of Ralph Adlave, the confessor of Henry I., first selected the retirement of Nostel,[c] from which, after a life full of romantic incidents, he was summoned in

[x] John of Hexham, col. 268. It is not quite clear that the offence here mentioned was perpetrated in Thurstan's life-time.

[y] Ailred, de Bello Standardi, col. 338. Dugd. Mon., vi., 210. Burton's Mon., Ebor., 373.

[z] Bromton, col. 1018. Dugd., vi., 267. Burton, 340. There is some doubt as to the date of this foundation.

[a] Burton, 212.

[b] Dugd. Mon., vi., 203-5. Burton, 115.

[c] Burton, 300. Hunter's South Yorkshire ii., 204, etc.

1133 to be the president of the new see of Carlisle. In 1130, or thereabouts, Thurstan himself established the first nunnery that had existed in the North since the Conquest, a house of Benedictines, at Clementhorp near York.[d] In 1131 the beautiful monastery of Rievaux was founded, in memory of his lost son, by Walter l'Espec, and some Cistercian monks, who had been sent to England three years previously by St. Bernard, found a resting-place in that charming valley.[e] William Paynel, at the instance of Thurstan, made a house for Austin canons at Drax, and another was erected at Wartre in 1132 by Geoffrey Trusbut, and was appropriated to the same order.[f] The religious colony, also, which found its way to Byland, was greatly indebted to Thurstan for its success. The abbat of Furness and his monks had fled before the Scots, and had found an asylum in York, where the archbishop welcomed and supported them. He recommended them to the kind offices of the widow of his old friend Nigel d'Albeni, who had assumed the well-known name of Mowbray, and she placed them at Hode till they were removed to Byland in 1138 by her son Roger, who was also the founder of the house of Newburgh.[g] Thurstan had a great deal to do with the affairs of Selby Abbey,[h] and he is said to have been mainly instrumental in restoring the church of Bardney.[i] The York historians inform us that he was the founder of eight religious houses. How far this is to be interpreted it is difficult to say; at all events he seems to have been the chief agent in the erection and the establishment of many of those noble monasteries which used to be the pride and the boast of Yorkshire. With the history of these retreats very few are acquainted. There are scarcely any who know the records of the adventures of their first inmates, which are invested with all the thrilling interest of romance; their struggles to maintain themselves; their simple and earnest piety, and their subsequent success. As long as the incurious reader turns away from subjects like these he will know very little indeed of the inner working, nay

[d] Dugd. Mon., iv., 323. This house was given by archbishop Geoffrey in 1192 to the nuns of Godstow (Benedict Petrib., 732).

[e] John of Hexham, col. 257, where the date 1132 is given. Ailred, col. 338. Bromton, col. 1028. Wm. Neubrig., i., 51. Dugd. Mon., vi., 274. Burton, 358. There is some interesting information about the early history of Rievaux in Opp. S. Bern., ed. 1690, i., 98-9. Martene, Thes. Nov. Anecd., iv., inter Statuta Capit. Gen. Ord. Cisterc.; Henriquez, Fascic. Ord. Cist.; Miræus, Chron. Cisterc., ed. 1614, p. 89. The Rescripts of pope Alexander III. in Labbe, Conc., x. Mabillon, Ann. Ben., vi., 158-9. Chron. Mailros.

[f] Dugd. Mon., vi., 297. Burton, 100, 381.

[g] John of Hexham, col. 259. Bromton, col. 1028. Wm. Neubr., i., 52-4. Dugd. Mon., v., 343-9; vi., 317. Burton, 328.

[h] Hist. Fund. Mon. de Selby, apud Labbe, Bibl., i., 608-10—a very curious historical tract with which few are acquainted.

[i] Lel. Col., iii. 263.

I will say, of the outward features of the Church in the middle ages. If he will only take the trouble to examine them he will find that, with all their faults, there were piety and devotion in times which too many have considered to be dark, and that there was some learning nursed and cherished within the cloister which later generations, with all their increased intelligence, have been unable to surpass.

There was another monastery, greater than any which have yet been mentioned, of which Thurstan, to a great extent, was the originator, and that was the far-famed abbey of Fountains.[j] The history of its foundation, as it has been described by Thurstan himself and the chronicler of the house,[k] is a most touching and charming narrative. In 1132 there was, what we may call, a rebellion in the monastery of St. Mary without the walls of York. That well-known abbey had been but for a short time in existence when the Benedictine rule, which its inmates professed to follow, was practically despised. Innovations had crept in. Want of discipline and neglect of duty had borne their bitter fruits. All, however, were not polluted by the taint. Richard the prior and Gervase the sub-prior, upon whom the charge of the monastery to a great extent devolved, groaned in spirit over the growing evil. Full of sorrow they sought counsel of their abbat, a kind-hearted but indolent man. Richard told him of his daily troubles, and of the insubordination of the monks. The inmates of the house were noisy brawlers. They chattered and quarrelled when not a word ought to be spoken. In food and dress and many minute points their rule was neglected. How different they were from the monks of Savigny and Clairvaux whom they had recently seen, and whose religious life was a mirror in which all might dress themselves for God. What was to be done? The abbat, like a timid man as he was, hesitated and delayed the matter, but rumours of the complaints which had been made reached the ears of the monks, who were excessively indignant. They banded themselves together against the reformers; threats were uttered, and there was malice written upon their faces. Fearful for the issue, Richard and his friends had an interview with Thurstan, to whom the state of things at York was not unknown. After some deliberation with the abbat and the officers of the house, a day was appointed on which the archbishop promised to visit the monastery and enquire into the alleged misconduct. When the time arrived,

[j] John of Hexham, col. 257. Ailred, col. 338. Bromton, col. 1028. Wm. Neubrig., i., 50-1. Mat. Paris, 59. Lel. Col., i., 54; ii., 338; iv., 105. Dugdale, v., 293, etc. Burton, 141. Henriquez, Phœnix Reviviscens, 69-70. Mabillon, Ann. Ben., vi., 204-5.

[k] The treatise, "De origine domus Font.," by Hugh de Kirkstall, is partly printed by Dugdale in the Mon., vi., 293, etc. It is now being printed *in extenso* by the Surtees Society.

he rode up to the gates with a goodly company which included several dignitaries of the minster, Hugh the dean, William the treasurer, archdeacon Hugh Sotevagina the historian and poet. William, the prior of the recently established monastery of Gisburgh, was also there, together with Robert, who appears to have been the master of the adjacent hospital of St. Peter. The party halted at the gate by which you still enter those sacred precincts, and, leaving their horses there, went on foot towards the chapter-house; at the door of that building, which was filled from end to end by monks, strangers as well as residents, the abbat of the house received them, and deprecated the presence of any one but the archbishop and his clerks. When Thurstan ventured to remonstrate, an uproar arose within which would have appalled a less intrepid man; they hooted and yelled like madmen. They rushed towards Thurstan with their arms stretched out as if they were eager for a wrestling match. They roared out that if he entered they would all of them depart. Thurstan's indignation was justly aroused. He told them that he had only come there to do his duty, and, as they interfered with him, he put their house under an interdict. What did they care! "Stop it for a hundred years!" was the shout of a fellow of the name of Symeon, and the rest yelled their assent. "Catch them, get hold of them!" was now the cry, and they seized the unfortunate prior and his comrades, and were going to imprison them or carry them off. The intended victims flung their arms around Thurstan and implored his aid. It was with some difficulty that the archbishop and his party, suppliants and friends, got away into the church, followed by discordant shouts of hatred and vengeance. The servants of the monastery were at every door and window, and the populace, aroused by the disturbance, was rapidly assembling. Thurstan ordered the cloister door to be secured, and, after a brief deliberation in the church, finding that action was impossible and the rioters impracticable, he returned home. The prior and twelve of his brethren accompanied him, and deserted their old abode to which they never afterwards returned. The archbishop now befriended these poor outcasts. He wrote a long and most graphic letter to archbishop Corbeil in refutation of the erroneous reports which were flying about,[1] in which he gave a full account of the insurrection at St. Mary's, and expressed simply and earnestly his own views on discipline and monasticism. He sheltered the wanderers for awhile, and then gave them a piece of ground for themselves in a rocky and

[1] This letter is being printed entire for the first time by the Surtees Society in their forthcoming volume on Fountain's abbey. It has already been published, in part, in Dugd. Mon., vi., 293, etc., and in S. Bernardi Opp., i., 386-91. Cf. Avesbury's Edw. III., appendix, 271.

secluded dell near his residence at Ripon. It was in the winter that they sought for the first time their solitary abode, but they cared not for the storm-winds or the snows. For awhile they were sheltered only by the rocks which hung over the waters of the Skell, and, afterwards, they nestled beneath a large elm, which was spoken of and cherished by their descendants in a far distant generation. They now communicated their sorrows and aspirations to the compassionate ears of St. Bernard, and placed themselves at his disposal.[m] That holy and intrepid man wrote to the abbat of St. Mary's, who had requested his advice, and desired that his former brethren should follow out the course which they had adopted. He expressed his gratitude also to Thurstan for the kindness which he had shewn to these afflicted monks.[n] There was much in common between those two noble-hearted and energetic men, and they had probably become acquainted whilst Thurstan was in exile. For two whole years the devoted and enduring monks subsisted merely upon roots and leaves;[o] but their poverty and self-denial were the parents of their wealth. They had obtained St. Bernard's permission to seek another sanctuary, where they could keep life together, when, most providentially, wealth began to flow into their empty coffers: a church was built, broad lands were given to endow it, and a noble abbey arose by degrees upon the scene of their sufferings and their triumph. From the many springs which bubbled up beside it they gave to their abode the suggestive name of Fountains,[p] and, by that title, one of the noblest monasteries in England was henceforward known. You may see its decaying walls in that beautiful valley which seven centuries have not robbed of its repose, and which reminds us, even in these latter days, of the munificence of Thurstan and of the piety and zeal of its first Christian colonists. The

[m] S. Bernardi, Opp., ed. 1690, i., inter notas ad finem, xl.

[n] Ibid., i., 99-100. At p. 292 there is another letter to abbat Geoffrey, censuring him for the want of discipline in his house.

[o] In this they resembled the monks of Clairvaux, "qui pulmentaria sæpius ex foliis fagi conficiebant" (S. Bern. Opp., ii., 1073. There is a long account of the trials of these poor monks in the narrative of Hugh de Kirkstall.

[p] Wm. Neubrig. (i., 51) says, "Et vocatur locus ille Fontes: ubi extunc et deinceps tanquam de fontibus Salvatoris tam multi hauserunt aquas salientes in vitam æternam."

St. Bernard, with his love of mysticism, drew a great many thoughts and images from the word Fontes. He speaks of the "quatuor fontes Salvatoris," the "quinque fontes Salvatoris," and the "quatuor fontes spiritualis Paradisi."

The name of his birthplace, Fontaines in Burgundy, was probably one great cause of his fondness for the word. The eldest daughter of Clairvaux, who was placed in the diocese of Châlons-sur-Marne, had the name of Trois-fontaines given to her by St. Bernard. Fontenay, Mellifont, and Font-Morigny were children of the same parent (S. Bern., Opp., i., 70-2; ii., 1087. Miræi Chron. Ord. Cist., ed. 1614, 35. Mabillon, Ann. Ben., vi., 27).

springs are still welling forth, and their waters are trickling into the Skell as they did when Richard saw them; but the voice of worship is no longer heard within those walls which it once consecrated to God. Roof and roof-tree have been torn away, although you gaze still with a saddened eye upon the overhanging rocks which covered many centuries ago a little band of Christian heroes.

Thurstan's day of life was drawing to its close. His health had been for some time failing. This prevented him from being present in 1138 at the battle of the Standard, and he was unable to attend the council which was held at London in the same year under the presidency of Alberic the legate. He had already given a hearty welcome to that dignitary, and he sent William, the dean of York, to represent him at the meeting.[q] He was too feeble to be there himself, for he was

"Jam propior leto fessusque senilibus annis."

He had been loved and honoured, he had done great things, but success cannot obliterate the effect of the trials by which it has been secured. Throughout his career he had been honest to his country and his see, but not without much suffering and affliction in body and in mind.[r] His heart would mourn within him when he beheld the blood which seemed destined to track the footsteps of king Stephen. Oh that he could lay aside the cares of office for which he was unfit, and enjoy a foretaste of that repose which the world-worn pilgrim shall one day find! He would see that others had already reached it, if it were to be found on earth, in the cells of Clairvaux, in the valley of the Skell, and by the waters of the Rie. In 1139 he was wishful to resign his see in favour of his brother Audoenus, the bishop of Evreux; and, to bring his desire to pass, he sent Richard, abbat of Fountains, to Rome, to secure what was uppermost in his mind, and to represent him at the council. A higher power brought everything to nought. Richard reached his destination, but he died there; and Audoenus followed him to the tomb, having assumed a little before his death the habit of a canon in the monastery of Merton.[s] What was Thurstan now to do? He communicated his secret thoughts and wishes to St. Bernard, and there is still extant a letter which that great man addressed to the aged and enfeebled prelate full of affectionate advice. He bids him retain his see, the wife to whom he had been so

[q] John of Hexham, col. 264. Ric. of Hexham, col. 327. Malmesbury, apud Savile, 103. Labbe, Conc., x., 992-4.

[r] "Pro salute patriæ, tam pro dignitate tutanda, et multa incommoda perpessus est et sæpissime in periculo fuit" (Polyd. Virgil, 210). Malmesbury, 156. Dachery, Spicilegium, iii., 506.

[s] Ric. of Hexham, col. 329.

long wedded, and from whom, without the sanction of the pope, he could not properly be divorced. Go, rather, and shew to the simple monk that he may find in a mitred bishop the pattern of a true ascetic. Dread not the nakedness or the poverty of that path. The barer it is the greater will be its purity. God be with you during the day, and may He give you in the evening that reward which lightens the toil and the heat, the penny which bears the image of the heavenly Cæsar.[t]

These words, so inspiriting and so sound, sank deep into the old man's heart. He set his house in order at York, rewarding his faithful followers, making restitution where it was required, and snapping link by link that chain which had bound him to the world. In his youth he had made a vow at Clugny that he would ally himself to the monks who there worshipped; and he now resolved to join a little congregation of Cluniacs, at Pontefract, which occupied the monastery of St. John. His parting from the ministers of his church in York was a most striking one. He called them to him in his chapel in the minster, and, after making his confession, prostrated himself with bared limbs before the altar of St. Andrew, and, confessing with many tears his past offences, he submitted himself to the scourge. When this was over he went to Pontefract, a great number of the clergy and the laity accompanying him. On the festival of the Conversion of St. Paul he took upon himself the vows and the garb of a monk within that little monastery, and devoted the remainder of his life to contemplation and devotion. He had only been there a few days when he felt the hand of death upon him; and he prepared to wrestle with the foe with that serene intrepidity which had characterized his life. The conflict took place on the fifth of February, 1140, and it was not one which the bystanders, and there were many there from York, would ever forget. The dying archbishop recited in solemn tones the service for the dead, whom he was so speedily to join. He chanted, with sobs and groans, the awful verses of the *Dies Iræ*; and then, whilst the rest were kneeling and praying around him, he passed away to await in the land of silence the coming of that day of wrath, so terrible to all, of which he had just spoken.[u]

He was interred, with befitting honour, before the high

[t] S. Bernardi Opp., i., 297.

[u] John of Hexham, col. 267, is the authority for this paragraph. Bromton, col. 1028. Gervase, col. 1350. Knyghton, col. 2385. Hemingford, apud Gale, ii., 485. Chron. Mailros, 71. Wm. Neubrig., i., 50. Stubbs, col. 1720-1. Trivet, 16. Dachery, Spicilegium, iii., 147.

There is some doubt as to the exact day on which Thurstan died. Gervase and Stubbs say that he died on Feb. 5. John of Hexham on the 6th. His obit was observed at Durham on the 8th (Liber Vitæ, ed. Surtees Society, 139). Hugh the Chantor places the altar in the monastery at Pontefract, and, after many years, when a party of too curious monks looked into his grave, they found, it is said, the body robed in its vestments without a symptom of decay.[v]

A few days after his decease Thurstan is said to have appeared in a dream to Geoffrey Trocope, archdeacon of Nottingham. It was in the stillness of the night, and there was his old master before him in his archiepiscopal attire. The thought of the fearful death-scene which he had so recently witnessed perhaps prompted the question, "Is there a hope of thy salvation, oh my father?" and, then, from the fleshless lips there issued the solacing reply, "To me to live is Christ, and to die is gain," which the listening friend thus turned into verse,

> "Vivere carne mihi fuerat, sed carne resolvi
> Est modo vera salus, vita beata mihi."[w]

Geoffrey, in conjunction with a person of the name of Hugh de Pontefract, drew up a life of Thurstan, partly in prose and partly in verse, which is preserved in the Cottonian library.[x] It adds nothing to the information which we possess from other sources, and is singularly meagre and uninteresting. A short extract will shew the calibre of archdeacon Geoffrey in the sweet path of poesy. It is a lament for Thurstan.

> "Gemma sacerdotum, jubar ecclesiæ, monachorum
> Dux, flos pastorum, claustri speculum, via morum,
> Semita justorum, supplantator vitiorum!
> In te cunctorum viguit mixtura bonorum.
> Transiit antistes ad gaudia summa polorum,
> Præmia sumpturus inde finita laborum.
> Proh dolor! Anglorum flos marcuit, aruit iste
> Mundo, sed celo vivat te præside, Christe.
> Heu nulli precio mors horrida, mors metuenda,
> Mors pietate carens, mors invida, mors fugienda.
> Incutis horrores, infers truculenta pavores,
> Fundis mœrores facis et post leta dolores.
> * * * *
> Ergo non doleat quisquis licet hic moriatur,
> Celica vita beat hunc qui Christo famulatur."

There is another account of Thurstan, also unpublished, by Hugh Sotevagina, the precentor and archdeacon of York.[y]

day on the Ides, meaning, I presume, the 13th.

[v] John of Hexham, col. 268. "Repertum est odoriferum et incorruptum" (Hugh de Pontefract, 55).

[w] John of Hexham, col. 267-8.

[x] Titus, A. xix. Vita S. Thurstani Archiepiscopi Ebor. partim oratione ligata, partim soluta, per Hugonem de Pontefracto monachum, et Galfridum de Nottingham. There is a life of Thurstan in Henriquez, Phœnix Reviviscens, 160—175. He says that the archbishop was a Cistercian monk, and that he died in 1136!

[y] In the Reg. Magnum Album belonging to the dean and chapter of York,—a splendid volume containing the most ancient privileges and evidences of the church. They have been transcribed at a comparatively late period, as the writer confesses his inability

Hugh was Thurstan's contemporary and friend, and he gives us, therefore, much information about his patron which is not elsewhere to be discovered. He restricts himself, however, too much to what may be called the foreign policy of Thurstan and his church. We should have been even more obliged to him had he told us a little more about the private life of the archbishop, and his work within his diocese. His account, also, terminates abruptly, and we know nothing from the writer about the battle of the Standard or of Thurstan's latter days.

Henry Murdac, abbat of Fountains, was the next actual archbishop of York, but his accession to the see was attended with much contention and generated much ill-feeling. I shall say in another place how it arose.

Murdac seems to have been a Yorkshireman by birth. His family was one of distinction, and he inherited from his parents both wealth and reputation. Through the kindness of archbishop Thurstan he was beneficed in the church of York.[c] He gave up everything, and assumed the humble cowl of a Cistercian to watch and pray by the side of St. Bernard within the walls of Clairvaux.[a] The letter by which the saint induced him to desert the world is still preserved. Murdac seems

to decipher the Saxon charters which he professes to give; indeed, he has made many blunders in his copy of Hugh. The lives, of which Hugh is supposed to be the author, occupy about seventy pages. Stubbs has availed himself, not always judiciously, of his labours. The concluding paragraph of Hugh's life of Thurstan is as follows: "Quanta audivimus et cognovimus, ea patres nostri narraverunt nobis, filii qui nascentur et exurgent et narrabunt filiis suis. Tu autem, Domine, miserere nostri." After this there comes a life of archbishop Murdac and the history of the famous controversy, taken from John of Hexham.

This "White Register" is the book on which archbishop Lee set such store. He lent it to Polydore Vergil as the greatest treasure belonging to his church. It still bears, I believe, in the margins the notes of the great archdeacon of Wells as well as those of the learned Wanley.

[c] Ric. of Hexham, col. 274. Hugh Murdac, a justice itinerant, became archdeacon of Cleveland in 1200. He was the founder of the Gilbertine priory of St. Andrew at York. There is a pedigree of the family of Murdac of Compton Murdac in Dugdale's Warwickshire, 404, and another among the Dodsworth MSS. at Oxford. Henry Murdac was a justice itinerant in 1189 (Foss's Judges, i., 404). Ralph Murdac was constable of Nottingham castle temp. Ric. I. (Hoveden, 419). Galfrid Murdac witnesses a charter granted by archbishop Thurstan in 1128 (Anglia Sacra, ii., 237).

[a] Vita S. Bernardi, apud Opp., ed. 1690, ii., 1112. Contin. Hist. Croyland, apud Gale, iii., 112. Wm. Neubr., i., 58. Trivet, 17. Recueil des Historiens des Gaules, xiv., 368. Rob. de Monte, 724. Dachery, Spicilegium, iii., 147. Mabillon, Ann. Ben., vi., 189, 223, where Murdac is called "nobilis Anglus," and "in schola præfectus."

to have had some communication with him before it arrived. How tenderly Bernard entreats him to taste of that fountain whose waters he himself had found so sweet! He pleads with the enthusiasm of a poet and the deep fervour of a saint. Oh! the charms of retirement which the Saviour himself delighted in, and which He left at last to join His fisher-brethren and evangelize the world! Believe me, thou wilt find more in woods than in books; the stocks and stones shall teach thee what a master cannot. Thinkest thou not that honey can trickle for thee from the rock, and oil from the flinty crag? Cannot the mountains drop with sweetness; the hills flow with milk and honey, and the valleys laugh and sing with corn? Oh, that thou wouldest become my fellow-learner in this holy school with Jesus for our master![b] Murdac was persuaded by these touching entreaties, and well he might be. They were made to others in the North of England with a like effect. The abbeys of Rievaux and Fountains were the fruits of that earnest pleading. It drew the robe of a Cistercian, within the walls of Clairvaux, over a prior of Hexham,[c] and all but induced Thomas, the provost of Beverley,[d] to resign his post.

Those who are well acquainted with the life and writings of St. Bernard cannot wonder at the influence that he exercised. Seven centuries have not lessened the feeling of veneration with

[b] S. Bern., Opp., i., 110. "O si semel paululum quid de adipe frumenti, unde satiatur Jerusalem, degustares! quam libenter suas crustas rodendas litteratoribus Judæis relinqueres! O si te umquam in schola pietatis sub magistro Jesu merear habere sodalem! O si mihi liceat purificatum prius tui pectoris vasculum supponere unctioni, quæ docet de omnibus! O quam libens tibi pariter calidos panes, quos utique adhuc fumigantes, et quasi modo de furno, ut aiunt, recens tractos, de cœlesti largitate crebro Christus suis pauperibus frangit! Utinam si quam mihi guttam quandoque de pluvia voluntaria, quam segregavit hereditati suæ, stillare dignetur in dulcedine sua pauperi Deus, mox eam tibi possem refundere, et rursus a te vicissim recipere quod senseris! *Experto* crede: aliquid amplius invenies in silvis quam in libris. Ligna et lapides docebunt te, quod a magistris audire non possis. An non putas posse te sugere mel de petra, oleumque de saxo durissimo? An non montes stillant dulcedinem, et colles fluunt lac et mel, et valles abundant frumento." St. Bernard addresses Murdac as "magister," which seems to shew that he was a graduate.

"Books! 'tis a dull and endless strife:
Come, hear the woodland linnet,
How sweet his music! On my life
There's more of wisdom in it.

"And hark! how blithe the throstle sings!
He, too, is no mean preacher:
Come forth into the light of things,
Let Nature be your teacher.

"She has a world of ready wealth,
Our minds and hearts to bless;
Spontaneous wisdom breathed by health,
Truth breathed by cheerfulness.

"One impulse from a vernal wood
May teach you more of man,—
Of moral evil and of good,
Than all the sages can."

[c] John of Hexham, col. 271.

[d] S. Bernardi Opp., i., 111-17, 363. Thomas changed his mind, and died, as St. Bernard tells us, "subita et horrenda morte." A new edition of the works of St. Bernard, properly corrected, is a great desideratum. The Paris edition of 1839 is merely a reprint of that by Mabillon, in which even his errors are perpetuated. Even that of Migne can be much improved.

P 2

which "the last of the fathers" is regarded. We still see before us that frail and yet striking figure attenuated by the most frightful discipline; we gaze upon that countenance with its unearthly pallor, and yet so beautifully transparent that you would deem it "lit with an inner light,"[e] and think that his soul in all its purity and holiness was looking through it; we may listen in fancy to that voice so touching and so earnest, that the very breath was held lest a single accent should escape. What multitudes flocked around him, to embrace him, to kiss his feet, to touch his very garment, and yet flattery and honours could not attract him. A simple, honest-hearted, self-denying monk he lived and died. But this was the man on whose word all Christendom used to hang in breathless expectation![f] This is he who preached a crusade, who elected a pope, chose bishops and archbishops, and chided kings! All these things our fathers have told us, but we can read for ourselves the words by which they were carried away, the heavenly contemplations, the almost divine musings with which they were fascinated. Surely the pen that handed them down to us

"Dropped from an angel's wing."

Never did any man's innermost thoughts and feelings colour his writings with a more vivid, a more speaking light. His whole soul shines through them like the sun at mid-day through his veil of clouds. The radiance appals us. We shrink, alas, too conscious of our own unworthiness and inferiority, from the presence of so much purity and holiness.

The life of Murdac is intimately connected with the history of Fountains abbey. The first abbat of that house was Richard, the quondam prior of St. Mary's, and to him, with the assistance of Geoffrey, St. Bernard's friend, is due the credit of the establishment and arrangement of that monastery, especially in

[e] Tennyson's Poems, ed. 1833, from a poem in one of the rare editions which has not been reprinted. Richard Crashaw, "poet and saint," thus expresses the same thought:—

"A soul sheath'd in a christal shrine,
Through which all her bright features shine,
As when a piece of wanton lawn,
A thin aërial veil, is drawn
O'er beauty's face, seeming to hide,
More sweetly shews the blushing bride."

[f] I cannot refrain from quoting bishop Foliot's eloquent description of St. Bernard (Epist., i., 149): "O quis ego sum, qui pastorem illum sanctum ovemque fæcundissimam, Clarevallensem abbatem clarissimum, digne commemorem? Quis mihi stilus aut quæ facundia, ut virtutis ejus, vel in modico, culmen attingam? Vir scientia clarus, sanctitate notissimus, sine fuco sanctissimus, scriptor insignis, prædicator egregius, ordinis speculum, ecclesiæ dilatatio, sui temporis sol, nebulæ dissipatio, abjectus sibi, mundo Christoque carissimus, sacerdos magnus, qui diebus suis Deo placens et justus inventus, iracundiæ tempore in ipso mirabiliter operante Domino Jesu, dissidentium factus est reconciliatio. Quem quum corporalis intuebatur oculus, mundo despicabilis habebatur. Quum spiritualis attendebat, nostri temporis hominem longe virtutum meritis antelbat. Quis ejus labores digne referat."

discipline. The saint, who during his life appears to have exercised over Fountains a protecting care, commended the progress that had been made, in a letter to the abbat and his brotherhood.[g] Richard was a man of no mean character and learning. In 1138, when Alberic cardinal-bishop of Ostia, the papal legate, arrived in England, the abbat of Fountains and the bishop of Hereford were the two persons whom he chose to accompany him on his tour.[h] In the following year Richard went to Rome on behalf of archbishop Thurstan, who was desirous of giving up his see, and it was at the eternal city that he died.[i] His place at Fountains was supplied by a namesake and a friend who had originally been a Benedictine at St. Mary's.[j] This person, who took some interest in the controversies about Thurstan's successor in the see of York, died at Clairvaux in 1143.[k] St. Bernard himself announced his decease to Alexander the prior of Fountains and his monks, and desired them to make choice of a fitting superior with the advice and assistance of William the Cistercian prior of Rievaux and the abbat of Vauclair.[l]

Murdac was the person who is last mentioned. After residing for some time at Clairvaux, and winning the confidence of St. Bernard, he was sent by him in 1135 to found a Cistercian house at Vauclair, in the diocese of Leon, and to be its first abbat.[m] When Richard, the second superior of Fountains, died, Murdac was engaged in a sharp controversy with Luke the abbat of the neighbouring monastery of Præmonstratensians at Cuissi.[n] St. Bernard intended him to move in a very different sphere. In the letter which he wrote to the prior and the monks of Fountains, he told them that Murdac was coming in his behalf to inspect their house, and that in the selection of their new head they were to be guided by his opinion.[o] Walter, the bearer of this epistle, would no doubt convey to them the wishes

[g] S. Bernardi, Opp., i., 101, and Dugd. Mon., v., 298.

[h] John of Hexham, col. 264. Ric. of Hexham, col. 325, where he is called "magnæ religionis et auctoritatis virum." Dugd. Mon., v., 299.

[i] John of Hexham, col. 265. Ric. of Hexham, col. 329.

[j] S. Bern., Opp., i., 101, annot.

[k] John of Hexham, 274, the place not being mentioned. Dugd. Mon., v., 300. S. Bern., Opp., i., 297-8. Mabillon seems to ignore the existence of this second Richard. He says that Richard died at Clairvaux on May 15, 1138, and that Murdac succeeded him.

[l] S. Bern., Opp., i., 297.

[m] Ibid., i., 298, annot. Recueil des Hist. des Gaules, xiii., 698, ex chronico Alberici. Gallia Christiana, ix., 633, where he is said to have been abbat 1135-8. Miræus, Chron. Ord. Cisterc., ed. 1614, 94. There is an account of Vauclair in the Voyage Litteraire de deux Benedictins, in which Murdac is mentioned. He was the greatest abbat of that house. Mabillon, Ann. Ben., vi., 223; where the year 1134 is given as the date of the foundation.

[n] S. Bern., Opp., i., 298, annot., ex Hermanno monacho Laudun', iii., cap. 16. There is nothing about this dispute in the account of Cuissi in the Ann. Præmonstrat. Ord., i., lxiii., etc.

[o] S. Bern., Opp., i., 298. Dugd. Mon., v., 301.

of the saint that Murdac should be the new abbat, and, at the same time, Bernard sent a letter to Murdac himself, entreating him to accept the post should he be appointed to it. Bernard spoke as if his election were a certainty, and promised, if he would go into England, to look well to the abbey of Vauclair, which he would be obliged to leave.[p] Murdac was appointed abbat of Fountains, and he accepted the proffered honour.

Murdac went to Fountains in 1143.[q] He was a rigid disciplinarian, for he had been brought up in a strict school. He was soon actively engaged in his new charge. He put everything in order; for although the Cistercians had only been at Fountains for ten years, the full severity of their rule was not entirely observed. It was otherwise now. The endowments of the house began to increase, and the revenues were administered in a noble manner. Before the monastery, still in the freshness of her youth, had come of age, she had become the parent of seven religious houses. Seven daughters had been born to her,

"All daughters of one mother."

Five of these, Woburn, Lisa, Kirkstall, Vaudy and Meaux, came into existence whilst Murdac was the abbat.[r] One of these cells,—that of Lisa, otherwise called the House of Light, was founded at the request of the bishop of Bergen, who came to see Murdac, and she carried the discipline and the fame of her parent to the wild shores of Norway. Meaux, the youngest of the family of seven, was born in 1150, and then the still youthful mother ceased to bear.[s] All her energy was henceforward devoted to the development of her own resources, and the purifying of the flame which arose to heaven from her own altars.

Where could there be a better place for a Cistercian monastery than that secluded valley? Here was their Jerusalem, their abode of peace; and they could say of it, as St. Bernard said of Clairvaux, "Lo, we heard of the same at Ephrata, and found it in the wood."[t]

"*Here man more purely lives, less oft doth fall,*
More promptly rises, walks with stricter heed,
More safely rests, dies happier, is freed
Earlier from cleansing fires, and gains withall
A brighter crown. On yon Cistercian wall
That confident assurance might be read."

[p] S. Bern., Opp., i., 298-9. Dugd. Mon., v., 301. John of Hexham (col. 274) says that St. Bernard appointed him.

[q] There is a chronological difficulty here. Richard, abbat of Fountains, died on Oct. 12, 1143. From John of Hexham it may be gathered that Murdac did not become abbat till 1145.

[r] A full account of the origin and progress of Fountains is to be found in the work of Hugh de Kirkstall, which is being printed by the Surtees Society. A great part of it is in Dugd. Mon., v., 298, etc.

[s] "Hæc novissima filiarum quas genuit mater nostra, et cessavit iterum parere" (Dugd. Mon., v., 302).

[t] S. Bern., Opp., i., 64.

Where could a place be found more fit to convince the recluse, if it were only by the force of contrast, that the retirement which he enjoyed was superior to the charms of the world beyond him? Where could he live more purely, more devotedly, to God? The great book of nature was daily open to the Cistercian there, and he would see in it what to other readers was meaningless and vain. The heavens looked down upon him with their many eyes piercing him through and through, and telling him that everything was visible to their viewless Lord. Strange voices seemed to commune with him from between the wings of the wind as it arose and fell in that solitary vale. In everything around him, pure and simple as it was, there was something to direct him heavenwards, a type or symbol of some better thing to come.

"Sum nemorum studiosus, ait."

"There was a spirit in the woods" through which he walked, and he would think of the green tree and the dry. The murmurings in the elm, the twinkling leaves of the beech which St. Bernard loved to watch, the wanton airs which ran in and out like sportive children among the branches of the oak, were as significant to him as the prophetic breeze which stirred of old "the tops of the mulberry-trees." In those rocks, once a shelter to him when he came for the first time into that "weary land," he would see a type of that great "spiritual rock" on which the Church was built, and he would beseech Him who had "poured down the stones into the valley," to be to him "a house of defence," and "a rock of habitation." The waters which bubbled up and sparkled among the clefts would remind him of the "pure fountain of life and the crystal sea;" and when he mused upon the perfections of Him who had sent those "springs into the valleys," he would join in the exclamation of the Psalmist, "All my fresh springs shall be in Thee. Benedicite, Fontes, Domino."

At the death of archbishop Thurstan in 1140, no small controversy arose as to his successor. The court was in favour of William Fitzherbert, the treasurer of York, who was actually elected and consecrated. As there was some suspicion of his having used undue influence in securing his appointment, William encountered the most strenuous opposition from all the reformers of the day. The whole of the Cistercian order seem to have been banded together against him, and among them were two abbats of Fountains, Richard[u] and Murdac. Murdac,

[u] S. Bern., Opp., i., 317. A letter to the pope on behalf of the monks of Fountains, who, as Mabillon thinks, had gone to Rome to oppose William in 1141. John of Hexham, col. 271.

indeed, seems to have led the opposition in England.[v] He was a sufferer for what he did. In 1146 pope Eugenius, instigated by St. Bernard, suspended William, and some of the archbishop's kinsmen in England determined to wreak their vengeance upon Murdac, whom they would consider to be the chief agent in the degradation of their master. They made their way to Fountains to seize the abbat. They could not find him. They burst open the doors, and sacked the monastery and its buildings. They then set the place on fire, and everything is said to have been consumed with the exception of a part of the oratory. All the while Murdac was stretched in prostrate adoration before the altar, expecting, momentarily, his end; but he was not observed. When the destroyers had departed he thankfully commenced the restoration of his house. Archbishop William, in after years, made amends for the excesses of his adherents, and expressed his deep sorrow for what had occurred.[w]

This act of violence created a great sensation at home and abroad. It was probably the immediate cause of the deprivation of William by pope Eugenius,[x] as Murdac was at Rheims when the sentence was passed.[y] This was done in 1147, and on the vigil of the festival of St. James in that year a great clerical assembly was held at the monastery of St. Martin, near Richmond, to elect a new archbishop. Robert de Gaunt the dean of York, and Hugh de Puiset the treasurer of that church, who had been preferred by William, were in favour of Hillary, one of the chaplains of the pope, who was afterwards raised to the see of Chichester. These two, in all probability, would express the wish of the court, as the former was the chancellor of England, and the latter the king's nephew. Opposed to them were the bishops of Durham and Carlisle, William de Augo the precentor, and the archdeacons of York, who were in favour of Murdac, and he seems to have been elected, although not without much controversy and opposition.[z] Murdac after this went to Clairvaux to pay a visit to St. Bernard, his old friend and adviser,[a] who had been actively employed in promoting his election.[b] From thence he went to the papal court at Trèves, where he had a hearty welcome. Eugenius put an end

[v] John of Hexham, col. 275. "Plurimum præsumens sibi de gratia Apostolici." Dugd. Mon., v., 302.

[w] Dugd. Mon., v., 302. Lel. Coll., iv., 108. John of Hexham (col. 275) gives a different account from the Fountains chronicler. He merely says, "Quandam possessionem monachorum de Fontibus cum copiis opum quæ ibi congestæ conservabantur incenderunt."

[x] S. Bern., Opp., i., 249. Bernard wrote to the pope on this occasion urging prompt action.

[y] Gervase, col. 1363.

[z] John of Hexham, col. 276. Miræus, Chron. Cisterc., ed. 1614, 122.

[a] Dugd. Mon., v., 302. Lel. Col., iv., 108.

[b] S. Bern., Opp., i., 298, annot.

to all difficulty and contention by consecrating him archbishop on the 7th of December, and giving him the pall.[c]

Murdac returned to England in the following year to find a scene of tumult and dissension, for which he was not prepared. The deposed archbishop was a cousin of the king, and a person of winning demeanour, and his sufferings had won for him universal sympathy. Stephen would not receive Murdac. He sequestred the stalls at York, and fined the inhabitants of Beverley for admitting the archbishop within their walls. The kinsmen of the deposed prelate were loud in their threats of vengeance, and caught the senior archdeacon, who escaped with difficulty alive. The citizens of York, however, were Murdac's bitterest opponents. They closed the gates of their city against him, and if any one went out to join him, the offender, if he were caught, was driven from the place and mulcted of all his property. The archbishop, upon this, excommunicated Hugh de Puiset, the treasurer of York, and all his enemies in that city. Puiset returned the compliment; and, as he was omnipotent in the minster, he would not allow the services to be suspended. They came, however, to an end, but Eustace, the king's son, made an order that they should go on; an act of interference which induced the archbishop to complain, formally, to the pope. Murdac took up his residence at Ripon whilst this unseemly disturbance was going on.[d] He would there be near his old monastery of Fountains, which he is said to have moderated during his life.[e] He made several excursions from Ripon. He paid a visit to the bishop of Durham; and at Carlisle he had an interview with king David, and was welcomed by his suffragan Adelulf.[f]

In 1150 there was peace at last between Murdac and his foes. Hugh de Puiset, at the request of the pope, was absolved from excommunication, and was reconciled to the archbishop at Yarm; and Eustace, the king's son, became his friend.* In the

[c] John of Hexham, col. 276. Ord. Vitalis, apud Duchesne, 983. Chron. Mailros, 73. Wm. Neubrig., i., 58. Trivet, 17. Bromton, col. 1029. Gervase (col. 1363) says that he was consecrated at Auxerre. In Dugd. (Mon., v., 302) it is said that he got the pall at Rome. Acta SS., Bollandists, June 8.

[d] John of Hexham, col. 277-8. Wm. Neubr., i., 58-9. Trivet, 17-18. Dachery, Spicilegium, iii., 147.

[e] Turold and Maurice were probably the principals of the monastery under Murdac. Cf. S. Bern., Opp., i., 286-7. John of Hexham, col. 274. Turold got into some trouble, and was removed from Fountains to Trois Fontaines. St. Bernard defended this appointment against the strictures of the bishop of Ostia, and said that if he had been an unworthy person Murdac would never have given him an office "*cui ipse præfuerat.*" This seems to shew the continuance of Murdac's connection with the monastery, but *not* in the capacity of abbat. There are lives of Maurice, Thorold, and Ric. Fastolph, abbats of Fountains, and their works, in Henriquez, Phœnix Reviviscens, 82, 159.

[f] John of Hexham, col. 277.

following year Murdac regained the favour of Stephen, and was solemnly enthroned at York on the day of the conversion of St. Paul. He laid upon the high altar on that occasion the ancient privileges, etc., of the church, which he had recovered and redeemed. They had been pawned, with many other treasures, by William to raise money to defray the expenses of his journeys to Rome. Murdac now invoked the curse of God upon any one who dared to alienate them again. He gave, also, probably at this time, several reliques to the minster.[g] Soon after this the archbishop crossed the seas, and spent his Easter with pope Eugenius at Rome. He went there in the capacity of an ambassador; and he was to procure from the chief pontiff, among other things, a formal recognition of the right of Eustace, king Stephen's son, to succeed to the throne of England.[h]

In 1153 Murdac was in another difficulty, into which he was forced by his conscientious wish to do his duty, regardless of consequences. William de St. Barbara, bishop of Durham, died, and Laurence the poet-prior, Wazo and Ranulph the archdeacons, and the rest of the clergy, chose Hugh de Puiset as his successor. This appointment gave great offence to Murdac and St. Bernard, not only on account of the character of Puiset, his youth, worldly-mindedness, and inexperience, but because, in their opinion, the metropolitan ought to have been consulted before the election was made. Wazo, and Nicholas the prior of Brinkburne, went to Beverley to announce formally to the archbishop what had been done. He astonished them by setting the election at naught, and by excommunicating the prior and the archdeacons. This act of severity gave much offence. When the offenders came to York to beg the mercy of Murdac, the citizens, indignant at the treatment which they had received, arose against their diocesan, calling him a traitor, and threatening him with their vengeance. He made his escape from the city, and never returned to it again. King Stephen and his son entreated him to be lenient, but, with the true Bernardine spirit, he scorned to please them by his compliance, at the expense of what he deemed to be his duty. The culprits followed him from York to Beverley, and there, at the request of archbishop Theobald, Murdac at length absolved them, but not before they had submitted themselves to his authority, and had been publicly scourged at the entrance of the minster. Puiset went to Rome, where he was consecrated by the pope. Laurence accompanied him, but he died on the journey as he was passing through France.[i]

[g] Fabric Rolls of York Minster, ed. Surtees Society, 152.

[h] John of Hexham, col. 279.

[i] Hist. Dunelm., Scr. Tres., ed. Surtees Society, 4-5. Symeon, Hist. Eccl. Dunelm., 293, and appendix, 385.

Murdac stayed for so short a time at York that he had not the opportunity of doing much. He spent a great portion of the summer of 1152 at Hexham, and tried to bring the canons of that place under a stricter discipline. In 1153 he removed the prebendaries from the church of St. Oswald, at Gloucester, introducing canons-regular in their room, and placing them under the charge of Humphrey, a monk from Lantony abbey. He was desirous also of effecting a similar change at Beverley on the death of Thurstan the provost, but his own decease prevented it being carried out.[j] Murdac, it will have been seen, was a most severe disciplinarian, and it was a matter of conscience with him to see that every one did his duty to the fullest extent. This unbending sternness made him unpopular, for the Cistercian rule was obnoxious, from its very strictness, to a great part of the Christian world. The church reformers of that age would hear of no compromise, and would not tolerate what they saw around them. A little judgment and common sense would have secured for them a strong and enduring position. As it was, the influence of the Cistercians, to a great extent, passed away when they lost St. Bernard. Excessive severity was not the way to secure the favour of the English barons. Whilst many of them were building and endowing monasteries, others seem to have been as careless of the simplest principles of religion; a strong reaction was, as it were, setting in against discipline and reform. The turbulent Comyn turned the church of Merrington into a fortress. Alan, Earl of Richmond, plundered the possessions of the see of York, and breaking with an armed band into the minster at Ripon, insulted archbishop William as he stood near Wilfrid's shrine.[k] The murder of Becket was the climax of this feeling of irreverence. Two strong waves were at this time meeting, and the collision was a startling one. But however indiscreet the Cistercians and the other church reformers may have been, no one can impugn the honesty of their purpose, or the sincerity and simplicity of their lives. If they censured others they did not spare themselves. In this respect Murdac resembled his master St. Bernard. He wore sackcloth continually, and practised the severest austerities.[l] Murdac died at Beverley on the 14th of October,

Gervase, col. 1375. John of Hexham, col. 281. Hutchinson's Durham, i., 166-7.

[j] John of Hexham, col. 280. Dugd. Mon., vi., 82. Fosbroke, in his History of Gloucester (p. 288), says that the priory of St. Oswald was built by Thurstan. There was a good deal of controversy about it in after years.

Murdac, also, made Germanus, prior of Tynemouth, abbat of Selby, to revive the discipline of that house (Matt. Paris, de S. Albani abb., 1018)—an appointment which caused a great uproar in the monastery (Hist. Mon. Seleb., apud Labbe, Bibl. Nov., i., 620.)

[k] John of Hexham, col. 273. Symeon, Hist. Eccl. Dunelm., 288.

[l] Stubbs, col. 1721. "Homo magnanimus et in causa (in)justitiæ omnino

1153. His remains were brought to York, and were interred in the minster in the place where the archbishops were laid.[m] Some time after his decease he is said to have appeared in a vision to an inmate of the nunnery of Watton, and to have miraculously assisted her.[n] It is unnecessary to make any farther allusion to this case. Ailred, in my opinion, has not added to his reputation by detailing, as meritorious, an instance of revenge of the most disgraceful and fanatical kind.

The same year in which Murdac died witnessed the decease of two men, to whom, of all others, he was under the greatest obligations, pope Eugenius and St. Bernard. The sun of the Cistercians set with their sainted leader. The historian of Fountains, when speaking of the death of the archbishop, makes a touching allusion to those flowers of the church which had been plucked before him. Murdac went to the tomb, he tells us, "sequens eos quos amavit. Dilexerunt se invicem in vita sua, in morte non separati, duces gregis Domini, columnæ domus Dei, luminaria mundi."[o]

William Fitzherbert, better known under the name of St. William of York, was a person of noble origin. His father was Count Herbert, who is said, by Stubbs, to have been chamberlain and treasurer to king Henry; and his mother, Emma, was a grand-daughter of the Conqueror, and was sister to king Stephen; from his infancy, therefore, William was brought up in the lap of luxury and wealth.[p]

About the year 1130 we find William, as treasurer of the church of York, witnessing archbishop Thurstan's charter of

invincibilis, eligens magis pro justitia periclitari quam ut justitia se presente periclitetur" (Dugd. Mon., v., 301).

[m] John of Hexham, col. 282. S. Bern., Opp., i., 298, annot. ex necrolog. Vallis Claræ. Symeon, Hist. Eccl. Dunelm., 294. Stubbs (col. 1721) says that he died at Sherburn, in which he agrees with the statement in the "president" book of Fountains, which fixes the date of Murdac's death on "prid. Id. Oct., 1153." Chron. Mailros, 75. Ann. Waverl., apud Gale, ii., 158. Rob. de Monte, 735.

[n] Ailredus, De sanctimoniali de Watton, col. 419. Murdac had something to do with the foundation of this nunnery (Dugd. Mon., vi., 955).

[o] Dugd. Mon., v., 303. Bromton, col. 1029. Wendover, i., 509. Wm. Neubr., i., 87. In Foliot's Letters (i., 92, 107) there is a letter to Murdac begging his kind offices on behalf of Gilbert, the precentor of York. Murdac is also mentioned in Opp., Joann. Saresber., i., 3.

[p] John of Hexham, col. 274. Bromton, col. 1029, 1040. Stubbs, col. 1721. Wm. Neubr., i., 58. I do not find count Herbert mentioned by any other writer as an officer of Henry; indeed, there is nothing known about him.

foundation of the nunnery of Clementhorp.[q] There is a deed, also, without a date, in which Henry I. grants the churches of Wallop and Wichtona, and the chapel of Grateleia, in which William the treasurer had a life interest, to be the *corpus* of a new prebend at York.[r] I have seen a charter of king Stephen, in which that monarch grants to William, the treasurer of York, his chaplain, the churches of Weaverthorpe, Londesburgh, Cleve, with their chapels, and the church of Stanton; all of which he held of the fee of his brother Herbert.[s] This probably is the nobleman whom Dugdale introduces in his Baronage,[t] and of whose parentage there has, hitherto, been nothing known.

Archbishop Thurstan died in 1140, and the chapter of York seem to have had great difficulty in selecting a person to succeed him. At the instance of Henry de Blois, bishop of Winchester, and the king's brother, they fixed upon his nephew, Henry de Sully. That ecclesiastic was the abbat of Fècamp in Normandy, and the pope would not allow him to become archbishop because he refused to give up his monastery.[u] In January, 1141-2, the clergy again met to choose a president, and the majority fixed upon William, the treasurer.[v] As he was one of the king's nephews, the court influence seems to have been brought to bear upon the chapter, and William, earl of Albemarle, was present at the election, in which he took an especial interest. That nobleman, unfortunately, shewed himself a hasty partizan, and did much mischief to the cause of William. Master Walter, of London, and the rest of the York archdeacons were opposed to the choice which the clergy had made, and were on their way to the king to state their case, when the stout earl arrested them and shut them up in his castle at Bytham. In the meantime the archbishop-elect went to Stephen at Lincoln, and was kindly received, and invested

[q] Dugd. Mon., iv., 323.

[r] Chartular. thesaurar. Ebor., apud Ebor. About the same time, "J, clericus, filius regis, canonicus Ebor," quit-claims to the treasurer the homage of Reginald, son of John, son of Sweyn (ibid.). Who could this be? The name is quite new.

[s] MSS. Cotton, Vitellius, A ii., 107. This charter is printed in Dugd. Mon., vi., 1196, where there are other deeds connected with the same places, giving some interesting information about the sons and grandchildren of Herbert the chamberlain.

[t] Dugd. Bar., i., 624. Herbert seems to have been the elder son, and to have succeeded to his father's estates in the fifth of Stephen. Herbert filius Herberti and William, treasurer of York, his brother, are mentioned as benefactors to Nostel priory in Rot. Chart., 215.

[u] John of Hexham, col. 268, where it is said, erroneously, that Sully was abbat of Caen. He was a Cluniac monk, and was the fifth abbat of Fècamp (Recueil des Hist. des Gaules, xiv., 384), and died, holding that office, in 1188-9 (Gallia Christiana, xi., 209). Mabillon, Ann. Ben., vi., 323, where he is called Coilli. Chronicon Fiscanense, apud Labbe, Nov. Bibl., i., 328.

[v] Diceto, col. 508. Bromton, col. 1028.

with the temporalities of the see. The bishop of Winchester, another uncle, who was at that time the legate in England, then sent him to Rome.[w]

The opposition, however, was not so easily quelled, and the harsh measures of the earl of Albemarle would not allay it. The discontented party determined to follow William to Rome, and make their appeal to the chief pontiff. It was a contest between the court and the most influential portion of the clergy. The clerical party was ably represented, and was backed by the reformers in the church, particularly by the Cistercians. The cause was heard in 1142 in the consistory of pope Innocent. Walter of London, the archdeacon, who had escaped from the clutches of Albemarle, presented the allegations against William, which were supported by William abbat of Rievaux,[x] Richard abbat of Fountains, Cuthbert prior of Gisburgh, Waltheof the famous prior of Kirkham, and Robert the master of the hospital at York. William was charged by them with having secured his election by bribery. Innocent listened to what was said, but would make no decision at that time. He ordered both parties to present themselves before him on the third Sunday in Lent in the following year.[y]

They came to Rome at the appointed time in 1143, and the case was heard. The main point against the validity of William's election was this, that the earl of Albemarle had come into the chapter-house, and had vitiated the proceedings by giving a message from the king that William should be chosen. The pope very properly declared that if, in addition to the personal denial of the imputation of undue influence by William himself, the dean of York would state on his oath that no such message from the king had been delivered, that then the archbishop-elect might be consecrated. The dean also, who was not present at the consistory, was to be allowed, if he chose, to take the oath by deputy. That dignitary had other things to think of, as he had just been nominated to the see of Durham by the

[w] John of Hexham, col. 268, 271. Ann. Waverl., ed. Gale, ii., 154. Waltheof, prior of Kirkham, would probably have been appointed archbishop of York on Thurstan's decease if king Stephen had not interfered. Waltheof was a great favourite of David of Scotland, and Stephen was afraid that, if appointed, Waltheof would play into his hands (Acta SS., Bollandists, Aug. 3).

[x] A person much concerned in the ecclesiastical reforms of the day. He was a great light among the early Cistercians, and Henriquez gives a life of him. St. Bernard wrote two letters to him exhorting him to bear "æquanimiter" the election of William (Opp., i., 320, 324). He died in 1145 (John of Hexham, 274), and his metrical epitaph, together with that of Robert, abbat of Newminster, is in MSS. Cotton, Titus D, xxiv., 81.

[y] John of Hexham, col. 271. Bromton, col. 1029, 1041. Stubbs (col. 1721) says that Osbert, the archdeacon of York, was the chief promoter of the attack on William.

prior and the clergy. William returned from Rome in September 1143, and following the advice of the legate, submitted his case to a council which was held at Winchester. Every one seemed, not to request, but to demand, his consecration; and not a murmur was heard against anything that he had done. The bishop of Durham had been expected to take the oath about the election in the chapter-house at York, which had been prescribed to him by the pope, but he was unavoidably absent. Ralph bishop of Orkney, Sanaricus the abbat of St. Mary's, York, and Benedict abbat of Whitby, took it in his behalf, and swore to the absence of simony and undue influence. What more could be required? On the 26th of September William was consecrated at Winchester by the bishop of that diocese, who was his uncle and his friend.[z]

In 1145 cardinal Hincmar, a legate from Lucius the new pope, visited England, and brought with him a pall for William. They did not meet, for William was a person of an easy and indolent disposition, and saw no reason for promptitude or haste.[a] In the meantime the pope died and was succeeded by Bernard, the abbat of the house of St. Anastatius at Rome, under the title of Eugenius III. He was a rigid Cistercian, and hung upon the lips of St. Bernard. The opponents of William now began most ungenerously to reopen the old sore. They could carry the day now, as they thought, and they resolved to try. They were decidedly in the wrong. William had complied with all the conditions which Innocent had laid down, and his consecration had been regular and proper. Why was he to be opposed? There must have been some personal feeling prompting his opponents, that curse which, under the colour of conscience and justice, has in every age instigated so many great men to be persecutors and maligners. William about this time shewed his love of peace by effecting a reconciliation between the bishop of Durham and the turbulent Comyn.[b] With Alan, earl of Richmond, he was not so fortunate.[c]

Hincmar returned to Rome in 1145, carrying the pall with him, and, in the following year, William went in quest of it himself to the court of Eugenius. The charges against him had been revived by the Cistercians, Henry Murdac, the abbat of

[z] John of Hexham, col. 272-3. Gervase, col. 1357, 1665, who says that archbishop Theobald declined to consecrate. Chron. Mailros, 72. Rob. de Monte, 714. I have used Mr. Stevenson's edition of the last-mentioned work. The original text may be found among the collected works of Guibert, and in Pertz, Monumenta Hist. Germ., viii., 475—535.

[a] John of Hexham, col. 274.

[b] Symeon, Hist. Eccl. Dunelm., 283-4, 292. There is a curious account of an adventure at St. Cuthbert's tomb, when William was there, in Reginaldus, De admir. B. Cuthberti Virtutibus, ed. Surtees Society, 198.

[c] John of Hexham, col. 273.

Fountains, taking a prominent part in the attack.[d] But William had a more serious opponent in St. Bernard. That great man, whose zeal in this instance overpowered his judgment, had been a constant opponent of the appointment of William. He wrote strong letters against him to popes Celestine and Innocent and the cardinals. He now exerted for the same purpose the immense influence which he exercised over Eugenius.[e] The cardinals, however, were in William's favour, and the pope was in a difficulty. At length Eugenius resolved to deprive him, until the bishop of Durham should take the oath which had been formerly required from him, and the cardinal-bishop of Ostia read the sentence of deprivation.[f] This was unfair treatment. It was tantamount to trying a person a second time for the offence of which he had already been acquitted. William left Rome in disgust, and spent some time at the court of Roger king of Sicily, as the guest of Robert, the chancellor of that monarch, who was an Englishman by birth. Whilst he was staying there, the indignation of Eugenius was aroused by the account of the attack upon Fountains abbey which had been made by some of William's indiscreet partizans. This unfortunate occurrence, together with the urgent appeals of St. Bernard, probably induced the pope to take summary measures against William. Murdac and the York clergy were present at a council which was held at Rheims in 1147, over which Eugenius himself presided, and there, in compliance with their request, William was removed from his archbishopric, and the bishop of Durham and the chapter of York were ordered to proceed to the election of another primate within forty days after the receipt of the papal mandate.[g]

Henry Murdac now stepped for awhile into the see of York, as has been already stated, and William, returning from the Sicilian court, found an asylum with his uncle at Winchester. The opposition that was made to Murdac shews the sympathy which was felt for the ejected prelate. At his uncle's palace William received all the honours that could be paid to an archbishop. High and low regarded him with affection and compassion. He made no murmur himself against the sentence of Eugenius.[h]

William, whilst he was at York, promulgated some orders about the trees and grass in churchyards (Wilkins, i., 425. Labbe, Conc., x., col. 1131).

[d] John of Hexham, col. 275.

[e] S. Bern., Opp., i., 229-37, 316. Baluzii Misc., ed. Mansi, i., 146. There is a long account of this controversy in Acta SS., Bollandists, June 8, 140; and in Alfordi Annales, iv., pt. ii., 35, etc. Mabillon, Ann. Ben., vi., 326.

[f] Gervase, col. 1363.

[g] John of Hexham, col. 275. Stubbs, col. 1721. Wm. Neubr., i., 58. Chron. Mailros, 73, the bishop of Durham "nolens eum sacramento purgare." Twisden's Historical Vindication of the Church of England in point of Schism, 58.

[h] John of Hexham, col. 276. Bromton, col. 1029, 1041. Hoveden, 278. Wm. Neubr., i., 58. Jo. Saresber., Opp., ii., 172. Dachery, Spicilegium, iii., 147. Trivet, 17.

"His duty is to stand and wait,
In resignation to abide
The shock, and finally secure
O'er pain and grief a triumph pure."

The luxury and inertness of his previous life seem to have deserted him. He was an altered man. He was sedulous in his devotions and study. Not a harsh word against those who had wronged him ever passed his lips. Affliction had wrought in him the end for which it was designed. It had given him

"A soul by force of sorrows high
Uplifted to the purest sky
Of undisturbed humanity."

William seems to have lived in retirement at Winchester during the whole of the archiepiscopate of Murdac. When that prelate died in 1153 the hopes of the sufferer again arose. The majority of the chapter of York elected him their superior, and he hastened at once to Rome, not to complain of his past wrongs, but to beg for present justice. All now seemed willing to befriend him. Gregory, one of the most influential of the cardinals, took up his cause with warmth, and William's cousin, Hugh de Puiset, who was then at Rome to expedite his own consecration as bishop of Durham, did what he could for him. Anastatius, the new pope, was moved by the account of his trials and the earnestness of his pleading, and restored him to the honours of which he had been deprived, giving him the wished-for pall.[i] William returned to England with a light heart, and kept the Easter of 1154 at Winchester, where he had so long resided.[j] Whilst he was in the South he is said to have paid a visit to Canterbury, and there he had much friendly intercourse with Roger the archdeacon. "That man shall be my successor," is said to have been his remark.[k] And so he was.

William now set out for York. Before he had entered into the city he was met by Robert the dean and archdeacon Osbert, who had withstood his election by the chapter, and they, hoping to prevent his approach to their church, announced their intention of appealing from the decision of their brethren to archbishop Theobald. William's progress, however, was not delayed by their opposition.[l] He reached the city on the 9th of May, a vast and rejoicing crowd accompanying him. As the party was crossing the Ouse, the bridge, which was then made of wood, gave way, and a number of persons were precipitated into

[i] Diceto, col. 510. Bromton, col. 1029. Stubbs, col. 1722. Hoveden, 281. Wm. Neubr., i., 86-7. Matt. Paris, 77. Chron. Mailros, 75. Ann. Waverl., apud Gale, ii., 158. Rob. de Monte, 736. Cotton's Chron., 69.

[j] Gervase, col. 1376.

[k] Stubbs, col. 1722.

[l] Wm. Neubr., i., 88.

the river. William is said to have wrought a miracle in their behalf. We are told that he made his prayers with tears to God for the sufferers, and, making over them the sign of the cross, they were all saved.[m] When a bridge of stone was erected at that place, a chapel upon it, dedicated to St. William, reminded the wayfarers of the legend.

William was in York but thirty days. On Trinity Sunday he officiated in the minster, and almost before the service was over he was seized with a very sudden and alarming attack of illness. He returned to his residence, which was hard by, and a banquet was prepared for his friends, whilst the archbishop sought his chamber, which he never left alive. Like many others, he had a presentiment of what was coming on.[n] For eight days he was on the bed of sickness, and then, on the 8th of June, he died.[o] There was a story current in the middle ages to the effect that he had been poisoned by something which his clerks or enemies had put into the eucharistic wine,[p] and on that account he was afterwards regarded as a martyr. There is, however, no allusion to this tale either in the MS. life of William, or in the account of him by Stubbs. William of Newburgh, also, speaks contemptuously of the report, and denies it on the authority of a monk of Rievaux of his acquaintance, who had been intimately connected with the archbishop, and had been present when he died. William died of a fever, and the suddenness of the attack made his friends imagine that he had been poisoned.[q] Archdeacon Osbert, who had constantly opposed William, was looked upon as the culprit. Symphorian, one of the clerks of the deceased prelate, charged him with the crime in the presence of the king and council, and was desirous that the matter might be decided either by the combat or the ordeal. Osbert professed his willingness to abide by the decision of an ecclesiastical tribunal. We are told by John of Salisbury that he failed to purge himself from the charge, but we do not know to what test he was subjected. Gilbert Foliot, however, expresses a strong opinion as to the innocence of

[m] Bromton, col. 1029, 1041. Stubbs, col. 1722 (on 7 Id. May). Polydore Vergil (210) makes the bridge at Pontefract.

[n] The following extract from the MS. life of St. William contains an allusion to his end:—"In omnibus, igitur, se exhibens ut Christi minister; post disciplinas diras quibus Domino mulctabat, post lugubrationes nocturnas et crebras, post fletus amarissimos quos præteritorum delictorum recordatio ex imis pectoribus eructabat, lorica justiciæ circumdatus, ad præparationem evangelii calciatus, sacris altaribus debitis horis libenter astabat, *ut patri filium immolaret.*"

[o] Stubbs, col. 1722.

[p] Gervase, col. 1376. Hoveden, 281. Chron. Mailros, 75. Fordun, Scotichronicon, ed. Goodall, i., 448. Mat. Paris, 77. Ann. Waverl., apud Gale, ii., 158. Rob. de Monte, 736. Serlo, the chronicler of Fountains, speaks of the report (Dugd. Mon., v., 303).

[q] Wm. Neubr., i., 88—90.

the accused person, and the injustice of the proceedings against him.[r]

William was interred[s] in the minster of York by his old friend bishop Pudsey.[t] His sufferings and character, the gentleness of his disposition and his untimely end, won for him general sympathy. The church of York had no saint at that time peculiar to itself, and the chapter were most anxious, if possible, to procure the canonization of William. Thirty-six miracles are said to have been wrought through the mediation of the deceased archbishop,[u] and a holy oil, one of the mediæval accompaniments of supposed sanctity, is said to have flowed from his tomb.[v] In 1227 the archbishop and the chapter of York entreated Honorius III. to enter William on the calendar, sending as their representatives Godard the penancer, Elias Bernardi, one of the canons, and Laurence, canon of Aquileia. Indulgences were also granted by the archbishop of Canterbury, the bishops of Rochester, London, Lincoln, Ardfert and Dublin, to those who visited the tomb;[w] the papal assent, however, was not immediately given, and a commission seems to have been issued to make a full enquiry into the circumstances of the case. The canonization was not completed until the pontificate of Nicholas III., when it was effected by the money and urgent entreaties of the bishop-elect of Durham, the magnificent Anthony Bek, who was represented at Rome by his cousin

[r] Foliot's Letters, i., 152. Joh. Saresb., Epist., i., 158, 170. The author of the history of the foundation of Selby abbey says that after Murdac's death archdeacon Osbert was degraded by the legate in synod assembled, for his conduct towards Selby abbey, and that he went to the priory S. Trin. at York (Hist. Mon. Seleb., apud Labbe, Bibl. Nov., i., 620).

[s] There is a story of there being an accidental fire in York on the night of his death. A part of the "domus orationis," in which the archbishop's corpse was laid, was consumed, but the body was preserved (Brev. in usum eccl. Ebor., pars hyemalis, ed. 1526, fol. cxiii).

There is a curious piece of evidence in a charter, by which Alice de Gant, widow of Roger de Mowbray, gives lands in Cave to the church of York. "Hanc donationem feci publice in ecclesia Beati Petri et præsentis cartæ attestatione confirmavi, anno Incarnationis Domini m° c° l° quarto, v Idus Junii, regnante rege Stephano, *vacante ecclesia post obitum archiepiscopi Willielmi, eodem etiam nondum sepulto*" (Dodsworth MSS. I am indebted for this information to my friend Mr. Walbran).

[t] Hoveden, 281.

[u] MSS., Harl., 2. York Breviary, 113. The thirty-six miracles are recorded by Dodsworth, who obtained his information from a table in the registry of York minster (MSS. apud Oxon., 125). In the book of chapter acts the following extraordinary circumstance is said to have occurred on St. William's day, 1290. I give it without comment. "Mutus quidam ad tumbam ipsius Sancti usum linguæ recepit in aurora diei, cujus lingua ante triennium per latrones fuerat amputata !"

[v] Stubbs, col. 1722. Brev. Ebor., 114 *b*. Recueil des Hist. des Gaules, xiii., 698. Chron. Joh. de Oxenedes, 148. Matt. Paris, 267, who seems to say that the oil began to flow in 1223.

[w] MSS. Cotton, Titus D. xxiv., 50 *b*, etc.

Stephen de Mauley, archdeacon of Cleveland.[x] The *depositio* of William was commemorated on the 8th of June,[y] and his translation on the 8th of January. At a council held in the minster on the 29th of October, 1478, the last-mentioned ceremonial was transferred to the Sunday next after the Epiphany, and it was ordered to be observed as a double and principal festival.[z]

The remains of William were interred in the nave of York minster, near the south-west pillar of the lantern; they were removed in solemn state to a nobler resting-place in the choir, on the 8th of January, 1283-4.[a] On no other occasion has the cathedral received within its walls a more illustrious assemblage. A double ceremony brought it there that day—the translation of St. William, and the consecration of that noble-minded man who had secured for the church of York the canonization of its archbishop. Bek, who was called

"Le plus vaillant clerk de roiaume,"[b]

was surrounded by the chief estates of England, including Edward I. and his gentle consort. The king had recently fallen from an eminence, and had escaped unhurt. He ascribed his good fortune to the agency of St. William, and hastened to York to shew his gratitude by being present at the translation of his body. The ceremonial on that occasion has been detailed with an interesting minuteness.[c]

On the night of the 6th of January, archbishop Wickwaine, attended by the dean and the canons, went into the minster, Anthony Bek, and his brother Thomas, the bishop of St. David's, accompanying them. The solemnity of the place and the time

[x] Miscell. Doc. penes Dec. and Cap. Dunelm., 495. The whole history was detailed on a table which was formerly kept in the minster. Stopford's Errors of Rome, 209.

[y] Martyrologium Usuardi, ed. 1714, 325. Acta SS., Bollandists, June 8th. A Memorial of ancient British piety, 88.

[z] York Breviary, *ut supra*, 113.

[a] Trivet, 260.

[b] Nicolas's Siege of Carlaverok, 53.

[c] This account of the translation is taken from a most rare volume, a copy of the York Breviary, which was given in 1733 by Rokeby Scott, clerk, to the minster library at York. I give a copy of the title. The words in italics are in red letters: "*Breviarium ad usum insigis* Metropolitane ecclesie *Eboracensis:* una cum *pica* diligentissime, accuratissimeque recognitum et emendatū: in preclara *Parrhisiensi* academia: ī edibus videlicet *Francisci Regnault* impressum: ac expensis honesti viri *Joannis Galcheti:* in predicta *Eboracēsi* civitate cōmorātis: hic suum capit exordium pro tempore hyemali. *Anno nostre reparationis* 1526." The class mark is X. P. 7. I have compared it with another edition of the same work (X. O. 24), which is imperfect at the beginning and the end. It contains a number of the festivals. The Bollandists have transferred the account of the translation of St. William to their pages (June 8). Cf. Hist. Dunelm. Scr. Tres., ed. Surtees Society, 64, where a curious circumstance is mentioned about Bek and St. William's remains. Prynne's Coll., iii., 307. Chron. Petrib., 154. Walsingham, apud Camden, 51.

did not appal them, for they were bent upon a holy work. They went to the tomb of William, and prostrated themselves in lowliest obeisance. When their devotions were finished, they arose and removed reverently the stone which served as a lid to the sarcophagus in which the archbishop was laid. The body still bore the vestments in which Puiset had committed it to the grave, and was steeped and redolent, as the narrator tells us, with an odoriferous oil. They began by removing the paten and chalice which lay beside the remains; and then the archbishop and his companions carefully and devoutly gathered together the bones from the head downwards, and rolling them up, with the other things which were there, placed them for the night in a capsule or case, which was sealed up and concealed until the morrow. On the following day the reliques were minutely examined, and everything that pertained to the body was deposited and secured in an appropriate feretory. On the day after this was the festival of the translation; and about the hour of prime the royal party, and a goodly company of lords and prelates, were assembled in the church. The archbishop preached a sermon in which he expatiated largely, no doubt, upon the merits of his now sainted predecessor. When this was over, the feretory was raised upon the shoulders of the king[d] and others, and was borne, probably with joyous music, around a portion of the choir to the elevated shrine in which it was henceforward to be preserved.

The place in which the feretory was deposited was in all probability behind the high altar, in the vacant space between it and the eastermost screen.[e] It was here that the shrine was erected and decked with the offerings of the worshippers. It seems to have been divided into two parts, one fitting into the other. The smaller part, in which the reliques were enclosed, could be lifted, and seems to have been borne processionally, on solemn occasions, through the minster and the city. There were appended to it the little gifts which piety or superstition had suggested—images, beads, rings, girdles, and jewels of every description, of gold, silver, or precious stone. The skull of the saint was kept by itself in a case of silver gilt. It was most richly decorated. When the storm of the Reformation broke over the church, this relique had a curious fate. On the 24th of October, 1541, the dean, Richard Layton, who was a minion of the king, caused a chapter act to be passed by which

[d] In the Liber Garderob. of Edward I., p. 39, etc., will be seen the offerings which he made at St. William's feretory and tomb.

[e] Willis's Architectural History of York Cathedral, 50-3. Fabric Rolls of York Minster, 152, 195, 221, 224. When Henry IV. stopped the influx of worshippers to archbishop Scrope's tomb, their offerings were transferred to that of St. William. Test. Ebor., ed. Surtees Society, ii., 233.

the head and its ornaments were to be appropriated to the use of the cathedral.[f] The bones of William were now unhoused. In May, 1732, Mr. Drake, the historian of York, removed the stone in the nave of the minster under which the remains of William were said to have been deposited, and found under it, in a leaden box, a number of bones huddled carelessly together without any order or arrangement. It seems probable from this that the reliques had been laid in their old resting-place after the feretory and the capsule had been destroyed.[g]

The chapter of York in the middle ages paid great honour to St. William, although, perhaps, his shrine had a less brilliant reputation than that of any other Northern saint. As early as 1230 a chantry was founded at the place of his interment by Elias Bernardi, one of the canons who had been most anxious to secure his canonization.[h] A chapel dedicated to him was erected upon Ouse bridge, to commemorate what had occurred when William came into the city before his death.[i] In the fifteenth century, a college, which bears his name, was built for the use of the ecclesiastics in the minster, at the east end of the cathedral. A considerable portion of it is now in existence.[j] There is still in the choir of the church of York "a storied window richly dight," detailing the principal events in William's life. The monks of Meaux treasured carefully among their reliques some of the hair of the sainted archbishop.[k]

St. William is not without his biographer. Some unknown writer has drawn up an account of his life, which is now preserved in the British Museum among the Harleian MSS., No. 2. It is in a hand of the twelfth century, and belonged at one time to Thornton abbey. The style is very inflated and diffuse, and the work contains nothing that we were not previously acquainted with through the pages of John of Hexham and William of Newburgh. There was another life of William among the MSS. formerly belonging to Sir Simonds d'Ewes, which I have been unable to trace.[l] Capgrave, also, gives a short account of him in his *Legenda*, which has been transferred by the Bollandists to their *Acta Sanctorum*.[m] The compilers of that invaluable

[f] Chapter Acts. This head was the greatest treasure that the church of York possessed. When Margaret, daughter of Henry VII., visited the minster, the head was brought for her to kiss.

[g] Drake's Eboracum, 420. Torre's MS. account of York Minster, 162. Gent's Ripon, 103. Drake gives an engraving of the sarcophagus which he found.

[h] Fabric Rolls of York Minster, ed. Surtees Society, 305. MSS. Cotton, Titus D. xxiv., 50 *b*.

[i] Drake's Eboracum, 280.

[j] Ibid., 570. Fabric Rolls of York Minster, 72. Dugd. Mon., vi., 1184.

[k] Poulson's Holderness, ii., 313.

[l] Smith's Catalogue of MSS.

[m] Capgrave's Nova Legenda, 310-11. Acta SS. June 8.

collection were unacquainted with the existence of any unpub-lished life of the saint.

I now give two hymns addressed to St. William. The first was discovered accidentally in the Cottonian library.[a] Alford in his *Annals*,[b] could only quote a few lines of it; and the writer of the life in the *Acta Sanctorum*, when he alludes to it says regretfully, "totum utinam dedisset." The second is gathered from the Responsoria, etc., in the service for the translation of St. William in the breviaries of the York use. To those who are accustomed to hexameters and pentameters the metres will be novel and refreshing.

I.

"Pasci greges de pastore
Aure discant, dicant ore
  Jubilum preconii;
Sit mel ori melos auri
Nomen nostri nunc thesauri
  Quondam thesaurarii;
Fraudulenter qui cassatus
Ab honore presulatus,
  Latensque septennio,
Vacat contemplacioni;
Magnum malum magni boni
  Sæpe fit occasio.
Statu causæ reformato,
Romam petit iterato,
  Nullis adversantibus.
Eboracum presul redit,
Pontis casus nullum ledit
  De tot turbæ millibus.
In octavis Penthecostes
Quidam malignantes hostes
  In eum pacifice,
Et ut ipsum privent vita
Celebrantis achonita
  Propinat in calice.
Toxicatur a prophanis
Ille potus ille panis
  Per quem perit toxicum.
Ambo presul amplexatur,
Ut per unum moriatur
  Et vivat per reliquum.
Vivit moriturque quidem,
Sed non agunt circa idem
  Fermentum et azima.
Corpus obit præ fermento,
Azimorum alimento
  Vegetatur anima.
Virus bibit nocuum risumque perpetuum brevi merearis lacrima,
Mortem subit optimam dum sacrando victimam fit et ipse victima.
  O Willelme, martir Christi,
  Per eundem quem bibisti

[a] MSS. Cotton, Titus A., 19, 150. [b] Annales, iv., part ii., 35, etc.

Salutaris calicem,
Fer solamen mundo tristi
Et quem tibi placuisti
Nobis placa judicem. Amen."

II.

"In Willelmi laudibus laxet clerus ora,
Sit in hymnis canticis concio canora.
Pii patris hodie corpus est translatum
Quod in imo jacuit in alto locatum.[p]
Quondam thesaurarius jam thesaurus cleri
Dedit opus medicum, nunc dat opem veri.
Cœlum solum sitiens gazas Christi miles
Ne scandentem retrahant calcat ut res viles.
In doctrina solidum cibum dat provectis
Et lactis dulcedinem miscet imperfectis.
Nostri patris in natalicio
Lætas laudes dictet devotio,
Cœli regem lactet oratio,
Ut jungamur ejus consortio.[q]
Ortus clari germinis hunc nobilitavit,
Et mentis nobilitas genus geminavit.
In agendis strenuus, fidus in commissis,
Ad censuram rigidus, firmus in promissis.
Mitis in consortiis, in loquela rarus,
In responsis providus, in sensu præclarus.
Voluntatis trutina non legis cassatus,
Virum novum induit cœlitus mutatus.
Juventutis januas claudit cassatio,
Sic malum sæpius boni fit occasio.
Vir ad sui gloriam redit inglorius,
Ut unguenti vasculum mundetur melius.
Lachrimarum lavacro purgatis personis,
Confert divinitus munus unctionis.
Laceratum exulem morsibus malignis
Nec faux frangit odii, nec livoris ignis.
Probat hunc exilium sicut hyems laurum,
In fornace ponitur, purum exit aurum.
Ne Samsonem Dalida faciat perire,
Hic carnem spiritui cogit obedire.
Agrum mentis seminat sementis virtutum,
Et mundi delicias spernit velut lutum.
Ne recentes flosculi virtutum marcescant,
Hos scripturæ rivulis irrigat ut crescant.
Factus Jacob vigilat extra supra gregem,
Nec minus interius regum sapit Regem.
Marthæ ministerio copulat Mariam,
Rachelis amplexibus fruitur post Lyam.[r]
Fragrat odor præsulis Romam venientis,
Occurrit fragranciæ plebs unius mentis.
Ex longinquis veniunt nec sunt fatigati,
Longa via visa est curta caritati.

[p] In the edition without date these two lines are substituted:—

"Pius pater hodie ex hac valle fletus
Ad supernum solium Syon transit lætus."

[q] In the edition of 1526 the lines, up to this point, come at the end of the service and not at the beginning.

[r] A Bernardine expression. There is something similar to it in Foliot's Letters, ii., 328, and in "Memorials of Fountains Abbey," ed. Surtees Society, 74.

Plebs occurrit præsuli, cadit pons dissutus,
Sed a casu populus ruens redit tutus.
Unda ruens populum recipit ruentem,
Et se pontem efficit per Omnipotentem.
Ne cursus ad superos animo claudatur,
Mens Dei dulcedini tota copulatur.
Servit elemosinis manus insopita,
Quibus se dat funditus vir Israelita.
In sublime levat, ut palma, comam spei,
Et imputrescibilis vivit cedrus Dei.
Fide fuit Finees, ut Job mansuetus,
Patiens ut Israel, ut Noe discretus.
Fidelis ut Abraham, ut Loth hospitalis,
Sagax ut Samuel, ut Joseph liberalis.
Vivum Christus oleo tam large linivit,
Quod adhuc in mortuo olei fons vivit.
Ut sit nomen præsulis oleum effusum,
Corpus fundit oleum ad ægrorum usum.
Adit Sancti tumulum languidorum cœtus,
Et qui plangens venerat plaudens redit lætus.
Præsulis antidotum præsens est egenis,
Quo devotos liberat pluribus a pænis.
Claudi recti redeunt, furor effugatur,
Epilepsis passio sanitati datur.
Purgantur hydropici, laudes fantur muti,
Datur paraliticis suis membris uti.
Lepre tergit maculas, membra dat castratis,
Lumen datur pluribus sine luce natis.
Rapiunt a pugile lex et hostis lumen
Quod per sanctum reparat cœco cœli numen.
Ab abyssi faucibus biduo submersum,
Mater natum recipit a morte reversum.
O Willelme, pastor bone,
Cleri pater et patrone,
Mundi nobis in agone
Confer opem, et depone
Vitæ sordes, et coronæ
Cœlestis da gaudia."

Roger de Pont l'Evêque, in Normandy, was the successor of William. We first hear of him in the family, or court as it was called, of Theobald, archbishop of Canterbury. That prelate had many clerks around him who were conspicuous for their abilities, and Roger was inferior to none of them. Theobald's residence seems to have been a little school of the prophets. Among the companions of Roger there was a youth who was destined in after years to surpass him in the vigour of his acts, and the splendour of his preferments. This was the well-known Becket. One of the many biographers of the martyred primate informs us, that at that time Roger was his superior in learning, but not in character and bearing. We are told that there was some jealousy between them, and that Roger on two occasions attempted to deprive Becket of the good opinion of the archbishop. He was successfully defended by Walter, archdeacon of Canterbury, who afterwards became bishop of Rochester.[s]

In 1148 the consecration of Walter vacated the archdeaconry of Canterbury, which was given by Theobald to Roger.[t] For the next six years we know very little of his life, with the exception of the fact that he was made one of the royal chaplains.[u] He was also involved in a controversy about his office at Canterbury, from which his friend, bishop Foliot, strove to extricate him.[v] In 1154 William of York died; and Robert the dean, and archdeacon Osbert, secured the election of Roger, even threats being used, as William of Newburgh states, to gain the suffrages of the chapter. This was brought about by Theobald, who was well acquainted with the merits of his archdeacon, and who would be glad to have a client and a friend at the head of the Northern province.[w] The archbishop consecrated him in Westminster abbey on the tenth of October, as many as eight bishops being present.[x] After this Roger went to Rome and received the pall.[y] He was present in December, 1154, at the coronation of Henry II.[z]

The ecclesiastical history of England during the early part of the reign of Henry II. centres in Thomas à Becket. It is very difficult even now to make a proper estimate of the character of that extraordinary man. Modern writers have weighed it with too much partiality or severity. They have been bewildered by the strong lights and shadows with which his life abounded. There were in him many noble impulses, a vigorous and independent will, a fearless intrepidity, swayed and marred occasionally by a waywardness of disposition, and an infirmity of temper to which exalted minds are too frequently subject. These defects very often set off a noble character. There is true strength occasionally in weakness. Every one, however, must admire that eight years' struggle for the privileges of his

[s] Becket's Works, ed. Giles, i., 10, 99, 184-5. Roger gave Becket the sobriquet of Thomas "cum ascia sive securi," or "Baillehache."

[t] Gervase, col. 1362. Somner's Canterbury, part ii., 150.

[u] Stubbs, col. 1722.

[v] Epist. Gilb. Foliot, i., 80, 124. Joann. Saresber. Opp., i., 175.

[w] Becket's Works, i., 10. Roger de Pontigny (ibid., 100) says that this was done with the connivance of the king, and that Becket was preferred to the archdeaconry of Canterbury and the provostship of Beverley "quæ Rogerius obtinuerat." Roger was never provost of Beverley. Wm. Neubrig., i., 90. Bromton, col. 1042. Rob. de Monte, 736.

Mapes mentions Roger in connection with Coxwold (De Nugis Cur., 50).

[x] Gervase, col. 1376. Diceto, col. 529—with no profession. Bromton, col. 1042. Anglia Sacra, i., 8. Ann. Waverl., apud Gale, ii., 158. Hemingford, ibid., 489.

[y] Trivet, 23. Bromton, col. 1042. Stubbs (col. 1722) says that the pope consecrated him.

[z] Rob. de Monte, 738.

church and his see, to which Becket sacrificed the ease and the enjoyments of his position, and, ultimately, his life.

Becket succeeded Roger in the archdeaconry of Canterbury in 1154, and in 1162 he was elevated, against his will, to the archbishopric. The two clerks of Theobald were now at the helm of the Church of England. They were soon placed in an antagonistic position to each other, not that there was any ill-will on the part of Roger towards his old friend, although many have laid that to his charge, but in those days even moderate and quiet men were obliged to take sides in the disputes of the time, and Roger must not be condemned because he was occasionally opposed to Becket. Becket was not a person who could at all times be supported, and it was too much the habit among the writers of that age, who were saturated with his spirit, to decry all who refused to render to their favourite their unreserved and unqualified assistance. Whenever there was a quarrel between the primate and the sovereign, the archbishop of York was in a peculiar and critical position, from which it was difficult for him to extricate himself without offending against his loyalty or against propriety. When Becket became archbishop, Roger offered to consecrate him, in accordance with the old custom, but his services were set aside.[a] Their friendship, however, was not then interrupted. About Whitsuntide 1163 the two archbishops went to Tours to a great council which was held by Alexander the new pope. That dignitary was then insecure in his seat, and was grateful for the support of the English prelates and their king. He shewed his appreciation of it in a manner which would scarcely please some of his friends abroad. At the council Becket, by his desire, sat on his right hand, and Roger, who was accompanied by the bishop of Durham, on his left.[b] When they returned from Tours there was a beginning of the troubles which embittered the remainder of Becket's life. Whilst he was chancellor no one could be more active in advancing the royal prerogative; his time and thoughts were frittered away in sports and levities which ill-beseemed an ecclesiastic, but as soon as he was placed at the head of the English church he was an altered man. He immediately adapted himself to his new position, and resolved to do his duty as archbishop, however painfully it might be contrasted with his previous life. He felt that he had been in the wrong, and cared not for remarks or consequences. He soon came into collision with royalty; he began to assert the privileges of the church, and to censure offenders of whom little notice had been hitherto taken. Henry

[a] Gervase, col. 1382.
[b] Matt. Paris, 84. Diceto, col. 512, 535. Wendover, i., 539.

was now nettled, and began to oppose Becket; he claimed for the crown the privilege of punishing ecclesiastics in the civil courts, but in this he was resisted by the whole bench of bishops. The king was clearly in the right. It was most improper that the clergy should have for their ecclesiastical tribunals the power of life and death, and it was most unseemly and wrong that any clerk who had been guilty of a capital offence should escape from punishment by sheltering himself under the privileges of his order. A case which illustrates the subject in dispute occurred within the province of York.

Henry was at York in 1158, when one of the burgesses of Scarborough came to him with a complaint. He said that he had been annoyed by a rural dean, who, without any witness, had condemned his wife as an adulteress, and had extorted twenty-two shillings from him on that account, contrary to the custom of the realm. The offender was summoned before the king, in the presence of archbishop Roger, the bishops of Lincoln and Durham, and John the treasurer of York, who afterwards became the president over the see of Poictiers. The rural dean asserted that the woman had been accused by a deacon and a layman, and that the husband, to secure mercy for his wife, had given twenty shillings to the archdeacon, and two to himself. He said, besides, in justification of the practice, that it was what the other archdeacons and rural deans, throughout the country, were accustomed to do. The king, with the barons and ecclesiastics, now began to think what should be done. John, the treasurer of York, recommended that the money should be restored to the burgess, and the dean handed over to his archbishop. Richard de Lucy then asked, "What satisfaction then shall the king have for this breach of the law?" "None," said John, "for the offender is a clerk." The ecclesiastics in this case seem to have carried the day, but not without arousing some angry feeling.[c]

The general question of the correction of the delinquent clergy was raised in 1163 at a council at London, and Becket and Roger, with the whole bench of bishops, asserted and maintained the privileges of their order.[d] The king and Becket were, consequently, enemies, but as long as the other prelates took the side of the primate, Henry could do little or nothing. About this time Arnulf, bishop of Lisieux, came over to England; he was most earnest in his attempts to reconcile the king and Becket, but without effect. At last he advised Henry to gain some of the bishops to his side, as by so doing he would have the best chance of making peace, or, at all events, of effecting

[c] Becket's Works, i., 213. [d] Ibid., ii., 251.

a compromise. Henry adopted this advice, and called several of the prelates to him at Gloucester. He talked quietly and reasonably with them, expressing his wish for peace and justice, and his disinclination to do any injury to the church. The archbishop of York, and the bishops of Chichester and Lincoln, assented to his views,[e] and Becket, after this, spoke of Roger with anything but kindness.[f] By the means of these prelates, and the entreaties of a papal messenger, and the nobles of the realm, Becket was induced to give way. The matter was then settled in a formal manner. The points in dispute were met and arranged in the well-known Constitutions of Clarendon, which were then drawn up. One of the three copies of these important enactments was placed in the hands of the archbishop of York.[g]

Henry was grateful to archbishop Roger for the assistance which he had given him. As a reward for his aid, and with the wish, no doubt, of humiliating Becket, he was desirous that the pope should make him his legate in Britain.[h] Roger, also, desired to have the power of bearing his cross erect in any part of England, and that he might crown the king. These were privileges which had been peculiar to the see of Canterbury for the last forty years. They depended upon the papal grant, and, therefore, the same hand that gave them could also take them away. They had been obtained in the first instance in a questionable manner, and Roger cannot be blamed for making an attempt to gain honours for his own archbishopric which were only accidents to the other. The old feud between York and Canterbury was revived, greatly to the indignation of Becket and his party, who censured Roger in the strongest language. The pope at first granted all that Roger sought for, but the unflagging resistance of Becket made him waver, and he changed his mind. The vacillation of Alexander was most remarkable. He gave leave, in the first instance, to Roger to act as his legate, then he requested him not to act for a while,

[e] Becket's Works, i., 25, 120; iii., 22. Jo. Saresb. Opp., i., 13. Hoveden, 282 *b*. Martene, Thes. Nov. Anecdot., iii., 655. Pertz, Monumenta Germ. Hist., viii., 458.

[f] Becket's Works, iii., 54, 68, 79, "Arch. Ebor., qui malorum omnium incentor et caput est." 202, "qui ex quo a Cantuariensi ecclesia in archiepiscopatum promotus est, ei quantas scivit et potuit, tetendit insidias." Becket's tongue was like a razor. Jo. Saresb. Opp., ii., 260. Gervase, col. 1394, 1412, 1459. Hoveden, 301, "diabolum illum!" Chron. Petrib., 104.

[g] Becket, ii., 10. Roger and the bishops of London and Salisbury are said by Fitz Stephen, in his life of Becket, to have prompted some of the conditions which were offered to him before the council of Clarendon (ibid., i., 217). Gervase, col. 1389.

[h] The king preferred this request through the bishop of Lisieux and the archdeacon of Poictiers. Becket, i., 32, 128; iv., 1, 2. Gervase, col. 1388. Hoveden, 282 *b*.

then he ordered him not to act at all, and not to bear his cross,[i] which last injunction, however, seems to have been occasionally disobeyed.[j]

Soon after this some farther negotiations took place between the king and Becket, between whom the bishops endeavoured in vain to mediate. Their own position at this time was peculiar and critical. They were divided in opinion, and scarcely knew what to do. Becket reproached them bitterly for joining his adversaries, and he charged them to take no part with the barons at the trial to which he was to be brought. He put himself under the protection of the pope, and when he came to court, was bold enough to carry his cross erect, in token of his authority. The archbishop of York and two or three others remonstrated with him on the folly and imprudence of the act, and told him that it would be considered as the beginning of an attack in which he was sure to be worsted. Becket's reply was that the spiritual sword could give a more deadly wound than any weapon which the king could wield.[k]

Henry was now in a towering passion; he was desirous that Becket should feel the full severity of the law, as he had broken the pledge which he had made at Clarendon. The bishops, however, would not venture to proceed against their superior in England, but they resolved to appeal against his conduct at Rome, and procure there, if possible, his deprivation. Soon after this Becket made his escape from England, and Henry sent a noble embassy to the pope to state his case against the primate, and justify his late proceedings.[l] Archbishop Roger was at its head. The ambassadors found the pope at Sens, and the bishops of London and Chichester, who were the chief speakers, opened the case against Becket with some asperity of manner. They endeavoured to exculpate themselves and defended the policy of their master. Roger spoke afterwards in a more moderate tone.[m] He shewed his good taste by appearing in the background. The efforts of the party were fruitless, although Becket was unable to return to England. He spent several years in exile, playing the courtier to Louis of France, or delighting his friends, the Cistercians, by living a retired life within the walls of Pontigny.[n] He wrote two expostulatory

[i] Becket, iii., 213; iv., 43, 46, 255. Matt. Paris, 93. Recueil des Historiens des Gaules, xv., 828-9. Labbe, x., 1194, 1219.

[j] Becket, i., 226; ii., 21.

[k] Becket's Works, i., 42-3, 137. Hoveden, 283 *b*.

[l] Becket's Works, i., 51, 139, 151, 237, 240-1, 347. Foliot's Letters, ii., 279. Hoveden, col. 284. Twysden, col. 714. Gervase, col. 1394. Labbe, Conc., x., 1436.

[m] Becket, iv., 270. Gervase, col. 1395.

[n] An anonymous friend, probably a Cistercian, told Becket in his troubles, "Apud Clarevallim, Cistercium et Pontiniacum, intercessione domini papæ,

letters to archbishop Roger about this time, chiding him for his opposition, and in one of them he enjoins him and the other prelates to suspend the services in their dioceses until justice should be done to their ecclesiastical superior.[o] The pope backed this letter by ordering Roger, on his obedience, to aid Rotro archbishop of Rouen, and Bertrand bishop of Nevers, his legates, who were to compel Henry, if possible, to make peace with Becket by the threat of an interdict, and by directing him to observe everything that they resolved upon.[p] Henry, on his part, was equally firm and energetic. Fitz Stephen says that he ordered his subjects to take an oath that they would neither receive, nor obey, any papal mandate about Becket, and that Roger and the other bishops allowed it to be taken within their dioceses.[q] In 1168 the king took a more violent step. He sent a letter to the archbishop of Cologne, stating that he was about to send an embassy to Rome, with Roger at its head, to demand the immediate removal of Becket, and to threaten the pope, if he withstood him, with his bitterest opposition. A partizan of Canterbury ascribed this obnoxious epistle to the pen of Foliot bishop of London, and gravely tells us that whilst that prelate was ruminating by night upon the subject, the evil spirit endeavoured, in vain, to startle him by crying out in a thrilling tone,

> "O Gilberte Foliot,[r]
> Dum revolvis tot et tot,
> Deus tuus est Ashtoroth!"

In 1170 Roger took a step which placed him in some peril, and caused him much difficulty and annoyance. At the desire of his royal master, in conjunction with the bishops of London, Durham, Rochester and Salisbury, he crowned prince Henry king of England in the middle of June.[s] Becket, upon whom that duty would have devolved, was not in England, and he took it much amiss. He protested against the act, and made great complaints.[t] Becket, who had heard of what was intended

oratur assidue pro vobis" (Works, iv., 255). Foliot's Letters, ii., 244, who says that Becket went to Pontigny at the desire of John bishop of Poictiers. Herb. de Boseham, ii., 246. Diceto, col. 539. Gervase, col. 1398.

[o] Becket's Works, iii., 227-9.

[p] Ibid., i., 55; iv., 47-8, 134.

[q] Ibid., i., 267-8.

[r] Wendover, i., 556. Mat. Paris, 90.

[s] Becket's Works, i., 56, 157; ii., 25, 112; iv., 159. Chron. Manniæ, ed. Stevenson, 394. Geraldus de Instit. Princ., ed. Stevenson, 177. Chron. Joh. de Oxenedes, 62. Chron. Mailros, 82. Matt. Paris, 101. Trivet, 54. Rob. de Monte, 773. Hemingford, apud Gale, ii., 497. Hoveden, 296.b. Wendover, ii., 11. Diceto, col. 552. Bromton, col. 1061. Gervase, col. 1412. Stubbs, col. 1722. Knyghton, col. 2396. Pertz, Monumenta Hist. Germ., viii., 413. Benedict Petrib., 4. Contin. Fl. Wigorn., ii., 138.

[t] Becket's Works, i., 274-5; ii., 26, 112; iii., 67-9. Bromton, 1061. Benedict Petrib., 6. Contin. Fl. Wigorn., ii., 141.

before the ceremony took place,[u] sent intelligence to the papal court, and Alexander wrote to Roger forbidding him to officiate.[v] If Roger received the letter he disregarded the injunction, and now paid the penalty for his rashness. The pope, at Becket's request, suspended him and his suffragan, Hugh de Puiset, whilst he excommunicated the Southern prelates who had officiated at the coronation.[w] He expressed, however, his willingness to withdraw the ban if the culprits would be obedient to Becket, and render satisfaction to him for their conduct.[x] The king, who was afraid of the papal censure, shewed some disposition to abandon the prelates, although it was to please him that they had got into this scrape.[y]

Roger and his brethren in trouble were undaunted, although somewhat dismayed. The pope's censure had not yet reached them, although it had been entrusted to Becket's charge. He was coming back to England, and they tried to prevent his landing. The exiled primate heard of their design, and took care that the letters should precede him, and they were delivered at Dover to those for whom they were intended. He himself, with some difficulty and risk, got safe to England. This was in 1170. When Becket arrived at Canterbury, the messengers of the archbishop of York and his friends who were in disgrace, came to him, and reproached him for trampling down his brother bishops, and for using fire and sword when he should have sought and practised peace. Becket laid upon their masters the guilt of the present strife. After this some persons came from the court with an order that he should absolve the condemned prelates. He told them that it was not in his power to reverse the decision of his superior, and that no one could do that; but if the bishops of London and Salisbury would pledge themselves to obey the pope's order, he would not object to absolve them.[z] This reply was brought to the bishops, who were on the point of giving way, till they were told by Roger that they could make no such promise without the king's permission, otherwise they would be guilty of treason. Their adviser is also reported to have said, "I have £8000, God be thanked, and I will spend it all to the last farthing to pull down the

[u] Becket, i., 268; iv., 287, 302. He had spies, "amici," as they are called, all over.

[v] Ibid., i., 268; ii., 26; iii., 64; iv., 47. Diceto, col. 513, 552. Labbe, Conc., x., 1219. Rymer's Fœd., n. e., i., 25-6. Wilkins, i., 459.

[w] Becket, i., 332; iii., 80; iv., 48—52, 64-5, 102. Chron. de Mailros, 83. Matt. Paris, 101-2. Peter Langtoft, 130. Chron. Petrib., 100. Wm. Neubr., i., 185. Hoveden, 297. Diceto, col. 553. Bromton, col. 1062. Labbe, Conc., x., 1219-22. Wilkins, i., 459. Benedict Petrib., 8. Contin. Fl. Wigorn., ii., 142.

[x] Becket, iv., 102, 283.

[y] Gervase. col. 1412.

[z] Becket, i., 280-4; iii., 83. Joh. Saresber., Opp., ii., 243. Gervase, col. 1413. Hoveden, 298.

arrogance of Becket, which is greater than his courage. Let us go to the king, who has hitherto stood our friend. If you return to Becket, the king, if he takes it amiss, will deprive us of our possessions. What will you do then?"[a]

Roger, and the two prelates who had been persuaded by his arguments, cross the Channel to Henry. They took with them, at the king's request, four or six clergy from the vacant sees to represent their chapters in the Norman court, with the strange expectation of being thus able to make a new election, and fill up the places of the suspended bishops. When the party came to the king, Roger was the spokesman. He protested against the sentence pronounced against them, which was the penalty of their loyalty to their sovereign. He spoke of the annoyance and the unmerited disgrace to which they were subjected. He told the king of Becket's present movements in England, how he was travelling about with guards and soldiers in a warlike guise. The hasty temper of Henry now burst out against Becket. Half angrily, half querulously, he deplored his own unhappy position.[b] The fatal fruits which were borne by that unfortunate speech are matters of history. Four daring and unhappy men, with the words of the sovereign still tingling in their ears, hastened across the seas to Canterbury, and demanded of Becket the absolution of the bishops. His reply was the same which he gave before, that it was beyond his power to do what they required.[c] Ere that day was over he was stretched in death before the altar of his own church. He was laid in the tomb within the walls of that noble cathedral which he had served perhaps too faithfully and too well.

A thrill of horror ran through all Christendom at this deed of wrong. Whatever Becket's faults may have been, and they were many, he made a full atonement for them in his death. Henry, the innocent cause of the murder, was stricken with sorrow and dismay, and Roger could not fail to be deeply moved. An enquiry was immediately made into the case, to see whether he was in any way the inciter of the crime; and he promised to abide by the decision of the pope. The archbishop of Rouen and the bishop of Amiens were the examiners. Roger met them at Albemarle on the feast of St. Nicholas, and he there swore that he was altogether innocent of the death of Becket. He also took an oath, that, before the recent coronation, he had not received the pope's inhibitory letter. He was unanimously acquitted from all blame, and his suspension was removed.[d]

[a] Becket's Works, i., 284; ii., 29-30.

[b] Ibid., i., 289-90; ii., 130; iv., 308. Benedict Petrib., 9-10.

[c] Ibid., i., 162-3. Jo. Saresb., ii., 244.

[d] Becket, iv., 67-8. Foliot's Letters, ii., 260. Wendover, ii., 19, 20. Di-

Roger wrote a long letter to his old friend, bishop Puiset of Durham, and to the chapters within the diocese of York, acquainting them joyfully with the result, and announcing his speedy return.[e] The style of the epistle is somewhat peculiar and inflated. The archbishop would have us believe, that during the recent enquiry the radiant figure of the Redeemer had stood on his right hand, shewing by His presence there the innocence of the accused. About the same time Roger interceded very warmly and kindly with the pope in behalf of Foliot, the bishop of London, who had been for a whole year under the ban of excommunication.[f] Roger was now enabled to return to his province; but the partizans of Canterbury never seem to have withdrawn the charge that he was one of the chief causes of the misfortunes of their now sainted favourite.[g]

Roger was not on the best of terms with Richard, Becket's successor in the see of Canterbury, indeed it was almost impossible for the two archbishops in those days, whoever they might be, to avoid bickerings and contention about privileges and position. In 1175 Roger was not present at the synod which Richard held at Westminster, nor did he explain his absence;[h] his clerks, however, were there, and made several claims on the part of their master.[i] They asserted the right of the archbishops of York to bear their cross erect within the province of Canterbury; and to have the spiritual control over the sees of Lincoln, Lichfield, Worcester, and Hereford. On these two points they summoned the archbishop of Canterbury to Rome. They appealed also to the same authority against the sentence of excommunication which Richard had passed against the officers of the conventual church of St. Oswald at Gloucester, which belonged to York, for refusing to pay him their obedience.[j] Nothing seems to have been done at the time, but soon afterwards, at Winchester, the king tried to act as a peacemaker between the two prelates. After a long debate he was partially successful. Richard of Canterbury consented to absolve the clergy of St. Oswald's, and to make that house as free and independent as a royal chapel. It was also agreed that with reference to the other points in dispute, especially that about the cross, that they should be decided by the archbishop of

ceto, col. 558. Stubbs, col. 1723. Matt. Paris, 104-5.

[e] Foliot's Letters, ii., 173. Joann. Saresber., ii., 264. Chron. Jo. de Oxenedes, 65.

[f] Foliot's Letters, ii., 171-3.

[g] Becket's Works, i., 10, 99, 370. Bromton, col. 1062.

[h] Diceto, col. 585. Matt. Paris, 109.

[i] Hoveden, 311. Rob. de Monte, 787.

[j] Diceto, 583. Bromton, 1100-2. Becket's Works, iii., 322. Foliot's Letters, i., 140. Opp. Jo. Saresber., i., 33. Benedict Petrib., 94, 106-7, 126-7. Cf. Prynne's Coll., iii., 984, 1026, and Reg. Ab. Corbridge.

Rouen, and the French bishops in that neighbourhood. They resolved, in addition, to have a truce for five years, and to start no new points of debate before the old were settled. This last engagement was not entirely adhered to. The legate Huguccio was unconsciously the cause of a rather amusing but unbecoming scene. In 1176 he had been with Roger at York, and he accompanied him to the court at Nottingham.[k] They were together, soon afterwards, at the council at Westminster. The old question of precedence in the presence of the legate was then revived. Which of the two archbishops was to sit on the right hand, a position which has excited angry feelings in nobler minds than theirs? Richard had taken the coveted place, when Roger seems to have pushed himself in between the legate and his rival—nay, he is even said to have sat down in Richard's lap; but this is probably only one of the Canterbury embellishments with which the story seems to be garnished. This was too much for the sensitive feelings of the friends of Richard. Ecclesiastics and laymen alike manifested a strange excitement, and even bishops

"Tantæne animis cœlestibus iræ?"

shewed that they could be subject to the same passions which run riot occasionally in less exalted minds. They pounced upon Roger and threw him down. They cuffed and beat him to their heart's content. They trampled him under their feet. When they were at length satisfied, the sufferer was permitted to rise, with a torn cope, and covered with dust and shame. They laughed at him when he remonstrated. When he went out to seek the king and demand redress, they shouted after him the old calumny, "Away, away, betrayer of St. Thomas. His blood is still upon thy hands." Roger was excessively indignant, and singled out from the others Geoffrey Ridel, bishop of Ely, as one of his most vehement assailants. Nothing, however, seems to have been done. The scene was far too ludicrous to necessitate any severe or vigorous remedy, but it was most discreditable and unseemly.[l] An end, however, was put, about this time, to the long-continued controversy about the profession. A bull of pope Alexander settled the question in accordance

[k] Hoveden, 313. Bromton, 1107. Benedict Petrib., 130. At another council at Nottingham in 1181 Richard of Canterbury carried his cross erect in the presence and within the diocese of Roger (ibid., 368).

[l] Diceto, col. 515, 589. Bromton, col. 1109. Gervase, col. 1483. Wm. Neubr., i., 232-3. Hoveden, 316. Anglia Sacra, i., 9. Geraldus de Instit. Princ., ed. Stevenson, 178. Fordun, Scotichronicon, ed. Goodall, i., 475. Hemingford, ed. Gale, ii., 506. Benedict Petrib., 139, 146. There is an amusing account of the scene, and a history of the controversy, in Fuller's Church History, book iii., 38-9.

with the old decree of Gregory the Great, forbidding altogether that token of submission. This was agreed upon at one of the many councils which were held at the Lateran, in 1179.[m]

Roger, like many of his predecessors, had frequent controversies with the Scottish bishops. During the life-time of Becket, he had a dispute with Richard, the bishop-elect of St. Andrew's, who had refused to be consecrated at York; and he appealed against him to the pope, desiring that he might be suspended, but without success. About this time Roger was invested with the legantine authority, a power which, although he was deprived of it in England, he seems to have always exercised in Scotland. He held a meeting at Norham, on the Tweed, and summoned thither the Scottish ecclesiastics, in the vain hope of inducing them to own their subjection to York.[n] One of the clergy who was there, Ingelram, the bishop-elect of Glasgow, set him still farther at naught by being consecrated by Alexander III. at Sens, in spite of the strenuous opposition of the representatives of York.[o] In 1174 Roger was at Falaise in Normandy, when William king of Scotland, then a prisoner, made a treaty of peace with Henry. In the following year the two monarchs met at York, and the conditions assented to at Falaise were solemnly sworn to and confirmed. They subjected the state of Scotland entirely to England, and the church, also, in all that was right and proper. In token of his submission the Scottish king deposited his spear and shield upon the altar of St. Peter in the minster, where they were for a long time preserved.[p] In 1176 there was a council held at Northampton;[q] at which the provisions of the treaty of Falaise were thoroughly examined and discussed in the presence of the Scottish king and his bishops. These prelates were required by Henry of England, on the strength of their allegiance, to own their subjection to the English church as they had hitherto done. Their answer was that they had never been subject to that church, and that the acknowledgment was unnecessary and unfair. Archbishop Roger led the argument against them, and produced documents which shewed, in particular, that the sees of Glasgow and Whitherne had always been dependent upon York. Upon this, the bishop of Glasgow asserted that his church was under

[m] Diceto, col. 589. Foliot's Letters, ii., 71. Labbe, Conc., x., 1553, 1689.

[n] Fordun, Scotichronicon, i., 461. Chron. Mailros, 79. The historian is not complimentary when he speaks of Roger as "delphinum illum." As soon as Roger had obtained the pall, Adrian IV. wrote a letter to the Scottish bishops charging them to obey him. Wilkins, i., 481.

[o] Hoveden, 283. Chron. Mailros, 79.

[p] Bromton, col. 1103-5. Hoveden, 311-12. Rob. de Monte, 786. Benedict Petrib., 113. Knyghton, col. 2396. Chron. Mailros, 88.

[q] Bromton, col. 1108. Knyghton, col. 2396. Hoveden, 314 *b*. Benedict Petrib., 137-8.

the especial protection of Rome, and that it was subject to no other power. No decision was then arrived at, principally, it is said, through the means of the archbishop of Canterbury, who was desirous of being the head of the Scottish church himself. Fordun gives a different account of the debate at Northampton. The bishops, he says, were summoned thither by the legate, who endeavoured to induce them to own the supremacy of York, and thus strengthen the efficiency of the Northern church. They were silent for fear of giving offence, when a young ecclesiastic of the name of Gilbert stood up, and combatted the arguments of the legate on behalf of his compatriots with so much boldness and ingenuity, that the demand was waived. "Well shot, master Gilbert," said Roger of York, laying his hand on the shoulder of the youthful orator, "but that shaft did not come from your own quiver."

"Ex propria pharetra non exiit ista sagitta."[r]

The truth of this story may be gravely questioned, at all events Fordun seems to be in error when he says that the youth, as a reward for his zeal, became bishop of Caithness; St. Gilbert, who actually presided over that see, did not die till 1245. Soon after the meeting at Northampton cardinal Vivian, the papal legate, held a council at Edinburgh, to which all the Scottish bishops were summoned. Christian bishop of Whitherne was not there, and the legate suspended him for his absence. Christian thew himself upon the protection of Roger, by whom he had been consecrated, asserting that he was the papal legate and the superior to whom his allegiance was due.[s] In 1178 a violent controversy broke out between the pope and William king of Scotland, in which Roger played a part. Richard bishop of St. Andrews died in 1178, and John Scotus was chosen by the chapter to succeed him. When the king heard of this selection he was excessively indignant. He expelled John from Scotland, and gave the see to Hugh, his chaplain, who was consecrated by the Scottish bishops. John, upon this, went to Rome and complained to the pope, who sent as his legate a person of the name of Alexis, to enquire into the case. The report was in favour of John, who was consecrated in 1180, the election of his rival having been cancelled. The king, however, drove John, for the second time, into banishment. Upon this, Alexander wrote to the Scottish bishops, confirming the proceedings of his legate, and excommunicating Hugh. He charged the king and his prelates to permit John to enter quietly into his see, otherwise the archbishop of York, who was

[r] Fordun, Scotichronicon, i., 476-8.

[s] Bromton, 1111. Hoveden, 324. Benedict Petrib., 211-12.

his legate in Scotland, would put the country under an interdict.[t] The warning, however, was despised, and, in 1181, Roger, by the desire of the pope, inflicted the threatened punishment, and excommunicated the king.[u] I shall mention in another place what was the conclusion of the difficulty.

From what has been already stated it will have been seen that Roger was one of the leading politicians of the day. There were other occasions on which he was engaged in the service of the state. He was very frequently in attendance upon the king.[v] In 1162 pope Alexander, through the means of Roger, and the bishops of Evreux and Lisieux, endeavoured to persuade Henry II. to ally himself to Louis of France.[w] In 1172 Alexander would not allow him to crown Henry and his queen, although he had officiated in that capacity before.[x] In 1174 he took a conspicuous part in the military affairs of the North. He entertained and aided Geoffrey bishop of Lincoln, the king's son, when he assaulted and captured the castle of Kirkby Malzeard; and, when he returned, the archbishop took charge of the fortress on behalf of the king.[y] He also welcomed the barons who were going against William of Scotland, and sent the news of his capture to Henry.[z] Ralph de Tilli, the constable of the archbishop's household, was at Alnwick when the Scottish monarch was taken prisoner, and was one of the party who rescued Prudhoe castle from the invading army.[a] In 1177 Henry gave to Roger the custody of Scarborough castle.[b]

Roger was a man of learning and ability. He was as ready with his pen as with his tongue. He wrote fluently and well. At the little court of Theobald of Canterbury, where the talents of Becket were of no repute, Roger had formed the acquaintance of most of the scholars of his day, among whom he occupied a distinguished place. With John of Salisbury he was on familiar terms.[c] Gilbert Foliot and he were great friends. They corresponded together, and when Foliot was under the papal censure, for his share in the opposition to Becket, he

[t] Labbe, Conc., x., 1239-41. Benedict Petrib., 346-9.

[u] Stubbs, col. 1723. Hoveden, 341-51. Benedict Petrib., 331, 370.

[v] Bromton, col. 1108, 1126-7, 1133. Benedict Petrib., 202, 231, 368.

[w] Recueil des Hist. des Gaules, xv., 785. There is a letter probably referring to this in Becket's Works, iv., 206.

[x] Diceto, col. 560. Gervase, col. 1421. Matt. Paris, 109.

[y] Bromton, col. 1093. Hoveden, 307 *b*. Vita Gerardi Archiep., apud Angl. Sacr., ii., 379. Benedict Petrib., 78.

[z] Chronique de Jordan Fantosme, ed. Surtees Society, 78-9, 91, 93.

[a] Hoveden, 308. Benedict Petrib., 74.

[b] Ibid., 323 *b*. Benedict Petrib., 203. Hinderwell (History of Scarborough, ed. 1832, p. 50) makes him hold that office till he died. Roger had also the custody of Roxburgh castle (Ben. Petrib.)

[c] Opp. Joann. Saresber., i., 75.

found an asylum at Beverley. Roger afterwards interceded in his behalf with the pope.[d] Hugh de Puiset, the famous bishop of Durham, of whom there is too little as yet known, and the archbishop of York, were intimately connected in prosperity and adversity.[e] Roger and pope Alexander III. corresponded on matters of discipline and on the public events of the day.[f]

It has been said that Roger was opposed to the monastic system, and that he expressed his opinion that Thurstan's greatest mistake had been the establishment of Fountains.[g] This is, probably, merely idle gossip. It is quite possible, however, that Roger discovered the inherent defects of the monastic system, which are not slow in developing themselves. He was a bold man, and was not afraid of checking what he thought to be wrong, and when we find him in collision with the canons of Newburgh, and suspending the prior of Gisburgh,[h] we well understand how his activity sharpened those weapons of abuse and railing which monkish chroniclers are too apt to use. It is also a remarkable fact that, with the exception of the abbey of Welbeck[i] and one or two other places, all the religious houses which were founded in the diocese of York during the archiepiscopate of Roger were Cistercian or Benedictine nunneries.[j] There was a superabundance of monasteries, and a reaction had begun. The age of great endowments and large ecclesiastical establishments was passing rapidly away. The system was being gradually refined, and consequently deteriorated.

Roger has also been charged with miserly and penurious habits, and with impoverishing his clergy and his diocese.[k] That he was a rich man there can be no doubt, for he had presided over a wealthy see for nearly thirty years, and he was a prudent husband of the fortune which he had amassed. We hear of him endeavouring to recover, at the papal court, the property

[d] Foliot's Letters, i., 135-45, 293; ii., 75. Becket's Works, iv., 308.

[e] There is an account of a miracle wrought on one of Roger's clerks at St. Cuthbert's tomb, in Reginald, de admir. B. Cuthberti virtutibus, ed. Surtees Society, 261.

[f] Hoveden, 325. Foliot's Letters, ii., 72, 75 *et seqq.* Labbe, Conc., x., 1245, 1488, 1564-7, 1573, 1585, 1590, 1603-4, 1612, 1620-1, 1666-7, 1684, 1698, 1706, 1724. Baluzii Misc., ed. Mansi, iii., 375. Wilkins, i., 487.

[g] Wm. Neubr., i., 268. Bromton, col. 1142. Hemingford, apud Gale, ii., 506-7.

[h] Labbe, Conc., x., 1597, 1626-7.

[i] Annal. Ord. Præmonstrat., ii., appendix, 711-12. Soon after 1172 Roger witnessed the charter of foundation of the monastery De Bosco Raherii, near Tours. (Martene, Thes. Nov. Anecd., i., 573.)

[j] At least a dozen of these nunneries may be reckoned up.

[k] Wm. Neubr., i., 267-8. Rob. de Monte, 805. Newburgh is outrageously violent against Roger, and says, "In vita sua tondendis magis quam pascendis ovibus Dominicis intendit." Benedict of Peterborough (149) says that he bought the chancellorship for Geoffrey, provost of Beverley, for eleven thousand marks. This person was Roger's nephew, and was drowned in 1177 (ibid., 250).

of which he had been deprived by the carelessness or waste of his two immediate predecessors.[l] Although in this respect he seems to have been unsuccessful, he took care that the deficiency was made up from other sources. He whom the lips of calumny have stigmatized as a miser, was the most munificent ruler that ever presided over the see of York. He made the archbishopric richer in every respect than he found it. Robert de Monte tells us how he added to the endowments of his churches and rebuilt all his residences so magnificently, that they could almost rival those in the Southern province.[m] He began a new basilica at Ripon, and gave to the work the very large sum of £1000.[n] At York he erected the archiepiscopal palace on the north side of the cathedral, of which scarcely any portion now remains. He decorated the minster with a new choir, worthy of the glorious work of Conrad, with which Canterbury had been adorned.[o] On the north side of the church, between his new palace and the cathedral, he founded the chapel of St. Sepulchre, which was dedicated to the Blessed Virgin and the Holy Angels. The endowment was a noble one. Eleven churches were appropriated to it, five of which he purchased with his own funds. A staff of thirteen officers belonged to it, all munificently provided for, and care was taken that there should be no jealousy or collision between the officials of the chapel and the dignitaries of the adjacent minster.[p] Roger gave also to his metropolitical church one of the bones of St. Peter, and a portion of the sandals of that apostle, which he brought from Rome. These, and some of the more precious relics which the minster of York possessed, were deposited in a hollow crucifix of gold, which was given to the chapter by the same prelate. This and other treasures belonging to the cathedral were given up to secure the ransom of Cœur de Lion from his Austrian captivity, but they were subsequently redeemed.[q]

In November, 1181, Roger, who had been prevented by illness from attending a council in 1177,[r] felt his end approaching. He was at a place called Cowda;[s] and he called around him the abbats, priors, and ecclesiastics of his diocese. In their presence he made the following munificent bequests. He gave more than five hundred pounds' worth of silver to William,

[l] Becket's Works, iv., 237.

[m] Rob. de Monte, 805. Hemingford, apud Gale, ii., 506-7. Trivet, 82.

[n] Walbran's Ripon, 25.

[o] "Fundavit chorum et testudines ejus, et capellam S. Stephani ad borialem partem templi" (Lel. Coll., i., 121).

[p] Stubbs, col. 1723. Lel. Coll., i., 38. Dugd. Mon., vi., 1181.

[q] Fabric Rolls of York Minster, 152.

[r] Bromton, col. 1122. Benedict Petrib., 181.

[s] Hoveden, 350 *b*. I cannot identify this place. Perhaps it was Cawood? Stubbs (col. 1723) says that Roger died at Sherburn. Antony à Wood makes him die at Osney abbey (Antiq. Univ. Oxon., i., 166).

archbishop of Rheims, and the French bishops, for the needy in their dioceses. A similar sum, for the same use, was given to the archbishop of Rouen and the Norman prelates; and a third, equally large, to his brother of Canterbury and his suffragans. All the rest of his treasure was also for the benefit of the poor. After this Roger was removed to York, and there he died at nightfall on the 22nd of November.[t] His noble bequests were altogether misappropriated,[u] and everything that he possessed came into the hands of the king, to whom he had been a faithful servant.[v] It was suggested to Henry that the deceased prelate had made a rule within his diocese, which had been sanctioned by the pope, to the effect that no will of an ecclesiastic should be valid which was made in his last sickness. Who could interfere with what a dying archbishop bequeathed but his sovereign? The king immediately sent his messengers, who seized upon the money, which was the property of the poor. But he did more than this. The archbishop, it was well known, had been possessed of immense wealth. He had died intestate; who was to have it? The bait was too tempting for an avaricious and ungrateful king; and he ordered everything that had belonged to Roger to be gathered together by the justices, and appropriated to his own use. The large sum of £11,000 of silver, and plate, and valuables of every description, thus found their way into the royal treasury. The curse of God, which settled upon Ahab, seems henceforward to have rested upon this plunderer of the poor. The gathering in of the spoil was not made without difficulty and controversy. The king's justices heard that the bishop of Durham had received three hundred marks of the archbishop's money, and they required them at his hands. Puiset told them, with the spirit which was native to him, that the money had been given for the weal of his friend's soul, in accordance with his desire, to the leper, the lame, the halt, and blind; that it had been spent in restoring churches and bridges. He had none of it, and those who wanted it must seek it for themselves. The king, upon this, was full of wrath, and seized upon the castle of Durham, regarding its high-spirited owner with the bitterest ill-will.

[t] Hoveden, ibid. Chron. Mailros, 91. Diceto (col. 613) makes him die on the 20th. Stubbs (col. 1723) on the 26th. Gervase (col. 1459) says in September. Cotton's Chron., 79.

[u] An account of the death-scene of Roger, and the misappropriation of his wealth, is to be found in Hoveden, 350-1. Wm. Neubr., i., 267, etc. Bromton, col. 1142. Matt. Paris, 116-17. Benedict Petrib., 371, 378. Diceto (col. 517, 614). He says that the confiscation was made when Roger was on his death-bed. This robbery actually makes Foxe enshrine Roger in his calendar of martyrs!

[v] Roger took the king's part when his sons raised a rebellion against him. Benedict Petrib., 58.

Puiset performed the last solemn rites for Roger, as he had done, nearly thirty years before, for his predecessor William. The remains of the archbishop were interred in the choir of the minster which he had rebuilt;[w] and when, after a lapse of nearly two centuries, it was again removed to make way for a more magnificent structure, the body of Roger was probably transferred by archbishop Thoresby to a new sepulchre at the easternmost extremity of the choir.[x] Tradition has for centuries ascribed to Roger the tomb in the north aisle of the nave, hard by the entrance into the chapel of St. Sepulchre.[y] The monument, however, is none of his. It is in a most debased style, and is not earlier than the reign of Henry VII.

When archbishop Roger died, the king of Scotland was under a sentence of excommunication, and his land under an interdict. William was overjoyed when he heard of his decease; and, after conferring with his council, sent off Joceline bishop of Glasgow, Arnulf abbat of Melrose, and others, to Lucius the new pope, to procure, if possible, a reversal of the sentence; and, rather than they should return without it, they were to promise that John, bishop of St. Andrew's, should be deposed.[z] The embassy was entirely successful. The ban was removed from king and country, and two papal commissioners, Roland bishop-elect of Dol in Brittany, and Silvan abbat of Rievaux, were despatched to Scotland to examine into the dispute about St. Andrew's. The difference was settled for a time, by both John and Hugh resigning their interest in that see into the pope's hands. Lucius then gave St. Andrew's to Hugh, and appointed John to Dunkeld. The quarrel was soon afterwards opened out again by the jealous and contentious disposition of the two prelates, and it ended at last, after much angry discussion, in another compromise, into which it is unnecessary to enter.

In 1191 pope Clement made a most important declaration respecting the position and independence of the Scottish church, at the request of the king. It refers to every see but that of Whitherne, which seems to have been given up to York by common consent. The Scottish church was made independent of every authority but that of Rome, and no one was to excommunicate or lay an interdict on the kingdom, unless he were the chief pontiff or his deputy. No alien was to act for the future as a legate within that district, unless he was a special emissary from Rome; and nothing relating to Scotland was to be settled in another country, except at the papal court. This

[w] Hoveden, 350 *b*. Stubbs, col. 1723. Benedict Petrib., 371.

[x] Preface to York Fabric Rolls, xvii.

[y] Torre's York Minster, MS., 135.

[z] Hoveden, 351. Ben. Petrib., 371, 372.

most important decree, it will be observed, disposes summarily of the claims of the see of York. The archbishopric, it will be remembered, was at that time vacant. It would have been more just and fair if this sentence had been delivered when there was a Northern primate. He would then have had an opportunity of asserting the claims of his church to the ecclesiastical control of Scotland, which his predecessors had always vindicated to themselves.[a]

The see of York was all this while vacant, the revenues flowing into the royal coffers.[b] Henry II., however, on more occasions than one, shewed some interest in the appointment of a primate, and the welfare of the Northern diocese. In 1184 the canons of York, and Hugh bishop of Durham, met at the king's request to fix upon an archbishop, but nothing seems to have been done.[c] In 1186 Henry sent Puiset back to England to be present at the festival of Easter in the province of York, in which there was at that time no prelate.[d] In September, 1186, the canons of York were present at the council at Marlborough, and nominated five persons in succession as archbishop; Hubert Walter their dean, Hamund or Hamo their precentor, Laurence archdeacon of Bedford, Bernard prior of Newburgh, and Roger Arundel. All of them were rejected by the king; for what reason we are not informed.[e] In the archbishop who was ultimately selected, Henry himself had an especial interest.

Geoffrey Plantagenet, an illegitimate son of Henry II. He was one of the king's elder children.[f] His mother is said to have been the well-known Rosamond Clifford, the Fair Rosamond of story; and this assertion gains some weight from the fact that in after years Geoffrey appropriated the religious house of Clementhorp, near York, to the nunnery of Godstow, in which Rosamond was interred.[g] There are, however, some

[a] For these Scottish affairs see Ben. Petrib., 371-2, 375, 379, 384, 510, etc., 528, etc., 538. Hoveden, 351-2, 354, 356, 360-1, 368, etc., 371-2. Labbe, Conc., x., 1735, 1743, 1753, etc. I have not gone into the subject at length, as it is not my purpose to write a history of the Scottish Church. That task has already been very creditably and honestly performed by Mr. Grub of Aberdeen. There are, however, omissions in that work which may be supplied by a careful examination of the minor English chroniclers and the writings of Foreign historians.

[b] Wm. Neubr., i., 270. Madox, Bar. Angl., 87.

[c] Ben. Petrib., 413.

[d] Ibid., 444. [e] Ibid., 453.

[f] Gerald Cambrensis, apud Angl. Sacr., ii., 378. The name of Geoffrey came from his paternal grandfather, Geoffrey comte d'Angers.

[g] Hoveden, 408 *b*. Ben. Petrib., 732.

chronological difficulties in the way,[h] and it seems probable that Geoffrey had for his mother some more insignificant person. Walter Mapes, if he is to be trusted, gives her the name of Ykenai, and a very low character.[i]

Geoffrey is said to have been born in 1159. When he was merely a child he was made archdeacon of Lincoln;[j] and in 1173, when, if the previous date be correct, he could not be more than fourteen years of age, his father procured his election to the bishopric of that see, and the appointment was confirmed by the archbishop of Canterbury at Woodstock.[k] The pope, also, seems to have winked at the irregularity. The youth, however, was not in priest's orders, and how could he be consecrated? Wikes tells us that Geoffrey himself was disposed to wait, because he aspired to something higher;[l] and there is probably some truth in this statement, when we remember that he had the same wish on a subsequent occasion. It was necessary, however, to conciliate the pope; and he crossed the seas in 1174, at his father's suggestion, to visit the papal court in

[h] Geoffrey was born, according to the Kirkstall Chronicle, in 1159, whilst Rosamond is called by Bromton a *puella* in 1173. The Kirkstall Chron., from the quotation from it which I have seen, appears to be singularly inaccurate. The question of Geoffrey's birth is discussed by Messrs. Bowles and Nichols in their History of Lacock abbey, 102. Cf. Sandford's Kings of England, 71.

[i] "Imposuit autem ei in principio regni sui meretrix quædam publica, nihil immunditiæ dedignans, filium quem a populo susceperat nomine Gaufridum, quem injuste minusque discrete tanquam suum acceptans, in tantum promovit ut hodie sit Ebor. archiepiscopus. Nomen autem matris ejus Ykenai" (Mapes, De Nugis Curialium, 228). Mapes, it must be remembered, was very bitter against Geoffrey.

The following illegitimate children of Henry II. were also connected with the North. Peter, brother of Geoffrey, was archdeacon of Lincoln from about 1190 to 1202 (Le Neve., ii., 43). In 1194 Geoffrey tried to get him made dean of York, but he was then at Paris, and the opportunity was lost (Hoveden, 415-16). A year or two after this we find the brothers bitter enemies (Ibid., 428).

Morgan, a brother of Geoffrey, and an illegitimate son of Henry II., by the wife of Sir Ralph Bloeth (Hist. Dunelm. Scr. Tres, 35; Sandford's kings of England, 72), was advanced by Geoffrey about 1201 to the provostship of Beverley upon the death of Robert (Hoveden, 468). In 1214 the monks of Norwich elected him their bishop, but the king knew nothing about it, and the election was set aside (Hist. Dunelm. Scr. Tres, 31). In 1223, being still provost of Beverley, the monks of Durham chose him as their bishop, and he went to Rome to be consecrated. His illegitimacy was the cause of the pope's refusing to confirm his appointment (Ibid., 35; and Lel. Coll., ii., 333.) Morgan was commemorated by the following epitaph (Camden's Remaines, ed. 1674, p. 495).

"Larga, benigna, decens, jacet hic stirps regia, morum
Organa Morgano fracta jacente silent."

"John clericus, filius regis, canonicus Ebor.," is mentioned in a chartulary of the treasurers of York: cf. p. 221.

[j] Ger. Cambrensis, *ut supra*, 378.

[k] Rob. de Monte, ed. Stevenson, 780. Gerald, 378. Diceto, col. 568. Contin. Fl. Wigorn., ii., 157.

[l] Wikes, apud Gale, ii., 32. Neubr. (i., 176-7) ascribes the delay solely to Geoffrey's cupidity, "oves Dominicas nesciens pascere et doctus tondere." This is a favourite phrase with Newburgh.

person, or by deputy.[m] The pope acted very properly, and deferred Geoffrey's consecration for three years.[n] Upon this, Henry, who seems quietly to have assented to this decision, sent his youthful son to be educated at Tours.[o]

Geoffrey must soon have thrown aside his books, as we find him back at Lincoln in the same year.[p] His filial affection was then put to the proof. An unnatural rebellion arose against Henry, fostered by three of his sons; but the young bishop-elect of Lincoln would not swerve from his allegiance and his duty.[p] At the suggestion of the lord chancellor he collected a very large sum of money within his diocese for his father's use, but having some doubt as to the propriety of the exaction, he returned every farthing that had been gathered together. He now exerted himself in a more useful, but in a somewhat unclerical way. He threw the money bags away to take up the sword. Roger de Mowbray, a neighbouring baron of great influence and power, was in rebellion, and Geoffrey never paused till he had stormed and pulled down his castle in the Isle of Axholme.[q] Flushed with his success, he now passed onwards into Yorkshire at the invitation of the sheriff and the archbishop, who were anxious to have his aid against William of Scotland, who was at that time invading England. He hastened at once to York, where he was the guest of the archbishop. He had a noble reception at the minster, and in the city. The next day brought the news of the retreat of William. Upon this Geoffrey led his troops against another of Mowbray's fortresses, that of Malzeard near Ripon, and forced the garrison to surrender after a short siege.[r] He then put the oath of allegiance to Hugh, bishop of Durham, who was suspected of treason. A rumour now reached him that the Scottish king was before the castle of Bowes, and he hastened to the rescue. The report, however, was a false one, and Geoffrey returned into the South. As many as one hundred and forty knights were in the train of the young soldier when he reached his father at Huntingdon. Henry was delighted at his loyalty and valour, and said of him before many bystanders, "All my other children are indeed base-born, but this is my true son."[s]

We hear little of Geoffrey after this for several years.[t] He seems, however, to have done a great deal for his diocese of

[m] Diceto, col. 582.

[n] Peter of Blois says this in a letter to Roger, dean of Lincoln. (Opp., i., 222-4.)

[o] Ben. Petrib., 111.

[p] Ibid., 58.

[q] Ger. Cambrensis, 378.

[r] Ger. Cambrensis, 379. Diceto, col. 577. Bromton, col. 1093. Ben. Petrib., 77-8. Matt. Paris, 108. Hoveden, 307 *b*.

[s] Ger. Cambrensis, 380.

[t] It is stated in the Chronicle of Kirkstall that Geoffrey was made a knight in 1179, and several modern writers have followed in its wake. Hoveden (351) says expressly that the person who received that honour was Geoffrey, earl of Brittany.

Lincoln, although he was neither priest nor bishop. He attended carefully to the property of his see, and promoted men of learning and reputation. He redeemed the ornaments of the church of Lincoln, which had been pawned for three hundred marks to Aaron, the Jew of Lincoln, and he added others, giving besides two large and fine bells to the cathedral.[u] But still he was unconsecrated, to the great injury of his diocese, although he was all the while enjoying the revenues of the bishopric. The three years prescribed to him by the pope had long since elapsed, when, in 1181, Alexander III. took the matter up, and wrote to the archbishop of Canterbury desiring him either to require his youthful suffragan to receive ordination and consecration, or to oblige him to give up Lincoln altogether. Geoffrey was now in a difficulty, but he did not shrink from doing his duty. After consulting with his father, brother, and several prelates, he wrote from Marlborough to the archbishop giving up the see, for which he modestly confessed himself to be unfit. He sent a letter also to the chapter of Lincoln, begging that body to annul his election.[v]

Geoffrey was no loser, in a worldly sense, by this change. His father made him chancellor, and gave him offices and rents to the yearly value of five hundred marks in Normandy and England.[w] Among these must probably be enumerated the castles of Beaugi and Langeis, the archdeaconry of Rouen, and the treasurership of the church of York.[x] For the next few years Geoffrey seems to have been generally with his father, to whom he was tenderly attached. He was present in 1182 when Henry made his will, in which his favourite son is made one of the dispensers of his charitable bequests.[y] He remained faithful to his sire in spite of the disloyalty of his brothers. In 1187,

[u] Ger. Cambrensis, Vitæ Episc. Lincoln., apud Angl. Sacr., ii., 418. There is a letter from him as bishop of Lincoln to a Mr. R. Blondus, censuring him for disobedience and neglect of duty. The writer seems to be Peter de Blois (Petri Bles. Opp., i., 184-5).

[v] Ger. Cambr., 380-1. Rob. de Monte, 802. Ben. Petrib., 354-5. Trivet, 82. Diceto, col. 517, 613. Gervase, col. 1458. Stubbs, col. 1724. Hoveden, 348-9. Matt. Paris, 117: Angl. Sacra, ii., 418. Fœdera, *n. e.*, i., 37.

[w] Rob. de Monte, 802. Trivet, 82. Ben. Petrib., 356. Hoveden, 349.

[x] Ger. Cambr., 380. Lel. Coll., i., 290, ex. Gualt. Coventr., where it is said that Richard I. gave these places and posts to Geoffrey. Gerald is the sole authority for his having been treasurer of York. The Beverley historians claim Geoffrey as one of the provosts of their minster. He had nothing to do with it. Geoffrey provost of Beverley was a nephew of archbishop Roger, and probably succeeded Becket in his office. In 1176 his uncle bought for him, for the large sum of 11,000 marks, the post of chancellor to Henry Fitz-Henry the young king. He was lost at sea in the month of October in the following year, as he was crossing from England into Normandy. He was also archdeacon of York (Ben. Petrib., 149, 249. Diceto, col. 589, 599. Hoveden, 315. Trivet, 73. Bromton, col. 1115).

[y] Gervase, col. 1459-60. Gerald de Instit. Princ., ed. Stevenson, 160. Fœdera, i., 47. Nichols's Royal Wills, 7. Nicolas's Test. Vet., 2.

when Philip of France raised the *oriflamme* against Henry of England, Geoffrey buckled on his harness, and the king gave him the command of a fourth part of his army.[z] He was with his father in the town of Mans when it was surrounded and fired by the French soldiery, and after many attempts to extinguish the flames, and a vigorous resistance, he made his escape with Henry and his men to the castle of Fresnelles. Many had fallen down by the way-side from fatigue, and Henry himself was worn out. Geoffrey desired him to repose, and wished to watch on the outside of the castle to protect his father from an assault. Henry would not permit him to do this; and replenished from his own stores the wardrobe of Geoffrey, which had been lost at Mans. On the morrow Henry got himself away to Angers; and Geoffrey, after a perilous journey, in which he was followed by a hundred knights, joined his father at Savigny. What a contrast to the baseness of John, the youngest and the best beloved of all his ungrateful children![a]

In June 1189 Henry was still abroad. After the capture of Tours a discreditable peace was made with France, at the making of which Geoffrey, full of indignation, would not permit his sick father to be present. The end of the king was now at hand, hastened as it was and embittered by the treachery of John.[b] He was in the castle of Chinon,

"Zu Chinon hält der könig seinen hof,"

and Geoffrey never left his side. One day the head and the shoulders of the sick man were resting on his breast; he was driving away with a fan the flies that buzzed around his father's face, whilst a knight at the end of the bed held in his bosom his master's feet. The eyes of the enfeebled monarch opened and fell upon his son. His harshness was gone, and he spoke, for at such times even stern and cold-hearted men cannot be silent. He told Geoffrey that, basely-born although he was, he had been a truer child than all his rightful children. Should his life be spared that filial affection should not be unrewarded. He bade him prosper and be blessed. The tears rushed from the listener's eyes, and muttering a few affectionate words he left the room and the scene which had caused him such poignant sorrow. The fever meanwhile increased in violence, and Geoffrey, unable to refrain himself, sought again the chamber of his sire. Henry was now dying. His eyes were closed, but when he heard the expressions of sorrow which his son was unable to repress, they opened upon him again. He knew him

[z] Ben. Petrib., 467. Bromton, col. 1133.

[a] Ger. Cambrensis, 381. Ben. Petrib., 452-3. Recueil des Hist. des Gaules, xviii., 216.

[b] Polydore Vergil, 276.

and faltered out his wish that he might become bishop of Winchester or archbishop of York. He blessed him for the last time, and stretched out to him, as a final token of his affection, a precious ring of gold, with a panther graven on it, which he had destined for his kinsman, the king of Spain. He gave him, also, another more costly jewel, a ring with a noble sapphire, which seems to have acted like a talisman.[c] After this the king passed away, and Geoffrey committed his remains most reverently to the tomb. The body was laid upon the bier in the church of Fontevraud, when Richard, one of the dead man's rebellious children, unexpectedly and hastily came in. He gazed for the last time upon the face of his injured sire. There he lay subdued at last, his countenance still retaining the stern expression which it had worn in life. In that awful presence Richard would remember that filial ingratitude had made that proud heart cease to beat.

> "Thy silver hairs I see,
> So still, so sadly bright!
> And, father, father! but for me
> They had not been so white!
> I bore thee down, high heart! at last
> No longer could thou strive;
> Oh! for one moment of the past
> To kneel and say—'forgive.'"

He groaned in spirit, and throwing himself on his knees beside the corpse, seemed to be deeply penitent.[d]

As soon as the funeral was over Geoffrey gave up the seals of the chancery, which he had held for several years. There seemed to be every prospect of peace and affection between him and Richard. Vain hope! Geoffrey, after visiting his possessions in the vicinity of Tours and Angers, rejoined his brother, who was then in Normandy, but he was met by cold and angry looks. Evil influences had been unhappily at work, and Richard's mind was warped. Geoffrey returned to England. When he arrived at London he was met by a large body of the York ecclesiastics, informing him that he had been elected to the see of York, which had been long vacant, and desiring him to come to them. He declined positively to accept the honour. He was not fit for it. He told them that he was fonder of dogs and hawks than of books and priests. The Yorkshiremen made a characteristic reply; they told him that it was not necessary that he should altogether abandon those tastes when he came

[c] A legacy which reminds us of the lines of Hugo Grotius in his Dactyliotheca,

> "Annule, cui moriens, et villas credit et agros,
> Tutelamque suæ prolis, opesque pater:
> Annule, qui pestem, fœdumque arcere venenum
> Pectore, qui philtri crederis esse loco."

[d] Ger. Cambrensis, 381-2. Ben. Petrib., 347. Hoveden, 372 *b*. Matt. Paris, 126.

into the North.[e] This temptation, and the recollection of his father's wish,[f] secured Geoffrey's consent. It may be well to observe that his election by the chapter of York had been by no means an unanimous one, and this division of opinion had been caused, to a great extent, by his own indiscretion. It would appear that Richard had promised him the archbishopric soon after his father's death, upon which Geoffrey had hastily sent his clerks to England to displace the custodiers of the temporalities and spiritualities of the see.[g] On the 10th of August the chapter of York met, in obedience to the royal mandate, to elect a new archbishop, and knowing as they did the wishes of the late king and his successor,[h] their choice, naturally enough, fell upon Geoffrey. Hubert Walter the dean, the bishop of Durham, and many of the canons were not present, and the election therefore was objected to as informal. Walter, who had at one time been himself nominated by the chapter, appealed to the pope, and with the assistance of the queen-mother, who had a stepmother's dislike to Geoffrey, he prevailed upon Richard to make an order that everything at York should continue as it was when his father died. The spiritual charge therefore of the diocese returned into the hands of the dean, and the temporal possessions to the care of their old custodiers.[i] This was the state of things when Geoffrey, after accepting the archbishopric at the hands of the representatives of the chapter, went to the court at Windsor. Every one seemed to be against him. After a long controversy the matter in dispute was amicably arranged. The coronation of the king took place, and, afterwards, on the 16th of September, when they were at Pipewell abbey,[j] Richard confirmed the election of his brother, and the fact was formally announced by Puiset bishop of Durham.

When this was over the king impressed upon his brother the necessity of his being ordained a priest, and threatened in the end, if he did not consent, to seize the revenues of the archbishopric. Geoffrey was now in a dilemma. He had some lingering hope of having a share in the kingdom; he would lose this if he became a priest; if he should not be ordained, he would be ejected from his see. After much hesitation he was admitted to the priesthood at Southwell, by his

[e] Ger. Cambrensis, 382-3.

[f] Hemingford, apud Gale., ii., 518. Fordun, Scotichronicon, i., 498.

[g] Ben. Petrib., 549. Wm. Neubr., 357. Chron. Jo. de Oxenedes, 72. Bromton, col. 1155. Hoveden, 373 *b*. Matt. Paris, 127.

[h] Wm. Neubr. (357-8) speaks of letters having been written to the chapter to that effect. Hoveden, 373 *b*.

[i] Ben. Petrib., 553-4. Diceto, col. 653. Bromton, col. 1156-7. Hoveden, 373 *b*.

[j] Ben. Petrib., 562. Wm. Neubr., 357. Diceto, col. 653. Bromton, col. 1161. Hoveden, 375 *b*. Matt. Par., 129.

suffragan, John bishop of Whitherne.[k] Puiset, the bishop of Durham, was an enemy of his, and Geoffrey would not allow him to officiate, a slight which Puiset never afterwards forgot.[l] Geoffrey had also made up his mind that the pope should consecrate him. In the month of October he paid a visit to York, but amid the festivities and gratulations which greeted his advent, he manifested his customary want of tact and infirmity of temper. The new dean and treasurer, Henry Marshall and Buchard de Puiset, a nephew of the bishop of Durham, besought him to install them, but he refused, inconsiderately, to do so till his own appointment had been confirmed by the pope. This added fuel to a fire which had been for some time kindled.

One incident in the long contention which followed is peculiar and amusing. Geoffrey was coming to the vespers in the minster, but being somewhat late, the dean and the treasurer ordered the service to begin without him. He arrived soon after with Hamo, the precentor, and several of the canons, and was very indignant at the slight. He and the precentor bade the service cease, the dean and the treasurer giving a contrary injunction. The singers, however, were silent, and Geoffrey began the vespers again. The treasurer then directed the tapers to be extinguished, and there was an end of everything. The archbishop-elect now put the church under an interdict. On the morrow when, according to their wont, for it was a high festival, the whole population of the city flocked to the minster to hear the service, Geoffrey, the dean and his brethren, were in the the choir endeavouring to come to terms, but the two culprits would render no satisfaction, and added insult to injury. The crowd would have rushed upon them if it had not been restrained by Geoffrey. Buchard and the dean were greatly alarmed. One fled to the deanery and the other to St. William's tomb. They were excommunicated and the interdict continued.[m]

Complaints of the conduct of Geoffrey were made to the king, and Richard, who for other reasons was annoyed at his brother, took possession of all his private property at home and abroad. When Geoffrey's messengers wished to go to the papal court, to obtain the pall for their master, the king would not allow them to leave the country.[n] The two brothers met again in December. William king of Scotland was summoned

[k] Ger. Cambrensis, 383. Ben. Petrib., 565. Bromton, col. 1162. Hoveden, 375 *b*. Matt. Paris, 131. Diceto (col. 653) said that the ordination took place in the presence of Fulmar, archbishop of Trèves.

[l] Ger. Cambr., 383.

[m] Hoveden, 378 *b*.

[n] Ben. Petrib., 569. Bromton, col. 1166. Hoveden, 375 *b*, who puts this occurrence in a somewhat different place.

to the English court, but he refused to come unless Geoffrey would escort him. Richard, upon this, desired the archbishop-elect to do so, and he attended the Scottish monarch from the Tweed to Canterbury.[o] He entreated the Scottish king to prevail upon his brother to restore his property, and William made a promise to do so, but forgot it. Soon after this Richard made a vain attempt, through the bishop of Durham and several other dignitaries, to induce Geoffrey to give up his archbishopric on the plea that his election had been an informal one, and when he refused to do so, he deprived him of the temporalities which were entrusted to Puiset. A few days afterwards the dispute came under the cognizance of John of Anagnia, the papal legate. Every attempt was made to dislodge Geoffrey, but to no purpose. Puiset and Hubert Walter, who was now bishop of Salisbury, brought forward the informality of his election; the new treasurer and the dean depreciated his character by saying that he was a homicide and born in adultery; the messengers of the king tried threats and bribes. The legate, however, was obdurate. At this crisis a compromise was effected, and a general amnesty was proclaimed. Money carried the day when reason and argument were powerless. Geoffrey promised his brother three thousand marks towards the expenses of the crusade, on which he was just embarking. Richard, on his part, restored Geoffrey's private property and the temporalities of his see, and prevailed upon him to confirm the privileges of the York chapter and Puiset, the dean, the treasurer and the bishop of Durham having relinquished the appeals which they had made against him.[p] His election to the archbishopric was solemnly confirmed by the legate and the pope.[q] Geoffrey's chief anxiety now was to raise the money for which he had pledged his word, and he was obliged to ask his clergy for a subsidy. It would probably have been given if the bishop of Durham had not opposed it. Soon after this, in the beginning of 1190, he was summoned abroad, and found his brother at Lyons. When Richard heard that he had come without the subsidy he was in a fury. It was in vain that Geoffrey gave him the reason for his insolvency, and requested him to take the revenues of his see till they satisfied his claims. This was not enough for Richard, who seized upon them all without reserve. He sent also the bishop of Bath and Wells, the dean of Mans and Buchard de Puiset to the pope, that Geoffrey's election might be annulled. In this he was too late, for the archbishop was a far readier politician, and had out-generalled

[o] Ben. Petrib., 575-6. Diceto, col. 649. Bromton, col. 1167.

[p] Ger. Cambrensis, 385. Ben. Petrib., 577-9. Bromton, col. 1169. Hoveden, 377-8.

[q] Diceto, col. 653. Matt. Paris, 131.

him. He had already sent some of his clerks to Rome, and the royal messengers met them as they were returning, bringing with them the official confirmation of Geoffrey's appointment as well as the pall.[r] Opposition was therefore useless, and the two brothers were reconciled at Tours. An arrangement was made about the payment of the money, and then Richard, who had already assumed the staff and the scrip of the pilgrim, went on his journey into the East. His favours, however, were always marred by some qualification or reservation, for he was full of mean subterfuges and petty jealousies. Before he went away he left a strict injunction forbidding any archbishop in his dominions to consecrate his brother. Geoffrey was all the while in possession of a general licence from the pope which authorized his consecration by any prelate of that high degree. Richard is also said to have extorted a promise from his brothers, John and Geoffrey, that they would not return to England for three years after his departure without his special permission. He subsequently withdrew this restriction in the case of John,[s] and Gerald Cambrensis informs us that Geoffrey had the like concession, but in this he seems to be mistaken.[t]

Geoffrey was now at peace with his brother, but he was not a man who could remain long quiet. His old feud with the family of Puiset seems to have revived. Geoffrey had excommunicated Buchard, the treasurer of York, but that dignitary, nothing daunted, had made his way to Rome, and pleaded his cause before Clement III., with such success, that not only was the bar removed, but the pope had refused to confirm the election of Geoffrey and to send him the pall. He had allowed, also, the bishop of Durham to be altogether independent of the see of York.[u] In the spring of 1191 the queen-mother seems to have gone to Rome, at the king's request, to beg the pope to reverse his sentence and to consecrate Geoffrey.[v] Soon after this Celestine III. ascended the papal chair, but Richard, as has been already stated, had changed his mind with reference to his brother. The archbishop-elect, however, dispatched Simon de Apulia,[w] one of his clerks, who was a Calabrian by birth, and a man of eloquence and learning, to the papal court. He was accompanied by Hamo, precentor of York, William Testard, archdeacon of Nottingham, and Ralph de Wigetoc,[x] canon of Ripon. They were so successful that

[r] Gerald Cambrensis, 386-7. Diceto, col. 663.

[s] Ben. Petrib., 584. Hoveden, 378 b. Ric. Divis. Chron., 15. Bromton, col. 1171.

[t] Ger. Cambrensis, 387.

[u] Ben. Petrib., 629. Hoveden, 387-8. Bromton, col. 1190.

[v] Hoveden, 392.

[w] Wm. Neubr., 405. He was afterwards dean of York and bishop of Exeter.

[x] There is an extraordinary story about this man in Hoveden (437). He was sick unto death at Rome in 1196,

not only was bishop Puiset deprived of his privilege and ordered to render obedience to York,[y] but, in addition to this, the church and diocese of York were exempted from the authority of any papal legate, unless he was some cardinal of high degree or honoured with some special mission. By the same messengers there arrived an order from the pope addressed to the archbishop of Tours, commanding him to consecrate Geoffrey without delay.[z] The ceremony, therefore, took place in the church of St. Maurice at Tours on the 18th of August, 1191. The archbishop himself officiated, and was assisted by eight other prelates with much pomp and circumstance.[a] The archbishop of Canterbury and his suffragans were greatly offended at what they considered to be an infringement on the rights of the English metropolitan. When Baldwin had first heard of Geoffrey's election, he had made an attempt to assert the old privileges of his see, and had made a fruitless order that the archbishop of York should be consecrated by no one but himself.[b]

We now come to one of the most extraordinary scenes in Geoffrey's life, a scene which possesses all the interest of a romance.[c] He was wishful to return to England, and his brother John urged him to embark, but there was his promise to the contrary to prevent him. England was then under the charge of William, bishop of Ely, who is said to have had some strong reasons for keeping Geoffrey out of the way;[d] and at his

and there he confessed to the pope and the cardinals that he had got many forged letters in the Roman court for himself and his master Geoffrey. The pope desired the archbishop of Canterbury to seize them. A man of the name of Roger de Ripon was caught at London with some of them in his possession, and poison was found on him, which had been given to him, as he said, to destroy Simon de Apulia, then dean of York, and several of the canons. Simon was sent for to London, and the poison, some gold rings and a beautiful zone, all poisoned, were handed over to him and were burned. The bearer was imprisoned. Geoffrey was blamed for all this by his enemies. Recueil des Hist. des Gaules, xviii., 77.

[y] Ben. Petrib., 694. Bromton, col. 1224.

[z] Ben. Petrib., 694. Gerald, 387. Bromton, col. 1222. Hoveden, 399. Knyghton, col. 2402. Wm. Neubr. (405) says that the bishop of Ely was the great cause of the delay in Geoffrey's consecration, having seized and wasted the archiepiscopal property whilst he was abroad. Bromton (1224) says that the bishop seized Geoffrey's goods in consequence of his consecration.

[a] Gerald, 388. Wm. Neubr., 405. Ann. Waverl., ed. Gale, ii., 164. Ric. Divis. Chron., 34. Diceto, col. 521, 663. Bromton, col. 1224. Contin. Fl. Wigorn., ii., 159. Matt. Paris, 136.

[b] Ben. Petrib., 563-4. Hoveden, 375 *b*. Bromton, col. 1162. Gervase. col. 1570-1. Anglia Sacra, i., 10. Henriquez, Phœnix Reviviscens, 20.

[c] This scene is described in Gerald, 389-92. Ben. Petrib., 695. Wm. Neubr., 406. Ann de Margan, apud Gale, ii., 10. Ann. Waverl., ibid., 164. Ric. Divis. Chron., 34-6. Diceto, col. 663. Bromton, col. 1224. Gervase, col. 1576. Hoveden, 399. Contin. Fl. Wigorn., ii., 159. Matt. Paris, 136. Polydore Vergil, 274. Recueil des Hist. des Gaules, xviii., 63.

[d] Too much abuse has been heaped upon the bishop for his share in this adventure. It seems to me that he was only doing his duty.

request the countess of Flanders and Boulogne forbade the archbishop to pass through her territories, or to sail from any of her ports. His suite might go, if they chose, but they must go without him, and they were to land at Dover. Geoffrey, who had resolved upon the journey, was not to be kept behind. His train reached Dover in safety, and whilst every one, no doubt, was examining it with curious eyes for the archbishop, Geoffrey was on the sea with a small party of his friends in an English fishing-smack. The constable of the castle was brother-in-law to the bishop of Ely, who seems to have ordered every one to keep a sharp look-out. The exile neared the shore very early in the morning, but he could not even then escape the vigilance of the garrison. He had disguised himself, but a royal face is not easily concealed. He was ordered into the castle, but he refused to go. He got upon a swift horse and galloped towards the priory. A horseman from the castle followed him in hot pursuit, and stretched out his hand to seize hold of Geoffrey's rein. The archbishop, still mindful of his old prowess in the field, gave the steed of his pursuer a kick with his right foot which nearly overthrew it, and then escaped to the monastery. It was immediately surrounded by a band of soldiers. The constable of the castle sent messenger after messenger in vain, ordering him either to take the oath of allegiance, or to return. What had they to do with it? He would do neither. The prince-bishop was undaunted, and confronted his foes with a fearless bearing from his chair beside the altar, arrayed in his stole and alb, and bearing in his hand his crozier wrought with ivory and gold. When the soldiers gazed upon him as he sat, they would think of the martyrdom and the intrepidity of Becket. A sudden movement now came over them. They threw themselves on their knees before the altar, and beat their breasts, as if to beg forgiveness for what they were going to do, and then they caught hold of Geoffrey by the arms and shoulders, and dragged him to the door. He resisted, and his head was dashed against the pavement, but they carried him out by the feet and arms. They tried to force him on his horse, but he would not mount it, so they pushed him along through the wet and mud, still bearing his crozier in his hand. They took him to the castle, where the constable received him on his knees with tears streaming down his cheeks. On that night a wind came roaring over the sea, and a storm arose which shook those massive walls to their foundations.

Geoffrey was in Dover castle for eight days without fire, water, or food, save such as his servants could buy for him in the town. His horses were sent off to the bishop of Ely, who was overjoyed at what had taken place, and he endeavoured to tempt his prisoner either to leave the country, or to take the oath of allegiance. He would do neither; for a grievous insult had been offered to him, and he knew that he would soon be in a position to dictate terms instead of accepting them. The tide of popular sympathy had already set in towards him. The mob, when they were carrying him to the castle, had shouted at the soldiery, indignant that a priest and the king's brother should be thus treated. The constable, who had been an unwilling tool, requested and obtained Geoffrey's pardon for what he had done. The news soon ran through the whole country, and caused much indignation and excitement. The bishop of Ely was anything but popular, and this freak made him more disliked than ever. The bishop of Lincoln at once excommunicated the perpetrators of the outrage. The bishops of London and Norwich threatened and remonstrated with their brother of Ely. Prince John, who was at Lancaster, took up the matter with great warmth. He ordered the regent, at his peril, to release his brother from his prison. The bishop of Ely did not dare to be disobedient. He sent Geoffrey's uncle, Hameline earl of Warren, to Dover to authorize his discharge on condition that he came to London to the council, and promised to abide by its decree. The pledge was given, and the captive left the castle in the same humble guise in which he entered it, passing through a rejoicing crowd. He halted for a while at Canterbury to visit the tomb of the martyred primate, and, soon afterwards, arrived at London. At Reading he met his brother John and many of the bishops and nobles of the realm, making his complaint against the chancellor, and begging for redress, which was soon promised. The bishop of Ely, however, would make him no amends. He set prince John's friends at naught; he would not meet them, and received all their overtures and proposals with the greatest contempt. He paid a bitter penalty for his folly and want of tact. He was excommunicated and deprived of his chancellorship, and was obliged to seek safety by an ignominious flight. Geoffrey now went on a visit to Northampton, where he had formerly been a student, and received a hearty welcome. He then set out for York, where he was solemnly enthroned in the minster on the festival of All Saints.[e]

Geoffrey was at this time in the middle of another controversy with the bishop of Durham. That restless prelate had left no stone unturned to procure the liberation of his see from its allegiance to York. He made appeal after appeal to Rome.

[e] Gerard Cambrensis, 392-407. Ben. Petrib., 697-700. Wm. Neubr., 406, etc. Ric. Divis., 37-42. Diceto, col. 664-5. Bromton, col. 1225-8. Knyghton, col. 2404. Hoveden, 399-400. Matt. Paris, 139-140.

He refused to pay the sums which were due from those churches within the diocese of York which belonged to Durham. Geoffrey wrote in vain to him to demand redress, and to require his submission. Puiset regarded his threats and his entreaties with contempt. He said that he had made his profession long ago to archbishop Roger, and that was quite enough. Geoffrey, upon this, thundered at him the sentence of excommunication from his minster, with candle, book, and bell.[f] His uncontrollable temper manifested itself in several ways. He overthrew the altars at which Puiset had officiated, and broke the chalices which he had used. He was very angry with his brother, prince John, because he had been at the same table with the bishop of Durham after his excommunication; and he held aloof from him till he had expressed regret for what he had done.[g] Puiset seems to have cared but little for these censures of his rival. In the following year, 1192, the ban was repeated, on the festival of the Purification, but it was looked upon with contempt. Puiset, however, was on his way to the papal court to prosecute his appeal, when he and Geoffrey had an interview at London, in the presence of the queen-mother. The case of each was heard, and Puiset expressed his readiness to abide by the decision of the queen and the archbishop of Rouen. Geoffrey would have none of this, unless his rival would first come to the church of York to seek for absolution, and to render his obedience. Puiset then said that he would make no peace with him unless he would solemnly proclaim, in the same place, the removal and the needlessness of the sentence which he had passed. Geoffrey of course refused, and the matter was at an end. It was during this visit that the archbishop excited the wrath of the Southern prelates by having his cross carried erect from his residence in the New Temple to Westminster. They would have broken the sacred symbol unless some royal personages had interfered, and the bishop of London forbade the celebration of divine service in the New Temple, which compelled Geoffrey to lower his cross and to desert his residence. Puiset now pushed his appeal at Rome.[h] He complained to the pope that he had been excommunicated whilst his appeal to the papal court was undecided, and Celestine revoked the sentence on the ground that it had been hastily and imprudently made.[i] He also sent a message to the bishops of Rochester and Lincoln, and the abbat of Peterborough, to the effect that if, upon

[f] Ben. Petrib., 716-17. Bromton, col. 1235. Gervase, col. 1580.

[g] Ben. Petrib., 727. Bromton, col. 1236.

[h] Ibid., 729-30. Bromton, col. 1237-8. Hoveden, 408 *b*.

[i] Ben. Petrib., 733. Wm. Neubr., 443-5. Bromton, col. 1238. Hoveden, 465-6. Labbe, x., 1769.

enquiry, they found that Geoffrey had really destroyed the altars and chalices, as was stated, that then Puiset should be altogether released from his subjection to Geoffrey during his life.[j] The two combatants met after this at Northampton; and then, at the request of the bishop of Lincoln, the farther consideration of the question was deferred to a future day.

The feud between Geoffrey and the dean and chapter of York had been temporarily settled, but this and every other armistice only seemed to inspire them with new vigour for assault and defence. The quarrel was now raging again, and Puiset, who was a man of war himself, did his best to see that the chapter were victorious. Henry Marshall the dean, Buchard the treasurer, Hugh Murdac and Adam de Tornovere, canons of the church, and Peter de Ros, clerk of the bishop of Durham, had been put by Geoffrey under an anathema. The archbishop of Rouen and the other justiciars of England ordered the Northern primate to restore to them everything of which they had been deprived, and, if he refused to do so, William de Stutevill and other powerful barons were directed to compel him, or to seize upon the temporalities of his see. Geoffrey was inexorable, unless the culprits would present themselves at the door of the minster in the guise of penitents, and receive absolution; promising, at the same time, to abide by the decision of the chapter in all future controversies. Wearied with delays and opposition they complied with his request, and another truce was made. The dean, however, a brother of William the earl-marshal, refused to stoop to the conditions, and spoke high words against his diocesan. Geoffrey met him with equal spirit. He put the city under an interdict, and would allow no divine service to be performed in it whilst the dean was within the walls.[k]

In 1193, whilst Richard I. was in captivity, prince John, it is well known, began to intrigue against his absent brother. His conduct aroused the indignation of Geoffrey. Whilst the barons in the South were taking up arms to protect the rights of their imprisoned sovereign, he collected together the forces of the North. Hugh Bardolf, the sheriff of Yorkshire, and William de Stutevill were with him, and they went to Doncaster, and began to fortify the town. Geoffrey, mindful of the exploits of his youth, was eager to invest the neighbouring castle of Tickhill which belonged to his rebellious brother; but Bardolf and Stutevill refused to accompany him, on the plea that John was their suzerain. The archbishop, full of wrath, called them traitors to their king and country, and withdrew

[j] Ben. Petrib., 741-2. [k] Ben. Petrib., 744-5. Bromton, col. 1239-40.

from them with all his men. Geoffrey, who with all his impetuosity had an affectionate heart, was much concerned at the misfortunes of his brother. Richard wrote to him from his prison, begging him, above all others, to watch over his kingdom, and to raise the necessary funds for his release. Whilst the Cistercians and the Gilbertines were surrendering their wool, and stripping their churches of their plate, to contribute their share towards the king's ransom, the canons of York refused to listen to their archbishop when he asked them to give up a fourth part of their income for the same purpose.[l] It was, no doubt, merely their personal dislike of the asker which prompted their refusal. In course of time this opposition seems to have been overcome, as the treasures and relics of the church of York were pawned for a while to alleviate the necessities of Richard.[m] When that monarch returned to England, there was on the whole but little friendship between him and his brother Geoffrey, for the children of Henry II. were united together by no strong fraternal ties. In 1195, after a visit to Sherwood forest, and an interview, as the legend tells us, with the famous outlaw Robin Hood,[n] Richard held his first council at Nottingham. Geoffrey sat at his right hand, and purchased, for the large sum of 3,000 marks and a rent of 100 marks per annum, the shrievalty of Yorkshire.[o] Many complaints were made at that meeting, by ecclesiastics as well as laymen, of Geoffrey's exactions and extortions, but he treated them with contemptuous silence, and no investigation seems to have been made.[p] He was not present at the coronation, as his brother would not allow him to bear his cross.[q] On the 23rd of April in the same year (1195), when Richard was at Waltham, he confirmed to Geoffrey his possessions abroad, and reconciled him to his old enemy, of whom we have lost sight for some time, the bishop of Ely. Soon after this the archbishop fell into disgrace for having injured the canons of York, and was deprived of the temporalities of his see, which remained for some time in the king's hands, being held for him by William de Stutevill and Geoffrey Haget.[r] Geoffrey was at this time suspended from his spiritual duties, and his fortunes were at their lowest ebb. The only place that was left to him was the manor of Ripon, at which he for some time resided; and it was here probably that he was brought into more immediate connection with the learned

[l] Hoveden, 412 *b*, 416.

[m] Fabric Rolls of York Minster, ed. Surtees Soc., 152.

[n] "The kynge came to Notynghame,
With knyghtes in grete arayo,
For to take that gentyll knyght,
And Robyn Hode, if he may."

[o] Hoveden, 419. Madox, Hist. Exchequer, i., 459.

[p] Hoveden, 419 *b*.

[q] Ibid., 420. Ben. Petrib. (556) says that he *was* there: so do Bromton, col. 1157; and Peter Langtoft, *n. e.*, 142.

[r] Hoveden, 420 *b*, 423.

Peter de Blois, one of the canons of that place, and incited him to commemorate, in a work addressed to himself, the life and merits of St. Wilfrid.[s] In the autumn of the same year Geoffrey went into Normandy to see his brother, and purchased his forgiveness for the sum of 3,000 marks, which restored to him all the temporal possessions of which he had been deprived.[t] He seems to have lost them again immediately for his intemperate language against the king for dispossessing him,[t] for he had not the slightest particle of discretion; and Fuller is not far wrong when he says that Richard was kinder to him "than his tumultuous nature did deserve."[u] The king was again in possession of the temporalities of the see. He would gladly have seen Geoffrey deposed, and it was with great regret that he heard, in 1196, of his being restored to the favour of the pope. He was more bitter against him than ever, and determined to let and hinder him as far as he possibly could. He persisted in giving away the stalls and offices at York, a course of conduct which brought the two brothers into collision. This state of things seems to have continued until 1198, when Geoffrey went to the court in Normandy at his brother's request, and they were again friends, Richard giving him back his temporalities, and promising to interfere no more with the appointments in his cathedral. He changed his mind a few days after this in consequence of the representations of the York chapter; and it was in vain that pope Innocent, by promises and threats, endeavoured to persuade him to be reconciled to Geoffrey.[v] Richard's sudden death, which took place shortly afterwards, put an end to all negotiations.

It has been already stated that the chapter of York refused to listen to Geoffrey when he urged them to contribute towards the ransom of his brother. Their disinclination to grant what he demanded was caused by the revival of the old feud, into which it will be necessary, although perhaps tedious, to enter. A second quarrel between friends who have been temporarily united is always worse than the first, and in this instance the trite observation was completely verified. In 1194 the promotion of Henry Marshall to the bishopric of Exeter vacated the deanery of York. Geoffrey, who was then at Ripon, gave the post to his brother Peter. Peter, however, was then at Paris, and the king urged his brother to bestow the dignity on John, provost of Douay. Upon this the archbishop strove to

[s] Bale, cent. iii., 231. Vossius, 426. There is a letter from Peter de Blois addressed to him exhorting him to resist heretics (Petri Bles. Opp., i., 350-1.

[t] Hoveden, 425, 428. Ann. Burton., apud Gale, iii., 203.

[u] Fuller's Church History, bk. iii., 45.

[v] Hoveden, 435 b, 442 b, 446 b.

extricate himself from the difficulty by giving the deanery to one of his clerks, Simon de Apulia. When the chance of a controversy seemed to be over, he endeavoured to prevail upon Simon to occupy it merely as the deputy, and for the benefit of Peter. As this was a very questionable transaction, the chapter of York shewed their opinion of it by electing Simon at once to the deanery. Geoffrey now made another move, and gave the office to a great favourite of his brother, Philip de Poictiers, archdeacon of Canterbury, who was subsequently bishop of Durham. The chapter were immediately in arms, and the battle begun. They held aloof from their archbishop, and claimed the right of electing their own superior. They would contribute nothing towards the ransom of king Richard. The messengers of Geoffrey were sent to make an appeal at the papal court. They were to halt, however, in Germany to see the king, and there they found that Simon had preceded them. Richard forbade either party to appeal to Rome. He would settle the dispute himself; and one of Geoffrey's friends was sent to England to bid him hasten to his brother. In the meantime the canons had put an end to the service in the minster, the bells were silent, and all the city was in a commotion. The archbishop's stall and the door which led into the nave from his palace were locked. When Geoffrey sent to require the continuance of the service, they paid no attention to his request. He went to the minster at Christmas, 1194, and finding it empty, filled it with his own clerks, and excommunicated four of the dignitaries of the cathedral for their contumacy. The sufferers, accompanied by the superiors of the houses of St Mary's, York, and Selby, and many of the Premonstratensian abbats, crossed the seas to Richard, who was angry at Geoffrey's disobedience, and obtaining his consent proceeded to the papal court, where the archbishop was also represented. The pope, on this occasion, set aside the claims of both sides, and gave the deanery, of his own authority, to Simon. The dean and his companions then laid many serious complaints against Geoffrey, relating for the most part to his mal-administration of his diocese. They said that he did nothing but hunt, and hawk, and busy himself with military affairs, whilst his spiritual charge was in the meanwhile uncared for. There were no ordinations, no consecrations nor synods; no abbat could obtain his benediction, although he might find himself excommunicated. The liberties of the minster of York were set at naught. Some of the canons had been put under an anathema; the vicars and officers of the church had been ejected. If any one talked of making an appeal to Rome he was thrown into prison. The archbishop would not institute clerks to benefices, but gave them to boys and base persons. He made livings vacant at his pleasure to obtain the revenues, and broke open the doors to get possession of the churches. These were very serious charges, and Celestine seems to have listened to them with attention. He determined to have them thoroughly investigated. He issued a commission of enquiry on the 8th of June, 1195, addressed to the bishop of Lincoln and two others, authorizing them to examine into the truth of these allegations. A few days before this, on the 31st of May, the pope had written to Hamo dean of Lincoln, and the archdeacons of Leicester and Northampton, authorizing them to reinstate the vicars and ministers of the church of York in their offices. The dean had told him that Geoffrey had ejected them, a statement which, if Hoveden, a contemporary, is to be relied upon, was certainly unfounded.[w] When the papal mandate arrived at Lincoln the bishop found that Geoffrey had already appealed to Rome, and that he was on his way to that city. The day of the examination, therefore, was deferred. Geoffrey never arrived at the papal court, as Richard forbade his progress; and he was afraid, besides, of the autumnal fevers which still ravaged the old capital of the world. His clerks, however, acted in his stead, and obtained a decree which frustrated every order that had been made in their master's absence. He was ordered to be at Rome to answer for himself at the following Martinmas; and when he failed to appear either in person or by deputy at that time and at Christmas, he was suspended from his office. He had, shortly before this, met with a sad reverse in England. Some of his servants had been brought, at the instance of the canons of York, before the archbishop of Canterbury, the king's justiciar, and his fellows, on a charge of robbery; and Geoffrey, failing to exculpate either himself or them, was disseised of the possessions of his archiepiscopate, with the exception of the manor of Ripon, and he lost his shrievalty as well.[x] A short time before Michaelmas, the dignitaries of the minster, who had been at Rome, returned to York. They brought with them the pope's absolution from the sentence of excommunication, which Geoffrey had pronounced against them; this was read solemnly in the cathedral by bishop Puiset, and then, with the assistance of the secular arm, they were restored to their preferments. Ralph, archdeacon of the West Riding, had died as he was returning, but Hamo the precentor and the archdeacons of Nottingham and Cleveland reached York in safety. Geoffrey appealed against all this to the pope, but Celestine merely suspended him on account of his non-appearance at Rome in contravention of his promise.[y]

[w] Hoveden, 415-17, 426-7. Labbe, Conc., x., 1773, 1775.

[x] Hoveden, 416 *b*, 423.

[y] Ibid., 417 *b*, 423, 425.

In the midst of this confusion, an event took place which under another state of things would never have occurred. This was nothing else than the presence of the archbishop of Canterbury at York, to hold a council in his capacity of legate, an honour which the pope had conferred upon him on the 18th of March, 1195.[z] Celestine, when he granted it, had stated that his commission was to override any privilege that Geoffrey might enjoy to the contrary, and this seems to shew that there was some understanding between the pope and the archbishop with regard to the council in the North of England. We may be sure that there was great need for such a meeting, and for the enforcement of discipline and order in the distracted diocese of York. Hubert of Canterbury would be proud indeed to visit the fair city of York as the representative of the pope, and to enter that cathedral over which he had himself presided. Geoffrey and he had come into collision on two or three occasions about the bearing of the cross,[a] but Hubert was a man of wisdom and discretion, and was more ready to allay contention than to excite it. It was clearly his duty now to go into the North. In the summer of 1195, he sent two messengers, Peter prior of Bineham and Master Geoffrey, to York to exhibit his credentials, and to make arrangements for his intended visit. In years gone by he would never have been permitted to enter within the walls of the cathedral, and even now, in spite of their dislike to Geoffrey, the dean and chapter still retained a shadow of their old independence. They told him that he might come to them as legate, but not as archbishop. Hubert arrived in the metropolis of the North on the festival of St. Barnabas, and for about a week was very usefully employed. He began by holding an assize in his capacity of justiciar. He then visited St. Mary's abbey, and deprived Robert the abbat for incompetency. After this he held a large assembly in the minster, at which the greater part of the ecclesiastics of the North were present. The legate shewed no ill-will towards his brother archbishop. Geoffrey's officers had, indeed, forbidden his approach, for which they were excommunicated; but he allowed them to resume their duties, and they took a part in the proceedings of the meeting. Every one seems to have been pleased with Hubert, who was courteous and obliging.[b] The decrees which were made at the two days' sitting at York have been preserved.[c]

[z] Diceto, col. 679-80. Hoveden, 429. Labbe, Conc., x., 1775.

[a] Gervase, col. 1584-6, 1679. Hoveden, 418-9.

[b] Diceto, col. 694. Hoveden, 430 b.

[c] An account is given in Wm. Neubr., 527, etc., together with the details of the controversy for precedence between Canterbury and York, and in Bromton, col. 1263, etc. Newburgh says that Geoffrey was then abroad, "ad placandam regis iram." Diceto, col. 693. Matt. Paris, 150. Hoveden, 429-30. Hist. Dunelm. Scr. Tres, 17. Labbe,

They relate, for the most part, to minute points of discipline and ritualistic observances, the administration of the sacraments, the dress and morals of the clergy, and the payment of tithes. Two or three of the enactments are rather amusing. No clerk was to drink in public, or to frequent taverns, and he was to avoid flirtations and their consequences. Great attention was to be paid to his tonsure. Any one who neglected it, and possessed a benefice, was to forfeit his cure. If he were not thus provided for, the rural deans and the archdeacons were to take the offender and deprive him, with their sacred fingers, of his flowing locks.

We must not lose sight of the bishop of Lincoln and his colleagues, whom the pope had empowered in June, 1195, to examine into the quarrel between Geoffrey and his chapter and clergy. The commissioners met at York, apparently to arrange how to proceed, and afterwards at Torkley and Ancaster; and the chapter proved in their presence that they had been losers through the archbishop of one thousand marks.[d] It was in vain, however, that they begged the arbiters to proceed to extremities against Geoffrey. "I would as lief be suspended myself as suspend him," was the bishop of Lincoln's[e] reply; and so little seems to have been done that the complainants were discontented, and sent messengers to Rome to tell the pope of the negligence of his representatives. Celestine, however, had anticipated their wishes, and had suspended the archbishop. At the instance of the chapter he committed the spiritual charge of the diocese to dean Simon and his brethren on the 23rd of December, and renewed the commission of enquiry which he had issued a few months previously to the bishop of Lincoln and his colleagues.[f] In February, 1196, the dean returned from Italy to York to take possession of his office, but some messengers of the archbishop met him, and protested against his being installed until the controversy about the deanery had been formally settled by the pope. Hot words and blows ensued which brought upon the offenders the sentence of excommunication. There was much angry feeling between the combatants. When Geoffrey's suffragan, John bishop of Whitherne, came to York to consecrate the chrism and the oil, the dean and chapter would not receive them; and when he hallowed them at Southwell, Geoffrey Muschamp, archdeacon of Cleve-

x., 1791. Wilkins, i., 505. Gervase, col. 1589. Hubert went to Durham, and the Northern monasteries seem to have been regularly visited.

[d] Hoveden, 426, 428.

[e] Hugh, bishop of Lincoln, died in 1200, and Geoffrey was at his funeral. (Matt. Paris, 172.) He was canonized in 1220 (Chron. Lanercost, 28). There is a life of him in Pez, Bibl. Ascetica, ed. 1723.

[f] Hoveden, 431-2. Labbe, Conc., x., 1781-3. Recueil des Hist. des Gaules, xviii., 77.

land, is actually said to have thrown them upon a dunghill. This was, indeed, a most unhappy time for the Northern church.[g]

Whilst matters were thus complicated Geoffrey resolved to pay the visit to the papal court which he had too long neglected. He went and was there a long time, as he could make but little progress in his business. The pope was greatly annoyed at him, and shewed his displeasure by the delays and impediments which he threw in his way, and by his unfriendly bearing.[h] At length he obtained a hearing, and the charges brought against him were thoroughly examined. The verdict was unanimously in Geoffrey's favour, and was a complete acquittal. He was restored to his archbishopric, and the accusations of his enemies were pronounced to be worthless and malicious. He would now be anxious to return to England, and to get possession of the temporalities of his see; but the king refused to see him, so he returned to Rome and resided there for some time.[i] In the year 1198 Geoffrey and his chapter were summoned to Richard's court in Normandy, as the king was most desirous that they should at length be reconciled. The dean and the chapter did not come at the appointed day, and the archbishop, who had made his peace with Richard,[j] went off to Rome on his own affairs as well as on those of his brother. Three days afterwards the York party arrived, and, with a bitter spirit of revenge, evoked Richard's feeling of jealousy against Geoffrey to such an extent, that the performance of his promise that the temporalities should be restored to him was for a while deferred. The dean and his friends returned home in high glee, boasting foolishly of their intimacy with the king, and of the mischief which they had effected. In the same year the archbishop and his opponents seem to have had another meeting in the presence of the king in Normandy, and Richard was most wishful that they should consent to abide by the decision of the archbishop of Rouen, and the bishops of Winchester and Worcester. Geoffrey was ready enough to do this, but the dean and his brethren would refer the dispute to a tribunal of secular canons, and to no one else; and they aroused the king's wrath by stating that the archbishop had not confirmed the appointments which he had made in their cathedral. It is impossible to reprehend in too strong terms the conduct of the dean throughout this long controversy. Geoffrey was indeed hasty and inconsiderate, but Simon shewed himself to be full of malice and mischief-making. In the same year the new pope, Innocent III., tried to mediate

[g] Hoveden, 426, 427 *b*.

[h] Gervase, col. 1590. Hoveden, 435 *b*.

[i] Gervase, col. 1597. Hoveden, 436.

[j] Matt. Paris (162) speaks of this reconciliation, and says that the cause of Richard's anger was the deposition of the chancellor during his own captivity.

in Geoffrey's behalf. The king sent the bishop of Durham and four other prelates to his brother, to say that the temporalities would be restored to him if he would confirm the presentations which he had made to offices in the minster at York. Their mission was fruitless, and the archbishop went again to Rome followed by the king's messengers. Innocent was now indignant, and threats of an interdict were made if satisfaction were not rendered to Geoffrey.[k] Even these appear to have been ineffective, and Richard's death, in all probability, prevented anything being done. About this time Innocent wrote to Geoffrey and the ecclesiastical dignitaries of his diocese, exhorting them to assist in the formation and equipment of a new crusade.[l]

The death of Richard I., which took place in 1199, placed his brother John upon the throne, and with him Geoffrey had hardly ever been on familiar terms. The archbishop was still without the temporalities of his see, and the quarrel with his chapter was unsettled. Geoffrey's first step was by no means favourable to the cause of peace. He was at Rome when Richard died, but the bishop of Durham was probably only acting in his behalf when he protested against the coronation of John taking place during his absence.[m] No notice, however, seems to have been taken of the slight; and John ordered Stephen de Turnham, who for two years had been the keeper of the temporalities of the archbishopric, to surrender them to Ralph de Kyme and two others for the use of Geoffrey. They were given up, although the king, full of avarice as he always was, retained them in his own hands beyond the stated time. Soon after this the two brothers met in Normandy, and many mutual assurances of friendship and affection seem to have passed between them. Whilst they were there a message came to the king from the archbishop of Canterbury, and Geoffrey Fitz-Peter the justiciar, entreating him, at the request of the York chapter, to detain Geoffrey in Normandy till he returned to England himself, as the coming of the archbishop would produce nothing but dissension. Their wishes were not attended to; and in the same year some propositions were made for

[k] Hoveden, 442 b, 444, 446 b. Baluz, Epp. Innoc. III., i., 369-70. Ibid., p. 647, the pope desires the bishop of Ely, the dean of Lincoln, and the archdeacon of Bedford, to examine into the charges brought against Geoffrey by his chapter, and (p. 746) there is a letter to Geoffrey begging him to shew his good offices to his nephew Otho.

[l] Hoveden, 447. Fœdera, i., 66. A somewhat similar letter in behalf of pilgrims to the Holy Land had been addressed some time before this by Hubert to the officials of the see of York (Hoveden, 434 b).

[m] Bromton, col. 1281. Hoveden, 451. Matt. Paris, 166. Geoffrey is blamed by Jordan de Brakelonda for speaking ill of the archbishop of Canterbury before the pope whilst he was at Rome (Chron., 15, 62).

making peace between Geoffrey and his chapter in the presence of cardinal Peter de Capua, the papal legate. They agreed to submit to the arbitration of Hugh bishop of Lincoln, and two others; and Geoffrey promised to forfeit to the chapter two hundred marks if he should act in contravention of this arrangement. The chapter demanded the payment of the penalty soon after this, when they were impleaded by the officials of the archbishop in obedience to a papal mandate. The referees seem to have done nothing, as in the year 1200 we find Geoffrey and his adversaries in Westminster abbey before the bishop of Salisbury and the abbat of Tewkesbury, who had been appointed by the pope to examine into the case. That high dignitary had done his best to make peace, and Geoffrey at length became reconciled to William Testard archdeacon of Notts, Reginald Arundel the precentor, and Simon the dean of York, on condition that they rendered satisfaction to him for his claims in their own chapter.[n] In the autumn of the same year Geoffrey was again in disgrace, and was deprived by his brother of all the temporalities of his see.[o] John was annoyed at him for several reasons. Geoffrey had refused to accompany him to France to be present at the making of a peace with that country, and at the marriage of the king. He had also declined to allow the sheriff of Yorkshire to collect the tax of a penny on each carucate of land, and had beaten the servant of that official. In addition to these offences, the sum of three thousand marks which he had promised to his late brother Richard was still unpaid. Geoffrey was excessively indignant at this treatment. When the sheriff of Yorkshire, James de Poterna, entered upon his manors, and wasted, it is said, all his goods, the archbishop excommunicated him and his men, together with all those who had counselled the king to inflict upon him this punishment. The same heavy sentence fell upon the burgesses of Beverley for breaking into his parks, and injuring his effects; and their town was placed under an interdict.[p] The king does not seem to have met the archbishop in the same violent spirit, as he restored to him his temporalities, merely appointing a day on which he should come to court to reply to the charges he had against him. We are told nothing of the result, but it does not appear that the ill-feeling that existed between the two brothers was removed. In 1201 John was in Yorkshire, which had been startled in the month of January by an earthquake. He went to Beverley, and shewed his contempt for his brother by becoming the guest of a person of the name of John Crassus, whom Geoffrey had excommunicated. The canons wished to

[n] Hoveden, 451 *b*, 452-3, 458. [o] Ibid., Rot. Chart., 102.
[p] Hoveden, 461. Matt. Paris, 170.

receive their monarch with all the ceremony that their church could afford; but it was still under an interdict, and the archbishop would not remove it even for the occasion. John was very angry. He ordered all Geoffrey's servants to be seized, and directed one of them, of the name of Henry de Capella, to be thrown into prison for refusing to give him access to the wine in his master's cellars![q] In the middle of Lent the king and queen were at York, and the archbishop made his peace by submitting to a fine; and it was determined that the subjects in dispute should be arranged by four bishops and four barons. John soon after this released his brother's servants, restoring his possessions, which he confirmed to the see; the archbishop buying that favour at the cost of one thousand marks, to be paid within a year.[r] At the same time Geoffrey, who was never quiet, was in the middle of another quarrel with his chapter about the appointments to two archdeaconries, in which he again availed himself of the thunders of excommunication. One of the two sufferers, Honorius archdeacon of Richmond, carried the story of his wrongs to the pope; and Innocent ordered that justice should be at once done to him, and chided Geoffrey in language which he seldom heard.[s] The archbishop's feud with the dean broke out again when he gave the provostship of Beverley to his brother Morgan.[t] John cardinal of St. Stephen, on the Cælian hill, chanced to be at York in the same year as the papal legate, and he tried in vain to settle the dispute. This high dignitary, who might, perhaps, at one time have occupied the papal chair, was what we call in these days a teetotaller and a vegetarian. The deficiency in one taste was supplied, as it very frequently is, by excess in another. The cardinal, as Hoveden quaintly observes, had a great thirst after gold and silver.[u]

It is refreshing to turn aside from the unceasing record of wranglings and dissensions to something of another kind, although it also reveals to us a weakness, and shews to what an extent credulity and folly may be carried. A fanatic of the name of Eustace, who was the Cistercian abbat of Flay, came

[q] In 1201 the burgesses of Beverley paid a fine of five hundred marks for the king's favour, and he promised to protect them from the encroachments of Geoffrey (Rot. de Obl. et Finibus, 375.

[r] Hoveden. Rot. de Obl. et Finibus, 146.

[s] Hoveden, 464 *b*, 465, 466, 468, *et seqq*. Matt. Paris, 170.

[t] It would appear that Simon obtained the office, as on the 14th of March, 1204, the king presented Simon, provost of Beverley, to the church of Cave (Rot. Pat., 39). Morgan perhaps got the post when Simon was made bishop of Exeter.

[u] Hoveden, 468. I now lose the assistance of this able and excellent historian. His name ought properly to be written Houeden.

into England as a peripatetic advocate of Sabbatarianism.[e] The minds of the men of the day must have been singularly hungry when they were willing to swallow the trash with which they were fed by this wandering divine. His credentials professed to be a letter found on Golgotha by the patriarch of Jerusalem, which contained, in our Lord's hand, a general command that no work whatever should be done between the ninth hour on the Saturday and sunrise on the Monday. On the strength of this injunction Eustace paid a visit to England, where he had a wonderful success. His subject was exciting, and it was something new, which was a great thing. The preaching of this apostle seems to have borne considerable fruit. In the course of his tour he found his way to York, and in their reception of him Geoffrey and the clergy and laity of his diocese seem to have been for once united. The people of the North were carried away by his words. They would sell nothing for the future upon Sundays save refreshment to the wayfarer. A portion of the profits of the vendor was to be devoted to sacred purposes, and every church was to possess an alms box in which it was to be deposited. Nothing was to be sold in or near a church, which had been too frequently made into a fair, and the wealthy were to be regularly taxed for the benefit of the poor. No one can object to the adoption of such reforms as these, but the means resorted to were objectionable, and the change, like all other sudden movements and hasty impulses, was not lasting. Eustace, however, seems to have done his best to bring about a better state of morals and manners, and to make it permanent. A flock of miracles is said to have attested the truth of what he said, like the references which, in these matter-of-fact days, bear witness to the potency of specifics of a less romantic kind. A certain carpenter of Beverley, poor man, disregarded the wholesome counsels of his wife, and made a wooden instrument, on a Saturday afternoon, for which he was struck with paralysis; and the like fate befel a woman who was weaving. Nafferton, in the East Riding, a place which in these days is proverbially famous for something very different, witnessed a strange scene. A man had baked himself a cake on the Saturday, and, when he broke it on the Sunday, blood came flowing from the fissure! But Wakefield saw the most striking judgment on the sabbath-breaker. Two worthies have already immortalized that merry town, but the pair must now be turned into a trio by the addition of a miller. He, unhappy man, was plying his trade on the sacred day, when, lo! blood rushed from between the stones instead of meal, and the wheel, in spite of the pressure of the

[e] Hoveden, 466-7. Matt. Paris, 169. Bromton, col. 1274. Chron. Petrib., 112.

water, refused to turn. Yorkshire is also said to have been remarkable in this year for the appearance, at one and the same time, of five moons![w]

A cloud hangs over the remainder of Geoffrey's life, although gleams of light break occasionally through the darkness. Had everything been clear and bright we should probably have found Geoffrey still embroiled in the dissensions of which he seems to have been so fond. The chroniclers unfortunately desert us, especially Hoveden; but the Patent Rolls give us a faint picture of what was occurring in the North. In 1202 there had been a quarrel between Geoffrey and the king, arising from something that had been done by the royal servants; and John informs the bishop of Ely that it was at an end.[x] In 1204 the archbishop was in arrear for his escuage to the crown, and measures were taken by the king to secure its payment.[y] In March, 1205, John was at York, and the bishop of Durham, the dean and chapter of York, and the great ecclesiastical dignitaries of the province, expressed their willingness to be obedient to Geoffrey; but as a matter of precaution for themselves and their estates they appealed against him to the pope.[z] This shews that the archbishop's unhappy temper had again been getting him into trouble, indeed his whole career seems to have been one of determined opposition to propriety and the law. In the spring of 1207 he was reconciled to his brother, and was restored to the possessions of which he had been deprived.[a] We are unacquainted with the cause of the quarrel which was thus terminated, but soon after this in the same year there was an irreparable breach between the king and Geoffrey. The archbishop set his face most stoutly against the unpopular tax of a thirteenth, which John extorted from his indignant subjects. He excommunicated those who ventured to collect it within his province, and finding probably that his personal liberty was in danger, he consulted for his safety by flight.[b] He left England, and never returned to it again. He appealed to the pope against his brother's conduct; but the interference of Innocent in his behalf appears to have been useless, although he went so far as to put the church of York under an inter-

[w] Knyghton, col. 2417.

[x] Rot. Pat., 5.

[y] Rot. Claus., 11. Prynne's Collections, iii., 9. Geoffrey is also mentioned in connection with payments, etc., to the king, in Rot. de Obl. et Finibus, 43. Rot. Claus., 35, 46, 65, 75, 90, 99.

[z] Rot. Pat., 51. In 1204 the king took the chapter of York under his protection. (Ibid., 40. Hutchinson's Durham, i., 189.)

[a] Ibid., 58, 62.

[b] Chron. Joh. de Oxenedes, 119. Cotton's Chron., 96. Matt. Paris, 186, 189. Contin. Fl. Wigorn., ii., 167. Hist. Dunelm. Scr. Tres, 23, 27. In Chron. Petrib. (115) the date is made 1208. In Stubbs (col. 1724) it is said that the thirteenth was exacted "usque ad dimidium baconem!" Rot. Curiæ Regis, ii., 196. Recueil des Hist. des Gaules, xviii., 166.

dict.[c] The remainder of his life, of which we know nothing, was probably spent upon his estates in Normandy that were given to him by his father, and which he would be permitted to retain. He died in 1212, it is said, at Grosmont in Normandy,[d] far away from the country which had looked so often with dismay upon the feuds and heart-burnings that he had originated. It is to be hoped that he learned in retirement what a blessed thing peace is.[e]

Geoffrey was a man who had warm friends and very bitter enemies,[f] upon whose animosity he looked with supreme contempt. He was passionate and regardless of consequences, like all the children of Henry II. It is quite possible that the slur upon his escutcheon, with which he was often taunted, would make him sensitive and impatient. It is a stain which all who are in his position have continually in their thoughts. Geoffrey, however, was capable of generous and patriotic actions,[g] and his filial affection is not to be forgotten. He had, unfortunately, been pushed into a path of life for which he was unfit. He ought to have been a soldier. He borrowed from the profession of arms his spirit and his energy. They were alien altogether from the quiet habits and the patient demeanour which ought to characterize a bishop. Who can fully estimate the mischief which was done to the cause of religion in the North by Geoffrey's reckless animosities, his thoughtless assaults on decency and order, and his jealousies and contentions? These were the things which made him miserable at home, and banished him in the end from his country and his see.

The story of the early part of Geoffrey's life has been written down by that courtly sycophant Gerald Cambrensis,

[c] Baluz, Epp. Innoc. III., ii., 175-6, 442.

[d] Ann. Waverl., ed. Gale, ii., 173. Stubbs, col. 1724. Matt. Paris, 194, 196. Lel. Coll., i. 295.

Godwin (*n. e.*, 677) is the sole authority for the statement that Geoffrey died at Grosmont. Recueil des Hist. des Gaules, xviii., 169.

[e] Contin. Fl. Wigorn., ii., 140. Mabillon, Ann. Ben., vi., 108. Prynne's Collections, iii., 23. Dugd. Mon., vi., 1088.

[f] Among them was Walter Mapes, who gives a long account of his feud with Geoffrey in his Nugæ Curialium, 235-7. Mapes alludes in a contemptuous way to his illegitimacy. The same slur and the pride of the archbishop evoked the following scurrilous lines, which may be seen in MSS. Cotton, Cleopatra, B, ii., 39 *b*:—

"Versus magistri Michaelis Malebuche de Galfrido archiepiscopo Eboracensi, qui filius Henrici regis genitus de quadam meretrice.

Spurie, quid jactas atavis te regibus ortum,
Polluit insignes titulos ignobile scortum.
Patris ad alta volans vel matris ad ima peribis,
Ergo tene medium, medio tutissimus ibis.
Spurius es regis, cleri fex, ordinis hostis,
Templi turbator, Veneris vas, presulis umbra.
Non es sufficiens ad tanti culmen honoris,
Sic mihi sufficiat Deus hac et omnibus horis."

In the Flores Historiarum, p. 253, it is said that when Geoffrey became bishop of Lincoln "extunc Deo et hominibus extitit reprobus et detestabilis."

[g] Stubbs (col. 1724) speaks of Geoffrey as "vir magnæ abstinentiæ et summæ puritatis."

and is printed by Wharton in his *Anglia Sacra*.[h] It was composed, in all probability, at the request of the archbishop himself, and it terminates with the controversy with the bishop of Ely. The writer probably found that he would injure his own popularity by extending the biography. The work contains some interesting historical information, but the style is ornate and heavy, and is more worthy of a courtier than of a chronicler. The character of the bishop of Ely is blackened in an extraordinary manner, whilst the archbishop is elevated into a hero. It is not to such men as Geoffrey that posterity will look for an example.

After the flight of Geoffrey the temporalities of the archbishopric came into the king's hands, and they remained in them until the appointment of Walter de Gray in 1216. Brian de Insula and Robert de Lexington had the charge of them,[i] and the bishop of Whitherne seems to have attended to the ecclesiastical requirements of the province.[j] The care of the spiritualities was in all probability committed to the dean and chapter of York.

Walter de Gray is next upon the list of archbishops of which he was a most distinguished ornament. More than six centuries have passed away since he was laid in the tomb within his own cathedral, but his name is still mentioned with respect and gratitude. We think of the cautious and wise statesman who was at the helm of England in times of danger and distress, and remember the piety and munificence of the prelate among the many memorials of his zeal and greatness which even now survive to us. He found the province to which he was translated a barren wilderness, he left it a fruitful garden.

Walter de Gray[k] was a scion of a family which in its many branches has accumulated both wealth and honours.[l] It has

[h] Anglia Sacra, ii., 374—408. Wharton says that it was written in 1193. There is a MS. of it in the library of C.C.C. Cambridge (Smith's Catalogue).

[i] Rot. Pat., 88. Rot. Claus., 208, etc., 222.

[j] Rot. Claus., 173, 181.

[k] I adopt the old mode of spelling this name. In his own roll at York the archbishop is always called Gray or Gra.

[l] The genealogist will find pedigrees and notices of the family in Dugdale's Baronage, i., 709; Baker's Northants, i., 140; Nichols's Leicestershire, iii., 682; Lipscombe's Bucks, i., 160; Blore's Rutlandshire, 165; Blomefield's Norfolk, *n. e.*, ii., 300-1; Archæologia, xxxii., 59; Frost's Notices of the Town of Hull, 59; Stapleton's Account of the Holy Trinity Priory, York, 151, etc.; Ashmole's Berks, ii., 280. The Close and Patent Rolls abound with information about the family.

given great men to England, and is still represented on the roll of peers. The member of it of whom we shall now speak was a younger son of John and Hawisia de Gray of Rotherfield.[m] His uncle, another John de Gray, who was a statesman of some note, became bishop of Norwich and a justiciar, and died in 1214. It was to his influence, no doubt, as well as to his own merits, that his nephew was indebted for his introduction and his success at court.

Walter de Gray received his education at Oxford,[n] and in after years that university, of which he was a distinguished member, established a solemn service to commemorate him on the anniversary of his decease.[o] In 1242, when Henry III. was going abroad, he made him the protector of that abode of learning,[p] and it was, no doubt, the consciousness of the advantages which he had reaped in Oxford that induced Gray to persuade Edmund de Abingdon to devote himself to the study of theo-

[m] This is a disputed point. Dugdale makes him a son of Henry and Isolda de Gray of Thurrock, and he is followed by MM. Léchaudé-d'Anisy et de Ste Marie in their Recherches sur le Domesday, i., 167. The objection to the archbishop's being the son of John de Gray is, that if this were the case, there were two Johns, brothers, in the same generation. This, however, is by no means impossible, and I prefer to follow Messrs. Nichols and Baker instead of Dugdale. The following pieces of evidence, which have never been applied to the pedigree of Gray, militate against Dugdale's view.

Hawisia de Grey, widow, grants the church of Cornwell to Oseney abbey, "pro animabus antecessorum et præcipue pro anima Johannis de Grey, fratris mei, quondam episcopi Norwicensis, assensu domini Roberti de Grey filii et hæredis mei. Teste Waltero de Grey episcopo Wigorn., filio meo." (Blomefield's Norwich, i., 478).

Sept. 17, 1235, archbishop Gray grants to Sir Robert de Gray, his brother, a carucate of land in Goukthorpe, etc., and on Sept. 15, with the assent of his brother, he grants to Thomas, son of R. de Marese, in marriage with Isabella, daughter of Robert de Monasteriis, lands in Everton and Beckingham (Rot. Gray. See Drake's Eboracum, appendix, 64).

In 1240 (24) the archbishop grants to his brother, Robert de Gray, "terram quam ex concessione dominæ Evæ de Gray habuimus in Rutherfeld, cum advocatione ecclesiæ, excepto tamen homagio et servicio dominæ Hawysiæ de Gray matris meæ (Rot. Gray). Hawisia is mentioned as the mother of the archbishop in 1227 (Excerpt. e Rot. Finium, i., 161).

June 5, 1238 (22), Walter de Gray was instituted "in eccl. de Semar ad pres. abb. and conv. de Whitby" (Rot. Gray). He was, I believe, prebendary of Southwell in 1242 and 1257 (Le Neve, iii., 461). Henry de Gray was canon of York in 1241 (Dugd. Mon., vi., 1195).

April 28, 1246 (30), Walterus de Gray, nepos domini archiepiscopi, habet custodiam Thomæ de Burgo qui sororem ipsius Walteri duxit in uxorem, cum omnibus terris suis; item custodiam terræ quæ fuit Alexandri de Hylton in Wyvestow (Rot. Gray.)

Walterus Gray, archiepiscopus, dedit homagium Walteri de Mikelfeud domino Waltero de Gray militi, nepoti suo (Reg. Giffard). Cf. Plac. de Quo Warranto, 665.

1268, Robert de Gray, son of Sir Walter de Gray, knight, presents his brother, John de Gray, clerk, to a moiety of the church of Linton (Reg. Giffard).

[n] Wood's Antiq. Univ. Oxon., i., 232.

[o] On April 30. Avesbury's Edw. III., 304. Rot. Hundred., ii., 805.

[p] Antiq. Oxon., *ut supra*.

logy.[q] His friend became archbishop of Canterbury, and a saint.

Walter de Gray's preferments in the church were all of them owing to the favour of king John. On the 23rd of January, 1206-7, that monarch gave him the prebend of Mallinges at Rochester,[r] and a stall at Exeter, with the archdeaconry of Totness, on the 10th of May.[s] On the 28th of August he was made vicar of a moiety of the church of Holkham.[t] On the 26th of March, 1208, he became rector of Stradbroke in Norfolk,[u] and on the 3rd of December, 1212, he obtained the living of Cossey in the same county.[v] In the following February he became the dean of St. Berians in Cornwall.[w] On the 14th of July, 1213, the king gave him the church of Kirkham for his life, but he almost immediately resigned it.[x] Gray was destined to sit upon the episcopal bench. Geoffrey de Muschamp, bishop of Coventry and Lichfield, died in 1208, and the chapter of Lichfield fixed upon Gray as his successor, in opposition to the nominee of the monks of Coventry. Pandulph, the papal legate, would admit neither of the two to the see, and after much angry feeling on the part of the electors a third person became the prelate.[y] Gray was more fortunate on another occasion. On the 20th of January, 1213-14, he was made bishop of Worcester, resigning the pieces of preferment which have been already enumerated. He was consecrated at Canterbury on the 5th of October. Of what he did at Worcester there is little known.[z] The see of York was all the while vacant, having been without a pastor ever since the retirement of Geoffrey in 1207, and several other bishoprics were in the same condition, as the king would not allow the chapters to elect in accordance with custom and law.[a]

[q] Martene, Thes. Nov. Anecdot., iii., 1788.

[r] Rot. Pat., 58.

[s] Ibid., 71, 75. Le Neve, *n. e.*, i., 401. Madox, Hist. Exch., ii., 42.

[t] Rot. Chart., 169.

[u] Rot. Pat., 81. Madox, ii., 42-3.

[v] Rot. Pat., 96. Blomefield's Norfolk, ii., 417.

[w] Rot. Pat., 96. Oliver's Monast. Exon., 7.

[x] Rot. Chart., 193. Rot. Pat., 102. On 7th June, 1238 (22), archbishop Gray instituted William de Ebor., canon of York, to the living of Kirkham on the presentation of Richard earl of Cornwall (Rot. Gray). The church was appropriated by Honorius IV. to the abbey of Vale Royal, and in 1287 Edward I. ordered that house to compensate Henry Newark, archdeacon of Richmond, for the loss which he thereby sustained (Prynne's Collections, iii., 373).

[y] Elected in 1211. Matt. Paris, 193.

[z] The king's assent to the election was given on the 26th of January, on which day he ordered the temporalities to be restored, and desired the archbishop of Canterbury to consecrate Gray (Rot. Pat., 109. Prynne, iii., 22). Mandate to the bishop of Winchester to give him seisin of his bishopric on July 7 (Rot. Claus., 168). Le Neve, iii., 51. Thomas's Account of the Bishops of Worcester, 123, etc. Reg. Sacr. Angl., 37. Matt. Paris., 212. Trivet, 161.

On the 28th of May, 1228, archbishop Gray granted an indulgence for the cathedral of Worcester (Rot. Gray).

[a] Chron. Petrib., 118.

The election of a new archbishop had been more than once suggested. In January, 1214, John wrote to the dean and chapter by the abbats of St. Mary's York, Beaulieu and Selby, William Briwere and William de Cantilupe his seneschal, giving them leave to choose a new primate with the assent of the bearers of the royal missive. As this was clearly an encroachment upon the privileges of the chapter nothing seems to have been done. It was most necessary, however, that the Northern province should have a superior, and on the 13th of May, 1215, the king wrote again to the chapter urging them to elect and demand no objectionable person.[b] This had reference to Simon de Langton, brother of the well-known archbishop of Canterbury, whom the dean and canons of York were most desirous to secure as their head in opposition to the wishes of the king.[c] On the 18th of June, 1215, the York dignitaries again received the royal permission to proceed to an election, and the monarch, perhaps too eagerly, expressed his desire that they should fix upon the bishop of Worcester.[d] The chapter were obdurate; and passing Gray by as an illiterate person they nominated their favourite Langton in direct contravention of the order of the sovereign. When the king heard of this, he sent at once to the pope to tell him that there would be no peace in England if the brother of a traitor should become the Northern primate. Innocent, upon this, wrote to the chapter on the 13th of September to say that he had rejected Langton, and had forbidden him to press the matter farther, and enjoined them to send their representatives to Rome by the 1st of November with some other nominee. Their spokesmen arrived at the appointed time, and clung to their old candidate, but the pope at once set him aside, and told them that if they would name no one else he should choose for them himself. The canons were provided against this contingency, and mentioned the bishop of Worcester whom they commended for his chaste life. "Per Sanctum Petrum," said Innocent, "virginitas magna virtus est et nos eum damus vobis." Gray was then at Rome, and when he had received the pall he returned to England. The king was

[b] Rot. Pat., 141. Le Neve, iii., 101. On the 23rd of May, 1215, pope Innocent wrote to the chapter of York urging them to select a proper person (Baluz, Epist. Innoc. III., ii., 822).

[c] Rot. Chart., 207. Rot. Claus., 269. Simon de Langton at the time of his disappointment was canon of Strensall at York (Rot. Claus., 178. Cal. Rot. Pat., 5). He afterwards was made chancellor of Dauphiny and archdeacon of Canterbury, and he took some part in state affairs. He was also a hard student and an author, and died in 1248. (Somner's Canterbury, ii., 152. Fœdera, i., 214, 218. Matt. Paris, 227, 230, 237, 254, 655. Rot. Claus, etc.) He is said to have been a Lancashire man (Baines's Lancashire, iv. 385), and, also, to have been born in Lincolnshire (Hist. Co. Lincoln, ii., 175). There is an account of the family of Langton in the Gentleman's Magazine for June, 1862.

[d] Matt. Paris, 227-8.

delighted at his promotion. It is said, however, that the archbishop was obliged to pay the immense sum of ten thousand pounds to procure the papal assent to his election.[e]

We must now turn to Walter de Gray's offices in the state, and his public acts which made him the favourite of two kings and enabled him to pass through life enjoying the goodwill of his contemporaries. With king John he was a great favourite, but he is said to have won his regard by the readiness with which he complied with his wishes.[f] We do not know when he was first introduced to that monarch's notice, but he must have gained a considerable position in society when, on October 2nd, 1205, John made him chancellor of England, he having paid a fine of five thousand marks to be permitted to hold that office for his life.[g] He seems to have retained it until the autumn of 1214.[h] On the 5th of August, 1206, his master made him a present of a hundred marks in consideration of his faithful services.[i] We are not told by the chroniclers that Gray was one of the advisers who counselled the reckless monarch to adopt the measures which degraded his kingdom and nearly robbed him of his throne; he was present, however, in 1213, when John resigned his dominions into the hands of the pope,[j] but, if Lord Campbell is to be credited, the chancellor refused to set his official seal to the conveyance.[k] In the same year Gray had a great deal to do with the foreign affairs of the country. On the 26th of June he and another received letters of credence from the king to carry them to the count of Flanders,[l] and in the following year he was in charge of the treasure which went with the English force that crossed the seas to support the count against the French.[m] During the famous controversy with the barons, that ended in the granting of the Magna Charta in 1215, Gray seems to have been on the side of the king, and he

[e] Ibid., 230. Ann. Waverl., apud Gale, ii., 183. Hemingford, ibid., 561. Hist. Dunelm. Scr. Tres, 29. Labbe, Conc., xi., 234. Recueil des Hist. des Gaules, xviii, 179.

He was translated to York on the 27th of March, 1216 (MSS. Cotton Vitellius A, ii., iii. *b*. Stubbs, col. 1724). The king ordered the temporalities to be restored to him on Feb. 19 (Rot. Claus., 248). Cf. Twisden's Historical Vindication of the Church of England in point of Schism, 45.

[f] "In omnibus regni agendis regis studuit facere voluntatem" (Matt. Paris, 192).

[g] Matt. Paris, 209, where a wrong date is given. Rot. de Obl. et Finibus, 368. His uncle, John bishop of Norwich, was his bondsman. Cal. Rot. Pat., 2. Fœd., i., 93. Madox, Hist. Exch., i., 63.

[h] Foss's Judges, ii., 79-80. Mr. Foss, in a paper in the Archæologia, xxxii, 90, etc., says that Gray gave up the office for a while in October, 1213, when he went into Flanders, but resumed it in the month of January following.

[i] Rot. Pat., 66. An order to pay him £40 on Jan. 20, 1214 (Rot. Claus., 161).

[j] Fœdera, i., 115.

[k] Campbell's Lives of the Chancellors, i., 123.

[l] Fœdera, i., 113. Rot. Claus., 160, 162.

[m] Rot. Claus., 206. Matt. Paris, 208.

was present with him at Runnymede, when that great deed of privilege was made, in which he is mentioned as one of the advisers of the sovereign.[n] He was also one of those whom John despatched soon afterwards, when he repented of what he had done, to collect forces abroad to resist the barons.[o] It is impossible to say what share Gray took in the many scenes of violence and peril which occurred during the next two years. His interests seem to have been bound up with the fortunes of John, and he did not desert him in his adversity. The king, who loved him well, was always showering his favours upon his trusty adherent. The public records contain many evidences of the regard that he bore to him.[p]

After the death of John, in 1215, the archbishop took the part of his son, Henry III., in opposition to the barons and their French allies. He was as great a favourite with the new king as with his father. In conjunction with the legate he anointed him sovereign.[q] In 1217 Gray was at Lincoln when the great battle took place between Henry and his enemies,[r] and the youthful monarch and his advisers shewed how highly they appreciated his counsel and support by giving him the lands of several of the rebels and many other favours in addition.[s] Shortly after this Gray removed the sentence of excommunication which the papal legate had passed against Alexander king of Scotland for doing homage to the invaders;[t] and in 1221, when William earl of Albemarle expressed his penitence for his rebellion against the young sovereign, the archbishop of York conducted him to Henry who pardoned him on account of his loyalty in bygone years.[u] Gray had previously been present at the reduction of his stronghold at Bytham.[v] The older Henry grew the greater was the confidence which he seems to have reposed in his father's friend, and the more numerous the kindnesses which he shewed to him.[w] In 1221 Gray formed one of the escort of Alexander king of Scotland to York when he was married to Joan the sister of the English monarch,[x] and the

[n] Matt. Paris, 215. Fœdera, i., 131. Statutes of the Realm, i., 8, 9.

[o] Matt. Paris, 222.

[p] Rot. Claus., 160, 176, 189, 248.

[q] Recueil des Hist. des Gaules, xviii., 845. In 1217 Gray was one of those who prompted the granting of the royal charter De Foresta (Statutes of the Realm, i., 20).

[r] Chron. Mailros, 131.

[s] The land of Robert Constable in Gloucestershire (Rot. Claus., 308) that of Robert de Everingham (ibid., 313). Rot. Claus., 297, 312, 341, 346, 351, 354. Excerpta e Rot. Finium, i., 59. Abbrev. Rot. Orig., i., 24.

[t] Chron. Mailros, 132.

[u] Matt. Paris, 261. Chron. Joh. de Oxenedes, 146. The earl got into trouble afterwards (Prynne, iii., 62).

[v] Rot. Claus., 475.

[w] Ibid., 361, 405, 421, 475, 497, 515, 535, 536, 573. Excerpta e Rot. Finium, i., 335.

[x] Matt. Paris, 263. Rot. Claus., 462, 476. Lel. Coll., ii., 536. Henry was there four days. Chron. Lanercost, 29. Chron. Mailros, 138. Scala Chron., 99.

archbishop officiated on the occasion.[y] The two sovereigns had been in York in the preceding year, when the preliminaries of the alliance were drawn up.[z] In 1224, when the barons were again disposed to be turbulent, Gray demanded of the earl of Chester the surrender of the castles and honours which he held of the crown, and they were unwillingly given up.[a] In 1225 he was at Alnwick when Roger Bigod was married to Isabel sister of the Scottish king.[b] In 1227 the diplomatic powers of the Northern primate were again called into requisition. The hasty coronation of the new king of France had given great offence to many of his nobles, and Henry believing it to be a fit opportunity for endeavouring to regain his influence among the magnates of Normandy, Anjou, Brittany and Poictou, who were bound to pay him their allegiance, sent Gray and others to make the attempt. The events of the last ten years had greatly weakened their loyalty to their suzerain.[c] In the month of January the ambassadors were sent to Hugh count of March and Angoulême, and they returned home about Easter; but in the following September they went again with letters of credence to the princes and prelates who were to meet at Antwerp.[d] Nothing, however, seems to have been done. In 1228 Henry kept his Christmas at York,[e] and he was there at the same time in 1230 with Alexander king of Scotland. The archbishop was also present with a large party of the nobility, and the great festival was observed with much splendour and rejoicing.[f] In 1233 Gray objected in a formal manner to Alexander being crowned in Scotland, to the prejudice of England and his own see; and, on the 6th of May, Henry III. endorsed his protest.[g] The result was probably unfavourable to the archbishop, and in a subsequent year Innocent IV. gave another blow to the privileges of York by sanctioning the opposition of the Scottish bishops.[h] In 1235 pope Gregory addressed Gray and the bishop of Carlisle in the bull in which he confirmed the treaty which had been recently made between England and

[y] Chron. Petrib., 124.

[z] Matt. Paris, 260, the archbishop taking a prominent part in the treaty (Prynne, iii., 51-2).

[a] Chron. Joh. de Oxenedes, 150. Gray had something to do with this nobleman in 1217 when he wished to leave England (Prynne, *ut supra*, 37).

[b] Excerpt. e Rot. Fin., i., 128.

[c] Matt. Paris, 282.

[d] Fœdera, i., 184, 187.

[e] Chron. Joh. de Oxenedes, 155. Matt. Paris, 290.

[f] Oxenedes, 159. Matt. Paris, 307. On 21st January, 1229, the king mentioned his intention of being at York in Lent with Alexander (Fœd., i., 193).

[g] Fœdera, i., 209. Prynne, iii., 85. Cal. Rot. Pat., 16.

[h] Chron. Lanercost, 61. There is a brief abstract of a letter from Gregory IX. to Gray about the patronage of the church of Gameford (Gainford ?) in Labbe, xi., 379. In 1238 I find it stated, that the pope had permitted the archbishop to grant dispensations to forty clerks within his province (Rot. Gray).

Scotland; and, on the 12th of December in the same year, Henry III. desired the archbishop and others to escort king Alexander and his queen to London, to be present at the celebration of his nuptials.[i] In 1237 Henry sent Gray with Richard earl of Cornwall to a large meeting which was called together by the emperor Frederick; and in that year he took a great interest in the election of his suffragan the bishop of Durham, and was present at the council in St. Paul's cathedral, which was presided over by the legate Otho. The archbishop of Canterbury occupied the seat on the right hand, and Gray made the usual protest and claim, which the legate adroitly put aside for the time, leaving the question still open.[j] There was a meeting also of the kings of England and Scotland at York, at which Alexander resigned his right to the counties of Northumberland, Westmerland and Cumberland, and the archbishop was present on the occasion.[k] In the following year Gray was again associated with the legate at a council which was held in the month of June,[l] and he was present in 1240 when a treaty was made between the king and David son of Llewellyn prince of Wales.[m] In 1241 he was at the court when Henry paid some extravagant honours to the representative of the pope,[n] and he was one of the prelates who met at Oxford and agreed that prayers should be offered up for the weal of the church which was at that time in a deplorable condition.[o] On the 9th of June in the same year he consecrated Nicholas de Farnham bishop of Durham at Gloucester, and received his profession of obedience, a concession upon which much stress was subsequently laid in the controversies between York and Durham.[p] In 1242 the king made up his mind to go to France, and the archbishop of York, Richard earl of Cornwall and William de Eboraco provost of Beverley were the exponents of his wishes to the council of the nation. When Henry set out on his voyage against the will of his subjects, archbishop Gray had the high distinction of being appointed the regent during his absence,[q] and he performed the many duties of his office in a manner which fully justified the confidence that had been reposed in him. During the king's stay abroad, which lasted for more than a year, the regent was variously employed. The wardens of the Cinque ports sought his aid when they had

[i] Fœdera, i., 214, 221. Wilkins' Conc., i., 630.

[j] Matt. Paris, 371, 377-8. Hist. Dunelm. Scr. Tres, 38; and appendix, lxviii.

[k] Matt. Paris, 377. Wilkins, i., 647. Fœdera, i., 233.

[l] Matt. Paris, 397.

[m] Fœdera, i., 239.

[n] Matt. Paris, 489.

[o] Wilkins, i., 682.

[p] Matt. Paris, 502. Nothing is said about this profession by the Hist. Dun. Scr. Tres, 41. When bishop Farnham resigned his see in 1249, Gray was one of the three prelates who made a provision for him (Matt. Paris, 658).

[q] Matt. Paris, 515, 517, 789. Chron. Joh. de Oxenedes, 170. Fœdera, i., 244. Cal. Rot. Pat., 19.

been roughly handled in their attempts to do mischief to the French shipping. He collected men, money and stores, and transmitted them to Henry. From the archbishopric of Canterbury and the other sees which were at that time in the king's hand, he gathered together a vast quantity of provisions, but he tried in vain to obtain a grant from the Cistercian houses in England of a year's income in the shape of the wool from their sheep, which, in point of fact, was nearly everything that they possessed. The king, however, to the archbishop's great astonishment, complained that scarcely any of the supplies had reached him, and it was Gray's belief that they had been lost at sea. A new and heavy tallage was therefore exacted from the citizens of London. In the meanwhile Henry repented of the hasty counsels which had led him beyond the seas, and ordered the regent to collect a fleet at Portsmouth and to be ready with the nobles for his arrival. They were waiting for him on the coast till they were all wearied. After many delays Henry returned at length to his own country which he ought never to have left.[r] In the same year the pope made the archbishop of York and the bishop of Durham his deputies to adjudicate in a controversy which had arisen between Grostête bishop of Lincoln and the monks of Canterbury,[s] and we also find Gray officiating at the marriage of the queen's sister to Richard earl of Cornwall.[t] In 1244 he was constable of the tower of London,[u] and he was mainly instrumental in allaying the quarrel that was likely to arise between the kings of England and Scotland;[v] and in 1248 he was present at the meeting of the parliament at London, at which great fault was found with Henry for his evil rule.[w] In the following year he and the bishop of Hereford were employed on a fruitless negotiation, an attempt to contract a matrimonial alliance between the royal houses of England and Provence.[x] In every important event which took place in the history of the nation Gray was more or less concerned; but the cautious wisdom which was able to preserve his own character from the reproaches of contempo-

[r] Matt. Paris, 519, 522, 527—529, 531. Prynne, iii., 100. Fœdera, i., 246-7, 250, 253. Wilkins, i., 683.

[s] Matt. Paris, 535. Grostête's Letters, 325. Grostête wrote again to Gray in 1245, urging him to advocate the claims of the bishop of Cervia (Ibid., 469, and Gratii Fascic. Rerum Expetend., ii., 427). About this bishop and his affairs there is an account in Ughelli, Italia Sacra, ii., 469. He had a quarrel with the archbishop and people of Ravenna.

[t] Ann. Waverl., apud Gale, ii., 203.

[u] Cal. Rot. Pat., 20. Fœdera, i., 256. On Nov. 2, 1220, Gray was ordered to take the charge of Newcastle-on-Tyne on the death of Philip de Ulcotes (Rot. Claus., 473); and in the twenty-second of Henry III. Kenilworth castle was given up to him as a residence for cardinal Ottoboni (Memoirs of Northumberland, 65).

[v] Chron. Petrib., 137. Chron. Mailros, 156.

[w] Matt. Paris, 646.

[x] Fœdera, i., 270, 277.

raries and posterity could not moderate the follies and the caprices of his master. After his decease, when the barons' war broke out, Henry would at length appreciate the merits of his faithful councillor and wish that he had adopted his advice. How often had Gray stood in the breach when the storm was lowering, and stilled it by his courteous and persuasive pleading and the serenity of his bearing.

The most brilliant scene, perhaps, at which the archbishop was ever present was witnessed at York in 1252. Henry III., his queen, and the whole court kept their Christmas in that city, and they were joined there by the royal family of Scotland. Then it was that Alexander, the youthful monarch of the Scots, was married to Margaret, Henry's daughter. He did homage for the territories which he held of England, and had been made a knight,

> "And on the morwe whan the day gan spring,
> Of hors and harneis noise and clattering
> Ther was in the hostelries all aboute:
> And to the paleis rode ther many a route
> Of lordes, upon stedes and palfreis."

The ceremonial in the minster at the celebration of the nuptials must have been a magnificent one. More than a thousand knights in silken attire were in the train of the bride, and, when the wedding was over, such a banquet took place that the historian of the occasion, conscious of his inability to describe it, shrinks altogether from the task. No bill of fare has been handed down to us, and we know nothing, most unfortunately, of the dresses of the ladies. The archbishop contributed as many as sixty oxen to the feast. Matthew Paris is most eulogistic when he speaks of his hospitality. He seems to have kept open house, and to have entertained his illustrious visitors over and over again with a princely grandeur. To the poor he was equally lavish of his charity and his munificence, and he is said to have expended on this occasion the large sum of four thousand marks. All this was done with a generous spirit, which befitted the time, and with a dignity which was characteristic of the donor.[y]

After this great meeting at York the archbishop seems to have taken little interest in state affairs. He was an old man, and stood in need of rest. There was another reason also for his quiescence. He could not approve of all the measures of the king, and he was too cautious to involve himself in difficulties and annoyance. It was for this reason, no doubt, that he stayed

[y] Matt. Paris, 715-16. Contin. Fl. Wigorn., ii., 183. Knyghton, col. 2444. Joh. de Oxenedes, 146. Chron. Lanercost, 56. Chron Mailros, 179. Chron. Petrib., 139. Fœdera, i., 278. Lel. Coll., iii., 6.

away from the parliament of 1252; at which there were some dissensions between Henry and the bishops, in which Gray, if he had been present, would have been obliged to take a prominent part.[z] He was absent also from the parliament in the following year, pleading as his excuse his old age and the length of the journey to London.[z] In 1254, however, the archbishop was drawn from his retirement, for when the queen went abroad to join her husband, who was in Gascony, he was made, for the second time, the regent of the kingdom.[a] There was no event of any importance to annoy the aged prelate, who accepted most unwillingly the responsibilities of office; but his serene wisdom could not fail to discern the tokens of the storm which was so soon to burst upon his country. In the beginning of 1255 the king returned to England, and a parliament was assembled in London at which Gray was present. The time was a melancholy one; for never had the monarch been in greater disrepute, or the nation in greater suffering. Henry was an obstinate and a thoughtless man, with little regard for the wishes and the welfare of his subjects, if he could give the rein to his own folly and extravagance. He was overburdened with debt, and he tried to free himself by starving his groaning and oppressed people. There were many angry words, and much murmuring and grumbling in that parliament, with great uneasiness and discontent. The whole country was in a state of sullen indignation. To add to the general alarm, the spring of that year was most ungenial. From the middle of March not a drop of rain had fallen, and any appearance of vegetation, which the sun mercilessly elicited, was scorched and withered by a north wind that never ceased to blow. It was in vain that the chief men of the country humiliated themselves by fasting to procure from the hands of the Great Giver the blessings of peace, and a fruitful season. The severity of the religious exercise, and the inclemency of the weather, only laid them on the bed of sickness, and the heavens were closed.[b]

The aged archbishop of York was one of these sufferers. He was borne down now with years, and was incapable of exertion and fatigue. The fasting, which he had daily practised, had affected his head; and his mind was oppressed with a heavy burden of anxieties and fears. The scenes in the recent parliament had annoyed him greatly; his life-long exertions for his country had apparently been fruitless, and the future, alas, was threatening and clouded. His heart gave way, and his

[z] Matthew Paris, 732, 745, 756, 765.

[a] Ibid., 765. Wikes (Gale, ii., 49) followed by Polydore Vergil (306) say that Gray and Richard earl of Cornwall were the regents.

[b] Matt. Paris, 778. Ann. Burton, apud Gale, iii., 341.

health accompanied it in its decline. His appetite was gone, and his days seemed to be at an end. The parliament had been dissolved, and, at the request of the bishop of London, the sick man went to seek for quiet and repose at the palace of Fulham. He had only been there three days when he died, on Saturday the 1st of May, 1255,[c] having prepared himself for his departure by receiving the last sacraments of the Church. His body[d] was borne honourably to York under the escort of Walter Kirkham bishop of Durham, who, to shew his reverence for the dead, distributed large sums every day in charity as the procession advanced into the North. The remains of the archbishop were interred in the minster at York, within the south transept, which he had himself erected. He had ruled over that church and diocese for nearly forty years, and they lost in him a munificent and an enlightened pastor, and England a true patriot, and an honest and an upright statesman.

We must now turn from archbishop Gray's faithful service to his country and her kings, to the works for which he is still remembered within the diocese of York. I am not giving him too high praise when I call him the greatest prelate of the century in which he lived. The same thoughtful care and watchful prudence which made all men like him,[e] in an age when there were many bitter enmities, and secured for him the uninterrupted favour of two kings, the same uprightness which moderated all his actions in the court and council-chamber, the same munificence which he manifested in all places, seem to have been the uniform characteristics of his archiepiscopal career. No one can examine the rolls on which his official acts are recorded, without being profoundly struck by the vigour of his pastoral rule, and the expansiveness of his charity. Everything seems to have been done on the most perfect system, and apparently under the personal inspection of the archbishop. The carelessness and the recklessness of his predecessor had turned the diocese into a wild; it was Walter Gray's high privilege to have the will and the means to till and sow the long barren field, and God gave him length of days that he might himself behold the harvest. It was the same in the temporalities as in the spiritualities of his see. He was a good husband of his revenues, and dispensed them nobly. Throughout his whole

[c] Stubbs, col. 1725. Knyghton, col. 2444. MSS. Cotton, Vitellius, A, ii., 111 b. Hemingford, apud Gale, ii., 561. Ann. Burton, ibid., iii., 341. In the Liber Vitæ of Durham (ed. Surtees Soc., 150) Gray is said to have died on May 6 (2 Non.).
Antony à Wood says that Gray died at Osney abbey. In 1221, singularly enough, Richard Gray became abbat of that house (Rot. Claus., 470).

[d] "Facta anatomia." The process need not be described. Matt. Paris, 778.

[e] Wikes, apud Gale, ii., 50. Polydore Vergil, 311.

diocese he seems to have been the great re-organizer of the parochial system, effecting subdivisions, and arranging the distribution of endowments. He held a provincial council at York, and promulgated some valuable constitutions relating especially to the furniture and ornaments of his churches, and to tithes.[f] He was sedulously attentive to the interests of the monasteries, and was their generous benefactor.[g] The subsequent archbishops of York had good reason to remember him. He made a rule that on each of the manors belonging to the see a certain quantity of stock should be reserved at the death of each prelate for the benefit of his successor, and he obtained the sanction of the king and pope for this arrangement, which he inaugurated himself.[h] He purchased the village of St. Andrewthorpe, which he appropriated to the see, charging it merely with an annual payment of twenty marks, half of which was to provide for the keeping of his own obit in the minster, whilst with the other moiety the chaplain within the manor of Thorp was to be supported.[i] This is the origin of the present palace of the archbishops, for the name of St. Andrewthorpe was soon changed to Bishopthorpe. It was to Walter Gray also that his successors were indebted for their house in London. The history of that palace is a remarkable one. It was the residence of the famous Hugo de Burgh, earl of Kent, who gave it in a fit of generosity to the Black Friars, from whom Gray purchased it, and presented it to his see. It bore the name of York-place until the time of Henry VIII., when that imperious monarch demanded it of Wolsey. It was given up, and we know it for the future as Whitehall.

> "Sir, you
> Must no more call it York-place, that is past;
> For since the cardinal fell, that title's lost;
> 'Tis now the king's, and call'd—Whitehall."

[f] These are given in Wilkins, i., 698-9. Cf. ibid., 755. The archbishop had a controversy with Robert de Thweng about the church of Lythe (Matt. Paris, 460).

[g] To give instances. In the charter in which he confirms the foundation of Healaugh, he speaks of the "novellam constructionem domus per sollicitudinem nostram" (MSS. Cotton, Vespasian, A, iv., 7, 8). He obtained from Henry III. a grant of fairs, and a market for Hexham (Ibid., Claudius, B, iii., 95). He granted to the canons of Nostell twenty marks per annum out of the church of South Kirkby (Ibid., 14 b). On June 10, 1250, he gave the monastery of Blyth an annual pension of five marks out of the church of Weston to enable the monks to keep hospitality (Rot. Gray). He made parks in Heeksgrave, Hockwode, and Nordwode, co. Notts (Rot. Hundr., ii., 311).

[h] These gifts are mentioned in Stubbs, col. 1724-5. The grant of Thorp is printed in Dugd. Mon., vi., 1194-5.

[i] The archbishop conveyed it to the chapter of York, and they engage to re-convey it to the future primates on the payment of the 20 marks. The chaplain was to pray, specially, for the souls of king John and archbishop Gray (Domesday Book, apud Ebor., 99).

If the walls of that palace could have spoken, they could have told a wondrous tale. They beheld in turn the intrigues and festivities of Wolsey and his master, the brilliant courts of Elizabeth, the fawning servility of Steenie, and the execution of Charles.

Archbishop Gray translated the remains of his predecessor St. Wilfrid at Ripon, and placed them in a befitting shrine.

> "Wilfridi reliquias de theca levavit,
> In capsam argenteam digne collocavit."[j]

He founded the prebend of Stanwick in that church,[k] and I agree with Mr. Walbran in ascribing to him the erection of the beautiful west front of that cathedral.[l] But it was upon the church of York that his benefactions were showered. The subdeanery and the subchantorship of the canons were established whilst he was archbishop, and it is quite possible that he founded them; at all events he attached the living of Preston to the subdeanery. The stall of Wistow was constituted about the same time, and he revived that of Weighton, which had fallen into decay. In 1218 he annexed the prebend of Newthorpe and the church of Acomb to the treasurership.[m] He appropriated the living of Mappleton to the archdeaconry of the East Riding, that of Wawne to the chancellorship, Tunstall to the newly established subchantorship, and Withernwick to the prebend of Holme. He had obtained these benefices from the abbat and convent of Albemarle, and he bestowed them upon the minster with the consent of the dean and chapter.[n] He gave to the same church thirty-two copes of blue and purple,[o] a valuable mitre, a chalice and paten of gold and precious

[j] From the metrical history of the archbishops in MSS. Cotton, Cleopatra, C, iv.

[k] Rot. Gray.

[l] Matt. Paris (343), under the year 1234, gives a curious account of an adventure at Ripon. It was a year of famine, and the archbishop had gathered together as much corn as possible, to the injury, as we are informed, of the poor. It was kept so long that it decayed, and the creatures that found a home in it were supposed to be special emissaries of the evil one, and to be sent to punish the avarice of the archbishop. The bailiffs at first ran away, and the rustics, whom they compelled to open out the stacks, were obliged to follow their example when they heard a strange voice out of the corn bidding them desist, "quia archiepiscopus et omnia quæ habebat diaboli possessio erat!" The whole thing is ridiculously absurd.

On the 21st of October, 1222, Henry III. ordered Galfrid de Neville to give to Gray ten bream out of the royal fish-pond on the Foss to stock his stew at Ripon. There is still a pond in Ripon parks which contains a number of this rare fish. Were they genealogists they might make out a very capital pedigree (Rot. Claus., 515).

[m] MSS. Torre. Rot. Gray.

[n] Rot. Gray. Dugd. Mon., vi., 1191-2. In Le Neve, iii., 102, it is said that Gray founded the subdeanery, the succentorship, and two prebends at York. He augmented the prebend of Grendale to 40 marks (Rot. Gray).

[o] Stubbs, col. 1725. In MSS. Cotton, Cleopatra, C, iv, the number is said to be twenty-six.

stones, a morse of gold in the shape of a rose, with a large ruby in the centre, and other choice stones, weighing more than a pound, and a tippet also decorated with gold and jewels.[p] But Gray's noblest work at York was the erection of the south transept, in which he is interred. It is the choicest portion of that glorious temple, and the early English style of architecture may there be seen in the supremacy of its beauty. In boldness of arrangement and design, and in richness of decoration, the south transept is without a peer. How many of those who gaze with curious and admiring eyes upon arcade and carving, are ignorant of the piety and merits, nay, of the very name of the prelate who called them into being more than six centuries ago.[q]

There he lies on the eastern side of the same transept, in the grave which received him on the vigil of the feast of Pentecost, 1255.[r] The place in which he is interred was in all probability selected by himself.[s] The altar of St. Michael, at which the archbishop founded a chantry in 1241 for the weal of his soul,[t] stood between the sepulchre and the wall; but all

[p] Fabric Rolls of York Minster, ed. Surtees Society, 213, 215, 222.

[q] From the fact that Gray granted an indulgence for the church of York in 1227, and that several other gifts to the fabric were made about the same time, it may reasonably be inferred that the building of the transepts was then going on (Fabric Rolls, 146-50). That on the south side must have been completed before 1241, the year in which Gray founded his chantry at the altar of St. Michael. Sewal de Bovill, who became dean about that time, confirms a grant of two bovates and two acres of land in Milford which the archbishop had made to Gilbert de Corbrigge, carpenter, "qui in ejus servicio diu stetit et tam pro ipso quam pro ecclesia Ebor. multum et fideliter laboravit" (MSS. Cotton, Claudius, B, iii, 113 *a*).

The north transept, which is ascribed to John Romanus, senior, was probably built shortly before Gray's work. It is less rich and probably, therefore, of an earlier date. Romanus became subdean in 1228, and died in 1256. He and Gray must have been great friends. On Nov. 27, 1237, the archbishop granted him an annual pension of 20 marks (Rot. Gray).

There is an interesting legend about the beautiful little church of Skelton near York. The antiquary Gent, writing in 1731, "mounted on his courser" to visit it, "because it is affirmed 'twas built with the stones that remain'd after the south cross of the minster had been finished by the archbishop Walter Grey" (Gent's Ripon, pt. ii., 3). There is an account of this architectural gem, I had almost said toy, in "The Churches of Yorkshire," and a work has been specially devoted to it, viz., "Architectural Illustrations of Skelton Church, by Ewan Christian, with an account of the building. Folio. London: 1846."

[r] Ann. Burton, apud Gale, iii., 341.

[s] As Professor Willis observes, "The pier arch under which the tomb stands is made wider than the others, apparently to give it importance." It was probably made so that the founder might rest beneath it (Architectural History of York Cathedral, 20).

[t] Founded March 22, 1241, for one priest, with two chaplains and a clerk under him, and liberally endowed (Fabric Rolls of York Minster, 297. MSS. Cotton, Claudius, B, iii., 76 *b*). Stubbs speaks of Gray ordaining three perpetual chantries at this altar (col. 1725). Gray had secured to himself the church of Millum, with which the chantry was endowed, between 1228 and 1230, but the actual deed of foundation was not drawn up till 1241, when the transept was probably completed. Archbishop Gray was also commemorated

traces of it have disappeared, save a figure of the archangel in the window above, still thrusting his spear into his prostrate foe. The monument on which you gaze is one of the most striking memorials of the age in which it was set up. The archbishop, who seems to have been of small stature and a slight frame, is stretched out at full length with his pastoral staff in his hand, which is thrust into the mouth of the serpent. The details of the figure and its adjuncts are full of simple elegance. Above the sleeping prelate, on ten light and graceful pillars, there towers a magnificent canopy, which terminates in finials of the most beautiful design. Many will be surprised to learn that these are of modern workmanship, and that they were moulded less than a century ago by an Italian of the name of Bernasconi, a sculptor of great merit. I cannot bestow too high praise on what he has done, for he seems to have been imbued with the true spirit of Christian art. He has crowned each finial with two thrushes in full song, wrought with exquisite skill, and resting upon wool-packs.[u] Had the carving been really old I should have ventured to suggest the meaning of the device. The packs would have been an allusion to the office of chancellor, which the archbishop once enjoyed, and in the thrushes there would have been, perhaps, a canting allusion to his name. The thrush in the North of England is at the present day frequently called the *gray bird*. It may well be singing, for what an offering of praise and worship is above it. The monument, I must add, is surrounded by a brazen screen of excellent and appropriate design. It was set in its present position by archbishop Markham, and his gift prompted the following lines from the earl of Carlisle:—

"From rude approach and from the touch profane
Thus gen'rous Markham guards this crumbling fane;
Revives just praise to Grey, makes widely known
A course of lib'ral actions like his own.
And should a baser age unmov'd survey
Our much lov'd prelate's mould'ring tomb decay,
View Time's coarse hand each grateful line efface,
Nor the broad tablet to his worth replace;
Yet on the spot where once was plac'd his urn,
Shall true religion ever weep and mourn;
A reverential awe around shall spread,
And learning point where rests his holy head."

at the altar of St. Stephen, which was founded by William de Langton, nephew and heir of William de Langton, late dean of York (Fabric Rolls, 301). When we recollect that the dean was also called William de Rotherfield, Gray's paternal estate, we can see at once to whom he was indebted for his preferment at York. Langton was interred in the sacred corner where the remains of archbishops Gray, Bovill, and Ludham were deposited.

[u] The finials are merely of plaster. Bernasconi has introduced a thrush on one of the ornaments of the north side of the tomb with less success. You

Walter de Gray is the first archbishop of York whose official acts have been handed down to us. These are registered upon two rolls of unequal size called the *major* and the *minor*, which have originally been one, and which ought to be re-united. They commence, most unfortunately, with the proceedings of the tenth year of Gray's archiepiscopate. They are of very great length, and exhibit documents of great interest and value.[v] The writing, which is on both sides, is singularly beautiful and minute; and no one can examine the roll without being deeply struck, not only with the caligraphy, but with the piety and energy of the archbishop, and with the perfect order and system which he observed in the management of his diocese.

Sewal de Bovill, dean of York, was Gray's successor. His origin appears to have been an humble one, and of his early life there is little known. He was one of the scholars who attended the lectures of Edmund de Abingdon, afterwards St. Edmund, at whose feet Grostête and Roger Bacon used to sit in the University of Oxford.[w] He would there be brought into contact with some of the most learned men of the day, among whom he is said to have distinguished himself by his works.[x] Bovill was greatly attached to his master, and, in after years, when the merits and sufferings of Edmund began to attract both sympathy and attention, he wrote to Innocent IV., urging him in strong terms to canonize his old instructor. He speaks of his former tutor in terms of the warmest praise and affection, and tells the

may see at once of what materials it is composed. In Drake's Eboracum (427) there is an engraving of the tomb before Bernasconi meddled with it. It is at present, I am sorry to say, in a dilapidated condition.

Drake mentions a curious story which was believed in his day, that the archbishop had died under a sentence of excommunication, and that his body therefore had not been laid in the sacred earth, but in the canopy over the pillars. The too curious antiquary made an incision into the stone-work, and soon found that there was no hollow within.

[v] Two or three extracts may be given. June 1, 1229, a pension of 5 marks from the church of Brancepeth to Peter de Vallibus, clerk. July 16, 1233, licence to the prior and convent of Wartre for a chaplain to pray for the soul of Robert de Percy in the chapel in which he is interred. Nov. 15, 1251, a pension of 40s. per annum to Roger Fitz Adam, clerk, nephew of our most dear friend, Fr. William, chamberlain of our lord the king.

[w] Martene, Thes. Nov. Anecdot., iii., 1838. Matt. Paris, 798. Wood's Antiq. Univ. Oxon., i., 196. Bowles's Lacock Abbey, 202. In Walter de Gray's roll the title of *magister* is given to Bovill, which shews that he was a graduate.

[x] Bale (Cent. iv., 311-12) makes Bovill the author of "Breviloquium ad Alexandrum; Statuta Synodalia; Ad suos Sacerdotes; Sermones et Epistolas."

pope that he had been his pupil in bygone days in the school of arts at Oxford.[y] Edmund, who seems to have had a deep insight into character, had told Bovill what would come upon him in after-life, and one part of his prediction had been already verified. He said that his scholar should be advanced to a high estate, but that he should be distinguished by his sufferings as well as by his temporal success.[z]

Bovill became the dean of York about the year 1240, holding at the same time the stall of Fenton.[a] He was also made archdeacon of York in 1249, on the death of Laurence de Lincoln, whose will he caused to be exemplified.[b] In compliance with the wish of his friend, whom he succeeded, he established a chantry at the altar of St. Laurence, in York minster, on the 16th of January, 1250.[c]

Upon the death of Walter de Gray the chapter elected their dean in his room, and the selection seems to have been a good one, as Matthew Paris speaks in high praise of Bovill's modesty, piety, and learning.[d] The king, however, was too fond of money to allow the temporalities of the see of York to pass so speedily from his hands. "I have never had them before," he is reported to have said, "and they shall not slip out of my fingers yet." He took possession of everything he could to the great grief of the archbishop-elect,[e] and justified his proceedings by saying that Bovill had been born out of lawful wedlock.[f] It was his wish, I believe, to secure the see for his brother Ademar, bishop of Winchester.[g] The chapter, however, supported their late dean with vigour and resolution. They borrowed two hundred marks of Peter the subchantor, to enable them to prosecute the matter at Rome; and on the 1st of October, 1255, they assigned to him as a security the churches of South Burton and Brotherton.[h] The proceedings at Rome were entirely in Bovill's favour. The pope sent him a dispensation which obviated the irregularity of his birth, confirming his election, and giving him the pall.[i] The chapter now brought the matter to a termination with the aid of Roger de Holderness, their representative.[j] It was useless

[y] Martene, *ut supra*.

[z] Matt. Paris, 798, 803, 827.

[a] From Rot. Gray it appears that he had a stall in 1237. MSS. Cotton, Claudius, B, iii., 8, 34, 45. MSS. Torre. Le Neve, iii., 121, 184.

[b] MSS. Torre. Le Neve, iii., 132.

[c] Domesday Book, penes Dec. et Cap. Ebor., 57 *a*. York Fabric Rolls, 292.

[d] Matt. Paris, 784. Wikes, apud Gale, ii., 50. Polydore Vergil, 311. Fuller's Worthies, *n. e.*, ii., 539. The temporalities had been in the hands of John Clarel and Adam de Hylton (Abbrev. Rot. Orig., i., 15).

[e] Matt. Paris, 779, 784, 786.

[f] Ibid., 786. Stubbs, col. 1725.

[g] Wikes, apud Gale, ii., 50. A person of great influence with Henry III. Cf. Mon. Francisc., 254.

[h] Reg. Giffard, 108 *b*.

[i] MSS. Cotton, Vitellius, A, ii., 111. Wikes, apud Gale, 50.

[j] Matt. Paris, 784. When Ludham was made archbishop, Roger de Hol-

for the king to resist. The royal assent to the nomination of the chapter was granted on the 4th of May, 1256,[k] and Bovill was consecrated archbishop at York on Sunday the 23rd of July.[l]

Soon after this ceremony took place Adam de Marisco, the learned Minorite, addressed the new prelate in a letter which assumes the character of a little treatise, as it extends to forty-seven chapters.[m] Bovill, who was a timid man, seems to have acquainted his friend with the doubts and fears which his new position aroused in his mind, and to have solicited his counsel. The reply of the celebrated friar reminds us of the letter which Beda wrote to Egbert. He begins by expressing the joy that all good men feel at Bovill's promotion,[n] and then he touches upon many points of great importance to a Christian bishop—the kind of life that he should adopt, the necessity for wise coadjutors, the care to be taken in making appointments and choosing clergy. All this is to be done with the aid of One above who is to be approached by prayer, upon the nature and degrees of which Marisco speaks at some length. He then turns to a subject upon which the Minorites were always eloquently indignant—the vices of the clergy, and he urges Bovill to repress them with a strong hand. After this the writer speaks of religion in its political aspect, and the wrongs which the church endured at the hands of the civil governors. All this is to be withstood temperately and firmly. Grostête is held up as a pattern worthy of imitation, and Marisco tries to cheer his friend by telling him that persecution is not only useful, but a blessing. We can well conceive that Bovill had been speaking to Marisco about the prediction of Edmund de Abingdon, to which the last piece of advice has an especial reference. The letter is an interesting document, and it is the key, no doubt, to Bovill's subsequent conduct.

Bovill's name occurs but once in connection with the state. On the 20th of July, 1257, he was one of the commissioners who were appointed to settle, if possible, the disputes between the king of Scotland and his nobles.[o] In the same year I find him mentioned as a worshipper at the tomb of St. Alban.[p] He

derness, *alias* de Skeffling, became dean.

[k] Le Neve, iii., 102, ex Rot. Pat.

[l] MSS. Cotton, *ut supra*. Stubbs, col. 1725. Anglia Sacra, i., 310. Hemingford, apud Gale, ii., 578. Wikes, ibid., 50. Knyghton, col. 2444. Matt. Paris, 804. Flores Hist., 363.

[m] Printed among the Monumenta Franciscana, 438-489.

[n] Marisco says of him, "Cujus indies usquequaquam per effectuum evidentias universis clarescit illustrius et virtus invincibilis, et sensus infallibilis, et zelus intemerabilis, et actus indefatigabilis" (ibid., 440).

[o] Fœdera. i., 362. Hutchinson's Durham, i., 210, where the date 1258 is given.

[p] Matt. Paris, 809.

did, however, some good work at York during his brief tenure of the archiepiscopate. He remodelled the constitution of the chapel of St. Sepulchre, which had been founded by archbishop Roger, changing the clergy into canons, and making provision for the management of the common property and the performance of the services.[q] Bovill, however, conferred a still greater boon upon the church, and his vigour and persistency in standing up for the rights of his cathedral when they were menaced by an insolent intruder, won for him the praises of his contemporaries, although they involved him in the troubles which his old master had foretold.

The deanery of York, which Bovill's own promotion had vacated, was given to Godfrey de Ludham, who succeeded him also in the archbishopric. Ludham's tenure of office was destined to be an uneasy one. One day three strangers found their way to the minster of York.[r] No service was being performed, for the priests and clerks at that time were otherwise employed. The men entered into the cathedral, and found a solitary worshipper at his devotions. They asked him which was the dean's stall? "This is it," he said, pointing to the place. The three then went up to it, and, one of them taking possession of the seat, the other two said, addressing him, "Brother, we install thee by the authority of the pope." The archbishop and his chapter, nay, the whole of England, were amazed and indignant. Without a word having been said to any one, the pope had given the deanery away to an Italian cardinal of the name of Jordan, who had got possession of it by this audacious and discreditable trick. Bovill, who seems to have been naturally of a quiet and retiring disposition, had a just cause to defend, and he would not submit to this dictation. The whole of England was being stocked with these Italian priests, who came over hungering after preferment. They had for some time made a prey of the church of York.[s] On this occasion Bovill exhibited such a determined front that the intruder went home, and made a complaint to the pope. The archbishop was now subjected to the rancour of disappointed and angry men, and endured a bitter persecution. He was suspended from his office; the minster was put under an interdict; Bovill's cross was taken away from him, and,

[q] Stubbs, col. 1725-6. Reg. Greenfield. Dugd. Mon., vi., 1182.

[r] Matt. Paris, 803, 820, 827. Ann. Burton, apud Gale, iii., 386.

[s] Many instances might be given. In 1255 Magister Rustandus, the subdeacon of the pope, came to England, and a stall at York was given to him by the king (Matt. Paris, 785). John Romanus, archdeacon of Richmond, is blamed for urging the Romans to enrich themselves in England (ibid., 792). Cf. Twisden's Historical Vindication of the Church of England in point of Schism, 61. In 1207 the king received 61*l*. 4s. 6d. "de prebendis Romanorum in dioc. Ebor." (Rot. Claus., 99).

finally, he and the dean were excommunicated. I cannot say whether these marks of the papal displeasure were ever altogether removed. It seems, however, probable that the sentence was rescinded, as Matthew Paris mentions an arrangement, which looks very like a compromise, that a pension of a hundred marks should be paid yearly to Jordan till some other preferment could be provided for him.[t]

These troubles and persecutions broke Bovill's heart, and he was soon upon his deathbed. At that solemn time the sinking prelate raised his hands and his eyes towards heaven, and appealed to the Redeemer from the unrighteous dealing of His pretended deputy upon earth. The dying man then thought upon the bold words of his old college friend Grostête, and resolved to follow his example and acquaint the pope with the evil he had done, protesting against the injustice. He bade him imitate the humility of his sainted predecessors, and not to tyrannize over the church, "for the Lord said to Peter, feed my sheep, and not, shear them, skin them, tear out their entrails, or eat them up." This was strong language; but it seems only to have provoked a smile of pity and contempt on the face of him to whom it was written.[u] There were many, however, who would be proud to think that men were not wanting to point out the evils of the times, and to lay the lash upon the real offenders.

Bovill died on the 10th of May, 1258.[v] On the Easter day before his decease he had made a great feast for the poor, and he left it and them to take a part in the services of his chapel. The memory of his virtues was long cherished in the North, and miracles, etc., are said to have attested the holiness of his life.[w]

Archbishop Bovill was interred in the south transept of the minster near the remains of Walter de Gray. A plain marble slab charged with a floriated cross, and elevated upon low pillars, still marks the spot. The ground was opened about 1735, and a gold ring was taken out of the grave, which is now preserved in the vestry. It is of simple workmanship, and without any ornament.

[t] Matt. Paris, 813. In the Anglia Sacra (i., 494) it is said that Bovill was excommunicated by the archbishop of Canterbury in obedience to a papal mandate. Another account is that Jordan suspended him, and that he was suspended at the time of his death, the pope knowing nothing of it—a most unlikely thing (Chron. Petrib., 142).

[u] Matt. Paris, 831.

[v] MSS. Cotton, Vitellius, A, ii., 111. Stubbs, col. 1726.

[w] Chron. Lanercost, 71-2.

Godfrey de Ludham, or de Kinton, probably derived his surnames from the villages of Loudham and Kinalton or Kinston in Nottinghamshire, of which county he seems to have been a native. The Christian names of his parents were Richard and Eda, and he had a brother, Thomas de Ludham, who was chaplain to the pope and a prebendary at York and Southwell.[x]

On the 17th of June, 1227, archbishop Gray granted to Mr. Godfrey de Ludham a pension of ten marks per annum, and on the 26th of August, 1229, he collated him to a moiety of the living of Peniston in the West Riding of Yorkshire.[y] About the year 1250 Ludham was precentor of York whilst Bovill occupied the deanery,[z] and when the dean was advanced to the archbishopric the precentor succeeded him in his office. He was immediately involved in the troubles that overwhelmed his diocesan. The pope, it will be remembered, attempted to thrust a cardinal of the name of Jordan into the deanery, and excommunicated Bovill and Ludham for opposing him.[a] There is, however, reason to believe that this sentence was soon withdrawn.

Bovill died in the beginning of May, 1258, and on the 29th of that month the king authorized the chapter to elect another archbishop.[b] They fixed upon Ludham on the 12th of July,[c] and the royal assent was given on the 25th.[d] Ludham took the precaution of going himself to Rome to secure the favour of the pope, and, after much trouble and expense,[e] he was consecrated there on the 22nd of September, and obtained the pall.[f] On his return to England he boldly entered London bearing his cross erect, and went to the court, where he was kindly welcomed by the king. After this, he set out for the North. On the 1st of December he received the temporalities of his see, and about Christmas he was enthroned with much rejoicing. He soon shewed his regard for Roger de Holderness by giving him the deanery. They had been friends for some time, and had been associated together at St. Albans.[g]

[x] Fabric Rolls of York, 293. It is mentioned in Melton's Register, in a document relating to the prebend of Wetwang, that Thomas and Godfrey de Ludham were brothers.

Walter de Ludham, knight, witnesses archbishop Gray's grant of Thorp (Dugd. Mon., vi., 1195). Cf. Thoroton's Notts, 289. [y] Rot. Gray.

[z] MSS. Cotton, Claudius, B, iii., 12 *a*.

[a] Ann. Burton, apud Gale, iii., 386.

[b] Le Neve, iii., 102.

[c] Chron. Lanercost, 66.

[d] Le Neve, iii., 102.

[e] Matt. Paris, 834, 839.

[f] MSS. Cotton, Vitellius, A, ii., 111. Cal. Rot. Pat., 31. Stubbs (col. 1726) says that he was consecrated on Sept. 23.

[g] Matt. Paris, 840. In 1260 the archbishop was ordered to find men to serve in Wales (Fœd., i., 399), and on Sept. 3 he was commanded peremptorily to collect the disme in his province (ibid., 445).

There is very little known of Ludham's conduct as archbishop. His register has not been preserved, and the chroniclers are silent about him. We learn, however, from Stubbs that in the third year of his archiepiscopate he put the city of York under an interdict, which lasted from the beginning of Lent to the festival of the Invention of the holy cross,[h] and the chronicle of Peterborough tells us that this severity was to punish the citizens for some injuries which they had done to their diocesan and the chapter of York.[i] In 1261 Ludham held a provincial council at Beverley,[j] and the people of that town were for some time under his displeasure for breaking into his parks. In the register of archbishop Giffard mention is made of some statutes which his predecessor drew up for the better management and discipline of the regular orders.[k]

Archbishop Ludham died on the 12th of January, 1265,[l] and was interred beside his predecessors Bovill and Gray in the south transept of York minster. A simple cross carved in stone marked the place of his sepulture. When the old pavement was taken up, about 1735, Ludham's monument was removed to the presbytery. It was injured in the fire of 1829.[m]

Ludham left a will, the provisions of which seem to have been neglected. On the 8th of March, 1268, the executors were called to account for their short-comings. They were four in number; the prior of the house of the Holy Trinity, London, William dean of York, Robert archdeacon of the East Riding, and John de Steinton, a layman. Thomas de Berneby, subdeacon of the pope, and John his brother, a layman, two of Ludham's creditors, made a petition to Octobonus the papal legate in England, that the executors should be obliged to pay the debts and legacies of their late master, and they were ordered to do so. On the 20th of February previous, archbishop Giffard had issued a commission to Nicholas de Wudeford, canon of Westbury in the diocese of Worcester, empowering him to enquire into the effects belonging to his predecessor in the see.[n]

Thomas de Ludham, the archbishop's brother, founded a chantry at the altar of the Blessed Virgin and St. John in York minster, at which the souls of the deceased primate, the founder, and their parents, were to be especially remembered. Three chaplains were to officiate at it, and it was endowed with lands in Skelton, Middleton and Boynton.[o]

[h] Stubbs, col. 1726. Chron. Lanercost, 71.

[i] Chron. Petrib., 143.

[j] Flores Hist., 379.

[k] Reg. Giffard. The rules which Ludham laid down for the management of the monastery of Hexham are preserved.

[l] Stubbs, 1726. Wikes, apud Gale, ii., 66. MSS. Cotton, Vitellius A, ii., 111 *b*.

[m] Browne's York Minster, 58.

[n] Reg. Giffard.

[o] York Fabric Rolls, ed. Surtees Society, 293, and MSS. D. and C. Ebor.

On the 30th of January, 1265, the king gave the chapter of York permission to elect a new archbishop, and they again fixed upon their dean, William de Langton *alias* de Rotherfield. This appointment was made on the 12th of March, and the king assented to it on the 1st of April. The pope, however, set it aside on the ground that Langton was a pluralist, although he held only a single living in addition to his deanery. Bonaventura, the famous Franciscan, was nominated by Clement IV. in Langton's place, but he seems to have waived his claim, as there was the prospect of a storm.[p] The diocese of York would indeed have been honoured if that illustrious man had been placed at its head. The piety and the works of the "seraphic" doctor were famous throughout the Christian world. They attained for him, among other honours, the rule of the order of the Minorites, the honours of the cardinalate, and a place in the calendar of the saints.

William de Langton, dean of York, who was rejected by the pope, was a great man. In 1265 he was summoned to parliament as dean, and in 1278 he declined the bishopric of Carlisle. He died in 1279, and was interred in the south transept near his friend and patron, archbishop Gray. He was commemorated by a very remarkable monument, which is now destroyed. Walter de Langton, bishop of Lichfield and Coventry, and a distinguished statesman, was his nephew.

Walter Giffard was the son of wealthy parents, and could boast of an illustrious ancestry. He was the son of Hugh Giffard of Boyton, in Wiltshire, by Sibilla daughter and co-heiress of Walter de Cormeilles.[q] The Christian name of the archbishop was probably derived from his maternal grandfather, but it would also remind him of Walter Giffard, lord of Bolbec and Longueville, a great Norman baron who came into England with the Conqueror, and fought by his side at Hastings.[r]

There is very little known of Giffard's early history. In 1256,

[p] MS. Vitellius, A, ii., 111. Knyghton, col. 2454. Stubbs, col. 1726. Chron. Petrib., 149. Le Neve, iii., 103, 121. Cal. Rot. Pat., 37. Wikes (apud Gale, ii., 74) says that Bonaventura resigned "timens pelli suæ."

[q] Hoare's Wiltshire—history of Heytesbury Hundred, 201, 238. Dugd. Bar., 59, 499, etc. The archbishop was probably the eldest son, as the estate seems to have come into his hands. There is a life of Hugh Giffard in Foss's Judges of England, ii., 351. Godfrey Giffard, bishop of Worcester, was the archbishop's brother, and I shall mention several others who were his kinsmen. Abbrev. Rot. Orig., i., 23.

[r] Master Wace's Chron., 256, etc.

Henry III. permitted him and his mother to reside in the castle of Oxford;[s] and on another occasion he was indebted to the good offices of Adam de Marisco, the learned Franciscan.[t] On the 22nd of May, 1264, Giffard was elected to the bishopric of Bath and Wells, being at that time a canon and an archdeacon in that church, as well as chaplain to the pope. Six days after this the king assented to the choice which had been made, and on the 1st of September Giffard received the temporalities of his see.[u] The archbishop of Canterbury was at that time abroad, and the new prelate crossed the Channel in quest of the rite of consecration, which he received at the hands of the bishop of Hereford in the church of Notre Dame at Paris on the 4th of January, 1265.[v] The English barons were most unwilling that he should leave the country for that purpose, and plundered his manors when he went, an act which he requited on his return by a sentence of excommunication.[w] Giffard was at that time, and throughout his life, of a handsome presence, fond of gaiety and humour, but of a luxurious disposition. He had afterwards a tendency towards corpulency, which is said to have affected both his temper and his health.[x]

Whilst he was bishop of Bath and Wells Giffard experienced many marks of the royal favour. In 1265 he was raised to the honourable position of lord-chancellor of England, receiving an annual pension of five hundred marks. He resigned the office when he was translated to York.[y] During the intestine troubles of the time the king made him the keeper of Oxford castle, and gave him instructions to furnish it with stores and munitions of war.[z] On the 15th of October, 1266, the pope promoted Giffard to the see of York, which had been vacant for more than a year.[a] He was enthroned on the festival of All Saints, and obtained restitution of the temporalities on the 26th of December.[b]

[s] Excerpt. e Rot. Fin., ii., 243.

[t] Monum. Francisc., 257-8.

[u] Prynne's Coll., iii., 224. Anglia Sacra, i., 566. Le Neve, i., 159. There is a life of him, containing nothing new, in Cassan's Lives of the Bishops of Bath and Wells, 139.

[v] Reg. Sacr., Angl., 44. In archbishop Giffard's register at York his acts as bishop of Bath and Wells are recorded from 1264 to 1266. These are arranged under archdeaconries in the usual way.

[w] Wikes, apud Gale, ii., 67.

[x] Chron. Lanercost, 71, 103. "Formosus et illustris clericus," or as Chaucer says,

"Now certainly he was a fayre prelat."

[y] Foss's Judges, ii., 353.

[z] Reg. Giffard, 76 *b*. On Aug. 12, 1266, Henry III. leased to him his manors of Pydingdon and Brehull, subject to an annual payment of £30. On Oct. 12, 1268, the king allowed him to add to the ground belonging to his palace in York a piece of crown land adjacent (ibid.) 56 Hen. III., licence to the archbishop of York, "kernellare domum suam de Garrode ad modum castri" (Cal. Rot. Pat., 44).

[a] MSS. Cotton, Vitellius, A, ii., 111 *b*. Wikes, apud Gale, ii., 77. Chron. Lan., 84. Matt. Paris, Addit., 859. Knyghton, col. 2464. Trivet, 228.

[b] Vitellius, *ut supra*. Wikes, 84. Stubbs, col. 1726.

Giffard still continued to take a part in public affairs after he came into the North. In the autumn of 1268, he had a quarrel with the archbishop of Canterbury about the right of bearing his cross erect, as on the 15th of October in that year Giffard's proctor, E. de Well, was at Lambeth, and in the presence of the archbishop made an appeal in behalf of his master to the pope.[c] With Edward I. Giffard was a great favourite. In August, 1270, when that monarch, then the heir apparent, was starting on his crusade, he drew up his will, in which he appointed the Northern primate one of the tutors of his sons.[d] In 1271, Henry III. made him custos of the counties of Nottingham and Derby, which his nephew Hugh de Babington superintended as his deputy.[e] In the spring of 1272 I find that he was constable of the tower of London; another of his nephews, Sir J. Neville, acting in his room.[f] On the 23rd of November in that year the archbishop was one of the persons who announced to the prince his father's decease,[g] and he was present at the coronation of the new king.[h] For some time after that Giffard was busily employed in receiving the oaths of allegiance to his master,[i] and in 1273 he was acting in his behalf in the affairs of St. Augustine's, Canterbury.[j] In 1275 he was one of those to whom the charge of the kingdom was entrusted during Edward's absence,[k] and in 1277 he sent his service against Llewellyn prince of Wales, according to his summons.[l]

The best account of archbishop Giffard's official acts is to be gathered from his register, which is preserved at York. It is full of novel and curious information relating to the ecclesiastical condition of the North of England. There are in it, among many other things, the earliest ordination lists that I am acquainted with; documents which have never yet been brought to bear, as they ought, upon the history of the clergy, and the annals of the church. The register gives us a very favourable idea of Giffard's attention to his diocese. In every respect he seems to have been a faithful pastor. He was a strict and fearless reformer of abuses, in days when there were many offenders, and startling deviations from discipline and order. Giffard made a regular visitation of his clergy, and shewed no mercy to

[c] Reg. Giffard.

[d] Fœd., i., 484. Test. Vetust., 9.

[e] Madox, Hist. Exch., ii., 153. He held it till 1st Edw. I. Cf. Fuller's Worthies. Archæolog., xxviii., 272.

[f] Reg. Giffard. [g] Fœd., i., 497.

[h] Wikes, apud Gale, ii., 101. We are told that the king would not allow him to be present when he was crowned in 1274, to prevent an outbreak about the cross with the archbishop of Canterbury (Ann. Waverl., apud Gale, ii., 227).

[i] Anglia Sacra, i., 499.

[j] Prynne's Coll., iii., 124.

[k] Cal. Rot. Pat., 46. Godwin (n. ed., 682), quoting the Close Rolls, says that Giffard was deputy in 1272, and again afterwards.

[l] Parl. Writs., i., 195, 197.

titled culprits. He reprehended William de Percy, canon of York and a brother of Sir Henry de Percy, for wasting his time among courtiers, and in undignified pursuits. He also attempted to grapple with Bogo de Clare, a son of the great earl of Gloucester, an ecclesiastic who gave much trouble to more than one archbishop of York. The history of this man is a most remarkable one. His noble blood, perhaps, made him spurn authority, and he paid no attention whatever to decency and discipline. At one and the same time he held as many as eighteen livings, in addition to the treasurership at York and the deanery of Stafford. On one occasion when a royal official served a writ at his house in London, Bogo's servants compelled the unhappy man to eat up the document, seals and all! Of course his parishes were grievously neglected, for Clare merely valued the income which they produced. The treasury at York was in such a state during his rule, that it was reported against him that the vestments and ornaments of the church were often used by women in childbed. In the church of Simonburn in Northumberland, whilst he was the rector, the chronicler of Lanercost observed in the place of the carving which ought to have been behind the altar some wicker work taken evidently from a stable, and still smeared with the dung of oxen. In striking and painful contrast to this parsimonious and guilty carelessness was the gift which Clare made to the queen of France, a coffer for her trinkets in the shape of a car on wheels. The coffer itself was of ivory, the wheels and all the exterior fittings, even to the smallest key, were of solid silver, whilst within everything was of gold or silk.

Archbishop Giffard paid much attention to the religious houses within his diocese. They stood at that time in great need of supervision. More than a century had elapsed since most of them were founded, but during this period the defects of the system were seriously and alarmingly developed. The following extracts will be the best illustrations of the subject. They are taken from the reports of the investigations which were made between 1274 and 1276.

Bolton in Craven. The whole convent conspired against the predecessor of William de Danfield, the present prior. Nicholas de Broc, the sub-prior, is old and useless. Silence is not observed, and there is much chattering and noise. John de Pontefract, the present cellarer, is incompetent. The cellarer and sub-cellarer are often absent from service and refections, and have their meals by themselves when the canons have left the refectory.[m] The house is in debt to the amount of 324*l*. 5s. 7d.

[m] These canons and many other ecclesiastics within the diocese of York

Swyne. The prioress cannot keep discipline. Sibilla de Bella and another nun are rebellious, and Alice de Scrutevile, Beatrix de St. Quintin, and Matilda Constable, abet them. The sick are neglected. The nuns have only a pair of shoes a year, scarcely a tunic in three years, and a *pallium* in twenty, but what their parents or friends may give them, or they are able to beg. The prioress is full of suspicions, and is credulous and hasty. The nuns and sisters quarrel, the sisters pretending to be equal to the nuns, and using black veils. There are two windows broken, through which victuals, etc., are carried out; and the nuns and canons meet together in an unseemly way. The household of Sir Robert de Hilton wander about through the cloister and parlour, and talk suspiciously with the nuns. The nuns have nothing for their fare but bread, cheese, and beer, and, on two days in the week, water instead of beer, whilst the canons live luxuriously.

Selby. The church of St. Germanus in the town is a chapel, and the rite of baptism was administered in it until children were carried to the monastery. The chapel and its altar are not dedicated, neither is the cemetery, because the dead are interred in the burial ground of the abbey. The chaplain was ordained in Ireland, but archbishop Gray allowed his orders. The abbat "mulierculas habet in maneriis suis et in villa de Selby."

Newbrough. The prior is too easy, and the superior too hot-tempered. A *camera* has been needlessly built at Thirsk. The cellarer traffics in horses like a dealer, and has a rough tongue. The keeper of the fabric is abroad at the cost of the house, and has not given in his account.

Felley. Ralph, the prior, laid violent hands on Ralph his brother-canon, and then took part in the service. He is old and infirm. He broke into the place where the common seal was kept, and took possession of it against the will of the monks. (He is deprived.) The canons lead very immoral lives.

Archbishop Giffard was bold enough to exercise his visitatorial power within the diocese of Durham, even within the walls of the potent monastery of St. Cuthbert. The see was at that time vacant, and, according to one of the Durham historians, the right of the archbishop of York to act within the bishopric during the interregnum seems to have been conceded. The chronicle of Lanercost, however, tells us that Giffard's visit was not unattended by dissension. The prior of Durham endeavoured to beguile his potent guest at his residence in the country with the dainty cates of which Giffard was so fond, but the archbishop did not forget the main object of his coming;

would be of the same mind as Béranger's Chanoine de l'Auxerrois :—

"Mon évêque, triste et bigot,
Prétend que je sens le fagot."

and a quarrel arose, which ended in Giffard's exclusion from the cathedral, and the excommunication of the prior and his rebellious brethren. We find also that Giffard was more or less mixed up in the controversy which preceded the election of bishop de Insula.[n]

Archbishop Giffard must be reckoned among the benefactors of the church of York. He augmented the chancellorship with the living of Acklam, and appropriated the benefices of Mappleton, Withernwick, Waghen, and Tunstall, to the archdeaconry of the East Riding, the prebend of Holme, the chancellorship, and the succentorship.[o] He gave also to the minster a fair mitre, a gold ring with a balas, two small saucers of gold, and two precious phials of silver gilt, wrought with cunning workmanship, and decorated with valuable stones.[p]

Among the grave and formal documents with which the archbishop's register abounds, there are several pages which are devoted to an interesting subject, the private expenditure of Giffard. From it we may gain what is of great value, a pretty fair insight into that prelate's character and life. I need make no apology for giving a number of extracts. There is, unfortunately, a provoking absence of minute details which is much to be regretted. We have a glimpse, however, of the archbishop's kindness to his relations, and his charities. The large sums which he gave for wine seem to shew that he was, as the Lanercost chronicler has described him, "*socialis et dapsilis.*" The expenses incidental to his taking possession of his see were in all probability so heavy that he was obliged to have recourse to the Italian bankers, or usurers as he appropriately calls them, to borrow money, and it is doubtful whether he was ever thoroughly extricated from their clutches. Many of their bonds, to which he was a party, have been preserved, and he might well complain of the "whirlpool" into which he had been plunged.

In addition to the special charges for providing necessaries, we find the record of large sums which were laid out for the expenses of the archbishop's hospice. Under these would be included the items of wages, provisions and travelling. For 1267 and 1268 the cost of the hospice amounted to 450*l.* per annum. In 1269 it was only 320*l.* In 1270 it was as high as 860*l.*, or 870*l.*, whilst in 1271, of which year we have only an imperfect account, it was above 600*l.* All this seems to point to an extravagant scale of expenditure, if we take into account the relative value of money at that time and the present.

The chief cause of this outlay must undoubtedly have been

[n] Hist. Dunelm. Scr. Tres, ed. Surtees Soc., 56. Chron. Lanercost, 103.

[o] Reg. Giffard.

[p] York Fabric Rolls, 213, 214, 216.

the great number of retainers that the archbishop was obliged to support. He had his regular officers to preside over each department of his household, with fixed and by no means small stipends. In addition to these, at each of his numerous residences, some of his servants were constantly living to take charge of the house, and at his various manors there were the farm-labourers and the bailiffs, all of whom depended upon him for their subsistence. The archbishop would thus be put to a very considerable expense. This would be greatly increased by the migratory life which the prelates of that age delighted in. A bishop, like his sovereign, was rarely more than three days at a time in one place. He was always passing from residence to residence with all the pomp and ceremony of a great feudal baron. Hawks and hounds were frequently his companions on his travels, and he would turn aside every now and then from the beaten causeway to flush the heron from its waterpool, or to chase the red deer through the woods. Behind the archbishop there rode a long train of domestics, who carried with them the wardrobe and the plate, and a great part of the furniture of their master. With these each of his manor-houses or castles was equipped, to be stripped again when the visitors deserted it. The bailiff of the place had little more to do than to provide the kitchen from his lands and streams, and to pay over, when it was required, the balance of his account. A pretty accurate itinerary of several of the northern prelates might easily be constructed, and it would be most interesting and suggestive.

The following extracts will give my readers some idea of the private expenditure of archbishop Giffard.

1267, Sept. 17. To Luranc Bom, citizen and merchant of Florence, the deputy of Reyner and Teclarius, merchants of the same city,[q] 1000 marks. Sept. 21. To Locco Hugolini and Gregory Sunelli, merchants of Sienna residing in London, 600 marks. Sept. 22. To our valet R. de Ascoc', 64*l.* 3s., to buy cloth in the fair of Bloccelegh.[r] On the Monday after Michaelmas day, to master Ruffinus,[s] archdeacon of Cleveland, 200 marks, in part payment of the debt that we owe to the merchants of Paris, contracted for the business of our church and ourself in the court of Rome, and, also, an order to N. de Wodeford to pay 350 marks for the same purpose. Nov. 3. To Sir Wm. d'Aubeny, knight, a robe of the value of 20s., and another to Roger Huse.[t] Nov. 9. To Hugh Everard, our clerk, 310*l.* 10s. 4d.,

[q] There is a valuable paper on the history of these foreign merchants and their dealings with England in the Archæol., xxviii., 207-326.

[r] Blockley, co. Worcester. In the fifty-fourth of Henry III. bishop Giffard was allowed to have a fair there (Thomas's Worcester, 136).

[s] Ruffinus died this year.

[t] Henry Hoese was one of the barons who fought against Henry III. He had lands in the counties of Wilts,

towards the expenses of our hospice. Dec. 9. To Paulinus, the Roman jester, 5 marks of our gift. To dame Alice,[u] our sister, 5 marks. Dec. 28. To Hugh de Cantilupe,[v] our precentor at York, 60*l*.

1268, Feb. 10. To the merchants for 21 casks of wine, bought at Hull,[w] 50*l*. 6s. 8d. April 12. To our valet, Richard de Button[x], for the expenses of our hospice, 80*l*. Apr. 27. To Ancherus, the cardinal,[y] 80 marks. May 6. To Henry le Waleys and Philip le Taillur, 100*l*. for wine; to Stephen le Munden, 26*l*. 13s. 4d., for jewels;[z] to Robert Neveracom, 73s. 4d. for wine; to Robert de Mumpaillars, 33s. 6d. for the debts of dame Sibilla Giffard our mother; to Anketill, the mercer, 10*l*. 8s. 4d. for cloth bought from him at Paris; to Edmund, the baker, at London, 6*l*. 13s. 4d. for corn; to Simon de Insula,[a] 40s. to repair our houses in London. June 7. To Philip, our constable at Oxford, for the expenses of Edmund de Mortimer,[b] 20*l*.; to my lord, the earl of Norfolk, for a palfrey and a saddle for his

Kent, etc. (Dugd. Bar., i., 623). In 1290 a Henry Hose was constable of Porchester castle (Rot. Parl., i., 25.)

[u] Alice de Mandeville, who is mentioned afterwards.

[v] A member of the noble family of Cantilupe. An executor of the will of Walter de Cantilupe, bishop of Hereford (Thomas's Worcester, 136), archdeacon of Gloucester 1256-1284 (Le Neve, iii., 77), rector of Stewkley, Bucks, 1246-1271 (Lipscombe's Bucks, iii., 472. MSS. Harl., 6950, 80 *b*). In 1285 Mr. Hugh de Cantilupe, a dignitary in Hereford cathedral, being dead, John de Clara, his executor, gave £20 out of his effects for poor scholars at Oxford (Antiq. Univ. Oxon., i., 324).

My readers must understand that these notes do not contain a tithe of what I could say about many of the persons they commemorate.

[w] A great place for wine-merchants. The archbishop had the prisage there, which will be alluded to afterwards.

[x] A kinsman, no doubt, of William de Button, Giffard's predecessor and successor at Bath and Wells. He was precentor of Wells (Cassan's Lives, 134). Cf. Abbrev. Plac., 152. Giffard gave a stall at York to Thomas de Button, afterwards bishop of Exeter (Anglia Sacra, i., 565-6).

William Button, the second, was nephew of his namesake and was Giffard's cousin (Cassan, 141). Giffard had the charge of the temporalities during the vacancy, and on March 8, 1267, he wrote from London to order the bailiffs of the manors, etc., throughout the diocese of Bath and Wells to surrender them to Button, whose appointment had been confirmed (Reg. Giffard, 81). On July 7, Giffard sold to him for 600 marks all the winter-corn on the manors belonging to that see, which he had of the king's gift, having sown it himself (ibid.).

Bishop Button made his will in June, 1275, from which it appears that the archbishop owed him money. Thomas de Button and Roger de Crukes, provost of Wells, were the executors (ibid.).

[y] A Roman cardinal, to whom the pope gave the stall of Wetwang at York. He resigned it, and a pension of 80, and subsequently 100, marks per annum was granted to him.

[z] "Jocalia" may be more appropriately translated ornaments.

[a] In 1265 Simon de Insula was presented by Henry III. to the living of Thornfagan (Reg. Giffard, Bath and Wells).

[b] I do not know who this person was. Edmund de Mortimer, a powerful baron, had a son Edmund who was rector of Hodnet (Dugd. Bar., i., 138). Edmund, son of Roger de Mortimer, was made treasurer of York in 1265 (Fœd., i., 458, and Reg. Giffard). Oxford castle had been in Giffard's custody.

fee at our translation,[c] 5 marks and a half; to Hugh de Babington to buy a robe "et penulas" for the use of our mother, 4*l.* 5s. 5d.; to James de Longeton to buy coffers and certain other necessaries for dame Alice de Mandevill, 28s. 9d.; a release to our valet, Walter le Barber, of his account of 100 marks which he carried for us to Paris when we were elected to the see of Bath and Wells.[d] July 20. To our beloved sister, dame Alice de Mandevill,[e] 10 marks, and to dame Matilda de Tywe,[f] 10 marks. Aug. 16. To Gilbert, our steward at Norton, 55s. 5d., which he has expended at our order for the staying of our dear sister, dame Matilda,[g] at Norton from the feast of St. Dunstan to that of SS. Marcellinus and Peter. Oct. 1. To our valet, R. de Ascoc', 83*l.* at St. Botulph's fair. Oct. 31. To Philip le Taillur and Henry le Waleys, citizens of London, 236*l.*

1269, March 2. To the friars preachers of Gloucester, two quarters of corn, and one quarter to a woman at Gloucester. March 4. To the bailiff of Norton, 28s. as a gift, and for the pigs which we had of him at Wykham. March 27. For the expenses of masters G. de Sancto Leofardo[h] and H. de Brandeston[i] and J. de Wudeford, chaplain, 9*l.* 10s.; to the clerks officiating in the church of York on Easter day in our presence, 18s. April 2. To Hugh de Babington, 100*l.* to lay out for us at St. Ives' fair. April 9. To Simon, bailiff of Cawood, 10*l.* to buy stock. April 20. To the dean of York, 120*l.*, which we borrowed of him for the king's use.[j] June 1. To Hugh de

[c] The earl marshal required a palfrey caparisoned as his fee.

[d] Giffard was consecrated at Notre Dame in 1266.

[e] An unnoticed sister of the archbishop. In 1279 Edmund de Mandeville resigned the stall of Stanwick at Ripon (Reg. Wickwaine). In 1301 bishop Giffard left 40s. to Edm. de M., a friar minor (Thomas, 80). Cf. Dugd. Bar., i., 206.

[f] John and Gilbert de Tywe were canons of York in 1241. In 1225 Sir John de Tywa, knight, presented Gilbert de Tywa to the living of Wathtunestre, dioc. Lincoln (MSS. Harl., 6950, 43 *b*).

[g] In 1301 bishop Giffard left to the church of Worcester a vestment which had been given to him by his sister dame Mabel Giffard, abbess of Shaftesbury, and he gave to her 20 "scutella" of silver and as many "salsaria" for the use of her monastery, a pot or pitcher of silver for wine, and another for water, etc. (Thomas's Worcester, appendix, 78-9).

[h] Official of the court of York (Reg. Giffard). On Oct. 22, 1274, Mr. G. de S. Leofardo had the archbishop's letters authorizing him to borrow 60 marks for the business of Mr. G. (ibid.). In 4th Edw. I., he, Thomas de Munkegate, official of the court of York, and Mr. Simon de Clervaus, etc., were in trouble for hearing matters not relating to wills (Rot. Hundred., i., 108). He held many pieces of preferment, and was bishop of Chichester, 1288-1305.

[i] Dean of Sarum, archdeacon of Dorset and bishop of Salisbury in 1287 (Prynne, iii., 359. Cassan, 197, etc.).

[j] On Feb. 6, 54th Henry III., the king acknowledges that the archbishop has lent him £120 in his great need. The sum of £20 has been repaid out of the profits of our mint, and we promise to pay the rest soon (Reg. Giffard, 76 *b*). Giffard, it will be seen, was obliged to borrow the money of the dean. He was frequently employed in raising supplies for the king.

Babington, 553*l.* to pay our debts. June 7. To Fr. Th. Thulus 20 marks for a palfrey; to dame S. de Heriz[k] three oaks from our woods at Sherwood.[l] June 25. An order to the bailiff of Chirchden to pay to Roger the miller of Oxford 20s. to provide necessaries for our kinsman William de Grenefeud[m] at Oxford, whilst he is studying there, because it would be difficult for us to send money to him on account of the perils of the ways. July 23. To Richard de Button, our valet, 20*l.* for the use of master William de Bolynton.[n] Sept. 22. To Wm. le Escoc' and Wm. le Waren', of Pontefract, 27*l.* 10s. for 11 casks of wine. Sept. 24. To William de Burdeaus, 32*l.* 8s. 8d., to Peter le Gascoyn, 72s., and to Galfrid de Maund, 4*l.* for wines bought of them. Nov. 25. To Gregory, prior of the friars of Mount Carmel at York, 30s. for certain things which we have ordered him to procure. Dec. 1. To Reyner, citizen and merchant of Florence, 200 marks.

1270, Jan. 16. To R. de Ascoc' the monies which Wm. Suwell has laid by, *i.e.*, 52*l.* of the temporalities, and 30*l.* which Clement, our clerk, placed with him out of the synodals, etc., for the expenses of our hospice. Feb. 10. An order to pay 200 marks to the merchants to expedite our affairs in the court of Rome "ut usurarum voraginem vitemus ad præsens." Feb. 19. To Simon, bailiff of Sherburn, 200 marks towards the expenses of our hospice. Feb. 27. To Mr. W. le Rus,[o] sub-dean of Wells, and the other executors of J., once sub-dean of Wells, 20*l.* for goods belonging to the said J., bought for our use. April 14. To Robert de Ascoc', 100s. from the goods of persons who have died intestate, for the use of our house. May 25. To Reyner de Luk, or Thomas his deputy, merchant of Lucca, 200 marks which we had of him at London for the expenses of our hospice. July 11. To Baldwin de Frivil,[p] our nephew, 60s.; to two valets

[k] In 1244 Jollan de Nevill paid 20 marks to the king for his leave to marry Sara, late wife of John Heriz, who seems to have died in 1241 (Exc. e Rot. Fin., i., 363, 426. Dugd. Bar., i., 685). Sarah, daughter and heiress of Sir John de Heriz, married Sir Robert Pierpoint, temp. Edw. II. (Coll. Top., viii., 346). Ab. Rot. Orig., i., 19.

[l] There are several notices of Sherwood in Giffard's register. Some one is excommunicated for taking a hawk's nest. The deer, however, were the chief care on the scene of the adventures of Robin Hood and his companions. Cf. Prynne's Coll., iii., 294.

"They were outlaws, 'tis well known,
And men of a noble blood;
And many a time was their valour shewn
In the forrest of merry Sheerwood."

[m] A very valuable entry. It refers, no doubt, to William de Greenfield, a kinsman of Giffard, and afterwards archbishop of York. Giffard, it seems, educated his youthful relation at Oxford.

[n] The archbishop's proctor at Rome.

[o] On Oct. 20, 1265, the subdeanery of Wells was given to Mr. W. le Rus, the prebend of Buckland, ibid., to John de Holteby, the prebend of Holecombe to Roger, seneschal of my lord of Exeter, but he refused it, and then it was given "in crast. S. Clem." to Mr. Wm. archdeacon S. Sereni in the church of Quercy (Reg. Giffard, as bishop of Bath and Wells at York, 70 *b*).

[p] An account of this family in Dugd.

of the earl of Warwick bringing deer to Scrooby . . . . ; to the messenger of my lord of Worcester,[q] 2s.; to J. Giffard, 60*l.*; to Stephen de Cormille for J. Giffard,[r] 66*l.* 13s. 4d.; to our cook, for his wages, 20s.; to A. Giffard, 20s.; to the valet of R. de Monteforti[s] at Henby, by the hands of H. Peverel, 13s. 4d.; to the messenger of my lord Octobonus,[t] 12d.; to repair our houses at London, 15*l.* 12s. 8d.; to the recluse at Doncaster, 6s. 8d.; to Spirioc going to the Holy Land, 12d.; to two recluses at Blyth, 12d.; to Bissop de Craucumb, 18d.; to a poor man at Wikham, 12d.; to R., our almoner, to buy shoes, 4s. 8d.; to friar William de Hothum,[u] 26s. 8d.; to the friars minors of Nottingham, 10s.; to a lame clerk at Iveden, 2s. Oct. 5. To our beloved nephew, Robert de Escoc',[v] 20*l.* to lay out for us in the fair of St. Botulph; to our nephew Hugh de Babington,[w]

Bar., ii., 103. Cf. Thomas's Worcester, appendix, 79-80. Exc. e Rot. Fin., i., 210, 227, 243, etc. Coll. Top., iv. 248.

[q] The archbishop's brother. The earl of Warwick was William de Beauchamp, who had just succeeded to the title (Dugd. Bar., i., 227). In his will, made in 1296, he left to his countess a cup which the bishop of Worcester gave him (Test. Vet., 52).

[r] Sir John Giffard of Brimmesfield, a kinsman of the archbishop, a soldier and statesman, of whom there is an account in Dugd. Bar., i., 501. In 1271 he carried off and married a noble lady, Matilda Longspe, and paid a fine of 300 marks for espousing her (Fœd., i., 488). He married, secondly, Alice Maltravers, and, thirdly, Margaret de Neville (Fœd., i., 663), by whom he had a son, Sir John Giffard. The father died at Boyton, 27th Edw. I. On "die sabb. p. f. S. Mich.," 1271, Sir Peter de Mauley, kt., pays to archbishop Giffard 20*l.*, part of the debt he owed to Sir J. Giffard, who made it over to him (Reg. Giffard, 72 *b*). In 1301 bishop Giffard left to John Giffard, his nephew, 10 marks; to dame Margaret de Neville, sometime wife of Sir John Giffard, his niece, a cup, etc. (Thomas's Worcester, appendix, 79). Ab. Rot. Orig., i., 107.

[s] A relation, probably, of the celebrated earl.

[t] A well-known officer of the papal court. During the contention between the king and his barons he took refuge in the Tower, and was rescued by the archbishop of York and others. The date of this is uncertain (Knyghton, 2438, 2455). In 1269 there is a letter from Ottobonus to the archbishop of York about the disme granted by the king to the pope (Wilkins, ii., 21). There is much mystery about the war with the barons. On Dec. 14, 1264, the archbishop of York was one of those appointed by Henry III. (then a prisoner) to treat with Simon de Montfort (Fœd., i., 449). When the rebellion was suppressed, Giffard, then bishop of Bath and Wells, was one of those who arranged about the forfeited lands (Dugd. Bar., i., 759).

[u] Some account of this great man will be given afterwards.

[v] In 1301 bishop Giffard left to Hugh de Escoce 10*l.* and armour, and a legacy to Joan his wife (Thomas's Wor., 80).

[w] Of Burghley, co. York, and Rolleston, Notts. Constable of Nottingham castle and sheriff of Notts and Derbyshire in 1271 (Coll. Top., viii., 313. Rot. Hundred., ii., 312), sheriff of Huntingdonshire, 23rd Edw. I. (Parl. Writs., i., 267), Inq. p. m. 25th Edw. I., dying seised of the manor of Burghley (Cal. Inq., p.m., i., 133), Richard de Babington being his son and heir (Abbrev. Rot. Orig., 95). In 1301 bishop Giffard left to Richard de Babington 10 marks and a horse (Thomas's Worcester, 79). On 12th September, 1312, archbishop Greenfield granted to Lucy, widow of Richard de Babington, who held of him the manor of Burghley by knight's service, the marriage of Hugh, son and heir of the said Richard (Reg. Greenfield). Cf. Coll. Top., viii., 313-15. Rot. Hundr., ii., 319. Thoroton's Notts.

11*l.* 18s. 3d., to expedite our business at Nottingham castle. Nov. 4. To the prior of Shelford three oaks from our wood of Sherwood, for timber. Nov. 7. At Nottingham, to Stephen de Norwich, of our alms, 6*l.* 2s. 9d., of the surplus of his account for the year when he was our almoner; to R., our chaplain, 4*l.* to announce our election; to friar H. de Misterton, 13s. 4d.; to our barber 2s. of our gift; to a certain clerk of Hedon to buy a shirt, 2s.; to the nuns of Wilberfosse and Brunnum (Nunburnholme), 20s. each; to the friars preachers and minors[x] on the day of the Nativity, B.M.V., 13s. 4d. each; to friar William de Hotham at St. Oswald's, 2s.; to the recluse of Eland, 3s.; to the nuns of Kirkeleye, 5s.; to the nuns of Thikkeheued, 3s.; to the friars preachers of Donestaple, 2s.; to J. de Neville, 133*l.* 6s. 8d. for the marriage of his wife; to Simon de Insula, 28*l.* 6s. 8d. to repair our houses and quay at London; to dame — Peverel 113s. 4d. from her son's church;[y] to William de Grenefeld 2s. for his expenses from London to Oxford; to Edward, the king's son, 66*l.* 13s. 4d. of our gift;[z] to Lucas de Luk, 7*l.* 7s. for silks;[a] to J. de Weston, 40s. for a silken zone for A. de Manndevill; to master J., called Le Romeyn,[b] 13*l.* 6s. 8d. of our debt at Paris; to the clerks officiating in the church of York at our mass on the festival of the Nativity, B.M.V., 18s.; to Agatha Giffard, 27s. 4d.; to two minstrels, 40s.; to master J. de Craucumb,[c] 40s. Nov. 14. To Roger Dousing, 8*l.*, and to

[x] Each of the four orders of friars had a monastery in York, and the Minorites an important one. The wardenship of York had within it seven houses, —York, Doncaster, Lincoln, Boston, Beverley, Scarborough, and Grimsby. Martin de Barton was the first custos of the Franciscans at York, Eustacius de Merc coming after him. Two ministers provincial of the order in England, John Mardiston and John Tysyngton, were buried at York (Mon. Francisc., 27, 43, 561, 579, 321). In 1277 bishop Giffard was admitted to the suffrages of the friars minors (Thomas's Worcester, appendix, 35). Cf. Wilkins, i., 762.

[y] I cannot find out to which branch of the Peverels this lady belonged.

[z] No doubt for the crusade on which Edward went, having previously appointed the archbishop one of the guardians of his sons. In 39 Hen. III. the friars minors were ordered to preach in favour of this expedition (Mon. Francisc., 620). There is in Giffard's register a long and very curious list of the *crucesignati* within the diocese of York. On oct., B. M. V. 1275, at Skefling, Sir S. dictus Constabularius, knight, confessed that he had committed adultery with Katherine, wife of Sir John Dentorp, knight, and he was fined 100*l.* The archbishop, in consideration of his contrition, gave him the sign of the cross (Reg. Giffard). We find the culprit in another character on June 26, 1281, when the primate decides in favour of a marriage between him and Catherine, daughter of Philip de Wynelesby (Reg. Wickwaine).

[a] "Pro sericis et sindon."

[b] Afterwards archbishop of York.

[c] A kinsman of the archbishop, and probably a son of Alice de Corneille, sister of Sibilla, who married — Craucombe (Dugd. Bar., i., 502. Hoare's Wiltes, *ut supra*, 201). He was a person of great consequence — archdeacon of the East Riding, canon of Grendale, and incumbent of Feliskirk, dioc. Ebor., and of Gousel (Goxhill), dioc. Lincoln (MSS. Harl., 6951, 19*a*), of Sutbraden in 1265 (Reg. Giffard, bishop of Bath and Wells). He was

Philip de Barton, 12*l.*, which they lent us at the fair of St. Giles at Winchester.

1271, April 2. To a certain writer for each quire[d] that he writes for my lord, 16d. June 2. To the friars preachers of Gloucester,[e] a mark, and two logs of wood for their fire, and to a poor matron there half a quarter of corn.

1274, July 13. To our clerk, E. de Well,[f] 100*l.* to buy goods for us at St. Botulph's fair.[g] August 11. We hear that the friars preachers are going to hold their general chapter at York on the feast B.M.V., an order to provide a banquet for them. Sept. 25. An order to the bailiff at Beverley to buy 13 casks of wine. Nov. 3. To the friars Carmelites of York, two quarters of corn and 30s.

1275, March 7. To Walter, our butler, 19*l.* to buy wine at Hull. To the marshal of our horses, six colts from our stud at Beverley. An order to the bailiff of that place to educate John Aucher[h] and his two companions, in the school of Beverley, providing them with every necessary, and spending 30s. upon three robes for them.

Archbishop Giffard died at York on the 25th of April, 1279,[i] and was interred in the minster, probably in the choir. When that portion of the church was rebuilt, the remains of Giffard and of several other archbishops were removed by the pious

summoned to parliament on several occasions, and in 26th of Edward I. had the temporary charge of the great seal at York. In 1295 he went to Rome in the king's business, and is called "a clerke gode and wys" (Parl. Writs, vol. i.. Cal. Rot. Pat., 59. Fœd., i., 817. Langtoft, ii., 262). He died in 1308, and there was a chantry at which he was commemorated in York minster (Fabric Rolls, 299).

[d] "Quaternus." Cf. glossary to "The Priory of Finchale," 440.

[e] Giffard resided occasionally at his manors, co. Gloucester. In 1217 king John gave archbishop Gray timber to build his houses at Escott and Otinton (Rot. Claus., 297).

[f] Edward de Well, vicar of South Kirkby, ordained deacon at York, in vigilia Paschæ, 1268 (Reg. Giffard).

[g] There is an account of an extraordinary scene at this famous fair in 1285 in Knyghton, col. 2466, and in Trivet, 266.

[h] Robert le Archer married Alice, niece of Alice de Craucombe. In 1244 Alice le Archer fined to the king for the custody of the lands of her heirs. In 1253 Archer's heir was a ward of Sibilla de Giffard (Dugd. Bar., i., 502. Exc. e Rot. Fin., i., 329, 411, 419; ii., 168). In 1301 bishop Giffard leaves 40s. to his niece, dame Margaret Aucher of Shaftesbury, 10*l.* and armour to his nephew, Sir Henry Aucher, knight, and 10 marks and armour to his nephew, Richard Aucher (Thomas's Worcester, appendix, 79). Abbrev. Rot. Orig., i., 3, 5, 6.

On Nov. 28, 1315, archbishop Greenfield, another kinsman, orders his receiver at Southwell to pay 20*l.* to dame Margaret Auchier, a nun at Shaftesbury, elected abbess of that house, and directs him to pay her every possible attention if she stays at the manor of Southwell (Reg. Greenfield.)

[i] MSS. Cotton, Vitellius, A, ii., 111. The date is doubtful. Wikes (Gale, ii., 108) says that Giffard died on the Vigil of St. Gregory soon after Easter. Peter de Ickham, on April 22 (Le Neve, iii., 103, and Reg. Sacr. Angl., 44). Stubbs, on April 29 (col. 1726). Inq. p. m., 27 April (Godwin, *n. e.*, 682. Le Neve, iii., 103).

Thoresby to the presbytery immediately before the great east window, and placed under monuments which had been prepared for them. It was there that Leland saw them when he came on his antiquarian tour into the North in the reign of Henry VIII.,[j] and they were there in the eighteenth century.

After Giffard's decease, on the 28th of April, the king committed the custody of the see, during the vacancy, to Thomas de Normanvill and Mr. Henry de Newark, who was afterwards archbishop. Giffard was in debt to the king, but his property was not seized, as the bishop of Bath and Wells and Nicholas Wudeford pledged themselves that everything should be paid.[k] One of the executors of Giffard's will was his brother Godfrey, bishop of Worcester. On the 21st of July, 1280, archbishop Wickwaine made a general order to his bailiffs, directing them to assist the executors in gathering in the effects of his predecessor. They were released from their trust on the 2nd of December, 1281.[l]

Archbishop Giffard died seised of great estates. He possessed, in a public or private capacity, manors in the counties of Wilts (Boyton), Somerset, Hereford, Gloucester, Southants, Notts, Oxford, and York.[m] His brother, Godfrey Giffard, bishop of Worcester, was found to be his heir.[n] The favour which the archbishop shewed to this kinsman excited some little murmuring and ill feeling. In 1270 one Adam de Filliby complained at Rome of the conduct of the Northern primate in making his brother archdeacon of York when he was only in minor orders, and in giving him many benefices without a dispensation, when he was deficient not only in clerical rank but in learning. The archdeaconry seems to have been the only thing that Godfrey Giffard held in Yorkshire, with the exception of the living of Adlingflete, to which he was presented by John de Eville in 1267.[o] I find, however, that he had much preferment in the South.[p] Godfrey Giffard was a great man both in

[j] Lel. Itin. The antiquary gives a rough note of the inscription, "Walter Gisfart obiit vii Kal. Maii"—*i. e.*, Apr. 25.

[k] Reg. Wickwaine, 41. Prynne's Coll., iii., 224. Abbrev. Rot. Orig., i., 33. The bishop of Bath and Wells was Robert Burnell, sometime archdeacon of York. In 22nd of Edw. I. letters of protection were granted to Mr. Nicholas de Wodeford, rector of Flatbury and Westbury (Prynne's Coll., iii., 599).

[l] Reg. Wickwaine.

[m] Cal. Inq. p. m., i., 67. Abbrev. Rot. Orig., 33.

[n] Thoroton's Notts, 390. Dugd. Bar., i., 501.

[o] Reg. Giffard.

[p] Coll. archdeaconry of Barum 6th November, 1265, res. 1267 (Le Neve, i., 405), canon of Wells (Newcourt, i., 59), rector of the greater mediety of the church of Atleburgh (Blomefield's Norfolk, i., 523), April 28, 1267, collated to the archdeaconry of York (Reg. Giffard). Nov. 1, 1266, installed to the living of Mells (Reg. Giffard, as bishop of Bath and Wells, at York). April 3, the archbishop gives him leave to borrow 60 marks in the court of Rome (Reg. Giffard). John Giffard

church and state. He was a justice itinerant, chancellor of the exchequer, and lord high chancellor of England. He presided over the see of Worcester from 1268 to 1301, with many vicissitudes of fortune. The will of the bishop is a remarkable document, and contains more than one allusion to his deceased brother.[q] He bequeaths to the church of Worcester his best mitre which archbishop Giffard had given him, with amice, stole and maniple, *en suite*, all covered with very precious pearls. To the altar of the holy cross in that cathedral he left a chasuble of red samite of his brother's gift.[r] To his brother, Sir William Giffard, he gave the ring of his chapel, a gemmel with a ruby and an emerald which the archbishop had left to him as an heirloom, five ancient and costly rings on a silk riband which belonged to his ancestors at Boyton, together with four bugle-horns at Boyton which were used as drinking cups, one of which had a foot of silver.[s] To his nephew, Mr. John de Ebroycis (Evreux),[t] he bequeathed a mitre covered over with pearls, which had once belonged to his uncle, the Northern pri-

was his nephew and heir (Abbrev. Rot. Orig., i., 120).

[q] Printed in the valuable collection of records in the appendix to the History of Worcester, by Dr. Thomas, pp. 77-81.

[r] In the Anglia Sacra (i., 494) it is stated that archbishop Giffard bequeathed to Worcester cathedral, "insignia capellæ pretiosa."

[s] These striking and beautiful objects were frequently the title-deeds of estates. Such was the noble horn of Ulphus, which is still preserved at York. There are others at Pusey and Queen's college, Oxford. Dr. Whitaker gives an engraving of one in the possession of lord Ribblesdale (History of Craven, ed. 1812, 36). In 1612 John Ireland, Esq., of the Hutt in Lancashire, bequeaths to Gilbert his brother and heir "my plate of silver and guilt, one chaine of gold, one sealinge ringe or signett of armes that was my father's, together with the Horne of Crotonn" (Reg. Test. apud Ebor.). Henry I. gave to the church of Carlisle the tithes of a part of the forest of Inglewood "et ecclesiam inde feoffavit per quoddam cornu eburneum quod dedit ecclesiæ predictæ, et quod adhuc (1290) habet" (Rot. Parl., i., 38).

[t] A son of — Giffard, the archbishop's sister, by William de Ebroicis, who was killed at the battle of Evesham. July 24, 1286, licence to him to be absent from his stalls at Southwell and Ripon, for three years, to study (Reg. Romanus). He resigned the prebend of Studley at Ripon in 1297, in which year he was holding the stall of Oxton, part ii., at Southwell (Le Neve, iii., 449. Reg. Newark). Archdeacon of Gloucester 1288-1295 (Le Neve, iii., 77). In 22nd of Edward I. he had letters of protection as archdeacon, canon of Ripon and Southwell and rector of Kempsey (Prynne, iii., 598). On July 23, 1295, bishop Giffard gave him the living of Tredington (Anglia Sacra, i., 517). Cf. Thomas's Worcester, 142, and appendix, 50. Angl. Sacr., ii., 509.

The family of Brun were connected with the archbishop by the marriage of Albreda, daughter and co-heiress of Walter de Cormeiles, with Richard le Brun (Dugd. Bar., i., 424). The primate gave the living of Schipwit (Skipwith) to N. de Brun his kinsman, and the prebend of Osbaldwick to R. de Brun his chaplain (Reg. Giffard). On Sept. 3, 1291, archbishop Romanus gave a pension of 5 marks per annum to William, son of William le Brun, till he provided him with a benefice (Reg. Romanus). In 1295 Mr. W. Brun was rector of Lake, dioc. Worcester (Angl. Sacr., i., 517). Archbishop Greenfield made Edmund le Brun succentor canonicorum at York.

mate, in the hope, perhaps, that it might sometime rest upon his brow. To the archbishop of Canterbury he gave a ring with a lion graven on it set with emeralds, to descend to his successors in the see. The testator then mentions, singularly enough, that he had received the sign of the cross in token that he had devoted himself to the conquest of the Holy Land, and he now leaves the sum of 50*l.* to equip a knight who is to cross the seas in his stead on that adventurous voyage.

William de Wickwaine seems to have been a native of the South, but of his parents and early history there is nothing known.[u] He occurs to us for the first time on the 4th of February, 1262, when he was instituted by the bishop of Lincoln to the rectory of Ivinghoe, in Buckinghamshire. He was then chancellor of the church of York, and held both these pieces of preferment till he became archbishop.[v] On St. Alban's day, the 22nd of June, 1279, the chapter of York met to choose a new diocesan;[w] eighteen of the votes were given to the chancellor, two to Thomas de Corbridge, who was afterwards archbishop, and one to Hugh de Evesham, a brother canon. This was the celebrated physician who obtained a place in the Sacred College in 1281. Wickwaine was of course elected, and obtained the royal assent to his appointment on the 4th of July.[y] He then went abroad to seek the pall. Nicholas III. referred the consideration of the matter to the cardinals of St. Mark and St. Mary in Porticu, and the decision of the chapter was thrown over, not from any flaw in their nominee, but apparently from some defect in the mode of procedure which they had adopted. The pope, however, solved the difficulty by appointing Wickwaine to the archbishopric of his own authority, as he had the majority of votes, and that the see might be no longer vacant. He consecrated him at Viterbo on the 19th of September, 1279, and wrote a long letter on the same day to Edward I. acquainting him with what he had done.[z] On the 28th of October the

[u] In 1282 Walter de Wykewone, cellarer of Winchcombe, became abbat of that house (Angl. Sacra, i., 506). There are several places called Wicken in the South of England.

[v] MSS. Cotton, Claudius, B, iii., 89. Lipscombe's Bucks, iii., 393. Le Neve, iii., 163.

[w] MSS. Cotton, Vitellius, A, ii., 111 *b.* Stubbs, col. 1727. Licence to elect an archbishop was granted May 7, 1279 (Le Neve, iii., 103).

[x] Prynne's Coll., iii., 225.

[y] Le Neve, iii., 103.

[z] Prynne, *ut supra.* Vitellius, *ut supra.* Reg. Wickwaine. Ann. Waverl., apud Gale, ii., 234, where he is erroneously called treasurer. Wikes,

king restored the temporalities of his see, and the new prelate was enthroned at York at the festival of Christmas.[a] A contemporary writer represents him as stern in disposition, careful in his habits, and emaciated in his personal appearance, yet a good and a most conscientious man.[b] The records of Wickwaine's life that are still preserved fully verify this description. He was evidently a strict disciplinarian, and the heart of a monk beat under the robes of an archbishop. He is said also to have been a man of learning and education, and to have written a work called the Memoriale.[c]

As soon as Wickwaine arrived in England on his return from the papal court, he came into collision with the archbishop of Canterbury on the old question,—the bearing of his cross erect. It was set up, according to ancient custom, when the travellers were in the middle of the sea and were in English waters, and it was carried in the same position into the province of Canterbury. The missives of the Southern primate had anticipated his arrival. The services were stopped in every parish in which Wickwaine halted; if he had been a heretic he could not have been treated worse, and, wherever he went, he could find no market, for the sentence of excommunication was hurled against any one who ventured to sell to him. But the worst has not yet been told. Adam de Hales, the official of the archbishop of Canterbury, and his party, made an assault upon Wickwaine and his friends. If the obnoxious symbol had not been hastily removed, it would have been broken into fragments. They abused and reviled the intruders to their hearts' content, affirming that they had their master's authority for what they did, and that he would bear them out. A large number of armed men were meditating a more serious assault upon Wickwaine when he entered London, but the archbishop was forewarned, and reached the court by a different route, and he there obtained the temporalities of York.[d] The king called Peckham, the Southern primate, to account for his violence, obliging him to recall his orders to his officials, and charging him to be more wary for the future.[e]

For the next five years Wickwaine was most actively and usefully employed in the laborious charge of his diocese. He seems to have devoted himself entirely to that work; for with the exception of his sending his service against the Welsh in 1282, and his being required to demand and collect several

ibid., 108. Trivet, 254. Stubbs, col. 1727. Angl. Sacra, i., 504. Walsingham, apud Camden, 49.

[a] MSS. Cotton, Vitellius, A, ii., 111 b. Le Neve, iii., 103.

[b] Chron. Lanercost, 102.

[c] Bale, Script., cent. x., 42-3. Fuller's Church Hist., book iii., 79.

[d] Reg. Wickwaine. Wilkins, ii., 43, 119. Wikes, apud Gale, ii., 108. Flores Hist., 409. Cotton's Chron., 158.

[e] Prynne's Coll., 235-6.

subsidies from the clergy of his province for the use of the king, we never find his name alluded to in connection with the state.[f] He stayed at home and worked diligently in his province. I find the bishops of Carlisle, Worcester, and Sens assisting him as suffragans on various occasions, but in his care for his flock he seems to have relied almost entirely upon his own exertions. He tried to do his own duty, and expected every one else to copy his example. As I have said before, he was a rigid disciplinarian, and he paid more attention, perhaps, than any other archbishop of York to the monasteries within his diocese. He arranged and carried out a systematic visitation of all that he had the power to reach. The reports of the commissioners have in a few cases only been entered on the register, but that volume contains what is of great importance,—the archbishop's injunctions to each house, based of course upon the result of the inquiries that had been made. These disclose a great laxity of discipline and a considerable falling away from rule and order. I shall give my readers a portrait of the abbat of Selby in December, 1278.

Thomas de Qualle (Whalley), abbat of Selby, does not observe the Benedictine rule; he does not sing mass, nor preach, nor attend chapter, nor keep discipline. He seldom eats in the refectory, and never sleeps in the dormitory. He rarely enters the choir, and scarcely ever hears matins but in his bed. He does not visit the sick. He has his meals before laymen within and without his monastery, and is quarrelsome, hot-tempered, and altogether incorrigible. He has alienated some of the property of his house, and gives its lands to the charge of grooms and ribalds. He is grossly incontinent. He is under sentence of excommunication for not paying the disme to the pope, but, notwithstanding, he comes to the church. He laid violent hands on brothers Robert of York and Thomas of Snaith, drawing blood from them, and he dragged with his own hands William de Stormeworth from the choir of his church. He employed Elias Faunell, a sorcerer, to seek the body of his brother when he was drowned in the Ouse, and gave him a large sum of money. This valuable official was of course removed from his post, but he was allowed to remain in the house, probably as a simple monk. Many months had not elapsed before he broke out of the monastery at night, carrying many things away with him!

In the year 1280 Wickwaine endeavoured to carry his visitation into the North, and to examine into the state of the

[f] Ibid., 275, 285-6, 289, 302. Parl. Writs., i., 11, 224, 228, 233. Wilkins, ii., 41-2. Fœd., i., 538. In February, 1276, he is ordered to excommunicate Llewellyn (Fœd., i., 541. Prynne's Coll., iii., 1212). Fœd., i., 607, 625.

priory of Durham. The prior and the monks most strenuously resisted him. I shall not attempt to lead my readers through the tedious mazes of the dispute, but shall content myself with some of the more salient points in the controversy.[g] The prior was anxious to shelter himself under the wing of the bishop, but the bishop went abroad and left the prior to his fate. He proved himself to be an adept in the art of defence. Wickwaine came to Durham, but he was met at the north gate which led into the priory by the knights of the bishopric, who would not suffer him to enter. Upon this he spoke to the crowd around, and excommunicated all the officials of the diocese. He then turned aside to Lanchester, appointing a day for his return. When the time arrived, the sub-dean of York and Robert de Pickering, who was afterwards dean, came to hold the visitation in the place of their master, but they were stopped upon Elvet bridge, and some partizans of the prior, catching hold of the reins of their horses, would not suffer them to approach. The contest, after this, went on with varying success for the remainder of Wickwaine's life. Either party excommunicated the other. Commissioners were appointed by mutual consent, who did little or nothing. Appeals were made to Rome, but they were of little use. In 1283 the archbishop paid another visit to Durham in the hope of inducing the noncontents to submit to him. The hope was a vain one. He went to the church of St. Nicholas, and after he had addressed the audience he was again on the point of excommunicating the prior and his adherents, when some young fellows of the city terrified him so much by their demeanour that he was obliged to desist. He fled from the church, descending the steps which still lead you towards the river, and, hastening across the Sands, never paused till he found a sanctuary in the neighbouring hospital of Kepier. The ear of his palfrey, oh profane act! was cut off, and its master would have been very roughly handled had not Guischard de Charron and Peter de Thoresby, two officers of the bishop's court, interceded in his behalf. After this he wisely kept away from Durham, and was never able to oblige the prior to submit to him. This resistance rankled in Wickwaine's mind as long as he lived, and it was the wish, as a Durham chronicler tells us, to bring the papal power to bear upon the offenders that induced him to set out in 1284 on that journey to Rome from which he never returned.

The following extracts from archbishop Wickwaine's register will give some idea of his life. In spite of his reputation for

[g] Hist. Dunelm. Scr. Tres, ed. Surtees Society, 58-69. Prynne's Coll., iii., 309. Chron. Lanercost, 120. There are many documents relating to it in Wickwaine's register.

abstinence and parsimony the charges for the maintenance of his household are large.

1279, Dec. 16. A bond to the executors of William Langton, dean of York, for 200 marks, 27*l.*, and 9*l.* for barley-malt sold to us.[h] Dec. 27. A bond to Thomas Guydysion' and the merchants of Lucca for 316 marks. A pension of 20*l.* per annum out of the stall of Knaresbro' to John de Metingham,[i] one of the king's clerks, till he be provided by us with some prebend.

1280, Jan. 16. We are indebted to the executors of Walter Giffard, our predecessor, in the sum of 95*l.* for hard corn *(bladum)* and a stack *(tassum)* of old hay, viz., for the hard corn of Scrooby, 18*l.*, for that of Askham, 43*l.*, for a stack and the corn at Southwell, 34*l.* March 17. A bond for 20*l.* to the executors of dean Langton for twelve dishes, twelve saucers, and two large dishes of silver. On the feast of the Holy Trinity, another bond to them of 6 marks for kitchen utensils, 10*l.* for wax, 16*l.* 6s. 8d. for 7 casks of wine. May 24. The abbat of Furness repays the archbishop 50 marks.[j] August 23. A request to the prior of Birstall to provide for us in his lands beyond the sea two dogs for the chase *(canes perdriarios seu culheros)*, and we will repay him for them. Nov. 14. A bond for 300 marks to Peter de Cestria.[k] Nov. 29. An order to the bailiffs of Otley and Ripon to find provisions for our huntsmen whilst they are within your bailywicks. Nov. 30. An order to the bailiff of Southwell to supply us with geese, hens and other birds against the festival of Christmas. Dec. 7. An order to the same officer to pay 100s. to Simon, our poulterer, for his use; and the bailiff of Beverley

[h] Nov. 8, 1287, the executors of Wickwaine have paid to those of dean Langton 350*l.*, which the archbishop owed them.

[i] On Jan. 20, 1281, he was collated to the prebend of Bole at York, which he held till 1301, when he died (Reg. Wickwaine, etc.). On April 13, 1301, the stall of Weighton was offered to him, but he declined it. He was born at Metingham in Suffolk (Fuller's Worthies, ii., 337), and held a prebend at Darlington in 1292 (Longstaffe's Darlington, 194). He was a great and an upright lawyer, and was justice itinerant, and, in Eyre, a judge in the Common Bench and of Pleas (Dugd. Orig. Jurid., 26, 44. Parl. Writs, *var. loc.*). He and Elias de Beckingham were the only two judges who, in a corrupt age, had the courage to remain honest (Ferne's Lacie's Nobilitie, 120. Fuller, ii., 337). Atterbury, however, charges him with injustice to the clergy, and says, "Look through all our history, and you shall find that wherever the clergy have smarted under any great hardship, some of their own order have been still at the bottom of it" (Rights of Convocation, 358). There is nothing to shew that Metingham injured the clergy in any way.

[j] The abbat was "scolaris et discipulus archiepiscopi" (Hist. Dunelm. Scr. Tres, 62). Cf. Beck's Ann. Furnesienses, 225.

[k] Supposed to have been an illegitimate son of one of the Lacies, earls of Chester. Prebendary of Bugthorpe at York, provost of Beverley, rector of Denford, Whalley and Slaidburn, etc. (Whitaker's Whalley, 50, 59; Whalley Coucher Book, i., 94, etc.; Bridges's Northants, ii., 232, etc.); a justice itinerant and a baron of the Exchequer (Dugd. Chron., 28. Madox, Hist. Exchequer, ii., 322. Foss's Judges, iii., 74). In the 22nd of Ed-

is desired to release the man and dog that he has captured, as Sir Roger Grymet has explained the matter to us.

1281, April 7. At Hornby in Lonsdale, a pension of 10 marks per annum to Mr. Walter le Breton,[l] the king's clerk, till we provide him with a benefice. April 14. A bond for 200 marks to Mr. Robert de Scarthburg,[m] dean of York. April 20. A bond for 120*l.* to Mr. H., archdeacon of Richmond.[n] We have taken, through our men, from the forest of Wervelmor, belonging to the lord Edmund the king's brother, three deer and five fawns. June 1. At Coverham; a bond for 100*l.* to Mr. Simon de Clarevalle,[o] rector of Bulmer. July 8. To Mr. W. de Bolington,[p] our clerk, 100 marks for his expenses to court. July 27. An order to the bailiff of Chirchden to pay his son Henry 52s., which we have given him as a mark of our affection. To Mr. Thomas, chancellor of the church of York, money for his expenses to Rome on behalf of our church.[q] Oct. 16. We have received from Mr. Roger de Holt a Bible which once belonged to Mr. Roger Pepyn.[r] Oct. 28th. An order to the bailiff of Ripon to provide provisions for our huntsman whilst he is in your district.[s] Nov. 17. An order to Wm. de Malton to make things ready for our coiners at York as he had promised. Nov. 19. We have made Mr. P. and Mr. G. Guydon masters of our mint.[t]

1282, Jan. 27. A pension of 10*l.* per annum out of our chamber to our clerk Master Robert de Ros.[u] March 14. To

ward I. he had letters of protection as provost of Beverley and rector of Rudby and Whalley, canon of Lichfield and Hereford, rector of Arksey, Easington and Slaidburn (Prynne, iii., 598-9). No wonder that he could lend money.

[l] The king wrote to ask this favour, Feb. 26, 1281 (Reg. Wickwaine). In 18th Edward I. Walter de Berton, clerk, was in the Tower on a charge of treason for counterfeiting the king's seal (Prynne's Coll., iii., 410). In 24th Edward I. Walter de Berton, rector of Bredon, dioc. Worcester, occ. (Rot. Parl., i., 227).

[m] Robert Ughtred, of Scarborough, dean of York from 1279 to 1290, a statesman and a great man. I shall not now describe his chequered life.

[n] Henry Newark, afterwards archbishop of York.

[o] A son of Robert de Claris Vallibus, citizen of York, by Eva, daughter of William Fairfax (Longstaffe's Darlington). In 18th Edward I. he, as official of the archdeaconry of Cleveland, was in trouble in the king's courts (Prynne's Coll., iii., 438). On 22nd April, 1301, he was allowed to be non-resident on the rectory of Lythe (which he had held for many years) on account of ill-health (Reg. Corbridge).

[p] He was subsequently rector of North Ferriby, near Hull.

[q] Thomas Corbridge, afterwards archbishop.

[r] Sub-dean of York. He died in 1267.

[s] By a clause in the forest charter of 1297 foresters were forbidden to take oats, etc., for themselves (Statutes of the Realm, i., 120).

[t] For an account of the York mint I must refer my readers to the able work of my kind friend, Mr. Davies. Cf. Rot. Claus., 361. Plac. de Quo Warranto, 8-9th Edw. I., 198. There is a list of the officers of the York mint, 32nd of Henry III., in Chron. Joh. Oxenedes, 322. Hugh de Sampson was mint-master in the time of archbishop Gray (Reg. Wickwaine).

[u] Prebendary of St. Pancras, London, a stagiarius of that church and arch-

our treasurer, Walter de Gloucestre,[v] 36*l.* 7s. 9d. for 15 casks of wine at Hull. March 30. To Walter, the goldsmith of York, 6*l.* 9s. 3d., the remnant due to him for 12 silver bowls, and for making them and the bowls of maser. April 16. To Sir Richard de Baunfeld, our seneschal, 20 marks for the expenses of our advocates *(narratores)* and servants in the next parliament at London, and for other matters of ours there. May 16. The bailiff of Ripon is ordered to pay 10*l.* to Walter, our clerk, to make provision against Pentecost. Oct. 7. To Mr. Robert de Scartheburg, dean of York, 100 marks. Nov. 19. To the warden and brothers of the friars minors of Beverley, 10 marks. Nov. 23. To John Roual, chaplain of the chapel of Thorp, 70s. for his stipend and for lights, for the term of St. Martin, 1281.[w] Nov. 26. To the friars preachers of Beverley, and their prior, 10 marks. Dec. 11. To dan Wm. de Capella, 20*l.* to make purchases for us in Cleveland.

1283, Jan. 4. To Robert de Exon,[x] our brother, 17 marks and a half which are in arrear for his payment in Bristol. Jan. 8. To Elias Drury, valet of Hamundy Box,[y] merchant, 33*l.* 5s. 9d. for wine bought of him. Jan. 15. To dan Simon, our receiver at York, 6*l.* 13s. 4d. for "jocalia," which we have bought, and 39s. 8d. laid out in "jocalia," and presents made to my lord of Dublin,[z] etc. Jan. 23. To William de Bolington, clerk, 100 marks to expedite our business in the court of Rome. Feb. 18. To Mr. H., archdeacon of Richmond, 200*l.* for goods

deacon of London, rector of Much Hadham (Newcourt, i., 60, 829-31). 22nd Edward I. he had letters of protection as rector of Hadham (Prynne, iii., 594).

[v] A great man. Canon of Beverley prebendary of Apesthorpe, archdeacon of York, and incumbent of Normanton on Sore. He held the livings of Norton com. Oxon. and Woodston com. Hunts (MSS. Harl., 6950, 37, 78), and was dean of Chichester (Le Neve, i., 256), eschaetor south of Trent, 1302-7 (Parl. Writs., i., 132, 379. Chron. Thorn, col. 2006), and frequently employed in state affairs. He was sometime archbishop Wickwaine's receiver. Cf. Foss's Judges, iii., 275.

[w] Cf. Prynne's Coll., iii., 674. He was appointed to Thorp on July 26, 1280 (Reg. Wickwaine).

[x] The only occasion on which this person is mentioned.

[y] A merchant of London, and a member of an honourable family in the city which was connected at the same time with Hull. Hamund Box was a sheriff of London in 1292 (Mon. Francisc., 503). July 22, 1289, licence for two priests to be chosen by Hamundus Box, citizen of London, to do service in our chapel at Hull for the soul of Robert de la Grave as long as the said Hamund chooses (Reg. Romanus). March 14, 1309, licence for John Boox, of Hull, to have service within his mause there (Reg. Greenfield).

[z] John de Darlington, a friar preacher, was the author of a Concordance, etc. (Chron. Lan., 156). He was confessor to Henry III., and in 1277 he was made collector of the disme in England against the rule of his order (Walsingham, apud Camden, 47). He was a friend of Wickwaine, and is mentioned in his register. He was consecrated archbishop of Dublin at Waltham on Aug. 27, 1279, by the archbishop of Canterbury, and died near London in 1284 (Contin. Fl. Wigorn., ii., 222, 231). Prynne's Coll., iii., 1230. Cotton's Fasti Eccl. Hib., ii., 12.

bought of him. Feb. 27. To Walter, the goldsmith, 111s. for two silver cups bought of him at Christmas. March 8. A pension of 50 marks per annum from our chamber to Gerard de Grandison,[a] nephew of Sir Otho de Grandison, counsellor of our lord the king. April 14. To Alexander de Kirketon, our seneschal, 100 marks to lay out for us at the fair of St. Ives. June 14. To Walter de Gloucester, our treasurer, 97*l.* 16s. 6½d. for wines. June 15. Twenty marks to him to buy silver pitchers. June 22. To Sir John de Eyvil,[b] 100*l.* for his expenses in making our service in Wales. July 1. To Mr. H., archdeacon of Richmond, 300 marks to advance our business in the court of Rome. August 9. To Robert, rector of Sutton-on-Derwent, 20 marks towards the reparation "pontis belli."

1284, March 6. A mandate against the ribalds and beggars who wander about our diocese, especially among the monasteries, seeking alms and pretending to be our messengers or kinsmen.[c] April 24. To Mr. John Clarell,[d] 100*l.* to buy robes for us at the fair of St. Ives. July 22. To Calmo, our baker, 180 marks to make purchases for us at the same place. August 11. To the prior of the friars preachers at York, 100s. of our gift. August 25. To Nicholas, of our chamber, 20*l.* to spend at St. Botulph's fair. Sept. 10. To master William, the notary, 40*l.* for the expenses of our clerks at Warwick. Nov. 25. To Mr. W. de Bolington, our clerk, 200 marks to advance our business at Rome. Dec. 13. To Alexander, our seneschal, 12*l.* 6s. 6d. to buy sheep. Dec. 14. To master Bartholomew carrying 20*l.* for the use of our lord the cardinal.

[a] He became prebendary of Apesthorpe in November, 1283. His brother Otho was recommended for a stall at York in 1301. It is impossible to give an account here of this noble and illustrious family, and of the great services which several members of it rendered to the state and to letters. The name of John de Grandison, bishop of Exeter, is quite enough to make it famous.

[b] An account of him and his family, which resided co. Notts, is in Dugd. Bar., i., 593. On 25th October, 1312, an oratory was allowed to dame Matilda de Eyvill in the manor of Galmeton for three years (Reg. Greenfield). Sir John was a justiciar (Prynne's Coll., iii., 412). He seems to have taken the part of the barons in the war with Henry III. (Abbrev. Plac., 227).

[c] These quæstores or brevigeri were very troublesome, and the archbishops of York frequently denounced them.

[d] Prebendary of Norwell Overhall at Southwell from 1256 till he died in 1293 (Le Neve, iii., 437). In 3rd Edward I. he and Henry le Vavasour were in trouble for making a park there (Rot. Hundred., ii., 311). In 1258-9 he was a messenger from the king to the pope about Sicilian affairs (Fœd., i., 379). In June, 1275, Clarell, being the pope's chaplain, was made a proctor to represent the king of England in the French parliament (ibid., 524). On July 2, 1282, archbishop Wickwaine made him and two others his representatives at Rome (Reg. Wickwaine), and he was engaged in the dispute between that prelate and the prior of Durham (Hist. Dunelm. Scr. Tres, 61-2, 66). He occurs very frequently on the public records. The following notice of him is startling.

In 22nd Edward I. he had letters of protection as prebendary of Southwell, rector of the chapel of Tickhill castle, and of Peningston, Harewood,

1285, Jan. 13. To Richard de Bannfeld,[e] seneschal of our house, to buy "jocalia," 14*l.* 7s. 4d. Feb. 17. To the steward at Wetwang, 100s. for oats and peas, and 15*l.* to the executors of Thomas de Ludham[f] for sheep. April 18. To Walter, the bailiff of Cawood, and dan Thomas de Sutton, everything necessary for the construction of our quay at Thorp. April 24. To Calmo, our chamberlain, 100 marks to spend for us at the fair of St. Ives, and 20*l.* more on June 4. June 4. To master John, called the Roman, 100*l.* in part payment of 1000*l.* we once received of him. June 9. To the prior of Watton a loan of 200 marks.

On the 23rd of December, 1283, Wickwaine made a provision for which his successors had good reason to be grateful. He had himself experienced the want of money when he came to York, and now he wisely and generously made an arrangement which bound each archbishop for the future to leave a certain quantity of stock and gear upon each of his manors for the benefit of the prelate that came after him. He made a rule, which the king confirmed on the 6th of October at Acton Burnell, that the amount to be kept should be 602 oxen, 54 horses and 1000 sheep, to say nothing of the carts and other necessaries, and these were to be distributed over twenty-three places. On the part of Wickwaine this was neither more nor less than a gift to his successors, and he evidently regarded it himself in that light, for he says that he made it for the weal of his own soul, and for those of the king and queen, Walter Gray, sometime archbishop of York, and William de Rotherfield, the late dean.[g]

We are told by Stubbs that Wickwaine was a great builder of churches, and that the greater part of the places of worship within his diocese were consecrated during his archiepiscopate.[h] He is also to be remembered for the part that he took in the translation of the remains of St. William in January, 1284. As I have already given a description of the ceremonial on that occasion, it is unnecessary to repeat it.

Wickwaine's life was now drawing towards its close. On the 24th of August, 1284, Edward I. states that he had given the archbishop leave to visit the papal court,[i] a journey which, as a Durham historian informs us, had for its object the expediting

Babboword, Wheteley, Estmarkam, Northwell, Walesby, Horeton, Edingeley, Briggeford, Ludham, Henningeford, Staneford and Ouston. Prynne may well call him "an execrable pluralist" (Coll., iii., 597). Cf. Hunter's South Yorkshire, ii., 52. Clarell was the founder of the friary at Tickhill (Coll. Top., iv., 73).

[e] In 4th Edward I. Richard Baumfeld, the archbishop's bailiff at Otley, was in trouble for some malversation about a robber (Rot. Hundred., i. 106).

[f] Canon of York, and brother of archbishop Ludham.

[g] Reg. Wickwaine, and Prynne's Coll., iii., 311. [h] Stubbs, col. 1727.

[i] Prynne's Coll., iii., 324.

of his suit with the great Northern priory.[j] The opposition which he met with from the monks of that house seems to have been the chief cross and trouble of his life. He would gladly have subjected them to himself, as his predecessor Murdac had done more than a century before, for he was animated by the same energetic and uncompromising spirit. To the latest hour of his life he regretted that he had consecrated Anthony Bek, bishop of Durham,[k] for he rendered him no assistance in his claim. Unable to obtain himself what he deemed to be right, he sought for redress from Rome. Whether he ever reached that illustrious city and court it is difficult to say, but as he went or returned he halted at the Cistercian house of Pontigny in Burgundy, a place of great renown in the twelfth and thirteenth centuries.

> "Est Pontigniacum pons exulis, hortus, asylum,
> Hic graditur, spatiatur in hoc, requiescit in illo."[l]

Becket had passed two years of his exile within those sacred walls; and more recently they had witnessed the death and the alleged miracles of St. Edmund of Canterbury. Pontigny was now the destination of many bands of pilgrims and a place of repute.[m] Wickwaine, who had all the feelings and much of the austerity of a monk, would gaze upon it with reverence. We are told, indeed, that he assumed the cowl in that monastery;[n] and he would have many incentives for doing so, for everything that he saw around him would reproach or attract him. Wearied and perplexed as he had often been, he would long for rest, and the time

> "When the spirit stoops
> To drink with gratitude the crystal stream
> Of unreproved enjoyment; and is pleased
> To muse, and be saluted by the air
> Of much repentance, wafting wallflower scents
> From out the crumbling ruins of fallen pride
> And chambers of transgression, now forlorn.
> O calm contented days and peaceful nights!"

A deeper and a more lasting repose than the poet pictures was soon to be Wickwaine's lot. He was seized with a fever at Pontigny, and died there on the 26th of August, 1285.[o] He was interred within those walls which overshadowed the tombs of Edmund of Canterbury and many of his countrymen, far

[j] Hist. Dunelm. Scr. Tres, 69.

[k] Chron. Lanercost, 122.

[l] Henriq., Phœnix Reviviscens, 46.

[m] Wickwaine himself granted permission to Roger de Malton and Hugh de Methley to make a pilgrimage to Pontigny, *s.a.* Malton was master of St. Leonard's hospital, York.

[n] Martene, Thes. Nov. Anecdot., iii., 1254. Stubbs (col. 1727) says that he resigned the archbishopric and retired to Pontigny.

[o] Stubbs, col. 1727. MSS. Cotton Vitellius, A, ii., 111 *b*, the 27th of August. Wikes (apud Gale, ii., 108) about Pentecost. Trivet, 263. Chron. Lanercost, 122. Contin. Flor. Wigorn., ii., 236. Lel. Coll., i., 179.

away from the harder skies of England, and his own cathedral beside the waters of the Ouse. The holiness of his life has led Stubbs to speak of him as a saint,[p] and he had that reputation among many people. His memory would be invested with additional renown by the fame of miracles said to have been wrought at his tomb,[q] which seems to have acted as a febrifuge.[r] If the church of York had been without a patron saint, the chapter in all probability would have tried to secure the canonization of Wickwaine.

On the 15th of September, 1285, Edward I. committed the custody of the temporalities of the see of York during the vacancy to Sir Otho de Grandison, who made Malcolm de Harcla his deputy. The proceeds, which amounted to the large sum of 1812*l.* 12s. 4d., were devoted to the construction of the royal castles in Wales.[s]

Wickwaine made a will, of which Walter de Gloucester, archdeacon of York, and Thomas de Wakefield, the sub-dean, were the executors. On the 18th of June, 1286, Roger Suayn, canon of Ripon, was authorized to sell the goods of the deceased prelate for the execution of his will. About Martinmas, 1287, archbishop Romanus acknowledged himself indebted to the executors in the sum of 1056*l.* for cattle, corn, etc., and on November 9 he received from them 220 marks on the score of dilapidations. On the 9th of April, 1293, he authorized Thomas de Corbridge, canon of York, and William de Blida, sub-dean, to make an enquiry about some of the chattels of his predecessor, which, it was alleged, had been deposited in the church of York, and had been carried away.[t]

John Romanus, or **le Roman**, was the son of the treasurer of York who bore the same names, and who seems to have migrated from Italy to England.[u] The father died at an ad-

[p] Stubbs, col. 1727.

[q] Chron. Lanercost, 122. Stubbs, col. 1727. Fuller's Church History, book iii., 79. Acta SS., June 8. The author of the notice of St. William of York in that collection, when at Pontigny at the end of the seventeenth century, heard nothing of any worship of Wickwaine, and supposed that his reputation had been obscured by that of St. Edmund. Liber de Melsa, inter MSS. Egerton, 1141, fol. 83.

[r] Chron. Lanercost, 122.

[s] Prynne's Coll., iii., 348, 433. Abbrev. Rot. Orig., i. In 1293 Malcolm de Harcley was one of the king's eschaetors (Rot. Parl., i., 92), and he was much employed in the service of the state.

[t] Reg. Romanus. In 1286 Harcley acknowledges the receipt of 100*l.* in part payment for corn sold to Romanus in the king's name.

[u] "Ex quadam pedissequa procreatus" (Knyghton, col. 2507). Stubbs, col. 1727. Prynne's Coll., iii., 542. Abbrev. Rot. Orig., i., 228.

vanced age in 1256, having held in succession within the minster of York the sub-deanery, the treasurership, and the archdeaconry of Richmond. Matthew Paris[v] speaks in disparaging terms of his avarice and peevish temper, but we must recollect, on the other hand, that the north transept and the central tower were erected by his munificence. The latter has been re-faced or destroyed, but the former still delights the eye with its grace and beauty. The treasurer was a friend of Grostête and archbishop Gray, and was a person of consequence and reputation.[w]

His son, John Romanus, the archbishop, received his education at the university of Oxford,[x] and was well versed in dialectics and theology.[y] An undated letter from Innocent IV. is in existence which may possibly refer to him. It is addressed to John, called Romanus, clerk, remembrancer of the papal

[v] Matt. Paris, 789, 792.

[w] Gray gave Romanus a pension of 20 marks per annum (Rot. Gray), and Grostête was his correspondent (Gratii Fascic., ii., 351. Grostête, Epp., 65, 203). He was a canon of York as early as 1228, and was the first subdean (MSS. Cotton, Claudius, B, iii., 16. Le Neve, iii., 127-8), in which year the pope empowered him to supersede an appointment to a stall at Sarum (Wilkins, i., 563).

He founded about the year 1240 a chantry at the altar of St. Andrew in York minster, which stood against the north-west pillar of the lantern. It was for the souls of the donor, John and Mary his parents, Cincius his priest, and Richard I. (Fabric Rolls, 217). Romanus also established an obit for himself (Domesday Book, 82), and granted land in Goodramgate, York, to the vicars choral (Reg. Magn. Album, part iii., 11).

This is probably the same Cincius, a canon of London, who was robbed, and carried off for five weeks, near St. Alban's in 1231 (Matt. Paris, 313-16). Romanus was appointed to enquire into the matter (ibid., 316). He may also be the Cincius "vir disertissimus Romanus," who is the author of a preface to Plutarch's treatise, De Virtute et Vitio, and who wrote a letter to Velleius about the translation of the De Contemnenda Morte of Socrates. These pieces are in the library of Benet College, Cambridge (Smith's Catalogue). The work ascribed to Socrates is of course the well-known Phædo of Plato, whom Daniel Heinsius commends in his poem on the same great theme,—

'Namque illi Graiorum omnis sapientia servit.'

Leland is quite wrong in saying that John Romanus the son was treasurer of York. The father held that post at his death, and, afterwards, the succession of treasurers can be regularly traced. This is an important fact for deciding the date of the north transept of York minster, which was erected by John Romanus, the treasurer. Stubbs (col. 1727) makes the father the treasurer, and says that he built the north transept and the lantern tower at his own cost, together with a great part of the hospital of St. Leonard. We are not necessarily to infer that he built them *whilst* he was treasurer: Stubbs merely calls him so to distinguish him from his son.

[x] In 1295 archbishop Romanus writes in behalf of the university, "Recolentes memoriter ac sincero animo recensentes, quod quasi a primis cunabulis scholastici studii ubera apud vos suximus in continuatione diutina donec ad majorem solicitudinem Divina providentia nos vocaret" [Wilkins, ii., 214]. On St. Stephen's day, 1289, the archbishop and the chapter of York assigned the house in the close at York belonging to the stall of Dunnington for a school (Reg. Romanus).

[y] Chron. Lanercost, 126. Knyghton, col. 2507. Trivet, 263. Polydore Vergil, 325.

penitentiary, and in it the pope desires him not to accept a bishopric without asking his permission.[*] It is quite possible that the person here alluded to was the young Englishman in whom the prescient eye of his master had already detected signs of future greatness. Many years, however, elapsed before it arrived. The first preferment that John Romanus seems to have enjoyed was in the cathedral of Lincoln. He became prebendary of North Kelsey in 1258, and resigned it for the stall of Nassington. In 1275 he was made chancellor,—a post which he gave up for the precentorship in 1279.[a] On the 7th of December in that year he was collated by archbishop Wickwaine to the prebend of Warthill at York,[b] the only piece of preferment in that church that he seems to have possessed.

Archbishop Wickwaine died in August, 1285, and on the 22nd of the following month the king authorized the chapter of York to proceed to a fresh election. On the 29th of October they chose Romanus, and on the 30th informed Edward I. of what they had done. He gave his assent on the 15th November, and Romanus went abroad to receive the pall and to be consecrated by the pope. The ceremony took place at Rome on the 10th of February, and the temporalities were restored to him on the 12th of April.[c]

When Romanus returned to England he was very nearly having a collision with archbishop Peckham about the bearing of his cross. On the 6th of April Peckham wrote from Saltwood to the dean of the Arches and Mr. William de Haverberg to inform them that he had heard that Romanus was to land on Palm Sunday following with his cross erect, and directing them to check him. An order was also given to the rural dean of Dover forbidding any clerks to approach the intruder, and commanding the services to be stopped in every parish where he halted, if he made use of the obnoxious symbol of his authority. The king had already heard that a quarrel was imminent, and had tried to prevent it, ordering that provisions and everything that Romanus and his suite required should be supplied to them on their journey. On the 11th of April Peckham again wrote to say that the archbishop, as he had heard, was in the priory of Bermondsey with his cross erect, and he forbade every one

[*] Baluzii Misc., ed. Mansi, i., 211.

[a] Le Neve, ii., 83, 92, 191, 196. Prynne, iii., 268. In his capacity as precentor of Lincoln, in 1285, Romanus came into collision with the king for bringing a suit against the prior of Huntingdon (Prynne, iii., 354). Jan. 1, 1288, quit claim to John Tebaud, chapter-clerk at Lincoln, of the monies received by Romanus on account of the choir boys at Lincoln during his precentorship (Reg. Romanus).

[b] Reg. Wickwaine, 58 *b*.

[c] Le Neve, iii., 104. Prynne's Coll., iii., 355. Stubbs, col. 1727. Trivet, 263. Chron. Lanercost, 121. Wikes, apud Gale, ii., 113. MSS. Cotton Vitellius, A, ii., 111 *b*.

to go near either the place or the prelate.[d] We hear nothing more of the quarrel at that time, but Romanus, in all probability, proceeded quietly into the North, the king interfering in his behalf to prevent any open dissension. The matter in dispute was afterwards the subject of some fruitless debate and negotiation.[e] The new archbishop was enthroned at York on Trinity Sunday, the 9th of June, 1286.[f] His installation banquet seems to have been on a magnificent scale. Several of the letters of invitation which Romanus sent have been preserved, and from them we learn that among many others the earls of Cornwall and Warren, the bishops of London and Carlisle, the dean of Lincoln, Sir R. Sutton and Sir William de Ros, knights, were asked to become his guests.[g] The Latinity of the archbishop was elegant and concise, and his epistles seem to have been regarded as patterns of composition by his successors in the see.[h]

Romanus, like some of his predecessors, was in want of money on his accession to office, and was obliged to fill his empty coffers by borrowing large sums. The following are some of the persons to whom he was indebted. My readers will observe how large a portion of the money-lenders were clerks, and they must draw their own inferences from the fact. The archbishop would naturally turn to them for assistance rather than to the foreign merchants. He was obliged, however, to have recourse to the latter.

1286, May 18. The archbishop authorizes Mr. William de Lincoln,[i] clerk, to contract a loan of 500 marks for him in the court of Rome. June 10. A bond to Robert de Scartheburgh, dean of York, for 1000 marks. A bond to Roger de Saxton for 50*l.*, and to Coppo de le Cotenne, citizen and merchant of Florence, of the company of the Frissinbaldi, and his fellows, for 200*l.* June 18. A bond to Mr. Thomas de Wakefeld,[j] sub-

[d] Reg. Wickwaine. Prynne's Coll., iii., 355.

[e] When Romanus was elected he endeavoured to get this point settled at Rome (Reg. Romanus). In May, 1287, archbishop Peckham ordered the bishop of Worcester to prevent the Northern primate from raising his cross within his diocese (Wilkins, ii., 128), and Romanus was obliged to seek for letters of safe conduct from the king (Reg. Romanus). On Oct. 9, 1291, Mr. H., dean of York, William, archdeacon of Notts, and Thomas de Corbridge were appointed to treat with the archbishop of Canterbury (ibid.). In 1295 there is a letter from archbishop Winchilsea on the subject (Wilkins, ii., 216). On June 12, 1295, Bertrand and Simon, the cardinals, offer to act as mediators between the two primates, and their proposition was accepted by Romanus (Reg. Romanus).

[f] MSS. Cotton, Vitellius, A, ii., 111 *b*.

[g] Reg. Romanus.

[h] Some of the letters of Romanus are inserted in the book which contains those of Thoresby. The epistles of these two prelates seem to have been regarded as models of orthography.

[i] Dec. 29, 1286, Mr. W. de Lincoln was collated to a stall at Beverley. In 1290 he was at Rome in the archbishop's behalf (Reg. Romanus).

[j] Prebendary of Botevant, chancellor and sub-dean of York, and canon of

dean of York, executor of William our predecessor, for 96*l.* July 12. A bond to Richard de Horton and Philip de Werkesworth, executors of the will of John de Wydington, canon of Lincoln,[k] for 100*l.* July 24. A bond for 200 marks to the merchants of Pystoria. July 27. A bond to Peter de Cestria, provost of Beverley, for 200*l.*; to Adam de Patrington for 100*l.*; to Mr. Thomas de Dalton for 20*l.*, and to Mr. Simon de Clarevall for 100 marks. July 31. A bond to William, dominus de Huks,[l] for 200*l.* Sunday before the festival of All Saints, an order to Henry, archdeacon of Richmond, to sell the archbishop's houses at Paris.[m] Nov. 3. A bond for 300*l.* to Mr. Thomas de Grimston,[n] archdeacon of Cleveland, Mr. William de Langton, rector of Croft, Walter his brother,[o] and Henry de Mileford, executors of William de Rotherfeud (Langton), late dean of York. 1287, Jan. 3. Authority to R. de Bamfeld, canon of Southwell and rector of Stillingfleet, to borrow for the archbishop 110 marks from the merchants. Jan. 24. A bond for 16*l.* 16s. to the executors of Mr. Henry de Skipton, archdeacon of Notts, for silver plate bought of them.[p] March 3. Authority to Mr. William de Lincoln, canon of Beverley, and Peter Durandi of Lincoln, to borrow 100 marks for the archbishop.[q] April 11. Bond for 200*l.* to Mr. Simon de Clarevall. May 10. Bond to Richard Guydicioniis for 200 marks. Nov. 24. Bond to Henry de Mileford, executor of dean Langton, for 100 marks. 1288, Trinity Sunday. A bond for 1000 marks to the dean of York. 1290, July 19. A bond for 200 marks to

Ripon. He was a favourite with the archbishop, who granted an indulgence of forty days to all who listened to his preaching. In giving Wakefield the chancellorship the primate spoke of "personæ tuæ nota probitas, meritorumque tuorum odorifera famositas."

[k] Prebendary of Lafford (Le Neve, ii., 160). Horton was treasurer of the same church. Executors at that time seem frequently to have acted as trustees of the estate of their deceased friend, and to have made the most of his effects by becoming money-lenders.

[l] He occurs in the Rot. Scotiæ, and was sheriff of Yorkshire 1305-7 (Drake's Eboracum, 351).

[m] On May 9, 1286, Romanus informs bishop Bek that he had let his houses in Paris to the nephews of Matthew the cardinal. On Jan. 6, 1289, he desires his clerk, Robert de Themlby to sell them for him, and, on August 15, 1290, he orders Mr. William de Haxeby to sell them, and to examine the accounts of William de Sens, citizen of Paris, who had had the charge of them.

Archdeacon Newark occurs as a money-lender. On Dec. 27, 1286, he lent the archbishop 20*l.* On March 16, 1287, he received from him 100 marks for first-fruits. On August 13 he lent the archbishop 47 marks, 6s. 8d.

[n] Archdeacon of Cleveland 1280-1289. Archbishop Wickwaine speaks of him as "amatissimus et intimus filius noster."

[o] The well-known bishop of Lichfield and a great statesman. He was a canon of York and master of St. Leonard's hospital.

[p] March 22, 1287-8, the archbishop buys sheep of his executors for 10*l.* April 1, he buys of the executors of Mr. Thomas de Barneby, rector of Barmston, for 20 marks, the corn in the laith and in the ground.

[q] The money was lent by Durandi de Lincoln, the father of Peter.

Richard de Horton, treasurer, and Thomas de Perar', canon of Lincoln, executors of Mr. W. de Hancton,[r] canon of that church. July 24. A bond for 40 marks to Sir John de Reygate, kt.[s]

Archbishop Romanus took but little part in public affairs after he came into the North; indeed, at no period of his life can we regard him as a statesman. In 1288 he had some dissension with the king, for which he lost the temporalities of his see; it was, however, of short duration; for, between the months of March and August,[t] he was in Gascony with Edward.[u] In 1290 he was present at the funeral of queen Eleanor, and at the king's request he ordered prayers to be offered up throughout his diocese for her soul.[v] In 1291 he was required to render military service against Scotland;[w] and in the following year he was mixed up in the negotiations about that kingdom.[x] On the 18th of June, 1294, he was enjoined to require the suffrages of the people of his diocese for the success of the king and his army on their way to Gascony, and on the 19th of August he was summoned to a council at Westminster about that country.[y] On two or three other occasions he was called to parliament;[z] but his name is not connected with any public office or with any important act in connection with the state.

The whole of the time of archbishop Romanus seems to have been devoted to his diocese. Henry, bishop of Whitherne,[a] acted for some time as his suffragan, and he was occasionally assisted by one or two other prelates, but he seems to have relied for the most part upon his own exertions. The annals of his life are to be derived from his own official registers which are preserved at York, and they certainly shew that he was a zealous and energetic archbishop.* The acts of our early prelates have been so little examined for biographical and historical purposes,

[r] Neither of these canons appears on the Lincoln Fasti.

[s] A commissioner of array in Yorkshire in 1300 (Parl. Writs., i., 345, etc.). On Dec. 10, 1290, John de Reygate was bailiff of Sherburn (Reg. Romanus). [t] Prynne, iii., 1293.

[u] Reg. Romanus.

[v] Chron. Lanercost, 137.

[w] Fœd., i., 753. Parl. Writs., i., 256.

[x] Fœd., i., 762. In 1292 Gregory IX. wrote to the archbishop of York and the bishop of Carlisle urging them to exhort the Scottish king to keep the peace (Chron. Lan., 146).

[y] Parl. Writs., i., 261. Fœd., i., 802, 808-10, 834.

[z] Parl. Writs., i., 25, 30-2. Fœd., i., 822. In 1286 the king begs him and the archdeacon of Richmond to procure a subsidy for him from the York clergy (Fœd., i., 673).

[a] On Sept. 9, 1286, he made his profession of obedience to the archbishop at Hexham, and had leave to go to Rome. He died Nov. 1, 1293 (Chron. Lan., 155), being at that time crucesignatus. He was at one time abbat of S. Crux. On Jan. 13, 1294, John king of Scotland wrote to Romanus about Thomas de Kirkcudbright, chaplain of Robert Bruce, who had been elected bishop by John, prior of Whitherne, and his convent. On May 30, 1294, the new prelate made his profession of obedience to Romanus, and the bishops of Carlisle and St. Asaph were asked to assist at his consecration, which took place at Gedling "die dom. in crast. B. Dionisii, 1294."

that a short series of extracts from those of Romanus will be interesting and novel. In the first place I shall give a list of those persons to whom the archbishop gave an annual pension. These sums were frequently spontaneously granted, either from affection or interest. Occasionally the king, in addition to the stalls and benefices which he filled up himself or begged, requested the prelate to place some court favourite upon his list of pensioners, or some foreigner gave a hint that he would like to be upon it, as the price of his good offices at the papal court. These persons became occasionally a very serious burden upon the archiepiscopal revenues.

1286, May 12. A pension of 20 marks per annum to Benedict, cardinal of St. Nicholas in Carcere Tulliano, for his good offices towards us and our church. 1287, Feb. 4. A pension of 10*l.* per annum to Ralph de Hengham,[b] clerk. April 18. A pension of 10 marks per annum to William de Burneton,[c] and on May 10 one of 100s. to William de Saham,[d] clerk. Another of 5 marks to John de Ousthorp,[e] clerk, at the instance of friar William de Hothum,[f] till we provide him with a benefice.

[b] Son of Sir Andrew de Hengham, of Hengham, in Norfolk. Chief justice, archdeacon of Worcester, chancellor of Exeter, canon of Hereford, Exeter, Lincoln and London. He occurs frequently in state documents. Foss's Judges, iii., 261. Weever, Fun. Mon., 367.

[c] A justice itinerant in 1302. Foss, iii., 68.

[d] A justice of the King's Bench. Ibid., 146.

[e] He was a prebendary of Howden (Reg. ii., Prior. and Conv. Dunelm., 69, 81).

[f] Prior-provincial of the friars preachers in England, and a person of very pleasing manners and of great piety and learning (Chron. Lan., 133-4. Fœd., i., 766. Cotton's Fasti Eccl. Hib., ii., 12). He was educated at Merton college, Oxford, and at Paris (Hist. Univ. Oxon., i., 324; iv., 14. Cotton *ut supra)*. In February, 1289, he is mentioned in connection with the king's intended expedition to Palestine (Fœd., i., 703. Prynne, iii., 428), and on May 8, *seq.*, he had letters of credence to the pope from the king (ibid., 708. Prynne, 389). In 1292 he was concerned in Scottish politics (ibid., 766). He was also intimately connected with Eleanor, the consort of Edward I., and had much to do in settling her affairs (Manners, etc., of England, 103, etc.). In 1298 he was preferred to the archbishopric of Dublin, and was consecrated abroad by bishop Bek. He died on Aug. 28, 1298, the year of his election, in the Dominican convent at Dijon in Burgundy. His body was brought to London, and was interred in the church of the Dominicans. Caius says that he was an author (Chron. Lan., 133-4. Trivet, 306. Prynne, iii., 772-3. Cotton, *ut supra)*.

And now for a romantic story to enliven a dull note. It comes from MSS. Harl., 912.

De Monte Chyviott. Dominus Johannes de Hothom Elyensis episcopus, audivit a fratre Willelmo de Hothom, avunculo suo, historiam quæ sequitur. Retulit vero quod erat in transmarinis partibus quidam nobilis qui omnia sua dimiserat propter amorem Dei, et duxit vitam heremiticam in nemore. Hic, ergo, audiens quod talis frater de Anglia transiret per patriam illam versus capitulum generale, misit ad eum rogans quod presenter ei loqueretur. Ad quem cum veniret (venerat?) quæsivit si novit aliquem montem in Marchia Scociæ qui vocaretur Chyviott? qui dixit quod sciret. Quare, igitur, quæro indicabo tibi. Una, igitur, nocte, audivi extra tigurium meum quasi magnus populus transiret, et, respiciens,

Dec. 9. A pension of 5 marks to James Simbaldi, clerk, till we can provide him with a benefice. 1288, Nov. 6. A pension of 10 marks per annum to Mr. Robert de Ros, archdeacon of London, and Mr. R. de Branndon,[g] canon of London, till we can give each of them a stall. 1290, May 13. A pension of 20*l.* per annum to Peter de Sabaudia,[h] clerk, on account of his noble birth and his relationship to the king, till we can find him a prebend. Sept. 23. A pension of 5 marks to Nicholas, son of Matthew Rugepall, merchant of Lucca, till we give him a benefice. 1291, July 24. A pension of 10 marks per annum to Mr. Richard de Herteford, till, etc. 1293, May 8. A pension of 100s. per annum to John de Vere, son of the earl of Oxford, till we find him a stall at York.[i] Mem. He died in the same year, and so the pension ceases. August 7. A pension of 100s. to Thomas Brabazon, rector of Hungerton, dioc. Lincoln, on account of the affection which his brother, Sir Roger Brabazon,[j] shews to us and our church, till we can give him a stall. 1295, May 13. A like sum to Hugh de Cressingham,[k] clerk, till we find him a prebend.

I now give in chronological order the following remarkable series of extracts from the register of the archbishop. Their

vidi pedites transire in maxima multitudine, deinque armigeros, deindeque milites, ultimo tres reges nobilitatis valde, unum a dextris et alium a sinistris equitantes et quasi ducentes tertium inter se. Et cum omnes transissent dolui nimis quod non conquisivi qui essent. Et cito pervenerunt tres miseri claudicantes a quibus conquisivi qui essent illi precedentes. Qui responderunt quod omnes erant demones excepto uno, scilicet illo ultimo, in medio, qui fuerat rex Arragoniæ,—ductus ad montem Chyviott, qui est locus frigidus valde, ut in frigido loco affligeretur qui delectabatur in calidis cibis et potis.

Oh frigid and most impotent conclusion! and yet it is an appalling fate for the disembodied spirit

"To reside
In thrilling regions of thick ribbed ice."

[g] Canon of Lincoln and London. 22nd Edward I. letters of protection to him as rector of Littlebury (Prynne's Coll., iii., 594).

[h] A son of Thomas prince of Piedmont, and cousin of Edward I. Prebendary of Newbald at York 1290-1309, dean of Salisbury and Lyons, and canon of Lincoln and Hereford. He was made archbishop of Lyons in December, 1308. Cf. Gall. Christ., iv., 161, 205. Baluzii Misc., i., 221, ed. Mansi. L'Art de vérifier les Dates, 8vo ed., xvii., 168. Guichenon, Histoire Generale de la Maison de Savoie, etc.

[i] A son of Robert earl of Oxford, unnoticed by Dugdale (Bar., i., 191-2). He was prebendary of Scamlesby at Lincoln (Le Neve, ii., 202).

[j] Sir Roger Brabazon was a justiciar and a person of consequence.

[k] A great man, justiciar and treasurer of England. In 21st Edward I. archbishop Romanus allows him and his fellow-justiciars to hold assizes at York in the time of Septuagesima and Sexagesima (Prynne, iii., 579). 22nd Edward I. letters of protection to him as canon of St. Paul's and rector of Enderby, Kingsclere, Hatfeld, Chalk, Berles, Barnton, Dodington, Cressingham and Reymerston, "an insatiable pluralist" (ibid., 597) Rector of Rudby, dioc. Ebor., in 1296.

The record of his pension is cancelled, for he was killed in Scotland, and so great was the hatred that the Scots had for him, that they actually flayed his dead body and tanned his skin, and, cutting it in pieces, kept them as memorials of their foe. Cf. Knyghton, col. 2519. Walsingham, 73. Chron. Lanercost, 190.

variety does not diminish from their interest. It would be difficult to find any historical notices of greater novelty and value.

1286, April 17. A letter from Edward I. to the archbishop, requesting the prayers of the faithful for the soul of Alexander, king of Scotland, who has recently died.[l] April 23. An indulgence for the brethren of the hospital of St. John Baptist and St. Thomas the martyr at the bridge of Stanford, for the repair of the said bridge, which has been destroyed by a flood, and for the perpetuating of the mass B.M.V. thereon.[m] An indulgence to those who visit the church of Mansfield at the dedication of two altars therein, viz., that of B.M. and S. Katharine, and that of SS. William and Margaret, and another for those contributing to the chapel of S.M. at Staner, near Selby. An indulgence for the cathedral of Carlisle, which has been destroyed by fire, and for the shrines of SS. Cuthbert and John at Durham and Beverley. An indulgence of 10 days for the soul of John dictus Venesun, whose body lies in the cemetery B. M. at Dover, on the north side. An indulgence of 40 days for the fabric of St. Saviour's church, Bermondsey, and one for the fabric of the house of the Augustinian hermits at Huntingdon, which has been burned down. An indulgence for the soul of Mr. William de Gyseley, who is buried in the monastery of Kirkstall, and for the health of Richard de Halton during his life and for his soul after his decease, together with the souls of Robert and Alice, his parents, who lie before the altar B. M. V. in the church of Halton, Lincolnshire. April 27. An indulgence for the soul of dame Christiana Ledet,[n] mother of Sir Gerard de Furnivall, whose body lies buried before the high altar of the priory of Byssemede, and her heart in the church of the friars preachers at Cambridge; also for the soul of that noble lady dame Alice de Ros, whose body is interred in the church of the friars minors at Lincoln. April 29. An

[l] Alexander was the king's brother-in-law, having married Margaret, daughter of Henry III. He fell from his horse in a dark night, and broke his neck (Knyghton, col. 2468).

[m] A series of extracts of great importance and novelty. It is impossible to illustrate each as it deserves; indeed I do not profess to do it, although I have a superfluity of materials.

[n] Cf. Dugd. Bar., i., 726. Plac. de Quo. Warr., 396. Hunter's Hallamshire. Thoroton's Notts, 455. Bishop Kellawe's register at Durham contains many entries of this nature. 1311, 15 Dec., ind. of forty days for the souls of Sir Walter Faucombrige and dame Agnes his wife. 1312, 23 Aug., ind. of forty days for the health of Hugh de Everesdon, abbat of St. Alban's. 1312, Nov. 14, ind. of forty days to all who listen to the preaching of the monks of Durham. Dec. 28, ind. of forty days to those who visit the church of Bliburgh, co. Lincoln, dedicated to St. Alkmund, and for the soul of Walter, sometime rector there, who is buried in the church. Ind. of forty days to those who visit the chapel of St. Leonard in Kirkstead abbey. Ind. of forty days for the souls of Thomas de Kellawe, Agnes his wife, and William their son.

indulgence of 10 days for the souls of Elias de Stapleford and Hawis his wife, who are buried in the church of Stapleford.[o] May 1. An injunction to the people of the diocese of York to pray for the good estate of the king and queen and their children.[p] An indulgence for the hospital of lepers dedicated to S.M. Magd., near Pontefract, and another for the hospital of St. Nicholas, near Beverley. Letters addressed by the archbishop to the bishops of Bath and Wells, and Durham, William de Luda and the archdeacon of Richmond, in behalf of John de Lithergrynes,[q] who is not at present in the king's service. June 15. A royal mandate to the archbishop to summon before the justices itinerant at York, Mr. William de Clifford, Mr. Thomas de Barneby, official of the bishop of Carlisle, and Mr. Henry Hay, rector of Aughton, his clerks, for a transgression in hunting.[r] July 6. An indulgence, to last for three years, for the brethren of the hospital S. Spiritus de Saxia, at Rome.[s] July 7. Administration of the effects of Sir Thomas de Huks, kt., to Adam de Derlington and Hugh de Collum, his executors.[t] Sept. 10. An indulgence of 40 days for the church of Whitherne containing the relics of St. Ninian, which has been burned down. Dec. 5. A gift of two oaks from our park of Beverley to Mr. J. de Penningston.[u] The following clerks, all having the first tonsure,

[o] Aug. 25, 1322, a chantry is founded in the church of St. Ellen, at Stapleford, for the souls of Hugh de Stapleford and Alice his wife (Reg. Melton). Cf. Thoroton's Notts, 213.

[p] Another order anno 3, and another anno 9.

[q] A person much employed in state affairs. A justice itinerant (Foss, iii., 124). 20th Edward I. he and Alice his wife founded a chapel in their manor of Lasenby, in which prayers were to be said daily for the souls of Edward I. and bishop Bek (Prynne, iii., 463). In the same year the king authorized him and the abbat S. M. Ebor. to choose a master for St. Nicholas's hospital, York (ibid., 470). Eschaetor north of Trent 25th Edward I. (Parl. Writs., i., 296). He was sheriff of Yorkshire between 1280 and 1286 (Drake's Eboracum, 351).

[r] Some of the archbishop's clerks are in trouble for hunting. They were of the same mind with Chaucer's monk—

"He yave not of the text a pulled hen,
That saith, that hunters ben not holy men."

[s] This was the hospital to which the pope wished to appropriate the stall of Fenton at York. It will be again mentioned.

[t] There are many of these valuable instruments in the early registers. 1287, Jan 24, administration of Sir Robert Sutton, knight, to Stephen de Sutton, his brother and executor. 1289, May 3, commission to receive the account of the executors of Sir Robert de Ros. May 10, commission to hear the account of Sir John Huse, Robert de Sherington, and Jordan de Stokes, executors of Sir Henry de Newmarch. 1293, July 13, commission to hear the account of the executors of Sir Robert de Ros, knight. 1293, Dec. 5, the will of Isabella de Fortibus, countess of Albemarle, is proved at Tottenham, and administration is granted to her executors, the priors of Brommore and Twynham and Sir William de Knouill, knight. 1294, March 1, commission to hear the account of the executors of dame Amy de Percy.

[u] Canon of South Muskham at Southwell, and probably of Beverley. William Clifford, who has been recently mentioned, was also a canon of Southwell.

are degraded this year; John de Hoveden for stealing 3s. 6d. at York; Henry de Novocastro for breaking into a house at Hoton in Bulmershire and stealing a tabard; John de Fainfoss (Fangfoss) for stealing 5 marks at Hoton-on-the-Wold; William de Baildon for stealing at York 4 silver spoons, and Robert de Karl' for stealing some decretals valued at 5 marks.[v]

1287, Jan. 27. Laurence de Crepings, rector of Hoton, acknowledges that he owes the archbishop 20*l.* as a punishment for incontinence. Feb. 16. Licence for the brethren of the hospital of St. Anthony, in the diocese of Vienne, to collect alms; another for the hospital B.M. without Bishopsgate, London; and a third, of twenty days, for the repairs of the bridge of Gloucester and the hospital upon it. August 17. A commission to the bishop of Whitherne to dedicate the churches of Oswaldkirk and Edstone, and to the dean of Bulmer to act as the archbishop's deputy in dedicating the churches of Thormanby, Dalby, Bulmer and Ellington. There remain to be dedicated those of Scalton, Whenby, Foston, Helmsley and Wheldrake. The archbishop binds the rector of Foston under a penalty of 5 marks to have his church built and ready for dedication within three years.[w] Sept. 24. Licence to Sir Robert de Baliol to have an oratory in his manor of Redness.[x] Dec. 27. An order to the bailiff of Southwell to give to the prior of the hospital at Jerusalem 10 wild animals, viz., deer, fawns, etc., as they come to the nets.

1289, Dec. 29. To Walter de Maydeston,[y] 400*l.* for the 30th, by order of the king.

1290, May 15. The archbishop grants the first-fruits of the archdeaconry of Richmond to Sir Otho de Grandison to enable him to go to the Holy Land.[z] June 11. A mandate of enquiry to the official of the archdeacon of York *ex parte* Sir Fulk Fitzwarren of Albebury, dioc. Hereford, kt. We have heard that Agnes Bacun, lady of Edlington, deceased, the late Fulk's sister, left him by will a precious stone called *asimu'*, which Agnes, daughter of Robert le Gru of Northampton, the maid of the

[v] These convictions of clerks are of painful frequency.

[w] Some valuable dates. It must not, however, be imagined that churches were always dedicated as soon as they were built. There are some valuable notices of this kind in the York Fabric Rolls, 235-242.

[x] An unrecorded member of a great house. March 23, 1273, licence from Gregory X. to Robert de Baliol to build a chapel in his manor-house at Redness on account of the inundations, etc., which keep him from the parish church (Reg. Wickwaine). Baliol was knight of the shire for co. York 25th and 29th Edward I. (Parl. Writs., i., 58, 94).

[y] Jan. 11, 1290, collated to a moiety of the church of Kendal (Reg. Romanus). May 5, 1307, to have the next vacant stall at York by papal provision (Reg. Greenfield). Bishop of Worcester 1313-1317. He was a great politician.

[z] This great man and his family have been already mentioned. Cf. Dugd. Bar., ii., 17.

said Agnes, has kept on the plea that there are two persons of the name of Fulk Fitzwarren; one the brother, and the other the nephew of her mistress.[a] June 13. The archbishop writes to the bishop of Ely expressing his regret that he cannot be present at his consecration.[b] Sept. 18. Licence to R., bishop of Bath and Wells, to hold a special ordination within the diocese of York to make J. de Langedon and Roger de Esserug, subdeacons.[c] Nov. 28. A letter from Edward I. to the archbishop, desiring the prayers of the faithful for the soul of queen Alianor, our wife, from our childhood.[d] Dec. 5. Purgation of dame Christiana, wife of Sir Nicholas de Menil, kt., from the charges of having prepared poison to kill her husband, and of having committed adultery with Mr. W. de Grenefeud and Walter de Hamerton.[e]

[a] A very curious story. On Jan. 12, 1290, administration of dame Agnes Bacun de Edlington, who died "in crastino festi S. Nicholai," and was buried on the Sunday after, to William de Bosevill and Richard de Rokeley, her executors (Reg. Romanus). For an account of the noble house of Fitzwarren, cf. Dugd. Bar., i., 445. The first. Fulk in the family was nearly killed by prince John, afterwards king, who broke his head with a chessboard.

[b] William de Luda (Louth), prebendary of Ampleford at York. "Vir magnificus et eminentis scientiæ" (Wikes, apud Gale, ii., 121). Consecrated at Ely, in the church B.M.V., by John archbishop of Canterbury, with great solemnity, on Nov. 23, 1290, having been ordained priest on Oct. 1 (Contin. Fl. Wigorn., ii., 243). A great statesman. On Oct. 31, 1291, on the marriage of a son of Sir John de Potthou to a daughter of Sir Gilbert de Luda, the archbishop ordered his official to pay over the money he held belonging to the lady (Reg. Romanus). In 1292 Henry Newark occurs as one of the executors of Gilbert de Luda (Rot. Parl., i., 86). Nicholas de Luda was his son and heir (Abbrev. Plac., 307). Gilbert de Luda was mayor of York in 1284 (Drake, 360).

[c] A great favour. The bishop had been canon of Grendale and archdeacon of York. He was lord chancellor, and was a very great man. He left a will, of which Mr. William Burnell, dean of Wells, and William de Hamilton, were the executors, and Philip de Burnell was the testator's nephew and heir (Act. Capit. Ebor., 22). Asherugge was a place in Bucks where Edmund, earl of Cornwall, founded a college. Walter de Asherugge was chaplain of Edward II. (Archæol., xxvi., 340). Roger de Asherugge was a clerk of the chapel of Edward I. (Lib. Garderobæ, 314). Langton is, I presume, the same person who became chancellor in 1293. He was prebendary of Fridaythorp at York, and held many valuable preferments, the highest of which was the see of Chichester, to which he was raised in 1305.

[d] The king says she died "die Martis proximo ante festum S. Andreæ apostoli" (Reg. Romanus). Ob. 4 kal. Dec. (28 Nov.). (Acta Capit. Ebor.). The chapter of York ordered a full peal to be rung when they heard of her decease (Lib. Garderobæ, 29), and on July 10, 1291, Edward sent to the church from Scotland, in memory of his late wife, a chasuble, alb, and amice (Fabric Rolls, 154).

Romanus at once granted an indulgence of forty days for those who should pray for the queen's soul, and this was repeated on Dec. 8, 1290. On June 7, 1291, the archbishop wrote to the king to say that his wishes had been attended to (Reg. Romanus). Cf. Prynne's Coll., iii., 448. Contin. Fl. Wigorn., ii., 244. Archæol., xxix., 167, etc.

[e] A curious episode in the history of this unhappy family. Greenfield afterwards became archbishop of York. On Jan. 29, 1293, Romanus writes to the king, who had ordered him to make an enquiry on the part of Menyl against his wife, and says that the husband

1291, Feb. 7. Roger de Wychton is made the archbishop's proctor to enquire of Mr. Giffred de Vezano, canon of Cambray and chamberlain of the pope, about the will of H. the cardinal.[f] April 4. Dispensation for Thomas de Multon and Margaret his wife. They have lived together, and a son has been born to them, they not knowing that Isabel, the former wife of the said Thomas, and Margaret, were first cousins.[g] May 29. Licence for Roger de Malton to go on a pilgrimage to Pontigny.[h] July 20. An order to pray for the soul of the queen-mother.[i] Sept. 4. A commission to Mr. John Clarell, canon of Southwell, to preach in behalf of the crusade.[j] Oct. 10. Licence to dame Margaret de Percy to reside for a year within the nunnery of Appleton, provided that her attendants are not disorderly.[k]

1292, Dec. 13. Licence to the archbishop of Dublin to use his pall within the diocese of York.[l]

1293, Jan. 12. Licence to William de Mortimer and Alice his wife to have an oratory at their pleasure within their manor of Sibthorp. May 4. The archbishop requests the king to give up to him Nicholas de Menill, clerk, who had been accused on the testimony of two felons, William Cokerel and Reginald le Hunter, of causing the death of William de Mowbray, Matilda his wife, and William and Hilda their children, by firing their houses and those of the vicar of Rudby. We have acquitted him

had driven his wife from his house and refused to maintain her. His old age made him dislike her (Reg. Romanus). He was ordered to provide alimony. On May 13, 1310, archbishop Greenfield granted to dame Christiana de Menyl, relict of Sir Nicholas de Menyl, the marriage of Richard, son and heir of Robert de Furneaux, knight, the archbishop's tenant at Lutterington (Reg. Greenfield). Cf. Dugd. Bar., ii., 110.

[f] Hugh de Evesham, among other preferments in the diocese of York, held the prebend of Bugthorpe and the livings of Spofforth and Hemmingburgh. He was a famous physician, and wrote several works on medicine and divinity. In 1281 he was made cardinal priest tit. S. Laur. in Lucina. He died of the plague in 1287. Cf. Knyghton, col. 2435. Ciacon., i., 773, etc.

[g] Cf. Dugd. Bar., i., 568. Nicolson and Burn's Cumb^{d}., etc., ii., 218.

[h] He had been there before. He was master of St. Leonard's hospital, York, and of the hospital B.M. Magd. at Ripon. He resigned the latter in 1294. On May 30, 1276, the chapter of York presented him to St. Leonard's hospital, Thomas, the former rector, having died on the Sunday after Ascension-day (MSS. Cotton, Claudius, B, iii., 18).

[i] Eleanor of Provence, widow of Henry III., who died in the nunnery at Ambresbury.

[j] This person has been already mentioned. A list of the places at which Clarell was to preach is given in the register. In 1291 a provincial council was held at York about the Holy Land, and the proposed union of the Templars and the Hospitallers (Chron. Lanercost, 143-4). William de Hotham was a great advocate of this crusade (Prynne, iii., 428), which came to naught.

[k] A privilege only granted to great ladies. Archbishop Wickwaine permitted the wife of Roger de Mowbray and her family to reside for awhile in the monastery of Newburgh.

[l] John de Saunford or Stanford, archbishop from 1284 to 1294. He was a Franciscan, and a person of consequence (Cotton's Fasti Eccl. Hib., ii., 12).

in our court. June 8. An order to use prayers for fine weather, that the great rains may be stayed.[m] August 27. Henry de Brumpton, an inhabitant of Scarbrough, about thirty years ago made a vow to go to the shrine of St. James of Compostella. On account of bodily infirmities he is unequal to the journey. An order to Laurence de Wetwang, warden of the friars minors at Scarbrough, to release him from his vow on the payment of 100s.[n] Dec. 8. A general letter from the king. It has been signified to us that William, son of Thomas de Lonesdale, lost his right ear by the bite of a horse. This is not to be to his prejudice.[o]

1294, Jan. 30. A mandate to pray for the soul of Margaret, some time queen of France.[p] March 1. A letter from the archbishop to the abbat of Fountains. We intend to pass a night within your monastery on our way to Otley, but this visit is not to be used as a precedent.[q] June 16. We have received from Robert de Percy 50 marks for the use of the hospital B.M. Magd. at Ripon. The said Robert is to reside in the hospital with one attendant, and to be maintained, and we give him a robe yearly. Dec. 20. Licence for the canons of Furness, Cartmell and Cockersand to be ordained by the bishop of Carlisle.[r]

Archbishop Romanus surpassed all his predecessors in his hospitality and munificence. He had a great number of knights among his retainers, and did everything in his power to advance the dignity and the fame of his cathedral. His name will always be remembered in connection with the fabric. On the 6th of April, 1291, he laid with his own hands the foundation-stone of the present magnificent nave. The dean and the canons were standing around him whilst he invoked the blessing of the Spirit upon the work which was then begun.[s] The archbishop was at the south-eastern corner of the nave, hard by the transept of Walter Gray, and in front of him were the tower and the northern transept which his father had erected. How many memories of bygone years would rush into his mind, even amid

[m] On July 12 there was an awful thunderstorm in the diocese of York (Chron. Lan., 154). "Transit annus iste multum frugifer nec famelicus" (Walsingham, 59).

[n] Cf. Monumenta Francisc., 406. Thus Piers Ploughman says,—

> "Pilgrymes and palmeres
> Plighten hem togidere,
> For to seken seint Jame."

[o] It might otherwise have been thought that he was a felon.

[p] A similar order was made by the king in January, 1296 (Prynne, iii., 680. Fœd., i., 836).

[q] These visits were very heavy burdens. In 1309 a statute was passed to prevent them (Statutes at Large, i., 153). The monastery of Fountains was at this time in a very bad state, and the visit was a matter of necessity.

[r] Dec. 10, 1289, licence to the bishop of Carlisle to ordain the monks of Furness, Cartmell, Conishead, and Hexham, and a commendatory letter to the abbat of Furness, who is going to the general chapter of the Cistercian order. Cf. Beck's Annal. Furnesienses, 238.

[s] Stubbs, col. 1728.

that concourse, when he looked and prayed! It was indeed a high privilege for a father and a son to call into being so large a portion of that noble and beautiful cathedral.

Romanus was the founder of the prebend of Bilton at York, which he established in 1294. He contemplated also the division of the stall of Masham into three and that of Langtoft into two. The arrangements for the last step seem to have been nearly completed, and canons were actually appointed, but the proposed scheme after all seems to have fallen through, and it was never attempted afterwards. The king put his veto upon the project,[t] and the life of Romanus was too short, and his influence at court too small, to enable him to obtain the consent of the sovereign. The archbishop was also a great benefactor to the church of Southwell, and founded several stalls in that cathedral.[u] One great point in the life of Romanus was the opposition that he offered to the encroachments of the papal power. His patience, which was never great, must have been considerably taxed by the system of provisions to which he was obliged too frequently to submit. Some of the best pieces of preferment in his church and diocese were given away by the pope to foreigners, regardless of the wishes and the cognizance of the archbishop, who saw that if this state of things continued his diocese would soon run to waste. These favourites of the pope were of course non-resident, and that feeling of annoyance and discontent was already springing up which resulted, after a time, in the order that no cardinal should be beneficed in England. In 1289 an event took place which made a great stir throughout the country. The pope, Nicholas III., had given the stall of Fenton at York, and that of Nassington at Lincoln, to his nephew Matthew Rubeus, cardinal deacon of S.M. in Via Lata, a man of great learning and distinction, and the protector of the order of the friars minors.[v] The cardinal obtained the consent of his uncle to the appropriation of the prebend of Fenton to the hospital of the Holy Spirit at Rome, of which he was the head. This arrangement was so novel, and was fraught with so much danger to the English church and her independence, that a great uproar was at once made. The king wrote a strong letter of remonstrance to the pope, in which he quietly hinted that what he proposed to do would not be tolerated. The nobles of the kingdom sent another missive couched in the same strain. But the

[t] Reg. Romanus. Prynne, iii., 783. Each of the divided stalls of Masham was to be worth 50 marks per annum (Act. Capit. Ebor., 15).

[u] Dugd. Mon., vi., 1314-15. Le Neve, iii., 421, etc. Thoroton's Notts, 313-14. An examination of the architecture of this church will throw great light upon that of York, especially that of the tower and chapter-house. The register of archbishop Romanus contains some documents relative to the fabric.

[v] Ciaconius, i., 721-2. The cardinal crowned five popes.

most striking document in the whole controversy is a letter addressed by Romanus to the cardinal himself, in which, without making a personal attack upon that dignitary, he reprehends in vigorous and remarkable language the wrongs which the church was suffering at the hands of the pope, who ought to have been her protector.[w] The examples of Grostête and Bovill, his own predecessor, were no doubt in the archbishop's mind, and he expresses himself with honest zeal and eloquent indignation. I shall not apologize for placing the letter of Romanus before my readers in the language in which it was written, as a proof of the energy of his character, and as a specimen of his scholarship.

"Domino Matheo Rubecard pro prebenda de Fenton, cui in annexionem hospitalis Sancti Spiritus de Urbe in Saxia de illa dicitur esse provisum.

"Domino M., Dei gratia Sanctæ Mariæ in Via Lata diacono cardinali, J., primas, ejusdem Ebor. archiepiscopus, etc., salutem. Tacti sumus dolore cordis intrinsecus, et tædio nobis est, nec immerito, vita nostra, quum, ut videmus, commissa nobis Ebor. ecclesia facta est nostris temporibus, utinam non nostris demeritis! sub tributo; tributo quidem gravissimo quo domesticis suis et notis contra cursum materni moris occultantur ubera ejus plena, et ignotis ac alienigenis mutato caritatis ordine suggenda nudantur, sicque cogitur esurientibus propriis panem porrigere alienis et lac sitientibus propriis extraneis propinare. Nec est ex omnibus revera quos genuit qui occurrat; non utique qui sustentet ex omnibus filiis quos nutrivit, dum inde imponuntur onera humeris ejus, unde velut ab arce refugii relevacionis dexteram implorare crediderat, inde gravamina venerunt unde profecto contra spiritum procellæ Dei auxilia proventura sperabat. Nec solummodo collo ejus jugum lamentatur impositum, sed et omnibus membris suis cum doloris ingeminacione deplorat. Ecce etenim quod præter provisiones factas vobis et fratri domini Portuensiis episcopi in ecclesia memorata, sanctissimus pater, dominus noster summus pontifex, nunc tercio in provisione cujusdam alterius eandem gravavit ecclesiam, et collegiatis etiam ab ipsa velut a matre dependentibus non pepercit, sed provisiones certis fecisse personis de vacaturis canonicatibus et prebendis asseritur singulis earumdem, per quod et eædem ecclesiæ divinis fraudantur obsequiis, cum non sit ex talibus personis qui pro tympano psalmum reddant, et nobis prejudiciale nimis existat cum collationes aliquæ per nos factæ personis idoneis per sedem apostolicam jam annullatæ dicantur, et providendi nostris clericis et aliis indigenis, qui personaliter residerent et divinæ hospitali-

[w] Reg. Romanus, 86.

tatis exhibitione debita septies in die laudis cantica personarent, vel adempta potestas, vel saltem ad longa tempora sit dilata. Porro de provisione vestra in prefata ecclesia a principio quando illud audivimus gaudebamus, sed nunc merito dolere possemus præcepto quod ad sustentationem hospitalis Sancti Spiritus de Urbe, cujus habetis custodiam, sicut fertur, facta vobis dicitur provisio memorata. Sic nostra prebenda, virtute provisionis hujus vobis in ecclesia ipsa collata, reputatur alienata perpetuo, cum verisimiliter presumatur quod futuri post vos custodes hospitalis ejusdem sint eidem prebendæ ad ipsius hospitalis supportanda onera quasi jure hereditario successuri. Ex quo provenit quod canonici valde perpauci ecclesiæ memoratæ deserviunt dum ejus peculium ad remotas nationes abducitur, et de ipsius spoliis alienis necessitatibus subvenitur. Fit quoque quod velut illa exigua corpore animalia, sed artis eruditione permaxima, gens apum, quæ non sibi sed aliis nectar melleum in thecis cereis thesaurisat, velut etiam quæ sibi non semper sed potius aliis vellera ferunt oves, non sibi quoque sed aliis juga boves . . . . propriam ecclesia prelibata, non sibi vel suis obsequiis, non proximis et vicinis, sed exterorum usibus et gentis ignotæ profectibus conquisivit. Spoliatur hoc modo Eboracensis ecclesia et Romanum hospitale vestitur; altare nudatur Eboracensis ecclesiæ et certum amictitur Sancti Spiritus hospitale. Tollitur Anglicis hospitalitas et transvehitur ad Romanos. His demitur, illis augetur. Hi denique seminant, illi metunt. Hi laborant, illi vero manducant. Sic, sic, pater et domine reverende, Eboracensis tractatur ecclesia, sic patrimonium ejus expenditur, sic proficit incrementis. Utinam sit qui adjuvet et non totaliter desoletur! Verumtamen non fuit hoc pia intentio ac devota claræ memoriæ catholicorum regum Angliæ et aliorum Christi fidelium, qui nedum prefatas nostras ecclesias, sed et totam ecclesiam Anglicanam ad dilatationem fidei orthodoxæ fundantes, eas temporalium bonorum largitionibus dotaverunt amplissimis, et libertatum immunitatibus munierunt, sed ea nimirum consideratione constat sic eos eisdem ecclesiis fuisse munificos ut, cum delictorum expiatione, consequerentur per hoc salubre remedium animarum, cultus divini nominis augeretur, servaretur hospitalitas, elemosinæ darentur pauperibus, et per ministros idoneos ad quos pro tempore ex eisdem bonis ecclesiastica stipendia devenirent, servire prefatis ecclesiis personaliter tenerentur. Ad hæc pietatis opera pietatis amici et misericordiæ sectatores in extructione sanctarum ædium lapides jactavere primarios, ad hæc bona dotalicia concesserunt, ad hæc immunitatem cirographa sunt largiti. Non fuit eorum in talibus cogitatus quod ipsorum elemosinæ in usus cederent exterorum, qui licet vellus evellere non tamen pecoris vultum agnoscunt, balatum nesciunt, linguam ignorant, et postes sacros nedum terere pedibus sed videre negligunt ædium sacratarum, quamquam ipsarum uberibus educentur. Sane mirari compellimur vehementer quod vos saltem, qui eidem ecclesiæ, presertim post vestræ promotionis eventum, jam eratis obnoxii, gravaminibus his subsecutis occurrere non curâstis, cum, sicut firmiter credimus, illis resistere vestræ circumspectionis industria potuisset, quæ ad obstacula majora tollenda et favoris exhibenda potiora suffragia vires habet, ad quæ nihilominus suffragari spes preconcepta debuerat, quam a longe retroactis temporibus et reposuimus in gratiæ vestræ sinu et adhuc nodis indissolubilibus repositam retinemus; reverendæ dominacioni vestræ devotissime supplicantes quod recommendatam habentes in caritatis visceribus ecclesiam memoratam contra persecutionum incursus et turbines, eidem vos, si placet, defensionis clypeum apponatis, et indempnitati ejusdem Eboracensis ecclesiæ quæ canonicis residentibus orbatam se fore conqueritur super alienatione prefatæ prebendæ, quam perpetuitatem, occasione clausulæ pro sustentatione predicti hospitalis apostolicis insertæ literis per quandam successionem quasi heriditariam in successores vestros deputandos ad custodiam hospitalis predicti transfundendam, quod absit, non absque gravi prejudicio ipsius ecclesiæ comminatur, pro futuris post vos temporibus tam pie quam misericorditer dignemini præcavere; exhibentes vos, si placet, inter tot gravamina quibus premimur, procuratoribus nostris in curia favorabiles et benignos super promotione propitia petitionum nostrarum quas ipsi vobis nostro nomine duxerint exponendas, ut qui gravamur in pluribus saltem per vos in aliquibus relevemur. Datum apud Jaccam, xij kalendas Octobris."

The opposition of the archbishop and the king to this scheme of alienation was successful, as the project was abandoned. The sovereign indeed put his veto upon it, which was decisive. The cardinal sometime afterwards endeavoured in vain to induce him to alter his determination.[x]

We must not shut our eyes to the defects in the character of archbishop Romanus. Persons with his energy and resolution are very frequently in extremes. He was subject to an unhappy infirmity of temper, of which the Italian blood that was flowing in his veins must have been to a great extent the cause. He was nearly always involved in some quarrel or dissension which had its origin in the clashing of contending interests, or some petty jealousy or dislike. It is painful to trace the path of an archbishop through the darkness of the past by the light of enmity and discord.

[x] Prynne's Coll., iii., 416-18, 625, 934. Rot. Parl., i., 33. Fœd., i., 740, 754.

The relations between archbishop Romanus and his chapter were by no means of an amicable kind. He had a feud with the dean, apart from his brother-canons. The dean, Robert Ughtred of Scarbrough, got into trouble, among other reasons, because he was a pluralist, holding, in addition to his office, the prebend of Husthwaite at York, a stall at Beverley, and the living of Adlingflete. In September, 1287, the archbishop deprived him summarily of his deanery and his canonry at York, and ordered the chapter to elect a new superior. A compromise seems to have been effected, as in May, 1290, the dean consented to resign all his preferments, the archbishop giving him, at the instance of the king, an annual pension of 400 marks for his life. He did not enjoy it long, as he died in the same year. At his decease he was in arrear to the archbishop, probably for some due or fine for non-residence, and the executors of his will, Sir Robert Ughtred, knight, and John his brother, were put under a sentence of excommunication, which was removed in May, 1293.[y]

The archbishop's contention with the chapter was on the question of his right to hold a visitation of the minster, and when he mooted this claim, he found that he was treading on very delicate and dangerous ground. The controversy seems to have been so warm that in 1287 the king authorized Edmund, earl of Cornwall, to act as mediator between the combatants.[z] On the 20th of May, 1288, they agreed to submit the matter to arbitration, the bishop of Norwich acting for the archbishop, and William de Corner, the precentor of York, for the dean. On the 24th of September the bishop of Chichester took the place of his brother of Norwich, who was prevented by illness from attending. In consequence, probably, of their award, an arrangement was made on the 21st of November, 1290, with reference to the power of visiting the chapter. It contains a great number of minute articles. The chief of them are as follows:—The dean was to pay the archbishop canonical obedience without infringing upon the privileges of the chapter. The archbishop might visit the minster once in five years, if he chose, but not by deputy. He must intimate his intention by letter to the chapter, and they were to give the formal notice. The archbishop alone was to enter the chapter-house, two members of the cathedral body, who were to be sworn to secrecy, acting with him. Any canon might then make his complaints. If any fault were detected, the archbishop was to allow the offender six months to amend it, and, in case of default or neglect, he was to award proper punishment in the chapter-house, with the

[y] The account of these quarrels is taken chiefly from the archbishop's register.

[z] Fœd., i., 679.

advice of the canons.—This is the sum and substance of the regulations about the visitation. Some arrangements were also made about the hearing of causes, which are of little interest.

The greatest struggle that Romanus was engaged in, and that which caused him most annoyance and anxiety, was that which he had with Anthony Bek, bishop of Durham.[a] There had been for a long time a soreness between Durham and York on the question of supremacy and the right to hold visitations, which had given much trouble to archbishop Wickwaine. The feud was running high when Romanus came to the see of York, but by the kind interference of cardinal Hugh de Evesham an arrangement was made with the prior and convent of Durham, by which the archbishop of York was allowed to have the control of the diocese during the vacancy of the see.[b] This seems to have given satisfaction, and the sentence of excommunication, in which Wickwaine had involved the monks of Durham, was now withdrawn. Romanus, however, was soon in the middle of another controversy with Bek, the wealthiest and most influential prelate of his day. It began, probably, about the question of the subjection of the see of Durham to York, which Bek was far too high-spirited to submit to. In 1290, when Romanus was at the funeral of queen Eleanor, the king in vain endeavoured to reconcile the two Northern prelates. On the 31st of July, 1291, when the archbishop was at Hexham, he sent his clerks, Henry de Tymparon and William de Thorneton, to bishop Bek to propose that the dispute should be referred to arbitration, but the offer was in all probability rejected. Romanus now resolved, if possible, to go abroad and plead his cause before the pope. The king, after much hesitation, allowed him to make the journey, and he started on the 1st of November, 1291. He was honourably received at the papal court, and continued there till the spring of 1292, but from the silence which exists about his mission we may conclude that it was unsuccessful. In the beginning of the following year, 1292, matters at last came to a crisis. John de Amelia, a notary, and William de Wrelton, alias De Piks, two of the archbishop's clerks, no doubt under his directions, went to Durham to deliver to Bek or his servants a citation from their master. Bek was then in Scotland with the king, but his officials acted as their lord would have done if he had been at home. John de Maydenstan treated the hostile mandate with contempt, and, seizing the luckless messengers,

[a] The authorities are, Prynne's Coll., iii., 456, 560-5, 1293; Rot. Parl., i., 102-5; Chron. Lanercost, 110-11, 137; Knyghton, col. 2502, 2507; Contin. Fl. Wigorn., ii., 267; Madox Bar. Angl., 150-1; Fuller's Worthies, *n. e.*, ii., 540; Drake's Eboracum, 430.

[b] Hist. Dunelm. Scr. Tres, 73, and appendix, 93, etc.

shut them up in the dungeons of Durham castle, of which he was the constable. Romanus was abroad when this adventure took place, but he wrote from Viterbo, where he was probably with the pope, on the 6th of April, 1292, to his official at York, commanding him to denounce the bishop of Durham as excommunicated. He sent also a request to Bogo de Clare, who, he probably thought, was bold enough to do anything, desiring him to beard the lion in his den by proclaiming the sentence in the priory of Durham, at the same time giving him a quiet hint that it would be well for him to say nothing at all about his being treasurer of York. Bogo would know Bek well, and would do nothing of the kind. The thought that he would refuse to act seems to have occurred to the archbishop, as on the 19th of April, a few days afterwards, he issued a like commission to the prior of Bolton, who published the sentence of excommunication. Like a wise man, with the fear of imprisonment before his eyes, he kept within sight of Yorkshire, for he performed the duty which was assigned to him at Northallerton and Darlington. Bek had been thrice warned, but he cared not a whit for the ban; he kept the two unfortunate officials in captivity, and set at naught their master.

In the following year the dispute came under the cognizance of parliament. It was laid before the king, in all probability, by Bek, and Edward took the matter up with vehemence. It appears that when the bishop of Durham was excommunicated, he was with the king in Scotland, and the monarch regarded the denunciation of his favourite prelate, whilst he was thus occupied, as a personal insult to himself. To obtain the release of his clerks Romanus ought to have proceeded against Bek in the king's court. The injury to the royal prerogative was assessed by the officers of the crown at the large sum of 20,000*l*. The archbishop pleaded his own cause, and tried to justify his conduct. It had never entered into his head, he said, to offer any slight to the king. The bishop of Durham was his suffragan; after repeated warnings he had been disobedient, and the archbishop in excommunicating him had merely acted in accordance with ecclesiastical law. In answer to this the royal advocate stated that Bek was a temporal as well as a spiritual dignitary; that he was prince palatine as well as bishop of Durham, and that a sentence of excommunication, which was an ecclesiastical censure only, would injure him in his secular character. Bek had a right to order the men to prison in his character of prince palatine, with which the archbishop had nothing whatever to do. The decision of the parliament was unanimous against Romanus, and he was committed to the Tower for his offence. The nobles, however, interceded for him, and he placed himself at the king's mercy. He was restored to the royal favour, but only after submitting to a fine of 4000 marks.

This was not the only reverse which Romanus experienced in the same parliament. Some time before this the king had expelled the Jews from England, and had appropriated their possessions. Among the sufferers was a person of the name of Bonamy, who had lived at York. When Romanus was on his way home from the papal court he halted at Paris, where he met Bonamy. The Jew told him that he had lent the prior and convent of Bridlington the sum of 300*l.*, which was still owing to him, and begged him to recover it for him. It was afterwards insinuated that the archbishop bought the debt; but this he denied, and it is only fair to believe him. When Romanus came back to England he made an official visitation of the priory of Bridlington, and the existence of the debt being proved the archbishop compelled the prior to pay the 300*l.* to one of his officers. It was an obligation, he told him, which the convent could not conscientiously disown. Quite true, my lord archbishop, but the money ought to have gone, not to yourself, but to the Jew or the king. Romanus, by receiving it, put himself at the mercy of the prior, who lost no time in complaining of his diocesan for concealing money which belonged properly to the crown. The case was of course decided against the archbishop, but we are not told to what penalty he was subjected.[c] His conduct, to say the least, was suspicious in the extreme; and most persons will be inclined to think that it was highly reprehensible.

The catalogue of mischief and contention is not yet exhausted. In 1294 Romanus quarrelled with the prior and sub-prior of the monastery of the Holy Trinity at York, and excommunicated them, taking possession of their goods, although they were exempt from his jurisdiction.[d] He had also a keen fight with Bogo de Clare, a well-known delinquent, and the notorious pluralist who has been already mentioned.[e] The archbishop was clearly a hot-headed and a most indiscreet person. Knyghton tells us that covetousness was his chief infirmity, and his conduct in the case of the Jew would certainly seem to shew that he had inherited that grovelling vice which is said to have characterized his sire.[f] The contests in which Romanus was perpetually involved bear a melancholy testimony to the way-

[c] Prynne's Coll., iii., 565-6. Rot. Parl., i., 99, 100, 120. [d] Ibid., 610.

[e] Reg. Romanus. Prynne, iii., 1284, etc. In 1293 he had suits with Thomas de Neville and Nicholas de Segrave (Rot. Parl., i., 93). He had also a serious affray with Boniface de Saluciis (Reg. Romanus. Rot. Pat., i., 138).

[f] Col. 2507. The words which Erasmus uses in his colloquy on "Opulentia sordida" are applicable to him, "Illi in hujusmodi sordibus educato præter lucrum nihil erat dulce" (Colloq., ed. 1650, 495).

wardness of his temper, his impatience of control, and his unwillingness to brook even the idea of a rival,

> "Nec quemquam jam ferre potest Cæsarve priorem
> Pompeiusve parem."

The archbishop died suddenly at Burton, near Beverley, where he had a residence, on the 11th of March, 1296. His remains were brought to York, and were honourably interred in the minster on the Saturday following.[g] It is not known where he was first laid; but when archbishop Thoresby began the rebuilding of the choir, he removed the bones of Romanus, and deposited them in the presbytery, placing over them a marble stone which was decorated with brass.[h]

Romanus died in the king's debt, and security was obliged to be taken that payment should be made as far as his effects extended.[i] Knyghton tells us that the archbishop's executors, of whom John de Leke was one,[j] refused to act, and that the charges of his funeral were borne by strangers, whilst no gifts for pious uses were made on the day of his interment, and not a prayer was offered up for the repose of his soul.[k] The charge of the temporalities of the see during the vacancy was entrusted to John de Lithegreynes.[l]

After the decease of Romanus his executors gave into the king's wardrobe a cup of white silver and a ring with a sapphire, which had belonged to him.[m]

Henry de Newark was a native, in all probability, of a little town in Nottinghamshire. Of his parentage there is nothing known, but he seems to have been a kinsman of William de Newark, who was a canon of Southwell and archdeacon of Huntingdon.[n]

[g] MSS. Cotton, Vitellius, A, ii., 111 *b*. Stubbs, col. 1728. Prynne's Coll., iii., 642. Knyghton (col. 2507) speaks of a mean funeral. In the Chron. Lanercost it is said that the archbishop died abroad (170).

[h] See Thoresby's Life.

[i] Reg. Melton, 18, 34. Cf. Knyghton, col. 2502.

[j] Reg. Newark. In 34th of Edw. I. John de Leke was the king's almoner (Prynne, iii., 1160). Chaplain of prince Edward, 28th Edward I. (Lib. Garderobæ, 31). There are letters to the pope in his behalf from Edward I. and II. in Fœd., i., 987, 1005, 1009, 1016; ii., 10, 46. He was bishop elect of Dunkeld in 1309 (Fœd., ii., 86), and in 1311 the pope elected him archbishop of Dublin (ibid., 132). He died in 1313, and was buried in Westminster abbey (Cotton's Fasti, ii., 14).

[k] Knyghton, col. 2507.

[l] Prynne's Coll., iii., 674.

[m] Wardrobe Accounts, 345. A gift of his to the king is mentioned, ibid., 348.

[n] He was archdeacon of Huntingdon in 1281 and 1282, and died in the latter end of 1286 (Le Neve, ii., 49). He

Newark appears to have risen in importance through his state services and his connection with the court. He was one of the clerks and chaplains of Edward I., and in that capacity he was sent by the king to the pope on the 12th of December, 1276, to announce the part which he intended to take in the proposed crusade, and in the following year he was acting as the king's proctor at the papal court, and was busily engaged in making preparations for that expedition.[o] In 1281 he was appointed to quiet the disturbances between the English and the Hollanders,[p] and in January, 1283, he was one of those who were ordered to collect the subsidy for the expedition into Wales within the bishopric of Durham.[q] On the 1st of February, in the same year, he was selected to arrange the amount of service that was due to the king from the knights to the north of the Trent.[r] In the summer of 1290 Newark was sent as an ambassador to Scotland to contract an alliance between the heir to the English throne, and Margaret, daughter of Eric king of Norway, queen of Scotland.[s] The year 1291 saw him with Edward I. at Norham, and he was deeply involved in the intricacies of Scottish politics.[t] In 1292 the king granted him letters of protection.[u] On the 1st of January, 1296, he was one of the commissioners who were deputed to make a truce with France, and treaties with Guelders and Flanders.[v] Indeed, he seems to have taken a very prominent part in public affairs during the reign of Edward I., and to have been a thorough man of business and a skilful and active statesman.[w]

Whilst Newark was thus engaged in the service of his country he was in the possession of numerous and important ecclesiastical preferments. In 1271 and 1275 I find that he

was also prebendary of Farrendon at Lincoln (Reg. Romanus). On July 11, 1287, archbishop Romanus denounced those who had abstracted a charter which testified to Thomas de Lincoln, clerk, being the heir of Mr. William de Newark. On Feb. 11, 1288, the same prelate ordered Mr. Henry de Newark, archdeacon of Richmond, to convert to its intended purpose the 100*l.* which Mr. William de Newark, archdeacon of Huntingdon, gave in his will to hire a chaplain to sing for his soul. 1289, March 24, the sum of 10 marks, which had been given to Matilda Adelyn, of Newark, deceased, is paid over to the archbishop by Mr. W. de Kelun and the other executors of William de Newark; 6 marks of it are ordered to be paid by the archdeacon of Richmond to the daughters of John de Egliston; and the other 4 to the nuns of Molseby by Mr. W. de Blida (Reg. Romanus). Cf. Thoroton's Notts, 197.

On June 18, 1298, archbishop Newark collated his chaplain, William de Newark, to the stall of North Muskham at Southwell, which he had himself vacated. He seems to have held it until 1340 (Le Neve, iii., 428-9).

[o] Prynne's Coll., iii., 193, 197. Fœd., i., 537, 542. [p] Fœd., i., 597.

[q] Prynne's Coll., iii., 303.

[r] Fœd., i., 625.

[s] Ibid., i., 734-6. Prynne, iii., 395, 398-9.

[t] Fœd., i., 767, etc. Prynne, iii., 504, etc. [u] Prynne, iii., 683.

[v] Ibid., 748. Fœd., i., 834-5.

[w] Knyghton (col. 2528) calls him "magnus clericus."

was prebendary of Brownswood in St. Paul's cathedral,[x] and in January, 1293, he occurs as a canon of the church of Wells.[y] In 1296 he vacated the living of Basingham, in the diocese of Lincoln.[z] But it was with the province of York that he was principally connected. On the 30th of March, 1270, he was presented to the living of Barnby, which he resigned in the same year,[a] and on the death of archbishop Giffard in 1279 the king made him and Thomas de Normanvill the keepers of the temporalities of the see of York.[b] With archbishop Wickwaine Newark seems to have been a great favourite. Soon after he became primate he made Newark archdeacon of Richmond, and on the 20th of December, 1280, he was collated to the stall of Holme, which he resigned for that of Strensal on the 9th of November, 1283.[c] In that year the archdeacon seems to have been advancing his master's interests in the court of Rome, and they were associated together in more than one pecuniary transaction.[d] Soon after archbishop Romanus came to the see we find Newark lending him money, and the archdeacon found a patron in that prelate, who gave him the stall of Great Muskham at Southwell on the 4th of June, 1287,[e] and appointed him his vicar-general on the 12th of March, 1288, during his absence with the king in Gascony.[f] In the spring of 1290 Newark was elected dean of York. The archbishop ordered the chapter to install him on the 12th of May, and that ceremony took place on the 10th of June.[g] Newark then resigned the archdeaconry of Richmond, but he held the stall of Weighton with the deanery till he was advanced to the primacy.[h] In his position as dean he had a collision with archbishop Romanus, who endeavoured to extort from him a profession of obedience, and an acknowledgment of his right to visit the cathedral.[i] I have already stated how this dispute was arranged, and it is unnecessary to refer to it again. Newark was present on the 6th of April, 1291, when Romanus laid the foundation-stone of the new nave of the minster,[j] and in the progress of that work he could not fail to be deeply interested.

[x] Newcourt, i., 120. Le Neve, ii., 365.

[y] Prynne, iii., 577.

[z] MSS. Harl., 6951, 32 *b*.

[a] Reg. Giffard.

[b] Prynne, iii., 224. Normanville was a justiciar and eschaetor beyond Trent (Rot. Parl., i., 38).

[c] Reg. Wickwaine, 3, 114. Torre says that he was made archdeacon of Richmond on Nov. 12, 1281.

[d] Reg. Wickwaine. In 1286 Newark farmed the prebend of Ulleskelf, and rebuilt the houses belonging to it near the minster (Reg. Romanus, 69 *a*).

[e] The stall was burdened with an annual pension of 50 marks to Adenulphus, a cardinal, by an old arrangement. Newark was one of the sureties of Romanus for the payment of his fine to the king (Drake's Eboracum, 430). Reg. Romanus, 70 *b*.

[f] Reg. Romanus.

[g] He was admitted on May 20 (Act. Capit.).

[h] Le Neve, iii., 137.

[i] Acta Capit.

[j] Stubbs, col. 1728.

Archbishop Romanus died in March, 1296, and when on the 26th of that month the king gave his permission to the chapter to choose a new primate, they responded by electing their own dean on the 7th of May.[k] The appointment appears to have satisfied the king, who gave his assent to what had been done, on the 5th of June. Edward also wrote to the pope, begging him to shew favour to Newark, and to give him the pall. He told him that he had made him a guardian of the kingdom during his own absence in Flanders.[l] For some reason or other, with which we are unacquainted, nearly two years passed away before Newark was consecrated. That ceremony at length took place in York minster on the 15th of June, 1298, Anthony Bek, bishop of Durham, officiating, with the assistance of the bishops of Lichfield, St. Asaph, and Cork.[m] The temporalities had been restored to him on the 22nd of June in the preceding year.[n] It was by the special permission of the pope that Newark was consecrated at York. He professed his inability to visit the papal court on account of the wars which were then raging abroad.[o]

Archbishop Newark has left very little at York by which he can be remembered. His life, after his accession to office, was so short that he had no opportunity of distinguishing himself in his new sphere of duty. In 1297 he was a member of the council of Edward the king's son,[p] and in that year and 1299 he was summoned to the parliament at London.[q] He is also mentioned in connection with the gathering-in of the taxes within his diocese,[r] and once or twice he came into collision with the royal prerogative in judicial matters; the cases, however, were of slight moment.[s] One pious act of the archbishop has been handed down. He covered with buildings a piece of waste ground at Hull, and with the rents he endowed a chaplain for each of the manors appertaining to his see, at Cawood, Burton, and Wilton, and a chantry priest, who was to perform service at the altar of St. William, in York minster, for the souls of the kings and queens of England, and the primates of the Northern province.[t]

Archbishop Newark died on the feast of the Assumption of the Blessed Virgin, 1299, and was interred at York.[u] He left

[k] Ibid. MSS. Cotton, Vitellius, A, ii., 111 *b*.

[l] Reg. Newark. Prynne, iii., 675.

[m] Reg. Newark. Stubbs (col. 1728) makes the day June 24, and MSS. Cotton, Vitellius, A, ii., 111 *b*, the 25th.

[n] Prynne, iii., 767. In Act. Capit. Ebor., 8 *b*, is a list of some stock belonging to the treasury which the archbishop had when he was first elected.

[o] Ibid., 642. Knyghton, col. 2507.

[p] Parl. Writs., i., 61.

[q] Ibid., i., 55, 78.

[r] Prynne, iii., 671, 692, 740-1, 789. Wilkins, ii., 235.

[s] Prynne, iii., 779, 793-4.

[t] Ibid., 862-3. Cf. Fabric Rolls, 236, where some work of his at Newark is perhaps alluded to.

[u] MSS. Cotton, Vitellius, A, ii., 111 *b*. Stubbs, col. 1728. Trivet, 316 —*circa*.

a will, of which two distinguished brothers, William and Robert de Pickering, both of them deans of York, were the executors. On the 18th of July, 1306, archbishop Greenfield appointed some commissioners to receive the account of their administration. The task of the executors seems to have been a thankless and a laborious one. They did not obtain their release till the 29th of March, 1311, and it was then found that they had received 5592*l.* 16s. 9½d.,[v] and paid 6010*l.* 2s. 0½d., so that they were actually losers by their executorship.

Thomas de Corbridge was born within the province of York, and was a native, in all probability, of the little village of Corbridge in Northumberland, which is situated on the Tyne.[w] It was formerly a place of so much importance that it sent members to parliament; but its incipient greatness was soon

[v] Reg. Greenfield. On "die Sabbati p. f. Assump. B.V." Newark's executors proved his will before the chapter. On "die Martis p. f. S. Gregorii," at the request of Peter de Ros and R. de la Ford, canons of York, the goods of Newark were sequestered on account of something due to the church. They were deposited in the house of the friars minors at York, and on the next day, G., the chamberlain, and H. de Newark, friars minors, brought nine large and four small chests to the chapter (Act. Capit., 9 *b*). On Nov. 21, 1301, a commission was appointed to receive the accounts of Newark's executors (Reg. Corbridge).

[w] Reg. Romanus. Several other persons of the name of Corbridge, who were probably related to the archbishop, occur in the registers of York.

H. Corbridge was a clerk of archbishop Giffard.

Thomas de Corbridge has licence to be ordained, being then an accolite, April 9, 1301. Sept. 25, 1301, Mr. Thomas de Corbridge, dictus de Malton, to the church of Brunum. Sept. 26, licence to him to be non-resident for seven years to study. Sept. 29, he, being the archbishop's clerk, was collated to a stall at Ripon, which, after all, he did not obtain (Reg. Corbridge). 1313, Oct. 4, licence to Mr. Thomas de Corbrig, rector of Kipask (Kippax), to be non-resident for three years (Reg. Greenfield). Feb. 28, 1318, a similar permission (Reg. Melton), and on Sept. 7, 1327, he was made collector of the money to be raised for the university of Oxford (ibid.). In 1318, Thomas de Corbridge, S.T.P., became canon of Thorngate, at Lincoln, and he was buried there. His arms, on a cross fitchè five escallops, were on his tomb (Le Neve, ii., 222). Prynne's Coll., iii., 903. Rot. Parl., i., 394. In 1313, Thomas de Corbridge was ordered to go abroad with the king (Fœd., ii., 212).

Robert de Corbridge, instituted on Sept. 25, 1301, to the living of Roos on the presentation of Kirkham priory. Sept. 26, licence of non-residence for seven years "ad scolas." On April 9, he had letters dimissory. He made his will on the Saturday after the feast of the Circumcision, 1347, being then rector of Roos. To be buried at the east end of the churchyard. 100s. for his funeral expenses, and 15 marks and his best portiphor noted to Peter de la Wardrobe to celebrate for him for two years. To the church a missal and his better vestment. My sister Alice and Stephen and Andrew her children, and Peter, son of my brother Richard, called Mareschall (Pr. Feb. 1, 1348).

absorbed in the wealth and influence of the neighbouring town of Newcastle. Hexham, with its stately monastery, was in the immediate vicinity, and young Corbridge would thus be brought into connection with the officers of the see of York, and their lord and master. He received an university education, and was a master in theology and a person of reputation and learning.[x] Stubbs commends his erudition in the highest terms, and speaks of him as a kind of admirable Crichton.[y]

The first piece of preferment that Corbridge held at York was the stall of Osbaldwick, but it is not known when he was first promoted to it.[z] This he gave up in 1279, when he was advanced to the chancellorship on the elevation of Wickwaine to the archiepiscopate.[a] On the 16th of January, 1280, he and Henry de Newark, archdeacon of Richmond, were appointed to enquire into the recent election of Robert de Scarborough to the deanery.[b] On the 25th of June he was collated to the prebendary of Stillington,[c] and in 1281 he was at Rome on some business connected with the minster, and archbishop Wickwaine defrayed the charges of his journey. On the 16th of June, 1290, he was made sacrist of the chapel of St. Sepulchre at York, and he resigned the chancellorship.[d] This office, which was an honourable and lucrative one, involved its occupant in no little difficulty and annoyance. It had become vacant by the death of Percival de Lavannia or Lavagna, an Italian of rank and wealth, and at his decease Nicholas IV. gave archbishop Romanus permission to bestow it upon an Englishman. Romanus offered it to Corbridge, who accepted it on the condition that he should have it without suit or annoyance of any kind. On these terms he gave up the chancellorship, to which Thomas de Wakefield, the sub-dean, was appointed, William de Blida succeeding him in that office. Corbridge, however, on taking possession of the manors of the sacristry, found that there was trouble and litigation enough,[e] and, availing himself of the condition that he had made, he again entered into his stall as chancellor. He ought really to have known what the condition of the sacristry was before he accepted it; by his present conduct he threw the chapter of York into confusion, dislocated

[x] Trivet, 316. Knyghton, col. 2528.

[y] Stubbs, col. 1728. "Sacræ theologiæ doctor egregius, et non solum theologiæ, immo quod raro uni mortalium accidit, omnium artium liberalium professor extitit incomparabilis."

[z] Reg. Wickwaine, 59. Cf. Le Neve, iii., 206.

[a] Le Neve, iii., 163.

[b] Reg. Wickwaine, 58 *b*. Dec. 17. 1279, licence to the chancellor and Mr. Hugh de Evesham to examine clerks (ibid.).

[c] Reg. Wickwaine, 59.

[d] For the account of this controversy cf. Acta Capit., i., 2. Reg. Romanus. Stubbs, col. 1729.

[e] The church of Calverley, the revenues of which John Scot claimed against Corbridge. On July 6, 1290, Romanus ordered James de Langtoft, his sequestrator, to seize them.

the arrangements which had been recently effected, and made Wakefield and Blyth his enemies. When his conduct, which was justifiable enough, came to the ears of the archbishop, he regarded him as an intruder and threatened to proceed against him. Blyth now claimed to be installed as sub-dean, but the chapter civilly declined, and the choir was watched lest the archbishop should come and bring about the installation. The precaution was a wise one, for Romanus came to the minster, and the door into the choir was not opened to admit him till he had promised to do nothing about Blyth until the dean, Henry Newark, had returned from Scotland. When the dean came back he visited the archbishop at Ripon, and the primate begged him to recal Corbridge who had started for Rome, and to get the dispute quietly arranged. Newark assented; but when he reached York and called the chapter together, he would be astonished when he saw Blyth present a citation from the archbishop, ordering the dean and canons to appear before him. This looked very like double dealing on the part of Romanus. The chapter now despatched Philip de Alnwick, their auditor, and Andrew de Tang, a notary, to the archbishop who was still at Ripon, to expostulate and to express their dislike of controversies and quarrels. The primate exhibited his usual infirmity of temper and spoke very angrily and indiscreetly, and the two emissaries of the chapter were thrown into prison. The dean and his brethren were now summoned to appear before Romanus at Cawood, but they were too cautious to pay any attention to his bidding. Corbridge in the meanwhile was pushing his case at Rome, but he was unsuccessful, and, refusing to cede his point, he was excommunicated on the 27th of July, 1290, and the sentence continued in force till the 24th of March in the following year.

On the 5th of September, 1299, Edward I. gave the chapter of York permission to elect a new archbishop in the room of Henry de Newark.[f] They met on the 12th of November, and John de Metingham, John de Cadamo and Robert de Pickering were appointed to scrutinize the votes. The majority fixed upon Corbridge,[g] and on the 16th the king assented to their choice.[h] He went to Rome and was consecrated by Boniface VIII., on the 27th of February, receiving at the same time the pall. The pope, however, obliged him to resign his right of election into his hands and afterwards gave him the archbishopric of his own authority. On the 30th of April Edward I. ordered the temporalities of the see of York to be restored to him. They

[f] Le Neve, iii., 104.

[g] Prynne's Coll., iii., 859. MSS. Cotton, Vitellius, A, ii., 112. Stubbs, col. 1729.

[h] Le Neve, iii., 104.

had been in the custody of Geoffrey Russell and Lambert de Trykingham.[i]

When Corbridge became archbishop of York he of course resigned the sacristry of the chapel of St. Sepulchre and the stall of Stillington. They were given by Boniface to his great-nephew Francis, son of Peter Gaetano, a noble Italian.[j] In 1304 Gaetano seems to have resigned the sacristry, and Corbridge, at the request of the pope, gave it to Gilbert de Segrave, a person of great learning and ability, who was afterwards bishop of London.[k] Edward I., however, was most wishful that one of his own clerks, John de Bush, should have not only that office, but the prebend of Stillington, considering that it was his right to give them away as they had become vacant by the archbishop's accession to the primacy. Corbridge was now in a difficulty; he refused to admit the king's right, and pleaded in his defence the wishes and claims of the pope. On the 6th of June, 1304, Bush came to the archbishop at Selby, bringing a letter from the king who was then in Scotland, in which he remonstrated with the primate for his disobedience. The archbishop replied that he was ready to appoint a commission to enquire into the merits of the case. Bush murmured at this, and denied the necessity of the proceeding, upon which Corbridge quietly observed, that the king, when he presented him, would of course do nothing contrary to the law. Bush now tried a legal remedy, and he was successful. The archbishop was brought before the king's courts and lost his cause, being deprived, as a punishment, of the temporalities of his see, which remained in the king's hands till his decease. Bush recovered the prebend of Stillington, for which he had been a petitioner. The sacristry came into his hands at a later period. As soon as Corbridge died, the chapter of York acted very ungenerously, and did an act of gross injustice. They removed Gilbert de Segrave from the control of the chapel of St. Sepulchre, and entrusted it to Bush.[l] The appointment, as the result shewed, was a most unsatisfactory one, for the new sacrist paid no attention to his duties.

[i] MSS. Cotton, Vitellius, A, ii., 112. Stubbs, col. 1729. Prynne's Coll., iii., 860. During this time the king and queen occupied the residences of the archbishop at their pleasure. We find them at London and Cawood (Lib. Garderobæ, 54, 93, 108).

[j] For an account of this controversy, see Prynne, 860, 1114, 1132. Fœd., i., 1000; ii., 21—24. Stubbs, col. 1729, where there are several statements which are not verified by historical evidence. Abbrev. Plac., 251-2.

[k] On Sept. 13, 1309, archbishop Greenfield empowered the abbat of St. Mary's, York, and Robert de Riplingham, the chancellor, to enquire into a claim for 40 marks which Gilbert de Segrave, archdeacon of Oxford, made on the executors of Corbridge (Reg. Greenfield).

[l] A clerk of the king 28th Edward I. (Wardrobe Accounts, 314); rector of Beckenham, Kent, in 1306 (Hasted,

This was not the only collision that Corbridge had with the king. There was a great deal of angry feeling between them about the church of Beverley. The archbishop gave great offence by his conduct whilst Edward was in that town, and, as a mark of his displeasure, the liberties of the place were taken possession of by the crown. They were restored on the 14th of June, 1301.[m] In 1304 Aymon de Carto, the provost of Beverley, and Corbridge, had a very serious quarrel on the subject of the visitation of the church, to which the king was made a party. The provost was anxious that the matter in dispute should be decided, not at Rome, but before the national courts, and Corbridge was as eager to prevent this. The archbishop had many charges against Carto for neglect of duties, extortion, etc., and besides all this, he was a pluralist, as he held, in addition to the superintendence of the church of Beverley, the precentorship of Lyons, the provostship of Lausanne, and the church of Duncarnayn in the diocese of Lismore. In June, 1304, Carto was excommunicated for his contumacy, and Robert de Alberwick was made provost of Beverley in his room. He was afterwards raised to the episcopal bench abroad.[n]

The debated point of the right of the Northern primate to carry his cross erect was not lost sight of whilst Corbridge was at York. On the 25th of April, 1300, the archbishop of Canterbury wrote to the bishop of London to say that his brother in the North had been following the obnoxious precedent which his predecessors had set, and he ordered that no one should stoop to receive his blessing. On the 25th of January, in the following year, he sent a deprecatory letter on the same subject to his suffragan the bishop of Lincoln.[o]

The name of archbishop Corbridge occurs very rarely among the state papers of the day. In 1294 he had the royal letters of protection.[p] In 1300 I find him attesting the exemplification of the bull of pope Boniface for the extension of the truce between France and England.[q] In 1301 he was summoned to the meeting of the parliament at Lincoln, and to those at Westminster and London in 1302. In 1303 he was requested to send his contingent to serve against the Scots.[r] The great Northern war was now raging, and the names of Wallace, Brus and Douglas would be ringing through the whole of Yorkshire. The city of York would thus become the great rendezvous of

—, 88); canon of St. David's in 1307 (Parl. Writs, i., 185); a public notary (Pell Records, 105); a trier of petitions in parliament, and much occupied in parliamentary work (Fœd., i., 973. Rot. Parl., i., 182. Parl. Writs, *var. locis, etc.)*. Stubbs, col. 1729.

[m] Prynne's Coll., iii., 861.

[n] Reg. Corbridge, 98-100. · Rot. Parl., i., 162.

[o] Wilkins, ii., 255, 264.

[p] Prynne, iii., 598. [q] Ibid., 872.

[r] Parl. Writs, i., 89, 112, 114, 116, 367, 370.

the English armies and a place of unusual importance. In 1298 the courts were removed to it from London, and they continued there for seven years.[s] The king and his family were frequently in the neighbourhood.[t] The following extracts from the archbishop's register will throw some light upon the history of the time as well as upon the proceedings of Corbridge within his own diocese.

1301, May 31. The archbishop receives from William de Newark, canon of Southwell, a missal of the York use, which we promise to restore to him when it is required. June 14. The will and codicil of dame Eva de Tibtoft[u] are proved before the primate in the house of the friars minors at Doncaster, and administration is granted to Roger de Wordham, rector of Arksey, and Adam de Radegrave, rector of Little Blakham in the diocese of Norwich. June 17. An indulgence of 40 days for the church of Ripon in which the relics of that glorious confessor, St. Wilfrid, are preserved.[v] June 19. The archbishop writes to Henry de Lacy, earl of Lincoln, allowing Michael de Merton and Reginald de Kington, friars minors, who are going with him to the wars of Scotland, to act as confessors for natives of the diocese of York.[w] Sept. 24. A dispensation of non-residence to Mr. Ralph de Nevill, rector of Middleham,[x] to enable him to study for two years. Oct. 3. A commission to Patrick de Braferton and Richard de Stowe to enquire for those who have deserted from the army in Scotland, having received their wages.[y] Nov. 2. John de Cave and Ralph, our bailiff at Beverley, appointed justices within that liberty to see into the use of bad money.[z] Dec. 17. Edward de Clement gives to the trea-

[s] Rot. Parl., i., 143.

[t] See the Wardrobe Accounts. Walsingham, 74. Knyghton (col. 2524) mentions the subsidy granted by the archbishop and the clergy towards the war.

[u] Daughter of Pain de Chaworth (Dugd. Mon., ii., 38). On Oct. 10, 1298, the administration of the effects of Sir Robert de Tipetoft, knight, was granted to dame Eva, his widow, Sir Baldwin de Manners, knight, and Roger de Wrtham, priest (Reg. Newark). Sir Robert was with Edward I. in the Holy Land (Test. Vetust., 8).

[v] Cf. Fabric Rolls of York, ed. Surtees Society, 235. Walbran's Ripon, 26.

[w] On July 15, 1300, William Namy brings the earl's will to Thorp with his seals appended, and delivers letters from his master begging that the archbishop's seal might be put to it, which was done. For the acts and deeds of this prince-like noble,—the greatest man in the North of England, see Dugd. Bar., i., 105, etc.

[x] On Sept. 19, 1306, licence to Mr. Robert de Neville, rector of Well, and deacon, to study for two years (Reg. Greenfield). These were, no doubt, members of the baronial house of Neville. On June 8, 1314, a confirmation of two chantries in the chapel of Thoraldeby par. Aysgarth, made by the king, the earl of Richmond, and Mary de Neville, lady of Middleham (ibid.).

[y] In 31st Edward I. the sanctuarymen at Beverley and many thousands of thieves and outlaws had been allowed to enlist. This accounts for the character of the army (Prynne, iii., 1010). Cal. Rot. Pat., 60.

[z] In 1299 a statute was passed against

surer and chancellor two piles and three ordinary trussels for the archbishop's mint.[a]

1301, July 19. The will of the countess of Warwick is proved at Sprotburgh before Reginald de St. Albans and William de Beverley, the archbishop's clerks, John de Wolfington, dioc. Worcester, representing two of the executors, Guy, earl of Warwick and Sir John de Hastings, and John de Schukeberewe appearing for Robert, prior of Kenilworth, and Mr. Thurstan de Keswick, co-executors.[b] Sept. 15. A general letter against those who have broken into Beverley park.[c] Oct. 24. Licence for George, rector of Dinnington in Morthen, to be absent from his living for a year at the request of Sir Brian Fitzalan.[d] Dec. 20. Sir William de Ros, jun., of Ingmanthorp, does homage to the archbishop in the chapel of Scrooby for the manor of Muskham.[e] Dec. 25. Licence to John de Drokenesford,[f] canon of York, to have a private confessor.

1302, March. Licence for Roger de Blida, rector of a moiety of the church of Rotherham, to be absent for a year in the service of the earl of Warren.[g] Nov. 29. A licence for Humphrey, son of Walter de Beauchamp, rector of Harewood, to be non-resident for a year to enable him to study.[h]

false money, pollards, etc. (Statutes, i., 131). In 1301 the use of foreign money was prohibited. Walsingham, 77. Fœd., i., 919. Wikes, apud Gale, ii., 127. Statutes of the Realm, i., 218.

[a] In 1300 liberatio cuneorum. Pontius de Couwers and Simon de Senis the archbishop's moneyers (Reg. Corbridge).

[b] Maude Fitz Geoffrey, widow of William de Beauchamp, earl of Warwick, died in May or June, 1298 (Dugd. Bar., i., 229). Cf. Test. Vetusta, 52-4.

[c] A statute was passed about breaking into parks in 1293 (Statutes, i., 111). The parks at Beverley gave the archbishops of York much trouble.

[d] For the splendid services of this great man see Dugd. Bar., i., 53. His monument in Bedale church is one of the finest sepulchral memorials in England.

[e] Ingmangthorp is near Wetherby. On Oct. 11, 1298, the archbishop received at York the homage of Sir William de Ros, jun., of that place, for the manor of Muskham, which he held by knight's service, and his brother, Thomas de Ros, did homage for the manor of Douseby, co. Lincoln, which he held by the same tenure. There is a good deal of information about this family in Thoroton's Notts, 346, 374. In 1300 Thomas de Ros, son of Sir William de Ros, of Ingmangthorp, did homage in the presence of Sir William de Ros, his brother, for the manor of Douseby.

[f] He never actually obtained a stall at York. A very great man, a courtier, and a statesman. Canon of Northwell, at Southwell, 1304-9 (Le Neve, iii., 440); rector of Dalston, Cumberland, 1292 (Reg. Romanus); rector of Childwall, 1307 (Reg. Langton, at Lichfield); canon of Lichfield, Wells, and Lincoln (Le Neve, i., 595, 638; ii., 191); keeper of the king's wardrobe, 1301-5 (Parl. Writs, i., 105, etc. Dugd. Chron., 34); lieutenant, treasurer, and chancellor of the exchequer (Cal. Rot. Pat., 68. Pell Records, 116. Madox, ii., 165, 305); cf. Parl. Writs and Fœd., in many places; chaplain to the pope; bishop of Bath and Wells, 1309-1329.

[g] A very great man, and the generalissimo of the army in the North. Trivet, 299, Knyghton, col. 2524, Rot. Scot., Fœd., and Parl. Writs, *passim*. Cf. Dugd. Bar., i., 80, etc., Hunter's South Yorkshire, and the History of the House of Warren by Watson.

[h] Walter de Beauchamp of Alcester was a brother of William earl of War-

1303, Jan. 11. An indulgence of forty days to all praying for the king and queen and their children, the peace of the kingdom and the good estate of the church.[i] Feb. 15. A mandate to the vicar of Thorp against those who have broken into the treasury at Thorp, and carried away, among other things, charters and muniments relating to our church. April 13. An order to pray for the king and queen, his son and the army going against the Scots. May 27. Licence to Sir William de Vavasour to choose a confessor whilst he is absent in the wars in Scotland.[j] August 4. We have received by the hands of Robelard, our valet, from Walter de Ailesbury, executor of the will of Edmund, late earl of Cornwall,[k] a ring of gold which was bequeathed to us in his will.

1304, Feb. 28. Mandate to the chapter of Beverley to prevent tournaments and duels in Lent.[l] March 30. Licence to Sir Geoffrey de Hotham, knight, to have an oratory for life within his manor at Cranswick.[m] March 30. Commission to consecrate the cemetery of the Carmelites who have lately taken up their abode within the boundaries of the parish of St. Saviour, York. June 11. An indulgence of forty days for the fabric of York minster.[n]

Archbishop Corbridge died at Laneham, Notts, on the 22nd of September, 1304. His remains were removed to Southwell, and were interred in the collegiate church on the 29th.[o] His

wick (Dugd. Bar., i., 229). Cf. Rot. Parl., i. 199. He was seneschal of the king's hospice (Lib. Garderobæ, 13, etc.)

[i] Prynne, iii., 1153. The papacy was now in trouble (Walsingham, 87-8). Mar. 26, 33rd Edward I., an order to the keepers of the spiritualities of York for prayers to be offered up for the soul of Blanche duchess of Austria, sister of Margaret queen of England (Prynne, iii., 1107-8. Fœd., i., 972).

[j] Of Haslewood, which he had leave to crenellate, 18th Edward I. (Cal. Rot. Pat., 53), custos civ. Ebor. 5th Edward II. (ibid., 73), and a great soldier. Cf. Dugd. Bar., ii., 19. His will is in the Durham Wills, ii., 13, etc. The church of York will long treasure his name. Jan. 1, 1300, Robert le Vavasour, subdeacon, son of Sir William le Vavasour, to the church of Freston (Reg. Corbridge). Walter le Vavasour was son and heir of Sir William. On Dec. 13, 1315, bishop Kellawe grants the marriage of Alienor, his widow, "ratione manerii de Cokefeld," to Nicholas, son of William de Holteby (Reg. Kellawe, 262 *a*).

[k] A cousin of the king. He died at Asherugge, Bucks, where he had founded a college, on Oct. 1, 1300, s. p., and was buried with great ceremony at Westminster abbey (Walsingham, 78). This ring was for the archbishop for the time being (Fabric Rolls, 214). On 28th August, 1304, the archbishop granted an indulgence of forty days for the repose of his soul (Reg. Corbridge). Fœd., i., 930. Lib. Gard., 32-3.

[l] These jousts, etc., generally marked the presence of the court or army. They were sometimes put down with a high hand. Dec. 30, 1299, mandate to the sheriff of Yorkshire to prohibit tournaments (Fœd., i., 917).

[m] Not mentioned by Dugdale or in any pedigree of the family. He was one of the collectors of the quindisme in Yorkshire in 29th of Edward I. (Rot. Parl., i., 242). Abbrev. Plac., 279. Abbrev. Rot. Orig., i., 249. Parl. Writs, *var. loc.* He was a partizan of Thomas of Lancaster (Fœd., ii., 230). In 1330 he founded a house of Austin friars at Hull (Coll. Top., iv., 132).

[n] Printed in the Fabric Rolls, 154-5.

[o] MSS. Cotton, Vitellius, A, ii., 111.

resting-place is beneath a large blue marble slab close to the pulpit. It was originally covered with a brazen effigy of the prelate which has been destroyed, but the inscription which ran around it might recently be deciphered.[p]

The archbishop left a will, of which Lambert de Trykingham, Mr. John de Nassington, senior, and William de Jafford were the executors.[q] On the 5th of January, 1311, archbishop Greenfield appointed William de Estden[r] and others to receive the account of their administration, and on the 24th they were released from their responsibility. The care of the temporalities of the see during the vacancy was placed in the hands of Lambert de Trykingham and John de Byron.[s] The dean and chapter, as usual, attended to the spiritualities.

William de Grenfeud, or **Greenfield**, was the next archbishop of York. He was in every respect a most distinguished man, being a wise and active prelate and an illustrious and useful statesman. The presidents of the see of York during the fourteenth century occupied a high position among the great men whom it was the policy of the Edwards to gather around them, and their good deeds will be long remembered in the North of England.

The birthplace and parentage of Greenfield have not been discovered, but we know that he was connected with several families of antiquity and distinction.[t] He was perhaps a native

Stubbs, col. 1729. Ob. Sept. 30 (Chron. Lan., 202).

[p] History of Southwell, 277.

[q] *Lambert de Trykingham.* A justiciar and a baron of the exchequer (Dugd. Orig., 36, 39, 41, etc.); rector of Harby, co. Leicester, 1275 (Nichols's Leicestershire, ii., 213); the king's tallager, 33rd Edward I. (Madox Ex., i., 741); canon of Halloughton, at Southwell, 1310 (Le Neve, iii., 423); master of Sherburn hospital, Durham, 1313 (Reg. Kellawe, 238). Cf. Parl. Writs, *var. loc.* Foss's Judges, iii., 533.

John de Nassington. A canon of York. It is impossible to speak here of this great man and the services and distinctions of his family.

William de Yafford was rector of Croft, to which he was instituted Nov. 2, 1300 (Reg. Corbridge); a canon in St. Sepulchre's chapel at York. On 22nd August, 1312, Nicholas, vicar of Topcliffe, and John de Eseby, the executors of his will, were released (Reg. Greenfield).

[r] June 2, 1308, commission to confer the next vacant stall at Beverley on our clerk, William de Estden. In 1310 he was holding the prebend which once belonged to Mr. Peter Eymerici. On Jan. 14, 1310, William de Estden, canon of Beverley, Mr. Nicholas de Calveton, Robert de Bluntesdon, and Nicholas de Molendinis, were ordered to receive the accounts of the executors of Corbridge (Reg. Greenfield). In 20th Edward I. he was treasurer of the exchequer at Dublin (Cal. Rot. Pat., 55).

[s] Prynne's Coll., iii., 1085-7, 1114-15.

[t] Mentioned in Hist. Co. Lincoln, ii., 149. In Carew's Survey of Corn-

of a little hamlet, which bears his name, in Lincolnshire, and he was related to the ancient houses of Giffard, Babington, and Freville. The university of Oxford was his *alma mater*, and the charges of his education were defrayed by his kinsman archbishop Giffard. Little did that prelate think that the youthful cousin whom he befriended would at a future time repay his pious care by governing the same see which he himself moderated, and surpass him in his zeal for the interests of his church and in his brilliant services to his country and his king. Greenfield was a student at Oxford in 1269 and 1270, and became a doctor of civil and canon law.[u] He was a courtier also as well as a scholar, and Stowe happily describes him as "an eloquent man and pithie in counsell."[v]

Greenfield obtained preferment in the church at an early age. On St. Thomas's day, 1269, whilst he was still at Oxford, his kinsman archbishop Giffard collated him to the stall of Halloughton at Southwell,[w] which he resigned in the summer of 1272, having been promoted on the 29th of July to a prebend at Ripon.[x] In the month of August, 1287, he occurs as canon of Laughton in the church of York.[y] He was also prebendary of Holborn in St. Paul's cathedral, and dean of Chichester in 1299 and 1303.[z] I also find that he was incumbent of Blockley in Worcestershire between 1291 and 1294,[a] and in the latter year, on the 22nd of September, he obtained the rectory of Stratford-on-Avon, which he held till he became archbishop.[b] He was also the temporal chancellor of the diocese of Durham.[c]

We must now turn to Greenfield's services to the state, which were numerous and valuable. He was one of the clerks of Edward I., probably in connection with the chancery. On

wall (ed. 1602, p. 59) it is said that he was a Cornish man. Fuller (Worthies, i., 212) makes the same assertion, probably confounding the name of Greenfield with Grenville. It must be remembered, however, that Richard de Grenville, the founder of that family, came into England at the Conquest with Walter Giffard, earl of Bucks, whose daughter he married. Cf. Quart. Rev., cii., 297; Wright's Essays, i., 134.

[u] Trivet, 339. Tanner, Bibl., 341.

[v] Annals, ed. 1615, p. 209. Fuller's Worthies, i., 212. "Vir eloquentia, consilio et curialitate præclarus" (Stubbs, col. 1729).

[w] Reg. Giffard. Le Neve, iii., 423.

[x] Coll. p. m. dom. Wm. le Vavacur. (Reg. Giffard). The stall is not mentioned, but it seems to have been that of Monkton, which was sequestered on account of Greenfield's non-residence. The sequestration was relaxed May 10, 1303 (Reg. Corbridge). In the taxation of pope Nicholas he is called canon of Studley, and, in the Nova Taxatio, of Skelton. The inaccuracy of these taxations is well known.

[y] Reg. Romanus. He held it till he became archbishop.

[z] Newcourt, i., 156. Le Neve, i., 256.

[a] Nash's Worcestershire, i., 104.

[b] Dugdale's Warwickshire, *n. e.*, 479. Greenfield had letters of protection in 1296 as canon of York and Ripon and parson of Stretford super Avenam (Prynne, iii., 682).

[c] MSS. Surtees. Hutchinson's Durham, i., 256.

the 3rd of February, 1290, he was one of the three persons whom the king sent to Rome about the subsidy for the crusade.[d] This was the adventure in which the celebrated friar, William de Hotham, took so great an interest, and Greenfield, possibly, was indebted to him for his introduction to the notice of the king. In 1291 Greenfield was engaged in treating with the kings of Arragon, Sicily, and France.[e] In the following year he was with Edward at Norham when he was busy with the affairs of Scotland,[f] and he and J. de Lascy were appointed to pay the debts which the king had incurred since his coronation.[g] In 1295 he received a summons to the parliament at Westminster, and he was called to the meetings of that body and of the council in 1297, 1298, 1299, 1301, and 1302, in his capacity as clerk of the council.[h] On the 1st of January, 1296, he and others were sent to make a truce with France and treaties with Guelders and Flanders.[i] On the 25th of April, 1302, he was made one of the king's proctors to carry on negotiations with France, and on the 15th of August he was empowered to treat for peace with that country.[j] On the 30th of September he was advanced to the honourable position of lord chancellor of England,[k] having been previously a clerk in the chancery. He held that office with credit and distinction for three years.[l]

On the 19th of October, 1304, the king authorized the chapter of York to elect another archbishop,[m] and on the 4th of December their choice fell upon Greenfield, who was at that time dean of Chichester and chancellor of England.[n] He received the royal assent on the 24th.[o] He told the king in the presence of his council at Lincoln that it would be necessary for him to go to the papal court, and on the 31st of December Edward wrote to the pope and cardinals in his behalf, speaking of his merits and services in terms of high praise.[p] The pontifical chair was at that time vacant through the decease of Benedict X., and, as some time elapsed before his successor was appointed, the stay of Greenfield at Rome was necessarily prolonged. Edward urged upon the new pope and the cardinals the necessity for haste, and on the 2nd of October, 1305, he granted letters of protection to Greenfield, which were to remain in force until the following Christmas.[q] On the 30th of January,

[d] Fœdera, i., 726, 741. Prynne, iii., 429.

[e] Fœd., i., 744-5.

[f] Ibid., i., 767. Prynne, iii., 506.

[g] Rot. Parl., i., 85.

[h] Parl. Writs, i., 29, 35, 65, 79, 91, 103. Fœd., i., 889. Prynne, iii., 884.

[i] Fœd., i., 834-5. Prynne, iii., 748.

[j] Fœd., i., 940, 942, 945. Cf. Lib. Garderobæ, 90.

[k] Cal. Rot. Pat., 63.

[l] Prynne, iii., 1010.

[m] Le Neve, iii., 105.

[n] MSS. Cotton, Vitellius, A, ii., 112. Stubbs, col. 1729.

[o] Le Neve, iii., 105.

[p] Fœd., i., 968. Prynne, iii., 1073-4.

[q] Prynne, iii., 1112. In Fœd., i., 1008, is a letter from the king to the cardinals, dated on the 25th of January, 1306, urging the consecration.

1306, the archbishop-elect was at length consecrated by Clement V. at Lyons.[r] On the 10th of February the king gave him a letter of safe conduct,[s] with which he returned to England, and he received the temporalities of his see on the 31st of March.[t]

The cost of Greenfield's residence at Rome, and the sums which he was obliged to disburse to hasten his consecration, were enormous.[u] He came back to England literally a beggar. On the 30th of May he required of the dean and chapter the profits which they had derived from their administration of the spiritualities of the see during the vacancy.[v] He was obliged also to borrow money on a very large scale, and his resources were thus crippled for several years. On the 21st of November, 1306, he wrote to William, cardinal priest of St. Potentiana, professing his entire inability to pay the money which he owed at Rome, and begging the pope to respite him till Christmas. He had not, he states, received any of the revenues of the archbishopric for the current year, as they had been assigned to a certain nobleman,[w] and he could neither pay the disme imposed by the pope nor the troisdisme for the expedition to Wales, to say nothing of the costly equipment of ten knights which he was required to provide. On the 15th of February Greenfield wrote to another cardinal to entreat for a little longer time, and pleading as his excuse the great straits he was in and his poverty.[x] On the 26th of June, 1307, Francis Rodolossi, and the company of the Bellardi at Lucca, of which he was a member, entered into an obligation to pay for the archbishop to the chamberlains of the pope and the college of cardinals the large sum of four thousand florins.[y] This sum, probably, would release Greenfield from his debts at Rome, but the borrowed money was to be raised and repaid, and to do this he was obliged to throw himself upon the kindness of his friends. On the 26th of December, 1306, the abbat of Selby lent him 20*l.* On the 29th he asked for the following loans, which he promised to repay in two months. Mr. Thomas Eadberbury,[z] canon of York, lent

[r] MSS. Cotton, Vitellius, A., ii., 112. Stubbs, col. 1729.

[s] Cal. Rot. Pat., 66. Prynne, iii., 1146.

[t] Prynne, iii., 1145-6. Le Neve, iii., 105.

[u] Fuller (Worthies, i., 212) says that Greenfield spent nine thousand five hundred marks, on what authority I do not know. He also says that Greenfield received two benevolences from his clergy in one year.

[v] Reg. Greenfield.

[w] John de Britannia, earl of Richmond.

[x] On Jan. 25, 34th and 35th of Edward I., the king wrote to J., cardinal of SS. Marcellin and Peter, in behalf of Greenfield (Prynne, iii., 1159).

[y] The archbishop might say with Piers Ploughman—

> "And with Lumbardes letters
> I ladde gold to Rome."

[z] Canon, successively, of Osbaldwick and Wetwang, and archdeacon of Cleve-

him 100 marks, and the prior of Kirkham the same sum; the abbats of Meaux and Whitby, the priors of Bridlington, Gisburgh, and Nostell, each 40 marks; the priors of Malton and Newburgh each 20*l.*; the prior of Watton and Mr. W. de Lincoln, canon of Beverley, each 40*l.*; the priors of Pontefract and Drax and Mr. H. de Carleton, canon of Beverley, 20 marks each, and Mr. J. de Markenfield 60 marks. On the 5th of March the archbishop was borrowing again; he obtained from Walter de Gloucester, canon of Beverley, 100 marks and 40*l.*; from the priors of Bolton, Worksop, and Thurgarton, from each 20*l.*, from the prior of Lenton 40 marks, for three months, and from Walter de Langton, bishop of Lichfield and Coventry, the large sum of 500 marks. On the 31st of May John de Drokenesford lent him 100 marks. He received 40*l.* from Stephen de Bella Aqua, his valet, on the 5th of June, and at Michaelmas, 1308, he borrowed 100*l.* from Walter de Bedwinde.[a] I have reason to believe that these were only a few of the archbishop's creditors who aided him in extricating himself from his difficulties. It will be observed that all the money-lenders were ecclesiastics. The Jews had disappeared some years before, and the greater part of the treasure of the country was now stored away in the chests of some wealthy clerk or in the coffers of the monastery.

The city of York at this time must have been a place in which any prelate would be glad to take up his abode, even though it cost him the ransom of an emperor before he could sit down in the chair of Paulinus. We should be much struck with the appearance of the capital of the North at the beginning of the fourteenth century. In the arrangement and building of its streets we should observe perhaps no difference between it and any other mediæval town. They resembled the close narrow wynds which may still be seen in Scotland, and the population, too large in proportion to the space that it occupied, as well for protection as from choice, was crowded within the walls. The houses would be principally of lath and plaster, jointed together by beams of wood turned and twisted in fan-

land. He was also precentor of Lichfield (Le Neve., i., 579), vicar-general and prebendary of Wellington, ibid. (Shaw's Staffordshire, i., 299). He died 35th Edward I., seised of manors, etc., in Oxfordshire and Berks (Cal. Inq. P. M., i., 216), and he left a will in which he bequeathed a cup of the value of twenty marks to archbishop Greenfield.

[a] Reg. Greenfield. Walter de Bedwin, rector of Catton and Aughton, co. York, treasurer of York, prebendary of Barnby at Howden, incumbent of Ripple (Nash's Worcestershire, ii., 299). In 1323 he exchanged Barnby for a stall at Crediton, and in 1329 he gave up the treasury at York for the living of North Ferriby (Reg. ii., Pr. and Conv. Dunelm., 80. Reg. Melton). A remembrancer in the Exchequer (Madox, ii., 267), and an assistant of the council to the parliament, 1310 (Parl. Writs, ii., part i., 42), etc.

ciful devices, and there would be much picturesqueness in the quaint gables and windows and buttresses that were around you. A residence of stone, from the difficulty of procuring it, must have been a great rarity. Here and there you would come upon the abode of some person of consequence, whose inn or hospice stood by itself in an enclosed court. The Jews had till very lately been the moneyed class within the city, but their recent banishment had directed the stream of wealth into other channels, and the class of rich merchants was springing up which made York so famous. The number of trades that existed there in mediæval times is indeed remarkable, and there was considerable traffic upon the river. But whilst the coffers of the citizens were being filled by honest exertion, art and religion were advancing with equal strides. The four orders of mendicant friars had recently established themselves in the city, and were begging their way, as fast as they could, to riches. Most of the churches were in existence which even at this day startle the traveller by their frequency, and they were being filled with chantries and other memorials of the living and of the dead. The number of the windows that they contain, and their height in the walls, shew how difficult it was to obtain light in the crowded localities in which they were erected. On the Northern side of the city you will see many signs of the progress that religion had made and of the wealth that had been lavished on her. Without the walls was the monastery of St. Mary encircled by the *haia* and *fossa*, the petty cause of too much bitterness and contention, and its stately church was now rising from the ground in all its glorious beauty. Within the fortifications, but in too close proximity to its neighbour, was the spacious hospital of St. Leonard, which had its origin in the munificence of Athelstan, and had recently been almost entirely rebuilt by John Romanus, the treasurer of the minster. Farther up the street you entered into the close containing the residences of the canons and their dean, and archbishop Roger's palace. In the centre of this space there was nothing now but bustle and confusion. The magnificent nave of the cathedral was rising inch by inch, and casting into the shade every edifice around it, and you could hear on every side the creaking of the wains as they rolled slowly up the narrow causeway from the river to the minster, with the voices of the masons and the chipping of the stone.

One great reason for this accession of wealth and influence to York was the political importance with which it had been invested. The wars with Scotland had converted it into a military position, and it became for a time, as it were, the capital of England. In 1298 Edward I. held a parliament in the city, and the archbishop and the clergy granted him a subsidy of a fifth.[b] The courts of justice were also removed thither from London, and they did not return for seven years. In 1299 a large army assembled at York under the command of John de Warren, earl of Surrey, for service in Scotland.[c] There were two more parliaments there in 1299 and 1300 in the presence of the king,[d] and Edward spent some time in the city in 1306. The position of the archbishop as a great potentate in the North would necessarily involve him in negotiations with Scotland and in the wars that too frequently interrupted them. He was obliged, at a great cost, to find a contingent for the army, and the presence of the court so near his own residence, although it enhanced his dignity, would add greatly to his anxieties and expenses. He would frequently be called upon to play the host to the distinguished men who were passing to and fro, and his assistance would be often sought for and required in the councils of the nation. Archbishop Greenfield was summoned to the parliament at Westminster in 1306,[e] and on the 2nd of July in that year he and the bishop of Lichfield were made the guardians of the kingdom.[f] In 1307 he was called to Edward's last parliament at Carlisle, and there he proclaimed the peace between France and England.[g] After the death of that intrepid monarch, which occurred shortly afterwards, his sceptre fell into very feeble hands. Greenfield, however, was closely connected with English politics during the reign of Edward II. On the 26th of August, 1307, the new king summoned him to the parliament at Northampton to deliberate, among other matters, about his coronation, and on the 18th of January he was invited to that ceremonial, which was to take place at Westminster.[h] In consequence of the suspension of archbishop Winchelsea the pope had desired Greenfield to officiate on that occasion, but a reconciliation was subsequently effected between the king and the Southern primate, who was thus enabled to maintain and exercise his privilege.[i] The reign of the new king was anything but a happy one. Greatness was always within his reach, for he was by no means destitute of ability, but he forgot it among the fops and fools who surrounded him. His partiality for Gaveston and the Despensers aroused the anger of his barons, and Yorkshire spoke out against his folly through the mouth of her favourite, Thomas earl of Lancaster. These

[b] Knyghton, col. 2528. Walsingham, 74

[c] Flores Hist., 431. Knyghton, col. 2530. Walsingham, 89. Rot. Parl., i., 35.

[d] Walsingham, 77.

[e] Parl. Writs, i., 164.

[f] Fœd., i., 989. Cal Rot. Pat., 66.

[g] Parl. Writs, i., 182-3. Chron. Lanercost, 206.

[h] Fœd., ii., 4, 27.

[i] Wilkins, ii., 295. Somner's Canterbury, ii., 62. In Flores Hist., 458, it is said that Greenfield and Bek consecrated Edward.

troubles and dissensions and the easy temperament of the king aroused the hopes of the Scots, who were eager to avenge their wrongs and vindicate their nationality. The war between the two countries broke out with redoubled fury, urged on by all the fiery energy of Robert de Brus. The weapons of the church were thrown into the scale against him, and the murder of Cumyn and his brother in the friary at Dumfries had brought upon him the sentence of excommunication which had been hurled against him by the pope. It is not probable, however, that "Carrick's outlawed chief" cared much either for his curses or his blessings. On the 12th of August, 1309, the bishops of Durham and Whitherne were desired to denounce the culprit, and when they did so they would hear around them the note of preparation and the clash of arms. On the 5th of August the king requested the archbishop to raise one hundred men on his manor of Hexham for Scottish service,[j] and about the same time Gilbert de Clare, earl of Gloucester, Edward's nephew, who afterwards fell at Bannockburn,

"—— Indignus quem sors tam sæva maneret,"

was Greenfield's guest at Bishopthorp, and his uncle, who was then at York, assured the primate that the visit should not be regarded as a precedent to the injury of his successors or himself.[k] In 1311 the archbishop was again asked to supply men for Scotland.[l] The Christmas of that year was spent by Edward in York, and he then ordered the walls of the city to be strengthened, and to be made ready for defence. He was now joined by Piers de Gaveston and his friends, whom his father had wisely removed from his society, and the old favourite was welcomed with open arms.[m] Among the frivolities of that court even the careless observer would detect angry looks and open murmurings. The nobles and the commons were watching their monarch in dismay. The disasters which soon fell upon the country would be regarded as a righteous punishment of weakness and evil-rule. The sword of the Scot became the avenger of the national wrongs of his foemen. The summer of 1314 witnessed the calamitous defeat at Bannockburn, when the pride of Edward was laid low.

"And the best names that England knew
Claim'd in the death-prayer dismal due."

[j] Fœd., ii. 83. Rot. Scotiæ, i., 70.

[k] Ibid., 95.

[l] Rot. Scot., i., 101.

[m] Walsingham, 99, 101. Trokelowe, Ann. Edward II., 10, 117. Carte's Gascon, etc., Rolls, i., —. Stowe's Chron., ed. 1615, 215. On May 1, 1313, the archbishop was peremptorily ordered to come to the king before he started for France (Fœd., ii., 210). Walter de Langton, bishop of Lichfield, was thrown into prison at York, for having been the means of driving Gaveston into exile (Adam Murimuth, 13).

It was with great difficulty that the English sovereign made his escape from that field, and he seems never to have paused in his flight till he found himself at York. He had there a large meeting of his council to discuss the affairs of the nation, and, on the Thursday before Michaelmas, Edward, in his own chamber within the palace of the archbishop, made John de Sandal, archdeacon of Richmond, lord chancellor of England.[n] Greenfield, like a loyal patriot, could not fail to be troubled at the reverse which his country had sustained, and he took an active part in the attempts to rescue her from her misfortunes. On the 4th of January, 1315, he and the bishop of Durham were excused from their attendance at parliament, as they were then busily engaged in protecting the marches of England against the Scots.[o]

Whilst this internecine warfare was raging in the North of England, a great, and I may call it an unhappy, movement was taking place within the church. The famous society of the Knights of the Temple was being destroyed. The leaders of Christ's flock manifested a strange ingratitude when they struck a fatal blow at that illustrious order. A period, comprising only two centuries, witnessed its creation and its ruin. It arose when the swords of the conquering Moslems were already gleaming over Europe, and it united against the bold invaders the soul of the chivalry of the West. The pilgrims who came out of the beloved but distant East had many a tale to tell of their sufferings and their wrongs, how the infidel trod upon the shrines which a glorious presence once ennobled, and the praises of Mahmoud were heard where Christ once walked and spoke.[p] A shiver ran through the whole Christian world when it heard the news. Uninvited and unaided a little band of knights devoted themselves to the dangerous task of protecting the travellers to Jerusalem, and they took their name from the holy temple, which was its chief ornament. The zeal for God's cause and the spirit of adventure soon increased their numbers, and they formed themselves into the sacred order of the Templars. The union in them of valour and devotion added greatly to their popularity. The chivalrous daring of the knights, their heroism in the field and in the cloister, the fascinating charm of the enterprize that they took up, the stirring praises of St. Bernard, soon won for them a position such as no religious body

[n] Fœd., ii., 255. Edward held a parliament at York in 1313 (Murimuth, 20).

[o] Ibid., 260. Rot. Scot., i., 137. Walsingham, 107.

[p] Their feelings are easily imagined.

"Al gran piacer, che quella prima vista
Dolcemente spirò ne l' altrui petto,
Alta contrition successe, mista
De timoroso, e reverente affetto.
Osano à pena d'inalzar la vista
Ver la Città, di Christo albergo eletto:
Dove morì, dove sepulto fue,
Dove poi rivestì le membra sue."

has since occupied. The heart of the whole of Christendom was yearning towards the East. The Templars were delighted to evoke this feeling, and to join in the energetic action that it prompted. They took the lead in every crusade, they were the first to carry the standard of the cross into the Moslem vanguard:—

> "Chieftains, lead on! our hearts beat high,
> Lead on to Salem's towers!
> Who would not deem it bliss to die
> Slain in a cause like ours?
> The brave who sleep in soil of thine
> Die not intombed, but shrin'd, O Palestine!"

The most dashing exploits were theirs; they could exhibit the most patient endurance. There were few places of note in Palestine and the East with which the Templars were not associated for some adventurous feat or some reverse heroically borne. We think of the holy city so often lost by them and retaken, we think of Antioch and Damascus, of the shores of Acre which have witnessed in a later day our own triumphs, and of that host of noble warriors who fell among the hills which overlook Gennesaret.

The close of the thirteenth century saw the last crusade, and the Moslems, against whose progress the Templars had so long been a successful barrier, were now unmolested in their advance. The Red Cross Knights were now unoccupied, and they flocked homewards to settle down upon their estates in Europe which had been given to them in bygone years by kings and nobles. They busied themselves with local politics, and amassed great stores of wealth. The more interest they took in secular affairs the more unpopular did they become. Men began to think, and with some reason, that they were not in their proper sphere, without remembering that it was not through the Templars' fault that the passage to the East was closed. The enthusiasm for the rescue of the holy places disappeared, and the exploits of those who had shed their blood to win and keep them from the infidel were forgotten. Avaricious monarchs heard with bated and then quickening breath of the hoards of money which the Templars had amassed, and Edward I. seized upon the treasure in their house in London; but, unmindful of the wrong, the leaders of the noble brotherhood fought and fell by his side at Falkirk. In 1307 a deliberate assault was made upon the body in France, where Philip le Bel was their opponent. The new pope, himself a Frenchman, was on the king's side. The commission of incredible crimes was laid to the Templars' charge—the most atrocious offences against decency and morality, and hideous blasphemy. Was it likely that a society which had especially devoted itself to the service of the cross, and had surrendered fortune and life for the sacred cause which it had adopted—was it likely that its members would belie their glorious traditions and their practice and their vows? It was impossible. Doubtless there were among the Templars many Bois Guilberts, half priests half soldiers, with too great a share of the spirit of the latter, but the conduct of the great mass of the order seems to have been irreproachable. It was doomed, however, to destruction, and the first blow was given in France with frightful vehemence. Evidence, which a modern court of justice would reject in derision, was listened to against the society, and noble gentlemen were led to the stake and the torture rather than confess themselves guilty of offences which they had never perpetrated.[q]

In the autumn of 1307 various attempts were made by foreign potentates to prevail upon Edward II. to enter into the league against the Templars. He discredited the stories which were narrated to him, and withstood for a time the importunities of those who besought his co-operation. At the request of the pope, however, he changed his policy, and acted with such secresy and vigour that in January, 1308, the greater part of the Templars, resident in England, and their property, were taken possession of by the royal officers. Clement V. was now eager for their punishment, and we must see how they fared in the North of England. On the 12th of August, 1309, the pope sent two bulls to the archbishop of York; the one was a general denunciation of the culprits, and especially of those within the province of York; the other was a mandate for the institution of an official enquiry. He also nominated the commissioners who were to act in that behalf. They were the archbishop himself, the bishops of Durham, Lincoln, Chichester, and Orleans, the abbats of Lagny and St. Germain des Champs in France, M. Sicard de Vaur, canon of Narbonne, chaplain to the pope and auditor of the causes of his palace, and Guy de Vichy, rector of Hesh *(sic)* in the diocese of London. The exhortations the pope were backed by a letter from the king of France, in which he earnestly requested the archbishop's co-operation.[r] Greenfield evidently did not like the duty which he was called upon to discharge. On the 26th of September he positively declined to take any part against the Templars within the province of Canterbury. He told the pope that the bishops of Lincoln and Chichester could not act in the affairs of the pro-

[q] There is an interesting account of this persecution in a volume entitled, "The Knights Templars, by C. G. Addison, Esq. 8vo. London: 1842."

[r] The original letter is in Greenfield's register. From that repository my account of the Templars is drawn, unless some other authority is given.

vince of York, and his peculiar relations with the Southern primate would not allow him to go into their dioceses. He expressed his readiness, however, to do what he could, and wrote to the bishop of Lincoln to suggest a friendly meeting at Laneham, Notts, on the 2nd of July, 1310, when the matter might be considered. The abbat of Lagny and Sicard de Vaur were in England, and for two years the clergy of the diocese of York were taxed for their support. They were, no doubt, the means of expediting the persecution. On the 11th of March Greenfield wrote from London to summon a provincial council to enquire into the allegations against the Templars. It was to be held at York on the 20th of May. Before it assembled, the culprits, who were confined in York castle, were examined. They were twenty-four in number, and came from Yorkshire and seven adjacent counties. They had been in the castle since the autumn of 1309, although they had been in restraint for a much longer period. The names of the sufferers must be perpetuated. They were William de Grafton, senior, preceptor of Ribstan, Ralph de Roston, Thomas de Stannford, Henry de Kereby, Thomas de Belleby, of Penhil, Robert de Langton, William de la Fenne, preceptor of Faxflete, Richard de Kesewyk, Stephen de Radenhalgh, priest of Westerdale, Michael de Sowreby, priest of Sorenty (?), in the diocese of Durham, Godfrey de Arches, preceptor of Newsham, John de Walpole, Ivo de Etton, Henry de Craven, Roger de Hugyndon, Henry de Rouclyf, Galfrid de Wylton, Walter de Gaddesby, Richard de Ripon, Thomas de Thresk, Richard de Shefeld,[e] John de Ebreston, William de Midelton, and Walter de Clifton. To these a twenty-fifth may be added, Thomas Streche. The examination of the prisoners lasted from the 28th of April to the 4th of May, but it produced no fruits. The knights had nothing to confess; they denied the charges of blasphemy, etc., which were brought against them, and asserted the orthodoxy of their faith.[f] They told but little of their own history. Grafton said that he had been admitted into the order at London, more than thirty-two years before, by Robert de Torvile, then grand preceptor in England. William de la Fenne took the oaths at Chaplay, in the diocese of Chichester, some fifteen years previously from Guy de Foresta, at that time grand preceptor. Stannford had been a brother for thirty years, having been initiated in Cyprus by William de Beaujen. Roston had been a member of the order for twenty-three years, and entered

[e] He is called Roger in another list. On May 17, 1311, the king wrote on behalf of John de Eberston, who had apostatized from the order through fear of death.

[f] Chron. Lanercost, 215.

it at Lentini in Sicily.[u] What stirring adventures and how much rough life such men must have seen!

The council met at York on the 20th of May, and most of the ecclesiastics of the North were there, with the exception of Anthony Bek, bishop of Durham, who was then seriously ill.[v] Nothing, however, was done, as the examination of the knights themselves had been unsatisfactory, and farther evidence was required. The meeting, therefore, was adjourned to a future day. In the meantime the archbishop was not idle. On the 25th of May he, in conjunction with the abbat of Lagny and Sicard de Vaur, cited the knights, who were still at large, to appear before them at Laneham on the 2nd of July. Only eight are mentioned, so it is evident that the exertions of the Northern sheriffs had been eminently successful. They were William de Grafton, jun., John de Usflet, Edmund de Latimer, otherwise called de Garvyle, John de Poynton, Richard Engayne, Ralph de Buleford, Stephen de Stapelbrigg,[w] and Walter le Rebel. On the 1st of June the archbishop commissioned Henry de Botelesford, his penancer, and John de Hemmingburgh, dean of the Christianity of York, to hear the confessions of the Templars in York castle, if anything farther could be extracted from them.[x] Every attempt was also made to secure fresh evidence. On the 20th of June Greenfield appointed several of the clergy to examine the servants and retainers of the Templars who had been with them at their houses or manors of Ribstan, Wetherby, Newsham, and Templehurst in the West Riding of Yorkshire, Faxeflete and Wythele in the East Riding, and Foukebrigg, Westerdale, Penhill, and Cowton in the North. What this enquiry produced we are not informed, but it is not probable that it brought to light anything of importance. The archbishop was at Laneham on the 2nd of July, and the bishop of Lincoln was with him by appointment. The Templars who were summoned never made their appearance, and they were excommunicated.

Before there was another meeting of the provincial council at York some evidence was taken in London relating to the proceedings of the Templars in the Northern province, which may be considered a fair sample of that which was generally produced against that body. It was mere hearsay of the most

[u] Wilkins, ii., 371. It is there said that this examination was taken in May, 1311.

[v] Bek seems to have been a friend of the Templars. On May 24, 1308, Wm. de la More, the English grand master, was placed in his charge (Fœd., ii., 45).

[w] Stapelbrigg was caught at Salisbury in 1311, and made a confession, after which he was reconciled (Addison).

[x] On July 8, 1311, a similar commission was issued to William de Langtoft and Mr. Philip de Boulton (Reg. Greenfield).

contemptible kind. Mr. John de Nassington,[y] the official of the archbishop of York, deposed that he was told by Sir Miles de Stapleton and Sir Adam de Everingham, that when they were once the guests of the grand preceptor at a banquet at Templehurst, they were informed that many of the knights had come there to pay worship to a calf! Sir John Eure, sheriff of Yorkshire, said that he had once asked William de la Fenne, the preceptor of Westerdale, to dine with him, and after dinner the preceptor took out of his bosom a book which he gave to Lady Eure to read, and she found a paper in it full of blasphemy against Christ. Like a prudent woman she shewed it to her husband, who spoke about it to his guest, and he laughed the matter off, and nothing more was said about it for six years. De la Fenne, in answer, said that he recollected the book, but knew nothing of the paper which it contained. William de la Forde, rector of Crofton, deposed that William de Reynbur, an Augustinian friar lately deceased, informed him that he heard the death-bed confession of Patrick de Rippon, Templar, son of William de Gloucester. He told him that on his entrance to the order he was stripped to the shirt, and taken to a secret chamber, where he was ordered to spit upon the crucifix and dishonour it in a more gross way, and, finally, to kiss and worship the image of a calf, which he did. The testimony of this witness was somewhat shaken when he acknowledged that he had only heard of this story after the institution of the proceedings against the knights. We find also that several of the Minorites came forward to give evidence which was of the most contemptible description. Robert de Oteringham asserted that he was once at Ribstan, and when grace was said after a meal, the chaplain turned round to the brethren, and made an observation which will read most appropriately in Latin, Diabolus vos uret! The same friar had a marvellous tale of something that he saw at Wetherby at midnight through a keyhole in the chapel, when he thought that he had surprised the inmates at their orgies. Another Minorite had heard that a Templar had been seen running about a field in a demented state, and crying out that he had sold himself to the evil one.[z] These creatures had a purpose to fulfil, and like their ancestors in baseness whom the Roman annalist denounces, "Sic delatores, genus hominum publico exitio repertum, et pœnis quidem numquam satis coërcitum, per præmia eliciebantur."

[y] On Aug. 19, 1311, Robert de Pickering, vicar-general, made him penancer for the Templars (Reg. Greenfield). On Aug. 18, the king ordered the sheriff of Yorkshire to place the Templars in Pickering's hands during the archbishop's absence (Fœd., ii., 167). Pickering probably sent them to the monasteries.

[z] Wilkins, ii., 358-9.

Greenfield, however he might dislike severity, was obliged to proceed against the accused Templars. On the 21st of Feb., 1311, he summoned another provincial council[a] to consider what was to be done. It was to meet at York on the 24th of May. All the prelates and dignitaries of the North were invited to it, together with several members of the mendicant orders, who took an especial interest in the crusade against the knights. They were Mr. John Gower, S.T.D., Mr. Thomas de Clifford, William de Okam, S.T.D., friar Thomas de Middleton, S.T.D., Friars Preachers, Richard de Wetwang, an Augustinian at York, and Adam de Lincoln, a Minorite from the same city. The council had eleven sittings, the last being on the 30th of July. The proceedings commenced with the celebration of the mass of the Holy Spirit, followed by a sermon from the archbishop, who stood at the high altar. When this was over the primate explained the object of the meeting, and the members then went to their work. The result was, on the whole, a proof of the good sense of the Northern clergy. The punishment of death was not awarded, as in other countries, and there was no cruelty nor torturing. The Templars, twenty-four in number, were brought from the castle, and were persuaded to submit themselves to the council. It was then ordered that each of them should be sent to a religious house within the province of York to do penance for his errors.[b] This decision gave some umbrage to the monasteries,[c] but the Templars, as a rule, appear to have conducted themselves with propriety, and before a year had expired the archbishop had released nearly the whole of them from the sentence of excommunication.[d] A due provision for their wants was agreed upon and was granted by the

[a] March 13, 1311, an order to the sheriff of Yorkshire to bring the Templars before him (Reg. Greenfield).

[b] Eperston was sent to Salley, Craven to Pontefract, Keswick to Kirkham, Langton to Bridlington, Gaddesby to Jervaux, Stannford to Fountains, Wilton to Whitby, Sheffield to Kirkstall, Kerby to Rievaux, Walpole to Byland, Radenachs to Worksop, Clifton to Shelford, Hughendon to Gisburn, Streche to Nostell, and Grafton to Selby. Stubbs (col. 1730) ascribes this arrangement to the kindness of Greenfield, but it did not, I think, originate with him.

[c] On March 1, 1312, a letter to the abbat and convent of Rievaux for refusing to supply food to Henry de Kerroby. They are ordered to do so. At the same time there is a letter from the vicar-general against the abbat and convent of Kirkstall for allowing, through their negligence, Roger de Shefeld to leave their monastery. Stannford gave some trouble at Fountains by using violent language and refusing to comply with rules, but a sharp reproof brought him to his senses.

[d] All were released in 1312 (Reg. Greenfield). They were kindly treated. On Aug. 15, 1312, the archbishop permitted William de Grafton, sen., to leave Selby abbey for a month, on account of business in the dioceses of York, Lincoln, and London (Reg. Greenfield). In the 4th of Edward III. William de Grafton was absolved from his vows, and was allowed to turn to a secular pursuit (Cal. Rot. Pat., 109).

king, amounting to a considerable sum, out of their sequestered estates.[e] Years passed away, and on the 31st of August, 1319, the pope made an order that any Templar, if he chose, might take the vows required by the monastery in which he was residing, but two only seem to have availed themselves of his permission within the diocese of York.[f]

Within a fortnight after the termination of the gathering at York archbishop Greenfield took his journey towards the South. Clement V. had convoked a general council, which was to meet in the month of October at Vienne in Dauphiny, and on the 1st of June Edward II. desired the Northern primate to come to London, as he was anxious that he should go abroad to be present at the great assembly in France, to which he had been summoned. On the 26th of July he directed him to remain at home, and to come to the parliament at London. Greenfield, however, after all, went to Vienne, the king giving him letters of credence and safe conduct on the 10th of October.[g] The archbishop was welcomed by the pope, and occupied an honourable position at the council, sitting next after the cardinals and the archbishop of Treves.[h] The affairs of the Templars and their offences were fully discussed. The meeting was prorogued till the month of April, 1312, and then, in the presence of Greenfield, the ancient order of the Temple was finally dissolved. On the 15th of August in that year the archbishop directed his official at York to make the announcement that it had ceased to exist.

A considerable light will be thrown upon Greenfield's archiepiscopal career by the following extracts from his register. They not only illustrate his public and his private life, but give

[e] On Sept. 30, 1312, William de Grafton receives from the archbishop the sum of 95*l*. 4*s*. for the stipends of himself and his twenty-three brethren within the diocese at York from the Sunday . . . the feast of St. Nicholas to the Sunday before the feast of St. Peter ad Vincula next ensuing. On Dec. 6. 1311, the king ordered Alexander de Cave and Robert de Amecotes, keepers of the lands, etc., of the Templars in the county of York, to pay the wages above mentioned, which were agreed upon at the general council (Reg. Greenfield). The Templars lingered for a long time in the monasteries. On April 2, 1335, an order was made to pay to Thomas de Streche, who was at Nostell, the arrears of his pension of five marks per annum (Reg. Melton). Rouclyf, Streche, and Gaddesby had an annual pension of six marks (The Knights Hospitallers in England, ed. Camden Soc., 209). June 6, 1321, a request to the prior of St. John at Jerusalem to pay to Ralph de Roston, formerly a Templar, the stipend assigned to him by the general council (Reg. Melton).

[f] Dec. 18, 1319, an order to the prior and convent of Gisburgh to allow Robert de Langeton, once a Templar, to enter their house, and on Sept. 29, 1320, a similar direction to the abbat of Selby in behalf of Henry de Kerby.

[g] Fœd., ii., 135, 141, 145. Cal. Rot. Pat., 73.

[h] Stubbs, col. 1730. Labbe, Conc., xi., 1557. Adam Murimuth, 15. Baronii Ann., Raynaldi, xxiii, 533.

us some curious glimpses of the state of manners and morals in the North of England.

1307, March 25. A commission addressed from Rose castle to the bishop of Lichfield and Coventry authorizing him to consecrate the bishop of Bangor at Carlisle.[i] April 9, at Beaurepayr, the archbishop certifies to a marriage having taken place between John, son of Sir John de Eglesclif, knight, and Juliana, daughter of William de Eglesclif. They were married in the church of St. Saviour in the Marsh in York on the 4th of June, 1294, by Stephen the rector.[j] A letter to the pope recommending the translation of St. Robert of Lincoln.[k] April 28. An order to cite Sir Nicholas de Meynell and Lucia, daughter of Sir Robert de Tweng, to answer to a charge of adultery.[l] May 23. A commission to liberate from prison Sir William Sampson, knight, who has been excommunicated for divers offences, amongst others, for incest with Isold and Clemence his own daughters. He is ordered to do penance at Nottingham, Newark, and Southwell. June 5. Licence to the official at York to sprinkle with holy water the churchyard of St. Martin in Micklegate, which has been polluted. Two boys were fighting in it, and the nose of one of them bled. August 7. An indulgence of forty days for the soul of Edward I. "Marcuit et aruit flos militiæ."[m]

1308, Jan. 9. An oratory to Sir John de Gray, knight, in the manor of Farewath. Jan. 21. An indulgence for the fabric

[i] The bishop, Griffin ap Yorweth, was consecrated on the following day by Walter de Langton, bishop of Lichfield. The court was then at Carlisle.

[j] When parish registers were unknown, ages, marriages, etc., could only be proved by some such document as this. The archbishop was at Beurepaire, near Durham, the country-house of the prior, of which some ruins still remain.

[k] Bishop Grostête. Archbishop Romanus wrote a strong letter to the pope in favour of his canonization (Reg. Romanus). On May 6, 1307, the king made the same request (Fœd., i., 1016. Prynne, iii., 1185)), but in vain. Grostête was not a person whom the papal court would be likely to canonize.

[l] A very singular story. Nov. 2, 1305, the chapter of York announce that William de Latimer has been excommunicated at the instance of dame Lucy, daughter of Sir Robert de Tweng. Sept. 4, 1309, commission to receive the purgation of dame Lucy de Tweng, wife of Sir William de Latymer, knight, for adultery and incest with Sir Nicholas de Meynyl. On the Friday after the Epiphany, 1309, Meynyl and the lady enter into a bond to pay 40*l.* each to dan Henry de Botelford, the keeper of the fabric at York. On July 8, previously, Meynyl as a punishment had been fined 10*l.* by the archbishop (Reg. Greenfield).

The frailty of Lucy de Tweng cast a doubt upon the legitimacy of her husband's son, but on July 1, 1328, it was found out, upon a formal enquiry, that Sir William, the reputed son of Sir William de Latymer, was not illegitimate, but the son of Latimer and Lucy de Tweng (Reg. Melton).

[m] The king died at Burgh on the Sands, not far from Carlisle, on the 7th of July (Fœd., i., 1018). On Oct. 28 the archbishop was desired to pray for the new king (ibid., ii., 9), "The floure of Cristendam" (Peter Langtoft, *n. e.*, 341).

of the church of St. Andrew at Bordeaux.[n] April 9. To Sir Godfrey de Melsa, knight, a gift of two or three deer out of our park at Beverley.[o] April 11. The archbishop writes to Stephen de Mauley, archdeacon of Cleveland, begging to see the deeds relating to the privileges of the prior and convent of Durham in Howdenshire and Allertonshire, about which he has spoken to him.[p] May 3. Commission to the bishop of Whitherne to dedicate the church of the Friars Preachers at Yarm which has been lately built. June 13. At Meaux, William de Rolleston of Beverley, Adam his servant, John Golding of Beverley, and John de Esingwald laying their hands on the archbishop's cross, promise that they will not again break into the park of Beverley.[q] July 17. An order to Robert de Bardelby, canon of York, and William de Threntoft, rector of Knesale, to fine to the king for five knights' fees, for which we are bound to find service in Scotland.[r] August 23. A mandate to the chapter of Ripon not to hold markets in the minster. Sept 10. A licence for the consecration of the altar B.M.V. in the church of the Carmelites at Nottingham.[s] Oct 6. An ora-

[n] A place of great consequence and value to England. There was more than one connection between it and York. In September, 1308, Bertrand de Fargis, a canon of Bordeaux, was made archdeacon of the East Riding. In 34th Edward I. Richard de Haverings, a canon of York, was constable of that town (Prynne, iii., 1094). This is the person who was elected archbishop of Dublin, but he never went there, for a very strange reason. He was so often prevented by stormy weather from making the passage to Ireland, that he gave it up, thinking that Providence was against him. The story reminds us of the famous De Courcy and his adventure.

[o] The most important of all the archbishop's parks. De Melsa was the head of a good Holderness family. In 5th Edward II. William de Melton paid three hundred marks to the king for the custody of some of the lands of Godfrey de Melsa (Abbrev. Rot. Orig., i., 190). Cf. Rot. Parl., i., 326.

[p] Mauley was a great man and a member of the Yorkshire house. A cousin of bishop Bek (Misc. Doc. treas. Durham, 495), prebendary of Bugthorpe, archdeacon of Cleveland, rector of Baynton and Hemmingburgh, co. York. He had the living of Ouston, co. Lincoln (MSS. Harl., 6951, 32), the deanery of Auckland, and the rectories of Houghton and Haughton, co. Durham (Reg. Kellawe, 22, 29). Seneschal of Durham castle, and vicar-general (MSS. Surtees), dean of Wimborne, and archdeacon of Lichfield (Hutchins' Dorset, ii., 534). He had much to do with the translation of St. William. He died on the Friday after the feast of St. Laurence, 1317, and was buried in York minster,—but see Prynne, iii., 1243. Abbrev. Plac., 258.

For the dispute about Howdenshire, etc., see Hist. Dunelm. Scr. Tres, 105.

[q] In 1323 a special commission was issued to try those who had broken into Beverley park (Parl. Writs, ii., part ii., 228).

[r] This service was a great burden to the archbishop. Bardelby was a clerk in the chancery. I shall speak of him afterwards.

[s] Nov. 23, 1310, licence to the Friars Minors of Nottingham to have their church and its altars consecrated. May 17, 1311, licence to the Carmelites of Hull to have their church consecrated (Reg. Greenfield). Sept. 17, 1314, licence to the bishop of Enachdune to dedicate an altar newly erected in the house of the Friars Minors at York (ibid.). John Bate was the chief ornament of the last-mentioned house (Lel. de Script. Brit., 434).

tory to Anora de Pirponnt in the manors of Holm, Wodehouse, and Weston.[f]

1309, Jan. 15. The archbishop grants to Thomas, son of Robert de Grenefeld, and Joan, daughter of John Attewell, and their heirs, two mesuages, four bovates, and eight acres of arable land, and six and a half acres of meadow in Sherburn.[u] May 21. Bull of Clement V. excommunicating Robert le Brus for many enormities, and for killing with his sword John and Robert de Comyn, of the diocese of Glasgow, knights, for refusing to join him in his proceedings against the king, one in the cloister and the other in the church of the Friars Minors at Dumfries, near the high altar.[v] Nov. 9. We have corrected, on her own confession, dame Joan de Corewenne, relict of Sir Thomas de Corewenne, knight, for adultery with Sir Simon Ward, knight.[w]

Among these friars there were many distinguished men who were natives of Yorkshire and of the North of England. Among the Carmelites were John de Eboraco, Galfrid Alievanti, Walter Kellaw, John Chelmerton, and John Goldston—all of them Yorkshiremen. Stephan de Patrington was the confessor of Henry V.* Robert Baston was a brother of Philip Baston, prior of the house at Scarbro', and was born at York. He wrote several works on Scottish politics. Bishop Scrope is well known (Bibliotheca Carmelitana, i., coll. 534, 581, 809, 836, 853; ii., 149, 686, 764, 829, 971-2).

Among the Preachers were Robert of York, John de Derlington, Thomas Stubbs, John de Heglescliff, and Holcot (Quétif, Scriptores Ord. Predic., i., prefat., xxv, 395, 625, 631, 671). Nor must archbishop Hotham, who has been already mentioned, be forgotten (ibid., i., 459-60). "Huomo da comparare con i più rari soggetti del suo tempo, nella dottrina et bontà della vita" (Pio, Huomini illustri di S. Domenico. Bologna, 1607. Part ii., 107). Cf. Ware's History of Ireland, ed. 1764, ii., 326. Touron, Histoire des Hommes Illustres de l'ordre de Saint Dominique, i., 603-8, ed. Paris, 1743. Tanner, Bibl. Brit., 414.

[f] Annora, daughter and heiress of John Manners, married Sir Henry Pierpoint (Coll. Top., viii., 345). Abbrev. Plac., 222.

[u] A settlement on their marriage. On Jan. 7, 1311, Thomas, son of Robert de Grenefeld, was made keeper of the woods and warren at Sherburn and Cawood. On Tuesday, the feast of the Purification B.V., Robert de Grenefeld and William his son were made guardians of the lands of Godfrey de Melsa at Hodeleston on account of the minority of John his son and heir (Reg. Greenfield). Robert de Grenefeld is mentioned in Abbrev. Plac., 250.

[v] A document, hitherto unknown, of much historical importance.

"The church of God saw Comyn fall."

The murder itself is described with painful minuteness. "In ejus refrigerare sanguinem calentem gladio non contentus, nisi sanguinem ipsum ejusque cerebrum, avulsum de capite, super dictum altare feritate diffunderet bestiali." Cf. Chron. Lan., 203. Fœd., i., 982, 987. Prynne, iii., 1024. On Jan. 14, 1315, an order to denounce as excommunicated Brus and his accomplices (Reg. Greenfield).

[w] On 21st September Ward promises that he will forfeit 20*l.* if it occurs again (Reg. Greenfield). On June 17, 1298, Sir Simon Ward did homage at Ripon for lands in Guiseley, Gevildale, and Kirkby Wharf, held by knight-service, and for Newby, held for the service of the fourth part of a knight's fee (Reg. Newark). On Nov. 21, 1306, Sir Simon le Warde, knight, jun., son of Sir Simon le Ward, deceased, did homage for Guiseley, etc. In July, 1309, he was a justice of assize for the liberty of Ripon (Reg. Greenfield). He will occur again. He was sheriff of Yorkshire 1315-1321 (Drake, 351).

1310, April 5. Licence for William de Ayketon, rector of Berewyk, to be absent from his living for a year in the service of Alesia de Lascy, countess of Lincoln.[x] June 8. To John le Warner, of Ripon, at the oversight of Sir Robert de Conyers, knight, two oaks from our wood at Thornton, one for our house at Ripon lately belonging to John Trenys, and the other to mend the bridge at Killingdall. June 9. A letter to William, bishop of St. Andrew's, in behalf of Beatrix de Hodsak, late a nun at Coldstream, which place she left on account of the war. She is now living at a house of anchorites near Doncaster, and the archbishop asks for her to be allowed to return.[y] June 22. Commission to receive the probate of the will of Beatrix, late wife of Geoffrey, son of Robert le Staunton, co. Notts.[z] July 22. A deer from our park at Hecksgrave to Sir John Lysours, knight, and another to William de Dogmerfield, our seneschal of Sherwood forest. August 24. Robert de Hendeley, Adam his brother, and Ythell his groom, have beat and wounded William Tyas, esquire of the countess of Lancaster, in the church of Pickering: a commission to the chapter to enquire and to exact satisfaction. August 28. Licence to John de Rolleston, one of the seven clerks in the church of Beverley, and chaplain of the chantry of the fraternity of St. Nicholas, to carry the standard of St. John of Beverley to the wars in Scotland, by the king's order.[a] Sept. 15. Licence to Margery, sister of the late Sir Brian Fitzalan, to have an oratory for three years in the manor of Baynton.[b] Oct. 17. The archbishop gives sixteen shillings from his tenement near Otley which the lepers hold of him, to repair the bridge of Otley. Dec. 31. An order to the bailiff of Ripon to provide the necessary materials for the construction of a chapel in our manor at Ripon.[c] The archbishop writes to the bishop of Norwich to say that Walter de Boynton,

[x] The wife of Henry the last earl.

[y] In 1296, when Edward I. was in Scotland, he made his headquarters in the nunnery of Coldstream (Trivet, 289). These wandering nuns are mentioned in Walsingham, 79.

[z] A good old family, co. Notts.

[a] Oct. 13, 1296, an order to John de Warren, earl of Surrey, and guardian of Scotland, to prefer to the next vacant benefice of the value of 20*l.* or marks Gilbert de Grymmesby, for bringing the banner of St. John of Beverley and staying with it in Scotland during the war (Fœd., i., 848. Prynne, iii., 667. Lib. Garderobæ, 51, 334). The banner was returned 29th Edward I. (Prynne, 910). The ensign was deemed to be the harbinger of victory, like that of St. Cuthbert of Durham.

> "And thus with girdle round his waist,
> Whereon the banner-staff might rest
> At need, he stood, advancing high
> The glittering floating pageantry."

Edward I. went to Beverley in 1289 to visit St. John's shrine (Walsingham, 75). He was frequently there, and Beverley was sometimes put in antagonism with York. The battle of Agincourt was fought on St. John's day. Cf. Lib. Garderob., 27, etc. John de Rolleston was master of the hospital of Newton in Holderness, 5th Edward II. (Abbrev. Rot. Orig., i., 195).

[b] Not mentioned in Dug. Bar.

[c] Oct. 15, 1314, ordination of a per-

rector of Ersham, in his diocese, a native of the East Riding, has broken with his servants into our park at Beverley, to hunt. The bishop is requested to correct him.

1311, Jan. 18. John Taukard, of Pontefract, layman, has struck and drawn blood from Henry, vicar of Aldbro'. He is to go to Rome for penance. Jan. 19. Letters dimissory, for minor orders, to John de Wyclyve, rector of Wyclyve.[d] March 30. Licence for Sir Ralph de Bulmer, knight, to choose a confessor. April 5. A relaxation of the sentence of excommunication pronounced against Mr. Robert de Baldock and Roger de Waltham for impeding the archbishop's visitation of the diocese of Durham. May 16. Proving of the will of Henry de Lacy, earl of Lincoln, and administration granted to Nicholas de Reding, Robert de Silkeston, John de Sandale, the king's treasurer, and Sir Henry le Scrop, knight, executors.[e] June 4. A gift to the prebendary of Wistow of ten loads of thorns and other brushwood to enclose his *placea* at Wistow. June 19. We have given to master Peter de Insula four or five bucks, now fat, in Cawood park, and three oaks there, and licence to Sir John de Insula, or some one in the name of the said Peter, to take and hunt the wild beasts within our liberty of Hexham.[f]

1312, Feb. 24. Licence to the parishioners of Newark to remove a certain chapel built by H., our predecessor, in the churchyard. It is useless, and the room is wanted: the mate-

petual chantry in the chapel built within the archbishop's manor of Ripon, and William Swaynby appointed the priest (Reg. Greenfield, and Acta Capit., 1343-1368, 50). The chantry was well endowed. Cal. Rot. Pat., 78. Abbrev. Rot. Orig., i., 212.

[d] A famous name.

[e] The great earl died in 1312 (Dugd. Bar., i., 105). On Sept. 27 Henry de Pluckele and Thomas de Folcardeby were appointed "coadjutores" of Joan, countess of Lincoln, a minor, for the diocese and city of York. She married Thomas, earl of Lancaster. On Dec. 22, 1313, she had leave to choose a confessor (Reg. Greenfield). Her shrift would be a long one.

[f] Peter de Insula was canon of Bole and sub-dean of York. He was probably born at Bywell in Northumberland, and, on that account, archbishop Corbridge, the native of an adjacent village, calls him "carissimus." Insula was archdeacon of Carlisle, Wells, Exeter, and Coventry, and dean of Wells. He died in 1311.

Sir John de Insula, his brother, was a baron of the exchequer and a great man. The public records contain much information about him. On March 19, 1323, Eudo de Crosgat, rector of Fyngale, Ralph de Dalton, of Whalton, and Richard de Knageston, executors of the will of Sir John de Insula, knight, are cited to say why they have not administered to his effects.

On Nov. 20, 1298, archbishop Newark gave Robert, son of Sir John de Insula, a stall in St. Sepulchre's chapel, York (Reg. Newark). Richard de Insula, another son, was precentor of Beverley and rector of Hotham. In 1306 and 1308 he had permission to be non-resident (twice) for two years at the request of his father (Reg. Greenfield). On Feb. 2, 1311, he was made penancer for the diocese of Durham (Reg. Kellawe). On Oct. 21, 1317, he gave up Hotham and the precentorship for the living of Long Newton, dioc. Durham (Reg. Melton). In 1313 Richard de Insula, rector of Stockton, was ordered to go abroad with the king (Fœd., ii., 212).

rials are to be used in the church. Feb. 26. A commission to Robert de Pykering, canon of York, to receive the vow of chastity of Alice, widow of Sir Richard de Bingham, knight. August 2. A general letter against those who detain the relics and muniments belonging to the hospital of St. John at Nottingham. Sept. 4. A mandate to the bishops of Durham, Carlisle, and Whitherne to pray for the king and queen and the peace of the kingdom. Sept. 13. Licence to J. de Amcotes, one of the seven clerks of the belfrey at Beverley, to be absent for a year in the service of Stephen de Mauley, archdeacon of Cleveland.[g] Oct. 24. A commission against Sir Richard le Waleys, knight, and Paulina, wife of Sir John de Graas, who is with him in his house, living in adultery.[h] Nov. 12. Licence for Cristiana, daughter of Nicholas de Cayli, to reside in the nunnery of Clementhorp till she is nine years old, at the request of her father and friends.[i] Nov. 13. A monition to the parishioners of Worksop to repair the north-west tower of their church, which is in decay.[j] Dec. 27. Purgation of Sir Gerard Salvayn, knight, and Margaret, wife of Sir Robert de Percy, knight, who were charged with adultery.[k] An order to the bailiff of Beverley to take twenty-four deer in our park there and give them to our friends in those parts, as we shall tell you *viva voce*. Dec. 31. Licence to the prior and convent of Hexham to sell a corrody to Sir John de Swinburn, for a lady a cousin of his.[l]

1313, Feb. 17. Citation of Mr. Francis de Luco, vicar-general of Francis Gaytani, archdeacon of Richmond, for extortions from the clergy, etc. He travels about with fifteen and

[g] April 13, 1313, licence for John le Porter, one of the seven clerks at Beverley, to be absent in the service of Sir Henry de Percy, knight (Reg. Greenfield).

[h] John le Graas, of Studley Royal, was sheriff of Yorkshire in 1309. On March 14, 1334, an order to pay the cost of an enquiry in a case of bastardy of Isabel, daughter and heiress of John le Graas (Reg. Melton). See Walbran's account of the lords of Studley. Aug. 22, 1313, a commission against dame Juliana, wife of Sir Roger de Grimston, knight, and, on June 8, another against Margaret, widow of Sir John de Grey, knight (Reg. Greenfield). Adultery, etc., were too frequent.

[i] March 24, 1312, the abbat and monks of Selby are prohibited from visiting Clementhorp or spending the night there. Nov. 13, 1314, licence to Agnes, daughter of Sir William de Colville, to stay at Swyne till she is twelve. Oct. 27, 1315, licence to Margaret, sister of Sir Nicholas de Meynil, sheriff of Yorkshire, to stay for a year at Clementhorpe (Reg. Greenfield).

[j] A valuable architectural notice. Another monition was given on Jan. 5, 1314. On May 7, 1314, the prior and convent of Worksop had the archbishop's permission to fell, for the use of their house, two hundred oaks in their wood of Roumwode (Reg. Greenfield).

[k] Salvin was high sheriff of Yorkshire in 1310, 1312, and 1313. Cf. Surtees's Durham, iv., 117. He was a hot-tempered man, and was frequently in trouble. Eschaetor ultra Trentam 1st Edward II. (Abbrev. Rot. Orig., i., 156), a soldier and statesman.

[l] Not mentioned in the pedigree of Swinburn in Hodgson's Northumberland, vol. i., part ii., 231, etc.

sometimes with twenty-four horsemen, each accompanied by a dog, for hunting. It is a great burden to the clergy to be obliged to entertain them.[m] April 9. The archbishop prohibits any adoration of an image of the Virgin lately set up in the church of Foston. There is a great flocking of simple people to it, as if there were any more virtue in it than in any other image.[n] April 16. At Burton, the archbishop absolves Sir Peter de Mauley, knight, for incest with Alyna, daughter of Sir Thomas de Furnivall, his wife's sister, on the condition that he pays one hundred marks to the fabric of York minster.[o] June 27. Mandate to Peter de Dene to summon Sir Ranulph de Nevyll, Anastasia, his daughter, Alexander and Sir Robert de Nevyll, knight, sons of the said Sir Ranulph, Maria their sister, and Christian de Sutton, to reply to certain articles.[p] June 28. Commission to enjoin penance on dame Alianor, wife of Sir Walter le Vavasour, knight, for divers excesses.[q] July 14. To Sir Robert Hastang, knight, of our special favour, eight oaks from our wood of Thornton, fit for timber. Sept. 19. The archbishop requests the abbat of St. Mary's, York, to give an annual pension to his clerk, Robert de Grenefield, on account of his confirmation.[r] Dec. 31. Licence to G., bishop of Enachdune, to ordain Robert de Holden, a domestic chaplain of the earl of Lancaster. Dec. 31. Licence to John de Stapelton to have service, for two years, performed by a competent person in a chapel of old foundation in the churchyard of Melsanby.[s]

[m] An official gets into trouble:—

"—— He was a prickasoure a right:
Greihoundes he hadde as swift as foul of flight:
Of pricking and of hunting for the hare
Was all his lust, for no cost wolde he spare."

Luco afterwards became canon of Laughton at York. Francis Gaetano, archdeacon of Richmond, was cardinal deacon of S.M. in Cosmedin. He was nephew of Boniface VIII.

[n] A very remarkable entry (Wilkins, ii., 423). On Feb. 20, 1314, sentence against those who worship an image of the Virgin in the monastery of Bridlington (Reg. Greenfield). This reminds us of the words of bishop Pecok. The Lollards in after years raised the same cry against images (Walsingham, 363).

[o] A titled culprit, who will be mentioned again. Fines of this kind were frequently devoted to the fabric.

[p] Bishop Kellawe is said to have made Sir Ranulph Neville do penance for incest with his own daughter (Lel. Coll., ii., 334). These are frightful revelations. On Sept. 13, 1312, dame Petronilla de Nevyll had leave to have service performed in her manor of Rudham. She was old and could not go to Danbywisk (Reg. Greenfield).

There is a long account of Peter de Dene, his romantic life and his strange fortunes, in the Journal of the Archæological Institute.

[q] This lady and her husband have been already mentioned. The early wills of the Vavasors disclose a curious state of morality. In 13th Edward II. Robert le Vavasour gives lands in Thorpunderwood and Elnewyk to Fountains abbey for the souls of Wm. le Vavasour, his father, and Walter, his brother (Abbrev. Plac., 335). In my extracts from the registers and other books of records I have preserved the spelling of the names and places as I found them.

[r] A customary claim. The king asked Greenfield to do the same thing for Robert de Cottingham on his own accession to the see (Prynne, iii., 1153).

[s] A chantry was founded in the church of Melsanby for the souls of

1314, March 25. Commission to Henry de Wilton, official, and John de Wodehouse, rector of Sutton-on-Derwent, to denounce in the church of York the insult done to us by some one on the part of Pandulph de Sabellia, throwing in certain papers at the gates of our manor of Cawood.[t] April 3. Commission to absolve Sir Ralph de Neville from excommunication for striking Alan de Morton, canon of Marton in Galtres, and for a matter relating to tithes. May 2. Licence to the prior and convent of Newburgh to receive into their house, as an act of charity, among the poor of Christ, a chaplain broken down with age, Stephen de Sandale, who officiated for a long time in the chapel of Sandbeck near Maltby. May 16. The archbishop pardons his tenants at Hexham 59*l.* 14s. 6d. on account of the losses they have sustained from the Scots by plundering and fire.[u] August 4. A mandate from the archbishop to Mr. J. de Nassington, jun., Mr. Philip de Nassington, and Mr. William de Stanes, proctors in the court of York, ordering them to plead the cause of Joan, daughter of the late comte de Bar, against John de Warren, earl of Surrey, in a suit for divorce.[v] Sept. 8. Citation of Joan countess of Surrey. John, earl of Surrey, tells us that when he was a minor and a ward of Edward I. he was obliged by certain noble men and women of England to marry her through fear, although related to her in the third and fourth degrees. The citation is to be made at the castles of Conisbro' and Sandal, and she is to be summoned to appear before the archbishop. Sept. 15. An oratory to John, earl of Surrey, at Clifton, near York, during the continuance of the present parliament, provided that Walter, archbishop of Canterbury, does not go there with his cross erect.[w] Oct. 18. Licence to Sir Henry de Percy to have service in his chapel at the Friars Preachers, York.[x] Dec. 10. Sir Nicholas de Menyl has sum-

Alan and Henry de Melsanby (Reg. Cart. Mon. de Easby). Alan de Melsanby and Adam and Henry his brothers are enshrined in the Liber Vitæ of Durham, p. 96.

[t] Some libellous papers. Savelli, an Italian, had a contest with Richard de Cornubia for the stall of North Newbald, which was decided at Rome in favour of the former. Great violence was used, and armed men were employed (Reg. Greenfield and Melton. Fœd., ii., 142, 202). Savelli was notary of pope John XXII., and died in 1320.

[u] There is an account of these destructive raids in the Chron. of Lanercost.

[v] An obscure and extraordinary incident, upon which these extracts throw much light. The lady was a daughter of Henry, comte de Barr, and a granddaughter of Edward I. The marriage was an unhappy one, but no divorce could be procured. The two, however, lived apart (Hunter's South Yorkshire, ii., 108, and Watson's History of the house of Warren, ii., 8, etc. Coll. Top. and Geneal., vii., 133).

[w] A cautious provision. York was now filled with persons of distinction, in attendance upon the court and parliament. The king gave the archbishop leave to erect his cross in the city (Fœd., ii., 253).

[x] The family of Percy had an "inn" in Walmgate. On Dec. 27, 1313, the archbishop appointed a commissioner

moned divers rectors, vicars, etc., to come to him at Easingwold with horses and arms for service in Scotland. We forbid them to go.[y] Dec. 19. Licence for Richard, bishop of Durham, to dedicate an altar transferred from one place to another in his chapel at Welhalle.[z] Dec. 25. Licence for Albreda, daughter of Sir Robert de Percy, knight, to have an oratory in her manor of Sutton-upon-Derwent, where she resides.[a]

1315, Jan. 9. Mandate to pray for the soul of Philip, late king of France, at the request of Edward II., who says of him that he has on all occasions been a well-wisher and a friend of us and our kingdom.[b] Jan. 14. A commission to Mr. John Gower, S.T.P., rector of Wheldrake, to preach at Northallerton on Monday, the feast of S.S. Fabian and Sebastian, before the army on its way to Scotland, and the Friars are desired to preach against the Scots.[c] Jan. 17. A letter to the abbat S.M., York, enjoining him not to exact 2d. in each mark from the dignities and stalls at York for the Scottish war.[d] Jan. 29. A mandate to the executors of Sir John de Barton, of Oswaldkirk, knight, who has been killed in Scotland, to prove his will.[e] March —. A commission to correct offences and misconduct in our household at Cawood. March 11. A commission to the parish priest of Birkin to hear the confession which a parishioner of his, Sir William de Holand, knight, is most anxious to make.[f] August 6. A general denunciation of those who with an armed force have taken possession of the church and manse at Egmanton. The corpse of Roger de Bergh, the late rector, is in

to hear the confession of Sir Henry de Percy (Reg. Greenfield). I shall not attempt to describe his greatness and his magnificent services.

[y] Menyl was high sheriff of Yorkshire. An array was being made to protect the Marches and to avenge Bannockburn.

[z] Bishop Kellawe built this manor-house near York (Hist. Dunelm. Scr. Tres, 97). Every trace of it has disappeared, but I have a portion of a minute survey of the place made in the reign of Elizabeth, when many of the residences of the bishop were allowed to fall into decay.

[a] Sir Robert, who is elsewhere mentioned, was the owner of Bolton Percy and Sutton-on-Derwent and a great benefactor to York minster (Abbrev. Plac., 210). In 21st Edward I. he had licence to crenellate his residences at Sutton and Bolton (Cal. Rot. Pat., 56).

[b] The father-in-law of Edward II. The praise he bestows was excessive (Walsingham, 77). April 13, 33rd Edward I., an order to pray for the soul of Joan, queen of France (Prynne, iii., 1107). Fœd., ii., 258.

[c] The Friars were the great preachers of the day. Gower was probably an orator,—

> "An specially aboven every thing
> Excited he the peple in his prechyng."

[d] Jan. 17, 1315, licence to the dean and chapter to take 2d. from each mark "contra Scotos" (Reg. Greenfield).

[e] He was summoned to serve in Scotland on June 30, 1314 (Rot. Scot., i., 145).

[f] A gallant soldier, who occurs as a partizan of the earl of Lancaster in 1316 (Knyghton, 2533). In 7th of Edward II. the king pardoned him for his share in the death of Gaveston (Parl. Writs, ii., 66).

the house and it cannot be interred, nor can service be performed.

It is through such materials as these that the past comes back to us with the lights and shadows with which it was once chequered. Great men who have long since mouldered into dust are again alive. We hear of the wars at which their hearts once beat. We see them in their homes,—their joys and sorrows are laid open; we know what they did and gave; we can criticize their virtues and their crimes, and we forget for awhile that these men lived and died more than five centuries ago.

It is very pleasing to have so many witnesses of archbishop Greenfield's piety and zeal. His register, a stout folio in two parts, speaks to us with many tongues. The primate was a most excellent and pains-taking diocesan. The details of monastic life which his acts exhibit are most remarkable. Greenfield tightened the cords of discipline around his monasteries in a way that none of them would like. He was constantly visiting them and correcting offences even of the most minute kind. He was very strict also with his clergy on the question of nonresidence, but he must have been much thwarted and annoyed by the number of foreigners who were sent over to him for preferment. It would be most mortifying to him to find that when he had collated one of his own clerks to a benefice, some stranger arrived with a provision from the pope which he could not venture to oppose, and that, occasionally, a third claimant would spring up for it in the person of the king. When this was the case, as it not unfrequently was, how could the archbishop reward the men who deserved his favour? He was dragged into the courts of justice or before the papal consistory, angry and disgraceful brawls took place in the churches themselves, and much scandal and bickering ensued. Greenfield, however, did his best to attend to the interests of his flock, and he laboured, for the most part, with success. It was almost impossible for him to do everything himself. I find therefore, without surprise, the bishops of Whitherne and Enachdune[g] acting as his suffragans, and he now and then was aided by his brethren at Carlisle and Durham.

The relations between Greenfield and the ecclesiastics within the diocese of Durham, although not entirely satisfactory, were generally amicable. The arrangement that had been made between Bek and Corbridge seems to have been adhered to. Greenfield and Bek had but little intercourse. We find them associated together in the enquiry about the Templars, to whom

[g] In 1306 and 1313 Thomas, bishop of Whitherne, was acting as suffragan. April 11, 1314, a commission to him to that effect. In 1314 G., bishop of Enachdune, was acting (Reg. Greenfield).

both were favourable. Bek died in the spring of 1311, and Greenfield then went into his diocese and ruled it during the vacancy of the see. He removed the sentence of suspension which the deceased prelate had laid upon some of the monks of Durham for their opposition to him during his visitation, but on the 26th of March he himself excommunicated William the prior,[h] Henry de Stannford the sub-prior, the sacrist, and Adam de Boyvill, one of the monks of Durham, together with Robert de Baldock[i] and Roger de Waltham,[j] two of the clergy of the county, for endeavouring to impede him in his work. With the exception of Boyvill, they were forgiven soon afterwards.[k] During his stay in Durham Greenfield visited the archdeaconries,

[h] Hist. Dunelm. Scr. Tres, 96, 98. Stannford became prior of Finchale.

[i] A great but unfortunate man. His preferments were numerous. In the North he was rector of Bradford (Reg. Melton) and Welton (Reg. ii., Prior. and Conv. Dunelm., 67), rector of Whickham and canon of Chester (ibid., 22-3). He had a pension of 100s. from the priory of Durham, which he gave up on the 4th of May, 1314, for one of 10 marks (ibid., 26). Richard de Baldock, prebendary of Weighton at York, was his brother. Robert de Baldock became lord chancellor of England. The chroniclers give an account of his unhappy fortunes and his end.

[j] Of this person some account may be acceptable. He was a native of Waltham (Fuller's Waltham Abbey, 20). Rector of Arksey 1294-1319 (?) (Hunter's South Yorkshire, i., 327). Mar. 31, 1304, Benedict XI. grants him a dispensation to hold the rectories of Long Newton and Egglescliffe, and canonries at London, Darlington, Auckland, and Chester, and bishop Kellawe confirmed it 23rd March, 1314 (Reg. Kellawe, 118). April 5, 1306, Clement V. allowed him, being then bishop Bek's private chaplain, to hold benefices of the value of 200 marks per ann. (ibid., 119). He was temporal chancellor of Durham (MSS. Surtees and Prynne, iii., 996), and a pensioner of the monastery there (Misc. doc. Pr. and Conv. Dunelm., 3439, 4562). He was prebendary of Cadington Minor at London, and a royal chaplain (Newcourt, i., 130), and on June 28, 1322, the king made him archdeacon of Bucks (Le Neve, ii., 68). In 1334 he had licence of non-residence on his rectory of Hatfield (Reg. Melton). He was keeper of the king's wardrobe at the time of his death, which took place in 1342 (Reg. ii., Prior. and Conv. Dunelm., and Reg. Kellawe, 347). He gave some messages, etc., in London to keep two priests to pray in the chapel of St. John Baptist for his soul, those of his parents, and bishop Bek, and gave it costly vestments, some of which were set with precious stones. He also founded an oratory on the south side of the choir, with a glorious tabernacle, splendidly carved and coloured (Dugdale's St. Paul's, *n. e.*, 21-2).

Waltham wrote a book called the "Compendium Morale," which was very popular in the middle ages. It is somewhat in the style of Valerius Maximus, and is pleasantly drawn up. There is a fine copy at Durham (B, iii., 24) in the library of the dean and chapter, which ends thus:—

"Explicit Compendium Morale de quibusdam dictis et factis, exemplaribus antiquorum, per Rogerum de Waltham canonicum London. compilatum, qui simplici opere suo hic concludens, cum Ovidio, libro de Ponto, ait

'Leta quidem letus cecini, cano tristia tristis,
Conveniens operi tempus utrumque suo.'

Sic Domino et Beatæ Mariæ Virgini se commendans. Amen."

I can trace six other copies of this book. Fuller says that Waltham wrote other works, especially one called "Imagines Oratorum." His account as keeper of the Great Wardrobe was among the Stowe MSS., and is now in the possession of lord Ashburnham. Cf. Lel. Comm. de. Script. Brit., 264, and Bale, cent. iv., 302.

[k] Reg. Greenfield.

and the call-roll of the clergy and the proceedings of the visitor are preserved at York. This is the earliest list that we possess of the incumbents of any district in the North. The archbishop took some interest in the election of Richard de Kellawe to the vacant see, the whole process of which he entered in his register. He consecrated him at York on Whit Sunday, 1311,[l] receiving from his new suffragan the profession of obedience, which he always carefully observed.

We must not expect to find that the old feud about the cross between the two primates had been given up. It broke out several times while Greenfield presided over the Northern province, but with no great violence. When the archbishop-elect went abroad after his election, the king wrote a letter to the pope begging that he might be allowed to carry his cross erect on his return.[m] In February, 1306, when Greenfield came back to England, Edward sent an order to the archbishop of Canterbury that no violence should be offered to him, although it had been intended.[n] On his route the Northern primate paid a visit to the abbat of St. Augustine's, Canterbury, but he took especial care that his presence should entail no annoyance upon his host.[o] In the spring of 1312, when Greenfield was on his way to the council at Vienne he met with such rough usage at the hands of the servants of the archbishop of Canterbury that the king again stepped in to protect him as he returned.[p] When he arrived in York, on the 1st of December, Greenfield empowered Adam de Osgodby, Robert de Bardelby, John de Markingfeld, William de Melton, and Mr. John de Franceys, canons of York, to state his position in the controversy to one of the cardinals. In the autumn of 1314, when the court was at York, there was a great risk of a collision. The archbishop of Canterbury was on his way to that city, and it was not likely that he would cede a single point to his rival in the North. On the 31st of August Greenfield ordered his official and the dean and chapter of York to resist him if he asserted the offensive privilege, and directed the services to be suspended at every place and church at which he halted, unless it were the royal chapel. Instructions were also given to the archdeacon of Nottingham to check the Southern primate on his entrance into the diocese.[q] The king, however, put an end to the danger by ordering Greenfield to allow his brother to carry his cross erect during his stay in York.[r] He would submit most unwillingly.

[l] Hist. Dunelm. Scr. Tres, 92. In 1311 Greenfield granted an indulgence of forty days to those visiting the shrine at Durham (Raine's St. Cuthbert, 103).

[m] Fœd., i., 969.

[n] Wilkins, ii., 284.

[o] Chron. W. Thorne, col. 2005. Prynne's Coll., iii., 1146.

[p] Fœd., ii., 167.

[q] Reg. Greenfield.

[r] Fœd., ii., 253. Trokelowe Ann., 29.

On the 12th of June in the following year, when there was a chance of Greenfield going into the diocese of Worcester, a strict injunction was given to the bishop by his superior that he should not permit the sacred symbol to be raised.[s]

The clergy of Yorkshire were indebted to archbishop Greenfield for some useful constitutions which were promulgated at a synod held at Ripon on the 30th of September, 1306. They are identical, as Wilkins observes, with those drawn up in 1289 by Gilbert, bishop of Chichester, one of Greenfield's oldest friends, and a kind patron to him. Some special injunctions were added to the effect that no appeal or obedience should be paid to Canterbury. The archbishop had another meeting of his clergy at Laneham in 1311, and he there gave them another set of constitutions.[t]

Turn we now from official duties and state employments to the private life of the archbishop. Let us look at him in his palace and home, and not in the council-chamber or on his throne. The following graphic details, which require little comment or illustration, give us an interesting picture of his everyday life.

1307, May 14. An order to pay to Thomas Dodington and John de Marcadel 34*l.* 14s. 9d. for wines. May 26. For 180 sheep bought of Thomas de Marston, 12*l.* 15s. June 4. To Mr. Robert de Rampton and the executors of Walter Oliver, 36*l.* for 300 sheep and 180 ewes reckoned by the greater hundred. August 13. To the abbat of St. Mary's, York, the collector of the disme for the relief of the Holy Land, 100*l.*[u] Dec. 29. We have received of John de Ripon, bailiff of Sherburn, 20*l.* in part payment of 100 marks for oaks sold out of Outwode.

1308, April 11. To William de Grenfeld,[v] our nephew, 120 marks for cloth bought at Stannford fair. May 12. To Richard de Pole[w] 55*l.* for 15 casks of wine bought of him. June 1. To John le Warnner, of Munketon, money to pay for 40 oxen and 80 sheep purchased for our larder. June 17. To Nicholas de Molendinis 20*l.* for certain business of ours which he has to transact at London. Oct. 21. To Mr. John de Nassington,

[s] Reg. Greenfield.

[t] Wilkins, ii., 285, 409-15.

[u] The money was never used for that purpose. The abbats of St. Mary's, York, were frequently collectors for the pope. On Dec. 5, 1307, there was another payment of 100 marks to him for the Holy Land. On May 2, 1308, Greenfield paid him 100 marks on account of the "decima biennialis" which was due to the king, and on Aug. 4 the abbat and convent received 100 marks from him as a subsidy to the church of Rome (Reg. Greenfield).

[v] On Nov. 1, 1318, William de Greenfield, one of the adherents of the earl of Lancaster, has a general pardon (Parl. Writs, ii., part ii., 131).

[w] One of the De la Poles of Hull, a family afterwards ennobled. He was knighted, and died in 1345. Cf. Test. Ebor., i., 7.

Mr. J. de Craucumbe, and dan Adam de Sheffeud, executors of Mr. John de Craucumbe, archdeacon of the East Riding, 34*l*. 13s. 2d. for sheep, lambs, and hay. Oct. 24. To Giles le Morton, our servant at Thorpe and at the granges at York, 12*l*. for corn for seed.

1309, Jan. 25. To Giles le Morton, servant at our granges at York, the money necessary for making a foss in the Old Baily,[x] for procuring plants to put in the said foss, and for repairing the road to the mills. Feb. 5. For six casks of wine, 18*l*. Feb. 18. To Eudo de Assarto, our chamberlain, 100*l*. for the expenses of our hospice. March 10. To John le Graas, sheriff of Yorkshire, four oaks for timber in our wood at Thornton. March 24. To Clement, shipman of the abbat of St. Mary's, York, 5s. which he spent whilst carrying timber to our manor at Patrington. July 21. To Richard de Wystowe 10*l*. to buy animals to give to our lord the king if he chances to journey to Scotland this way. July 27. To Lambert de Trikingham, seneschal of our lands, 20*l*. in part payment of his fee (which was 40 marks). August 7. Matthew, rector of Little Sandal, pays to Eudo, our chamberlain, 40s. for the reconciling of the churchyard of Little Sandal.[y] August 9. To Toctus, brother of Frysotus de Monte Clare, 64*l*., in which John de Britannia, earl of Richmond,[z] says that he is bound to him for corn during the vacancy of the see. The letter was dictated by the archbishop.

1310, March 24. To Giles le Morton, keeper of our granges at York, 66s. for hay bought of John de Pelham,[a] keeper of the king's oats. The said John has intimated to us that he has oats for horses to sell at York at 4s. a quarter, and that he can sell as much as we want. April 11. To Thomas, bishop of Whitherne,[b] 100s. as a gift, and an honest hospice at York against the time of our general council. May 2. To Giles le Morton, keeper of our granges at York, money sufficient for the repairs of our manor at Thorp and our palace at York.

[x] The Old Bailey is in York on the Micklegate side of the Ouse, in the direction of Clementhorpe. It will be again mentioned (Drake's Eboracum, 265).

[y] A slip of parchment inserted in Greenfield's register tells us that the following churches, etc., were reconciled during the year 1309. June 30, the church of West Retford; July 8, the churchyard of Little Sandal; August 3, the chapel of Laxton Morhous; Oct. 10, the churchyard of Dunham; Sept. 24, the churchyard of Bramham; Nov. 4, the churchyard of Bardesey; Nov. 5, the churchyard of Harewood. 1310, April 16, the churchyard of S.M. at the gate of York castle. The shedding of blood was the cause of the pollution. The cost of reconciling a churchyard was, it appears, 40s.

[z] Cf. Dugd. Bar., i., 51.

[a] He is mentioned once or twice in the Parl. Writs.

[b] He made his profession of obedience at Scrooby on the 26th of June, 1306 (Reg. Greenfield). On 20th September, 1314, the king gave Thomas, bishop of Whitherne, leave to visit his diocese (Rot. Scot., i., 131).

May 19. To Nicholas de Molendinis 57*l.* to make provision for us in the fair of St. Ives. May 24. To repair our mills at Ripon 17 oaks, under the supervision of Sir Robert de Coygners[c] and the bailiff of Ripon. June 1. To William, son of Robert de Grenfeld our kinsman, 20*l.* for the repairs of the houses of the manor of the church of Bolton Percy. July 4. To John de Wynton our butler, 71*l.* 7s. 11d. for wines bought at Hull. August 25. To Sir Thomas de Colville, knight, lord of Cokewold, 100*l.* for the service due from us to the king in the Scottish war. Oct. 14. To Sir Robert de Coyners, knight, 50*l.* for a horse sold by him to us at Ripon fair for the use of John Giffard.[d]

1311, March 4. An order to pay the expenses incurred by our messengers holding a provincial council at Durham.. July 4. To the bishop of Whitherne 20*l.*, for acting as our suffragan during our absence. July 8. An order to pay the money for building our study in our *camera* at Cawood, and for repairing the front of our chapel at Burton.

1312, August 21. To William de Langtoft, keeper of the fabric of the church of York, 100*l.*, which we have promised and graciously conceded for the said fabric.[e] Sept. 12. To H. de Wodhouses, servant of our manor of Cawood, money sufficient to carry on our work there to its completion. Nov. 13. For wines bought at Hull, 8½ marks. Nov. 15. An order to Henry de Henney, canon of Ripon and our receiver there, to pay 10*l.* to the keeper of the fabric of two bridges near Ripon which have been broken down. Nov. 23. To Roger de Thornton, our receiver at York, 24s. 11d. for repairing our old crozier.[f] For

[c] Probably of Ripon. On June 15, 1304, he and Adam de Middleton, clerk, were made justices of assize for the liberty of Ripon. On Aug. 30, 1310, he, Adam de Middleton, rector of Arncliffe, and Thomas de Fyssheburne, had a similar commission, and Conyers had another on Jan. 18, 1314. On Nov. 11, 1309, he was appointed to enquire into a dispute between the archbishop and the abbat of Fountains about the boundaries of the moor or pasture near the vill of Colhou (Reg. Corbridge and Greenfield).

June 7, 1313, dom. Thomas le Conyers occurs as the sequestrator of the archbishop within the archdeaconries of Notts, Cleveland, and the East Riding (Reg. Greenfield).

On August 11, 1336, a loan of 10 marks to Sir Robert Coigners, knight. June 25, 1338, another of 20*l.* to his executors. August 3, another of 25*l.* to Robert Coigners (Reg. Melton). This is, I presume, the person whose marriage archbishop Melton bought in 1333 for Joan his niece for the sum of 60 marks. He is a witness in the Scrope and Grosvenor Roll (ibid., ii., 317).

[d] Probably Sir John Giffard of Brimmesfield, the archbishop's kinsman, or one of the Giffards of Weston. On Feb. 10, 1309, Greenfield gives an acquittance to dame Margaret Giffard for 50 marks, part of a debt of 100*l.* in which she was bound to us for Sir John Giffard of Weston (Reg. Greenfield).

[e] On May 21, 1306, Greenfield granted an indulgence of forty days in behalf of the minster. In the preface to the Fabric Rolls, p. xi, I have stated erroneously that he gave a donation of 500 marks to the fabric. The real donor was his successor Melton.

[f] The parcels are, " In cruce domini

making a new one, 40s. For furs to set upon our mantle bought by Thomesyne, 12s. For the York fairs on the feast of St. Peter ad Vincula, 26s. 8d. Dec. 16. A loan of 40*l.* to the prior of Watton in his great necessity. Dec. 21. To Peter de Baddefosse 16 marks for four casks of wine.

1313, Jan. 5. To the Friars Preachers at York 40s., to the Friars Minors 2 marks, to the Augustinians 20s., and to the Carmelites 20s., to enable them to keep the festival to-morrow.[g] Jan. 14. To Adam Munketon, goldsmith of York, for making our new crozier, 20s., and 16d. for testing the silver used thereon; for quicksilver 6d., and for three gold florins bought for gilding the said crozier, 12s. 10d. For a saddle bought for John Fauconberge,[h] 5s. 6d. Jan. 29. To Walter de Brikynhale, 5s. 7d. for the cost and *apparatus* of our Bible. Feb. 11. To Nicholas de Molendinis 40*l.* for certain matters which we told him to do. Feb. 13. To the goldsmith for making the cover of our cup, 12s.; for one florin bought to gild it, 4s., and for making it, 3s. March 5. To a wine merchant 9½ marks for two casks of new wine. March 29. To Adam de Munketon, goldsmith, 14*l.* 7s. 9d. for the making and the metal *(pondere)* of seven salvers *(scutellarum)* and six cups of silver. April 27. To Gaylard de Laden, 10*l.* 16s. 8d. for four casks of wine bought for our use at Hull, and to Arnald de Leulk, 40*l.* for 16 casks of wine bought there. June 7. To Margery de Wyghton for straw *(literia)*[i] bought for our use, 10 marks. June 13. To William de Grenefeld, our nephew, 40 marks on our business. June 19. To John de Sandwich 40 marks to make provision for us at London. July 26. We have pardoned Robert de Mering, of Southwell, 40s. in consideration of a colt we have bought of him. July 15. To Robert de Bluntesdon, 200*l.* to make provision for us at the next fair at St. Botulph's. Sept. 3. To Mr. John de Weston,[j] the king's chamberlain in Scotland, or to

facienda; in pondere, primo, 7s. 3d. In diminutione operis, 8d.: in vivo argento empto pro eadem, 4d.: in factura ejusdem crucis, 6s. 8d.: in ij florinis et di. auri emptis, 9s."

[g] In the Wardrobe Account of Edward I. (44, etc.) similar gifts occur. The Friars were not ignorant of good living if Piers Plowman, Chaucer, and Buchanan are to be believed. Their migratory life was one of their chief characteristics: that they would justify in the words of Erasmus, "Tales errones erant apostoli; talis erat et Dominus Jesus;" and for their fasting, etc., the lines of the poet might be their warrant:—

"Our Lord Jesu, as holy writ deviseth,
Yave us ensample of fasting and praieres.
Therfore we mendicants, we sely freres,
Ben wedded to poverte and continence."

Their life, soon after their introduction into England, must have been anything but pleasant, as Eccleston speaks of their crowding together for warmth "like a litter of pigs."

[h] A son of Walter de Fauconberge and a ward of the archbishop of York. He will be again mentioned.

[i] Lib. Garderobæ Edward I., 33.

[j] Paymaster at Berwick 1299, 1300 (Lib. Garderobæ, 145). An eschaetor and much concerned in Scottish affairs (Fœd., ii., 499. Rot. Scotiæ, i., 61

Peter Bonavicta, merchant, of the company of the Bardi, 100 marks. Oct. 25. To the abbat of St. Mary's York, 100*l.* which we are compelled to pay in these days in behalf of our predecessor J. Romayn for a certain disme imposed in his time. Nov. 16. A loan of 120 marks to Mr. P. de Dene[k] which he has borrowed from us in the time of his great need. Dec. 23. To the goldsmith at York for the metal and the making of six silver cups, 4*l.* 18s. 7d. To Peter de Badefos, 15*l.* for five casks of wine which he sent to Cawood.

1314, Jan. 25. An order to pay the money required for making a new gate in our manor of Hexham and for other works there. Feb. 11. A loan of 40*l.* to the prior and convent of Hexham on account of the frequent incursions of the Scots. Feb. 20. To John de Sandwich money sufficient to buy half a web of cloth of the suit of our winter livery, and a thick variegated fur for dan William de Melton.[l] To the Friars Preachers and Minors of York, 40s. each, and to the Augustinians and Carmelites, 20s. each, of our alms, and let each convent be asked to permit every priest in their houses to say a mass for the soul of Robert de Grenefeld, our brother, lately deceased. March 22. To John the goldsmith at York, and others, 7*l.* 7s. 6d. for certain small things. May 12. To Thomas Frere, William Curtays and Roger de Upton of Doncaster 20 marks for the repairs of the causeway between Doncaster bridge and a bridge outside the town called Wylghebrigg. May 26. To the keepers of the fabric of the church of St. Peter, York, 50 marks, of our special favour. May 28. To William de Vasconia, wine merchant, 25*l.* 2d. for 8 casks of red wine bought of him, and to Peter de Badefosse, 33*l.* 16s. 1d. for 10 casks of red, and 1 pipe of white wine bought of him. May 31. To the repairs of 2 bridges at Ripon, 10*l.* June 18. To John de Merkingfeld 100*l.* as a loan to restore his fortunes, with God's help, for we are much concerned at his unhappy case.[m] July 18. To John

etc.). Constable of the Tower of London (The French Chron. of London, 55). Constable of Bordeaux, 1st of Edward III. (Cal. Rot. Pat., 99).

[k] Prebendary of Grendale at York, which he gave up in 1322, when he took the cowl in the monastery of St. Augustine, at Canterbury. He made a will in favour of that house, but tiring of his profession, ran away. Thorne gives an amusing account of his recapture.

[l] Afterwards archbishop.

[m] Prebendary of Warthill at York and Studley at Ripon, and rector of Escrick. In the 5th and 6th of Edward II. he was chancellor of the Exchequer (Madox, ii., 326), having been appointed to the office two years before, when he had the royal permission to crenellate his house at Markenfield, near Ripon, which still remains (Cal. Rot. Pat., 70). He was occupied occasionally in state matters (Rot. Scot., i., 70. Rot. Parl., i., 449. Fœd., ii., 249, 409), and lent money to the monastery of Durham (Reg. Kellawe, 71). He was executor of William de Hamilton, dean of York and lord chancellor of England, with whom he had been long connected. He got into trouble and was excommunicated on account of his

de Okham,[n] the king's cofferer, 100 marks for our service in the Scottish war in 1313. July 22. To Nicholas de Molendinis, 10*l*. 16s. 8d. for cloth and furs for our use, and to Peter de Badefosse, 40*l*. 6s. 8d. for a pipe of wine. July 12. To Henry de Cawod, our poulterer *(poletario)*, 17*l*. 3s. 5d. to buy oxen, sheep, and pigs for gifts to the king and queen.[o] August 6. To Nicholas de Molendinis, 200*l*. to provide for us at St. Botulph's fair. August 14. To John de Sandale, lieutenant of the treasury, 40*l*. which we have granted to the king for the wages of forty footmen who are to be sent to Berwick to guard that town in its great need.[p] August 19. To a goldsmith at York, 69s. 2d. for the metal and the making of four silver cups. To a certain baker at York for consecrated bread *(panis Dominicus)* lately sent to Sir Hugh le Despenser, and Ralph de Mehermer.[q] Sept. 22, To Sir John de Wylmerton, knt., 200 marks which we have granted to our kinsman Sir John Giffard of Brymmesfield to help towards the payment of his ransom in Scotland. To Sir Henry de Wylmerton, knight, 100 marks which we have given to Sir Baldwin de Fryvill, knight, our kinsman, towards his ransom in Scotland. Oct. 3. To Sir Simon Warde, knight, 20*l*. for the same purpose.[r] Sept. 24. To John de Sulle,[s] 10*l*. which we have lent him in his great need. Nov. 6. To William de Ponteburgi, our bailiff at Sherburn, money to pay for fifty furs bought at Pontefract for our winter livery. Nov. 21. To the Friars Preachers of Beverley three quarters of corn. Dec. 9. To the bailiff of Sherburn money to pay the wages of John Lousing our carpenter. Dec. 10. To Peter de Badfos 50 marks

maladministration of that trust, and this, probably, is the "miseria" to which Greenfield alludes. Markenfield's will was made in 1321, and is in the registry of the dean and chapter of York.

[n] A baron of the Exchequer.

[o] Walsingham, 104.

[p] Cf. Chron. Lanercost, 224, etc. Fœd., ii., 248.

"England was roused—on every side
Courier and post and herald hied,
To summon prince and peer,
At Berwick bounds to meet their liege
Prepared to raise fair Stirling's siege
With buckler, brand, and spear."

[q] It is impossible to speak here of these great men. The panis may be thus explained, "Quoque appellata sunt eulogia ea panis κλάσματα, quæ in veteri ecclesia ad alias parœcias, aut ad peregrinos ἐπιδημοῦντας, ut dictum, mitti solebant. Similiter etiam Latini eulogias dixere frusta panis benedicti quidem, sed non in usum eucharistiæ, quæ et absentibus et catechumenis, jus sumendæ eucharistiæ non habentibus mittebantur, ut ipsis essent vice sacramenti. Fractio panis dicebatur eulogiarum benedictio, quæ a presbyteris vel episcopis fiebant ante cibi sumptionem seu prandium; quas eulogias amicis vel convivis in communionis symbolum distribuebant." See also Ducange *sub voce Eulogia*.

[r] The consequences of the defeat of Bannockburn. We see from this how the ransoms of the prisoners were raised. Wylmerton had been a captive himself, and Ward is, erroneously, said to have been killed on that fatal field. Wylmerton is probably the same person that was executed for treason at Bristol in 1322 (Murimuth, 37). Miracles are said to have attested his excellency.

[s] Chamberlain of Edward I. in 1306 (Fœd., i., 998). Abbrev. Rot. Orig., i., 36.

for red vestments of "siklatun,"[t] which belonged to Sir Henry de Percy, with parures, stole, and maniple, embroidered.

1315, Jan. 14. To Hugh Saunterre,[u] our valet, and Giles de Morton, "domicello nostro," money to buy for each of them the following arms, "one aketun, one haubergeon, and one bacinet," and gauntlets and a lance. Jan. 27. To Gaillard Cessime, wine merchant of Gascony, 20 marks 13s. for 4 casks of wine. Feb. 13. To Stephen de Bella Aqua,[v] bailiff of Southwark, 74s. 8d. which he paid for stone and flint bought for making a certain chamber in our manor of Scrooby. To John de Moubray and Peter de Mauley 50 marks each, as captains of these parts, appointed by us and our clergy for the defence of this province against the Scots.[w] March 30. Mandate to the receivers at Chirchedon to buy 3 casks of good wine, as we intend to come there this summer. April 8. To the bailiff of Sherburn for 55 lambs' furs, bought for our use at Pontefract, the necessary money. April 18. To Wm. de Grenefield, our nephew, 50 marks for certain business of ours. April 26. To William de Thorp, our baker *(panetario)*, 20*l.* to buy horses for our use at Ripon fair. May 5. To Sir Robert Coigners, 20*l.* which we have lent to him. May 6. To Peter de Badefos, 49*l.* 14s. 2d. for 15 casks of wine at Hull. May 17. To the keeper of the bridges at Ripon,[x] 20*l.* To our steward at Scroby, money to buy certain things required to build a chamber in our manor there. May 28. To the keeper of the fabric of the church of York, 50 marks for the more expeditious progress of the work this summer, August 11. A loan of 50 marks to Sir Ralph Fitzwilliam.[y] August 23. A loan of 20*l.* to Henry de Knaresburgh minister of the house of St. Robert of Knaresburgh and his convent on account of their great need. August 31.

[t] In 1295 the cope of John Mansel "de panno aureo qui vocatur ciclatona" was in the treasury of St. Paul's (Dugdale's St. Paul's, *n. e.*, 1318). Other instances occur in Ducange under the word *cyclas*. Cf. Knyghton, col. 2740.

[u] Walsingham, 107. There was a great levy about this time in Yorkshire (Rot. Scot., i., 165).

[v] He was bailiff of Ripon in 1307. The family belonged to Nottinghamshire. Cf. Thoroton's Notts, 321. John de Bella Aqua (Bellew) married Laderina, one of the daughters and co-heirs of Peter de Brus (Madox, Bar. 51). On "die Dom. in crast. Omn. Sanct.," 1309, Isabella de Bella Aqua granted to William, son and heir of Sir John de Bella Aqua, her son, his own marriage which she bought of Sir William le Vavasour for 200 marks (Reg. Greenfield). Plac. de quo Warranto, 188, 193, 212.

[w] On 16th March 200 marks more were given to four captains, and a like sum on the 26th (Reg. Greenfield).

[x] On 26th August another sum of 10*l.* for them to William le Littester, burgess of Ripon (ibid.).

[y] In 24th of Edward I. he occurs as brother and heir of Geoffrey Fitzwilliam (Abbrev. Rot. Orig., i., 96). He was custos of Newcastle and Carlisle in 1315 (Rot. Scot., i., 140), and was much employed in the service of the state. For an account of him and his princely fortunes, see Hodgson's Northumberland, vol. ii., part ii., 274. Foss's Judges, iii., 89.

To the prioress and convent of Clementhorpe, 40s. of our alms. and to a poor man, who made a ditch in the garden of our palace to carry off the superfluous water, 2s. Sept. 5. To the prior of St. Mary's York, 20*l.* for the covering of our houses at Westminster. Sept. 10. To Stephen de Bella Aqua money to buy 50,000 or 60,000 turves, and 6 marks for making a certain mill of ours at Laneham. Nov. 18. To the Friars Preachers and Minors of York, each 5 marks, and to the Augustinians and Carmelites 40s. each, on account of the excessive dearness at the present time.[*]

Archbishop Greenfield died at his manor house at Cawood on the festival of St. Nicholas, Saturday, December 6, 1315,[a] and was interred within the minster of York to which he was a generous benefactor. He lies in the north transept on the eastern side, in the corner adjacent to the choir aisle. The monument which commemorates him, although much mutilated and injured, is a very striking one. The marble slab that covers his remains has been plated with brass, of which nothing is in existence save a portion of the figure of the archbishop which time and neglect have almost entirely obliterated. He wears his mitre, and is clad in full canonicals, and his hand is raised in the act of benediction.[b] Above the figure there towers a lofty overarching canopy of rich decorated work surmounted by a statuette of Greenfield who is seated in his chair.[c] This is a valuable memorial of the skill of a recent master mason of the cathedral. Between the tomb and the wall there once stood the altar of St. Nicholas, for, as the decease of the archbishop occurred on the festival of that saint, this place, most happily and appropriately, was selected for his interment. At the time of Greenfield's death two chantries were in existence at that altar, and on the 28th of April, 1346, Richard de Cestria, canon of York, added a third at which the soul of the archbishop was especially commemorated.[d]

About 1735 the tomb was opened and a fine gold ring with a ruby was taken from the dead man's finger. It is now deposited among the treasures in the vestry. The lines of Hugo Grotius may be applied to it :—

[*] Knyghton (col. 2532) speaks of the "caristia tritici" in 1307, but he does not allude to this year. Murimuth, however, mentions it (p. 24), and says that a quarter of wheat was worth 30s. and more. Cf. Sprotti Chron., 77, and Trokelowe, 34. The corn could not ripen in consequence of the wet weather.

[a] MSS. Cotton, Vitellius, A, ii., 112. Stubbs, col. 1730.

[b] Engraved in Waller's Sepulchral Brasses, and in Drake, 432.

[c] It was behind this tomb that the wretched fanatic Jonathan Martin secreted himself in 1829 when he set fire to the minster. In 1434 the archbishop's tomb was enclosed (Fabric Rolls, 53).

[d] Fabric Rolls, 299. Domesday book penes Dec., and Cap. Ebor., 52 *b*.

"Annule, qui thecam poteras habuisse sepulchrum,
Hæc, natalis erit nunc tibi, theca, locus."

I find also that Greenfield bequeathed another ring to the dean and chapter to decorate the feretory of St. William. This came into their possession on the 7th of January, 1316.[e]

Goodwin tells us, without stating his authority, that the archbishop bequeathed his library to the monastery of St. Alban's,[f] which at that time was in very high repute. His will has not occurred to me. Thomas de St. Albans', canon of Southwell, and William, son of Robert de Greenfield, the testator's nephew, were the executors.[g] They were released from the responsibility of their charge on the 16th of August, 1322.[h]

William de Melton, the forty-second archbishop of York, was a person of whom all contemporary writers speak with respect and admiration, and he must be regarded as one of the greatest prelates that ever presided over the Northern province. He was of humble origin, but he raised himself to distinction by his natural abilities and his unflagging energy, and became one of the most conspicuous and useful statesmen of the age in which he lived. Nor were his services to the church less remarkable from his connection with the court.[i] It is, indeed, difficult to do full justice in a narrow space to so illustrious a man.

He was a native of a little hamlet, called Melton, in the parish of Welton near Howden,[j] which is situated about five miles from North Cave, and nine from Beverley and Hull. The district in which he was born was under the control of the see of Durham from very early times, and the prior and convent of that renowned monastery were the patrons of the church in

[e] Fabric Rolls, ed. Surtees Society, 214. There was in the treasury, by the gift of Greenfield, a pontifical ring with an emerald in the middle surrounded by four rubies and four large pearls (ibid.).

[f] De Præsulibus, *n. e.*, 685. He probably derived his information from the famous Golden Book of St. Albans' which is in the Cottonian library.

[g] Drake's Eboracum, 432.

[h] March 4, 1319, commission to Mr. Dennis Avenel, canon of Beverley, and Thomas de Cave to receive the accounts of the executors. Oct. 10, 1324, the king orders Mr. Thomas de St. Albans to be summoned to pay the sum of 193*l.* 17s. 5½d. to archbishop Melton (Reg. Melton).

[i] "Licet de curia regis esset assumptus, religiosam tamen vitam habuit et honestam" (Lanercost Chron., 233).

[j] Mr. Nichols makes him a native of Melton Mowbray (History of Leicestershire, ii., 259). There are pedigrees of the family in Baker's Northants, i., 673; Poulson's Holderness, ii., 199; Hunter's South Yorkshire, ii., 162.

which Melton would worship in his boyhood. They befriended him in his struggles with the world, but it was in all probability to bishop Bek and archbishop Greenfield that he was mainly indebted for his rapid progress in the court and church. The neighbourhood from which he sprang produced another great man about the same time, John de Hotham, lord chancellor of England and bishop of Ely.

In 1300 Melton occurs as one of the ostiarii of the wardrobe of Edward I., and he was comptroller of the same department at the accession of his son, an office which he was holding in 1315.[k] In the spring of 1308 he went abroad with Edward II., being at that time the secretary of that monarch, in the charge of the temporary seal.[l] On the 20th of April, 1310, the king sent a commendatory letter in his favour to the pope, praising him highly, and saying that he had been in his service from his boyhood. This seems to shew that there was then some prospect of Melton's rising to greatness, and this is the more probable from the fact that Edward wrote in the same strain to the pope and cardinals on the 12th of November, 1312.[m] On the 12th of August, in the same year, he went as a commissioner from the king to the barons and *probi homines* of the Cinque ports,[n] and he was sent abroad on May 3, 1313, with letters of protection, on the king's business, and the constable of Dover was ordered to make arrangements for the passage of Melton and his companions.[o] On the 1st of August, in the same year, Melton was one of the commissioners who were to look to the protection of the marches of England against the Scots, and on the 12th of June, 1314, he and others had letters of credence to archbishop Greenfield, as the representatives of the king, in the convocation of the clergy that was to meet at York to consider the subject of the expedition into Scotland which ended in the disastrous defeat at Bannockburn.[p]

Whilst Melton was thus employed, he was a pluralist of the first water. He seems, indeed, to have been beneficed in every part of England, but it must not be inferred that he held all his pieces of preferment at the same time. In 1299 he was presented to the rectory of Refham, in the diocese of Lincoln, which he was holding in the following year.[q] On the 10th of

[k] Liber Garderobæ, 45, 87, 95, 166, 181, 332. Madox, Hist. Exch., i., 74. Rot. Scotiæ, i., 143. Pell Records, 118. Parl. Writs, vol. ii., part ii., 10.

[l] Fœd., ii., 29. Parl. Writs, vol. ii., part ii., 11, 43. In 1343 he gave the great seal to the keepers thereof by the king's order.

[m] Fœd., ii., 107, 187.

[n] Parl. Writs, vol. ii., part ii., 43.

[o] Fœd., ii., 211.

[p] Ibid., 249. Rot. Scotiæ, i., 113. Parl. Writs, vol. ii., part i., 421; part ii., 77. On August 13, 1313, he was sent to various prelates within the province of York to ask for loans against the Scots (ibid., vol. ii., part ii., 65).

[q] MSS. Harl., 6951, 33. Cal. Inq. Post. Mort., i., 165.

July, 1301, he was instituted, at the presentation of the abbat and convent of St. Mary's York, to the rectory of Hornsea in Holderness.[r] On the 2nd of January, 1305, he obtained the first part of the prebend of Oxton cum Crophill at the church of Southwell,[s] and on the 13th of March, 1308, he was instituted to the rectory of Lythe, at the presentation of Sir Peter de Mauley, and he made a diligent enquiry into the dilapidations of his living.[t] On the 27th of August, 1308, he was made dean of the college of St. Martin-le-grand,[u] and archdeacon of Barnstaple, in the church of Exeter on the 13th of October.[v] In 1309 he became prebendary of Louth at Lincoln.[w] On the 3rd of May, in that year, he gave up his stall in the collegiate church of Westbury, in the diocese of Worcester, to Mr. William de Lincoln for his prebend at the altar of St. Michael at Beverley, to which he was collated. On the 2nd of June he was presented by Edward II. to the stall of South Cave at York, but it was found upon enquiry that Neapolio, a Roman cardinal was in possession of it in virtue of a papal provision, and Melton did not obtain it.[x] On the 30th of July he was collated by archbishop Greenfield to the prebend of Northwell at Southwell which John de Drokenesford had held, and on the 6th of October he was preferred, by the same prelate, to the provostship of Beverley.[y] In the same year he was presented by the king to the rectory of Thorpland in Norfolk.[z] On the 23rd of March, 1310, he was collated to the stall of Driffield at York, exchanging for it, with John de Cadomo, his prebend in the collegiate church of Darlington, and he was installed by the chapter on the 15th of August.[a] On the 4th of August he was instituted to the rectory of Spofforth at the presentation of Sir Henry de Percy.[b] In 1312, on the 4th of July, Richard Kellawe, bishop of Durham, granted him an annual pension of 20*l.* for the good service he had rendered him,[c] and Melton was in the receipt of a similar gift of ten marks per annum from Walter de Langton, bishop of Coventry and Litchfield, which he gave up on the 12th of November, 1318, when he no longer needed it.[d] On the 8th of April, 1312, the prior and convent

[r] Reg. Corbridge, 33 *b.* Reg. Greenfield, part i. Instituted again May 7.

[s] Le Neve, iii., 447.

[t] Reg. Greenfield.

[u] Newcourt, i., 426. Kempe's St. Martin-le-Grand, 102. Mon. Francisc., 506. Plac. de quo Warranto, 452. Cal. Rot. Chart., 140.

[v] Le Neve, i., 406.

[w] Ibid., ii., 180.

[x] Reg. Greenfield, part i., 12-13.

[y] Ibid., part i., 46 *b.* He was collated to it previously on Oct. 22, 1308. Oliver's Beverley, 390. Cal. Rot. Chart., 141, 147. Plac. de quo Warranto, 636.

[z] Blomefield's Norfolk, vii., 98.

[a] Reg. Greenfield. Acta Capit., 16 *b.* In August, 1311, when Robert de Pickering was elected dean, Melton received the vote of Robert de Rippling-ham, the chancellor.

[b] Reg. Greenfield, part i., 80 *a.*

[c] Reg. Kellawe, 4 *b.*

[d] Reg. Melton. He had also a pen-

of Durham gave him the rectory of Welton, his native parish, but he resigned it on the 14th of September following,[e] and on the 13th of January he is said to have been preferred to a stall in the church of Howden.[f] On the 21st of November, 1314, he received the living of Castre, Northants, which he gave up in 1316,[g] and in September, 1317, he resigned that of Brigham, in Cumberland, upon his promotion to the archbishopric of York.[h]

The death of archbishop Greenfield in December, 1315, vacated the see of York, and on the 13th of that month the king gave the chapter leave to proceed to a new election. On the 21st of January they fixed upon Melton at the king's request, and on the 5th of February Edward assented to their choice. On the 8th the king wrote in Melton's behalf to the pope and gave him letters of safe conduct to enable him to leave the kingdom.[i] On his arrival at the papal court he was subjected to a lengthy and tedious delay occasioned, no doubt, to a great extent by the death of Clement V. His wishes, however, were thwarted by some *attachés* of the papal court, among whom may be mentioned Pandulph de Savelli, George de Poregia, and Francis Gaetano, all of whom were beneficed in Yorkshire and had some grudge, in all probability, against the archbishop-elect. On many occasions the king wrote to the pope and cardinals in Melton's favour, at one time protesting against the delay, and expressing the mischief which it might occasion in consequence of the incursions of the Scots, at another time remonstrating with the opponents of the confirmation and imploring that it might at once be made.[j] Smooth words, however, as well as rough were impotent, and the consecration was actually delayed until the 25th of September, 1317, when it took place at Avignon.[k] On

sion from the prior and convent of Coventry. There is a singular letter from prince Edward relating to it in 33rd Edward I., which certainly shews that Melton was fond of money (Ninth Report of the Deputy Keeper of Public Records, appendix, ii., 247-8).

[e] Reg. ii., Prior. and Conv. Dunelm., i., 111 *b*. When Melton was elected archbishop he wrote a kind letter to the prior asking him to be present at his enthronization. He also lent the convent 100 marks (Misc. Documents penes Dec. and Capit. Dunelm., 4603, 4967).

[f] MSS. Torre. Hutchinson's Durham, iii., 451.

[g] MSS. Harl., 6951, 57 *b*. Bridges' Northants, ii., 501.

[h] Reg. Melton. He resigned at the same time the rectory of Hornsea, valued at 50 marks per annum; the prebend of Driffield, taxed at 100*l*. per annum; the stall of St. Michael at Beverley, worth 17*l*.; and the provostship worth 40*l*.

[i] Stubbs, col. 1730. Le Neve, iii., 106. Fœd., ii., 285. Cal. Rot. Pat., 79. On 19 kal., Jan., 1315, the chapter asked the king's leave to proceed to a new election (Reg. Dec. and Cap., sede vac.).

[j] Fœd., ii., 297-8, 300, 305-7, 310, 312-15, 318-19, 327, 332-3, 341. Edward calls Melton "prædilectus clericus et familiaris noster." On April 20, 1317, the pope wrote to the king to say that he had ordered a cardinal-bishop to hear the matter (Fœd., ii., 326). Carte's Gascon, etc., Rolls., ii., 6—9.

[k] Stubbs, col. 1730. MSS. Cotton, Vitellius, A, ii., 112.

the 8th of October Edward restored to Melton the temporalities of his see.[l] The new primate was at Beverley during the celebration of the next Advent, and on the 14th of February he was solemnly enthroned at York, the festivities on that occasion lasting for three days.[m]

When Melton returned into the North he was plunged into the vortex of Scottish politics which occupied his attention for the remainder of his life. The peace of the Borders was being continually broken, and it was necessary for the English soldiers and statesmen to be always on the alert. On the 27th of January, 1318, the archbishop was summoned to a meeting of the parliament at Lincoln,[n] and on the 18th of March he was one of the commissioners appointed to make a truce with Scotland.[o] Negotiations, however, were thrown aside, and on the 8th of June the proposed meeting at Lincoln was deferred in consequence of the news that the Scots were at that time in England. The restless marauders broke into Yorkshire in the month of May, plundering and burning what they could as they passed along. The towns of Northallerton, Boroughbridge, Knaresbrough and Skipton in Craven were destroyed, and Ripon was only saved from ruin by the tenants paying down to the invaders the large sum of 1000*l*.[p] On the 5th of June the archbishop excommunicated the Scots for the mischief they had caused at Ripon and Otley. They had done very serious injury, besides, to a large portion of his diocese. The value of church property in Yorkshire was depreciated by that raid to the large amount of 1000 marks, and as many as sixty benefices were injured. The church of Tadcaster was destroyed, and that of Pannal burned, as the invaders had tarried at that village. The tower of the church of Knaresbrough still bears the marks of the fire that was kindled around it in the vain hope of bringing it to the ground and destroying the fugitives whom it sheltered. The abbey of Fountains was for some time the head-quarters of the Scots, and, as may be expected, the substance of that noble house was entirely wasted or taken away.[q] Corpses and smoking villages marked the path of the retreating foe. The utmost vigilance was required to prevent the recurrence of the inroad. The archbishop was made one of the keepers of the marches,[r]

[l] Fœd., ii., 344.

[m] Stubbs, col. 1731. The bishops, abbats, justiciars, etc., were invited to the enthronization (Reg. Melton).

[n] Parl. Writs, vol. ii., part i., 173, 175, 178.

[o] Fœd., ii., 358. Rot. Scotiæ, i., 179.

[p] Chron. Lanercost, 235. Parl. Writs, vol. ii., part i., 181. Fœd., ii., 437. Reg. Melton, where there is a list of the places injured. On Jan. 1, 1319, the archbishop ordered his own tenants at Ripon to pay their quota. In Leland (Coll., i., 250) it is said that the Scots killed many of the clergy, etc., at Ripon. This information is in Murimuth, 38.

[q] Reg Melton. Cal. Rot. Pat., 83.

[r] Cal. Rot. Pat., 83.

and on the 10th of June and the 25th of August he was ordered to array his servants and send them against the Scots.[s] On the 20th of October he was summoned to the parliament at York, and, on the 16th of December and the 13th of January following, he was again desired to prepare his tenants for service across the Tweed.[t]

The year 1319 found Edward II. keeping his Christmas at Beverley, as he was eager to punish the Scots for their recent foray into England. The attempt of Edward Brus upon Ireland had ended in a signal failure, and his brother Robert had been formally excommunicated by the pope. On the 6th of May the archbishop was summoned to a parliament to be held at York.[u] The king was gathering together for his expedition all the forces that he could collect, when he was distressed to hear that the governor of Berwick had treacherously surrendered that town to the enemy, and he hastened northwards to recover it. On the 21st of July archbishop Melton wrote to the bishop of Durham, the dean and chapter, and the official, of York, soliciting the prayers of the faithful on behalf of the expedition, and granting an indulgence of forty days to those who offered them. On the 4th of September the primate wrote to the abbat of St. Mary's and other dignitaries requesting them to meet him on the ensuing Friday at the church of the Holy Trinity in Micklegate, York, and to join in a solemn procession, with its customary litany of supplications, for the success of the royal forces.[v] On the same day a very different order was issued by the king, and it came to York—the herald of alarming news. It told the archbishop that whilst the English monarch and his chivalry were at Berwick, Randolf, earl of Moray, and the famous Douglas were making a raid into the kingdom in another direction, and Melton and the chancellor, John de Hotham, bishop of Ely, were ordered to array and lead against them the *posse comitatus*.[w] The crozier seems to have been thrown aside for a more potent weapon, and the warrior-bishops seem to have taken all the precautions that civilians could adopt.[x] The soldiers were absent

[s] Parl. Writs, vol. ii., part i., 502, 505, 511, 512.

[t] Ibid., 182, 511-12. Fœd., ii., 382. Rot. Scotiæ, i., 190. Wilkins, ii., 485.

[u] Parl. Writs, ii., part i., 197.

[v] Reg. Melton. On March 10, 1318, Melton enjoined the people of his diocese to pray for peace, there being at that time dissensions between the king and his barons (ibid.). On the 20th of July the king asked for their prayers (Fœd., ii., 402), and, on October 3rd, Melton granted an indulgence of forty days to those who complied (Reg. Melton). What a contrast to the spirit and the temper of the present age! In 1321 Melton granted another indulgence of forty days to all who prayed for the king, and another in July, 1319 (Hist. Dunelm. Scr. Tres, appendix, 123).

[w] Parl. Writs, ii., part i., 525. Rot. Scotiæ, i., 202.

[x] We think of the archbishops of Orange and Poggio in the Gierusalemme Liberata :—

in the North, but the exhortations of their diocesan would bring the clergy into active service with as many of their parishioners as they could persuade to accompany them. A motley crew of 10,000 men is said to have been collected, many of whom were better acquainted with the breviary than the sword, and all seem to have been completely ignorant of discipline and military array.[y] Parsons, vicars, friars of divers orders and hues, citizens of York who left unwillingly their merchandize, grooms and ribalds were sent into the field. The invaders had made a daring but unsuccessful attempt to seize the queen in the neighbourhood of York; they had actually destroyed the suburbs of that city, and were now lying about twelve miles off on the promontory between the Swale and the Ouse, near the little village of Myton where the two streams unite. On the 12th of October the English 10,000 came up to them in disorderly array and shewing a front that any enemy would rejoice to encounter. The Scottish forces must have watched them with eager satisfaction till they crossed the river by which their retreat was intercepted. Several haystacks were now fired, and the smoke drifting into the eyes of the Englishmen blinded and bewildered them. In the middle of the confusion and right through the smoke, the Scots came down upon them, and they turned and fled to the right hand and the left. They were thrust into the river to be drowned, or perished by the sword upon its banks. Great numbers were killed, whilst others were carried away into captivity, amongst whom was William de Armin who was subsequently bishop of Norwich. Nicholas de Fleming, the mayor of York, was one of those who fell, and the fugitives seem to have been rescued from complete destruction only by the night. The marauders now made their way homewards and escaped from the English army, carrying with them an immense booty. The Scots, in memory of the profession of a great number of their opponents, gave to that contest, if such it may be called, the title of the white battle; and the English soldiers, in bitter ridicule of the prowess of the clerical warriors, called that meeting and its debate "the chapter of Myton."[z]

"Poi duo pastor de' popoli spiegaro
Le squadre lor, Guglielmo ed Ademaro.
L'uno, e l'altro di lor, che ne' divini
Uffici gia trattò pio ministero,
Sotto l'elmo premendo i lunghi crini,
Essercita de l'arme hor l'uso fero."

[y] There is an account of the battle in Chron. Lanercost, 239. Lel. Coll., ii., 462-474. Buchanan, Rerum Scot. Hist., 8vo, Francofurti, 263. Murimuth, 30. Walsingham, 112. Trokelowe, 45.

[z] Rot. Scot., i., 204. In Barbour's The Brus, ed. 1856, p. 404-5, the following lines occur:—

"The archbishop of York tha mad
Thar capitane, and till consale
Has tane that tha in plane battale
Wald assale the Scottismen,
That fer fewar then tha war then.
Than he displait his baner,
And other bischopis that thar wer.
* * *
Of tha yhet thre hundreth war
Prestis that deit intill that chas;
Tharfore that bargane callit was
The chaptour of Mytoun, for thar
Slane sa mony prestis war."

If archbishop Melton was present at this disastrous adventure, it was the first and the last time that he tried his fortunes in the field. How the English soldiers would laugh at his puny and unsuccessful efforts when the army came back from Berwick! Edward returned to York with all speed as soon as he heard the news. On the 15th of September Melton and several other commissioners were sent to Carlisle to propose an armistice, to which the Scots, who had secured everything that they desired, very readily assented.[a] In the following month the courts of justice were removed from London to York, and remained in that city for half a year. The hopes of England seemed now to centre in the metropolis of the North. The king was there, full of indignation at the recent mishap and yet fearful for the future. He was dealing with a subtle and potent enemy, and time was necessary to bring together another army. On the 15th of January, 1322, Melton was ordered to explain Edward's intentions by causing his declaration to be read in the churches,[b] and on the 19th he was authorized to treat with Robert de Brus.[c] On the 7th of February, and on two other occasions in the same year, he was directed to supply men or money for the Scottish war and to provide his customary service.[d] His diplomacy, therefore, had been unsuccessful. In the autumn of 1322 there was another inroad of the Scots into Yorkshire. They swept over much of the same ground which they had devastated in 1319. The king sent John de Britannia, earl of Richmond, with a body of soldiers to watch their movements, but he incautiously allowed himself to be surprised among the hills between Byland and Rievaux. The invaders, who were at home among the rocks, made prisoners of the English commander and a number of his men. Edward, never dreaming that danger was so near, was all the while in the monastery of Rievaux. He fled in haste, two of the monks serving as his guides, leaving all his plate and treasure behind him, of which the enemy possessed themselves. After scouring the country towards the east and south as far as the Wolds, and receiving a large sum of money from the inhabitants of Beverley for sparing

In Hardyng's Chronicle, *n. e.*, 309, there is the following description of the battle:—

"To Boroughbrydge by East and West he brent,
And home agayne with many a prysoner,
Without harme or lette of his entent,
With mykell good, but in Myton medowe, nere
To Swale water, laye then with great power
Walter Wareyn among the hay kockes bushed,
Upon (the byshop) sodenly with Scottes yssued.
And xv hundreth Englyshe there he slewe,
And home he went with kyng Edward full glad,
With prysoners many, mo then men knewe,
The byshop fled fro the felde full woo bestad,
With his clerkes that then were full mad."

[a] Fœd., ii., 434. Parl. Writs, ii., part i., 230.

[b] Parl. Writs, ii., part ii., 17.

[c] Fœd., ii., 441.

[d] Parl. Writs, ii., part i., 544, 558, 568, 620. Wilkins, ii., 514.

their town, they returned leisurely into Scotland.[e] They carried off with them the earl of Richmond, and several years passed away before he could be ransomed. He had already become acquainted with the troubles of captivity, as he had been taken prisoner in his youth in the wars in France.

A very distinguished man comes prominently forward about this time in the history of the North of England, and plays a conspicuous part in the annals of the nation. It was long before Yorkshire forgot one of the greatest of her favourites, Thomas, earl of Lancaster. Royal blood was flowing in his veins, for he was a grandson of Henry III., and he had a spirit far more fitted to control an empire than that which animated his feeble-minded cousin who now sat upon the throne. An alliance with the heiress of the Lacies gave him unbounded influence and a princely fortune. He was far too powerful to look with indifference upon the busy world of politics around him, and too honest to countenance the follies of the monarch and his courtiers. When the hireling Gaveston was in the flush of his ambitious career, Lancaster was one of the nobles who drove him into exile and set themselves to work to correct the abuses in the administration of the kingdom; and when that haughty minion subsequently returned, the stout earl was one of those who took him prisoner and sentenced him to death. After this event there was a turn in the tide of the fortunes of Lancaster. The king regarded him with the most bitter hatred; but domestic affliction was the thorn which rankled in his side. His wife dishonoured her ancient name by her disloyalty to her husband, and the monarch rejoicing at his trouble, contemptuously rejected his demand for redress. The indignant noble, when he looked around him, found that other peers were as discontented as himself. He rushed into rebellion, for he was a man with a vast number of friends and retainers and a fearless spirit. He raised a large army to vindicate his rights, but a little subtle diplomacy on the part of Edward caused it to be disbanded. In 1321 the ridiculous partiality of the king for the Despensers again aroused the anger of the nobles, and there was a meeting at Sherburn in Elmet where a confederacy was organized which resulted in the banishment of the favourites. Untoward circumstances, however, produced the dismemberment of the league,

[e] Walsingham, apud Camden, 113. Chron. Petrib., 163. Chron. Lanercost, 247. In Leland (Coll., i., 250) it is said that the burgesses of Beverley paid down the sum of 400*l.*, Buchanan, Rerum Scot. Hist., 8vo, Francofurti, 265. Fordun, Scotichronicon, ii., 279. Barbour's The Brus, ed. 1856, 434.

"Schir Johne of Bretane thar was tane
And richt fele of his folk war slane."

The Buik of the Croniclis of Scotland, iii., 256. Murimuth, 38. Walsingham, 113. Galfr. le Baker, 66. Otterbourne, i., 62, 110, "apud Bydland bankes." Trokelowe, 64.

and in the following year Edward had the opportunity presented to him, which he had so long coveted, of effecting the ruin of Lancaster. The earl and his followers came into collision with the royal forces at Boroughbridge and were compelled to submit to them. The captors led him in triumph to Pontefract with every mark of ignominy, and there, on the 22nd of March, he was put to death in the sight of his own castle.[f] The circumstances attending the execution were calculated to impress the scene upon the beholders, and encircled the memory of the dead with fond and affectionate regrets. The victim had always been a favourite, and when he died, as the people thought, in his country's cause, their sympathy was exhibited in a remarkable way. The same sufferings which led the people of the North to desire the canonization of archbishop Scrope, and Henry VI., induced them to regard Thomas of Lancaster as a saint. His mutilated body was interred in the parish church of Pontefract, and, on the 7th of October, 1322, archbishop Melton issued a mandate forbidding any one to approach his tomb for the purposes of devotion. He found it necessary to repeat his injunction on the 24th of August in the following year. On the 24th of February, 1327, when the tide was turned in favour of the friends of Lancaster, he adopted a very different tone. The concourse of worshippers to Pontefract had not slackened, and the country was ringing with the report of miracles which had attested the sanctity of the deceased earl, when Melton wrote a letter to the pope to mention what had occurred, and to request the appointment of a commission to enquire into the circumstances of the case.[g] Nothing in all probability was done, but the fame of the great nobleman was not soon extinct. On the 30th of October, 1343, archbishop Zouche, at the earnest entreaty of Henry, earl of Derby, set at nought the prohibition of Melton, and permitted service to be done by a monk in a chapel on the hill at Pontefract,[h] and on the 21st of May, 1354, archbishop Thoresby made a similar concession.[i] The chapel

[f] Lel. Coll., ii., 464-5. Chron. Lanercost, 244, etc. Trokelowe, 10, 53-63. Mon. Malmesb., Vita Edward II., 124, 178, 220. Knyghton, col. 2539-41. Froissart, ed. Johnes, i., 4, etc. Scala Chron., 148-9. Fœd., ii., 478, etc. Walsingham, 116. Galfr. le Baker, 65. Hardyng (n. e., 310) says,—

"There he was headed anone upon the hyll,
And buryed was there in a chapell fayre."

[g] Reg. Melton. Leland says that lord chancellor Baldock "caussid xiiij Gascoynes well armid to watch the hille a certen tyme" on account of reported miracles (Coll., ii., 466). The beads of the earl were treasured in the monastery of Durham (Raine's St. Cuthbert, 122).

[h] Reg. Zouche. On Dec. 15, 1327, a royal order was issued prohibiting any unauthorized person collecting money for the chapel on the hill where the earl was beheaded (Fœd., ii., 726. Cf. ibid., 707). On 7th March, 1330, and April 3, 1331, the king wrote to the pope requesting that he might be canonized (ibid., 782, 814). Cal. Rot. Pat., 100.

[i] Reg. Thoresby. On 24th of May,

was on the place of the earl's execution, and was perched on an eminence adjacent to the town.

I have just alluded to archbishop Melton's attempt to check the expression of the feelings of the people of the North towards their favourite. He had previously done what he could to assist him, having induced his clergy to make a grant of 2000 marks to Lancaster. On the 9th of April, 1322, the king censured him for his conduct and desired him to express his contrition by making a similar gift to himself.[j] Later in the same year Melton was ordered to array his tenants beyond the Trent, and was summoned to the parliament at York, which was to have met in the first instance at Ripon.[k] It was on this occasion that all the enactments against the Despensers were annulled. The monarch and his court spent their Christmas at York, and preparations were being made for the renewal of the campaign against the Scots. On the 5th of April, 1323, the archbishop desired the people of his diocese to put up their prayers in behalf of the proposed expedition.[l] There seems, however, to have been little cordiality between Melton and the king. Edward would not forget how the primate had aided Lancaster, and he would see that he looked with disgust upon his follies and misgovernment. The feeling of the monarch towards Melton was shewn in the tone in which he addressed him. On the 21st of May the archbishop was peremptorily summoned to attend a council at York early on the morning of the 23rd, and on the 30th he was at a similar meeting at Bishopthorpe, when the subject of a truce with Scotland was mooted and considered.[m] It was on this occasion that Henry de Beaumont was guilty of rudeness to the king, for which he was sent to prison.[n] On the 18th of June, 1323, Melton was made a justiciar for the county of Notts, to try the commissioners of array who had been guilty of malversation and oppression.[o] On the 2nd of February, 1324, he had letters of protection to carry him to the parliament at London.[p] On the 6th of August he was requested to give his aid in arraying soldiers within the county of York, and on the

1361, the archbishop confirms the ordination of a chantry made by Simon Symeon on the hill near Pontefract, in the chapel where Thomas, earl of Lancaster, was beheaded (169). 20th Nov., 1361, ordinatio novæ vicariæ de Pontefract et cantariæ pro anima Thomæ quondam comitis Lanc. (ibid., 109). Cf. Test. Ebor., i., 281.

[j] Parl. Writs, ii., part i., 566. On the 28th of February Melton had been ordered to raise soldiers to oppose the earl (ibid., i., 550).

[k] Fœd., ii., 496. Parl. Writs, ii., part i., 567. Between 1317 and 1325 Melton was frequently summoned to parliament (ibid., ii., part i., 173, 175, 178, 182, 197, 215, 219, 234, 245, 261, 290, 317-18, 329, 334, 350).

[l] Reg. Melton.

[m] Parl. Writs, ii., part i., 286. Murimuth, 37.

[n] Fœd., ii., 520. Abbrev. Plac., 342.

[o] Parl. Writs, ii., part i., 634.

[p] Ibid., part ii., 268.

8th of November he was desired, with others, to treat with the representatives of Robert le Brus.[q] On the 21st of December he was summoned to send his service into Gascony, and on the 30th he was called to the council at Winchester.[r] Melton seems now to have recovered altogether the good opinion of the king, for on the 3rd of June, 1325, he received the honourable appointment of lord treasurer of England.[s] There are some letters in his register relating to the fortifying and the victualling of the castles of Dover and Rockingham,[t] which shew that his office was no sinecure, but it does not appear that he held it long.

A deep mystery is hanging over the history of the period, and we know but little of the latter days of Edward II. and of the intrigues which placed his youthful son upon the throne. Upon the imprisonment of his old master, Melton seems to have looked with great displeasure. The archbishop owed everything to Edward's kindness, and he did not forget him in his adversity. He refused to be present at the coronation of the new sovereign,[u] and although he did not desert the court, he would regard its proceedings with vexation and distrust. On the 12th of May, 1326, he was ordered to prepare himself and his retainers to defend his king and country,[v] and in the following year on the 15th of April, he had letters of safe-conduct to enable him to join the court at Stamford.[w] At Christmas he was at Wallingford with the young monarch and his mother,[x] and he was one of Edward's guardians.[y] Soon after this the archbishop was implicated, to all appearances, in a very dangerous intrigue, an attempt to upset the government of the new king. Edmund, earl of Kent, was the leader, and he is said to have been abetted by several prelates, of whom Melton was one. The archbishop, according to the confession of one of the delinquents, entered with heart and soul into the enterprize, and promised to supply the earl with men and money. He was arrested, and obliged to answer for his share in the conspiracy. The verdict was one of acquittal, and Melton brought an action against his accusers, assessing the damages for the wrong which had been done to

[q] Fœd., ii., 565, 578.

[r] Parl. Writs, ii., part i, 326, 684. He was also ordered to send his service into Gascony on May 17 and August 2, 1325 (ibid., 697, 714).

[s] Ibid., pt. ii., 272. Dugdale (Chron. 38) says that he was elected on July 30. Cal. Rot. Pat., 96-9. He had a lieutenant in that office (Madox, Hist. Exch., ii., 41). "Eboracensis ille, Willelmus nomine, olim curialis, in omni commisso fidelis extitit, et quamvis inter curiales diu conversatus, mores tamen a convictu non traxit, set, obviatus Anglorum cupiditati, per Dei graciam impolutus semper permansit" (Mon. Malmesb., Vita Edward II., 237).

[t] Reg. Melton.

[u] Anglia Sacra, i., 367.

[v] Parl. Writs, ii., part i., 749.

[w] Fœd., ii., 703.

[x] Walsingham, 126.

[y] Barnes's Edward III., 4.

him at 1000*l*.[e] This is scarcely reconcileable with the statement of the author of the Peterbro' chronicle, that the archbishop fearlessly acknowledged his participation in the scheme, and said boldly that for the good of the state he would emperil his own life and everything that he possessed.[a]

In the spring of 1327 the young monarch and his court were at York making ready for an expedition into Scotland. He and the queen-mother were residing in the monastery of the Greyfriars, and around them were all the luxury and pomp which that rich century could produce.[b] The city was filled with soldiers and their captains, eager to avenge the reverses of past years, and among them were the men at arms from Hainault under the guidance of their gallant count. Every village, also, in the neighbourhood was thronged with fighting men, many of whom, as if in mockery of their profession, "were cloathed all in cotes and hoods embrodered with floures and branches verie seemelie, and used to nourish their beards," a practice which tempted a Scottish wag to fasten the following "rime" to one of the church doors in the city,

> "Longbeards hartlesse, painted hoods witlesse,
> Gaie cotes gracelesse, make England thriftlesse."

I shall not detail the quarrels of that army in the camp, or its adventures in the field among the forests and moors in the wilds of Durham. The march was full of picturesque incidents, sudden alarms,

> "When those behind cried forward,
> And those before cried back;"

the startled deer leaping in and out among the spears and ensigns, and the bold and gallant Douglas charging among the English tents in the silence of the night.[c] Whilst these things were going on in the North, the queen-mother and her younger children were the guests of archbishop Melton in his palace at York, and the city was strictly guarded, the primate aiding the mayor and citizens in rearing and manning the fortifications.[d] On the 23rd of November, after the return of the army,

[e] Walsingham, 129. Chron. Lanercost, 265. Knyghton, col. 2555. Froissart, i., 83. Rot. Parl., ii., 31-2, 54. Murimuth gives the evidence against Melton from the lips of the informer. "Ly dit, qe le ercevesque de Everwik ly manda per un chapelyn, Sir Aleyn, une lettre de credence, et fut la credence tiele: q'il ly aidroyt a la deliverance soun frere de v mille li et outre quant q'il aveit, e quant q'il pareit rendre."

[a] Chron. Petrib., 165.

[b] Lel. Coll., ii., 307-475. Froissart, i., 39-45.

[c] Froissart, i., 62, etc. Chron. Lanercost, 260. Knyghton, col. 2552. Scala Chron., 154. Lel. Coll., ii., 475. Barbour's The Brus, ed. 1856, 456-7. Murimuth, 54. Hardyng's Chronicle, *n. e.*, 316.

[d] Fœd., ii., 709-11. There was some controversy between the archbishop and the corporation about the walls (Reg. Melton). Stubbs, col. 1731.

Melton was empowered by the king to treat for a peace with Scotland, and he and the bishop of Lincoln were authorized to grant letters of safe conduct to the ambassadors from that country.[e] On the 10th of December the archbishop was summoned to a parliament which was to meet in York.[f] Soon after this that fair city witnessed a more brilliant spectacle than the sight of an army eager for the field or the assembling of the council of the nation. This was the marriage of the youthful monarch to Phillippa of Hainault which was solemnized in the minster at the end of January 1328. Archbishop Melton and John de Hotham, bishop of Ely, officiated at the ceremony, and the whole country was wild with joy and excitement.[g] Of this alliance an illustrious offspring was the fruit. There flowed from it the noble chivalry of the Black prince, the generous greatness of the progenitor of the royal house of York, and the sage and cautious wisdom of "time-honoured Lancaster."

In 1330 the conspiracy of the earl of Kent occurred which has been already alluded to. Melton's assumed participation in that rash attempt must have exposed him to no little danger and must have lost him the favour of the king. Edward, however, was too generous to be malicious or revengeful, and he was too well aware of the merits and services of Melton to allow him to continue in disgrace. On the 16th of February, 1331, the archbishop was made a conservator of the peace between England and Scotland,[h] and on the 28th of November he was again advanced to the post of lord-treasurer of England which he held till the month of April in the following year.[i] On the 26th of June, 1332, the king asked him for an aid towards the marriage of his sister to the duke of Guelders, and, in the autumn, Melton seems to have been present at the parliament at Westminster.[j] On the 1st of December he, Robert de Stratford and Geoffrey le Scrope, or any two of them, were empowered to open the council of the nation at its meeting in York.[k] The parliament seems to have been summoned again to York in the spring of 1334,[l] and on the 12th of June in that year Melton was desired to ask the clergy of his diocese to give their assistance against the Scots who had recently been signally worsted at Halidon Hill. After this Melton appears to have taken but

[e] Fœd., ii., 723-4. Rot. Scotiæ, i., 223.

[f] Knyghton, col. 2552. Fœd., ii., 725. On two occasions, on 18th Aug. and 23rd Sept., orders were given for the removal of the treasury to York (Fœd., ii., 713).

[g] Different dates are assigned to this ceremony. Knyghton, col. 2552. Chron. Lanercost, 260. Lel. Coll., ii., 476.

[h] Fœd., ii., 809.

[i] Dugdale, Chron. Jurid., 40. Cal. Rot. Pat., 109.

[j] Knyghton, 2560. Fœd., ii., 840, 844.

[k] Fœd., ii., 848. Knyghton, col. 2562. Chron. Lanercost, 270. Jan. 4, 1333, breve regium pro parl. apud Ebor. (Wilkins, ii., 570). Rot. Parl., ii., 67. Walsingham, 133.

[l] Barnes's Edward III., 83.

little interest in public affairs. We find him now and then engaged in the collection of subsidies and aids for the king,[m] and in 1339 he was on several occasions made a commissoner of array to gather men together for the wars in Scotland.[n]

The great variety of Melton's avocations in connection with the state did not cause any delay or neglect in the administration of his diocese. He seems to have been a man who did with all his might whatever he took in hand, and this, no doubt, was the main cause of his success in life. His archiepiscopal register, which extends to more than 1200 pages, shews that he was an energetic prelate, prompt in action, zealous in the suppression of vice and irregularity, and a good shepherd of his flock. He lived in an eventful period and witnessed changes around him such as no archbishop of York perhaps has ever beheld. Two monarchs died whilst he was connected with the court, the one surrounded by the warriors who were to fight their country's battles, the other terminating an unhappy existence by a still more unhappy end. Melton saw the rise and the fall of Lancaster; that drama so rich in incident and misfortune was acted before his very eyes. He would hear with joy or grief of the exploits on the Borders, of the fatal rout at Bannockburn and of the triumph at Halidon Hill, of the chivalrous daring of Brus and Douglas, Fitzalan, Bohun, Percy and D'Argentine. The story of their gallant deeds would be frequently recounted in the halls of Bishopthorpe and York, and many a mass would be said and many a prayer would be offered up for the champions and the cause of England. The archbishop, however, had anxieties of his own in Yorkshire. He would grieve bitterly over those oft-recurring incursions of the Scots which turned his diocese into a wilderness. He was obliged to welcome within the walls of York the troops who were continually streaming towards the North bent on conquest or revenge, and the city presented, far too frequently, all the pomp and bustle of a camp. Their presence portended, as he was well aware, a long succession of subsidies from his afflicted

[m] Fœd., ii., 888. On Oct. 23, 1334, and on July 5, 1335, Melton was desired to have prayers offered up for the king (Reg. Melton, and Fœd., ii., 896). On 26th March, 1336, he was requested to procure a subsidy from his clergy in the convocation at York against the Scots (Fœd., ii., 935). On Aug. 21 and 28, 1337, he and others were made commissioners to raise money in Yorkshire for the French war (ibid., 991, 994). On Nov. 1 the king asked him and his clergy for a loan for that purpose (ibid., 1005). On Feb. 8, 1338-9, a mandate to him to call upon the clergy for a subsidy (1069), and again, 10th Oct. seq. (1092).

[n] On Feb. 16, May 4, and Oct. 10 (Fœd., ii., 1070. Rot. Scotiæ, i., 564, 573). In 1338 Melton gave the king five hundred quarters of wheat towards provisioning the Scottish army (Rot. Scotiæ, i., 554). Wilkins enumerates the meetings of the clergy at York during Melton's archiepiscopate, ii., 519-20, 546, 583, 623, 629, 673, 711, 727, 735.

clergy. The court also was very often in York, for it followed after the army, and Melton had kings and queens under his roof. He had been an attendant upon royalty from his youth, and had long since discovered with Sejanus that

"The way to rise is to obey and please,"

but still when he became a courtier he did not forget to be a patriot. The wish to advance the interests of his country led him to support the cause of Lancaster, and, perhaps, all but wrecked his prospects and position in the conspiracy of Edmund earl of Kent.

Archbishop Melton had a good deal of trouble with his brethren of Canterbury about the bearing of the cross. I do not find that there was ever any actual outbreak, but care was always necessary to prevent it. It is needless to enumerate the many occasions on which precautionary measures were adopted; suffice it to say that neither primate ever left his province unaccompanied by some order from the king to direct that no violence should be used towards him during his progress.[o] But this was not the only contention which Melton was involved in on behalf of the privileges of his see. In 1327 he had a quarrel with the dean and chapter of York about the visitation of the church, which was of so violent a character that the king wrote to the pope to beg him to interfere. In the following year the dispute was amicably settled through the intervention of John XXII., and the visitor was not impeded in the performance of his duties.[p] In 1328 and 1329 Melton had a fierce controversy with Louis de Beaumont, bishop of Durham, about his rights in the peculiar jurisdiction of Allertonshire. The men of the Bishopric and the borderers from Northumberland and Tynedale were arrayed on the side of their diocesan, and were ready, if necessary, to take the life of the intruding primate, who laid them under a sentence of excommunication,

[o] Fœd., ii., 499, 544, 574, 604, 716, 739, 766, 844, 888, 904. Parl. Writs, ii., part i., 263, 291, 318-19, 352. Ibid., part ii., 274-5. Cal. Rot. Pat., 115. Aug. 7, 1318, a letter to the archdeacon of Notts to desire the archbishop of Canterbury "ne crucem deferat in prov. Ebor." June 3, "1334, litera officiali Ebor. ad tractandum cum arch. Cant. pro bajulatione crucis." July 4, 1335, "relaxatio sequestrationis interpositæ in ecclesiis Ebor. pro bajulacione crucis Cantuar" (Reg. Melton). Wilkins, ii., 525, 526. There is a curious story about Melton and archbishop Reginald in the Anglia Sacra, i., 365. Mon. Malmesb., Vita Edward II., 237. Carte's Gascon, etc., Rolls, ii., 8.

[p] Stubbs, col. 1731. Fœd., ii., 725. Wilkins, ii., 547. In 1327, "visitatio thesaurariæ Ebor." The chapter resist. Nov. 25, a letter to the king "ad amovendum vim laicalem ab eccl. Ebor." 1332, "compositio inter Dec., et Cap. super formam visitationis" (Reg. Melton). 1333, Feb. 3, letter to the pope from the king asking him to take away his sentence of suspension from the church of York, on account of the quarrel between "P. S. Stephani in Cælio Monte Card.," and Mr. William de la Mare (Fœd., ii., 849).

for which they cared not. The church of Leek seems to have been the centre of the attack, and it was regularly garrisoned; but at length the king stepped in to prevent the shedding of blood, and the controversy was stayed.[q] On the death of Beaumont, Melton was for some time in disgrace with the sovereign, for advocating the claims of Robert de Graystanes, the historian, to be his successor, and for consecrating him at York.[r] The appointment, however, was subsequently set aside, and none can regret it who know that the great scholar Richard de Bury was the prelate who was selected. Archbishop Melton had also a long controversy about the dues in the port of Hull.[s]

The following brief notes of some of the more remarkable documents in archbishop Melton's register will give some idea, at all events, of the variety of his official duties. I have taken no pains to extract the ordinations of livings, the foundations of chantries, etc., which that noble volume contains. There is no lack of materials for history and biography; their very multiplicity obliges me unwillingly to pause.[t]

1318, Jan. 21. Licence to John de Hotham, bishop of Ely, to have service performed in a fair chapel recently built at Threhouses, his birth-place.[u] May 1. We have received from the executors of our predecessor, 100*l.*, in part payment of the sum

[q] Hist. Dunelm. Scr. Tres, 104-6. On Oct. 29, 1329, the king interfered (Fœd., ii., 774-5). Melton had excommunicated the bishop (Reg. Melton, 491). Cal. Rot. Pat., 106.

[r] Hist. Dunelm. Scr. Tres, 120. Chron. Lanercost, 276. Anonym. Hist. Edward II., apud Hemingford, ed. Hearne, ii., 404. Fœd., ii., 882. Cf. Murimuth, 74, where it is said that peace was made between the king and Melton at the intervention of Bury and the nobles.

[s] Fœd., ii., 697, 710, 850. Rot. Parl., i., 431-2; ii., 39, etc. Reg. Melton, 420, etc. Frost's Port of Hull, 120. Tickell's Hull, 73, etc. Cal. Rot. Pat., 108.

[t] I well remember placing this noble volume some years ago in the hands of my kind friend the late historian of South Yorkshire. His words and looks of astonishment are not forgotten. "I have ventured," he said, "to write a work on Yorkshire topography without consulting this book, which I never saw before. It would take me six months to examine it properly."

[u] A very great man. He was a Yorkshireman by birth. The names of his parents were Alan and Maude, and his uncle was archbishop of Dublin. He was canon of Dublin, rector of Rowley and Cottingham in Yorkshire, and prebendary of Stillington. In 1316 he became bishop of Ely, and he held that post for twenty years. His offices in the state were numerous and his services considerable. He was successively chancellor of the Irish and the English exchequer, lord treasurer and lord chancellor of England. It is impossible to enumerate his acts in this place. Cf. Fœd. *var. loc.* Cal. Rot. Pat., 69, 74, etc. Rot. Scot., i., 113, etc. Anglia Sacra, i., 647. Fasti Eccl. Hib., ii., 193. Thoroton's Notts, 449, 452. Bentham's Ely, 156-7. Newcome's St. Alban's, 412. Reg. Kellawe at Durham, 115. Reg. Langton at Lichfield. Foss's Judges, iii., 265, 444. Carte's Gascon, etc., Rolls, i., 70.

On Dec. 7, 1318, archbishop Melton authorized him to dedicate the church of North Cave "de novo constructa." It had probably been built by Hotham himself. On 24th September, 1314, bishop Kellawe, of Durham, whilst at Naburn, granted an indulgence of forty days in behalf of the chapel B.M.V.

of 200 marks due to us for oxen and horses appertaining to the stock of the archbishopric, which is deficient.[v] July 26. Letters testimonial in behalf of Aveline, daughter of Peter de la Twyere, who has been unjustly defamed.[w] August 24. A pension of 40s. per annum to Wm. le Cossale.[x] August 31. A commission to dedicate the church of the Augustinians at Hull. Oct. 11. Licence to the abbat and convent of Selby to have the chapel of Armyn consecrated. Nov. 3. Permission to Sir John de Segrave, knight,[y] and Christiana his wife to have as their confessor William de Drayton, a Friar Preacher. Nov. 8. An indulgence for the cathedral of Carlisle which has been burned by the Scots. Dec. 7. To John de Fontibus, the queen's clerk, four marks for his annual pension.[z] Dec. 16. Leave to J., bishop of Glasgow, and J., bishop of Ely, to hold an ordination within the diocese of York.

1319, Feb. 12. Bond from Walter de Fauconberge, son and heir of Sir John de Fauconberge, knight, deceased, to keep the archbishop and the executors of his predecessor harmless. Dame Ela de Fauconberge, his mother, is dead, and he promises to divide her substance with John and William Fauconberge, his brothers, and Arnebrough and Joan his sisters, of whom the archbishop is the guardian.[a] March 18. An indulgence of 30 days to all who hear the mass of Robert de Bardelby,[b] canon of

in the church of South Cave, for the good estate of Alexander de Cave and Joan his wife, and for the souls of Peter and Elen de Cave, his parents, who are buried in the church of All Saints at South Cave (Reg. Kellawe, 133).

[v] Soon afterwards the archbishop buys a number of sheep. 190 wethers and 33 ewes are bought at Wilton, 8 wethers and 19 ewes at Patrington, the price of each being 2s. 1d.,—28*l.* 2s. 6d. 41 lambs at Patrington and 172 lambs at Wilton, the price of each 20d.; sum 19*l.* 8s. 4d. On the death of Greenfield, Melton, then keeper of the king's wardrobe, Walter de Norwich, the treasurer, and John de Insula, bought the corn and wine belonging to the deceased primate (Abbrev. Rot. Orig., i., 223).

[w] A Holderness lady. On 28th Nov., 1318, the king writes to the archbishop and complains that some malicious citations and charges for adultery, etc., have been made in his diocese. He requests they may be stopped (Fœd., ii., 379). Cf. the Frere's Tale in Chaucer.

[x] A native of Cossale, Notts, and a baron of the Exchequer. Cf. Thoroton's Notts, 228. Foss's Judges, iii., 418.

[y] A great warrior. Custos Scotiæ (Trivet, 340. Knyghton, col. 2530), where he shewed great valour (Walsingham, 87). He was taken prisoner at Bannockburn.

[z] Elsewhere called John de Fonteneio. John de Fontenay, the king's clerk, had a controversy about the living of Ufford, in the diocese of Lincoln (Fœd., ii., 449). A John de Fontibus, the physician of queen Margaret, was advanced to a stall at Rouen in 34th of Edward I. (Prynne, iii., 1159).

[a] Cf. Thoroton's Notts, 448-9. Coll. Top. and Genealog., iv., 262.

[b] Prebendary at Dunnington at York, which he exchanged in 1323 with Gilbert de la Bruere for a stall at Chichester; canon of St. Sepulchre's chapel, and incumbent of Moor Monkton (Reg. Melton. Cal. Rot. Pat., 86). He was a clerk in the Chancery, and was much employed in parliamentary work (Parl. Writs, Fœd., Madox, Cal. Rot. Pat., etc.). In 1316 he founded a chantry at the altar of St. Michael in

York and the king's clerk, on Easter day, and pray for the good estate of the said Robert and his father and mother. April 26. Sir Wm. le Constable is allowed to have an oratory in his manors of Holm and Flayneburgh during the archbishop's pleasure. May 26. The archbishop grants time to dame Margaret, relict of Sir Geoffrey Maucovenant, to enable her to rebuild the chancel of the church of Esington, in "Wytbistrande."[c] July 26. An order to pray for fine weather, on account of the excessive rains. Oct. 1. Licence for Martin de Alnewick,[d] S.P.P., a Friar Minor, to hear the confessions of Sir Henry Fitzhugh and Sir Robert de Hastang, knights, Garnius de Weston, Nicholas de Ask, Lady de Charmues and Sara her *domicella* in the parts of Richmond and Hexham. Oct. 22. Elen, widow of Nicholas Flemyng, mayor of York, takes the vow of continence before the archbishop in his chapel at Bishopthorp.[e]

1320, Jan. 29. An order to the bailiff of Chirchdon to give three oaks for timber to Mr. William, the queen's chandler.[f] Feb. 1. Letters testimonial in behalf of John, bishop of Glasgow, who can receive nothing from his see on account of the war with Scotland. March 1. Licence for Roger de la More, rector of the moiety of the church of Ketilwell, to be absent from his living in the service of Sir Henry le Scrop, knight, justiciar of the king. May 16. A dispensation, "super defectu natalium," to William, son of Henry le Scrop, knight. May 19. An order to prevent tournaments and jousts near the city of York.[g] June 17. The abbat and convent of Rufford enter into an obligation to entertain for a day and a night each archbishop of York on his first coming into his diocese. July 24. John de Pickering, chaplain, is absolved from the sentence of greater excommunication for breaking into the close of the manor of Mr. Dennis Avenel, canon of Beverley.[h] August 18. An indulgence for the conventual church of Pontefract. Sept. 9. An annual pension of 40 florins to Oldred de Laude, and another of 20 florins to Mr. John de Rocca, advocates in the Roman court. Sept. 10. Licence of non-residence to John de Mauley, rector of

the church of St. Dunstan in the West (Newcourt, i., 336). Cf. Foss's Judges, iii., 50, 226.

[c] Sir Geoffrey is mentioned in the Rot. Scotiæ.

[d] Alnwick was divinity reader at Oxford among the Friars Minors (Mon. Franciso., 553), and an author (Bale, cent. v., 401).

[e] Fleming was mayor of York, and was killed at the battle of Myton. Aug. 22, 1320, an indulgence of forty days for the soul of Nicholas de Fleming, whose body is buried in the church of St. Wilfrid at York (Reg. Melton). This church, which is now destroyed, was in Lendal. A chantry was founded for Fleming in it (Drake 337).

[f] April 24, 1318, to William de la Mare two oaks for timber from our wood of Outwode, and, on May 1st, timber to mend the church of Cawood.

[g] The usual accompaniments of an army.

[h] Avenel was archdeacon of the East Riding, an office to which he was preferred in 1322.

Baynton, that he may make a pilgrimage abroad.[i] Sept. 26. The archbishop announces the canonization of Thomas, late bishop of Hereford.[j] The 10th of October is the day appointed for his commemoration.

1321, Jan. 2. An order that no toll or custom be taken from the citizens of York when they come to Beverley. Jan. 8. Bull of Pope John XXII. for the safe conduct of Robert de Brus and the Scottish bishops to the papal court.[k] Jan. 12. A letter of safe conduct to our valet, John de Mar, to go to Newcastle to provide hay, fuel, oats, etc., for us, and a missive to Richard de Emeldon, the mayor, in his behalf. Jan. 23. An indulgence for the fabric of the church of York.[l] March 24. Leave to the Carmelites of Scardeburgh to erect a chapel and set up a tower with a bell in it in their house.[m] May 28. An indulgence of 20 days in behalf of the church of St. Patrick at Lameley in the diocese of Durham, which has been destroyed by the Scots.[n] July 2. Licence to Margaret Malbys, a young girl, sister of Sir Wm. Malbys, knight, to stay in the nunnery of Swyne till she be ready for the veil. Sept. 3. An order to break the seal of Peter de Wyverthorp, prior of Bridlington, who has resigned his office.[o] Dec. 21. Absolution of John de Whiteby, clerk, for using necromancy.[p]

[i] He is mentioned as seised of the manors of Doncaster and Mulgrave in the Ninth Report of the Deputy Keeper of the Public Records, p. 76. What was the motive that led Mauley across the seas?

"—— μέγας δέ με θυμὸς ἐπείγει
Δῆμον ἐς ἀλλοδαπῶν ἰέναι."

[j] The archbishop grants an indulgence to those who visit his tomb. The bull of canonization is given in Melton's Register. The king was very anxious for the canonization (Fœd., ii., 355, 363, 385, 443). The bishop, of course, was Thomas de Cantilupe. Cf. Wilkins, ii., 651. The canonization was solemnized in 1348 in great state (Barnes's Edward III., 420-1).

[k] Brus was anxious that the sentence of excommunication that had been passed on him should be recalled. For this object he sent Randolph, earl of Murray, to Avignon in 1323. In Fœd., ii., 413, is a bull of John XXII. excommunicating Brus. In the Buik of the Cronicles of Scotland, iii., 258, are these lines:—

"Quhen all this thing es brocht to sic an end,
Ambassadouris this ilk king Robert send,
Greit men of gude wer greitlie till advance,
Ane to the paip and uther unto France."

[l] Another was granted on Jan. 6, 1324-5. On Feb. 12 there was a letter for the quæstores. Cf. Fabric Rolls of York, p. 159-60.

[m] Richard I. gave the church of Scarbro' to the abbey of Citeaux. The Cistercians at Scarbro' were very jealous of the Friars (Beck's Furness, 88), and there was some contention between them. The rector of Scarbro' seems hitherto to have been desirous that the Carmelites should worship

"Withouten noise or clatering of belles."

[n] A little nunnery in the upper part of Tynedale. It was destroyed by the Scots in 1296 (Chron. Lanercost, 174), and the marauders seem to have penetrated again into that wild and romantic neighbourhood.

[o] The seal was broken, especially on the decease of a dignitary. There is much information on this point among the muniments at Durham.

[p] What hadst been at, sir clerk? at what forbidden arts

"The time when scritch-owls cry, and ban-dogs howl,
And spirits walk, and ghosts break up their graves?"

1322, Feb. 7. Licence to Joan de Lacy, countess of Lincoln, to have John, chaplain of Melcheburn, for her confessor. March 22. Thomas de Brounetofte, a monk of Blyth, is sent to the court of Rome to be absolved for consecrating Christ's body twice over.[q] March 25. A commission to absolve Humphrey de Bohun, earl of Hereford, from the sentence of excommunication.[r] July 5. Sir Wm. de Brus, knight, is absolved from the charge of drawing blood from Michael de Harcla. He denies it.[s] July 8. Licence to Thomas de Wake, lord of Lydel, to build a monastery of Augustinians in his vill of Cottingham, by the leave of the pope.[t] July 16. Administration of the effects of Sir Nicholas de Menill, knight, to Nicholas de Menill and John de Menill, brother of the deceased.[u] A general sentence against those who have concealed the deeds of Sir Henry le Vavasour.

1323, Feb. 4. Sir Geoffrey de Upsale,[v] knight, is ordered to maintain his wife. April 4. An order to receive the purgation of Sir Peter de Mauley, knight, who is charged with having committed adultery with Alice Deyvill. April 21. A commission to dedicate the altars in the monastery of Thurgarton, which has been constructed *de novo*.[w] June 23. A general sentence against those who have dragged Philip de Deen from

[q] A very heinous offence. The culprit said that he did it ignorantly. On June 8, 1323, the archbishop ordered Bruntoft to be expelled from Blyth for rebellion and insolence. There seems to have been a great lack of discipline in Blyth abbey.

[r] He was killed on the 16th of March, 1321, at Boroughbridge, whilst he was arrayed on the side of Thomas, earl of Lancaster. He died in a very peculiar way (Dugd. Bar., i., 184. Coll. Top. and Geneal., iv., 76). He was buried in the church of the Friars Preachers at York. Knyghton, col. 2540. Galf. le Baker, 65. De la Moor, 596.

[s] Sir William Brus founded a chantry in the church of Pickering for the souls of himself and Matilda his wife, Adam and Matilda, his parents, Mr. William and Mr. Robert de Pykering, his ancestors and heirs, his uncles and aunts, and William and Alexander de Bergh (Domesday Book, apud Ebor., 152). The Pickerings were cousins of the founder. "In Pykering chirch I saw two or three tumbes of the Bruses, wherof one with his wife lay in a chapel on the south syde of the quier, and he had a garland about his helmet. Ther was another of the Bruses biried in a chapel under an arch of the north side of the body of the quier, and there is a cantuarie bering his name" (Lel. Coll., i., 6. Lel. Itin., i., 65, ed. 1769).

[t] The public records are filled with notices of this great baron. See Dugd. Bar. The establishment at Cottingham was soon transferred to Hautenprize. The pedigree of the Wakes recently published by the Architectural societies is by no means a correct one. See Rot. Parl., ii., 194, etc.

[u] On August 23rd the vicar of Ormesby was made the coadjutor of Nicholas Menyl, who was a minor.

[v] A commissioner of array N.R.Y. in 1318 (Rot. Scotiæ, i., 185). He had a pardon given to him for his share in the death of Gavestou, being a retainer of the earl of Lancaster (Fœd., ii., 230).

[w] A monastery co. Notts, which was erected in the twelfth century by Ralph Deyncourt. Its foundation ought to have been mentioned among the good deeds of archbishop Thurstan (Thoroton's Notts, 302).

the church of the Augustinians at York, where he had taken sanctuary, and removed him to the marshal's prison.[x]

1324, Jan. 22. Dame Beatrix, widow of Sir Robert de Percy, lord of Sutton-on-Derwent, took the vow of chastity before the archbishop at Cawood. June 24. Commission to the archbishop of Armagh to confer the first tonsure, and to confirm children within the diocese of York.[y]

1325, Sept. 3. Absolution of Roger de Mora for saying mass in the presence of the Scots who are excommunicated.[z]

1326, March 3. Licence to Thomas Wake, lord of Lydell, to transfer his monastery from Cottingham to a place called Hautenprise.[a] March 17. An order to Robert, servant at the Grange at York, to give to John de Waltham, the king's messenger, a quarter of wheat, of our special favour. April 1. The king writes to the pope to say that thieves have broken by night into the archbishop's chapel, and have carried off his pall and other ornaments. He begs for another pall for him.[b] April 18. An order to our bailiff at Beverley to give to Thomas Whiteheade, our servant at Kynalton, two strong but not valuable colts, and nine three-year-old colts, to work at Kynalton in ploughing and waining, and the bailiff at Southwell is directed to give him timber to repair the chancel of our church at Kynalton. June 12. Certificate of the baptism and conversion of a Jew, viz., Walter de Notyngham, in the church of St. Mary, Nottingham, on Monday after the Octave S. Trin., 1325. Sir Walter de Goushill and Richard de Whatton, knights, and

[x] In 33rd of Edward I. William, son of Richard de Whitgift, fled for protection to the churchyard and altar of the church of Whitgift, and was dragged away. The king ordered him to be released (Prynne's Coll., iii., 1105).

[y] The following suffragans of archbishop Melton have occurred to me. April 28, 1318, commission to David "Recreensis episc.," to reconcile the churchyard of Masham. He had been acting for two years (Reg. Sacr. Angl., 143). On Nov. 19, 1326, Rowland, late archbishop of Armagh, was commissioned to celebrate orders. On 27th October, 1332, the bishop of Carlisle was made suffragan. In 1335 the bishops of Lincoln and Norwich assisted the archbishop. March 28, 1340, the bishop of Corbavia was licensed to act.

[z] Some tale hangs upon this entry, but what was it? More received a licence of non-residence in 1320 to join the suite of Sir Henry le Scrope. Every orthodox churchman would now regard Brus with the utmost detestation;—

"—— A wretch beneath the ban
Of pope and church for murder done
Even on the sacred altar-stone!
Well mayst thou wonder we should know
Such miscreant here, nor lay him low,
Or dream of greeting, peace or truce
With excommunicated Bruce."

[a] Removed thither from Cottingham. John XXII. sanctioned the change on Jan. 1, 1327. On Oct. 31, 1327, the archbishop granted a licence for the performance of service at Hautenprize. The founder nominated Thomas de Overton, a monk of Broune abbey, dioc. Lincoln, as the first prior (Reg. Melton). In the 15th of Edward II. Thomas Wake, the king's cousin, had leave to found a religious house at Newton (Cal. Rot. Pat., 90), and to crenellate his manor-house at Cottingham in 1st of Edward III. (ibid., 99).

[b] Fœd., ii., 624.

Orfrannia, wife of Robert Ingram of Nottingham, were his sponsors.[c]

1327, Jan. 28. Licence from the abbat of Westminster for the bishop elect of Whithern to be consecrated in a chapel in that abbey.[d] Feb. 24. Leave for dame Joan Luterel, lady of Gameleston, on account of old age, to eat whatever kind of pulse and stuffed meats she pleases. May 5. An agreement between the archbishop and Robert le Constable of Flaynburg. Constable is to perform the archbishop's service in Scotland, receiving for it 100*l.* May 26. An indulgence of 40 days to those who hear the preaching of the monks of Durham.[e]

1328, Jan. 4. Penance enjoined by the archbishop to Sir Peter de Mauley, knight, for adultery with Sara de London. On every Friday in Lent, the Ember days and Advent, for seven years, he is to fast on bread and small beer, and on Good Friday and the vigil of the festival of All Saints, to use only bread and water. He is to make a pilgrimage to the shrines of S. William of York, S. Thomas of Hereford, B.M. at Southwell, S. John of Beverley, and S. Wilfrid of Ripon, and is to be "fustigated" seven times before a procession in the church of York "in sola basna, capucio deposito."[f] July 29. An indulgence of 40 days for the fabric of the church of Ripon. Sept. 1. Licence for Sir Wm. de Malbys, knight, to remove the bones of his father and mother, Sir John and dame Agnes de Malbys from the church of Acaster Malbys to Rievaux abbey, where the remains of his ancestors are interred.[g] Oct. 11. An indulgence for the dedication of the altar in the house of the Friars Carmelites at York. The archbishop dedicated it on Tuesday, Oct. 5. Oct. 24. Licence for Wm. de Boyton, rector of Lockington, to take the body of Wm. Danyel from the churchyard into the church.

[c] On March 21, 1334, the archbishop certified that Walter Conversus, formerly called Hagyn in the Hebrew tongue, was baptized at Nottingham on June 30, 1325.

[d] Commission to John, bishop of Carlisle, to consecrate him, which he did "die Dominica in vigilia purif. B.M.V.," the new prelate making his profession of obedience to York. In 1323 the archbishop wrote letters against his being consecrated at Rome.

[e] There is a mandate from bishop Hatfield in the same behalf issued in 1346 (Hist. Dunelm. Scr. Tres, appendix, 135). In 1334 archbishop Melton granted an indulgence of forty days to those visiting St. Cuthbert's shrine (Raine's St. Cuthbert, 103).

[f] A salutary example. Mauley was an old offender, and the archbishop, probably, was glad to catch him. In the 9th of Edward II. the king ordered an enquiry to be made into an affair in which he, Mauley, and others were concerned. They had opened and carried off a car containing as many as seven nuns from Watton abbey! (Cal. Rot. Pat., 80).

[g] The little church of Acaster still remains, and would, probably, have sheltered at the present day the monuments of the Malbis. The abbey of Rievaux is in ruins, and there are no memorials of the dead to be espied within its walls.

1329, May 30. Licence for Sir Robert de Eccleshale, knight, to enter a religious order with the consent of dame Matilda de Codenoure, his wife.[h] August 10. The archbishop dedicated and consecrated the church of Wakefield, the great altar in honour of All Saints, and that of B.M.V. on the south side, the altar of St. Nicholas on the north, and that of St. Peter in the middle of the church.[i]

1330, March 8. Appropriation of the church of Stretford to Eggleston abbey, the annual revenues of which before the war used to be taxed at seven marks, but now, in consequence of the war, they cannot be taxed at all.[j] Sept. 24. Licence of non-residence to Mr. Robert Baldock, rector of Bradford.

1331, May 3. A loan of 100 marks to Wm. de Cusance.[k] August 21. A letter in behalf of John Akerman of Bruges, who has taken sanctuary at Norwich for killing Sir John Nele, knight, at Courtrey.[l]

1332, Sept. 19. Acquittance from Cardinal Neapolio[m] for his pension of 80 florins. Dec. An acquittance to the abbat and convent of Whitby for a pension of 100s. to Wm., son of Henry de Melton.[n]

1333, Feb. 12. A loan of 50 marks to dan Richard de Bury,[o]

[h] On Jan. 30, 1469, in the church of Manfield, Joan, wife of William Coke, of that village, gave formal permission to her husband to take orders (Orig. penes Tho. Witham, cler., de Lartington).

[i] A valuable architectural date.

[j] This house was at all times borne down with poverty. The remains of the abbey exhibit the plainest workmanship. Their chief charm is derived from the glorious combination of scenery, the hill and wood and water that are around them.

[k] Canon of Thorp at Ripon 1311-1338, when he exchanged it with Wm. de Dalton for a prebend at Auckland and another in the chapel of Bridgenorth. Prebendary of Lincoln and London, archdeacon of Cornwall, etc. (Le Neve, i., 398; ii., 161, 444). He was also keeper of the king's wardrobe 15th Edward III. (Pell Records, 149), and treasurer of the exchequer, and was much employed in state affairs.

[l] Some interesting adventure of which we know nothing. The lists of those who took sanctuary at Durham and Beverley have been published by the Surtees Society.

[m] Neapolio Ursinus, cardinal of S. Hadrian in Tribus Foris, a Roman by birth, was one of the leaders of the Sacred College, in which he had a seat for nearly sixty years. He died at Avignon in 1347 (Ciaconius, i., 904, etc.). He was canon of South Cave at York and Sutton at Lincoln. Cf. Fœd., ii., 577, etc. He had many benefices in England.

[n] The archbishop's nephew and brother, who will soon occur again.

[o] The illustrious bibliomaniac, and the gem and grace of the North of England in the fourteenth century. Statesman, bishop, scholar, "nihil tetigit quod non ornavit." How few in that age would throw aside the cares of office, for Bury had been chancellor and treasurer of England, and solace themselves in the untrodden paths of literature and taste. What a delight it must have been to the bishop to find himself at Auckland with such companions as Bradwardin, Fitz-Ralph, Burley, and Holcot, and refreshing himself among the many tomes which he had collected,

"Ducere sollicitæ jucunda oblivia vitæ."

"Prélat pieux et charitable, politique fin et habile, bibliophile savant et spirituel, il sut se faire aimer par ses contemporains, non pour ses dignités, ni pour sa fortune, mais pour les pre-

canon of York. Feb. 24. A loan of 200 marks to John, bishop of Winchester.[p] Oct. 19. A dispensation from John XXII. to Sir Geoffrey Luterell, knight, and Agnes, daughter of Sir Richard Sutton, knight, who have married, not knowing that they are related in the third and fourth degrees. Dec. 3. A licence to baptize, bury, etc., in the chapel and chapel-yard B.M. at Hull.

1334, Feb. 23. A licence of non-residence to Robert de Creyk, rector of Ackworth, as long as he officiates in the chapel of queen Philippa. April 9. A commission to the abbats of Fountains and Kirkstall to absolve the body of Sir Simon Ward, knight, late deceased, from certain sins which he had committed.[q] August 5. An order forbidding any one to listen to the teaching of friar Henry de Staunton, hermit. Oct. 7. A licence to beg for the fabric of Whitby abbey. Oct. 23. A similar licence in behalf of the house of St. Sepulchre, at Jerusalem.[r] Oct. 24. A loan of 1000 marks to the king.

1335, June 6. To Robert de Malton, domestic chaplain of

cieuses qualités qui le distinguaient à la fois, comme homme de Dieu, comme homme d'Etat et comme homme de science" (Philobiblion par Richard de Bury, ed. Paris, 1856. Notice Biographique, xvi).

[p] A very great man and a native of Yorkshire (Hunter's South Yorkshire, i., 54. Cal. Rot. Pat., 72). Archdeacon of Richmond, prebendary of Gevendale and Riccal, canon of Beverley and Southwell, incumbent of Stillingfleet and Lockington, in Yorkshire, and Radcliffe-on-Sore, co. Notts, canon of Lincoln and London, and treasurer of Lichfield (Le Neve, ii., 417; ii., 140; i., 581). Prebendary at Howden (Reg. ii., Pr. and Conv. Dunelm., 10). Rector of Simondburne, Northumberland, 6th Edward II. (Reg. Kellawe, 177 *b*). Rector of North Mimms, Herts, 1312 (MSS. Harl., 6951, 73. Clutterbuck's Herts, i., 460). Chancellor of the exchequer, treasurer and lord chancellor of England, chamberlain of Scotland, and much employed on state business (Fœd., Cal. Rot. Pat., Parl. Writs, and Rot. Scotiæ, *var. loc.* Dugd. Chron., 34, 36. Madox, Hist. Exch., ii., 53, etc. Liber Garderobæ, 5. Rot. Parl., i., 266-7. Introd., Pell Records, 44th Edward III., xxiv., etc. Foss's Judges, iii., 296).

[q] Late sheriff of Yorkshire and a man of importance. On 12th August, 1336, the archbishop says that Sir Simon de Ward, late deceased, owed him 22*l.*, and desires that the sum should be raised out of his effects at the oversight of Sir John le Ward. Melton was very careful in looking after his debts. On April 7, 1337, he ordered the goods of Sir John Mauleverer, deceased, to be sequestered, to recover 20*l.* which he owed to him. This system of money-lending would give the archbishop extraordinary influence. Stubbs, indeed, says as much.

Monsieur Johan Warde is one of the witnesses in the Scrope and Grosvenor controversy. "Et dit auxi qil ad une chambre en un manoir q'homme appelle Gyvendale oue lez armez de Scrop sont mys et depeyntez o[r] la pareye en quelle chaumbre sount les armez du S[r] de Nevyll, les armez du S[r] de Percy, les armez du S[r] de Clifford" (i., 118). An interesting picture of an old manor.

[r] On Sept. 16, 1336, Melton granted a licence for begging to the representatives of the hospitals of the Holy Spirit at Rome and St. Anthony at Vienne, and, on Nov. 20, another was given to the master and brethren of the hospital of St. Thomas the Martyr at Eastbridge near Canterbury. The whole country seems to have been overrun by these peripatetic mendicants, among whom, necessarily, were many impostors.

John, earl of Cornwall, the king's brother, 200 marks as a loan for the use of the said earl. Oct. 15. Licence for John de Bampton, rector of Foxholes, to be non-resident. He is a tutor in the family of Sir Geoffrey le Scrop, the king's justiciar.

1337, March 11. Licence to remove the ancient and disused chapel of St. Peter, in the churchyard of Dewsbury, employing the materials on the fabric of the parish church.

1338, April 10. A mandate to the bishop of Carlisle to pray for the king.[s]

1340, March 18. Licence to enclose Isold de Knesall in a house contiguous to the wall of the church of Knesall.[t]

In the time of archbishop Melton ecclesiastical architecture was at its full perfection, and great works were going on in all the cathedral churches within the province of York, to which the primate must have been more or less a patron. No one should shrink from rendering his homage to the age which produced these masterpieces of Christian art.

> "—tibi res antiquæ laudis et artis
> Ingredior, sanctos ausus recludere fontes:"

Piety, surely, could not be dead, when she bore such fruits as these. It was to no momentary impulse or capricious influence that our cathedrals owed their origin. They were the offerings of men full of devotion and self-sacrifice, who, if they gave largely in the cause of God, never thought that they gave too much. What they did was well done, and they built for their spiritual descendants rather than for themselves. Arch-

[s] Fœd., ii., 1026. William de Hatfield, one of the younger children of Edward III., died about this time, and was interred in York minster. He was born in 1336. The monument ascribed to him is in the north aisle of the choir. The marble effigy of the youthful prince is wrought with wonderful skill and beauty. It has been said that the niche in the wall in which it is laid was not made for it; this is an error, as the canopy above and behind the figure is powdered, as I discovered, with the *plantagenista*. The effigy, however, had been removed to another part of the church, and was restored to its present position about eighty years ago by the poet Mason when he was precentor (Corr. of Mason and Gray, ed. Mitford). The fact that one of her children was interred in the minster probably accounted for the gift of the richly embroidered bed of queen Philippa which was made to the chapter (Fabric Rolls, 125).

[t] During the latter years of each archbishop the documents in his register generally become less numerous. The reason is an obvious one. The documents were not transcribed when they were drawn up, but were kept till a certain number had been collected. At the death of any archbishop many of these would be frequently lost, and some would be necessarily regarded with less interest, especially such as related to private matters. The various parts which constitute a register were not bound together till after the decease of the archbishop, and then, occasionally, original documents which had been missed were inserted between the leaves. Even in those years with which most care has been taken omissions may sometimes be detected, when a comparison is made with some contemporaneous register.

bishop Melton gave at one time to the fabric of the church of York a sum which, in the money of the present time, is equivalent to many thousands of pounds.[u] He restored the tomb of St. William. He finished the western portion of the nave of the minster,[v] and on the exterior, in the most conspicuous position, on that glorious façade, his munificence is strikingly commemorated. He sits above the central doorway, graven in stone, in his archiepiscopal attire, with his hand still raised in the attitude of benediction. Over his head is the finest Gothic window in the world, built in all probability by himself, and still beaming with the glowing colours with which he adorned it. On either hand is an effigy of a benefactor of the church, the heads of the noble houses of Vavasor and Percy, bearing in their arms the wood and stone which they once gave. Any one might be proud of a monument like that! But this is not the only architectural memorial which archbishop Melton has left behind him. His name is traditionally connected with the erection of the noble church of Patrington in Holderness. He helped to raise the glorious minster, of which Beverley may still be proud, and at Ripon[w] and Southwell he is not yet forgotten. Great indeed was he in the offices which he filled and in the gifts that were prompted by his munificence; but, with the true spirit of the age in which he lived, he did not forget the little hamlet in which he was born and the humble parents from whom he sprang. He built and endowed a chapel in the village of Melton, in which father and mother and son were to be commemorated. The worshipper in that tiny shrine would muse with no little pride upon the noble fortunes and the piety of his compatriot.

Many pleasing traits in the character and disposition of Melton have been handed down to us, and the historian Stubbs speaks of the archbishop in a manner which shews that he was well acquainted with the prelate whom he commends. He made great additions to the dignity and the revenues of the archiepiscopate, without trespassing in any way upon the patrimony of the needy. His poor tenants had no oppression to complain of. The fines imposed by Melton's seneschals were not exacted, rents were lowered, and debts and arrears were frequently forgiven. Affluence and plenty were around him, and the servant was revelling in abundance whilst the master

[u] When archbishop Zouche visited the chapter in 1343 this sum of 500 marks was still unpaid (Acta Capit. Ebor.).

[v] Tumbam Sancti Willelmi sumptibus xx librarum renovabat. Occidentalem partem navis ecclesiæ beati Petri Ebor., DCC libris argenti appositis consummabat (Stubbs, col. 1731).

[w] In 1331 Melton made statutes for the church of Ripon (Dugd. Mon., vi., 1368).

was as frugal as a hermit. Courtier although he was, Melton would fast and pray so often that his chaplains and officers were worn out when they tried to copy him. Matins he never missed, and the mendicant never appealed in vain to his charitable heart. His diocese was most sedulously attended to. For many years he held in person or by deputy as many as five ordinations. He frequently confirmed and visited the sick. It was not unusual for him to absolve the bodies of the dead, and he would leave his chariot, and, taking his stole and book, release them from the guilt of the offences of their past lives.[x] When the chronicler mentions this circumstance, our thoughts wander unconsciously to the scene of the disaster at Myton. We see the archbishop, full of grief at the mishap, passing hastily and anxiously among the dying and the dead, speaking words of peace to those on whom the light of life was still resting, and pardoning or trying to pardon those who had gone into that land of silence where earthly defeats as well as victories are forgotten.

There is no evidence to shew that Melton was a person of any literary distinction. He was too sagacious, however, and too good not to pay due respect to the scholar and his work. Bred as he had been in the service of his country, he could value well the peace which the student covets and creates. Melton was a kind friend to the university of Oxford. On the 5th of March, 1324, when that illustrious abode of learning was at a low ebb from disturbances within its own walls, the archbishop took it under his protection, and, on the 7th of September, 1327, he authorized the making of a collection throughout his diocese for its relief.[y] On the 7th of March, 1331, he appropriated the church of Aberford to University College. It is

[x] Stubbs, col. 1731.

[y] Reg. Melton. On Nov. 11, 1346, Amandus de Hauwyk, clerk, proctor for the master and scholars of University hall, Oxford, received from the chapter of York the sum of 20*l.* in part payment of a bequest in the will of Mr. Robert de Riplingham, late chancellor of York (Acta Capit., Ebor.).

Riplingham by his will, dated Jan. 14, 1331-2, left 100*l.* to secure the prayers of several priests for the souls of himself, Walter de Merton, bishop of Rochester, archbishop Newark, and others. To the scholars of Merton college he gave his silver spoons, a cup and a goblet, his books of Concordance, his book of Sentences, the Summa of master Henry de Mandario, and all his other books save those which belonged to John de Hesele. He left the munificent sum of 300*l.* to purchase advowsons or lands to maintain perpetual scholars or masters of arts in the university of Oxford, or in whatever place the university should be transferred to (Reg. Test. Ebor.).

Riplingham was a fellow of Merton college, which had been founded about sixty years before by the bishop of Rochester. Merton college was first established at Maldon, in Surrey, and it was from thence removed to Oxford. The troubles which had recently assailed the university suggested to Riplingham's mind the possibility of its removal to some other place. The legacy above mentioned seems to have been lost (Wood's Antiq., Univ. Oxon., iv., 43. Smith's Annals of Univ., Coll., 99).

pleasing also to know that a member of that illustrious seminary, the learned author of the *Philobiblion*, held a stall at York during Melton's archiepiscopate, and to see that the great scholar found a patron in his diocesan. A halo rests around the memory of Richard de Bury, the scholar-bishop of Durham, who first kindled the lamp of learning within the classic walls of Auckland, where a Tunstall, a Morton and a Butler have since worked and thought. The annals of his life, his wanderings in quest of books, the avidity with which he devoured them, the number of his literary friends and his intimacy with Petrarch, form a bright spot in the history of the North. What a contrast to the unlettered pride of Louis de Beaumont his predecessor in the Palatinate, who, although he was allied to kings and princes, was ignorant, strange to say, of the Latin language. On the day of his consecration, when he was making his profession of obedience to the archbishop of York, he stumbled, with a readiness which a refractory suffragan might envy, at the word *metropoliticæ*, and passed it over with the convenient words, *Seyt pur dit*. On another occasion, whilst he was officiating at an ordination, he faltered at the words *in ænigmate*, and confessing himself to be a Davus when he ought to have been an Œdipus, he astonished the listening clerks by the observation, *Par Seynt Lowis, il ne fu pas curtays, qui c'est parole icy escrit.*[a]

In spite of the disasters of the nation and of the warfare which reduced many of the clergy in the North to beggary, archbishop Melton was a very wealthy man. He was a cautious and prudent person, and was very frugal and sparing in his tastes and requirements. His register presents him to us as one of the great money-lenders of the day. Scarcely a year seems to have elapsed without some thousands of marks passing through his hands in the way of loans. The archbishop had debtors in every class of society. The monarch himself required money, and he found it in Melton's coffers. The barons and knights stood in need of it to provide their equipment for the wars, or, perchance, to pay their ransom, if they were unfortunate enough to be captured, and they got it from the northern primate, occasionally leaving behind them as a pledge for its repayment some of the plate which formed almost the sole ornament of their castles and halls. The poor abbat, or prior, whose granges had been destroyed by the marauding Scots, received a loan from his diocesan which enabled him to provide subsistence for his distressed brethren. The ability to supply the wants of so many petitioners, shews that Melton was a man of great wealth and substance. It would make him courted and treated

[a] Hist. Dunelm. Scr. Tres, 118.

with respect by all, and would add very greatly to his influence.[a] It is quite possible that the possession of these riches would dull some of the finer lines in Melton's character,

"Φλεόντων δωμάτων ὑπέρφευ
Ὑπέρ τὸ βέλτιστον—"

It enabled him, however, to befriend his kinsmen, whom he was, perhaps, too fond of advancing and providing for. The archbishop was desirous of "making a family," and he made it. The greater part of his wealth seems to have come to the children of his brother Henry. He was fond of purchasing and trafficking in land for their use; and the knightly house of Melton of Aston, which was fostered and upreared by his munificence, took its place soon after its founder's decease among the greatest families in Yorkshire.

Archbishop Melton maintained his household and lived in a style which befitted his high position. The number of his retainers was very considerable, and there was no want of hospitality or munificence in his palaces. The following extracts will give a more graphic picture of the requirements of the times in which he lived and of the domestic economy of his household, than any remarks or observations of mine.

1318, Jan. 22. To Simon Rose, our attorney, 100s., if necessary, to provide counsel for the archbishop. Nov. 4. To John de Ecclesclif, bishop of Glasgow, 5 marks towards his expences.[b]

1319, March 10. To Thomas Deyvill, our bailiff at Ripon, 40s. for the use of our tenants in the bailywick of Ripon, who are coming to York to go with the king into the North for the defence of the kingdom, and 20s. for a standard of silk for the said tenants.[c] July 30. To Walter, the clerk, of Beverley, 79*l.* 16s. 8d. for cloth bought of him. Nov. 11. To Henry de Melton, our brother, 20*l.* as a gift.

1320, Jan. 7. An order to the park-keepers at Beverley to give to Mr. Richard de Melton, rector of Brandesburton, a deer. August 5. To Mr. Richard de Melton,[d] rector of Lythe, 200*l.* to make provision for us at St. Botulph's fair.

1321, July 25. To William Lumbard, 112s. 3d. for our summer

[a] Stubbs, col. 1731.

[b] There is no bishop of this name in Keith's Fasti of the Scottish church. The bishop of Glasgow at this time was a person of the name of John Wiseheart. He was probably acting as a suffragan for Melton like the Irish prelate who is mentioned below. Ecclescliff has been mentioned before. He was a Friar Preacher, and was successively bishop of Bethlehem, Connor, and Llandaff (Quètif. Scriptores Ord. Predic., i., pref., xxv).

[c] It was in this year that the Scots ravaged the Ripon country.

[d] He occurs, also, as rector of Gilling and seneschal of the archbishop's hospice. On Jan. 19, 1327, Richard de Melton, rector of Brandesburton, was collated to a stall in St. Sepulchre's chapel at York.

liverey.[e] August 8. To the Friars Preachers in their general chapter at Pontefract assembled, 100s. August 20. An order to repair the kitchen of the manor of Otley at the oversight of John, vicar of Otley.

1322, Jan. 23. To John, bishop of Clonfurt, 20s. as a gift. May 22. To Gregory de Thornton, knight,[f] 20 marks in part payment of 100 marks due to him for our service to be rendered in Scotland to the king, which he is to do. May 23. Sir Thomas Ughtred, knight, releases the archbishop from the payment of his wages due for the same service.[g]

1323, June 1. To Thomas de Escrik and Richard de Warwick, our household servants, for the use of the king and queen and their servants, 94*l.* 6s. 8d., and for the use of Sir Hugh le Despenser, jun., the best silver cup in our chest, of which we send you the key, and a smaller cup to Eleanor his wife.[h]

1324, July 12. To Henry de Melton, our brother, two stots. July 24. To Robert Valeyns,[i] canon of York, two deer for his feast during his residence.

1326, Feb. 2. To Henry de Melton, our brother, a gift of ten marks. June 18. To Richard de Gretford, our bailiff at Hull, the money for ten casks of wine. July 19. An order to pay ten marks for the expenses of the archbishop's horses in London. Oct. 20. To Mr. Robert de Dufton and Mr. William de Carleton, 40s. for their expenses in going to Scotland in our behalf. An order to give to William de Ayton, brother of Ralph, late perpetual vicar of Sherburn, 4½ marks of silver, a silver piece, a cup *de murro*, a portiphor of the Sarum use, and a pix covered with pearls, and he to enter into a bond to answer to us about the dilapidations of the vicarage. Oct. 21. An order to Roger de Somervill, sheriff of Yorkshire, to pay for the archbishop forty marks for the wages of Sir Henry Fitzhugh, knight, who is going to the aid of the king in the train of John, earl of

[e] In Stubbs (col. 1731) it is said that Melton gave out his liverey twice a year.

[f] A farther sum of 60*l.* was paid to him on July 4, 1322.

[g] The agreement between him and the archbishop was made Sept. 9, 1318. Ughtred was to serve with "x hommes d'armes od x chevaux covertz." There is an account of several members of the house of Ughtred of Kexby in Dugd. Bar., ii., 144, and in the public records. Sir Thomas was summoned to parliament 18-38th Edward III. He died in 1365, and was buried at Catton, his son Thomas administering to him on the 4th of July.

[h] The archbishop is playing the courtier to a royal favourite.

[i] Robert de Valoignes, precentor of York 1317-1320, in which year he exchanged it with Thomas de Berton for the rectory of Clive in the diocese of Worcester. In 1323 he became canon of Warthill, which he held for twenty years. He died in 1343, and was buried in the chancel of the church of Northfleet, of which he was rector. He was probably a residentiary of York. In 1343, when archbishop Zouche visited the minster, it was reported to him that there were "dissensiones et discordiæ detestabiles" between Valoignes and John de Giffard, a brother canon (Acta Capit. Ebor.).

Surrey, and, on the same day, a loan of 200 marks to Sir William de Ros, lord of Hamelake.

1327, June 30. To dan Nicholas de Hugate,[j] 100*l.* to give to the king and queen. July 2. To Robert de Wodehous,[k] keeper of the king's wardrobe, for the king's use, 500 marks in money and gold florins "de agno, cathedra et mace,"[l] to the value of 300 marks, as a loan. Nov. 9. The archbishop desires Mr. Alan de Conyngesburgh, his proctor at the court of Rome, to make a present for him of 1000 florins to the pope. Nov. 25. To Mr. John de Thoresby going to the court of Rome, 20*l.*[m]

1328, August 12. To the king fifty marks to buy him a palfrey. August 29. To Philip de Redmere, our valet, 20*l.* for certain works of ours at Hull.

1330, April 9. An order to pay to Mr. Robert de Bridlington for the use of William,[n] son of Henry de Melton, 1000*l.*,

[j] Provost of Beverley 1315-1338. Prebend of Barnby at York 1317. Archdeacon of Gloucester 1317 (Le Neve, iii., 77). Canon of Howden and Saltmarsh at Howden (Reg. ii., Pr. and Conv. Dunelm., 107). Master of St. Nicholas's hospital at York (Dugd. Mon., vi., 710). Incumbent of Lythe and Welwick. In 17th Edward II. he occurs as receiver of monies to be spent in Aquitaine (Pell Records, 136: Abbrev. Rot. Orig., i., 276). In 2nd of Edward III. he was appointed to superintend the preparation of the apartments in the palace of the archbishop of York for the celebration of the king's marriage (Pell Records, 140). He was canon of Asgarby at Lincoln (Le Neve, ii., 101), and his will was proved on the 12th of July, 1338 (MSS. Harl., 6954, 55 *b*). A chantry was founded for his soul in York minster in 1357 at the altar of SS. James and Katherine (Fabric Rolls, 286).

[k] A younger son of Sir Bertram de Wodehouse, of Kimberley, by the heiress of the Feltons (Blomefield's Norfolk, ii., 543). Chaplain to Edward II., clerk of the wardrobe, chancellor and baron of the exchequer and lord treasurer of England (Fœd., ii., 398, 419, 787, 1040. Cal. Rot. Pat., 105-6, 109, 132. Rot. Scot., i., 139. Rot. Parl., ii., 79. Madox, Hist. Exch., ii., 327. Dugd. Chron., 39-42. Lib. Garderobæ, 73. Foss's Judges, iii., 314, 539). Prebend of Knaresbro' and archdeacon of Richmond, canon of Hereford, Lincoln, Southwell, and Lichfield, incumbent of Boney and Tyverington. In his will, which was made in 1345 (Test. Ebor., i., 13), he desires to be buried in the church of the Austin canons at Stamford. The author of the metrical pedigree of the family of Wodehouse tells us, whilst speaking of the nephew of the treasurer,—

> "His uncle Robert, being High Treasurer
> Of England, one who had sometime before
> Bin Richmond's dean and chaplain to the king,
> So pious and discreet his life had bin."

[l] A most valuable description of these coins, which, in the absence of gold at home, English bankers, etc., were most anxious to procure. I believe that coins of all these three types are not now in existence. Peter de Dene in his will made in 1322 mentions Florins "de agno et mas" (Chron. W. Thorn, col. 2037).

[m] Afterwards archbishop. He arose into importance through his skilful diplomacy at Rome. A farther sum of 30*l.* was given to him by Melton on Dec. 2nd at Newcastle. In 1326 he occurs as receiver of Melton's chamber and his private chaplain.

[n] Afterwards Sir William de Melton, knight, of Aston, the archbishop's nephew and heir, æt. 23 in 1340. He died in 1362, leaving a son and heir, Sir William, æt. 23, whose mother was Joan, sister and co-heir in her issue of Thomas lord Lucy, who died July 4, 1369 (Baker's Northants, i., 673. Hunter's South Yorkshire, ii., 162). I make some additions to the pedigree.

The will of Sir William Melton, the

and for the use of Thomas, John and Joan the brothers and sister of the said William, 100*l.* each. April 24. An order to Simon de Swanlond to buy 10,500 small florins of Florence to prosecute our cause in the papal court against the bishop of Durham.[o] June 1. To dan. John de Elghton, chaplain, celebrating at Melton for the souls of our parents, a wage after the rate of five marks per annum. June 8. Thomas Fox, the receiver at Hexham, is ordered to construct a good and a stout gaol at that place.

1331, May 17. An order to the receiver at York to have made for the archbishop a silver cup of the price of 40s., and another of 2½ marks or 30s. May 21. To Adam Coppendale of Beverley, 100*l.* 4s. for cloth bought of him for our summer liverey. May 24. To Walter de Kelstern, 185*l.* 8s. 1d. for plates of white silver, and to Henry de Belton,[p] 327*l.* 18s. 9d. for plates of white silver received from him through the hands of Mr. Robert de Bridlington and John de Nottingham.[q]

second, is printed in Test. Ebor., i., 246. He died in 1398, having been a witness for the Scropes in 1386 (Scrope and Grosvenor Roll, ii., 301), and his widow, shortly afterwards, took the vows before archbishop Scrope in the following manner:—

"In the nome of Jhesu Crist, Amen. Y Katerine de Melton de Aston, of the erchebisshopricke of York, byfor you hier, worsshepful fader in God and lord Richard by the grace of God erchebysshop of York, primat of Engelond and legat of ye court of Rome, in the wyrsship of Gode and hys moder Seinte Marie maiden and al seintz of heven, in your holy handes make avowe and byhot that y shal kepe my body henforword in chastitee, and in token of this avowe y make this seyne of the holy cros whith my owne honde +."

A Mr. William de Melton was sometime the archbishop's receiver at Hexham. Possibly he was the issue of the following marriage which is entered in archbishop Melton's register. Jan. 13, 1307, Clement V. grants a dispensation to William, son of Nicholas de Melton, and Christian his wife, who had married although they were related, and had had four children. The consanguinity was thus shewn. A person called "Anketinus diaconus," had two children, Thomas and Agnes. Ralph "dictus clericus" was the son of this Thomas. Ralph had a son Ralph, the father of Maud, mother of William de Melton. Agnes, daughter of Anketinus above named, was the mother of Alexander Paslewe, who was the father of Geoffrey, the sire of Christian. I scarcely think that this document relates to the parents of the archbishop.

On Oct. 4, anno 22, archbishop Melton writes to the bishop of Durham to enquire about an exchange of benefices as proposed by William Melton, rector of Alston, and John de Bridlington, rector of a moiety of the church of Roxby in the diocese of Lincoln (Reg. Bury, 311). June 22, 1370, ind. Mr. William de Melton in vic. de Withornse, having exchanged for it his rectory of Brandesburton with Thomas de S. Martino (Reg. Thoresby). Mr. William de Melton was ordained priest at York on the Saturday after St. Lucy's day, 1358, William de Ferriby giving him a title (ibid.).

[o] The contest between Melton and bp. Beaumont is elsewhere alluded to.

[p] Mayor of York 1334-7 (Drake, 360-1). On July 2, 1336, the prior and convent of Durham allowed him and the other parishioners of All Saints, Ousegate (Pavement), to build houses in the churchyard, where the dead were not interred, to support a chaplain in honour B.M.V. in the said church (Reg. ii., Pr. and Conv. Dunelm., 107 *b*). Belton founded a chantry there on 4th of July, 1347 (Drake, 294).

[q] A John de Nottingham was dean of Lincoln in 1340 (Le Neve, ii., 32).

August 9. To Richard de la Mare[r] and Thomas de Ergom their expenses, etc., in taking the fattest of the deer in our parks, co. Notts. August 20. To Mr. Richard de Snoweshull and Richard de Grimeston of York, goldsmith, 100lb. of silver plate.[s] August 31. To Willliam de Cliff, the money necessary for himself and men, his horses and dogs, whilst taking the feræ in our park at Beverley, and salt for salting what he takes.[t] Sept. 22. To William de Melton, son of Henry de Melton deceased, our brother, 1000*l*. as a mark of our affection. Nov. 22. To Mr. Richard de Eryom,[u] canon of York, 100 marks to ex-

[r] A cousin of the archbishop. I shall notice several other members of the family.

[s] The York mint was in full play during this archiepiscopate, and I shall give some new and valuable notices of its progress. A great quantity of money seems to have been struck at York, but there are few peculiar mint-marks, such as are observed on the coins of the bishops of Durham. Their absence may be easily accounted for by the fact that York was not a palatinate like Durham; such a privilege, therefore, as the use of mint-marks could not properly be assumed.

Mr. Richard de Snoweshill was Melton's mint-master. Melton made him his receiver, and he became rector of Huntington near York. He made his will on the 27th of August, 1349, in which he desired to be buried in the choir of the church of All Saints at Huntington, near the vestry-wall, if he dies in the diocese of York. He gives a legend to the church, and leaves 10s. to buy a stone coffin in which his body is to be laid. Pr. 7th August, 1349 (Reg. Zouche).

The following extracts relate to the operations of the York mint at this time. August 7, 1331, an order to Mr. John de Notyngham, the archbishop's receiver at York, to give to Mr. Richard, the goldsmith, of Grimesby, whom we have appointed our *magister cuneorum*, all our silver plate in your keeping. August 8, Mr. Richard Snoweshill appointed *custos cambii*, and on the same day, Nottingham, the receiver, is directed to give him 200 lb. of silver to hand over to Richard, the goldsmith, to coin into money. Aug. 28, 1331, the receiver is ordered to pay Snoweshill 100*l*. for the use of the mint, and on August 31 the same officer is ordered to place in his hands the archbishop's silver plate. Dec. 28, 1331, to Mr. R. de Snoweshill, our receiver at York, the money he has spent "circa missionem cuneorum nostrorum apud London et pro ipsis cuneis ibidem fabricandis," and for bringing them to York, and, also, for making a chasuble for our chantry in York minster. March 13, 1333-4, acq. of the accompt of Snoweshill as keeper of the mint, 3110. lib. arg. 4s. 11d. remaining in his hands. The accounts run from August 8, 1331, to Michaelmas, 1333, and are passed. Jan. 12, 1337-8, an order to the receiver at York to buy silver plate for our use.

[t] August 5, 1334, an order to pay to William de Cliff and his companions the money they require for hunting for us at Ripon.

[u] Prebendary of Ulleskelf, which he held from 1322 to 1338, when he died. His history is a remarkable one. He made his own way in the world, as in June, 1304, he is mentioned in archbishop Corbridge's register as "Richard de Eryum super Tees, pauper clericus." He soon rose into importance, Kellawe, bishop of Durham, having taken him by the hand. In 1313 he was prebendary of Lanchester, and in receipt of an annual pension of 66s. 8d. from the convent of Durham (Reg. ii., Pr. and Conv. Dunelm., 35, 61. Hist. Dunelm. Scr. Tres., appendix, 107). On Dec. 3, 1315, the dean and chapter of York ask Kellawe to ordain Mr. Richard de Erium, rector of St. Nicholas's, Durham (Reg. Kellawe, 155 *b*). In November, 1316, he was made canon of Saltmarsh at Howden (Reg. ii., *ut supra*, 79 *b*). He is very frequently mentioned among the acts of bishop Kellawe. In June, 1322, he exchanged his stall at Howden with Richard de

pedite the business of ourself and our church at Rome. Nov. 28. To Mr. John de Barneby, our domestic chaplain, 1500 florins for our affairs in the court of Rome. Nov. 29. An order to the receiver at Howden to give to John de Haytefeld as many hens "de lak" at this time, and whenever he comes to you, as the sumpter horses of our poultry store, can carry to us at York, and the wheat and barley "de doddes," which are due to us from Howdenshire, to be brought to our manor of Cawood.[v]

1332, Jan. 18. To Mr. John de Notingham, the expenses of his journey to and from St. Oswald's, Gloucester. Jan. 19. To Mr. Thomas Sampson,[w] official of our court at York, two deer from our park at Beverley. Feb. 21. An order to pay 100s. for building a grange at Boulton. April 5. To John le Waryner, money to repair our *camera* at Ripon. May 14. An order to Mr. Robert de Bridelington,[x] seneschal of our lands, to pay 1000 marks of the money of our cousin which is in your hands to David earl of Athol.[y] May 25. To dame Margery de Mel-

Osgodby for the prebend of Ulleskelf. In April, 1323, he was presented to the living of Brompton in Pickering Lyth, which he held till he died (Reg. Melton). On July 8, 1324, he was one of the persons appointed to settle the disputes between France and England "ratione castri de Monte Pessato" (Fœd., ii., 558). He died in 1338. See Hist. Dunelm. Scr. Tres, 104.

[v] Some curious customary rents. In Best's Farming Book, which has been published for the Surtees Society, there is the following explanation of "doddes." "Many have alledged y[t] white wheate is ye best to mingle and sowe with rye and y[t] it will bee ye soonest ripe, but wee finde experimentally y[t] Kentish wheate is ye best or y[t] which (hereabouts) is called *dodde* reade, and besides it is a larger corne, and a wheate y[t] will sell as well amongst rye as ye other."

[w] A distinguished man. He was son, I believe, of John Sampson, who was knight of the shire for Yorkshire in 1298, and was closely connected with the families of Sutton and Malbys. He held at various times the livings of Acaster Malbys, Halmby, and Misterton, and was warden of the chapel of Sutton in Holderness, canon of Holme at York, and a residentiary and prebendary of Beverley. In 1342 the canons of York elected him their dean, but the appointment was set aside by the pope after a long and angry controversy. Sampson was employed in state affairs (Fœd., ii., 794, 870, 947; iii., 116. Rot. Scot., i., 590-1. Rot. Parl., ii., 105). There are letters from him in existence describing the victory at Neville's cross (MSS. Bodl., 2086, 18), and he was very useful in advancing the building of York minster. He died in 1349, having made a noble will which is still unpublished. His wealth was enormous.

[x] Private chaplain of Melton. In February, 1320, he exchanged his stall in the church of All Saints, Derby, for that of Welton at Lincoln (MSS. Harl., 6951, 77 *b*). He was canon of Nunwick at Ripon, Woodburgh at Southwell, and South Newbald at York, the last of which he obtained in 1330 in exchange for the stall of Parva Cestria at Derby. He held, also, the livings of North Ferriby, Claworth, and Elneley. He died in 1332. On Dec. 29, 1331, the custody of the marriage of Richard, son and heir of Richard de Forneus, was entrusted to Bridlington. Robert and William F., his brothers, are mentioned (Reg. Melton).

[y] This was for the manor of Gainsborough. The bargain was cancelled. On March 15, 1333-4, the archbishop desired the money should be received back from the earl, together with the deeds.

ton, our kinswoman, three quarters of wheat and five of malt. June 16. To Richard de Danport, tanner of Pontefract, 107s. for thirty-one hoods and twenty-one super-tunics furred with budge, and forty-four lambs' furs for our summer liverey. June 24. To Mr. Ivo, the mason, five marks for stone bought at Tadcaster for our work at York. August 1. To the Augustinians at Lincoln, in their general chapter there, two marks. August 24. To dan Richard de Melton, seneschal of our hospice, 200 marks to make provision for us at St. Botulph's. Sept. 29. To Mr. Robert, our cook, money enough to buy 2000 stockfish in the next fair of St. Botulph's, with his expenses. Nov. 12. To John de Dyock, the money necessary to hire a ship to bring "plastre ston" from Gainsbro' to Southwell.

1333, May 4. To William de Fereby,[z] our domestic clerk, 100*l.* for the expenses of our hospice. Oct. 18. An order to Mr. Richard de Snoweshull, our receiver at York, to repair and make a glass window in our chapel, the east window of our chamber, a new window in our study, and a new partition *(particula)* in the west end of the great hall of our palace, and to pay 40s. for a silver gilt cup. Oct. 21. An order to pay 100s. for a pontifical ring. Oct. 23. To Adam de Coppendale of Beverley, 39*l.* 17s. for spices. Nov. 1. To Simon, master of the schools at Newark, for the expenses of our kinsmen William and Thomas de Melton and their tutor as long as they are there, 2s. 5d. per week. Nov. 2. To John de Esk, 24*l.* for two bovates of land bought for the use of our beloved kinsman Thomas, son of Henry de Melton.[a]

[z] A kinsman of the archbishop, and a member of a great clerical family which held many preferments in Yorkshire. Ferriby is near the archbishop's birthplace at Melton. It would be tedious to enumerate minutely the preferments of William de Ferriby. Suffice it to say that at one time or other he held the archdeaconry of Cleveland, the chancellorship and the stalls of Bilton, Holme, and Dunnington at York, where he was a residentiary. He was also canon of Ripon, Southwell, and Salisbury, dean of Hereford, chancellor of Beverley, and prebendary at Chester and Osmunderley. He held the livings of Brompton, Claworth, Stokesley, North Ferriby, Hugate, Carleton in Lindrick, Kippax, Acaster Malbys, the mastership of Bawtry hospital, and the rectory of Watford, Northants. He was executor of archbishops Melton and Zouche, and dying in 1379 was buried in York minster. His will is in Test. Ebor., i., 103. Cf. Fabric Rolls, 123, 286, etc. Ferriby leaves to the fabric of York minster 20 marks, and all the books which formerly belonged to archbishop Melton.

[a] A very interesting notice of the education of the archbishop's nephews. The eldest has been already mentioned. His uncle seems to have allowed him 100s. a year after he left school.

On May 30, 1332, Mr. William le Burton, vicar of Kirkby Moorside, received the charge of Thomas, son of Henry de Melton, a boy. On May 14, 1335, the care of Thomas and John, sons of Henry de Melton, was entrusted to Mr. William de Yafford, parson at the altar B.M. Magd. in York minster. On Dec. 5, 1335, William de Ferriby, the archbishop's domestic chaplain, was made their curator (Reg. Melton). On March 30, 1351, there was a commission to ordain Mr. Thomas de Melton, rector of Hotham (Reg.

1334, Jan. 15. To Roger de Monketon, jeweller of York, 52s. 11d. for a cup and two pieces of silver. April 12. To Adam de Coppandale of Beverley, 10*l.* 21d. for two ells of canvass. May 10. An order to reward Robert Parvyng, William Basset, John de Trevanyon, William Scot and John de Anlaghby, advocates, of York, for their advice and assistance in our business. May 19. To William de Popelton, seneschal of our hospice, fifty marks as a gift to our lady Philippa the queen, and money to buy two carcases of oxen, three of pigs, and six of sheep to give to the king.[b] June 3. To Mr. Thomas Sampson, official of our court at York, sufficient money for our cause against the archbishop of Canterbury.[c] July 10. To Richard Lune, steward at Otley, 20*l.* for building and repairing our houses in the manor there. August 1. To John Levenyng,[d] our valet, the money required for hunting for us, and storing what he takes, at Southwell and Scrooby. August 10. An order to pay the money for the silver chain of our seal, and for a case to it. August 13. To Robert the plumber, money for lead nails used in our chapel and oriole at York. August 21. An order to Nicholas de Siglesthorn, our receiver at Beverley, to pay ten marks to the keeper of the fabric, towards the fabric of the high altar there, and twenty marks towards the fabric of the nave.[e] August 31. To John de Worne, 100 marks for the charges at the custom-house and the expenses connected with our wool which has been exchanged in Flanders. Oct. 31. To Thomas de Ougtered, knight, who is about to go to Scotland, 40*l.*, and he requires for the present the use of some part of his silver vases. His request is granted.[f]

1335, Feb. 19. Release of the accompt of Richard de Snoweshill, our receiver at York. He has in hand belonging to us, 1712*l.* 14s. 6d., thirty-six "florinos regales," forty-nine "de agno," and forty-six "de Florentia," with a silver cup gilt and enamelled, an ewer gilt and enamelled, pledged by Sir John Cromwell[g] for twenty marks, and two "inpele," pledged by Sir

Zouche). In 1358, on the Saturday after St. Matthew's day, he was made deacon at York, his title being a chantry to which he was appointed by William de Ferriby. He was ordained sub-deacon on the vigil of the feast of Trinity preceding (Reg. Thoresby).

[b] In this year Edward III. won his great victory at Halidon hill.

[c] No doubt arising from the *bajulatio crucis*.

[d] A cousin of the archbishop. In 1336 a Richard de Cardoyl is mentioned as standing in the same relationship to that prelate.

[e] A very valuable date. About the year 1324 there was a papal indulgence issued in behalf of the church of Beverley. Cf. Cal. Rot. Pat., 104.

[f] Sir Thomas Ughtred has borrowed money of Melton, leaving his plate as a pledge for its repayment.

[g] Apr. 11, anno pont. 16, a loan of 20 marks to Sir John Cromwell, who gives as a pledge a cup and ewer of silver.

Fulk Fitzwarren, for 20*l.* April 21. To William de Wirkesworth, 200 marks and more for our summer livery.

1336, April 5. To the prior of Wartre, 100*l.* at the oversight of John de Melton, to the use of the said John and Margery his wife our kinswoman. July 13. An order to Mr. Richard de Snoweshill to give out fourteen ells of silk for our summer livery. Dec. 11. We have received from our receiver at York, 842*l.* 11s. 10d. of our new money.[h]

1337, Jan. 8. To Thomas Fox, our receiver at Hexham, 23s. 4d. for making our mill at Alwenton.[i] April 27. To Sir William de Erghom, knight, ninety marks for a mesuage, a bovate of arable land and the advowson of the church of Aston, which we have bought of him.[j] May 8. To Roger de Middleton, 100 marks for the manor of North Milford bought of him.

1338, June 7. To Mr. Thomas Sampson and dan Nicholas de Hugate, canons of York, 500 marks to the use of the fabric of the church.[k] Sept. 21. To dan Richard de Melton, rector of Brandesburton, 30*l.* for the making of the work of our chapel at Melton, together with the sum of 20*l.* due from the executors of Nicholas de Hugate.

1339, Feb. 4. To Mr. Thomas Sampson or Thomas de Ludham, keeper of the fabric of the church of York, 100 marks for the glazing of the window newly constructed at the west end of the cathedral.[l] May 14. An order to Mr. Giles de Reddmere[m] to provide for us some good parchment at Lincoln, paying for

[h] Was this the produce of the York mint or Florins, etc., which had been obtained in the way of exchange?

[i] Aug. 24, 1351, Thomas Fox, rector of Gilling in Ridale, and John Luk, rector of Haltwhistle exchange (Reg. Zouche).

[j] The manor of Aston, W.R.Y., came into Melton's hands in 1332, when Thomas de Aunby passed it over to him (Hunter's South Yorkshire, ii., 162). "Aston's secret shade" was in subsequent years the patrimony of the family of Darcy, and, in still later days, sheltered the poet Mason, who became precentor of the minster of York.

In 1334 Melton granted letters of attorney to Thomas de Lelom, his valet, to take possession in his name of the manor of Killom from Peter, archbishop of Rouen, and his chapter. The archbishop knew in what peril the property of aliens in England was placed; and he was wisely selling his lands in that country (Reg. Melton). In 8th Edward III. Melton was enfeoffed by the archbishop of the manors of Ottery St. Mary, co. Devon, Kingsclere, and Buntworth, Hants, and Killom, co. York (Cal. Inq. P. M., ii., 62).

[k] Stubbs (col. 1731) says that Melton gave 700 marks, and there is no reason to doubt his accuracy, although the whole amount is not accounted for in the register. No one can suppose that all the items of the primate's expenditure are entered in that book.

[l] The beautiful west window, the glass of which is still perfect.

[m] A kinsman of the archbishop. Canon of Hungate at Lincoln (Le Neve, ii., 99). He made his will on the Wednesday before the feast of St. Barnabas, 1347, in which he desired to be buried in Lincoln cathedral, before the great cross in the nave, near the tomb of Sir William de Boloyn. To the fabric he gave 40s. To Juliana, his sister, a nun at Irford, 2 marks. To Thomas de Geynesburgh, chaplain, vicar in the cathedral, 20s., and his portiphor of the Lincoln use, and to him and Wm.

it 40s. or 50s. July 25. To dan Richard de Melton, 25*l.* for our chapel at Melton.

1340, Jan. 7. We have received from Sir Antony de Lucy,[n] knight, 200*l.* in part payment of 400*l.* due to us for the marriage of William de Melton our kinsman, and this money the archbishop gives on the 13th, as a special favour, to his cousin Richard de la Mar.[o]

Archbishop Melton died at Cawood on the 4th or 5th of April, 1340, and was interred in the north aisle of the nave of York minster, near the font.[p] Mr. Drake, the historian, thus describes the opening of his tomb in 173 . "On the laying the new pavement of the church the stone which covered the grave of this prelate was taken up. It was of blue marble, very large, but quarterly cloven, and had been plated with brass on the borders, and all over the middle part of it. Upon trial for a vault the workmen came, at about two yards depth, to six large unhewn stones, which laid cross and cross, as a drain is covered. Upon removing two or three of them we discovered a curious walled grave of ashler stone, in which the archbishop was laid. He had been put in a lead coffin, and afterwards in a mighty strong oaken one; but both were so decayed that it was easy to get to his bones. On the top of the uppermost coffin, near his breast, stood a silver chalice and paten which had been gilt. On the foot of the chalice was stampt a crucifix of no mean workmanship, and on the inside of the paten a hand

de Redmer, his brother, all his books which are not set apart for the Friars Preachers at Lincoln. Pr. 20th June, 1347 (Reg. Zouche).

Philip de Redmer "consanguineus arch[i]" is mentioned in Melton's register. Philip, son of John de Redmer, occurs in Abbrev. Rot. Orig., i., 156.

[n] A great warrior and statesman. Melton married his nephew to Lucy's daughter.

[o] The family of De la Mare were connected with the archbishop, and were preferred by him. The name is a suggestive one.

William de la Mare "consanguineus noster," once called W. de la Mare de Melton, held many offices. At various times he was canon of South and North Newbald and Ulleskelf and treasurer at York, prebendary in St. Sepulchre's chapel, All Saints Derby, provost of Beverley, incumbent of North Ferriby, Wath, and Waltham. On Jan. 1, 1319, he was made seneschal of all the archbishop's manors and lands. He died 25th November, 1365, and was buried in York minster.

Thomas de la Mare, brother of William, also called *"consanguineus"* by the archbishop, was sacrist of St. Sepulchre's chapel. In 1338 he became canon of Weighton, exchanging for it his rectory of Stratford, dioc. Lincoln. He died at Clareburgh, Notts, on 6th of October, 1358, and was buried there. His will is in Test. Ebor., i., 68. *It* is a valuable document, and several of the Meltons are mentioned in it.

[p] His obit was observed on the 4th (Reg. Magn. Album, part iii., 112). It is said that he died on the 5th in Stubbs, col. 1731. MSS. Cotton, Vitellius, A, ii., 112. On April 6, 1340, the dean and chapter of York send William de la Mare and two others to the king to tell him that the archbishop died on the 5th, and to ask leave to choose a successor (Act. Capit.). Bur. "in crast. S. Georgii" (Chron. Lan.). Mr. Baker (Hist. Northants) is wrong in saying that Melton died on April 14,

giving the benediction. We could not find that he had been buried in his robes; his pastoral staff laid on his left side, but no ring could be met with. His bones, as they laid together, measured six foot, which argues him to have been a very tall man. His grey hairs were pretty fresh; after we had taken a short survey of the *exuviæ* of this once famous man, the grave was closed up in the manner it was before; but the chalice and paten were carried to the vestry."[q]

Archbishop Melton left a will, of which William de la Mare, canon of York and provost of Beverley, William de Ferriby, canon of York and rector of Stokesley, and William de Wyrkesworth, rector of Slaidburn and prebendary in the chapel of St. Sepulchre, were the executors, and they had their release on the 6th of November, 1345. It appears that with all his wealth the archbishop had not paid proper attention to the buildings, etc., belonging to his see, as on the 14th of November, 1342, the executors bound themselves to pay to his successor the large sum of 4000 marks on the score of dilapidations.[r] Melton, however, left great wealth behind him, of which perhaps he was a little too fond, and his nephew William de Melton of Aston was found to be his heir, being at that time twenty-three years of age.[s] The archbishop died seised of the manors of Kingsclere and Buntworth, co. Southants, Killam, Aston and Towton, within the honour of Pontefract, North Milford, Kirkbywharf, Abholme and Sherburne in Yorkshire, and Upston, co. Notts.[t] All these estates came into the possession of his nephews, whose descendants were among the highest knightly families in Yorkshire.

On the 1st of February, 1355, William de Ferriby, an executor of the deceased prelate, and probably in accordance with his wishes, established two chantries to commemorate his benefactor and kinsman. The endowment consisted of twenty-six marks per annum out of lands in Hotham, Northcave, Melton, Ferriby, Swanland and Elveley. The first of these chantries was in the chapel of St. James at Melton, which the primate himself had erected. The other was at the altar of the Holy Innocents in York minster. Two priests officiated there and made special mention of the soul of the archbishop and that of Edward of Carnarvon, king of England, through whose means he had risen to greatness. Each of these chaplains received the sum of five marks per annum.[u]

[q] Drake's Eboracum, 433.

[r] Reg. Zouche.

[s] Baker's Northants, i., 673.

[t] Cal. Inq. P. M., ii., 94. The names of the keepers of the temporalities after Melton's death are given in Abbrev. Rot. Orig., i., 224.

[u] Reg. Thoresby. Domesday book, penes Dec. et Cap. Ebor., 55-7. Fabric Rolls of York minster, 286. Hutchinson's Durham, iii., 477.

On the 20th of January, 1359-60 Elias de Walkington, the sub-chantor of the vicars choral, made an arrangement with Ferriby and De la Mare, by which the obit of the archbishop was to be annually observed on the 4th of April.[v]

William la Zouche is said to have been a younger son of William, lord la Zouche of Haringworth, Northants, by Maude daughter of John lord Lovel, and to have been born at his father's seat.[w] But whether these were his parents or not, his very name bears witness to his illustrious birth. The lords of Haringworth were famous for their hospitality, and in Kennet's time the proverb, "to go a Zouching, was commonly applied to an unbidden but welcome guest."[x]

Zouche was probably engaged in the service of the king in early life, as we find him acting as a clerk of the wardrobe in 1332.[y] On the 8th of May, 1329, he was sent to France to make provision for the king against his arrival; and on the 6th

[v] Reg. Magnum Album, pt. iii., 112. MSS. Cotton, Claudius, B, iii., 297.

[w] Bridges' Northants, ii., 318. There are pedigrees of the family of Zouche in Dugdale's Baronage, i., 688, etc.; —Warwickshire, 42; Nichols's Leicestershire, ii., 372, but the archbishop is not mentioned in any of them. The name Zouche is of French origin "de stirpite sicco," as Camden says (Remaines, ed. 1674, p. 191), the "durum ex stirpe genus" of Virgil, and the primate fully verified the derivation by his prowess in the field.

On the 4th of November, 1344, archbishop Zouche made his brother, Sir Roger la Zouche, knight, his seneschal at Hexham (Reg.). In February, 1346, he was retained by him, with six others, to defend the Marches of Scotland, and on that account he was excused from going abroad with the king (Fœd., iii., 69). On the 4th of July, 1345, Sir Roger, who is described as belonging to Leicestershire, had orders to cross the seas with the sovereign (ibid., 52), and on 12th of January, 1359, he and three others were desired to raise an hundred archers for service (ibid., 416, 441).

Henry la Zouche, perhaps a brother of the archbishop, was presented in 1346-7 by Sir William la Zouche, of Haringworth, to the rectory of Barby, Northants (Baker, i., 264). In the year 1350 he was made prebendary of South Cave at York, which he exchanged for the stall of Ampleford with Henry de Ingleby on the 12th of Aug., 1351. He died holding it in March, 1361-2, being at that time archdeacon of Sudbury, having been appointed in January, 1351 (Reg. Zouche. Le Neve, ii., 491).

[x] Kennet's Par. Ant., ii., 472-3. The following testimony is borne to the hospitality of the Herberts: "It was an ordinary saying in the countrey (Montgomeryshire) at that time, when they saw any fowl rise, 'Fly where thou wilt thou wilt light at Black-hall'" (Life of Edward lord Herbert of Cherburg, ed. 1770, p. 5). The inscription, which was formerly engraved upon the village cross at Sprotborough, was an honour to the Fitzwilliams (Hunter's South Yorkshire, i., 348).

"Who so is hungry and list well eate
Let him come to Sprotburgh to his meate,
And for a night and for a day
His horse shall have both corne and hay,
And no mane shall aske him where he goith
away."

[y] Pell Records, 142.

of June, 1335, he was present in the camera of the Friars Minors at York, when the great seal was given to the archbishop of Canterbury. Before this time, however, he had obtained church preferment. On the 10th of December, 1329, he was collated to the archdeaconry[z] of Barnstable in the church of Exeter, which he must have given up on the 12th of July, 1330, when he was advanced to the archdeaconry of Exeter.[a] He exchanged this office with Thomas de Nassington for the rectory of Jakelee on the 10th of June, 1331.[b] On the 9th of March, 1334, he was admitted by archbishop Melton, on the provision of the pope, to the next vacant prebend at Southwell, but it does not appear that he ever actually enjoyed one. On the 11th of February, 1336, he was promoted in a similar way to a stall at York. In 1336 the canons of that cathedral elected him their dean, and he was installed on the 12th of November. On the 29th of June, 1338, Zouche made his obedience to archbishop Melton in the chapel of the palace at York in the presence of a goodly company of ecclesiastics.[c] He was collated to the prebend of Ufton at Lichfield, of which he had only a brief tenure, on the 9th of April, 1340.[d]

The deanery of York was an honourable and an arduous office, but Zouche had still time to spend in the service of his country. The post which he held had been already occupied by several distinguished statesmen, for the deans of York had rare facilities for making themselves useful in the controversies and the wars with Scotland. Zouche, in this respect, was no exception to his predecessors, and he rose in early life to greatness. In 1337 he was made lord treasurer of England, and he seems to have held the office in the 15th Edward III.[e] On the 23rd of April, 1337, he was one of the persons who were to arrange about the wages of the soldiers who were on their way to Scotland, and, on the 26th of June, he and others were directed to summon the army to York.[f] On the 28th of the same month he was ordered to be present at York to state the king's intentions about his turbulent neighbours in the North. On the 28th of August he was one of the commissioners who were appointed to raise money in Northants for the French war,[g] and on the 6th of October he was requested to act upon the Borders, in fortifying the towns, treating with the Marchmen

[z] Fœd., ii., 762, 909.

[a] Le Neve, i., 393, 406.

[b] MSS. Harl., 6951, 101 b. Nassington was canon of South Newbald at York, and died in 1346.

[c] Reg. Melton.

[d] Le Neve, i., 633.

[e] Cal. Rot. Pat., 128, 131. In 1339 Zouche, as treasurer, was abroad in the king's behalf (ibid., 134). Dugd. Chron., 42. Avesbury's Edward III., 46. Fœd., ii., 964, 1094.

[f] Rot. Scot., i., 489, 494.

[g] Fœd., ii., 979, 994.

and other necessary business.[h] On the 19th of January, 1340, Zouche, in his capacity of treasurer of England, together with several others, was deputed to open the parliament at Westminster in the absence of the king.[i]

Archbishop Melton died in the spring of 1340, and, on the 13th of April, the king issued his congè d'elire to the authorities at York. On the 2nd of May, the chapter assembled, and two candidates were proposed, the dean and William de Kildesby, Edward the Third's secretary and favourite, who was a notorious pluralist. The wishes of the sovereign seem to have been openly expressed in Kildesby's behalf, but they were disregarded; as out of eighteen voters who were present, Zouche obtained the suffrages of all but five. The archbishop-elect and his friends seem to have suspected that some controversy would ensue, and Zouche took the singular but wise precaution of being installed on the day of his election.[j] A vehement contention now broke out; Kildesby leaving no stone unturned to carry his point, and the king vigorously assisting him.[k] On the 14th of March, 1341, Edward wrote to the pope entreating him to support his favourite against Zouche.[l] The quarrel had the effect of delaying the settlement of the question for more than two years, but it ended in the defeat of Kildesby, as Zouche was consecrated by Clement VI. at Avignon, on Sunday the 7th of July, 1342.[m] On the 8th of September the king granted him letters of safe conduct to enable him to return home, and, on the 19th, the temporalities were restored to him.[n] On Sunday the 8th of December, the festival of the Conception of the Virgin, the new archbishop was solemnly enthroned in his cathedral, and there was a banquet in the palace for which great preparations were

[h] Ibid., 1100. Rot. Scot., i., 503.

[i] Fœd., ii., 1106. Rot. Parl., ii., 107.

[j] Stubbs, col. 1731. MSS. Cotton, Vitellius, A, ii., 112. Le Neve, iii., 106. [k] Stubbs, col. 1732.

[l] Fœd., ii., 1118.

[m] Stubbs, col. 1732. MSS. Vitellius, *ut supra*. After a long delay, for the pope "electos Eboracensem et Lincolniensem tenuit in curia languentes, et nullatenus expeditos" (Murimuth, 115). The same writer says that Clement VI. appointed Zouche to York on June 26, whose election had been hindered on account of an alleged resignation (p. 133).

[n] Fœd., ii., 1210-11. William de Kildesby was a great man. On Dec. 2, 1340, he was made master of the rolls (Fœd., ii., 1143), and between that year and 1342 he was keeper of the privy seal (ibid., 1129. Rot. Parl., ii., 132. Rot. Scot., i., 625. Cal. Rot. Pat., 138). He was canon of Wetwang and treasurer at York, warden of the chapel in Tickhill castle (Hunter's South Yorkshire, i., 236), prebendary of Darlington 20th October, 1341 (Reg. Bury, 347), rector of Worfield, dioc. Lichfield (Willis, i., 175), canon of Southwell, Bath and Wells, Howden, Lincoln, London, etc. In 1343, after his disappointment at York, he had the king's permission to make a pilgrimage to Jerusalem, and was allowed to retain all his preferments (Fœd., ii., 1220-2). He died at Caen on the 20th of July, 1347, after an active life. Robert de Kildesby, canon of South Cave at York, was his brother. Cf. Angl. Sacr., i., 22, 40. Carte's Gascon, etc., Rolls, i., 111.

made. One incident in the programme of that great day was the presence of Hugh, the abbat of Jorevaux, to render his submission to his diocesan.[o]

For two or three years after archbishop Zouche's arrival in the North he seems to have devoted himself entirely to the requirements of his diocese, and it is probable enough that his collision with the king on the question of his appointment was the cause of his being temporarily unoccupied in the service of his country. Before long, however, he had an opportunity of displaying in a pre-eminent degree his patriotism and his valour, There began to be some uneasiness on the Borders, and all eyes were turned towards their troublesome and restless neighbours. In the autumn of 1345 a Scottish army broke into Cumberland and did much mischief, but this foray was only the prelude to a more serious campaign. In the beginning of the following year, when the danger became imminent, the king shewed that he had forgiven the archbishop by making him one of the wardens of the Marches, and Zouche, in his new capacity, was most actively employed.[p] In the month of July Edward went abroad and began his career of victory in France, and, about the same time, David king of Scotland made another raid into Cumberland, but it was not of a grave character. The news of the glorious triumph at Cressy came across the seas to England,[q] but the conqueror's mind was ill at ease when he heard of the attitude which the Scots were assuming. On the 2nd of July the archbishop was ordered to go to the Marches with all his power,[r] and, on the 25th, the king sent his clerk, Richard de Saham, to bring him some news from the Borders. On the 20th of August Edward desired the mayor of York and others to levy men at the oversight of Zouche, Henry lord Percy and Ralph lord Nevill whom he had made commissioners of array.[s] All these precautions were salutary and wise. In the month of October the Scots broke into England with a large army bent upon something more than plunder. They rolled down Tynedale, scattering the inmates of Lanercost and Hexham, and wasting the country as they came. They passed from thence into the bishoprick of Durham, and drew themselves up upon the green hills which overlook the Wear from the west, and within view of the stately towers which still adorn the capital of the palatinate. The news of their arrival had run through York-

[o] MSS. Cotton, Vitellius, A, ii., 112. Reg. Zouche.

[p] Rot. Scot., i., 663, 670. Zouche had given the king great offence, and, as Seneca says in his Medea, "Gravis ira regum est semper."

[q] The king wrote to Zouche announcing the victory. The letter is printed in the Retrospective Review, *n. s.*, i., 120.

[r] Ibid., 672.

[s] Fœd., iii., 87, 89.

shire, and the archbishop, nothing daunted by the peril of the undertaking, immediately took the field. Queen Philippa remained behind at York whilst the primate went forth to the battle,

> "Infula cui sacra redimibat tempora vitta,
> Totus collucens veste atque insignibus armis."

The heads of the great houses of Percy, Mowbray, Neville, Scrope and Rokeby went with him, and an army was soon collected. It rested for awhile at Richmond, and then entered the Bishopric at Barnard castle, under the command of the archbishop. On the night of the 16th of October they were in Auckland park, the troops being divided into three bodies, one of which was led by Zouche.[t] Early on the morning of the 17th he had a sharp skirmish with Sir William Douglas and a troop of horsemen in which the Scots were worsted. On the morrow, the 18th of October, the two armies met on the hills to the west of Durham which look down upon the city. It must have been a striking sight to see the warrior-prelate going among his men, cheering and encouraging them and giving them his benediction. His prayers were heard; for before that day was over the royal invader was a prisoner, and the flower of the chivalry of Scotland was torn and dead. That was a victory which the monks of Durham never afterwards forgot. The chronicler of that noble house has told us a romantic story of what then occurred to them.[u] A vision is said to have warned the prior and his brethren to be present at the fight, but they were not in warlike guise, with spear and panoply and sword. They elevated on a spear one of their most precious relics, the corporax cloth of St. Cuthbert, and, fearless of injury or wrong, they went to pray for their countrymen in the middle of the battle.

> "—The prior of Durham with holy hand
> Raised, as the vision gave command,
> Saint Cuthbert's relic—far and near
> Kenned on the point of a lofty spear."

Some sacred influence seemed to hover around the suppliants, for the foemen touched them not. They would hear the ringing shouts around them, the cries of the vanquisher and the wounded. They could see, when they looked up, the ebb and the flow of the fight, until at length the enemy was pushed off the green rounded hills, among which they stood, and driven in

[t] For an account of the battle, etc., see Chron. Lan., 346, etc.; Knyghton, col. 2590; Stubbs, col. 1732; Lel. Coll., ii., 470. Murimuth (177) and the Monk of Malmesbury (250) say that the battle was chiefly won by the York clergy. Walsingham, 167. Minot's Poems, 39-44. Arch. Æliana, *n. s.* Hardyng's Chron., *n. e.*, 328. Galf. le Baker, 172. Avesbury, 145. Fordun, ii., 341.

[u] Rites of Durham, ed. Surtees Soc., 20-5, 50. Hist. Dunelm. Scr. Tres, appendix, 434-5. Durham Wills, 29-30.

wild confusion towards the North. With what joy and gratitude would the delighted monks welcome the conquerors when they returned to them! They would lead them down the narrow pass which opened out into the city, and there before the sacred shrine the knees of the wearied soldier were bent in thankful acknowledgment of his triumph. It was probably the first time that archbishop Zouche entered that stately temple. When he visited it again he would see the trophies of the battle which he had done so much to win, the famous black rood of Scotland, and the banners of the slain or captured nobles waving over St. Cuthbert's shrine.

The disgrace of archbishop Melton's defeat at Myton was now wiped out, and Zouche had won for himself not only commendation for his energy and patriotism, but the reputation of a successful general. He sent his valet, William de Hugate, to the king with the news of the victory,[v] and Edward was profuse in his thanks and praises. He begs the archbishop to continue his hitherto successful care in guarding the Marches. The monarch speaks, in a spirit characteristic of that noble age, of the mercies that had been vouchsafed to him, how thankful he was for God's goodness, of which he was unworthy.[w] The cloud which had hung between Edward and Zouche seems now to have been removed. On the 10th of December the king requested the archbishop and several of the great men in the North to give him their presence and their advice at Westminster, where the war might be discussed,[x] and, on the 18th of November, 1350, he shewed his especial favour to the Northern primate by condoning all his past shortcomings on account of his great services, particularly in the battle of Durham.[y] This concession is partly, no doubt, of a general character, but it also has reference to the offence which Zouche had given to Edward when he was elected to the see of York.

The archiepiscopal career of Zouche was not a long one, but it was signalized by activity and a painstaking attention to his duties. His was essentially a reign of peace, and no controversy seems to have disturbed it.[z] He received a subsidy from his

[v] On Dec. 11 the king orders him a reward of 10*l.* (Fœd., iii., 98). Some two or three prisoners who had been captured in the battle fell to the archbishop's share, and there is some correspondence about them in Fœd., iii., 95, 105; Rot. Scot., i., 687.

[w] Fœd., iii., 91-2. Rot. Scot., i., 675.

[x] Fœd., iii., 97. Rot. Scot., i., 679. On Sept. 5, 1348, the king desired Zouche "procurationes cardinalium colligere" (Fœd., iii., 170), and on March 1, 1351, he was asked to convoke his clergy, and obtain from them a subsidy in aid of the French war (ibid., 214).

[y] Cal. Rot. Pat., 160. Fœd., iii., 210.

[z] Feb. 18, 1343, commission to Mr. Thomas Sampson, jur. civ. prof. and official, John de Aton, canon of Lincoln, and Robert de Askeby, our domestic chaplain and rector of Washing-

clergy on his accession to office, and, at the same time, he requested the heads of the various religious houses within his diocese to give a benefice to some poor clerk. The register of the see during this period mentions the establishment of a large number of chantries and the appropriation of many livings. It also contains the following entries.

1342. On the Sunday after All Saint's day, the archbishop, at the request of the king, grants a pension of 100s. per annum to Reginald de Donynton,[a] clerk, till he can provide him with a benefice. Nov. 17. An order to the receiver at York to pay, at the oversight of William de Popelton, the money required to repair our houses at York to be ready for our installation banquet.[b]

1343, June 15. To the nine canons in residence at York two oaks each and their fagots, from our wood of Langwath. August 4. Bull of Clement VI. denouncing Louis, duke of Bavaria, as an enemy of God and an excommunicated heretic.[c] August 27. An order to pray for fine weather.[d]

1344, July 18. Ralph, bishop of Lethlyn,[e] appointed suffragan. Oct 21. Licence to John de Stafford, rector of St. Michael's, Ousebridge, York, to be absent for a year in the service of the earl of Derby. Nov. 10. To Thomas Wadilove, the runner of our treasurer at York, a stipend of a penny a day.

1345, Jan. 21. To Mr. Robert de Askeby and John de Sutton, clerk, our domestic chaplains, their expenses whilst absent on the business of our mint. June 23. A mandate to pray for the king and his army.

1346, April 17. Licence to the abbat of St. Mary's, York, to hear the confessions of his monks. June 26. A general sentence against those who have entered Aberford church and killed John de Byngham, clerk, whilst he was on his knees

ton in the diocese of Durham, to treat with the archbishop of Canterbury "super bajulatione crucis." In Zouche's Register, 253-4, are some statutes made at a synod at York.

[a] In 1347 the king presented him to the stall of Barnby at York, and he died holding it in 1349. Cf. Fœd., ii., 988, 1060. In 1325 Reginald de Donington was sheriff of Lincolnshire (Parl. Writs, ii., part i., 339).

[b] On the 9th of February the receiver, Mr. William de Wirkesworth, was desired to pay for the provision that had been made for the banquet, at the oversight of John de Thorp "dilecti clerici nostri."

[c] Cf. Chron. Lanercost, 253, 304, etc. Knyghton, col. 2553, 2565. Murimuth, 60. The duke was mixed up with the affairs of the anti-pope and was made emperor. Barnes's Edward III., 410. Cf. Baronii Ann., Raynaldi, xxiv.

[d] On Oct. 24, 1345, the chapter of York grant an indulgence of forty days to those who pray for the removal of the "aëris intemperies" (Acta Capit., Ebor.).

[e] Another commission to him on Sept. 10. The archbishop gives him a pension of 40 marks per annum and the fees. Jan. 20, 1344-5, 10 marks to him for his salary.

praying. August 9. An order to pray for the king and his army going to France.[f]

1347, May 3. To Mr. Thomas Sampson, official of the court of York, 50*l*. for his fee.[g] October 5. Licence for Simon de Stowe, rector of a moiety of the church of S.M. Castlegate, York, to be absent in the service of dame Joan Fitzwauter, lady of Egremont.

1348, Feb. 21. Commission to John de Coniston, a Carmelite friar, to hear the confessions of Sir John de Haryngton, knight, and his wife.[h] March 5. Hugh, archbishop of Damascus, is appointed suffragan with a pension of 40 marks per annum and the fees.[i] April 11. Letters testimonial to a marriage between Robert de Swylington and Avora, daughter of Sir Stephen Waleys, knight, deceased. They were contracted on the Monday before the feast of St. Thomas the Apostle, 1347, in the house of Thomas Basy in Micklegate, York, and were afterwards publicly married. May 11. Sentence against those who have hindered the procession at Southwell on the feast of Pentecost, coming up to the high altar with swords, clubs, etc. June 11. The feast of St. Bartholomew: the provost and scholars of Queen's college, Oxford, put themselves under the protection of the archbishop and his successors.[j] July 28. An order to pray for the removal of the mortality and infection of the air.[k]

1349, Feb. 4. A commission to the official of the archdeacon of York to hear confessions, on account of the mortality and pestilence in various parts of our diocese. April 28. Mandate to the bishops of Carlisle, Durham, Whitherne, etc., to publish the letters of the pope about the indulgence on behalf of the mortality. June 26. Commission to Hugh, archbishop of Damascus, to dedicate the cemeteries of the chapels of Egton and St. Thomas near Beverley. July 10. To dedicate in haste, on account of the pestilence, the chapel and cemetery of St. Oswald at Fulford. July 15. The cemetery and chapel of

[f] The year of the famous battle of Cressy.

[g] Feb. 13, 1350, a similar sum to the official, Mr. Gilbert de Welton, doctor of laws.

[h] There are many other licences for the friars to hear confessions and preach. On Nov. 16, 1348, Hugh de Warmesby, a Friar Minor of Doncaster, was authorized to act as confessor to dame Margery de Hastinges and her family for a year.

[i] There are other commissions to him dated on June 5, 1349, Jan. 27, 1349-50, and March 4th, 1351-2. March 6, 1347-8, a payment of 10 marks to him in part payment of his salary. On August 27, 1344, Simon, bishop of Whitherne, made his obedience to the archbishop at Cawood. There is an interesting notice of archbishop Hugh in the Fœd., iii., 229.

[j] This college will be mentioned afterwards.

[k] There is a dreadful account of this pestilence in Knyghton, col. 2598, etc.; Murimuth, 178; Walsingham, 168; Fœd., iii., 198, where it is said that a great part of the people, especially the operatives and servants, died of the plague.

Cleseby par. Staynwegges. July 17. The cemetery at Wilton. July 23. The chapel and cemetery of Semer par. Rudby, and the chapel of Brotton par. Skelton. August 1. The cemetery of the chapel of Barton par. Gilling, to be used during the pestilence, and, on August 7, the chapel of Eseby par. Stokesley.[l]

1350, Feb. 20. To John de Acome, canon of St. Sepulchre's chapel, York, 20*l.* for our business in the court of Rome. Feb. 27. To Sir Henry Percy, sen., 50 marks for his fee. April 9. To Sir Thomas de Rokeby, knight, late sheriff of Yorkshire,[m] 20*l.* July 24. Licence of non-residence for a year to William Neuport, rector of Arncliff,[n] in the service of lord Percy.

1351, Jan. 7. A letter to the chapter of York enjoining them to make Roger de Ledes, a vicar-choral, do penance for drawing blood from a clerk of the cathedral in the minster. Feb. 5. Licence for John de Chesterfield,[o] rector of Foston, to be absent from his benefice for 2 years in the service of Sir William la Pole, knight. June 7. To John de Flete of York 44 marks of

[l] Stubbs (col. 1732) tells us that the plague began at Michaelmas. In 1349 there was a great mortality in the city of York, which continued till St. James's day. Avesbury (257) says,

"Mors prima communis MC ter L minus uno."

The scourge, it will be seen, extended to the most remote and the healthiest villages in the county of York. These orders for the consecration of cemeteries tell a sad tale. Cf. Galf. le Baker, 189. Fordun, ii., 347. The clergy suffered very severely (Statutes of the Realm, i., 378).

[m] Sir Thomas Rokeby of Rokeby, sheriff of Yorkshire 1337, 1343-50 (Drake, 352), a great soldier, and one of the leaders at Neville's cross. For an account of him see Scrope and Grosvenor Roll, ii., 308-9. In 1327 he brought Edward III. in sight of the Scots at Stanhope park (Fœd., ii., 717. Barnes's Edward III., 12. Œconomia Rokebeiorum).

[n] A retainer of the noble house of Percy. Rector of Arncliffe 1349, which he gave up for Spofforth. This he exchanged in 1359 for the rectory of Bishopwearmouth, co. Durham. In 1362 he again acquired the living of Spofforth, and was allowed to hold that of Bishopwearmouth with it. In 1365 he gave up Spofforth for the prebend of Ulleskelf at York (Reg. Zouche and Thoresby. Reg. Hatfield, at Durham, 43, 52, 58). Newport died in 1366, and his will is in Test. Ebor., i., 80. A chantry was founded for him at the altar of St. Gregory in York minster (Fabric Rolls, 284).

The love of non-residence was increasing. The words of Piers Ploughman may appropriately be cited :—

"Parsons and parisshe preestes
Pleyned hem to the bisshope,
That hire parisshes weren pouere
Sith the pestilence tyme,
To have a licence and leve
At London to dwelle.
* * *
Some serven the kyng,
And his silver tellen
In cheker and in chauncelrie,
Chalangen hise dettes
Of wardes and of wardemotes,
Weyves and streyves.
And somme serven as servauntz
Lords and ladies,
And in stede of stywardes
Sitten and demen
Hire messe and hire matyns
And many of hire houres
Arn doon un-devout licke."

[o] The king's chaplain. Canon of Grendale at York. Ordained accolite, sub-deacon and deacon in 1349, being then rector of Pleslay and Foston (Reg. Zouche). He had leave to be non-resident at Foston in 1352, 1353, and 1361. Chesterfield was prebendary of St. Stephen's, Westminster, 1348-58 (Newcourt, i., 747), and canon of Chalk at Wilton, dioc. Sarum (Phillips's Wiltshire Incumbents, 40).

silver for wines bought of him. Sept. 6. The archbishop orders the use of a new service in honour of the Virgin, and others for the translation of St. Thomas of Hereford and St. Ambrose.[p] Oct. 4. A letter against the begging friars, ordering them not to seek alms in the churches "libris apertis more quæstus." Dec. 11. Commission to William, bishop of Sodor and Man, to celebrate orders.

1352, Feb. 1. A mandate to pray for Henry, duke of Lancaster, who is going abroad against the enemies of the faith and cross.[q] March 9. General letter against those who have dragged William de Echardeby from sanctuary at Wetheral. April 11. Licence to the dean of Pontefract to exhume the bodies of three men interred in the churchyard of All Saints, Pontefract, who were condemned by the justices, and to inter them "in loco de Sancto Victore," near the town, which is said to be dedicated, where it has been the custom to bury criminals who have been hung. May 6. Commission to William de Bokenham, prior of the Carmelites at Coventry, to wash away with holy water a stain of blood in Beverley minster. May 7. Licence for Thomas de Percy,[r] rector of Catton, to be non-resident for two years to study. May 14. An acquittance to William de Newport, rector of Arncliffe, an executor of the will of Sir Henry de Percy, sen., knight, for a horse called Lyarde de Patrington, in our hands at the time of our decease, as a mortuary on account of the church of Catton, and also for a gold ring with a stone called an *emeraude*;[s]' and, on the same day, the executors release the archbishop from the pension of 100 marks granted by him to the said Henry, the archbishop paying 100*l.* for all arrears.

For some time before his death archbishop Zouche was afflicted with a very serious bodily infirmity, and it was the

[p] Both to be with *Novem Lectiones*, and the hymn *Salvator, mundi domine*, to be said on each double festival instead of that *Te lucis ante terminum*. On Feb. 11, 1343-4, the archbishop makes some alterations in the services for the feast of the Conception B.M.V., Good Friday, and the feast of St. Martha. They are to be specially kept.

[q] Zouche calls him "regni Angliæ membrum nobile et columpna una." Whilst on his way to Palestine, he was arrested at Cologne by the emissaries of Otho, duke of Brunswick. This originated a duel, which will soon be alluded to (Barnes's Edward III., 465). He was called the good duke of Lancaster, and was a famous warrior.

[r] March 31, 1352, inst. in rect. de Catton, "ad pres. regis, custodis terrarum patris tui dom. Henrici de Percy." On June 17, the pope allowed him to hold a stall at Chester-le-street, he being then but 19, in respect for Edward III. and Isabella his mother, Percy being their cousin (Reg. Zouche). Percy was bishop of Norwich from 1355 to 1369 (Le Neve, ii., 464-5. Test. Vet., i., 84).

[s] In his will made in Sept., 1349, Henry, lord Percy, leaves the archbishop 100 marks, which he owes him, and "unum annulum pontificalem cum ameraude" (Test. Ebor., i., 61), and he bequeaths to Sir Ralph Neville "duos bacinos quos dominus archiepiscopus mihi dedit."

consciousness of its presence and the recollection of the perils from which he had escaped, that induced him, we may believe, to make the last disposition of his worldly substance and commit himself into the hands of his God. His will is dated at Ripon on the 28th of June, 1349, and seems from internal evidence to have been drawn up in one of those blessed intervals of health which sick persons are occasionally permitted to enjoy. There is little in the document to interest my readers, indeed it seems to have been prepared for the special purpose of securing the foundation of a chantry. The testator simply directs his remains to be interred within his cathedral, and leaves the sum of 300 marks for the establishment of a perpetual chantry in York minster, which is to be served by two chaplains who are to do service for his soul, and it is to be dedicated to God, his mother the Blessed Virgin, All Saints, and especially to SS. Mary Magdalene and Martha. The remainder of his estate is left to the disposition of his executors, Ralph lord Neville of Raby, Sir Roger Zouche, knight, his brother, Sir Marmaduke Constable, Sir William de Place and Sir Christopher Mallory, knights, Mr. Gilbert de Welton, William de Ferriby and Roger de Stiendby, clerks, and Anketil Mallory, esq., the two last being placed in the most responsible position, as nothing is to be done by the executors without their cognizance. There is an allusion in the will to the archbishop's parents, which shews that they were then alive.[t]

The erection of this chantry, although mentioned in the archbishop's will, was not altogether left to the care of his executors. The founder began the building of it himself. He wished it to be contiguous to the south wall of the choir, without detracting in any way from the beauty of that part of the fabric, and he was desirous, as the best means of carrying this into effect, that the master-mason at the minster should have the management of the work. It is pleasing to observe the affectionate way in which the consent of the chapter of York was sought for and granted. They speak to each other with the kind and touching sympathy of old friends, and in those words, few although they are, the melancholy conviction seems to be expressed that their intercourse in this world would ere long be at an end.[u]

The erection of the chapel seems to have been begun in 1350,[v] and it was the founder's intention to have been laid in it,

[t] Printed at length in Test. Ebor., i., 5-78.

[u] York Fabric Rolls, ed. Surtees Society, 168-9.

[v] Nov. 16, 1350, Roberto de Swetmouth, rectori alt. S. Laurencii in eccl. cath. Ebor., 40*l.* pro diversis expensis circa constructionem capellæ nostræ ibidem. April 25, 1351, a similar sum for the same purpose, to John de Acome,

but before it was completed he was called away to his account. He died at Cawood on the 19th of July, 1352, and on the 8th of August he was interred before the altar of St. Edward, in the nave, hard by the remains of his predecessor archbishop Melton.[w] When Stubbs wrote his chronicle, no monument had been erected to commemorate him; "a proof," as the historian sarcastically observes, "of the noble disposition of his parents and of those whom he had benefitted exceedingly." But he needs no memorial of that kind, when you gaze upon that glorious nave with its triumphs of sculpture and of art, which the prelate, who is now sleeping beneath your feet, once assisted in creating!

The chapel which archbishop Zouche began was probably completed after his death; but its subsequent history is involved in mystery and doubt. Within eight years after his decease the rebuilding of the eastern portion of the cathedral commenced; and as the Norman choir was gradually removed, the chapel which was appended to it could not occupy the same position. The new choir was wider than its predecessor, and the archbishop's chapel, therefore, must have been taken down. After that time no trace whatever of the chantry has occurred to me. There might possibly be some difficulty about the rebuilding, and the chapter may have appropriated the endowment to that purpose; perhaps the executors of Zouche's will were as careless of their trust as they were of erecting a memorial over their benefactor's grave, and the endowment was neglected. The present office of the chapter clerk, which was at one time the vestry of the cathedral, is supposed to be Zouche's chapel; at all events it cannot be far from the position which that building originally occupied. At the east end there are still traces of an altar and its accompaniments, but their presence in this place proves but little, as we know that the service was transferred for awhile from the minster to the vestry in 1394. The room is now the depository of the records of the dean and chapter, which remind me of the courteous attention that laid them open to me, and of the many long hours that have been spent upon their pages. The labours of past years, which have filled these volumes, rise

canon in the chapel of the B.V.M. and the Holy Angels. Nov. 18, 1351, another sum of 40*l.* to Swetmouth and Acome. On May 10, 1352, the account of the two is passed. They are called "custodes novæ fabricæ capellæ nostræ juxta latus australe ecclesiæ nostræ cathedralis Ebor. noviter inchoatæ." The account runs from April 23, 1350, to April 28, 1352, and they have spent 25*l.* 9s. 7d. more than they received.

[w] Stubbs, col. 1732. Acta Capit. Ebor. His end is thus described in the metrical chronicle of the archbishops of York in MSS. Cotton, Cleopatra, C, iv.:—

"Hic Willelmus pontifex anno suo nono
Quievit a laboribus suis fine bono,
Apud villam propriam Cawod vocitatam,
Eboracus habuit glebam tumulatam."

vividly before the writer when he accidentally finds himself on this scene of his exertions,

> "And as a hare whom hounds and horns pursue,
> Pants to the place from whence at first he flew."

On the 2nd of April, 1353, archbishop Thoresby empowered Mr. William de la Mare and John de Wodehouse, canons of York, John de Crakhall, doctor of decrees, and Adam de Twysilton, commissary general, to enquire into the dilapidations of the houses and woods belonging to the see, and into the damages done by the executors of his predecessor. This strengthens the inference that there was some neglect of duty on the part of those officials.

John de Thoresby was one of those great and good men who were the glory of the fourteenth century. That was indeed, in every respect, an illustrious age. Whilst the chivalry of England was winning renown in the wars in France, every liberal art was being fostered and cherished at home, and John de Thoresby stood in the front rank of that band of worthies who signalized themselves by their taste and learning. It is with a feeling almost akin to veneration that I look back upon his many services to his country, his pious zeal and his open-handed munificence.

We are indebted to a scion of the family of Thoresby, in a later age, for an account of his ancient house of which he was so proud. The name of honest Ralph Thoresby, the Leeds antiquary, would be a credit to any pedigree in Yorkshire. There is a little hamlet of the name of Thoresby hard by the well-known castle of Middleham in Wensleydale, and there, in all probability, it was that the archbishop of York was born. His father, Hugh de Thoresby, was the owner of the place, and his mother was Isabel, daughter of Sir Thomas Grose of Suffolk.[x]

[x] Thoresby's Vicaria Leodiensis, 185, etc., where there is a life of the archbishop. Ducatus Leodiensis, ed. Whitaker, 69. Diary, i., 225, 366. Thoresby gives an engraving of a figure of the archbishop taken from a window in the minster. He is holding a church in his right hand.

The following persons were, no doubt, related to the archbishop, but in what degree I cannot say.

Richard de Thoresby, incumbent of Bugbrooke, Northants, 1348-9, and rector of Oundle 1352 (Bridges's Northants, i., 487; ii., 408). May 16, 1355, coll. preb. at St. Andrew's altar, Beverley, exchanging for it with Thomas de Helwell, his prebend of Hatherdon in the chapel at Wolverhampton (Reg. Thoresby). June 25, 1355, collated by the archbishop to the free chapel of Ferrybridge, which, on July 2nd, he

Far be it from me to question a genealogy of which a herald of some note has said, "In my opinion, I never saw any descent so well travelled, nor so truly set down." It would ill become me to differ from the decision of my *compater*,[y] and the illustrious authorities by which he is supported.

John de Thoresby was probably induced to take up the profession which he adopted, by the good fortune of his uncle Peter, who held several important offices in the bishoprick of

exchanged with John de Donyngton for the stall of Sharow at Ripon (ibid.). There is a letter extant from the archbishop in behalf of his cousin, Richard de Thoresby, canon of Beverley, "super travis sibi debitis," in MSS. Cotton, Galba, E, x., 80. On May 12, 1350, there is an order from the king to Richard de Thoresby, keeper of the hanaper of the chancery, to pay for him certain monies (Fœd., iii., 106).

John de Thoresby, doctor of laws, instituted on Oct. 24, 1353, to the rectory of Lilford (Bridges's Northants, ii., 242), which he resigned in 1373 for the provostship of Beverley (MSS. Harl., 6952, 6). On Dec. 7, 1367, he was admitted on the authority of the pope to the stall of Grendale at York, and on 19th of December, 1369, he exchanged his stall of Offley at Lichfield with Mr. John Turke for the prebend of Nunwick at Ripon (Reg. Thoresby). On August 20, 1360, he and others were appointed to treat with David Brus (Fœd., iii., 506). The archbishop wrote to the bishop of Lincoln asking him to grant a licence of non-residence to his kinsman, John de Thoresby, rector of Lilleford, "ad scolas" (MSS. Cotton, Galba, E, x., 85). He was one of the archbishop's executors (Test. Ebor., i., 90).

Elias de Thoresby, on Nov. 7, 1361, exchanged the hospital of Bawtry with John de Grantham for a stall in St. Sepulchre's chapel at York. On May 26, 1362, he exchanged his rectory of Northcoles, dioc. Lincoln, with the same person for the rectory of S. Trin., Goodramgate, York. On Feb. 9, 1362,3, he exchanged the last-mentioned living for that of St. Dennis in Walmgate, which, on July 10, 1367, he exchanged for the rectory of Gamelston, Notts. This he again exchanged on Nov. 27 for the rectory of Weston. On Aug. 2, 1371, he was collated to a stall in St. Sepulchre's chapel, York (Reg. Thoresby). On December 16, 1391, Elias de Thoresby, rector of Weston, makes his will, desiring to be buried in the church of Weston. He leaves 7 marks to be given to the poor on the day of his burial, and 10 marks for the expenses of the funeral and the entertainment for his neighbours, besides the corn and malt and everything that can be provided at the rectory. To the fabric of the church of York he leaves 20s., and he leaves 40*l*. to three chaplains who are to celebrate for him at Weston. To William Thoresby he gives 40s. To the fabric of the bell-tower of Weston church, 20s. To John, rector of Wilford, a silver cup with a cover. To the prior of Bridlington, two silver cups. To the prisoners at Lincoln, 40s. He appoints as executors, John, rector of Wilford, John, vicar of Wheatley, John Golias, chaplain, and Robert de Thoresby. The will is dated at Stretton, and was proved at York on Jan. 14, *seq.*, Thoresby, one of the executors, renouncing (Reg. Arundel).

William de Thoresby, rector of a moiety of the church of Cotgrave, made his will on Friday, the feast of S.S. Vitus and Modestus, 1347. To be buried in the cemetery of the church of All Saints at Cotgrave. To Juliana, his sister, 5 marks. To Isold, his sister, 10 marks. To John, son of Beatrix de Thoresby, 40s. and 10 ewes. To his brother John, 20s. To his brother Adam, a horse, etc., at Thoresby. Pr. June 21, 1347 (Reg. Zouche).

In 1344 *John de Thoresby*, a friar preacher, was ordained priest at Newark (Reg. Zouche). On July 20, 1349, John, son of Cecily de Thoresby, was collated, at the presentation of the king, to the living of Aldwalby, and died in 1355 (MSS. Harl., 6951, 110 *b*.)

[y] Mr. Surtees, in his History of Durham, iv., 94.

Durham, in addition to the rectory of Aysgarth in his native vale.[z] The young Yorkshireman went to Oxford, where he became a scholar of repute and a great lawyer.[a] His learning and his energy soon made for him a pathway through the world. He became beneficed in Yorkshire, being instituted whilst he was merely an accolite, on the 15th of October, 1320, to the living of Bramwith on the presentation of Thomas, earl of Lancaster. We know not to what extent the youthful clerk was interested in the fortunes of that ill-fated nobleman, but we soon find him connected with archbishop Melton, and he was made one of the members of that prelate's household who were in close attendance upon his person. In 1326 he was receiver of the archbishop's chamber and a domestic chaplain, an office which he filled in the autumn of 1328. In 1327 he went in his master's behalf to the court of Rome, and, in 1334, he is described as his attorney, being evidently a person wise in counsel and learned in the law.[b] He became a great ecclesiastical advocate and a proctor to the papal court, an employment to which he was indebted for his reputation and his advancement.

Thoresby soon became possessed of high clerical preferment, and archbishop Melton was not his only patron. A clever and an active lawyer would gain many friends. Between 1325 and 1335 he was incumbent of Honington in Warwickshire.[c] On the 17th of June, 1327, he was admitted by archbishop Melton, on the provision of the pope, to the next vacant prebend at Southwell, which seems to have been that of Norwell Overhall, which he was holding in 1329.[d] In August, 1335, he resigned his stall in the chapel of St. Sepulchre at York.[e] In March 1338-9 he occurs as archdeacon of London.[f] On the 4th of January, 1339-40, I find him, as rector of Elwick in the diocese of Durham, making a grant of a messuage near his church to the priory of Tynemouth, and in the spring of the following year he resigned the mastership of the hospital of St. Edmund at Gateshead.[g] On the 22nd of May, 1340, the king appointed

[z] Rector of Aysgarth, a son of Hugh de Thoresby, and the archbishop's uncle (Ducatus Leodiensis, 69). Temporal chancellor of Durham in 1289, and constable of Durham castle (MSS. Surtees, ined.). Master of Kepier hospital in 1311 (Reg. Kellawe). Cf. Abbrev. Rot. Orig., i., 38).

[a] Vicaria Leodiensis, 189. A *dirige* was performed for him at Oxford on penult. Feb. (Avesbury, 302). Bale, cent. vi., 493. Godwin (687) says that Thoresby was a great benefactor of the University of Cambridge. He must mean Oxford.

[b] Reg. Melton.

[c] Dugdale's Warwickshire, *n. e.*, 427. He appropriated this living on Feb. 25, 1350-1, to the priory of Coventry (Thomas's Worcester, 180).

[d] Reg. Melton. Le Neve, iii., 437. Plac. de Quo Warr., 648.

[e] Reg. Melton.

[f] Le Neve, ii., 320. Did he ever enjoy it?

[g] Reg. Bury at Durham, 321 *b*,

him to the stall of South Muskham at Southwell,[h] and he is said to have held that of Warthill at York in 1343,[i] but I have seen no documentary evidence of the fact. On the 29th of September, 1343, he was instituted to the rectory of Oundle, Northants, which he held till 1347.[j] In 1343 he resigned the living of Sibbesdon in the same county.[k] He was prebendary of (Thorngate at) Lincoln in July, 1345, when the pope wrote to inform him that he had advanced Thomas Lisle to the see of Ely.[l]

Thoresby, it will be observed, was indebted to Edward III. for more than one piece of preferment. We know not when he was first introduced to that monarch's notice, but it is probable that his abilities as a lawyer were the cause of his rapid advance in honours and position. He seems to have been the king's proctor in the court of Rome, and to have won the good opinion of all with whom he was connected by his diplomatic skill and his integrity. On the 7th of March, 1330, Edward sent a letter by Thoresby to the pope and cardinals, begging for the canonization of his father's foe, Thomas, earl of Lancaster,[m] who had given the ambassador his first living. In 1336 Thoresby's friendly relations with the pope were imperilled by a singular adventure. A summons to appear before the pope on some question of appeal was served upon him in open court in England; the papal messengers were at once thrown into prison as guilty of a contempt, and were only set free when queen Philippa interceded in their behalf.[n] This seems to have done Thoresby no permanent injury, as on the 16th of March, 1340, he went again to the papal court to procure a dispensation for a marriage which was to take place between Hugh le Despenser and a daughter of the earl of Salisbury.[o] In the same year he was a trier of the petitions which were presented to the parliament from England and Flanders,[p] and he is said to have gone as one of the royal envoys to Rome on the question of a peace with France.[q] On the 21st of February in the following year he was appointed master of the rolls, and he held that office till the month of July, 1346.[r] In 1343 and 1345 he had the temporary charge of the great seal of England.[s] In 1344 he was

340 *b*. On March 1, 1340-1, Mr. Walter Faucomberg was presented to the hospital of St. Edmund at Gateshead, then vacant by the resignation of Mr. John de Thoresby. Mr. Gibson, in his Tynemouth Priory, gives a different date to this grant to that house (i., 149).

[h] Le Neve, iii., 431.

[i] Ibid., iii., 220.

[j] MSS. Harl., 6951, 103 *b*. Bridges's Northants, ii., 408.

[k] MSS. Harl., *ut supra*.

[l] Fœd., iii., 55. He was canon of Lincoln in 1347 (Le Neve, ii., 222).

[m] Fœd., ii., 782.

[n] Foss's Judges, iii., 523.

[o] Fœd., ii., 1119.

[p] Rot. Parl., ii., 112.

[q] Barnes's Edward III., 207.

[r] Dugd. Chron., 45. Newcourt, i., 339. Fœd., ii., 1151. Le Neve, i., 294.

[s] Cal. Rot. Pat., 146. Fœd., ii., 1231; iii., 53. Carte's Gascon, etc.,

sent to the pope to tell him how the truce with France had been broken.[t] In 1345 he was present when John, duke of Brittany, did homage to the king.[u] On the 25th of November, in the same year, Clement VI. addressed him in a friendly letter in which he besought him to assist with all his energies the two cardinals who were coming to England in the vain hope of preserving the peace between that country and France.[v] In 1345 and 1346 Thoresby had the charge of the privy seal,[w] and in the latter year he was variously employed. I find that he was one of the collectors of the quindisme, and on the 8th of September he was one of those who were desired to announce the king's wishes to the parliament. On the 22nd of October he was made one of the commissioners who were appointed to treat with France at the instance of the pope and cardinals, and Clement wrote to him a letter full of gratitude for his services in the cause of peace.[x] They had been attended hitherto by little success. The crowning victory at Cressy, which had just been won, scattered the pride and the hopes of the chivalry of France, and was a bitter mortification to the chief pontiff and the court of which he was the centre. Ten years after this, after the defeat at Poictiers, which the cardinal of Périgord had done his utmost to avert, some wag wrote the following verses in which he treated with derision the partizanship of the pope:—

"Ore est le pape devenu Franceys
E Jesu devenu Engleys,
Ore serra veou qe fra plus,
Ly pape ou Jesus."[y]

In 1347 Clement VI. shewed his regard for Thoresby by appointing him bishop of St. David's. The king gave him the temporalities on the 14th of July, and he was consecrated on the 23rd of September.[z] There is nothing known of what he did in his Welch bishoprick, but we hear of Thoresby in another character and in a more conspicuous position. In the year in which he was elevated to the episcopal bench he was in attendance upon the king at Calais with ninety-nine persons in his retinue,[a] and he, no doubt, took part in the stirring incidents of that romantic siege. On the 16th of June, 1349, Thoresby had a still loftier step, for he was raised to the woolsack as lord chancellor of England.[b] On the 4th of September in that year

Rolls., i., 114. Kalendars and Inv. of the Exchequer, i., 158, 160.
[t] Barnes' Edward III., 313. Foss's Judges, iii., 523.
[u] Fœd., iii., 39.
[v] Ibid., 64.
[w] Ibid., iii., 53, 86.
[x] Fœd., iii., 89, 92. Rot. Parl., ii., 160.
[y] Knyghton, col. 2615.
[z] Le Neve, i., 294. Jones and Freeman's History of St. David's, 303.
[a] Vicaria Leodiensis, 189.
[b] Le Neve, i., 294.

a papal bull translated him from St. David's to Worcester, and the temporalities were restored to him on the 10th of January, and the spiritualities on the 11th.[c] The duties of his office in the state delayed his enthronization until the 12th of September, 1351,[d] and Thoresby's connection with Worcester must have been brief and unsatisfactory. He was destined to fill a higher and a more honourable position. The Northern primacy was vacant in 1352 by the decease of archbishop Zouche, and on the 25th of July the king desired the chapter to proceed to the election[e] of his successor. With one voice they fixed upon Thoresby, and sent Gilbert de Welton to acquaint him with their decision and to urge him to assent to their postulation which had been forwarded to the pope. He gave them his reply from London on the 6th of September, and his letter is couched in that graceful and flowing Latinity which Thoresby had always at his command. He expresses his extreme surprise at the intimation which he has received, and wonders that the electors have passed over better men among their own body. Without giving them a decisive reply, he is profuse in his expressions of gratitude and longs for an opportunity to shew his kindly feeling towards his benefactors and their church. At the same time Thoresby seems to have despatched another letter to his patron Clement VI., desiring his advice. He thanks him for his past goodness to him in raising him to two sees in succession, and, mentioning what has occurred, he refers the matter to the pope's judgment. He will abide altogether by his decision, relying upon that kindness which has so often been shewn to him. The letter was one with which Clement would be pleased, and no one could better appreciate the merits of the writer. The wishes of the chapter of York were acceded to. The pope, however, appointed Thoresby of his own right, and not as the person postulated by the electors. Clement wrote from Avignon on the 22nd of October, 1352,[f] and the temporalities were restored by the king on the 8th of February.[g] Thoresby, it will be remembered, was at this time chancellor of England, and was unable to disengage himself from the official claims upon his time. On this plea he made William de la Mare his vicar-general in the diocese of York, on the 20th of January, 1352-3. Like many of his predecessors, Thoresby was in want of money at his accession to his new dignity, and

[c] Ibid., iii., 57-8.

[d] Thomas's Worcester, 180. Anglia Sacra, i., 534-5.

[e] On July 20 the chapter write to the king to say that Zouche died on the 19th, and to ask for leave to choose his successor. A meeting for that purpose was held on August 16 (Acta Capit. Ebor.).

[f] Printed in the appendix to Thomas's History of Worcester, 116-19. The bull is in Fœd., iii., 249. Reg. Thoresby.

[g] Fœd., iii., 251-2. Le Neve, iii., 107.

he complained of his necessities to the pope. The clergy, however, assembled in synod on the 8th of May, and granted their diocesan a very liberal subsidy, the seculars giving him 8d. and the religious 12d. in each mark.[h] The new primate was all the while engaged in the South, and from an order which the king made on the 1st of April that he should bear his cross erect without being molested,[i] we can see that the old quarrel with Canterbury had not yet died out. A few months after this Thoresby turned his face towards the North. On the 8th of September he was solemnly enthroned at York, and the ceremony was witnessed by a great concourse.[j] The archbishop then laid upon the high altar as an offering a small gilt crucifix of great value, containing, among other relics, a portion of the true cross. This was returned to him on the 10th of October, that he might have the use of it for the remainder of his life, an engagement having been made that it should be restored after his decease under a penalty of 100*l.*[k]

Thoresby, like a faithful pastor, devoted for the future the greater part of his time to the duties of his diocese, and gradually disentangled himself from all state employments. It was some time, however, before he could release himself, and even after his resignation of office his services were still occasionally required. Men were loath to lose him, for he was one of the most able and most popular statesmen of the day. He was one of the sponsors of Philippa the infant daughter of Lionel duke of Clarence,[l] and Edward III., whom he very faithfully served, held him in high esteem. In 1355 Thoresby was one of the wardens of the cinque ports, and on the 1st of July, when the king was starting on his French campaign, he was made one of the regents of the kingdom during the absence of the sovereign.[m] On the 27th of November, 1356, the archbishop resigned the charge of the great seal, which the king received with many expressions of affection and regret.[n] On the 16th of August, 1357, Thoresby was one of the commissioners appointed to treat with the Scots for the ransom of their king who had been a prisoner since the disaster at Neville's cross in 1346, and the primate was engaged on several occasions in after years in the same tedious negotiations.[o] On the 20th of July, 1359, the

[h] Reg. Thoresby.

[i] Fœd., iii., 257. This date ought, perhaps, to be 1353.

[j] Stubbs, col. 1732.

[k] Fabric Rolls, ed. Surtees Society, 186-7. The treasury of York possessed also of Thoresby's gift, "Una mitra cum appendiciis bene ponderans (ibid., 213).

[l] Hardyng's Chron., *n. e.*, 333.

[m] Fœd., iii., 305. Cal. Rot. Pat., 165.

[n] Fœd., iii., 344. In this year Thoresby begins to hold his ordinations at York himself. It is probable, therefore, that before this he was generally non-resident. The pall seems to have been sent to him from Rome (Stubbs, col. 1732).

[o] Ibid., 365, 367-8, 372, 382, 506, 659. Rot. Scotiæ, i., 809, 864.

king, as a compliment to Thoresby, released his tenants in Hexhamshire from the payment of tenths and other state dues in consequence of the good service which their lord had rendered to his king and country.[p] There is something very touching in the manner in which Edward speaks of his faithful and affectionate subject. He mentions his loyalty and goodness, and the prayers which the trusty prelate had offered up in his behalf to One who is mightier than man. He is now on the brink of old age, and is eager for contemplation and repose, and the good wishes and the blessings of his grateful sovereign are with him in his retirement.[q]

That retirement was merely a new field of duty, holier indeed and more peaceful than that which he had deserted. A good man like Thoresby will find work for himself to do, wherever he may be placed. Great and noble as were his services to the state, we find the striking features of his character still more pleasingly and usefully developed in his attention to his diocese. He was truly great in everything that he attempted. He possessed a very practical mind, a thorough aptitude for business, much energy and zeal, and a very kind and considerate heart. These are qualifications which in any age are almost sure to command success. Honest exertion, aided and set off with habits of personal piety, and modulated by Christian charity, is a noble gift. It was conspicuous in everything that Thoresby did, and gave him an influence over others of which he could scarcely be unconscious. Whenever money and labour were required for others, he was always ready to bestow both without any regard to his own ease or comfort, for he was thoroughly unselfish. It is not often that we find a great statesman and scholar surrendering his country for his flock, and making his intellect subservient to the interests and welfare of his diocese. I shall point out, one by one, the good deeds of the archbishop, and shew with what success he moderated the great Northern province. I shall first regard him in the light of a peacemaker "lites et contentiones ubique delevit."[r] *Μακάριοι οἱ εἰρηνοποιοί.*

The contention about the right to bear the cross erect had been for several centuries a fertile and a painful source of controversy between the Northern and the Southern primates. This Thoresby very happily brought to an end. On the 20th of April, 1352, a meeting took place, at the intervention of the king, in the palace of Westminster, between archbishops Thoresby

[p] Fœd., iii., 436. On June 8, 1355, the archbishop was commissioned to array Hexhamshire (Rot. Scot., i., 777).

[q] There is a letter extant from Thoresby to the king's secretary, in which he asks him to present for him to the king "chariotam cum attilio et sex equis de melioribus quos habemus, et duobus valectis et duobus garcionibus:" he sent them by R(ichard) de R(avenser) (Reg. Neville, part ii., 20).

[r] Stubbs, col. 1733.

and Islip, and the following arrangement was effected. Each primate was to be allowed to carry his cross erect in the province of the other, but, as an acknowledgement for this concession, Thoresby, within the space of two months, and each of his successors within the same period after his election, was to send a knight or a doctor of laws to offer in his name at the shrine of St. Thomas of Canterbury an image of gold of the value of 40*l.*, in the fashion of an archbishop holding a cross or some other jewel. At parliaments and councils the Southern primate, as the tenant of the most ancient and dignified see, was to sit on the right hand of the sovereign on the higher seat with his cross erect, the archbishop of York being on the left. The bearers of that *insigne*, when they met in the open street, were to walk abreast, but in a gateway or a narrow passage the cross of Canterbury was to have the precedence.[s] The pope, also, had his share in the arrangement, and, as Fuller says, "to end old divisions, made a new distinction, primate of all England and primate of England, giving the former to Canterbury, the latter to York. Thus, when two children cry for the same apple, the indulgent father divides it betwixt them, yet so, that he giveth the bigger and better part to the childe that is his darling."[t] It seems rather to me, pace Master Thomas Fuller, to be a distinction without a difference. The papal confirmation was made in 1354,[u] and the king, who must have been delighted at the result, shewed in the same year how highly he was gratified by Thoresby's acquiescence. There is an order for the payment of 7*l.* 8s. 5d. to Richard de Grymesby, goldsmith, for certain images made in honour of St. Thomas of Canterbury, and delivered to John archbishop of York, of the king's gift, for his oblation at Canterbury.[v]

The good offices of archbishop Thoresby were also employed in effecting a reconciliation between the mayor and citizens of York and the abbat and monks of St. Mary's abbey. There had been many disputes between them on the question of boundaries. As early as 1262 there was an affray in which some of the servants of the abbey were killed, and in 1315 and 1316 there was an active and violent renewal of the quarrel. It broke out again soon after Thoresby became archbishop, and a suit was begun in the king's courts. The primate was fortunate enough to allay it, and an agreement was drawn up to prevent any recurrence of the disturbances.[w]

[s] Reg. Laur. Booth, 77 *a*. Printed in the Anglia Sacra, i., 43, 75. The year 1353 is also given as the date of this arrangement. Stubbs, col. 1732. Wilkins, iii., 31, 54.

[t] Church History, book iii., 39.

[u] On Feb. 22 (Anglia Sacra, i., 77).

[v] Pell Records, 161.

[w] Stubbs, col. 1733. Drake's Eboracum, 581, 597.

I shall now gather some flowers from the archbishop's official acts.

1352. An order to the official at Worcester to solicit the prayers of the faithful in behalf of Henry duke of Lancaster, who is to be at Paris on the 4th of December to prove his innocence and the justice of his cause in a single combat with the duke of Brunswick.[x]

1353, April 11. A licence of non-residence for three years to Stephen Maulyon,[y] rector of Sandal, in the suite of the queen. May 4. Licence to Sir John Meaux, knight, to have the bones of Godfrey Meaux his great-grandfather, John Meaux his grandfather, Godfrey Meaux his father, and Scolastica and Joan his sisters removed from the church of Aldbrough to the priory of Hautemprise in consequence of the encroachments of the sea: they are to be buried in a place, in which, as we understand, Sir John himself intends to be interred.[z] August 16. Sentence of excommunication at the instance of John de Clone,[a] our domestic chaplain, custos of the free chapel at Ferrybridge, against those who have plundered the said chapel of its books and ornaments. Sept. 12. A commission to Gilbert, bishop of Carlisle,[b] to bless chalices, etc. Oct. 21. A commission to William, bishop of Sodor, to confer orders, etc.

[x] Lancaster charged the duke with having arrested him whilst he was at Cologne on his way to Palestine, and challenged him to mortal combat. Cf. Knyghton, col. 2603. Barnes's Edw. III., 465-7. Froissart. Wilkins, iii., 27, 52.

[y] A Fleming, rector of Sandal and canon of Wetwang. In 1343 he was archdeacon of Winchester (Le Neve, iii., 25). In 1357 he was dean S. Gaucherii, and, afterwards, in 1364, of Cambray (Gallia Christiana, iii., 71).

[z] A valuable entry in more respects than one. It completely overthrows the pedigree of the family of Meaux which is given in Poulson's Holderness. It also shews us the date of the present church of Aldborough, as Sir John Meaux, to whom the present licence was granted, was buried in it and not at Hautemprise, in 1377. A rich altar tomb, which bears his effigy, commemorates him, and the church in which it stands is at the distance of a mile from the still encroaching sea. Aldbro' church, therefore, was built between 1353 and 1377. Sir John de Meaux in his will (Test. Ebor., i., 100) desires to be buried in the aisle of B.M.V. in the church of St. Bartholomew at Aldbrough, and orders his corpse to be dressed for the grave in the garb of a Friar Minor, he having become a brother of that order.

[a] Chaplain and executor of archbishop Thoresby. On July 5, 1371, he was instituted to the rectory of Kirkby Ravenswath, exchanging for it his living of Birkin with John de Middleton (MSS. Harl., 6978), 4 *b*). On Feb. 5, 1379-80, he exchanged Ravenswath with Robert de Wycliffe for the rectory of St. Crux in York (Reg. Hatfield at Durham, 169 *b*), and on the 26th of the same month he was instituted to the stall of West Witton at Auckland, a part of the above-mentioned exchange (ibid., 170 *b*). On April 30 he was admitted to a prebend in St. Sepulchre's chapel at York (Reg. Neville). A John de Clone was the king's attorney 1339, 1340 (Dugd. Chron., 43).

[b] Gilbert de Welton exchanges in 1343 his rectory of Wistow, dioc. Lincoln, with Thomas de Ripplingham for the stall of Eton at Southwell and the rectory of Claworth. In 1347 he was made canon of Osbaldwick at York, and in 1348 he gave up Claworth to be

1354, Jan. 25. An indulgence of 40 days in behalf of the monastery of Helagh park, which is in great decay.[c] May 16. Licence for Alan de Corbrigg, rector of St. Peter the Little, York, to be absent for two years from his benefice, to visit the sepulchre of our Lord and the *limina* of S.S. Peter, Paul, and James.

1355, Feb. 7. A bull of pope Innocent VI. granting an indulgence of a year and forty days in behalf of the monastery of St. Augustine, Canterbury, and another, ordaining that the feast of St. Augustine be observed as a double festival through the whole of England.[d]

1356, March 19. Licence of non-residence to Thomas de Langetoft, rector of St. Helen's in Stonegate, at the request of the prince of Wales in whose suit he is. August 14. An order to pray for the prince of Wales and Henry duke of Lancaster.[e] August 28. Commission of enquiry to Mr. John de Crakall, doctor of decrees and canon of Ripon. Hugh Knyght, priest, informs us that he was attacked at Wath by certain armed laymen, and that he killed one of them in self-defence.

1357, Jan 11. Licence to Sir Henry le Scrop,[f] knight, to have service in an oratory in his manors, and a commission to consecrate the area, etc., for the conventual church, etc., of the Carmelites at Northallerton. Feb. 18. Indenture between the archbishop and Laurence de Florence about the making of sterlings in the palace at York.[g] Dec. 20. Dispensation for Mr. William de Carleton, canon of St. Sepulchre's chapel, York, to

the chantry priest in the archbishop's manor of Ripon. In 1349 he obtained the prebend of North Leverton at Southwell, and was appointed an executor in archbishop Zouche's will. He was bishop of Carlisle from 1353 to 1363. Cf. Reg. Zouche. MSS. Harl., 6951, 103*b*. Test. Ebor., i., 56. Fœd., iii., 116. Le Neve, iii., 236. Nicolson and Burn's Cumberland and Westmerland, ii., 266, etc.

On Feb. 28, 1353-4, bishop Welton was empowered to celebrate orders, and, on the 28th, to consecrate the oleum and chrisma.

On Jan. 17, 1358, the king gave leave to Michael, bishop of Whitherne, suffragan of the archbishop of York, to come to England on business relating to his church and himself (Fœd., iii. 387). In the same year a strange prelate, Thomas, bishop of Chrysopolis, was attacked at Kexby, near York. He charged the bishop of Durham with the assault, but he was acquitted (ibid., 389).

[c] A monastery at a short distance from York, of which some remains are still in existence. It seems to have been rebuilt about this time.

[d] Cf. Chron. W. Thorn, col. 2120. Labbe, Conc., xi., 1930. Wilkins, iii., 33.

[e] The year of the battle of Poictiers. Thoresby was desired by the king to order thanksgivings throughout his diocese for the victory (Barnes's Edw. III., 517). In MSS. Bodl., C, iv., 2080, are letters from him reciting the order of the king for the thanksgiving (Smith's Catalogue).

[f] First lord Scrope of Masham and father of Richard Scrope, archbishop of York. He died in 1391, æt. 76 (Scrope and Grosvenor Roll, i., 134).

[g] On May 2, 1353, the king allowed Thoresby "duos cuneos monetales" at York (Fœd., iii., 258). On July 18 there is a valuable order from the king about the York mint (ibid., 261. Davies's York Mint, 33-4).

be absent from canonical hours on account of illness, still receiving his distributions as a residentiary.

1358, Feb. 21. Absolution of William de Roston and John his son. They were going through the fields at Esterton to their work when John Pie, chaplain, lept upon them, being armed. William Roston ran away, but a great dog belonging to Pie pursued and caught him, and his master gave him a grievous blow on the arm with a weapon called a *gisham*. Upon this, the wounded man, to save his life, struck Pie on the head *cum blado*, and his son wounded him with an arrow. Sept. 6. A mandate to pray for the soul of Isabella the queen-mother.[h] Sept. 17. Permission to Sir Robert de Hilton, knight, to remove the bodies of Matilda and Margery his daughters, who have been dead for some time, from the lower part of the porch or aisle of the Holy Trinity in the church of Swyne to a higher place in the same porch, where the said Sir Robert intends to be interred with others of his kin.[i]

1359, July 3. A commission to Geoffrey archbishop of Damascus[j] to act as suffragan. Oct. 20. To William de Burton, citizen and merchant of York, 8*l.* 6s. 8d. for a long woollen cloth bought of him for our use.

1360, Jan. 15. To our kinsman, Robert de Thoresby, 10*l.* for different works in our manor of Thorp. Sept. 14. To William de Hovyngham, goldsmith of York, 10*l.* in part payment of the price of a silver dish which we bought of him to lay alms in at our table. Nov. 3. To Richard de Leven, citizen and tanner of York, 20 marks in part payment for furs for our livery.[k]

1361, June 9. Mandate to the prioress and convent of Molseby to re-admit to their house Elizabeth de Neville some time an apostate. July 12. An order to pray for the removal of

[h] She died at Risings, near London, on 22nd of August, 1358, and was buried at the Grey Friars (Barnes's Edward III., 550-1). From April 30 to May 14, 1358, she was residing in London at the house of the archbishop (Archæologia, xxxv., 453). Murimuth, 191. Coll. Top. and Geneal., v., 278.

[i] Extensive alterations were being made in this curious old church. In January, 1361-2, there is a monition to the parishioners of Swine to contribute to the new work of the nave and tower of their church (Reg. Thoresby). The monuments of the Hiltons are a conspicuous feature in the Trinity aisle.

On April 24, 1347, a chantry was founded in the church of Wynestede by Sir Robert de Hilton, for the souls of himself, Margaret his wife, his ancestors, and Sir Ralph de Greystock (Reg. Melton). Curiously enough, the manor of Swine afterwards came into the possession of the Meltons with the heiress of Hilton (Poulson's Holderness, ii., 198).

[j] On August 10, 1359, Thomas, bishop of Norwich, was authorized to confirm for the archbishop. He was a Percy, and was, therefore, connected with the North. Some suffragans of the archbishop will be mentioned afterwards.

[k] June 10, 1361, 20*l.* more to him for our livery against Christmas. Oct. 3, to Richard de Wateby, citizen of York, 40*l.* to provide our liverey, and, on Feb. 4, 33*l.* 6s. 10d. to him for the same purpose. 1362, April 18, to Richard Wardrober, 40*l.* for our liverey.

wars, pestilences, and other troubles of the kingdom.[l] July 21. To the Friars Minors and Augustinians of York 5 marks each for their general chapter to be celebrated at York. Oct. 1. To Elias de Thoresby, receiver of our chamber, 1000*l.* for the expenses of our hospice. Oct. 3. To Mr. Walter de Skirlawe,[m] our beloved clerk, 21*l.* 15s., for our expenses in the court of Rome.

1362, Feb. 1. Licence to the inhabitants of Staynburn, par. Kirkby Overblows, to have service in the cemetery of their chapel there during the continuance of the pestilence.[n] Feb. 26. Commission to absolve Sir Adam de Everingham,[o] knight, who has been excommunicated for laying violent hands on Richard de Halghton, rector of a moiety of the church of Derfeld. May 6. To John Boys, 57*l.* 16s. 9d. for 567 sheep bought at Ripon.

1363, April 18. An order to pray for the prince of Wales and his army, they being detained by contrary winds. July 20. An order to pray for fine weather on account of the harvest. Oct. 2. William Strother, canon of Kirkham, is absolved from the sentence of greater excommunication for giving the eucharist to Robert Corbet, chaplain, without the leave of his curate. The relaxation is to last till Michaelmas, 1364, on condition that he goes to Rome for absolution.[p]

1364, June 29. To Robert de Thoresby, our esquire, 100s. for the building of a new chamber in our manor of Thorp.[q] An

[l] There was a great pestilence this year which carried off three bishops and Henry, duke of Lancaster (Murimuth, 195). In Hardyng's Chron., 330, it is said,—

> "In that same yere was on Sainct Maury's, day,
> The greate winde and earthquake mervelous,
> That greately gav the people all affray,
> So dredfull was it then and perelous,
> Specially the wind was so boistous
> The stone walles, steples, houses and trees,
> Were blow downe in diverse ferre countrees."

[m] The great and good bishop of Durham. He was a Yorkshireman by birth, and was a great benefactor to his native county. He gave largely to the choir and central tower of York minster, and a chantry was founded for him at the altar of St. Cuthbert. He was one of the greatest builders of his day, and was a man of prince-like munificence. My collections for his life are far too numerous even to abbreviate here. I saw him about fifteen years ago at Durham, when his tomb was disturbed, swathed in lead, through which the outline of his crozier could easily be traced. He now lies in the north aisle of the choir, between the organ and the wall, before the stone seat which he erected for the aged men who were to sit thereon and offer up their prayers for his soul. A gorgeous brass, fifteen feet in length, once covered his remains. The matrix is now laid before the altar-steps, and is erroneously ascribed to bishop Beaumont.

[n] Walsingham (179) says of this year, "Moriebantur plures morbo litargiæ, multa infortunia prophetantes: mulieres insuper decessere per fluxum, et erat communis pestis bestiarum." Great winds also prevailed.

[o] 28th Edward I. Prob. æt. Adæ de Everingham fil. et hær. Roberti de Everingham (Abbrev. Plac., 242).

[p] "To wash this blood from off my guilty hand."

[q] 1364-5, 10*l.* more for it on Feb. 13. On March 22, 10*l.* more. On May 2, 10*l.* more. On June 10, 100s., and 100s. on July 15.

indulgence of 40 days to those who relieve two brethren of Armenia whose monastery has been destroyed by the Saracens.

1365, March 14. Lease of the archbishop's mint, for two years, to Andrew de Florencia, at a rent of 20 marks per annum. April 27. Absolution of John de Gaytford, Gervase de Pecco, etc., for cutting off the head of John de Wynteworth, chaplain, till they can go to Rome for absolution. July 2. Excommunication of those who have broken into the monastery at Pontefract and carried away plate, jewels, and a pix before the altar of St. Leonard. August 5. Licence of non-residence for two years to William Wyclyf,[r] rector of Wyclyf, to enable him to study. Sept. 9. An order to the parishioners of Worksop to

[r] An interesting extract. In 1361 a William de Wycliffe was one of the fellows of Balliol whilst John de Wycliffe, the reformer, was master of that college (Fascic. Zizan., prefat., xi). This licence of non-residence was, in all probability, to allow him to return to Oxford. He is probably identical with William de Wycliffe, who was instituted on the 7th of August, 1363, on the presentation of John de Wycliffe, to the rectory of Wycliffe in Yorkshire (MSS. Harl., 6978, 1, 2, extracts from a register of the archdeacons of Richmond which is now lost), and with Mr. William de Wycliffe, rector of Wycliffe, who was ordained accolite at York on the Saturday after St. Matthew's day, 1363 (Reg. Thoresby). After this we hear nothing of him.

In 1368 another William de Wycliffe was ordained accolite, sub-deacon, deacon, and priest at York, Easby abbey giving him a title (Reg. Thoresby).

We now come to two greater personages, who accompany each other through life, as they began it, in the most perplexing propinquity. One of them is the celebrated reformer.

On Saturday before St. Mark's day, 1350, John de Whytecliff was made an accolite in the house of the Friars Minors at York, and John de Wycliffe an accolite at the Friars Preachers in the same city on the Saturday after St. Lucy's day in the same year. In 1350-1, also, John, son of William de Wykliff, and John, son of Symon de Wycliff (the names of the fathers being fortunately given to distinguish the two), were ordained sub-deacons at the Friars Preachers, deacons at Pentecost, 1351, in St. Mary's abbey, and priests in York minster on the Saturday after St. Matthew's day, 1351, the officiating prelate being Hugh, archbishop of Damascus (Reg. Zouche). This information is entirely new.

Mr. Shirley has spoken about these two persons in a note to the Fascic. Zizan. I agree with him that an argument can be drawn with difficulty from the spelling of an old name. It is still remarkable that one of the two John Wycliffes, *i. e.*, the prebendary of Chichester, was called John Whytcliff in his will and before it. One of the accolites at York is also "Whytecliff," but only in that instance; and as Wyklif is much more akin in sound to Whytcliff than Wycliff (the name of the village is always pronounced hard), the presumption is that in John, son of Symon de Wycliff, we have the master of Balliol and the reformer. I do not, however, set much value upon this inference.

It may, I think, be safely assumed that the reformer is one of these two. Both of them had their title from Eggleston abbey, which is within three miles of the little village of Wycliffe. They were both, therefore, Yorkshiremen. The genealogy of the Wycliffes at this early period is beset with difficulties, and I shall not now weary my readers with a long piece of genealogical criticism. The little church of Wycliffe, with the sparkling Tees rushing by it, will well repay a visit. It contains some interesting sepulchral memorials of the family, including one to an only son, the last hope of that ancient house, which was erected by his father, who reared it, as he observes with much feeling, "non sine summo

desist from wrestling, archery, indecent dances and singing, in their churchyard.[s]

1366, Jan. 16. To John de Beverley, tailor, for a long cloth, "de tanneto," 11*l.* 4s. April 20. Sentence against those who have laid violent hands on the dean of Pontefract, and killed John de Whittheued, his servant. July 7. To John de Helwill,[t] canon residentiary of York, two oaks in our wood of Langwath, and their faggots, our accustomed gift at this time. Oct. 9. A commission to absolve Adam de Wordelworth, chaplain, for killing John de Staynton, at Berneslay, in self defence. Nov. 17. An order to pray for the prince, who is going abroad to help the king of Spain.[u]

1367, April 13. Licence of non-residence for two years to John de Ledcombe, rector of Castleford, to be in the king's service, and, on May 5, a similar licence to Elias Brithewell, rector of Bramwith, in the service of John, duke of Lancaster. Dec. 6. An order stopping markets being held on Sundays in the porch and churchyard of Whitgift, and prohibiting eatings and drinkings there.

1368, Oct. 26. An order to pray for the removal of the pestilence.

1369, March 3. John, son of William Chapman, of Great Driffield, aged 8, was giving hay on the feast of St. Edmund the king, 1363, to a certain horse belonging to William Ichon, of Crauncewyk. The horse being unbroken, bit off the greater part of the boy's right ear. A certificate to that effect. May 8.

rerum humanarum fastidio." As Waller says of the only son of lord Andover,—

"'Tis not a single corpse alone does lie
Under this stone, but a whole family;
His parents' pious care, their name, their joy,
And all their hope, lies buried with this boy."

My father was born within a mile of the village of Wycliffe, and I have often heard him say that at the beginning of the present century the dialect of the neighbourhood was so identical with the language of the reformer's version of the New Testament that he would undertake to read any chapter of it to an old person, and it would be understood thoroughly, with the exception perhaps of a word or two.

[s] A practice which had arrested the attention of Giraldus Cambrensis in the twelfth century. He speaks, in terms of reprobation, against the saltationes and cantilenæ then prevalent in churches (Gemma Ecclesiastica, 119).

[t] Canon residentiary of York and prebendary of Barnby from 1349 to 1387. He was also rector of Misterton and Rowley. By his will, dated on the 3rd of March, 1386-7, he desired to be interred in York minster, and gave the sum of 100s. to the fabric.

[u] The famous expedition into Spain in behalf of king Pedro,

"For whiche the prince with all his hole power
Rode into Spain to helpe hym to conquer."

The great battle of Najara and the exploits of Sir John Chandos and his illustrious leader are matters of history. There is a long account of the fight in "The Black Prince," edited for the Roxburghe Club, 250, etc. The prayer of the victor is a striking one:—

"Que je ne sui pas cy venuz
Fors pur droit estre sustenuz
Et proesce et pur franchise
Qe mon coer semonte et attise
De conquestre vie de honour
Jo vous supplie qeu cesti jour
Voillez garder moy et ma gent."

An order to pray for the king, queen, and prince, and for the removal of the pestilence.[v] May 20. To Mr. J. de Waltham,[w] for his expenses in going to London, to the parliament to be held at Westminster on the octaves of the festival of the Trinity. June 5. An order to repair the nave of St. Peter the Little, York. July 7. To Mr. Robert de Patrington, master-mason, 14 marks for repairing the windows in the chapel of our manor at Cawood, and to Henry de Miryman as much as is due to him for the custody of our manor of Thorp.

1370, May 31. A commission to receive the vow of chastity of Beatrix wife of Andrew Gower.[x]

1372, Feb. 18. Licence to Nicholas de Swanland, rector of St. Cuthbert's, York, to pull down some houses at the east end of his church, built at his own cost, and to use the materials in enlarging and repairing the choir. Nov. 9. Licence to Isabel de Faucomberge, widow of Walter de Faucomberge, knight, to remove his body from before the image of the Holy Cross in the church of Gisburgh to that part of the church in which his ancestors are interred.[y]

1373, Nov. 5. A grant of the wardship and marriage of John son and heir of John de Langton of York to William Gray, citizen of York, and Robert de Wyclif,[z] rector of St. Crux, York.

[v] There was a great pestilence, and the corn was much injured by floods (Walsingham, 184).

[w] A person who had many preferments in the church. Canon of Lichfield, York, Southwell, and Bromyard, sacrist of St. Sepulchre's, York, official of the court of York, master of the hospitals at Bawtry and Beck, Norfolk, canon of Lanchester, incumbent of Hunmanby, Cortenale, Saxby, Steeple-Langford, Towcester, and Heversham (Reg. Thoresby. Nichols's Leicestershire, ii., 312. Blomefield's Norfolk, viii., 190. MSS. Harl., 6952, 4, 10; ibid., 6978. Le Neve, i., 603. Misc. Doc., penes dec. and cap. Dunelm., 4196). He was an executor of archbishop Thoresby in 1373 (Test. Ebor., i., 90), and was his kinsman (MSS. Cotton, Galba, E, x., 85).

He was probably the uncle of John de Waltham, archdeacon of Richmond and bishop of Salisbury, one of the favourites of Richard II., "who hadde pleased the king so greatly that (though many murmured at it) he commanded him to bee buryed at Westminster among the kings." His brazen effigy is still gleaming over his resting-place on that sacred platform.

[x] A name to which the poet Gower has given a great interest. Would that his origin could be safely traced to the county of York! On Dec. 17, 1342, archbishop Melton allowed Alice, widow of John Gower, of Cold Ingleby, to have an oratory for three years in her manor there (Reg. Melton). The question of the origin of the poet has been discussed by Sir Harris Nicholas in the Retrospective Review, second series, ii., 111, and by Dr. Reinhold Pauli in his introduction to the Confessio Amantis. Their researches prove that the poet lived in the South, and had estates in Suffolk, but nothing more. He might still have been a native of Yorkshire, as Leland says he was. One of the persons mentioned in the transfer of the Suffolk estates, Guy de Rocliffe, who was also interested in them, was a Yorkshireman, and it must not be forgotten that Gower had a lease of the manor of Southwell, co. Notts.

[y] Some notices of this family have already occurred.

[z] The Langtons and the Grays were

The following horrible crime was committed at Beverley in November, 1372. A shoemaker of the name of William de Watton, who had been for some time deranged, came into the church of St. Mary in that town. The poor creature observed a priest of the name of Peter de Aldegat, and went up to him, as if to make his confession, with his hands folded after the guise of a penitent. "Woe is me that ever I was born," he said: "by God's heart I will go and drown myself." "Far be this from thee," said the priest, "for then thou wouldst be lost both in body and soul." The lunatic then cried out, as if some sudden idea had flashed across his mind, "He wanted to kill me unless I would be friends with Adam de Coppandale. I will kill myself." Aldgate replied, "Away with the thought. Hope in God and pray here, and I will soon make Adam de Coppandale and all his people thy friends." He then went away, and told the master and the kinsmen of the madman to come and take him away, saying that he was insane. On his return, Watton, who no doubt had

two wealthy and distinguished families in York.

Of Robert de Wycliffe, who was very probably a near relation of the reformer, perhaps a nephew, some account may appropriately be given. He was a man of wealth and influence. On the 2nd of August, 1362, he was instituted to the rectory of Wycliffe on the presentation of Katherine, widow of Roger Wycliffe. He held it only for a year (MSS. Harl., 6978, 1 *a*). In 1368 he was ordained sub-deacon at York, being rector of St. Crux in that city (Reg. Thoresby). On May 14, 1375, he was collated to a prebend at Auckland (West Witton), vacant by the death of David, son of Sir Thomas de Ingilby, knight (Reg. Hatfield, 79 *a*). On Feb. 5, 1379-80, he exchanged the rectory of St. Crux, York, for that of Kirkby Ravenswath with John de Clune, and on the 26th of February Clune was inducted into Wycliffe's stall at Auckland, which was part of the exchange (ibid., 169, 170). From 1377 to 1423 he was rector of Rudby, having been appointed by Philip, lord Darcy (Graves's Cleveland, 165), and on Jan. 17, 1382-3, he was instituted, at the king's presentation, to the rectory of Romaldkirk, which he held till he died (MSS. Harl., 6978, 10 *b*), having obtained it in the way of exchange with Richard de Middleham for the living of Ravenswath.

He was closely connected with bishop Skirlaugh. From 1399 to 1402 he was constable of Durham castle. On Feb. 3, 1390-1, he occurs as temporal chancellor of Durham, and he continued so till Skirlaugh's death. He was also his receiver-general (MSS. Surtees, and Hutchinson's Durham, i., 324), and one of his executors (Test. Ebor., i., 311). Wycliffe died at Kepier hospital, near Durham, of which he was master, in 1423 (Surtees's Durham, iv., 65).

Wycliffe was connected as executor or trustee with several great personages. He was an executor of Margery, widow of Sir William de Aldeburgh, in 1391 (Test. Ebor., i., 152), of Philip, lord Darcy, in 1399 (ibid., 255), and of Sir John Depeden, in 1402 (ibid., 299). His own will and schedule of bequests, full of interesting and valuable matter, are in Durham Wills, i., 66, and Test. Ebor., i., 403.

From notices of the Wycliffes which have been given before it will be seen that they were a great clerical family. I can scarcely identify the following person with the ecclesiastic of whom I have been speaking. On March 28, 1338, Robert de Wycliff was ordained priest in the priory of Durham by Boniface "Corbavien' episc.," Walter de Stapelton giving him a title of 5 marks (Reg. Bury, 307 *a*). On the vigil of the feast of the Trinity, 1363, Nicholas, son of John de Wycliff, was ordained priest at York (Reg. Thoresby).

suspected his errand, stabbed him in the breast with his knife, and the priest died of the wound. The bailiffs, who were in the church hearing mass, at once seized the murderer, but his victim adjured them by Christ's body to do him no harm as he did not know what he was doing, and he forgave him before God. The prisoner was shut up in the house of Thomas de Waghen and went raging about during the night with a drawn knife, saying that he heard and saw his enemies devising his death. It was discovered that on one occasion he had cut off his mother's hair. She submitted in fear and trembling to the operation, and the maniac afterwards thanked God that he had not choked her. This is a fearful picture. It is dreadful to think of the times when there were no receptacles for lunatics; who were permitted to wander about at their will among their friends and kinsmen.

It will be seen from the extracts which have just been given, that several violent assaults upon ecclesiastics are mentioned. They are a very fair criterion of the spirit of the times. Those are indeed evil days when the garb of a clergyman cannot protect him from insult and wrong. But, as a general rule, when such is the case, the fault is to a great extent to be ascribed to the church itself. The cords of discipline have been slackened till it becomes perilous to draw them tighter. An evil example has been set by those who profess to teach,[a] and, as Dryden tells us,

> "If they be foul on whom the people trust,
> Well may the baser brass contract a rust."

The trumpet has been giving an uncertain sound. And so it was in the middle of the fourteenth century. There was, in many respects, a great decline in morals and in devotion. We find laymen and clerks killing and wounding one another, churches desecrated, the privileges of sanctuary abused, and all the grades of society distorted and confused.[b] The church seems to have been powerless to correct or regenerate. Internal weakness and corruption made her voice very weak, if it could be heard at all. It is a very grand sight to see a man like Thoresby push himself boldly forward in such a crisis into the fore-front of the battle, with the skill to originate, the energy to carry out his plans, and the honesty to scourge offenders whether

[a] Gower is not complimentary when he is speaking of the pastors of his day in the prologue to his Confessio Amantis. After many severe words he says,—

> "Lo, thus to-broke is Criste's folde
> Wherof the flock withoute guide
> Devoured is on every side
> In lacke of hem, that ben unware
> Shepherdes, which here wit beware
> Upon the worlde in other halve.
> The sharpe pricke instede of salve
> They usen now, wherof the hele
> They hurte of that they shulden hele.
> And what sheep, that is full of wulle
> Upon his backe, they toose and pulle."

[b] For an account of several cases of sacrilege, see Knyghton, col. 2628.

they were friends or foes. The archbishop of Canterbury made bitter complaints to him about the wretched state of the church of England; how the high and mighty gave her no support, and how her influence had departed.[c] Thoresby spoke to his brother primate some strong and earnest words of comfort, and prepared himself for the battle. His eagle eye saw at once that this was the time for action, and his zeal for God's cause induced him to withdraw himself from the clash of party warfare in which he had honourably achieved so many brilliant successes, that he might strive to win a bolder victory, the reformation of the church. There is nothing to prove the assertion which has been made, that he was dissatisfied with his creed; he merely endeavoured to purify and not to overthrow what was before him; and yet there are many points in his character that remind us of Wycliffe, and it would be curious to know if there were any connection between the primate and his compatriot. Both were natives of the North Riding of Yorkshire, and it is possible enough that they were kinsmen. Both were animated, in matters of discipline at least, by the same earnest and fearless spirit, but Wycliffe stepped out of his way to do what Thoresby attempted to effect through the ordinary paths which the church suggested to him. It was indeed a time for energetic action, and Thoresby knew it. The country around him had been desolated by the plague and the wars, and the spirit of irreligion had crept in and established itself too securely. The people were in a state of gross ignorance, and many of the clergy, if they were disposed to work at all, were not fit to teach. Some were wandering away from their parishes in the trains of knights and nobles, or haunting, in quest of secular preferment, the purlieus of the court. Many livings were held at the same time by one man, whilst others, through the system of papal provisions, were possessed by foreigners.[d] A fierce fight was raging on this point between the king and pope, in which the ecclesiastical sovereign and his party were ultimately worsted. At the close of the reign of Edward III. the power of the cardinals in this country came to an end.[e] It had been dominant for many years in the church

[c] Reg. Al. Neville, part ii. Among Thoresby's letters.

[d] The poet Occleve gives strong evidence (De Regimine Principum, ed. Roxburghe Club, 1860; p. 51):—

"A dayes now, my sone, as men may see,
O chirche to o man may nat suffise;
But algate he mote have pluralitee,
Elles he han not lyve in no wise.
Ententyfly he kepethe his servise
In court, ther his labour shall not moule,
But to his cure loketh he full foule.
"Thoughe that his chauncelle roof be alle to-torne,
And on the hye awtere reyne or snewe,
He rekkethe not, the cost may be forborne
Cristes house to repaire or make newe;
And thoughe ther be fulle many a vicious hewe
Undir his cure, he takethe of it no kepe:
He rekkethe never how rusty ben his shepe."

[e] In the same register there is a strong letter from Edward III. to one of the cardinals reprehending him for calling him a fool! It was probably

of York to its exceeding detriment. Since the commencement of the fourteenth century, more than thirty of these dignitaries had held the highest offices in the minster whilst they were of course non-resident. Between 1343 and 1385 the deanery was in their hands. The first of the three who occupied it, Hélie Talleyrand,[f] cardinal-bishop of Alba, the fruitless intercessor at Poictiers, might have been the "lucidum ecclesiæ sidus," as his friend Petrarch called him in Italy, but he never shone at York. He was far better acquainted with the intrigues of the sacred college at Avignon, the vineyards of his ancient house at Périgord, and his college at Toulouse. His successor at York and in the cardinalate, Anglicus Grimaldi, adopted the cause of the anti-pope, and was ejected from the deanery which he never once saw. The wisdom and the learning of Adam de Eston could not preserve him from the same fate, although they saved him from the vengeance of Urban VI., when five of his brother-cardinals, who had joined him in a conspiracy against the pope, were fastened up in sacks and thrown into the sea. When the heads of the cathedral at York were thus non-resident, it was not to be expected that there would be much order or discipline observed in the church that they neglected. It was not in the power of Thoresby to check the system of provisions; he was indeed too closely bound to the papal court by the strongest ties of gratitude to attempt to do so even if he had possessed the power; and there was a continuous influx of cardinals into his diocese whilst it was under his care.[g] He did, however, what he could to see that the church of York was properly attended to. On the 12th of May, 1362, he visited the chapter, and there he reprehended the system of non-residence, of which archbishop Melton had formerly complained to him.[h] The dean, of course, was not there, and the forty poor

addressed to one of those dignitaries who had a stall at York.

[f] "Consanguineo di presso che tutti i Principi della Francia, uomo di gran-senno e valore pe' suvi tempi, e assai lodato dagli Scrittori di quell' età, e sopra gli altri dal Petrarca, e da altri molti, per la dottrina e prudenza" (Cardella, Memorie Storiche de' Cardinali, ii., 133).

[g] In the letter and common place book which is called the second part of archbishop Neville's register, fol. 6 *b*, is the following sentence which would express Thoresby's feelings about the cardinals, and it is probably from his pen:—

"Heu michi quia incolatus meus prolongatus est ad extraneos et alienigenas, qui velut surdi et muti suorum ovium balatum non intelligunt, de morsibus luporum non curant, sed velut mercenarii videntes lupum venientem fugiunt, auferunt vellera lac et lanam, lucra captantes, semper dorsa ab oneribus divertentes, prout dolor ymmo immensus dolor, sed utinam ejus doloris auferatur occacio potentia Salvatoris."

[h] The letter is in Neville's register, part ii., 16 *b*. The archbishop speaks of the non-residence of the canons at York, and wishes to have the poor stalls augmented with the rich. It is possible that Zouche was the writer, and not Melton.

persons, to whom he was bound to supply food, were forgotten. The sub-dean, also, was non-resident, and his house in the close was in decay. Branktre, the treasurer, had never been in York since he was appointed, and the sacristans and clerks of the vestry had received from him no wages. The vicars experienced a more than common share of blame. Many of them had bad voices, and those who could sing sang wrong. When they left the Beddern and went into the city they were dressed after the fashion of squires, in very unclerical attire, with knives sticking in their girdles, and baselards dangling between their legs.[i]

Thoresby was not a man to be daunted by difficulties and obstructions. Ignorance was one of the great vices of the age, and he resolved to assail it. He caused to be drawn up, in the form of a catechism, a brief statement of what he deemed to be necessary for salvation, comprising the articles of belief, the ten commandments, the seven sacraments, the seven deeds of bodily and ghostly mercy, the seven virtues and the seven deadly sins, and in them we see the first faint shadowings of an English ritual. These were prepared in a twofold form, and were issued from Cawood on the 25th of November, 1357. The first was in Latin, and was apparently to be perused by the clergy, to the neglect and ignorance of whom the archbishop boldly and sharply ascribes the existence of the evils of the times.[j] The

[i] Acta Capit. Ebor. Fab. Rolls, 242.

[j] The preamble runs as follows:—"Johannes, etc.; dilecto filio archidiacono nostro, etc. Quia nonnulli Christi fideles, quibus, licet immeriti, præsidemus, non sunt, quod dolenter gerimus, saltem in grossis et necessariis Christianæ legis observantiis instructi, quod tam ex nostra, quam ex rectorum, vicariorum et sacerdotum parochialium, qui ipsos juxta susceptæ curæ debitum haberemus instruere, incuria, ne dicamus ignorantia, dicitur evenire, per quod, quod Deus avertat, de facili via patere potest erroribus et gravibus periculis animarum. Nos volentes, ut tenemur, super hoc remedium apponere salutare, sacro approbante cleri nostrarum diocesios et provinciæ consilio, super hoc sic duximus ordinandum, ut quilibet rector, vicarius, capellanus parochialis et curatus alius, saltem diebus Dominicis, sine exquisita verborum subtilitate exponant, seu exponere faciant, populo in vulgari, articulos fidei, præcepta tam Novi quam Veteris Testamenti, opera misericordiæ, virtutes principales, gratiæ sacramenta et peccata mortalia, cum sua sequela; et quod vice nostra injungant parochianis suis, viris et mulieribus, quod ipsi et eorum singuli præmissa omnia diligenter audiant et addiscant, et quod hæc parvulos suos, filios et filias, clare doceant, et ipsos ad hæc addiscenda compellant: et quod saltem in singulis quadragesimis dicti curati parochianos suos, an hæc sic didiscerint et sciverint et sic liberos suos instruxerint, examinent; exquisite injungentes non parentibus in hac parte pœnitentiam salutarem, quam pro tempore, prout eorum requirit inobedientia, studeant aggravare. Et ne quis super hiis per ignorantiam se valeat excusare hæc sub verbis planis et incultis, ut sic levius in publicam deducantur notitiam, fecimus annotare."

We gather from this that the English of the document that will be shortly given was of the plainest and rudest kind.

There are copies of this mandate, the creed, etc., slightly varying from the above, among the MSS. at Lambeth, 408, 577 (Tanner, Bibl. Brit., 711). Cf. Wharton's note ad. Hist. Dogmatic., Archiep. Ussher, ed. 1690,

other was in English verse, which is so uncouth that it is difficult to distinguish it from prose. This was translated from the Latin by John de Taystek (Tavistock or Garrick?), a monk of St. Mary's abbey, and it is entered on the register of archbishop Thoresby's official acts. Mr. Halliwell has printed it in his Yorkshire *Anthology,* and it is also to be found in the *Vicaria Leodiensis* of Ralph Thoresby, who did not know, however, that it was in verse.[k] The English version was intended for the benefit of the laity, and, that it should be properly understood and appreciated, the archbishop gave it as wide a circulation as he possibly could. Copies were multiplied and dispersed in various forms, and the primate "sent them in small pagyantes to the common people to lerne it and to knowe it; of whiche yet manye a copye be in England."[l] So wrote some one in the fifteenth century. The word "pagyantes" opens out a very interesting field of speculation. It is the name applied to the miracle plays which were once so popular and so common. Was the North of England indebted to Thoresby for the introduction of these instructive, yet somewhat profane, representations? It is very probable indeed that he would press them into his service to arrest the attention of the wayfarers in the streets, and please the eyes and ears of the unlettered crowd. The Crede or Belief play was one that was once acted and recited in York.[m] It will,

pp. 430-1. See also Harmer's Specimen of Errors in Burnet's History of the Reformation, part i., 56-7.

[k] Yorkshire Anthology, 297-314. Vicaria Leodiensis, 213-35. Mr. Halliwell derived his copy from MSS. Harl., 1022, 74-80. At the end of the poem in this MS. is the following account of its authorship :—

"Transumpta erat ista predicacio a lingua Latina in nostram maternam linguam de mandato domini Johannis de Thoresby, Ebor. Archiep., per venerabilem et discretum virum Johannem de Taystek, monachum monasterii beatæ Mariæ Ebor., anno Domini millesimo trescentesimo quinquagesimo septimo."

[l] "Syr William Thorsby, archebishop of Yorke, did do drawe a treatise in Englyshe by a worshypful clerke whose name was Garryk. In the whiche were conteyned the artycles of belefe, the vij dedly sines, the vij workes of marcy, the x comaundements; and sent them in small pagyantes to the common people to lerne it and to knowe it, of whiche yet manye a copye be in England" (Dibdin's Typogr. Ant., iii., 257). Fascic. Zizan., prefat., xiii. Foxe's Book of Martyrs, i., —.

[m] By will, dated August 2, 1446, William Revetour, of York, chaplain, leaves "fraternitati Corporis Christi in Eboraco quemdam librum vocatum le Crede play, cum libris et vexillis eidem pertinentibus" (Test. Ebor., ii., 117). Tavistock's verse would certainly require all the paraphernalia of the banners, etc., to render it attractive.

For an account and specimen of these plays at York, see Mr. Davies's volume of York Records of the Fifteenth Century; Drake's Eboracum, appendix, 29-32; (Croft's) Excerpta Antiqua, 105-10; Camden Miscellany, iv., No. 3. The manuscript collection of the old York miracle plays, which was formerly in the possession of the corporation of York, is now in the library of the earl of Ashburnham. Among the many treasures from Stowe which that nobleman has gathered together is the following work :—

"A poem on the Trinity by William of Nassyngton, a proctor or advocate in the ecclesiastical court of York. 4to. A curious MS. of 640 pages, partly on vellum and partly on paper, written

I think be some day discovered that this is the poem by John de Tavistock.

The poem, if such it can be called, is, with a few exceptions, without rhymes. It was drawn up, as the archbishop tells us, with studied plainness, and it is very uncouth and quaint. As it has been printed twice before, although by no means accurately, I shall only give on the present occasion the preamble and the Ten Commandments. The document is a valuable one, not only for philological purposes, but also as the creed of the inhabitants of Yorkshire in the fourteenth century. The writings of Buonaventure and St. Thomas Aquinas, the Seraphic and the Angelic doctors, and those of that now almost forgotten scholar, from whom they derived so much, Peter Lombard, the Master of the Sentences, have supplied the author with many of his materials, another verification of the words of the earliest of our English poets,

> "Out of olde fieldes, as men saithe,
> Cometh all this new corne from yere to yere;
> And out of olde bookes, in good faithe,
> Cometh all this new science that men lere."

My reader must tax his own ingenuity and patience to explain the many curious words that are presented to him.

Als that a gret clerk[n] shewes in his bokes, *et est secundo Sentenciarum, distinctione prima*, of all the creatures that God made in heven and in erthe, in water, or in ayre, or in ought elles, the soveraigne cause and ye skill whi that he maide thaime was his owen gode will and his godenesse, thurgh whilk godenesse, als he is all gode, he wold y[t] som creatures of thas that he made were communers of that blisse that evermore lastes. And for no creature might come to that ilk blisse withouten knawyng of God, als that clerk techis, *ubi supra*, he made skilwise creatures angels and man of witt and of wisdome to knawe God al myghten, and thurgh yaire knawyng love him and serve him, and so come to that blisse that thai were made to. This maner of knawyng had our forme fadirs in ye state of innocentz that thai were made in, and so shuld we have had if yai had noght synned noght so mikell als hali saules has now in heven, bot mikel mare than man has now in erthe; for our forme fadirs synned, sais the prophet, and we bore ye wickednesse of thaire misdede.

Treñ ultimo. For ye knawyng that thai had of God Almighten, thai had it of Goddes gift at thaire begynnyng with outen travaile or trey or passyng of tyme, and all ye knawynge yat we have in yis

about the year 1480." I should conjecture that the date is a century earlier, and Nassington, in all probability, assisted Thoresby in his religious work.

[n] Petri Lombardi Sententiæ, fol. Lovanii, 1566. Lib. ii., distinctio prima, 157-161. Peter Lombard owed many obligations to the works of the famous Abelard, for there were other things thought of besides love

> "Near Paraclete's white walls and silver springs."

This preamble is in metre, but I print it, as a curiosity, in prose. It is written so.

world of him is of heryng and leryng and techyng of othir of the lawe and the lare yat langes till hali kirk, ye whilke al creatures that loves God Almighten awe to knawe and to kun and lede yaire lyve aftir, and so com to yat blisse yat never more blynnes. And forthi that mikell folke now in yis world ne is noght wele ynogh lered to knawe God Almighten, ne love him, ne serve him als thai suld do, als thair dedis oft sithe openly shewes, in grete peril of thaime to lyve and to saule, and peraventure ye defaute in thaime that has thaire saules to kepe, and suld teche thaime, as prelates, persons, vikers and prestes that er halden be deit for to lere thaime, oure fadir ye erce bissshop, yat God Almighten save, that als Saint Paule sais of Jhesu Crist (Paulus ad Thimo^{m}, secundo capitulo), will that al men be saufe and knawe God Almighten: and namely thas undirloutes that to him langes has treted and ordayned for commune profet thurgh the consaile of his clergie, yat ilkane that undir him has kepyng of saules, openly on Inglis opon Sononndaies teche and preche thaim, that thai have cure of, the lawe and the lore to knawe God al mighten, yat principali mai be shewed in yis sex thinges. In the fouretene poyntes that falles to ye trouthe. In ye ten comandementez that God has gyven us. In ye seven sacrementez that er in hali kyrk. In seven dedis of merci until our even Cristen. In ye seven vertues that ilk man sal use, and in ye seven dedely sinnes that man sal refuse. And he comandes and biddes in al that he may, that all that haves kepynge or cure undir him enjoygne thair parochiens and thair sugettes that thai here and lere this ilk sex thinges, and oft sithes reherce tham til that thai kun thaime, and sithen teche them thair childer, if thai any have, what tyme so thai er of eld to lere tham. And that persons and vikers and all paroche prestes enquere diligently of thaire sugettes in the Lentyn tyme, when thai come to shrift, whethir thai kun this sex thinges, and if it be funden that thai kun thaim noght, that thai enjoygne tham opon his behalve and of payne of penaunce for to kun them. And forthi that nane sal excuse tham thurgh unknalechyng for to kun them, our fadir the ercebissshop of his godenesse has ordayned and bidden that thai be shewed openly on Inglis omanges the folk. * * * *

The secund thyng of the sex to knowe God Almighten,
Is the Ten Comandementz[o] that he has gyven us.

[o] See Petri Lombardi Sent., lib. iii., distinct. xxxvii. De decem preceptis quomodo contineantur in duobus mandatis charitatis. Cf. Opp. S. Bonaventuræ, ed. 1609, v., 414-27. Opp. S. Thomæ Aquinatis, vi., 142, etc., ed. 1594.

In the library of the dean and chapter of York, xvi., L, 12, is a curious MS. in English written soon after Thoresby's period, and no doubt with the same object that was so dear to his heart. A brief summary of the contents may be given. "Here bigynneth ye ten comanndementis. Of feith, hope and charite. The Paternoster. The Ave Marie. The Crede. The werkis of bodili mercy. The werkis of gostli mercy." An account of the creation, baptism, etc., follows.

In a copy of the York Breviary, printed at Paris by Francis Regnault, some one had written the following couplet, the meaning of which is obvious:—

"Keep ten,
Flee seven,
Use well five,
And win heaven."

Of the whilk ten, the thre that er first
Augh us haly to hald onentes oure God,
And the seven that er aftir onentes our even Cristen.

The first comandement charges us and techis
That we leve ne loute nane false goddes:
And in this comandement is forboden us
Alkyns mysbeleves and al mawmetries,
All fals enchauntementez and all sorceries,
Al fals charmes and al witchecraftes,
All fals conjurisons and all wicked craftes
That men of mysbyleve traistes opon,
Or hopes ony help in withouten God Almighten.

The secund comandement biddes us noght take
In ydelship ne in vayne the name of oure God:
So that we trow noght in his name, bot that is stedefast,
That we swere noght be his name but bihovely,
And that we neven noght his name but worshipfully.

The third is that we sal hald and halowe our haliday,
The Sononnday and all othir that falles to the yhere,
That er ordayned to halowe thurgh halikirk.
In whilk daies all folk lered and lawed,
Awe to gyf tham godely to Goddes service
To here it and say it aftir thair state is,
In worship of God Almighten and of his gode halowes;
Noght than for to tent to tary with the world,
Ne lyve in lykyng ne lust that the flesh yernes,
Bot gladly to serve God in clennesse of lyfe.

The ferth biddes us do worship to fadir and to modir,
Noght anely to fleshli fadir and modir
That getes and fosters us forthe in this world,
Bot til our gastely fadirs that has hede of us,
And teches us how to lif til hele of oure saules,
And til our gastely modir that is halikirk,
To be buxom tharto and save the right of it,
For it is modir til all that Cristenly lyfes,
And als swa til ilk man that worshipfull is,
For to do worship aftir that it is.

The fift biddes us that we sla naman,
That is at say bodily ne gastely nouthir,
For als mony we sla in that at we mai
Als we sklaundir or bacbite or falsly defames,
Or fandes for to confound tham that noght serves,
Or withdrawes lyvelade fra tham that nede haves,
If we be of haveyng for to help tham.

The sext comandement forbedes us to syn,
Or for to foly fleshli with any woman,
Outhir sib or fremmed, wedded or unwedded,
Or any fleshly knawyng or deid half with any
Othir than the sacrement of matermoyne excuse,
And the lawe and the lare of halikirke teches.

The sevent comandement biddes us noght stele.
In whilk is forboden robbyng and revyng,
Al wrangwise takyng or withhaldying,

Or hiding or helying of othir men godes,
Ogayne thaire wit and thaire will that has right to tham.

The aughtand biddes us we sal bere
No fals wittenes ogayne our even Cristen :
In whilk is forboden al maner of lesyng,
Fals conspiracie and forswerying:
Whare thurgh our even Cristen mai lese thair catell,
Faith, favour or fame, or any thyng elles
Whethir it be in gasteli or bodili godes.
The neynd is that we noght yerne oure neghtebure house.

In whilk is forboden al wrangwise covatise,
Of land or of lithe or of ought elles
That mai noght be lifted ne raised fro the ground,
Als thing that is stedefast and that mai not be stirred.

The tend and the last is that we yerne noght
The wife of our neghtebure, ne of our even Cristen,
Ne his maiden ne his knave, his ox nor his asse.
In whilk is forboden us to yerne or to take
Ony thing that may be stirred of othir men godes,
Als robes or richesse, or othir catell,
That we have no gode title, ne no right to:
For what thing so we gete, or tas in othir wise,
We mai not be assoiled of the trespas:
Bot if we make assethe in that at we may,
To tham that we harmed withaldand thaire godes.
And in cas that we have thurgh false athes,
Als in assises or othir enquestes,
Wittandly and wilfulli gert oure even Cristen
Lese thaire patermoyne or thaire heritage,
Or falsly be desesed of land or of lithe,
Or fals divorce be made, or ony man dampned,
Of al we do that we may unto the party,
Yit may we noght be assoiled of oure fals athe,
Bot of our bisshop or him that has his powere,
For swilk eas is rively reserved til him selven.

This teu comandementz that I have nowe rekend
Er umbilouked in twa of the godspell (*Luce* x° *ca*°)
The tane is that we love God over al thinges,
The tothir that we love oure even Cristen als we do oure selven;
For God augh us to love halye with hert,
With al oure might, with al oure thought, with word and with deid:
Oure even Cristen alswa augh us to love
Un to that ilk gode that we love us selven:
That is that thai welefare in bodi and in saule,
And cum to that ilk blisse that we think to,
Who so dos this twa fulfilles all the othire.

There is no evidence to shew what reception the remarkable formulary met with, of which a specimen has been given, or what effect it had upon the religious belief of the North of England. But when the people looked at their archbishop, they could see that he was in earnest. His practice was as pure and simple as his precepts. He could be seen going about his diocese exhorting and correcting, neglecting no portion of his varied and extensive duties. His private life seems to have been one continued round of work and devotion; the day began with the celebration of matins, and the services for the hours were regularly observed. The archbishop and his almost exhausted clerks were present at them all.[p] The clergy and the primate frequently met for deliberation in synods and councils,[q] and many wise enactments were then made. On the 18th of April, 1364, Thoresby promulgated a set of constitutions which met some of the errors of the times.[r] One of them was to prevent the holding of markets, wrestling matches and archery meetings, etc., in churches and churchyards. Another forbade games and sports at wakes. Mothers and nurses were ordered to keep their children out of their own beds for fear of overlaying them. Priests and clerks were to be attired in a seemly dress. All fraudulent assignments of property were reprobated, and some minute directions were given about tithes, the stipends of chaplains and others, and clandestine marriages.

It was of course Thoresby's great desire to improve the tone and character of his clergy. Whilst archbishop Zouche presided over the see, some thousands were admitted into orders, but a great number of them were in all probability laid low by the pestilence in 1349. A visitation of this severity is generally followed by a great deterioration of morals and manners. When Thoresby, therefore, came to York in 1352 he would find not only a paucity of clergy, but much ignorance and inattention to their duties among the ecclesiastics of Yorkshire. One of his chief endeavours was to add to their numbers and increase their efficiency. His ordination lists, which have been preserved, shew us how he laboured. He very rarely permitted any one to assist him in this part of his episcopal duties,[s] and the care which he bestowed upon it would soon bear its fruits. To give some idea of the extent of his work, the proceedings of a single year may serve as a specimen. In the year 1369 the archbishop held three special and four general ordinations, at which he officiated himself. At these, as many as 306 became accolites, 187 sub-deacons, 163 deacons, and 161 priests. They were to officiate in Yorkshire, a part of Nottinghamshire, and in those portions of Lancashire and Westmerland which were comprised in the archdeaconry of Richmond. When we contrast such numbers as these with the scanty lists sent forth by the prelates

[p] Stubbs, col. 1733.

[q] Wilkins, iii., 39, 85, 91, 96.

[r] Reg. Thoresby, 144. Wilkins, iii., 68.

[s] From 1356 to 1361 Thoresby officiated himself. In 1361-4, "fr. Galf. episc. Milien'" acted once in each year. In 1365 "Thomas episc. Magnassien'" officiated thrice, and "Robert episc. Lambren'" twice in 1366. From 1370 to the end of Thoresby's life the labour of the ordinations fell entirely on "Ric. Sermen' episc."

at the present day, we may well be startled at the difference. But we must not forget the reasons which, in the middle ages, made so many throng into orders. Canons, and monks, and chantry-priests, in addition to the regular parochial clergy, come then before us. The light is now quenched in the chapel and the oratory, and the monastery, which once perhaps had a hundred inmates, is now untenanted by one.

These ordination lists are a perfect study for the thoughtful and enquiring mind. There are four or five of them in each year of Thoresby's archiepiscopate, and the ceremonial usually took place in York, at the minster, Bishopthorpe, St. Mary's abbey, one of the houses of the friars, or, perhaps, now and then, elsewhere. We have no means of knowing to what examinations the candidates were subjected; but the test, in all probability, was a slight one, and considering the humble origin and the almost necessary ignorance of many of those who submitted to it, it could scarcely be otherwise. If a man was desirous of a degree in an university, he frequently obtained the permission of his diocesan to desert his living for a year or two in after life. Comparatively few, it will be observed, became either deacons or priests: the duties of a cantarist could be performed by persons of an inferior grade, and, possibly, the two higher steps necessitated a stricter examination, from which the majority would shrink. A benefice, indeed, could be held by a person who was in no orders whatever, although of course he could take but little part in the sacred duties that devolved upon him. A mediæval ordination list is a suggestive picture of clerical life which very few have looked upon. The youth comes before his diocesan frequently without a patronymic, and finding for the first time in his life that he stands in need of a surname, he adopts the title of his birthplace. Richard the son of William the baxter would convey a perfect notion of identity in Ravenser, but not beyond it; and, when he assumed the higher orders, he called himself Richard de Ravenser, by which appellation he was long honourably known. William or John Thomas's son, was not deemed euphonious or distinguishable by the world in which he wished to rise. The patronymic, also, was occasionally discarded for the name of the birthplace. Henry Daniel of Wakefield became Henry de Wakefield bishop of Worcester and lord treasurer of England. The prefix *dominus, dan* or *Sir,* which so frequently meets your eye, is applied more frequently, I think, to the possessor of a benefice than to a graduate who comes before you with the word *magister*. Here is a rector or a vicar from another diocese with letters dimissory from his bishop, and next to him, perhaps, is a graduate of Merton or of Baliol with his fellowship for his title. The question of what constituted a title to orders is full of interest. No one required one till he wished to become a sub-deacon; and then a canon, or a monk, or a beneficed clergyman had enough when he mentioned his monastery or his living. No difficulty was raised when the candidate had some means of his own or was in receipt of a stipend of five marks, about 80*l.* per annum of our money, from his father or a friend. Any one who did not come under the above category sought a title from some religious house, for it had the privilege of giving one. We sometimes see a little monastery containing, perhaps, ten or a dozen monks, giving five or six titles in a year. In all probability they could be bought. Some indeed might say that the recipient had been subjected to some preliminary course of training within its walls. This, no doubt, was in many instances the case, but it could scarcely be so when the religious house was a nunnery.

Another way in which it was in the power of Thoresby to improve the tone of his diocese was by the encouragement of learning and by promoting persons of eminence and reputation. He was himself a man of no mean or ordinary attainments. He received his education at Oxford, where he was well acquainted with Divinity and the canon law.[t] The ease and happiness of his Latin correspondence are great. His letters were regarded as masterpieces of composition by his contemporaries,[u] and if a selection from them were published in the present day, they would be read with pleasure even by those who have derived their style from the purest models of classical antiquity. A few specimens of them will excite the interest and curiosity of my readers.

I. *Archiepiscopus significat abbati Ebor. qualiter monachus suus jam redit ad monasterium.*

Salutem, etc. Venit ad nos,[v] quasi columba suam rediens ad fenestram, confrater vester frater J. de G., commensalis noster carissimus, qui jam in præterito festo Nativitatis Dominicæ nedum Divini verbi pabulo sed gestus honesti modestia tam salubriter quam laudabiliter nos refecit, quem nostri consideratione habere velitis propensius commendatum. Sibi fraternæ caritatis dulcedinem et spiritualioris communionis habundantiam petimus, impendentes per quod nos ad votiva vestra inveniri volumus pro tempore promptiores. Et quia quidam, ut dicitur, murmurant contra eum, fingentes eum quædam sinistra nobis contra vestrum aliquos prædicasse et correctiones in

[t] Bale, cent. vi., 493.

[u] There is a large collection of them in that farrago of curious matter, the second part of the Register of archbishop Alexander Neville. There are many of them, also, in MSS. Cotton, Galba, E, x.

[v] This, probably, was the monk, Garrick, or Tavistock, who was busy with the creed, etc.

capitulo vestro fieri procurasse, ipsum ab impositis hujusmodi sub verbo veritatis plenius excusamus, quia revera super hoc totaliter est immunis, et ideo nullus vestrum sibi improperet ex hac causa. Circa vero principium quadragesimæ ipsum libenter haberemus, nobis ad magnum nostrum solatium assistentem, quem ad hoc licenciare velitis cum scripserimus pro eodem. Feliciter in Domino valeatis.[w]

II. *Archiepiscopus eleganter scribit cardinali.*

Beneficiorum affluentia multiplicium quæ nobis, licet inmeritis, tam liberaliter impendidit vestra dominatio gratiosa eidem dominationi supra vires nos efficit obligatos. Sed cum non habeamus quicquam temporale condignum quod vobis digne possimus rependere pro receptis, Ille, quæsumus, vobis tribuat, qui supra meritum præmiat universos. Quoddam tamen memorale, licet modicum, affectionis, et obsequii debiti verum signum, unam videlicet capam, vobis transmittimus per dilectum clericum nostrum W. de S(kirlaugh), presentium portatorem, cui in dicendis ex parte nostra velitis credulam, si placuerit, dare fidem.

III. *Archiepiscopus eleganter significat alteri episcopo qualiter cura ecclesiæ divisa est pluribus pastoribus in partem solicitudinis vicarii Christi scilicet papæ, ut sic quisque agnoscat gregem suam.*

Convalescente dudum statu sanctæ matris ecclesiæ, cooperante semine verbi Dei, fides sibi cultores allexit, sicque propagante sobole distinctæ fuerant per sanctos patres in ecclesia prelaturæ, ut sub plurium pastorum vigiliis qui in partem solicitudinis capitis ecclesiæ vicarii, videlicet Jhesu Christi, sunt vocati, gregi melius provideretur Dominico, et dum suum quisque pastorem agnosceret, salus proximior cuilibet pararetur. Sed revera admirationem nobis jugiter multiplicem *(sic)* quod vestra circumspectio fines sic distinctos excedens, in alienam segetem falcem mittit, non contenta terminis quos posuerunt patres nostri. Nostis enim quod talis prioratus nobis et non alii præter Romanam ecclesiam insolidum est subjectus, tamen, ut dicitur, voluntarie minis opprimitis, subtrahendo, etc.

IV. *Archiepiscopus eleganter commendat magistrum Thomam de Nevill*[x] *iturum ad curiam Romanam cardinali Petragoricensi et rogat corditer pro eo.*

Reverendissimo in Christo patri et domino domino Taillere Dei gratia episcopo Albanensi Eboracensis ecclesiæque decano, Johannes ejusdem ecclesiæ archiepiscopus, Angliæ primas, cum votiva sua recommendatione reverentiam omnimodam et honorem. Generis claritas et morum gravitas ordinata quibus filius in Christo carissimus magister T. de Nevill, natus nobilis et præpotentis baronis domini Radulphi de Nevill, canonicus Ebor. et magister in artibus, qui etiam

[w] Erasmus in his book, "De conscribendis Epistolis," would scarcely coincide with Thoresby in his liking for short letters, "Illic mihi blatero quispiam arrepta censoria virgula, Solonis leges dictabit, clamabitque delendam esse epistolam quæ non intra duodecim versiculos constiterit." It will be remembered how Pliny discusses this point with his friend Tacitus. Of course he is against brevity, and covets the ingens copia verborum.

[x] Of Thomas de Neville something will soon be said. The cardinal to whom the letter was addressed was dean of York. He died in 1364.

in jure civili laute studuit et profecit eminenter, noscitur insignitus, digne proveniente intuitu attolli laudibus, et fidelis testimonii suffragio propalari. Sane cum idem magister Thomas sacrosanctam Romanam curiam ex certis de causis, per Dei gratiam adire disponat, ipsum quem ex familiari notitia sic fore scimus genere, moribus, et sciencia conspicuum, dominationi vestræ reverendæ, quæ ex mirata vobis nobilitatis et bonitatis exuberantia libenter intelligitur super dignos, votiviori quo possumus recommendamus affectu: corditer supplicantes quatinus ipsum nostri consideratione habere velitis, si placet, propensius commendatum et gratiosoribus prosequi consiliis et auxiliis in agendo paternitatem vestram.

The following letters shew that the archbishop was not devoid of humour.

V. *Litera testimonialis missa per archiepiscopum alteri episcopo quod talis clericus est superstes, et lætus, et non mortuus, prout fama laborat.*

Reverendo in Christo patri et amico nostro carissimo domino A. de B., Dei gratia Exon. episcopo, J. eadem permissione, etc., salutem et semper excrescentia fraternæ fœdera caritatis. Quia locorum distantia et relatorum levitas inconsulta plerumque veritatem obnubilant, et vias aperiunt ad errores, pium et meritorium fore credimus fidum veritati testimonium perhibere. Cum igitur, ut audivimus, quorumdam in partibus vestris habeat assertio socium nostrum carissimum venerabilem virum magistrum W. de Ex(on.)[y] canonicum ecclesiæ nostræ Ebor. diem suum clausisse extremum, scire velit vestra sinceritas pro constanti quod die datæ præsentium idem magister W. ad nos venit apud manerium nostrum de Cawode, sanus, hillaris, et jocundus, et pro nobis, qui quandam discrasiam habemus, aptam ordinavit sui gratia medicinam, et pro certo eum a magno tempore non vidimus ita lætum; quod vobis sub verbo veritatis fideliter contestamur. Incolumitatem vestram diu conservet, etc.

VI. *Archiepiscopus congratulatur cuidam seni per verba jocosa, et regratiatur sibi de literis sibi missis, et rogat ut habeat eum in precibus suis.*

Seni senex salutem, et in senectute bona diutine prosperare. Venit nobis in suavitatem odoris recensita memoria specialis amicitiæ, ac gratæ liberalisque familiaritatis, quas semper in vobis præ ceteris invenimus, et valde cedenter votis nostris præsentialiter vos videre ut mutuis possemus colloquiis, et solatiis confoveri. Sed cum hoc locorum distantia commode non permittat, suppleat, quæsumus, defectum corporalis præsentiæ mentalis præsentiæ plenitudo, quæ latius se diffundit; nam sicut scribitur "*non ubi animat est anima, quin verius ubi amat.*" Unde consideratione amoris antiqui, quem inter nos non antiquatum esse credimus, velitis in devotionibus vestris memores esse nostri, requirentes vos semper cum fiducia, si quæ volu-

[y] William de Exonia, master in theology, arts, and medicine, became prebendary of Riccal in 1336. He held stalls at Lincoln and Exeter. He died about 1360. Cf. Fœd., ii., 1104. Fuller's Worthies, ii., 305. Fœd., iii., 82. Queen Philippa presented him in 1339 to the rectory of Castleford.

eritis nos facturos, ad quorum placabile complementum inveniètis ex animo nos paratos. Sit diu vobis ætas valida, quæ, licet pruinosa insenescat in capite, virtuosa tamen insenescat incremento.

VII. *Archiepiscopus recommendat se magistris de cancellaria regis.*[a]

Socii et amici carissimi, cederet nobis ad augmentum lætitiæ de prosperitate vestra audire placentia, et quia de nobis similia libenter, ut confidimus, audiretis, dilectioni vestræ arridentem jam nobis, laudetur Deus, sanitatem corpoream nuntiamus, gerentes in votis vobis et vestrum singulis facere quæ sciverimus fore grata. Et quidem jam rem novam aggredimur, nunc laboribus, nunc solatiis, indulgentiis, plus quandoque vacantes in visitatione nostra venationi Veneris quam ferarum. Et sic caveat dominus W. de L., ne commissa sua præterita jam in lucem erumpant; quod si forsan contigerit, propter reliquias antiquæ familiaritatis agemus mitius cum eodem. Alia non occurrunt jam scribenda, sed agenda nostra penes nos, cum emerserint, habere velitis affectione solita, si placuerit, commendata, nos semper in votivis fiducialiter requirentes.

VIII. *Archiepiscopus scribit cuidam veteri amico suo, jocando, et rogat eum visitare eum et habebit bonum vinum.*

Venerunt ad nos in exultatione spiritus dilectionis vestræ literæ pluries nobis missæ, quæ, licet de veteri dicamus, innecata procedant pharetra, cum juvenem et lætum animum repræsentant, dum in eis apta connexione jocosa sapidis ministretis. Et quidem merito dici debet placabilis hæc mixtura per quam avida mens scientia instruitur et hillaritas provocatur, sed cum hillaritas floridam producat ætatem debet potissime senibus esse grata. Et quia bonum vinum cor exhillarat, ut alludamus potatorum proverbio, *vinum subtile facit in sene cor juvenile,* ipsius usum moderatum jocundo vobis consilio sancimus; ut cum ad partes veneritis nos personaliter visitetis, ut de antiquis possimus communicare præludiis, et de vino nostro cum appendiciis ad recreationem vel renovationem juventutis mutuæ vobis participabimus læta manu.

We acquire from these letters a very pleasing impression of Thoresby's powers of composition, and they shew us, also, that their benevolent writer was neither a bigot nor a fanatic. A man who could use his pen with so much facility and in so pleasing a manner, could speak no doubt with the same ease and readiness. There must have been in him the voice and the bearing of a courtier. The skill which he had manifested in diplomacy must have aided him in his diocese, and there would

[a] An amusing and familiar letter, written probably soon after Thoresby became permanently settled in the North, to his old friends in the chancery office. Several of them held preferments at York. David de Wooller, master of the rolls, whom Thoresby speaks of as "socius noster carissimus," was prebendary of Fridaythorp from 1352 to 1370. Henry de Ingleby held, in succession, the stalls of Ampleforth and South Cave. Richard de Ravenser was a canon of York and provost of Beverley. The list might be increased. Who the delinquent was to whom Thoresby humorously alludes I know not.

be many even there to admire the learning which had attracted the attention of Edward III. and Clement VI. John Baconthorp inscribed to the archbishop his commentary on the Ethics of Aristotle,[a] and Thoresby himself was not unknown in the world of letters. He is said to have entered into the lists with the Mendicant Friars,[b] who had been bold enough to preach that mortuaries ought not to be rendered to the priest. Against them, as Bale informs us, Thoresby wrote "*Processum quendam*" in one book, commencing with the words "*Pridem sanctissimus in Christo pater.*" The second part of archbishop Neville's register contains several pieces which may perhaps be ascribed to his predecessor. They consist of a series of extracts from the Vulgate and the Patristic writings, some fragments of letters, and a portion of a Catholicon, or dictionary of difficult terms.[c] It does not go beyond the first letter of the alphabet.

Among the great men who became beneficed in York minster during Thoresby's archiepiscopate, it is enough to mention the names of Alexander de Neville, his successor in the see, Robert Braybrook, bishop of London, Henry de Wakefield, bishop of Worcester and treasurer of England, cardinal Simon de Langham, archbishop of Canterbury, William de Courtney, of whom it is unnecessary to speak, and John de Waltham, bishop of Salisbury. But there are two others with whom Thoresby was intimately connected at York who must not be forgotten, Walter de Skirlaugh,[d] bishop of Durham, his private chaplain and

[a] Vicaria Leod. and Bale. Cf. Bibl. Carmelitana, i., col. 750. It is there said erroneously, that Thoresby died in 1474, and Bacon in 1346.

[b] In Antiq. Univ. Oxon., i., 475, John Toresbie is mentioned as an opponent of the begging friars, who by their meddling had become an intolerable nuisance. Wycliffe, Fitzralph, and others, took the same side. Cf. Walsingham, 173. I do not suppose that Thoresby's encounter with the friars was an angry or a serious one. His will is enough to shew that there was no ill-feeling towards them remaining in his mind. See the prefaces to the Fascic. Zizan., and the Monum. Francisc., by Messrs. Shirley and Brewer. Bale says the friars were "ad id invitati ac concitati a quibusdam primoribus, qui talia solvere jure debebant."

[c] This account of Thoresby's works is taken from Bale, cent. vi., 493. Vicaria Leodiensis, 189. Tanner Bibl. Brit., 711.

"Incipit tractus, catholicon dictus, abreviatus, in quo reperies omnes difficultates sacræ scripturæ, quæ consueverunt legi et recitari communiter in ecclesiis, expositus, quantum ad intellectum literalem ac moralem, secundum ordinem alphabeticum." There are two or three leaves of it.

[d] In MSS. Cotton, Galba, E, x., 74, is a letter from Skirlaugh to the archbishop excusing, for many reasons, his long stay at Rome. Thoresby writes, and says that Skirlaugh has told him that Peter, cardinal bishop of Præneste, archdeacon of York, has left by will 100 florins to the church of York; and he desires that measures be taken for securing it for the fabric (ibid., 82).

In 1354 and 1356 Skirlaugh was Thoresby's domestic chaplain. In 1358 he was ordained accolite, deacon, and subdeacon at York, by letters dimissory, his title being the rectory of Preston Bisset, co. Bucks. In 1361 he was made archdeacon of the East Riding (Reg. Thoresby).

Skirlaugh's connection with Thoresby

correspondent, and the well-known William of Wykeham.[e] From these two distinguished ecclesiastics, so renowned for their architectural taste, Thoresby, in all probability, derived many hints for the work that he effected in his own cathedral, and it is likely enough that the beautiful structure which Skirlaugh and Wykeham would gaze upon as it arose from the ground at York, would awaken that zeal in the same cause which led them to imitate the example of their patron at Winchester and Durham.

This brings before us the glorious choir which Thoresby commenced at York, and which was far superior in beauty to that which Conrad once raised in the sister-church of Canterbury. Years had passed away since archbishop Melton completed the western façade, uncrowned still by its two stately towers, and glazed the noble window which is its chief grace, whilst, towards the east, the choir of archbishop Roger, insignificant as it must have been in size and decoration, was still

and with York made him take great interest in the rebuilding of the choir. His arms, six osiers, in cross, interlaced, are cut in stone in the north choir transept, which, perhaps, he helped to build.

They also occur in the lantern tower, "magnam partem campanilis, vulgo lantern, minsterii Eboracensis construxit, *in medio cujus operis arma sua posuit*" (Hist. Dunelm. Scriptores Tres, 144). This, however, was done after his death. In his will, dated in 1403, Skirlaugh bequeathed 100 marks to the fabric of the minster (Test. Ebor., i., 309). In addition to this sum, I suppose, his executors paid to the keeper of the fabric in 1415 the sum of 52*l.* for the wages of six masons for a year (Fabric Rolls, 32). The lantern, probably, was being built in this year.

I look, I must confess, with much distrust upon the inferences drawn from the appearance of shields of arms in churches, and other heraldic devices. They were frequently carved, I believe, as is the case in the present day, long after the part of the building which they ornament was completed. The person to whom they carry us, was a benefactor to the church, and probably to that part of it, but the inference as to the exact date is unsafe. These shields, I believe, were often left blank till the building was finished, and for a good reason. A work, for example, extends over twenty years. If during the first five all the stone shields were covered with the bearings of those who had contributed up to that time, there would be no room left to commemorate, perhaps, some far greater benefactor at a later period, or towards the close of the work. When everything was done, a proper and a fair selection could be made. Much caution also should be used in inferring dates from stained glass.

[e] This great man was prebendary of Laughton at York, when he was advanced to the see of Winchester. He had also been a canon at Beverley and Southwell. Thoresby wrote to congratulate him when he became a bishop (Reg. Neville, part ii., 26 *a*); and between him and Wykeham there was much intimacy and friendship.

In 1357 Wykeham was custos of the royal works at Windsor castle, and at the same time he was actually the keeper of the king's dogs at that place! Eleven years after this he was bishop of Winchester. The story of his life is part of the history of England, "neither do I doubt," says Stowe the chronicler, "but he that thus lived is now with God, whom I beseech to raise up many like bishops in England." Had not his birth-place been ascertained, I should have tried to fix it in Yorkshire, and yet Fuller says, "How can his *cradle* be certainly fixed in any place, when it is equally rockt betwixt *twenty* villages of the same denomination."

untouched. The contrast would be deemed a painful one, and would excite many a remark. On Trinity Sunday, 1348, Thomas Sampson, a wealthy canon who had had somewhat to do with the erection of the nave, left the sum of 20*l.* to the new choir, if the work was begun within a year after his decease, thus fulfilling a promise which he had frequently made to Thomas de Ludham and Thomas de Patenham the keepers of the fabric.[f] The time passed away and the legacy was unclaimed, and it is probable enough that the French wars, the pestilence, and the long continued illness of archbishop Zouche were a great bar to the commencement of the building. When Thoresby came to the see in 1352, he found the minster overburdened with debt,[g] another reason for delay, but he was not a man to be long satisfied with inactivity, and, as soon as he could disengage himself from his state employments, he threw himself with heart and soul into his work at York. The unfinished and neglected condition of the cathedral caused him much grief.[h] On the 25th of January, 1354, he granted an indulgence of 40 days to those who contributed to the fabric, and on the 19th of January, 1356, the chapter wrote to ask him to give them timber to complete the ceiling of the nave.[i] In 1359 and 1360 the archbishop gave several sums of money to the fabric fund of the church.[j] The chapter and the primate had now made up their minds to begin the erection of a new choir, the old one being removed by degrees as it could be dispensed with. On the 20th of July, 1361, Thoresby aided the good work by ordering his manor-house at Sherburn to be pulled down, that the stone, a scarce and valuable article, might be made use of in the minster.[k] Ten days after this, he laid the foundation-stone of the new choir, accompanying the act by a gift of 100 marks towards the under-

[f] Test. Ebor., i., 54.

[g] MSS. Cotton, Galba, E, x., 61.

[h] Among the observations in Neville's register, part ii., is the following which I refer to Thoresby and his church. He is using the Vulgate. "*No^a ecclesia Ebor.* (in margine). Capud meum doleo, conturbatus est in ira oculus meus, anima mea, et venter meus, quia corona capitis fere deciditur, fere deficit in doloribus vita mea. Nam ubi in primaria fundatione fueram in reverentia, sicut domina gentium, princeps provinciarum, libertatibus et privilegiis radiata et dotata, facta sum opprobrium gentium serviens sub tributo; facies mea quæ aliquando fuerat formosa præ singultuosis suspiriis et nimium effusis lacrimis supra carbones denigratur, dum dispersi sunt lapides sanctuarii in capite omnium platearum. Et quæ olim fueram formosa corruo tristis et anxia, etc." (6 *b*).

[i] Most of these documents, and others connected with the fabric about this period, may be found in the York Fabric Rolls, published by the Surtees Society.

[j] 1359, April 20. To John de Codyngham, master of the fabric of the Church of York, 20*l.* for the more rapid completion of the said fabric. 1360, Nov. 24. An order to pay the like sum to him. The same on Jan. 7, seq., and 30*l.* on April 14, 1361. This money was probably spent in completing what was wanting in the nave, or in making preparations for the commencement of the choir.

[k] Fabric Rolls, 174-5.

taking.[l] In addition to this sum, he prompted and stimulated the munificence of others by indulgences granted by himself and obtained from the chief pontiff, and during the remainder of his life he gave yearly to the fabric fund the generous benefaction of 200*l*.[m] I cannot estimate the amount of Thoresby's gifts to the choir only, in the money of the present day, at a lower sum than 37,000*l*., and this, in all probability, is considerably under the mark. When, in addition to this, we take into consideration the money which must have been derived from other sources, it is impossible to doubt the accuracy of the historian when he tells us that the Lady-chapel or presbytery was finished in the archbishop's lifetime.[n]

In confirmation of the accuracy of the chronicler, we have

[l] The order to pay it is dated on Aug. 1 (Reg. Thoresby). "*In primi positione lapidis centum marcis de suo proprio dotavit*" (Stubbs, col. 1733).

[m] "*Postea annuatim, dum vixit, fabricæ prædictæ ducentas libras persolvebat*" (Stubbs). The following extracts from Thoresby's register shew the regularity of his payments, and the accuracy of the chronicler. 1361. Oct. 3, 50*l*. 1362. April 13, 100*l*.; Aug. 9, 100*l*. 1363. April 16, 100*l*.; Nov. 3, 100*l*. 1364. July 6, 100*l*.; Dec. 4, 100*l*. 1365. June 13, 100*l*.; Oct. 16, 100*l*. 1366. June 24, 100*l*.; Nov. 5, 100*l*. 1367. May 7, 100*l*.; Oct. 23, 100*l*. 1368. April 20, 100*l*.; Nov. 14, 100*l*. 1369. Aug. 15, 100*l*. 1370. Jan. 28, 100*l*.; July 28, 100*l*.; Nov. 25, 100*l*. 1371. June 15, 100*l*.; Nov. 1, 100*l*. 1372. March 10, forty marks in full payment of 100*l*.; 25 —, 100*l*. 1373. Feb. 11, 100*l*.; July 24, 100*l*. The keepers of the fabric during this period were John de Codyngham (Cottingham), John de Sandale, Adam de Henedlay (Henley), John de Laghton or Leghton, and John de Ferriby.

The sum total of the above gifts is no less than 2,376*l*. 13*s*. 4*d*., which was bestowed entirely upon the choir; in addition to which there is the following gift: April 5, 1362, To Robert de Rithre, lord of Rithre, 20*l*. for twenty-four oaks which we have bought of him for the fabric of our church at York. To bring this large sum to the money of the present day we cannot multiply it by less than fifteen, and this produces nearly 36,000*l*.

[n] "*Et ut operi prædicto subvenire devotionem fidelium ardentius excitaret, omnibus ejusdem fabricæ benefactoribus indulgentias largissimas a sanctissimis patribus apostolicis concessas, sua petitione impetravit, et ad remedium animarum suorum subjectorum et aliorum quorumcunque manum adjutricem præbentium, cum propriis indulgentiis et benedictione miro affectu illas participavit*" (Stubbs). This is borne out by the Fabric Rolls, 175-6, and other places. Everything was done that could swell the fabric funds. The brevigeri were sent about even into the diocese of Lincoln to beg (Fabric Rolls, 178; Lit. quæst. pro fabrica Ebor., 21 Oct., 1356, etc.). In 1360-1 the chapter made a tax of a twentieth, to last for three years. On Oct. 12, 1365, the dean of the Christianity of York was ordered to levy the recent subsidy to the fabric of 4d. in each mark from the clergy of his deanery; and on the 20th a commission was issued to collect 2d. in every mark from all spiritual and temporal benefices in the diocese, towards the fabric fund. In the eighth of Richard II. the value of the church property alone within the province of York was taken at 40,000 marks per annum (Chron. Thorn., 2164). By these means large sums would be gathered together, and I cannot think that the fabric fund would in any year in Thoresby's lifetime, after the choir was begun, be under 600*l*., and this is a low estimate when we recollect that a third of it was contributed by the archbishop. With such a sum as this wielded by active hands the presbytery could easily be finished in less than twelve years.

decisive evidence that the presbytery was in use within a short period after the decease of its alleged builder. On the 17th of August, 1384, John de Waltham, sub-dean of York and Thoresby's kinsman, in a codicil to his will which was made at Newbald near York, left the sum of 20*l.* to two chaplains who were to perform service in *the new work of the church of York,* for the souls of his master, archbishop Thoresby, Henry de Ingelby and others. The new work was the choir, as is shewn by many documents and wills, and here we have an intimation that a portion of it, which was of course the presbytery, was so far complete that services could be done in it which were to extend over two years. It may be inferred from the mention of this period of time that the work was finished, as the chaplains could not, nor would they, be asked to sing for two years continuously in a place where they might be interrupted by carpenters and masons, and stone and wood. It is well known that these masses, for obvious reasons, were performed immediately after the decease of the testator. If the presbytery had not been ready to allow the priests to officiate in it, or if there was likely to be any delay in carrying out the wishes of Waltham, the sub-dean, of all people, would have known that, and would have expressed himself differently. The conclusion, therefore, is irresistible that the presbytery was finished in 1384. Where could Thoresby be more appropriately commemorated than at the altar which he had founded in that place? Otherwise, some different altar must have been in use in the same part of the cathedral at that time, and why should it not? In my memoir of archbishop Arundel I shall give some new and decisive evidence as to the date of the western portion of the choir.

One of the main wishes of Thoresby in all this labour and expense was to provide a place where the mass of the Blessed Virgin might be daily celebrated.[o] Accordingly the work began

[o] "In ecclesia Ebor. non fuerat aliquis locus congruus ubi missa gloriosæ Dei genetricis et Virginis Mariæ cotidie in ipsa ecclesia celebranda decenter poterat celebrari" (Fabric Rolls, 174. Thoresby's words). This document has reference to the choir only, and Stubbs gives us the result when he says, "*Idem archiepiscopus, ut verus amator Virginis capellam ejusdem Dei genetricis et Virginis Mariæ—peregit*" (Stubbs). The only portion of the church which is or has been called the Lady chapel is that at the east end, where there was an altar of St. Mary; and in 1557 Sir Leonard Beckwith desired to be buried "*in our Lady queare wher they singe messe behynde the highe aulter;*" and he was buried at the east end of the church, as is said in his wife's will. This proves where the Lady chapel was and is: most certainly it was not the chapel, once adjacent to the north wall of the nave, of the foundation of archbishop Roger. That was always called the chapel of St. Mary and the Holy Angels, or that of St. Sepulchre, and never at any time the Lady chapel. What Thoresby of Leeds and Gent of York say on this point is of no value, and no argument can be drawn from the fact that some richly sculptured stones have been discovered in houses

at the extreme east and proceeded westward, and there he constructed a Lady chapel or presbytery, full of rich sculpture and painting, in the centre of which the altar to the Virgin was set up. This chapel occupies four bays of the choir towards the west, and the munificent founder, as Stubbs informs us, had the privilege of seeing it thoroughly completed in his lifetime.[p] Before that altar of the Virgin he caused six marble stones to be laid to commemorate six of his predecessors who had been interred in the old choir, which was farther westwards. He was well aware that in course of time, as the old building that was around them was removed, their remains would be disturbed. He therefore took up their bones and placed them in the Lady chapel under the six stones which were wrought for him by the master-mason of the cathedral.[q] When Leland was making his

at a little distance from the site of St. Sepulchre's chapel. In the first place, no one can say that they belonged to it, or to the minster at all, and, if they did, they cannot be brought forward to shew that archbishop Thoresby built it, for they are not of Thoresby's time. They prove nothing. Stubbs has described minutely the foundation of St. Sepulchre's chapel by archbishop Roger, and its re-formation by Sewal de Bovill in a way that leaves no doubt as to its identity. Would he not have been equally clear and precise in telling us about Thoresby's alterations in it, if he had made them?

[p] "*Idem vero archiepiscopus, ut verus amator Virginis, capellam ejusdem Dei genetricis et Virginis Mariæ mirabili artis sculptura, atque notabili pictura peregit*" (Stubbs). Nothing can be more decisive than this. Thoresby began a Lady chapel and he *finished* it. If, therefore, this Lady chapel is the easternmost part of the church, or the presbytery, and it can be no other place, that part of the minster was altogether built by Thoresby, and, putting aside the corroborative documentary proofs of this which are given in the Surtees Fabric Rolls, the architecture itself tells the same tale.

It has been said that the life of Thoresby by Stubbs is not to be relied upon, because it does not appear in every MS. of that chronicler, and because there are blunders in it.

If criticism is of any value, internal evidence will shew that the hand that wrote the lives, for instance, of Corbridge, Greenfield, and Melton, the authenticity of which has not been questioned, wrote that of Thoresby also. The circumstance of Thoresby's life not being in every MS., which is easily accounted for, would be regarded by many as a proof of its authenticity. There could be no possible reason for ascribing it falsely to Stubbs, and not a doubt was thrown upon it till the controversy about the choir began. Even if Stubbs was not the author of it, it is taken from a MS. of undoubted antiquity, and it would possess, therefore, an independent value of its own.

With regard to the alleged errors in the life, they remain to be proved. There is no chronicle, I believe, which will bear in every place the searching test of collateral information, and minute points are often discarded. I will say this, however, for Stubbs: no one could have submitted the work of an historian to a more searching examination than I have that of his, and, though occasionally inexact, he is on the whole wonderfully correct, and his life of Thoresby is perhaps more correct, as it is also more interesting, than any other. I have given my readers an opportunity in these notes of seeing this for themselves. It could not have been written by any one who was unacquainted with the person that he speaks of, as is the case with the life of Melton also, and there is strong corroborative evidence of almost every fact that he narrates. With regard to the building of the choir Stubbs is very decisive, and his testimony is incontrovertible.

[q] "*Idem archiepiscopus — capellam Virginis Mariæ — peregit.* IBIQUE

tour in the beginning of the sixteenth century he observed the stones where Thoresby placed them,[r] and they still occupied the same position at the close of the seventeenth century when they

plurimorum venerabilium pontificum, prædecessorum suorum, corpora, a choro superius translata, propriis expensis fecit tumulari" (Stubbs).

It has been shewn *where* this chapel was. We are now told that Thoresby interred *in it* the remains of six of his predecessors. The following evidence and that in the succeeding notes will again shew the exactness of the chronicler, and fix decisively the position of that chapel and the tombs in it even at the beginning of the eighteenth century.

1369, Feb. 18, an order from archbishop Thoresby to pay to master Robert de Patrington, master mason of the fabric of the new choir of our church at York, for the making of six marble stones for the tombs of our predecessors, for which we have entered into an agreement with him, 10*l.* Aug. 23, 1369, 10 marks more to him for the same purpose, in part payment of 40*l.* 1373, June 12, 100s. more to him (Reg. Thoresby).

In the Fabric Roll for 1434 (ed. Surtees Society, 54), among the smaller expenses, there is an entry which shews that the stones had been laid down before the altar of the Virgin, and that the brazen imagery was then fixed in them or re-set. "In vadio j hominis firmantis ymagines episcoporum in petra coram altare B.M., 6s. 8d." *Petra* clearly refers to the stones in front of the altar. Petra never means a pier, and, besides, there is no pier *before* the altar of the Virgin in which they could be placed, supposing them to be statues or images, nor are there traces of any fixings in the lateral piers.

[r] In Leland's Itinerary, viii., 14, ed. 1769, is the following passage:—

"Sepul. Archiepiscoporum in orient. parte ecclesiæ.

1277. Walterus Gisfart obiit 7 Cal. Maii, anno Dom. 1277.

1153. Henry Murdak obiit anno Dom. 1153.

1108. Gerardus obiit 12 Cal. Jun. anno Dom. 1108. Defuit inscriptio

1373. Johannes de Thoresby, quondam Menevensis, postea Wigorn. et Ebor archiepiscopus, qui fabricam . . . . obiit 6 die Novembris anno Dom. 1373.

1113. Thomas junior obiit anno Dom. 1113, 5 Idus Mart.

1295. Johan. Romanus obiit anno Dom. 1295."

We thus see that in the reign of Henry VIII. Leland saw at the east end of York minster the tombs of seven archbishops, of whom Thoresby was one. The altar of St. Mary is in that part of the church, and nowhere else were there the tombs of six primates together. The position of Thoresby in the middle shews clearly that the place of his interment was marked before these stones were laid down, for, as Torre draws them, they were contiguous to each other, and as Thoresby tells us himself in his will that he had fixed upon the place in which he was to be laid *(in loco alias ordinato)*, it seems naturally to follow that the tombstones of his predecessors, and perhaps his own, were then in their proper position.

The evidence of Leland is strongly confirmatory of what has been said already. But an attempt has been made to throw discredit upon his testimony. The grounds taken for this are the confused state of the MS. where this passage occurs; the fact that the passage occurs, not in Leland's own MS., but in a copy of it made by Stowe the antiquary. It is also asserted that from the nature of the information itself, it was not taken by Leland from personal observation, but from a MS. of lord Scrope's. 1. It is well known that the omissions and misplacements in Leland's MSS., which are very numerous, were caused not through Leland's carelessness, for he was very accurate as far as he professed to go, but from the neglect of those who arranged and bound his MSS. after his decease. Proper allowance should be made for this. 2. Even if it was copied by Stowe, it was copied from Leland's MSS., and it is therefore trustworthy, for Stowe was a careful and learned man, and would copy faithfully as far as possible

were sketched and described by James Torre, the well-known and laborious antiquary.[s]

At that altar of the Virgin in the new choir, before which the remains of Thoresby himself were laid among those of his predecessors which he had so honourably entombed, a cantarist, who bore the same rank as the *personæ* of the minster, offered up prayers for the archbishop's soul. Stubbs tells us that he derived his income from houses and lands of the primate's own procuring, but the history of this altar is a somewhat remarkable one.[t] Henry lord Percy, who died in 1351, expressed a strong wish to his executors that chantries should be founded by them

what was before him. 3. Supposing, for the sake of argument, that it *was* copied, as is said, from a book belonging to lord Scrope, no family would be better able to know what was in this part of York minster, as it was their burial-place. But Leland was in York himself, as his Itinerary several times shews, and it was unnecessary, therefore, for him to take from others what he could see himself, for if Torre saw these monuments in 1700, much more could Leland almost two centuries before. The notes are roughly taken, after his fashion, and they must not be criticized as if their writer intended to give a full and accurate account of what he saw. The objection proves too much. If these notes are not Leland's making, the whole of his work, nay, his works, I may say, are an imposture. They are Leland all over. Many passages might be given very similar to this about York, for brevity and meagreness of description are his failing, although he was a shrewd and close observer. Take the following notice of Hereford cathedral (Itin., viii., 55):—

"In australi parte chori.

1198. Gul. de Vere episcopus Hereforden: præfuit 12 annis. Obiit 9 call. Januarii anno Dom. 1198.
Dominus Robertus Foliot episcopus Hereforden.

1147. Robertus de Melum sedit annis . . . tempore Henrici 2 filii . . . Hic fuit in omni genere literarum insigniter eruditus. Obiit anno Dom. 1147.
Dominus Robertus Betune episcopus Hereforden.
Dominus Reinelmus episcopus Hereforden.

1516. Dominus Richard Maiew episcopus Hereforden., doctor theologiæ, rector turbæ Magdalenensis, archedecon of Oxford, chanselar of Oxforde, elemosinarius Henri the 7, præfuit Hereforden. eccl. 11 annis et amplius. Obiit 8 die April. anno Dom. 1516."

[s] Torre measured the stones, marked their places in his map of the pavement of the minster, and sketched them in pen and ink. There were mitres upon them, and other signs of archbishops, formerly in brass, as he tells us, and they were laid right in front of the old altar of St. Mary, before the great east window. An engraving of his drawings and his verbal description of them is given in the preface to my Fabric Rolls, xviii. It will be seen therefore, by an irrefragable chain of evidence, where the altar of St. Mary and the chapel and the tombs were of which Stubbs speaks, and thus we know what part of the church it was that Thoresby completed before his death (*perfecit*—Stubbs). Leland also tells us the same thing when he says that Thoresby "de novo struxit chorum," and "perfecit navim" (Lel. Coll., i., 45, 121).

[t] "*Ibidem* (*i. e.*, at St. Mary's altar) *pro anima sua et animabus omnium fidelium defunctorum capellanum pro suo perpetuo celebratarum constituit. Quem quidem capellanum suosque successores habitum personalem in ecclesia cathedrali prædicta gestaturum, ad perpetuam ejus memoriam composuit, domos et possessiones de suo proprio acquisitas, perpetuam eleemosynam prædicto presbytero et successoribus suis pro suo perpetuo contulit duraturas*" (Stubbs).

for the weal of his soul, but it was not apparently until 1362 that his son, Sir Henry Percy, and two of his executors, William Newport, rector of Spofforth and Sir Richard Tempest, knight, carried his desire into effect. On the 10th of December in that year the archbishop, in a very interesting and carefully constructed document, gave his consent to the establishment of four chantries and laid down rules for their management. Three were to be at Alnwick castle and one in the minster of York, and they were all to be endowed with the profits of the church of Kirkby Overblowers, which were ceded for that purpose by Sir Henry Percy. Between the chantries at York and Alnwick there is a marked and peculiar distinction. The three chaplains at Alnwick were to pray for Henry lord Percy who was interred in Alnwick abbey, Mary lady Percy, etc., and they were to be presented by the executors to the archbishop, and he was to admit them. The cantarist at York, on the other hand, was to be nominated by the archbishop and his successors, and presented by the executors. He was to pray for the good estate of Thoresby and the canons during their lives, and for his soul after his decease, together with the souls of his predecessors and successors, *and* for those of lord Percy, etc., and others of his family. There is no record here, it will be observed, of any endowment in the shape of lands or houses by Thoresby himself, but still the peculiar and prominent manner in which his name is connected with the York chantry, makes it plain to me that he must have been in some way or other pecuniarily interested in its foundation.[u] The fact, which we learn from Stubbs, that he built and ornamented the place in which the chantry was erected, is sufficient to account for this. Thoresby gave the executors a position for the chantry chapel to which it was necessary to add nothing in the way of decoration and appendages. Hence it was that it was called the Thoresby-Percy chantry, and sometimes that of Thoresby only.[v] It is impossible to suppose that the archbishop would be allowed to take the lead in a chantry in which he had no right and claim. The family of Percy would not have tolerated such conduct. He could not be doing a wrong or an injustice when the king, the chapter and Sir Henry Percy sanctioned his proceedings, whilst the executors of the deceased noble gladly accepted the arrangement, "scienter et gratanter voto unanimi cum omnibus suis articulis acceptârunt,

[u] That this circumstance was not publicly declared is no proof against its existence, and other feelings than those of shame might easily prompt its concealment, as Pliny says to his friend Saturninus, "Si qui benefacta sua verbis adornant, non ideo prædicare quia fecerint, sed ut prædicarent, fecisse creduntur. Sic quod magnificum referente alio fuisset, ipso qui gesserat recensente, vanescit."

[v] York Fabric Rolls, 295, etc.

applauserunt et emologârunt."[w] This looks as if the archbishop had been doing them a favour instead of receiving one.

The shades of evening may be for a long time delayed, but they must come at last: the sun must at length set.[x] And yet we may apply to the pious and now aged man the words in which Beza addressed Tiraquellus, when in his friendly warmth he spoke of him as the Varro of his time,

> "Fortunate senex! te nulla oblivio mortis,
> Te nunquam totum tollet avara dies."

The good archbishop, who must have been more that seventy years of age, fell into his last sickness in the autumn of 1373, at his palace at Bishopthorpe. On the 12th of September, a notary was summoned into the sick prelate's bedchamber to draw up his will. The sentences are evidently written down as they fell from Thoresby's lips. There is no display, and nothing can be more matter of fact and concise. There are in the will as many as forty-four legacies, all, with the exception of five, in money, the highest sum bequeathed being that of 40 marks. The following legacies are probably to relations. To Agnes and Margaret de Thoresby, 80 marks. To John de Thoresby, 40 marks. To Robert Thoresby, 20 marks. To Elias de Thoresby, 10*l.* Robert de Hackthorpe, notary, the writer of the will, Henry de Greymsby, John de Cloune, Elias de Thoresby and Thomas de Midelton, are each rewarded with a silver cup with a cover. The domestics of the dying prelate, the butler, barber, brewer, the keeper of the pantry and the larder, and the page of the chamber are all of them remembered. Two friars, John de Thoresby and William de Haynton, were to have five marks apiece, and Idonea de Brunnom, a nun at Hampole, 100s. To each house of begging friars in York a bequest of five marks was made. The following persons were then appointed executors, Sir Richard le Scrop,[y] knight,

[w] Domesday book penes Dec. et Cap. Ebor., 62 *a*, etc. This contains the elaborate foundation of the chantries from which the information in this paragraph has been mainly derived. Thoresby was very anxious, as he tells us, about these chantries, "desideranter cupimus, quantum cum Deo possimus, quod cantariis hujusmodi de cætero laudabiliter deserviatur." The place, time and manner of celebrating the service at York were left to his discretion, and we can easily imagine, therefore, why the altar of St. Mary in the presbytery was selected.

[x] The beautiful lines of Waller suggest themselves :—

> "The seas are quiet, when the winds give o'er.
> So, calm are we, when passions are no more.
> For then we know how vain it was to boast
> Of fleeting things, so certain to be lost.
> Clouds of affection from our younger eyes
> Conceal that emptiness which age descries.
> The soul's dark cottage, batter'd and decay'd,
> Lets in new light, through chinks that time has made:
> Stronger by weakness, wiser men become,
> As they draw near to their eternal home:
> Leaving the old, both worlds at once they view
> That stand upon the threshold of the new."

[y] First lord Scrope, of Bolton. A great soldier, and lord treasurer and lord chancellor of England. He died in 1403, æt. 75, and in his noble will made in 1400 he left 10*l.* to the new

Mr. John de Waltham,[c] and Mr. John de Thoresby and dan Henry de Barton,[a] canons of York, and Mr. Henry de Greymsby, and, as a last request, they were desired to make a further acknowledgment of the services of the servants of the testator, if his estate should permit of it. There is nothing to shew that Thoresby was a wealthy man, or that he had a large and expensive household. He had probably laid his treasure up where alone it can be found.

John de Cloune and Elias de Thoresby were standing by whilst the notary took down these words, and on the 31st of October the three were summoned into the archbishop's presence to listen to a codicil which he wished to make. He had but little to say and add. If it happened that he went the way of all flesh by reason of the infirmity which afflicted him, he desired that his body should be interred within four days after his decease in the place which he had otherwise arranged. To John de Cloune, who was standing by, he gave one of his better cups of silver, and he begged his executors to reward with his silver plate those clerks belonging to his household who had small benefices. He forgave Robert de Thoresby 10*l.* which he owed him. To Agnes and Margaret de Thoresby, daughters of the late Galfrid de Thoresby,[b] he gave 100*l.* due to him from Henry de Barton. To the vicar of the church of Leeds he left a robe which he had worn.[c] The sick man said nothing more, and this is our last glimpse of archbishop Thoresby. On Sunday the 6th of November,[d] being St. Leonard's day, he passed away, and his good deeds went with him.

They laid his remains before the altar of the Virgin, for whom he had a profound veneration, in the lady-chapel at York, the "novum opus chori" which he had himself constructed.[e]

work at York minster (Test. Ebor., i., 275. Scrope and Grosvenor Roll, i., 59).

[z] The archbishop's kinsman. Thoresby asked the bishop of Lincoln to allow John de Waltham, rector of Cortenhale, bachelor of laws, to be non-resident, that he might go to the schools (MSS. Cotton, Galba, E, x., 85). Mr. John de Waltham, rector of Cortenhale, was ordained sub-deacon by Thoresby at Westminster, by letters dimissory, on April 23, 1356, at a special ordination, deacon on the vigil of S. Trin., 1361, having the sacristry of St. Sepulchre's chapel at York as his title, and priest on Saturday after the feast Exalt. S. Crucis, 1361 (Reg. Thoresby).

[a] Thoresby's domestic chaplain in 1360. Treasurer of York, prebendary, in succession, of Riccal and Osbaldwick, and rector of Bolton Percy. Master of the hospital of St. Mary Magd., near Southwell, and canon of Lincoln.

[b] In 1350 Geoffrey de Thoresby received the dilapidations due to bishop Thoresby at Worcester (Thomas's Worcester, 179). In the 11th of Edward III. he was made "assaiator monetæ regiæ" (Cal. Rot. Pat., 130).

[c] The will and codicil are in Test. Ebor., i., 88, etc.

[d] Acta Capit. Ebor. On the 7th the chapter order Robert de Newton, their chamberlain, and John de Feriby, to sequestre Thoresby's effects. Stubbs, col. 1734. There is a short notice of Thoresby in Stowe's Chron., ed. 1614, 270.

[e] "*Sepultus est coram altari beatæ*

His predecessors in the see, whose bones he had honourably placed there, were sleeping on either side. It was a noble sepulchre for a noble-hearted man. The brazen imagery that once decorated his tomb, nay the stone itself, has disappeared; but his good deeds, so numerous and so apparent, will perpetuate his memory better than either brass or marble.

Mariæ Virginis in novo opere chori, die Jovis, in vigilia Sancti Martini" (Stubbs). He was thus connected in death with that altar which he had constructed and honoured during his life. This makes the chain of evidence about the choir complete. Speaking of his place of sepulture in his will, Thoresby merely desires to be interred "in loco per ipsum patrem alias ordinato." There was no reason for him to say more, as the place would be well known, and the blank stone or space among the graves of his six predecessors would shew to all for whom it was intended.

That Thoresby was laid there is evident from the statement of the metrical chronicler of York (MSS. Cotton, Cleopatra, C, iv.). This writer mentions some facts which are not in Stubbs or any other writer, and he has therefore an independent authority of his own. The work seems to be in two parts, the first stopping with archbishop Scrope, the other, in a rather different style, coming down to the time of archbishop William Booth. A person who lived in the time of archbishop Scrope is a valuable witness as to what happened thirty years before.

The poet thus describes Thoresby's burial-place and death:—

> "Apud Thorp defungitur mundanis exutus
> Eboraci ponitur scenosis indutus,
> *In capella Virginis Matris graciosæ,*
> *Inter coepiscopos præsul gloriose*
> *Quos de fundis operis fecit hic levari*
> *Et sic honorifice ibi tumulari.*"

Leland describes the position of the archbishop's tomb even more minutely. Torre, Thoresby (Vic. Leod., 193), Drake (Eboracum, 435), and Godwin (687), give it the same position.

It has been suggested that a tomb on the north side of the nave of the minster commemorates Thoresby. From the strongest and the most indisputable evidence it has been shewn that he was buried at the east end and not in the nave. It has been said however (for Stubbs's statement has now been admitted to this extent) that the Lady chapel in which he was interred was that of St. Mary and the Holy Angels, or that of St. Sepulchre, appended to the nave. In answer to this I assert that this chapel was never known as the Lady chapel, and that the tomb, now ascribed to Thoresby, is on the *outside* of that chapel and not within it, so that the words of Stubbs do not apply to it at all.

It may be said that the remains may have been inside the chapel of St. Sepulchre, but that they have been *removed* out of it. When could that have been done? Clearly not before the Reformation, for the chapel was then in existence. Who, I should like to know, ever heard of the reforming iconoclasts preserving or translating a man's bones that were in their way? Nor could the removal have taken place in queen Mary's days, because then there would have been no wish to destroy the chapel in which they were placed. If Thoresby's remains were removed at all from St. Sepulchre's chapel, the change must have been made at the Reformation, and then either a new monument must have been constructed for them, or a portion of the old one set up in a new place. If this were the case, the date of the stone-work of the present monument would be either 1373, the year of Thoresby's death, or at the period of the Reformation. Both these hypotheses are completely overthrown by the fact that the architectural features of this sepulchral memorial prove it to have been erected between 1480 and 1510, and they shew that it is not a portion of an old tomb, but a new one specially constructed for the position that it occupies. Some years after 1510 Leland saw Thoresby's gravestone, with its inscription, in the presbytery at the east end.

In December, 1862, this monument, which had been injured, was completely

There seems to have been some little controversy between the executors of Thoresby and archbishop Neville on the question of dilapidations. On the 4th of October, 1374, those officials met the archbishop in a chamber in his palace, called Pountenysyn, and there, in the presence of his brother John, lord Neville, they submitted themselves to his decree. On the 13th of April in the following year, the executors Waltham, Thoresby and Barton, paid to the primate 2350 marks on the score of dilapidations, and 612 marks to supply the deficiencies in the stock which was to remain on the archiepiscopal manors.[f] The safest and wisest course, perhaps, that any prelate could adopt was to leave the adjustment of these claims to his successor and his executors.

It has been said that Thoresby was raised to the cardinalate by Urban V. Bale is the first person who makes this statement, and he gives him the title of St. Sabina.[g] Torre goes farther than this, and gives a rough drawing of his seal with this inscription, *S. Johis tt Sci P. ad Vincula presbyteri cardinalis.*[h] There is no documentary evidence whatever of Thoresby's ever having been a cardinal, and Ciaconius and the other biographers

restored, and the restoration has been such as to give it a much earlier date than belongs to it. Some liberties also have been taken with the sculpture, as, for instance, two birds holding scrolls, on either side of the central figure of the Virgin, have been metamorphosed into eagles with ears of wheat in their mouths. I cannot say a word, however, against the skill displayed by the masons, but no ancient monument, in my opinion, ought to be restored.

When the tomb was examined, a long box, more than six feet in length, was found containing bones and fragments of vestments. It was too narrow to admit of the reception of a body, so that these bones must have been gathered together and translated to this place at the latter end of the fifteenth century. Tradition, for the last century and a half, has ascribed this tomb to archbishop Roger. It, no doubt, contains the bones of some ecclesiastic, perhaps an archbishop, whose grave was disturbed, and as there was no stone elsewhere ascribed to Roger, who was buried originally in the choir, it may perhaps be his. The point cannot at present be settled, for even the fragments of robes, if their date could be ascertained, could prove nothing. Adhuc sub judice lis est.

[f] Reg. Neville.

[g] Cent. vi., 493. Thoresby, Godwin, and Tanner quote Torre. Godwin, however (*n. e.*, 687), questions the authority of Bale.

[h] Through the kindness of my friend, Mr. C. Sykes, I have been allowed to examine the drawing made by Torre, which is in the library at Sledmere. The seal is a large oval one. In the centre are the Virgin and child, under rich canopies. To the right is a figure of St. Peter with his keys, and below him the letters *S. Petrus*. To the left is a figure of pope Urban, with *Urbanus* under his feet. Below the Virgin is a kneeling figure of a cardinal holding a crozier, and on either side is a shield of arms. The charge on both is the same, viz., two stags, one above the other. The inscription in the text occupies the usual position. Different arms are assigned to Anglicus by Ciaconius (ed. 1677, ii., col. 561). The one bearing is probably that of his see, the other that of his family. "Che fu Decano della Metropolitana di York, nato, o almeno oriundo dall'Inghilterra per parte del padre, o sia dell'avo" (Cardella, Memorie Storiche de' Cardinali, ii., 208). Cf. Gallia Christiana, i., 823, etc.

of the members of the Sacred College never mention his name. The person to whom the seal refers was not Thoresby at all, but John Anglicus Grimaldi, who was created cardinal-priest of St. Peter ad Vincula, in September, 1366, by his brother, Urban V. In the month of November, in the same year, he was made dean of York, an office of which he was deprived in 1381. The archiepiscopal seal of Thoresby, of which there is a fine impression in the British Museum, and at least a dozen at Durham, is a glorious specimen of sigillary art, and is very much richer than that of his contemporary the dean.

END OF VOLUME I.

ADDENDA ET CORRIGENDA.

pp. 13-15, etc. *The Culdees.* This peculiar name cannot be traced, I believe, earlier than the ninth century, and the Christians of Iona, etc., should, perhaps, be called Columbites. As far as the creed and the practice of the Culdees and Columbites can be ascertained, I find no substantial difference between the two, and I have used the word Culdees as a generic term, the followers of Augustine and Wilfrid being of course excluded from it. It is a very remarkable fact that the canons of York were called Culdees in the reign of Henry I., another reason why I should use that word.

p. 37, note *j*. *Bromton.* The surname of the chronicler ought to be *Brompton.* This error runs through the volume.

p. 44, line 22, and note. *Akebargh.* "I never could think that Aykburgh or Ayksburghe was the place alluded to by Bede, and called after James the Deacon. If it is Jakesburgh, what are we to say to Aykescarth, Aykescough, Aikby, and Aikton? and could the same process transmute Jakeswell into Hawkswell? Why should not Hackford, near Hawkswell, have not been changed? In Gale's map, Aikburgh is placed between Hawkswell and Tunstall, near Catterick, but in reality, Aikber, as it is now called, is near Fingall, a farmhouse by the side of Fingall beck. As to Hawkswell, I think I have seen the Saxon personal name of Havoc in Domesday book, at all events it is called Havocswell there. I examined the cross at Hawkswell most minutely on the 17th of November, 1834, and several times within four years afterwards, and I am willing to make an affidavit that there was no inscription upon it then."—J. R. W.

p. 63, note *y*. For *clearly*, read *perhaps*.

p. 67, note *i*. For *Chron. Petrob.*, read *Chron. Petrib.*

p. 72, line 4 from foot of page. For *Ætla*, read *Oftfor.*

p. 77, note *i*. For *Cænob.*, read *Cœnob.* So also in the note on the next page, in note *g*, p. 125, note *i*, p. 133, and note *l*, p. 134.

p. 78, bis. For *Medhamstead*, read *Medeshamstead.*

p. 80, line 5 from foot of page. For *Grey*, read *Gray.*

pp. 91-2, notes. For *Fædera*, read *Fœdera;* also p. 240, note *v*, and p. 254, notes *v* and *y*.

p. 96, note *t*, and p. 97, line 1. For *pænitentiale*, read *pœnitentiale.*

p. 97, note *d*. For *Alcuini Op.*, read *Opp.:* this also occurs at pp. 98, 101-3, 106-11, 121.

p. 99, line 9 from foot of page. For *Ceonwulf*, read *Coenwulf.*

p. 106. The hexameter line at the foot of the page should be,

"I tamen, i pro me, tu, cui licet, aspice Romam."

p. 109 and note *u*. Aclete is very probably Auckland, co. Durham. Sochasburg is either Sockburn or Sadberge in the same county. W. H. D. L.

p. 118, note *g*. For *Servatus*, read *Senatus*. The same correction may be made at pp. 117, 121, 127, 128.

p. 134. One of the pins found in Wulstan's grave is in the collection S. A., London.

p. 162, line 19 from top. For *two*, read *four*.

p. 203. Ralph Deincourt founded the monastery of Thurgarton, Notts, by the advice and at the entreaty of Thurstan (Thoroton's Notts, 302).

p. 209, line 6 of the poem on Thurstan. For *inde finita*, read *indefinita*.

p. 214. Fountains was the mother of *eight* religious houses, and not of *seven*.

p. 220, line 7 from foot. There is a different account of the parentage of St. William in Coll. Top. and Genealog., i., 219. It is there said that his mother was Adela, daughter of Sir Robert Corbet, a concubine of Henry I.

p. 227, line 6 from foot. Honorius III. decreed the canonization of St. William by bull dated 15 Kal. Apr. anno x. (Addit. MSS., Br. Mus., 15351, fol. 311). The translation took place as I have stated, and this may be regarded as the final act of the canonization.

p. 230. In the treasury of York, circa 1500, there was "unum feretrum de berill" adorned with silver gilt, and precious stones, containing part of St. William's hair (Fabric Rolls, 221). By will, dated April 24, 1506, Margaret Norton, of Bilbrough, widow, left to Chr. Norton, "unam cathedram quæ fuit Sancti Willelmi Ebor. archiepiscopi" (Reg. Test. Ebor.).

p. 241, line 21 from top. For *unhappy*, read *impious*.

p. 245, line 25 from top. For *thew*, read *threw*.

p. 291, note *i*. On "die Sabbati, qua cantatur Scicientes, 1221, apud Blidam," the archbishop ordained Richard de Popeleswurch, priest, the master and brethren of the Temple giving him a title, "ad celebrandum in capella Novi Templi, London., pro anima Johannis quondam regis Angliæ illustris" (Rot. Gray).

p. 292, line 12 from top. In Gray's roll I find these most important notices: "Anno 19, 9 Kal. Dec. Indulgentia pro fabria ecclesiæ Southwell. On 5 Kal. Dec., pro ecclesia Ripon. On 17 Kal. Aug. 17, pro ecclesia Beverlacensi 'miserabili ruina enormiter deformata.'"

p. 295, note *v*, last line. For *king*, read *pope*.

p. 313, note *a*. Read *sindon'*.

p. 321. '*Canes perdriarios*—(?) pointers or setters.

p. 328, note *w*. Archbishop Gray instituted Chinchius, Romanus clericus, to the living of Elveley.

p. 394, line 16 from top. In 1306 Sir John Giffard made over to his kinsman the archbishop the manor of Boyton, co. Wilts. He was to stay with the archbishop and to be maintained by him, together with two esquires, six horses, and six garciones.

CPSIA information can be obtained
at www.ICGtesting.com
Printed in the USA
LVHW110931160522
718424LV00013B/61

9 783375 006754